THE CRAB APPLE CREEK ANTHOLOGY

Set 1 – The Crab Apple Series
Safe in Crab Apple Creek
Return to Crab Apple Creek
The Other Crab Apple Creek

Set 2 – The Legend of The Crystal Caves
The Crystal Dragon
Dragon Myths
The Dragon Dance

Set 3 – Mists Over the Meadow

Set 4 – Secrets of the Mountains

Set 5 – The Applewood Grove

The Legend of the Crystal Caves

The
Crystal Dragon

Dr. KARMLE L. CONRAD

DEDICATION

I dedicate this to The Special Ones. Keep The Magic alive!

~Karmle L. Conrad

ACKNOWLEDGEMENTS

Thanks to my sweet friend Denise Mooers for brainstorming with me to name "Q," the dragon. It was all her idea!!! I love ya' Barnaby!

Thanks to my fabulous artist and friend Jay Mooers for his input on starting this book. He gave me the ideas that are the first three pages. Love you, Jay!

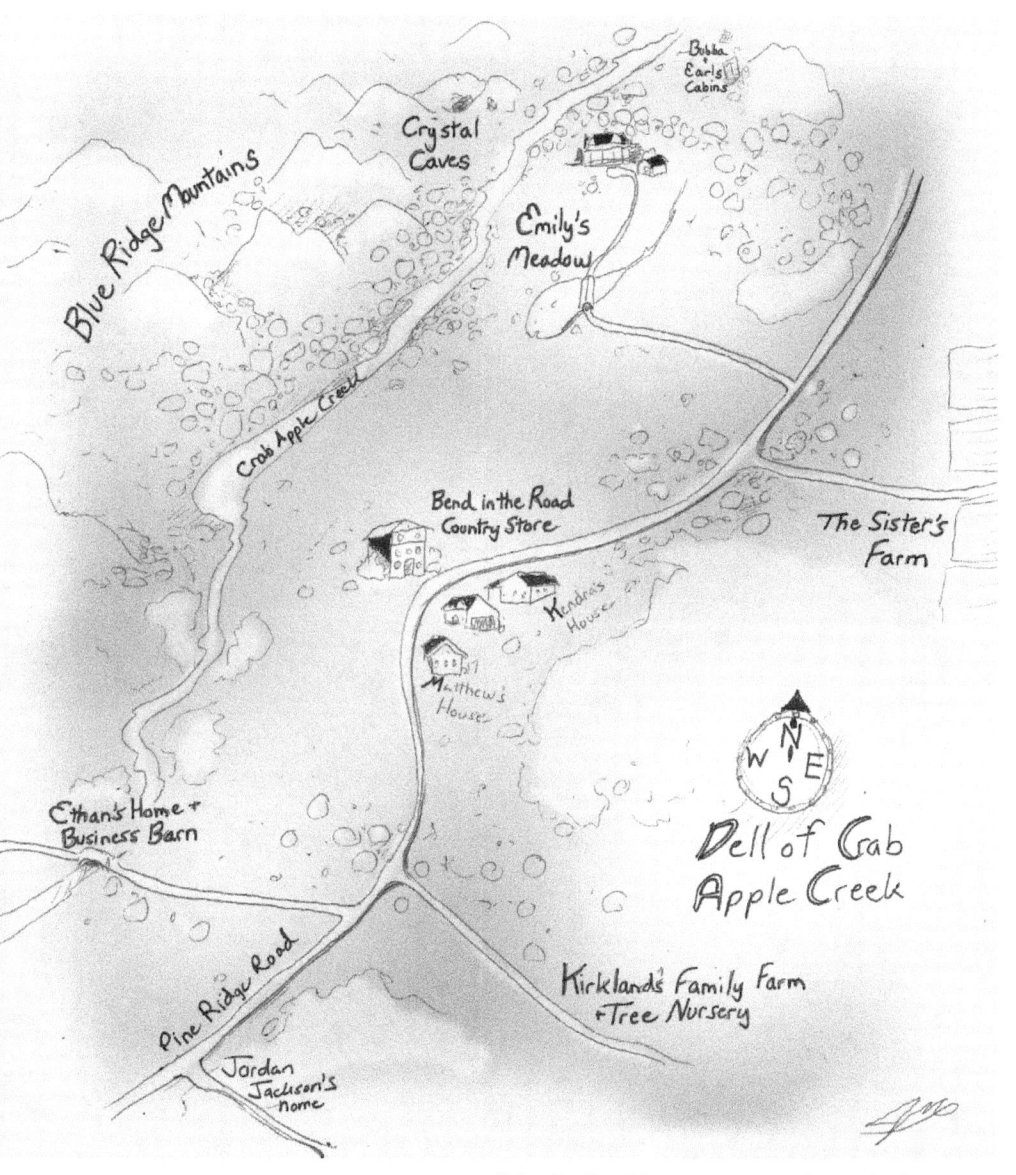

Map by Jay Mooers - www.edenparktales.com

The Legend

There are powers in those crystal caves—strong and ancient powers guarded by a fierce creature. The creature will let some enter the caves to look around for only a minute; then it scares them with fire, ice, and horrible sounds until they leave, never to return.

Legend says there are a few special ones that are made to become one with The Crystal Caves. They've been around as long as The Crystal Caves. And no one knows how long those caves have been around. Some folks found notes written about those caves and that creature from eons ago. Some found drawings of them. There are a few cave paintings in the mountains that show those caves and a strange creature standing in the middle of the crystals. Some say it's an alien. Others say it's a creature from ancient fairy tales put there to scare the kids so they won't look for The Crystal Caves.

Legend says most can't even find those caves. They are protected by strong powers. Some say it's The Ancient Magic that protects them.

Legend says those caves only become alive when their powers are needed to protect Mother Earth and Father Sky and to save The Special Magic and Special Powers.

Legends are made up of truth and speculation, some would say.

The Legend of The Crystal Caves is surrounded by mystery and Magic.

The Caves

He'd been traveling for an eternity, it seemed. Day turned into night, then turned into day again. He'd walked through swamps and fields that reminded him of the highland moors, forests, and streams. He climbed up one mountain to be greeted by another. He was near death when he collapsed at the edge of a clearing. He knew he had slept when the light shining in his eyes made him wake up. He moved a bit and looked out into the clearing, trying to remember where he was and what had happened to him.

He slowly sat up and took a good look around. He saw something shining across the clearing just inside the trees. He was a curious man. He stood up, swayed a bit, got his bearings, and set out across the clearing. It was a small clearing, and when he arrived at the tree line, he saw the light that had awoken him from his death sleep shining on a rock outcrop. He stepped over to it and saw that it was the opening of a cave. Maybe he could use this cave as a shelter for the next while. He stepped into the entrance and saw an incredible sight.

The cave was filled with crystals of all colors, shapes, and sizes. Some hung from the cave roof, others looked to have been set down, and others jutted from the walls and floors. As he stood there, he became aware of a sound. A soft humming sound. He didn't see anything that could make the sound, so he just stood still, watching the crystals. It only took him a minute to realize the humming was coming from the crystals themselves.

The crystals began to glow as they hummed, and some began a rhythmic pulsing kind of glowing. He was mesmerized and didn't know how long he stood there until the crystals became quiet. He looked around and saw a tunnel of sorts leading away from the room. It was in the back of the room, and it was tall and wide. He hadn't seen it before. He knew it hadn't been there when he first entered the cave. He was about to take a step to cross the room and have a look into that tunnel when a shadow appeared on the back end of the tunnel just where it curved.

The man stood watching as the shadow grew larger and larger until the creature came around the curve. It was huge. Its eyes were glowing purple and looking right at the man. The creature walked into the room and stood in the center of the crystals as they made a place for it.

The creature spoke to the man. "Thank you for getting here. We know it has been a long and hard journey. We are pleased that you have listened to the wind and the earth and made your way here. You are home. Now, eat, drink, and sleep. We will teach you a great many things as you step into your life as a protector of The Magic."

The creature vanished before the man's eyes, and a table and chair appeared. There was food and drink set for the man. He gave himself a shake, then sat at the table and ate.

When he finished, a palate of straw and animal skins appeared next to him. As he lay down, his last thoughts before sleep took over and his new life began were: I know there's Magic in Middle Earth, but I never thought I'd be a part of it. I accept my new life and will honor and serve as long as I live.

And the man slept.

The Special One

It took a long time to come up out of the deep unconsciousness of eons. A really long time. As she became aware that she was no longer in a deep sleep, she tried to return to her unconscious state. It didn't work. It never had before. She tried to ignore the voices of those awakening her. That didn't work, either. She finally gave up and became fully awake.

She stretched while lying down, rolled from side to side, and finally sat up. She gave her head a gentle shake and looked about.

"All right already!" she hollered. "I'm awake! What'd he do this time? Or was it his assistant that screwed up?"

As she stood up to her full height, she saw the usual light shining in the main room. She walked in and found the usual assortment of beautiful crystals, all shining and humming along.

"You all look and sound so very beautiful, as always," she said.

The crystals blinked a thank you.

"Do ya' know what's going on this time?"

No response.

"Okay, then. I guess I'll have to wait for the Ancients to fill me in on the latest news," she replied. She walked to the cave entrance and stuck her head outside to have a look around.

"Well, we're in a different place this time. Wonder where? It sure does look nice out there. Nice field, and it looks like a structure of some kind a ways off. Oh-oh, I hear the Ancients arriving. Time to go back inside."

As she walked into the main room of the cave, she saw the Ancients gathered in the center. She bowed to them and waited for them to speak.

"Hello, Penelope. Thank you for finally waking up. We are in need of your Special Gifts. It seems there is some evil afoot, and we need you and the others to put a stop to it."

"Thank you for coming to me. I am honored to be asked to help. I accept, as always. Do the others know who they are yet?"

"No. The assistant is very aware of her Gifts and has just fought a horrific battle, sending The Dark into the outer universes in a greatly diminished capacity. The other does not know who he is at all. He accepts The Magic and that he was a part of the battle. However, he believes it was just to get the sword to her. That's okay for now. Soon, he will learn his true identity with you helping him. Are you ready for this new adventure?"

"I am, and I am blessed to be chosen for this challenge," she responded as she bowed again.

"As it is, so shall it be. We will be watching as always. If need be, we will help, but only as a last resort."

"Understood," she responded. And as she watched, the Ancients vanished into thin air as they always did.

"Well," she thought aloud, "I guess we've got some work to do."

She returned to her special place in the caves to await the time she would make her presence known to him...again.

CHAPTER 1

Jordan Jackson was working in his home office on the URR project on Tuesday. He loved the whole abbreviation thing. URR stood for Underground Railroad. He got lost in remembering how he came to The Creek as a delivery driver for a familiar company, found and bought his farm, then left the company to work for Katelyn's best friend Sami as a researcher. He was working on the history of the Underground Railroad in all the cities where Sami was renovating hotels. What an amazing progression of events.

All of that reminiscing brought him to the dragon. Had he really seen a dragon flying over the barn? It couldn't be. Dragons were fantasy. But, then, he argued with himself, The Creek was full of The Magic. After all, he had been made to fly in that huge Battle on The Rise just a few weeks back. Now, that was unbelievable by all means. People don't fly. Except he had flown. His mind was racing. So, if people could fly and all, then The Magic that had happened was real. So, why couldn't he have seen a real dragon? What the hell was a dragon doing flying over his barn? Where had it come from? What was it doing here? That is, if it were really real.

He shook himself. It was all just too much for him. It had been an unbelievable time, for sure. Time to get back to his research. He loved history, and being able to research history wasn't work. It was an adventure. Maybe he could lose himself in his work and not think about all The Magic stuff. He truly knew he couldn't take any more Magic right now.

As he focused on his screen, it flashed, and he was looking at something that was not a part of his research. It was a room made up of large, life-sized crystals. Then it was gone, and his research was back on the screen.

This was just too much for him. He jumped up from his chair and yelled, "What the hell was that? More Magic? No more Magic! I can't do this right now.

1

I'm still trying to figure out how I flew a crystal sword to Katelyn. You guys need to leave me alone. And, what was that thing I saw flying around outside? I know I saw a dragon. What the hell is going on around here? Leave me alone! Dragons are not real!"

Jordan kicked the kitchen door open as he burst outside. He was beside himself. He was still trying to work through that whole Battle on The Rise thing and the tattoo on his shoulder, which he knew he never got. It had just appeared right after The Rise thing.

Jordan walked around his barn a few times to try to calm down. Being outside was what he loved. He was walking through the barn and yelling when George, his eagle, flew in. George settled on a high timber and watched Jordan. George was worried that Jordan was having a meltdown. He was yelling and walking very fast. He was kicking at anything that happened to be in his way, including the wheelbarrow full of tools. The wheelbarrow fell sideways, and everything scattered around. This made Jordan stop and look at the mess.

Jordan stood there staring at his tools. He was breathing fast and felt hot. He didn't know he had made fists with both hands until he opened them, and they felt weird. He didn't remember going outside. He didn't remember going back into the barn. He knew he was angry with The Other Side for flashing that room full of crystals on his laptop.

He felt defeated. He dropped down onto the floor, feeling empty.

George was watching from his lofty place on one of the cross beams near the top of the barn. He knew if he flew over to Jordan and talked with him, Jordan might go nuts. So, he just watched and waited for Jordan to call out to him.

Jordon sat there lost. He didn't really know what to think was real. He needed someone to talk to who knew about all this stuff. Katelyn. He'd call Katelyn. No, wait a minute. He couldn't talk to Katelyn. She didn't know about the dragon. Shit!

Jordon lifted his head and looked up into the rafters of the barn. He saw the eagle.

"George? Get down here right now!" Jordan demanded.

He watched George swoop down and stand in front of him.

"The one thing I know to be true is that you can talk," Jordan said, looking directly into George's eyes. "Now talk!"

George morphed into his human self and sat down to face Jordan.

"What the hell is going on? No double talk, just the truth," Jordan demanded of George.

George took a minute and replied, "Jordan. Uhm. I don't know where to start. I'm so sorry for how this has happened. I understand why you're angry right now."

"Oh, yeah. And, one more thing. I have a pet eagle who can talk to me and change into a human being at will," Jordan said sarcastically. "What the hell?"

"That you do," George said.

"Wiseass," Jordan said. "Don't give me that line about how I agreed to this. I most certainly did not. I am not suicidal! I'm surprised I haven't gone completely off the deep end already. Crystal swords, flying around, you, and my Crystal Cave with all its magical doings."

"I'm rather impressed that you've held it together this long," George said.

Jordan gave George the death look.

There was a loaded silence in the barn for the longest time. Jordan got up and paced around while George just sat there.

"Well," Jordan said, stopping next to George. "What the hell is happening to me?"

George stood up and walked around the barn for a minute.

"Jordan, you are not going crazy," George began as Jordan kicked straw at him.

"Like hell, I'm not," Jordan said. "I'm just trying to forget about this Magic stuff and get lost in my research. I love my research. And, just like that, an image of a space full of life-sized crystals appears on my laptop for just half a second, then vanishes. What the hell is that all about? Ya need to tell Them to leave me alone. I've done my job for Them. I need my space and peace so I can get back to normal."

"Have ya had any Reiki lately?" George asked.

"Don't!" Jordan replied, looking like he was going to punch George.

"Just a thought," George replied, stepping further away from Jordan. "I think we need some help right about now."

"Keep it up, and you're the one who's going to need help," Jordan replied.

"Got it," George said.

"I do remember they said I could quit any time I chose to," Jordan said.

"They did," George answered.

"Good. Hear me loud and clear," Jordan said. "Since you won't leave me alone, I quit. I resign. I'm done with all this Magic stuff. Now, leave me alone!"

"They have heard your plea," George said. "Just one thing: I'm staying here just like I am in case you want to talk to me about anything."

"I accept that," Jordan said, bowing to George. "I am so tired. I'm going in to crash. Thanks, George."

"You are welcome, Jordan," George replied. "Rest easy."

As Jordan left the barn, George morphed back into his eagle self and took to the air. He flew a wide circle around The Creek. It was at peace. For now.

Jordan found his bed and collapsed onto it. The last thing he remembered was that space with those huge life-sized crystals.

When Jordan woke up Wednesday morning, he felt rested. He was still not sure about all that had happened. He set to work and kept focused for the day. It felt good to work. He had a video meeting with Sami after supper.

"Hey, Sami," Jordan said when they connected.

"Hey, Jordan," Sami replied. "How's the research comin' along?"

"I love this stuff," Jordan said. "I know we're about to hit the mid-Atlantic properties, so I've set up a spreadsheet of the hotels and am researchin' their involvement in the URR. There are a lot of slave states in this bunch, so findin' the URR sites is kind of tricky."

"I figured as much," Sami said. "The URR safe houses were very well hidden. So I think a lot of readin' is gonna happen."

"I agree," Jordan said. "It seems that even though Virginia was a slave state, there were factions that hated slavery. I suspect these folks had to live a double life. Sort of like a double spy thing."

"I got the same impression from the few things I've read," Sami said. "The old family names should have some colorful histories to investigate. Share your spreadsheet, and I'll add whatever I find to it."

"That's a great idea," Jordan said. "Any plans to come for a visit? I know Katie would be thrilled."

"As a matter of fact, yes. I should be in The Creek in just a few days. My bosses said I need a long break," Sami replied.

"I like the sound of that, and The Creek will be thrilled to have you home again," Jordan said. "Does Katie know yet?"

"That's my next call. You'll probably hear her hollerin' all the way to your farm," Sami said, laughing.

"I'll step outside so I don't miss it," Jordan replied, laughing with Sami.

"I love the research you do. Keep it up. Is there anything you need as far as supplies go?" Sami asked.

"I sent a list to you a few minutes ago," Jordan replied.

"I'll send it along to the business office, so you should have it within the week," Sami replied.

"Great. Now, go call our Katelyn," Jordan said.

"Will do. Later," Sami said as they ended the chat.

Jordan stepped outside to close the barn for the night. George was waiting for him on the back porch.

"So, Sami's coming home," George said as he looked up at Jordan.

"She is," Jordan replied, looking out over the farm.

"I'm gonna take a walk around the barn. Come with me," Jordan said.

Jordan and George walked around the barn and then out to the front porch to look at the crystal by the door. Every night, without fail, when the sun hit that crystal, it shot beams of light all over the place. It was awe-inspiring to behold.

"Not a word, George," Jordan said.

George nodded in reply.

Jordan walked the dirt tract a ways before returning to the barn. George flew in and settled on the roofline timber. Jordan closed his eyes and stood in silence. This is what he needed: silence and no Magic.

"Good night, George," Jordan said as he closed the big barn door.

"Good night, Jordan," George replied.

The Magical Creature heard everything and felt sad for Jordan. He would need to come to terms with all this Magic stuff soon. He was needed once again to balance the forces of good and evil.

Jordan slept peacefully that night. The Creek was quiet as well.

"Sami's comin' home," Katelyn said as she entered the shop Thursday morning.

Ethan, Finn, and Ian looked up at her and laughed.

"We like that news," Finn said.

"I can see that you love the news," Ethan said.

"Well, yeah," Katelyn replied.

"When?" Ian asked.

"She'll be here late tomorrow night, then for a week and both weekends. Her bosses demanded that she take the week off," Katelyn replied.

"I'm all for that," Finn said. "I'd take the week off if my bosses told me to."

"Wiseass," Ethan and Ian said at the same time. Then laughed.

"I've already texted Ted, Emily, and Miss Cora. They're excited, too. Ted said he'd get the word out for a Saturday night supper at The Store."

"I love when this happens," Ian said. "My family will be thrilled."

"Did we get the new client that wants to build up north of town?" Katelyn asked as she put her things in her office.

"They're on their way over now," Ian said. "They have a few more questions for us about the land use in the area. Most of it is privately owned or part of the National Forest. They want to make sure no one is gonna build a big neighborhood anywhere near them."

"Fat chance the private land owners will sell to a development company," Finn asked.

"True. Well, Emily owns a lot of the land north of her place along the road. So no worries there," Ethan explained. "The other fifty-acre parcel is owned by the Kirkland's. They are not sellin' it. Period," Ian explained. "As a matter of fact, the

Kirkland's have plans to plant cherry trees in that huge meadow along the road. They said there will be about fifty trees planted in the spring."

"I heard some talk about that the last time I was out at the nursery," Finn said. "Scott said they'd been thinkin' about that meadow for a couple of years. They tested the soil and found it perfect for fruit trees. He said they'd start work in April. Karl is all set to build the road, and I know Scott's talked to the two of you for plans for the orchard house."

"He has," Ian said. "We're getting the details worked out over the winter. You'll be lookin' at geothermal possibilities before the snow flies."

"Yes, sir," Finn said, saluting Ian.

"That's right," Ian said. "Good to see you know who the boss is around here."

Katelyn and Ethan laughed at the two of them.

"Looks like our clients have arrived," Ethan said as he saw a car drive by the window.

They all spent most of the morning working with the clients. By the end of their meeting, the clients were ready to sign on with Ethan's company to build their forever home in the Blue Ridge. Contracts were signed, and their next meeting was set for the next day.

"I like these two," Ethan said after they left. "They know exactly what they want and what they don't want. No neighborhoods!"

"I agree," Katelyn said. "It's great that the land they have has been passed down through the generations. Gina said it's been in the family for over two hundred years. I'll bet Miss Cora knows all about that."

"Gina and Terry Bancroft," Ian said. "I have a faint memory of that last name from a long while back."

"Me, too," Ethan said. "It sounds familiar, but I can't place it. Miss Cora will know for sure. We'll have to ask her about it at supper on Saturday."

"Good idea," Finn said. "Now, how about some lunch? I've got leftovers from Mom's pot roast last night."

"Crockpot pot roast?" Ian asked.

"Yes, sir," Finn said. "She sent enough for all of us."

"I do love your mom," Ethan said as they set about preparing leftovers.

"Mmmm. So good," Katelyn said. "Tell your mom thanks from me."

"Ditto," Ethan and Ian said.

Lunch was cleared, and they got back to work.

Folks were busy all over The Creek for the rest of the day. Kendra was looking at two pieces of land north of The Creek for interested parties. Jenna was busy with several commissions for artwork for local folks. Ted and Michael were trying a few new products at The Store. Ted was busy creating new dishes and letting anyone who walked in at the right time sample them. Most were good. A few were not to see the light of day again.

Matthews was busy with his usual work. He had just gotten a text from Ethan and was talking to him about the Bancroft's.

"Hey, Ethan," Matthews said. "I see you're busy as usual."

"Hey, Matthews," Ethan replied. "I am. They signed the general contract today, and we're meetin' with them again tomorrow mornin'. We've got pictures from the drones to show them how their land looks from up above. You know we do that with all of our clients. It gives them a good idea of how things look and helps them choose where to build. I know we need a security check, and that's why I texted you."

"I appreciate your promptness," Matthews said. "Email me a copy of the general contract, and I'll get the process started. Are they locals?"

"The name sounds familiar to Ian and me, but we can't quite place them. We're gonna ask Miss Cora at supper Saturday night. Did you get the email about Sami comin' home Friday night for a long week?"

"I did," Matthews replied. "I'll bet Katelyn is all excited."

"Oh, she is," Ethan said. "She hasn't stopped smilin' since she got the news from Sami last night."

"We need a gatherin'," Matthews said. "It's been a while since the Battle at The Rise, and we haven't even talked much about that. This will be good for everyone."

"Always is when The Creek gets to cookin' and bakin'," Ethan replied.

"Later, then," Matthews said as they ended the call.

Ethan went back to work, and Matthews looked at the contract he had just received. Then, he started the security check, which usually took about a week or so.

Emily was busy with her farm. The fall harvest was in full swing. She and Ethan had planted a large pumpkin patch, and it seemed that every seed had sprouted and every plant had at least two pumpkins on it. Orange ones, white ones, and some were even striped. There were all sizes from very little to huge. They were talking about having the locals pick their own pumpkins. The two of them were having a blast with the garden that fall. So was Trouble, the mutt that had wandered onto the building site while the place was under construction. He still loved chasing birds and butterflies every chance he could.

Emily's pond was getting more and more settled. There were a couple of families of ducklings, a pair of swans, and even a bunch of wild turkeys that visited every day. If you were lucky, you would see wildlife at dawn and dusk. The deer loved the pond along with foxes, rabbits, raccoons, and even an eagle from time to time. Emily's Farm was settling into the Blue Ridge just fine.

It was late afternoon while Emily was busy picking veggies when she felt a soft breeze blow through the place. It wasn't so much a breeze as a change in the energy in the air. She was familiar with this shift all too well. She stood up, closed her eyes, and tuned in to the energy around her. She felt a knowing that things were going to change a bit in the near future. A good change. Nothing bad. But a change nonetheless. She opened her eyes and saw an eagle soaring overhead. She bowed to the eagle; it swooped down close and squawked, then lifted up into the thermals and rode them out of sight.

And so it continues, Emily thought. She smiled and returned to her veggies. She had already filled two baskets. First, she would put most of them on the farmstand at the end of the driveway. Folks looked forward to this and enjoyed her veggies. Then, she would take some of them to The Store for Ted to use and give away to those in need.

Miss Cora was rocking on her front porch when she felt the energy shift. She closed her eyes and tuned in to the energy the same way Emily had tuned in. She, too, felt at peace with the energy and knew the coming change was a good one. She thanked The Divine for the message and went back to rockin' and watchin' the day go by.

Mo and Lanie were busy harvesting their latest batch of plants. Their farmstand was a busy place, too. Their special blends of marijuana were a huge hit with everyone. They were taking care of the batch that would be ready just before Thanksgiving. It was a special high-potency blend they had designed. The solar panels they had designed and patented had made all this possible. They were excited to see what this plant would produce.

Bubba and Earl were thrilled with the cabins Emily had built for them. They loved them. They felt like they were in cabin paradise. The geothermal heat was especially enjoyed. They would bank a fire for the night and not have to get up and stoke it in the middle of the night at all.

Jordan had been working straight through the day, grabbing something to eat at lunch and never stopping his research. He needed a break when he realized he had gone off daydreaming about nothing in particular. He grabbed a juice and went out back to walk his land. George flew overhead, circled, and kept up with Jordan as he walked along the dirt track. He didn't want to go near his Crystal Cave. No more Magic.

He kept walking without paying any mind as to where he was until he got to the forest at the end of the dirt track. He looked around and was surprised he was at the most eastern point of his farm. He hadn't been out here since he built his house. So he decided to walk through the forest a bit to see what he could find.

The forest was full of pine trees and hardwoods. The leaves were beginning to change color on some of them. He heard a rustling to his right and stood still. He saw a fox family looking at him. He bowed his head ever so slightly, and the foxes went on their way. He heard the sound of water and remembered a stream flowing through these woods. It was the one Finn had tapped into for his geothermal energy source. He found the stream a minute later and watched the water flow around rocks and boulders. He walked along its bank upstream and found a small waterfall. It was so peaceful here. He sat down on a flat rock and enjoyed the place. George flew in and perched on a branch close to Jordan.

As Jordan watched the water, the sun sent rays onto the stream. There were rainbows everywhere you looked. It was surreal. It only took a second for him to realize The Magic was around when he saw faeries flying along the stream in the sun's rays.

"No Magic!" Jordan hollered. "Leave me alone!"

"Oh, Jordan," George said. "They just wanted to give you peace and beauty to enjoy."

"I want to be left alone," Jordan said. "I appreciate the beauty of Mother Earth. I don't need to be reminded about the Magic."

As Jordan was talking, a figure appeared, hovering over the stream. It was an apparition of a man dressed in flowing robes.

"Jordan, we are truly sorry for dumping all The Magic on you that has happened these past few weeks. We have left you alone for a few hours as you demanded."

"I said no more," Jordan replied. "What part of NO don't you understand?"

"We hear you loud and clear. We sent this gift to you just now to give you a few moments of peace."

"How can it be peaceful when I know it's The Magic making all this happen?" Jordan said.

"Good point," the apparition replied. "We didn't think of it like that."

"Duh," Jordan replied.

George laughed at this.

"George, quiet," Jordan said, looking at his eagle.

"You accept The Magic in George but won't allow any other Magic to happen around you. Why?" the apparition asked.

"Too much to understand. I can't even begin to comprehend that this Magic is real. I know it is in my head, but the rest of me is beyond overwhelmed with it all. How the hell did I fly? And what about that crystal sword? What's that all about? And, while we're on the subject of bizarre shit happening, what the hell was that thing flying over my barn? It looked exactly like a dragon. Dragons don't exist. Answer me that."

The apparition was silent for a minute, then said, "Why do you say dragons aren't real?"

"Seriously?" Jordan replied. "Seriously? They only exist in stories. Fiction stories. There has never been any valid proof that dragons ever existed. No fossils ever found."

"That would seem to be all true," the apparition replied. "I can understand your thoughts better now."

"What kind of double talk is that?" Jordan said, looking at the apparition. "Wait. I don't want to know. I am not having this conversation with a ghost."

"Fair enough," the apparition said. "Will you accept the faeries and rainbows from us as a token of our thanks for all you've done?"

"Jordan," George started to say.

Jordan silenced him with a look that would kill an elephant.

"No. No Magic," Jordan said, feeling confused and deflated.

"We understand," the apparition said. The faeries flew around Jordan and then disappeared. The sun kept shining on the water, though.

"The sun's doing its own thing," the apparition said.

Jordan remained silent as he focused on the water. The Magic knew he was at his breaking point. They sent healing energy to him and then left him alone. The apparition vanished.

"Jordan, I'm very worried about you," George said as he morphed into his human form.

"George, I'm at my wit's end. I can't do this anymore," Jordan said quietly. "I need my normal life back. No more Magic."

"They do understand," George said as he stood beside Jordan. "They sent the faeries and sunbeams to give you some peace."

"Didn't work," Jordan said, looking at George. "It was more Magic. I feel so tired."

"How about we keep walking downstream for a bit? No more Magic," George suggested.

"Okay. I do like these woods. They are beautiful," Jordan said as they walked along the stream crossing his property from north to south. "Look, there's a beaver lodge in the middle of the stream. It's split the stream in two."

"These beavers sure are industrious," George said.

"This has created a kind of marsh around here," Jordan said as he sunk into the soggy soil. He stepped back until he was on firm ground.

"Let's go back to the house," Jordan said. "This walkin' thing has made me very hungry. I didn't realize it was this late in the day."

"I hear ya," George said as he returned to his eagle self. He flew off over the field and met Jordan as he walked up onto the back porch.

"Thanks for the company, George," Jordan said as he went inside and fixed his supper.

"Later, Jordan," George said as he flew into the barn.

Jordan and the rest of The Creek spent their evening doing the usual end-of-day stuff. A few folks stopped by Jordan's farm to watch the sun hit the crystal on the front porch. It surely was magnificent. They chatted for a minute afterward, then went on their way.

Jordan settled in his living room, watching a few shows before he went to bed.

The Magic called an emergency meeting. It was really The White Light. Jordan knew it as The Magic. They were very concerned about his state of mental health.

"We must stop bothering Jordan for a while," the priestess said. "He is very fragile right now."

"I am concerned he may not be able to fulfill his destiny this time," a White Light Paladin said.

They all agreed with this statement.

"We will send him healing around the clock as they say," the priestess said. "This must be done gently and quietly. It is imperative that he be healed and ready to continue with The Magic. We are all aware of what would happen if his destiny is not fulfilled."

"This is the worst it's been for him," the White Light Paladin said. "I wonder if he took on too much this time?"

"That doesn't matter now," a voice said from beyond the mists. "He is needed, and we will be with him and take care of him."

"I stand with him," the White Light Paladin said.

"As I do," all of the others pledged.

"He will soon begin to remember. That's when he'll need us the most," the priestess said.

"And his assistant? Is she ready?" another asked.

"Yes, she is. Although this will be a lot to take in, she is ready," the priestess stated.

"Then so are we," said those gathered as they bowed toward the priestess.

"And so we begin," the priestess said, dismissing them to carry on the work of The White Light.

Friday dawned clear and warm. The Creek was busy with work, school, and the harvest of gardens and vineyards. The Store was a popular spot for breakfast ever since Ted had created his famous bagel breakfast sandwiches. That's where Finn and Katelyn were to be found on this fine day.

"Finn, great idea to come here for breakfast before work," Katelyn said as she grabbed napkins and sat across from Finn.

"I agree," Hal said as he walked up the steps to the dining room. "I love these things."

"What's got you up so early this mornin', Hal?" Finn asked as Ted took Hal's bagel order.

"Doesn't matter as long as he's here," Ted said.

Hal laughed as he gathered his things and joined Finn and Katelyn at the table.

"I'm workin' on some of the tables from all the trees that came down a while back. The maple and oak are beautiful. I've got a bunch of frames from the smaller pieces. I put them up on eBay, and they're sellin' like hotcakes," Hal explained as Ted brought their breakfast out.

"There's one right here," Ted said, pointing to the menu board. "I asked Hal to make a new frame, and this is what he created."

"This is beautiful," Katelyn said. "The lines in this piece of oak are beautiful."

"Thanks, Katelyn. Red oak does have some spectacular patterns," Hal said.

"And you always seem to find them," Finn said. "You are a true master craftsman, Hal. How about you bring some over to the shop for our clients to look at? I bet they'll all want a few for their new homes."

"Thanks, Finn. That's a great idea," Hal said. "I appreciate your thoughtfulness. Now, time to eat."

Talk turned to Sami's supper for the following evening.

"Hey, Ted, you been creatin' again?" Hal asked.

"I sure have," Ted replied. "You'll get to sample it tomorrow night. Michael says it's heavenly."

"He would know," Katelyn said. "I take it it's a new desert?"

"Sure is, darlin'," Ted replied, winking at her. "You bringin' your mayonnaise cake?"

"Sure am. I wouldn't want to disappoint you," Katelyn said, winking back at Ted.

"Are you flirtin' with my girl right in front of me?" Flinn said as he wrapped an arm around Katelyn's shoulders.

"Who me?" Ted said, acting all innocent.

Folks laughed at the two of them as breakfast was finished.

"Has Sami left her hotel yet in Maryland?" Hal asked.

"She texted me about an hour ago. She's on her way," Katelyn told everyone. "She said she's gonna stop at an artist's studio along the way. She loves his work and wants to show it to us for our thoughts. She should be here around nine-ish tonight."

"I love it when she comes home," Ted said. "I get to have her sample all my new stuff."

"And she loves to help you," Katelyn said. "She said she's ready for her breakfast bagel tomorrow mornin'."

"I'll be ready to prepare it for her whenever the two of you get here," Ted replied.

"What does that mean?" Finn asked.

"Those two have been known to stay up into the dark of night talkin' about anything and everythin'. Then, they sleep in a bit and show up here in need of love and food," Ted replied.

"So true," Katelyn said, laughing. "We look a sight when we get here, but by the time we leave, Ted has managed to revive us for the day."

"I hear Miss Cora is makin' her famous cornbread," Hal said.

"She is," Ted replied, and they talked a bit more about Saturday's supper event.

"Well, it's time to move on," Hal said. "I'll stop by today."

"Great, Hal," Finn said. "Time for us to get to the shop."

"You know how Ethan can be," Katelyn said. "He's a taskmaster for sure."

"Just like me," Michael said as they paid their bill.

"Yeah, right?" Ted said, snapping a towel at Michael.

"Payback is hell, my friend," Michael threatened.

"I love your payback," Ted said, blowing a kiss to Michael.

"Later," Katelyn said as they left.

"Those two are a blast," Finn commented as they drove off down the Pine Ridge Road to the shop at The Soaring Mountains Builders. "They have a special love for each other that allows them to grow as their own person and together as partners. That's a rare thing."

"I agree," Katelyn said as they parked Finn's truck. "My folks and yours have that special thing goin' on, too."

"They certainly do," Finn said as he opened the door.

Ethan and Ian were ready for them.

"The Bancroft's will be here shortly. They moved their appointment up to first thing," Ian told them. "They want to see the drone footage, and then we're all drivin' out to their property, so you might want to change into your field clothes, Katelyn."

"Thanks for the update," Katelyn said. "I'll be right back."

She was changed and walking back into the shop when the Bancroft's pulled in. They looked at the drone films on the big wall screen, and the landowners were thrilled.

"This is amazin'," Terry said. "I love what digital technology can do."

"Wow!" Gina added. "Where do we begin to look?"

Ethan and Finn explained about the land and where the creeks flowed. There were three creeks on their property. Two were small, and the third was bigger than most in the area. It almost looked like a small river.

"This creek called The Crystal Creek flows underground from within the mountains and surfaces north of your property about two miles up, "Finn explained. "We discovered a hot spring on the west side of your property. I've been monitoring the temperature from a digital setup I put in place Monday. Yes, Ethan, I went up Monday after we talked. The temperature has been a steady 100 degrees Fahrenheit. Just right for people to use. The Crystal Creek flows around the spring, so the geothermal source for the hot spring water is well underground. I can tap into it to heat your house and barn. I've had the engineers we use begin their preliminary plan for that already. If you decide on that area, we will need to build a bit away from the hot spring."

"We have a hot spring? Awesome," Gina said.

"I'm lovin' this already," Terry added.

"Let's walk over to the screen, and I'll explain the land layout in detail," Ethan suggested.

Ethan pointed out all the things on their land: the forest, meadow, animal paths, the hot spring, and the location of their boundaries in relation to the Kirkland's and Emily's land and the National Forest. He explained that Scott Kirkland was going to plant about fifty cherry trees in their meadow. Although the meadow did not border the Bancroft's land, it was within sight of the eastern boundary.

"I like the cherry orchard a lot," Terry said. "It will add to the land and help the animals and all."

"You a farmer in disguise?" Finn asked.

"I sure am," Terry replied. "Even though I design software for private industry, I love the land and want to add animals and all to the place in a year or so."

"That sounds fantastic," Katelyn said. "I'll be sure to design your home with lots of windows so you can enjoy the landscape."

"I love that idea," Gina said. "And, of course, the world-famous Sutherland wrap-around porch with a porch swing and dormers. I love doghouse dormers."

"I just put that in your design portfolio," Katelyn said.

"So, with everythin' we've shown you, let's get up to your property so you can see the land in real-time," Ethan said.

They took Ethan and Finn's trucks, waving at folks at The Store as they drove north. They passed Emily's Meadow and Laine and Mo's place and soon came to the Bancroft's land.

"I had Karl, our excavation guy, cut a rough track to the meadow. We will replace all the small trees that were taken down. You can see them along the track," Ethan explained as they drove onto the meadow.

"This is bigger than I imagined," Terry said.

"Look to your right, and you'll see a few trees with red tape. They mark the boundary between you and the Kirkland's land. Their meadow is about a half mile through those trees. So, there's a good border for privacy along your meadow."

"Okay," Terry said. "Let's walk the meadow."

They set out walking west and north and covered the meadow in about a half hour.

"This will be perfect for our horses," Gina said. "We plan on having four of them."

"How about that small group of trees over there? Let's take a look," Ian suggested.

As they walked through the trees, a beautiful surprise greeted them.

"Would you look at that?" Katelyn said.

They had walked into a clearing about the size of four big barns. In the middle of that clearing, a large crystal sat on a raised bit of ground. It was purple and pink and glowed brightly.

"This is where we build," Gina whispered.

They all stood silent and knew she was right. Katelyn and Finn looked at each other and nodded, knowing The Magic was at work once again.

"We agree," Ethan said. "We'll leave that crystal where it is until we absolutely need to move it. Then, you two can decide where it will be placed. We know how to handle these special gifts from Mother Earth."

"The Creek is a special place with lots of Magic happenin'," Terry said. "We chose you as our builders because we had a gut feelin' that you know about The Magic around here."

"You are correct in that thought," Ethan said.

"I think we should have the chiefs walk your land to make sure there aren't any sacred areas. We always do that to be respectful of their ancestors," Ian said.

"Oh, absolutely," both Terry and Gina said at the same time.

"Great," Ian said. "I'll text them right now so they can make time in their schedules to walk the land."

"What direction will your house face?" Finn asked.

"South, southwest," Terry replied.

"Good idea," Katelyn added. "That way, you'll get the evenin' sun on your porch and the mornin' sun in the kitchen."

"Exactly," Gina said.

"Follow me to the hot spring," Finn said.

A few minutes later, after walking through the forest, they came upon the hot spring. It had a cleared area around it but was set into the woods as if it were being kept hidden.

"This is ethereal," Terry said.

The steam rising from the spring folded into the sunbeams and shot little rainbows all around the clearing.

Gina knelt next to the spring and put her hand in. "It feels heavenly."

"They always do," Finn said.

"And it's only a few minutes' walk from where your farmhouse is gonna be built," Katelyn added. "Very nice."

"I've lived here all my life and never knew this hot spring was here," Ethan said. "Always somethin' new to learn."

"That's the truth," Ian said, agreeing with Ethan.

"I like the bit of rock edging around the spring," Terry said. "It almost looks like it was put there."

"Could have very well been built there," Ian said. "Probably by the natives. I'll be sure to ask the chiefs. They said they'll stop by Saturday mornin' and walk the land. I'll text them about the hot spring now."

A minute later, Ian said, "They said they had heard stories about the spring but never knew they were true. They also think that their ancestors would have been the ones to build the rock edge. No one has owned this land since their ancestors were here except the Bancroft families."

"This is so cool," Terry said. "A bit of history to add to our new home."

"It sure is," Katelyn said as she ran her hands through the water. "I'll bet Miss Cora will have a thing or two to say about this hot spring at supper tomorrow night."

"By the way, since you two are the latest folks to return to The Creek family, you are invited to supper at The Store tomorrow evenin'. Katelyn's BFF and a member of The Creek since this summer, Sami, is comin' home for a long visit."

"We'd love to be here for that," Gina said. "I love the sandwich I got from The Store yesterday. That Ted is a master chef for sure."

"He most definitely is," Finn said. "His creations are addictive. Be warned."

"Come on, Katie," Ethan said. "Time to move along."

"This is so calmin' and soothin'. I could get used to havin' a hot spring nearby," Katelyn said.

"You do have one nearby," Ian said as they began walking back to the trucks. "Just up behind The Store."

"That's right. Thanks for remindin' me," Katelyn said. "I do believe Kendra and I will be visitin' it this evenin'. She just texted me a big yes."

"There's one behind The Store?" Terry asked.

"Yes, indeed," Ethan replied as they walked past the crystal in the clearing.

"This day is only gettin' better," Gina said.

"I don't remember my grandparents mentionin' that hot spring. I was a kid when I came back to The Creek after we moved away. We came for visits every summer for about a month. Love this place. When we learned we had inherited the land after my grandmother passed, I was thrilled to get back here," Terry explained.

"Terry brought me here when we started datin' years ago, and we both said we'd love to live here one day," Gina said.

"Now, we're gonna do just that," Terry said, looking around. "This place is special. I can feel it in the air."

"We know," Katelyn said. "Can we walk to the northern boundary?"

"Sure," Ethan said as they set out.

It was about a mile to the boundary. They walked through thick forests, following animal paths most of the way. They found the northern boundary by following the GPS coordinates from the drone survey.

As soon as they stopped walking, Katelyn noticeably shivered for all to see.

"You okay?" Finn asked, looking at Katelyn.

"I think so," Katelyn replied. "Look over there," she said as she walked ahead of the others to a place in the trees. There, set between two huge old oaks, was a crystal as pure white as could be. It was the size of a bushel basket and glowed softly.

"Oh, my God!" Gina said. "I've never seen anythin' like this before."

"Me, either," Terry said.

"Don't take any pictures," Ian said as he saw the two of them getting ready to do just that.

"Why not?" Terry said.

"We don't want strangers all over the place up here. If you send that picture around, The Creek will be overrun with people tryin' to take that crystal for themselves and any other ones they might find. It would be a nightmare."

"I never thought of that," Gina said. "No pictures and no texts about what we find around here. I feel the need to protect this place."

"Why?" Terry said.

"I don't understand it, but I have a gut feelin', again, that we should not tell anyone about this place. There's somethin' magical about The Creek," Gina said.

"That's weird," Terry said, looking right at Gina. "My grandmother used to say the same thing. She was very protective of this place. Their farmhouse is a bit north of here. It borders the National Forest as well. We'll go by it later."

17

"Who lives there now?" Ethan asked.

"A second cousin and his family," Terry said. "They're kin to us and distant kin to the MacKinnon's."

"We know them," Ian said. "They grow some of the most beautiful mountain plants in the Blue Ridge."

"That's them," Terry said. "We haven't visited them in a long time. I mean, I haven't. Gina hasn't met them yet."

"I will today," Gina said.

Katelyn was staring at the crystal and hadn't really heard much of what had been said.

"Earth to Katelyn," Finn whispered in her ear.

"Oh, sorry," Katelyn said as she focused. "I got lost in the energy of that crystal."

"We know how you love crystals," Ethan said. "Time to get goin'."

They were back at the shop setting appointments for the Bancroft's to meet with Ian and Katelyn to begin the detailed process of designing their new home and barn.

"See you tomorrow at The Store," Ethan said as Gina and Terry took their leave.

"Sure thing," Terry replied.

"That crystal in their field was amazin'," Finn said.

"The one in the forest was hummin'," Katelyn said softly.

"Really?" Ian asked.

"Yes," Katelyn replied. "Its energy rippled out into the forest for quite a ways."

"Ya know," Ethan said, "Those crystal caves aren't too far from there. I wonder if those crystals are from The Crystal Caves?"

"You know where they are?" Ian asked.

"Not specifically. Miss Cora has always said they're up aways from Emily's place. And, since we didn't see them on the Bancroft's land, they must be north of there," Ethan said.

"Makes good sense," Finn agreed.

"I'll look at the land maps and see if I can pinpoint them," Ian said.

"You won't find them," Katelyn said. "They're a part of The Magic here. Only those that need to find them will be shown where they are."

"You're probably right," Ian said. "The Magic is in charge around here, and we protect The Magic. Enough said."

"Time to eat," Finn said. "All that walkin' has made me hungry."

They had lunch and kept busy the rest of the day. Suppertime found folks relaxing and getting ready for the weekend. Kids finished their homework; chores were done, then The Creek settled in, watching the evening come along.

Katelyn was wrapped in a soft blanket, rocking on her porch, waiting for Sami to arrive.

"Hey, Katie girl," Kendra said from her porch next door. "Waitin' for Sami?"

"Yes, Ma'am," Katelyn replied. "This is a gorgeous evenin' we have here. It was nice and warm today, close to bein' hot. And, now, the evenin' is bringin' cool air to our mountains. Love it."

"Me, too," Kendra said as they waved at folks leaving The Store. They watched Ted and Michael bring in the furniture and things, getting ready to close for the night.

"Give our Sami a hug and kiss from us," Michael called over to Katelyn.

"I sure will," Katelyn replied. "Sweet dreams, you two."

Ted and Michael waved as they went inside, locked the doors, and lowered the lights.

"Time for me to call it quits," Kendra said. "It's been a busy day."

"I hear ya," Katelyn said. "We walked the Bancroft's land all mornin'. I was ready for a nap after lunch. No deal, though. The boys kept me busy. I love my work."

"Try to get some sleep. I know you and Sami will be talkin' most of the night," Kendra said.

"Probably. Sleep well," Katelyn said as Kendra got up and opened her door. "You, too."

The night came on in all its glory, and it wasn't long before Sami drove into The Creek. Katelyn was up and out of her rocker before Sami was even in the driveway. She was pulling at Sami's door the minute Sami turned off the engine.

They grabbed each other and hugged, laughed, and cried all at the same time.

"I thought I'd never get here," Sami said when they finally separated.

"Same here," Katelyn said.

They grabbed Sami's stuff and headed inside. They put her things in her room and then made a beeline for the kitchen.

"Hungry?" Katelyn said. "There's lasagna in the frig."

"Starvin'," Sami said as she made a plate and put it in the microwave. "You make this?"

"Yup. Yesterday for Finn and me," Katelyn said. "I told him we had to save some for you."

"He agreed because he didn't want you to get after him," Katelyn said.

"You know I would," Sami said as they sat at the table. "This is heavenly."

"So, what's new with you?" Katelyn asked as they settled in the living room.

They talked for about two hours; then, both yawned deeply at the same time.

"I need some sleep," Katelyn said.

"It's no wonder after stompin' around in the woods all mornin'," Sami said.

"You, too, being up since five with last-minute emergencies," Katelyn said as they turned off the lights and walked down the hall.

"Breakfast at The Store?" Sami said when they got to her room.

"Yes, Ma'am," Katelyn replied. "Sleep well, my Sami. You're home safe in The Creek."

"Love you forever and always," Sami said as she flopped onto her bed.

"Love you forever and always," Katelyn said as she went into her room. The last thought in Katelyn's head was of that huge crystal in the woods. There was something familiar about it. She knew that crystal but couldn't remember ever being in that part of the forest in her life. Probably The Magic at work again. Always The Magic.

The girls slept deeply. The Creek was surrounded in protective energy as always.

CHAPTER 2

It was the weekend, and Saturday found Sami and Katelyn walking into The Store around nine for breakfast.

"Look who's finally home," Ted hollered out as he and Michael saw the girls at the same time.

They scooped Sami up into a huge hug that seemed to last forever.

"Now, this is what I call a homecomin'," Sami said, hugging the guys.

"You look great," Michael said when they finally separated.

"She's lost weight," Ted declared. "Time to start feedin' this girl some down home-cookin'."

"I agree," Sami said as they walked into the dining room. "Ted, you know what I like."

"Yes, I do, darlin'. I'll get things goin' right now," Ted replied.

"I'll grab the juice and coffee," Katelyn said.

"Looks who's darkened our doorway," Finn said, coming up the steps into the dining room. "Give a squish, girl."

"Good to see your handsome self again, Finn," Sami said. "You are definitely easy on the eyes."

"You got him blushin', Sami," Ted said, carrying orders to the table. "Breakfast for you, Finn?"

Yes, sir," Finn said. "You got the fixin's for a good ole country breakfast back there?"

"You know I do," Ted said. "Get yourself some coffee, and I'll be right back."

"Grab one for me, too, Ted," Hal said as he joined the group at the table. "Sami, great to see you back home."

21

"Thanks, Hal," Sami said. "Good to see you, too. Katelyn tells me you're designin' frames from the downed trees from the summer. Great idea."

"I am," Hal said. "I've got a couple in my truck. I'll go fetch 'em."

Hal was right back, and everyone took a look at his designs.

"These are beautiful, Hal," Katelyn said. "I love the different shapes. It really shows the lines of the wood."

"Here," Michael said. "Put this behind it and see how it looks with the picture in it."

"Oh, my God," Sami said. "This is magnificent."

"It truly is," Finn said. "That frame makes the picture come alive."

"I love this picture," Ted said, laughing with the others. "I think Ted and I look great next to our crystal selves."

"That was some day," Hal said.

"It sure was," Finn said. "And those crystal Ted and Michael statues are still out there. They look brand new."

"That's The Magic for ya'," Hal said.

"Here's your big breakfast, boys," Ted said, placing dishes on the table. "I figured y'all might want to sample a few things, so have fun."

"Ted, you always know what we're thinkin' when it comes to food," Sami said, scooping up some hash.

"Yes, I do. I'm the food psychic hereabouts," Ted said, taking a bow.

"Oh, boy. Now you've done it," Michael said from the front room." I'm gonna have to enlarge all the doorframes in this place."

"Wiseass," Ted hollered back.

Folks ate, talked, and enjoyed themselves with anyone who came into the place. Sami got a text a bit later as some folks were leaving.

"Katelyn, Jordan wants to know if we want to come by in a bit," Sami said.

"Fine with me, as soon as I can move," Katelyn said, laughing and pointing at Finn and Hal. "Can you guys even breathe after eatin' that big breakfast?"

"Not much," Hal replied, laughing. "I think I'm gonna sit here and have another cup of coffee."

"I'll do the same," Finn said. "Say 'Hey' to Jordan from us."

"We will," Sami said as she and Katelyn went to the register to settle their bill.

"Later, girls," Michael said as they left The Store.

"I'll drive," Katelyn said as they freshened up before going to Jordan's. "You had a long drivin' day yesterday, and I love to pamper my best friend."

"I like your plan," Sami said as they got into Katelyn's SUV and set off for Jordan's farm.

Jordan was waiting for them on the porch.

22

"Sami," Jordan said as he hugged her. "It's great to have you back home."

"Great to be back home, Jordan," Sami said. "I love travelin' around and learnin' about the history of the towns and cities we're workin' in. I love redesigning each place with special touches just for that location. I do. But I love comin' back home again the best. Back to this home."

"Speakin' of that," Katelyn said, winking at Jordan.

"I saw that," Sami said. "What have you two been up to?"

"Well, Sami," Jordan said. "We've been talkin' about you bein' home here, and we think you should relocate to The Creek permanently."

Sami looked at Katelyn and then hollered out, "Yes. I love the idea. I'd be happy to make this place my permanent home."

"I was hopin' you'd say that," Katelyn said with tears flowing down her cheeks.

"Katie," Sami said, crying, too.

"Now you two got me cryin'," Jordan said as George flew over to join them.

George gave a squawk as well.

They laughed as Katelyn said, "Looks like George approves of the idea, too."

Jordan winked at George as he said, "Oh, he does, for sure. I'm learnin' eagle-speak rather well."

George squawked a few times at this, making them all laugh.

"Let's celebrate a bit before we get down to business," Jordan said as they walked into the kitchen.

"You joinin' us, George?" Katelyn said, holding the door open for him. He walked right in and settled near the end of the breakfast bar.

"I swear that eagle knows just what we're sayin'," Sami said, winking at George. He lifted a wing at Sami, making Jordan and Katelyn laugh.

"What do you ladies want to drink?" Jordan asked. Juice was handed out to everyone, and Jordan made a toast. "Sami, welcome home. I love ya. Katelyn loves ya, and it seems George does, too. This is where you belong."

They raised their juice bottles, clanking them together, and took a drink.

"I gotta' tell ya, this feels perfect," Sami said. "Just one thing, where am I gonna live?"

"With me," Katelyn said. "We'll figure out the rest later."

"I've got too much stuff for your place," Sami said. "Is Kendra's other house free?"

"I believe it is," Katelyn said. "Let's ask her."

"Hey, Katelyn," Kendra said, answering her phone.

"Hey, Kendra. I have you on speaker with Jordan and Sami," Katelyn replied. "We have a question for you."

"Hey, Sami. Welcome home," Kendra said. "Hey, Jordan. Is George behavin' himself.?"

Jordan looked over at George, saying, "Most of the time." George squawked at Jordan.

"I heard that; hey, George," Kendra said. "So, what is your question for me?"

"Kendra, is your other house free right now? The one on the other side of yours?" Sami asked.

"Yes, it is," Kendra replied. "Why?"

"I'd like to rent it from you. I'm movin' to The Creek permanently as soon as possible," Sami said.

"Hot damn!" Kendra hollered, jumping all over the place. "Best news I've heard all day."

"I take it that means I can rent the house?" Sami said, laughing with Jordan and Katelyn.

"Of course," Kendra said. "I'll help you arrange for movers and all when you're ready."

"Oh, my God. I haven't even begun to think about that. I accept your offer and all the advice you can give me," Sami said.

"You're in good hands with Kendra," Katelyn said. "We'll stop by after we're finished at Jordan's."

"I'll be waitin'," Kendra said. "You tell anyone else yet?"

"No, this just happened," Sami said. "Hey, don't tell anyone. I'll tell them at supper tonight."

"Great idea," Kendra said. "See ya later."

"Bye," the three of them said as the call ended.

"Oh, my Sami, I don't think I can take this," Katelyn said. "I've wished we could be together again since we left The Crystal Village in Alabama, but I never dreamed this could happen. Best news I've heard all day, too."

"It sure as hell is," Jordan said. "Now, I get to collaborate with the exquisite mind of our Sami right here at home. That's whenever she's here."

"True that," Sami said. "I've been talkin' with my bosses, and we've figured out a tentative schedule for me to work from home every three weeks. They said I need to keep some semblance of sanity about me."

"I agree with them," Katelyn said. "Especially now that home is here in The Creek."

"Ditto," Jordan said, and George squawked with him.

"You said it, George," Sami said, raising her juice bottle in a salute to George.

"I can't even think right now," Katelyn said. "So, Jordan, was there a specific reason you wanted us to come over?"

"Oh, yeah. There is," Jordan said. "I know you were on The Rise with me, Sami. I haven't been able to think that whole thing through without fallin' to pieces." Jordan stopped as he began to cry. "I know it all happened, but it all seems so bizarre that I can't get a handle on it. So I told The Magic to leave me alone from now on. I don't know what else to do. Can you two help me?"

George walked over to Jordan and rested a wing on his leg.

"George knows how upset you are," Sami said. "The creatures of the wild have a special way of focusin' in on us humans."

"I know they do," Jordan said. "Thank God for George. I talk to him all the time. Sometimes, I even think he understands me. Either way, he listens, and sometimes that's all I need. Someone to listen to me."

"Jordan, it's been weeks since The Battle on The Rise. You could have called me over anytime," Katelyn said, going over to Jordan and laying her hand on his arm.

"I know, but I didn't want to burden you," Jordan said.

"I'm havin' a bit of trouble understanding the whole thing myself," Katelyn said. "I try to think about it for only a few minutes at a time. More than that, and I think I'm goin' crazy."

"But you understand The Magic. I don't. I don't have any of the powers or gifts you have. I'm just a guy livin' on a farm with an eagle with attitude," Jordan said.

"I know I've been given these sacred gifts or powers or whatever they call them," Katelyn said. "I don't really know how all this works, either. I just found out about this whole thing when I came back to The Creek a few months ago. All new to me, too."

"And, Sami, what about you? Flying around and all. You're a warrior if ever I saw one," Jordan said.

"Spill, girl," Katelyn said. "After all, we all have that tattoo on our shoulders."

"What the hell is that all about? It looks like a dragon's tail," Jordan said. "Dragons aren't real. They're just fantasy. I swear I'm asleep and woken up in a different dimension."

"Nope. This is the real dimension we've all been born into," Katelyn said, being a wise ass.

"Funny girl," Jordan said. "How am I supposed to go on with all this stuff in my head?"

25

"Okay, Jordan. I do understand," Katelyn said. "I talked with Sami about it, and that seems to help. I also accept the fact that The Magic is real. Those two things are helpin' me cope with everythin.' So, we need to talk about this a lot. Just like we are now. Sami and I are here for you."

"That makes a huge difference. I can feel my anxiety level gettin' lower as we talk," Jordan said.

"Good. Now, about The Magic. What are your thoughts there?" Sami asked. "Only answer if you want to."

Jordan was quiet for a minute, then said, "Well, I know it must be real. I've seen stuff in The Creek that can only be explained because of The Magic. Miss Cora helped a lot of us understand the mystery of The Magic just before the battle. I accept that. This is my one big question: Why me? Why did they give me that crystal sword and make me fly it over to you?"

"Good question," Katelyn said. "I don't have an answer. I think it must have somethin' to do with balancin' the energy in the universe. That's all I got."

"That's a hell of a lot more than I've come up with," Jordan said. "I'll accept that for now."

"Me, too," Sami said. 'It doesn't explain everythin', but it's a start."

George squawked a lot, showing his approval.

"Thanks, George," Jordan said. "This all helps. It's good to hear you guys don't really know why, either. I don't feel so alone. Thank God you're here."

"We feel the same way about you," Sami said. "We'll keep talkin about all this every day if that's what it takes."

"Agreed," Katelyn said. "Jordan, I do believe you seem more relaxed now."

"I do, Katie. Thanks to you, Sami, and George, who wants to go out flying right now," Jordan said as he followed George to the door, opening it for him. George flew off into the sky with a squawk of thanks.

"I love that eagle," Katelyn said as they settled around the island once again.

"So do I," Jordan added. "Now, Sami, I have those printouts for us to look at on Monday. Not now. I do believe you're on vacation."

"I agree," Sami said. "You're comin' to supper tonight, right?"

"I wouldn't miss it," Jordan said. "I feel much better and will be able to enjoy myself more than I thought I would before we talked. I have an idea, Sami. How about we make my den our headquarters? That way, we can be in the same place when we come up with our crazy ideas."

"I like that idea," Sami said. "Once I tell the bosses about my move here, I'll have them send new computer equipment for me to your house, along with furniture and all."

"That sounds great," Jordan said, slapping a high five with Sami.

"There will be no working during Sami's vacation," Katelyn said, trying to sound stern.

"Yeah, right," Sami and Jordan said, laughing at Katelyn. "We need to spend a little time together on Monday, as we planned, to finalize a few things so the next phase of plans can be put into action for the property I'm currently workin' on."

"Okay, just this one thing," Katelyn said. "I'm gonna count on George makin' sure you two don't go crazy with work."

"I'm sure he'll keep an eye on us," Jordan said. "He seems to know a lot about stuff in general."

"He sure does," Sami said as they saw George peeping in the window.

"I swear that bird has sonar capabilities," Jordan said, making a face at George. George squawked loudly at Jordan.

They talked about other things for a bit; then, it was time to leave.

"So glad you two came by today," Jordan said. "I do feel more at ease with the whole thing."

"Good," Sami said.

"Time for lunch, then we need to run a few errands into Pine Ridge," Katelyn said.

"Later," they all said as the girls drove off.

"George, I know you heard every word," Jordan said. "Thanks for bein' my confidant. I love ya. George."

"Same here, Jordan," George said as he brushed his wing against Jordan's leg.

The man and eagle stood side-by-side, lost in silence for a spell.

"Well," Jordan said quietly, "Time for some lunch for both of us."

"Later, Jordan," George said and took to the sky.

Jordan spent the afternoon cleaning house and watching a soccer game before getting ready for the gathering at The Store.

"Boy, Jordan sounds like he's about to crash and burn from his experience in the battle," Katelyn said. "I'm worried about him."

"So am I," Sami said. "It seems talkin' with us helped, though."

"I got that impression, too," Katelyn said as they parked on the street near the diner in Pine Ridge.

"Diner food?" Sami said.

"Absolutely. No reason to go home then come back this way," Katelyn said as they walked into the diner.

They enjoyed their lunch, ran their errands, and were back in The Creek by mid-afternoon.

"Hey, girls," Kendra said from her porch.

Katelyn and Sami walked over to chat with Kendra.

"Hey, girl," Kendra said, hugging Sami.

"Hey, yourself," Sami replied.

"Welcome home for good," Kendra said as they sat down.

"I am over the moon excited about movin' here," Sami said.

"Me, too," Kendra said. "Here's your house key and garage remote."

"Don't we need to sign papers and all?" Sami said, looking excited.

"No. We're all set. Your rent is the same as Katelyn's," Kendra said. "You can tell her."

"One hundred dollars a month, everything included," Katelyn said, laughing at the expression on Sami's face.

"Really? Why?" Sami asked.

"Because I said so," Kendra replied.

"Okay, I accept," Sami said, taking the keys and remote from Kendra.

"Let's talk about movin' from one state to another. How much stuff do you have?" Kendra asked.

"I have a two-bedroom apartment. One room is my artist center. I have a drafting table and chairs for the art studio and the regular house. I will give most of the regular furniture to charity. The mattress and upholstered chair will be thrown out. My personal stuff will need to be packed and shipped with my art studio stuff. No appliances besides my Keurig will come home with me," Sami said.

Kendra laughed at this. "I love my Keurig, too."

"I love my whistling tea kettle," Katelyn said.

"I know packers and movin' companies in the Montgomery area. I'll contact them and get the best deal I can. When are you thinkin' of going back there?"

"I have to inform my bosses of my move first. I'm sure they'll be thrilled," Sami said. "I have about two months of vacation, so I don't think getting' time off will be a problem. I can always work from Montgomery while I'm packin' the place."

"That sounds good," Kendra said. "I can't wait to see people's faces when you tell them you're comin' home to The Creek for good."

"I still can't believe this is happenin'," Sami said with tears in her eyes. "It feels so right, like I should have been here all along."

"Funny how that happens," Kendra said, sneaking in a wink that Katelyn didn't see.

"I love the whole thing. All of it," Katelyn said. "Kendra, Sami, and I spent some time over at Jordan's, as you know. He is confused, angry, and a bit scared about all that happened to him on The Rise. We talked for a bit, and he said he's not so anxious now. George is there for him as well. I swear that eagle knows exactly what we're sayin'. Anyway, Sami and I need your help with ways to help him."

"I wondered about him," Kendra said. "He hasn't been around much. That's what got me wonderin'. I'm glad you two spent some time with him. The Magic can be overpowerin' for the good guys sometimes. First, we need to send Reiki every day. Then, we need to ask The White Light to surround and protect him. I'll stop by in a day or two and see how he's doin'. Is he comin' to supper?"

"Yes," Sami replied. "He said he wouldn't miss it for anythin'."

"That's a good sign," Kendra said. "Now, are you bakin' for tonight, Katelyn?"

"Yes, I am," Katelyn said, standing up. "That's our next chore."

"Well, get to it," Kendra said. "I can't wait to smell all the good scents waftin' over here from your house.

"I'm sure we'll need a taste tester," Sami said as they crossed the lawn.

"Finn has his radar on. He'll be over in about an hour to grab some cookies," Katelyn said. "You can set your watch by him."

Katelyn and Sami got busy making cookie dough, the mayonnaise cake batter, and frosting. The cookies were baking for about ten minutes when they heard Finn's truck pull in.

"I told ya he'd be here about now," Katelyn said as the back door opened and Finn walked in.

"Just in time," Finn said, kissing Katelyn. "Gotta pay the baker."

"Smooth move, Romeo," Sami said as Finn picked her up, swung her around, and hugged her.

"Great to see you, Sami," Finn said, setting her back down on the floor.

"Ditto, Mr. Finn," Sami said, curtseying as the women from the old days did.

"Oh, you two," Katelyn said as she took the cookies from the oven and placed them on cooling racks. "Don't even think about it, Finn. They're way too hot right now."

"I'll give them five minutes," Finn said.

"Deal," Katelyn said as she put two more pans of cookies in the oven.

"This frosting is great," Finn said.

Katelyn looked over at him, and he was holding a spoonful of frosting in his hand.

"Go ahead, then leave the rest alone. I need it for the cake," Katelyn said, laughing with Sami at Finn's antics.

"So good," Finn said, taking his time eating the frosting.

"Is your mom bakin' apple pies?" Sami asked.

29

"Yes, Ma'am," Finn answered. "Four of them. She's got dad peelin' apples."

Katelyn looked at Finn and saw Jay pretending to peel apples. "I see Jay is helpin' out as usual."

"Dude," Finn said. "Ya look a little thin to me."

"Always the wise guy," Jay replied.

"I love seein' and hearin' spirits," Sami said.

"I would hope so after The Battle and all," Jay replied. "I love mom's pies, and your cookies are decadent, Katie girl."

"Thanks, Jay," Katelyn said. "Love you to pieces, too."

"Anythin' new in the spirit world?" Finn asked.

"We're a bit concerned about your Jordan. He isn't takin' all this Magic stuff well," Jay said. "We saw you two talkin' with him. That definitely helped calm him a lot. We like the Reiki thing and are already surroundin' him with protective energy. We don't want to lose him. He's helped The White Light so much, we think of him as one of our own."

"Thanks for the update, Jay. It means a lot to us here on the Earth plane," Katelyn said.

"Bro, leave the cookies alone," Jay said, watching Finn. "If I can't have any, then neither can you."

Katelyn and Sami laughed at Jay and Finn.

"Go ahead, Finn. Have a couple of cookies. The cold water's in the frig," Katelyn said as Finn started in on the cookies.

"No fair," Jay said. "I haven't had real food in months."

Katelyn placed her hands in front of her as she said," I humbly ask The White Light for Jay to become human again for a little while to enjoy the cookies and get smothered in hugs and kisses from us. My eternal thanks for your compassion."

In an instant, Jay was human again.

"Bro!" Finn said, grabbing his brother in a big hug.

"Hey, don't hog the guy," Katelyn said, elbowing Finn to make him let go of Jay.

"Katie, girl," Jay said as he wrapped her up in a big hug.

"My turn," Sami said as Jay hugged her.

"Thanks to the Divine for this special time," Finn said, bowing respectfully.

A flash of soft light went through the room.

"These are heavenly," Jay said with his mouth full.

"There's a little left-over lasagna in the frig," Katelyn said.

"Mine," Jay said, putting the lasagna in the microwave. "Eatin' is one of the things I miss the most, besides all the people around here."

"We know," Finn said, punching his brother in the arm.

"Right back at cha'," Jay said, returning the favor.

Jay winked at Sami as he said, "Sami, it's a good thing you're here for a while. Katelyn really misses you."

"I miss her, too, and everybody in The Creek," Sami said. "Y'all are really special people to me."

"How's the work on the URR comin' along?" Finn asked.

"It's amazin'," Sami said. "Jordan is a first-class researcher, and his articles are perfect. Easy to read and understand by the general public. We've had lots of great comments about the URR displays in each of the hotels we've finished."

"Sounds great," Finn said.

"Jay, is there anythin' goin' on we need to be aware of?" Katelyn asked.

"Not that I know of. You know I don't know everythin'. They do keep me informed about y'all down here, though. It seems this is a time of rest and quiet. Katelyn sent The Dark into the nether regions for a long, long time. No wonder Jordan is feelin' helpless. He'll recover in time with your help," Jay answered.

"Good to know," Katelyn said.

"Thanks for the update," Finn said. "We are in need of rest and positive energy around here for everyone. It's been a busy year battling The Dark Force."

"Amen to that," Sami said.

"Tonight's gatherin' will be a great way to have fun and enjoy each other," Katelyn said.

"You're comin' tonight, right?" Finn asked Jay.

"I am," Jay said. "Wouldn't miss it."

"So, Jay, I gotta ask this question," Katelyn said.

"We knew you would," Jay replied.

"Where in the blazes did that tattoo come from? What's it for?" Katelyn asked,

"I can't tell you because I don't even know," Jay answered her.

"It is really cool," Sami said. "I like mine. Jordan's not too sure about it. He knows he didn't get it on his own. He said it looks like a dragon's tail and that dragons aren't real. He is angry about havin' it, especially without bein' given any reason for it."

"I can understand that," Jay said, agreeing with Sami. "I don't have any other information about the tattoo you three share. I'm sure you will be told about it when the time is right. That's all I got."

"Not much, but thanks anyway," Katelyn said, sticking her tongue out at Jay.

"That's gonna cost you another cookie," Jay said as he bit into one. "Absolutely sensuous."

"Time for me to go back to being a ghost," Jay said as he hugged each of them.

"Have Mom and Dad seen you lately?" Finn asked.

"No. I'm headin' over there now to watch them make those pies," Jay replied as he became his ghost.

"Maybe The Divine will let you be human with them for a while, too."

Another flash of light filled the room.

"Thanks so much, " Finn said. "Our folks are gonna love this."

"Later," Jay said as he vanished.

Diane and Hank were working on the third pie when Jay appeared in the kitchen.

"Hey, Mom, Dad," Jay said. "Yes, I'm real."

"Oh, my stars," his mom said as she grabbed him and cried, holding him for the longest time.

"Join in, Dad," Jay said, holding his arm out to wrap around his dad.

"This is beyond wonderful," Diane said. "Is anythin' wrong with you bein' here for real.?"

"Nope," Jay said as they all sat down. "I was over at Katie's watching Finn steal her cookies. She saw me pretendin' to peel apples and asked if I could be real for a while. So, I was. She makes the most delicious cookies, Mom."

"Yes, she does," his dad replied. "Did you and Finn leave any for tonight?"

"We did. Katelyn cut us off," Jay replied, laughing. "Finn asked if I had been over recently, and I said not in a while. So, he suggested I stop by, knowin' how much I love your pies, Mom. He asked if I could be real for you for a while, and They said yes. So, here I am."

"Thanks, everyone over there," Diane said, kissing Jay on the cheek.

"I love what you did with my blue flannel shirts. Making pillows out of them and giving a few to Finn was genius," Jay said.

"Thanks, Jay," Diane said. "I got the idea on the web. You know how much I love to sew fun stuff, and your dad helped, too."

"I do believe two of the pies are done," Jay said, looking in the oven.

"They are," Diane said as she put them on cooling racks on the stovetop. "You need to wait a while until they settle and cool down some."

"I know," Jay said. "Need some help, Dad?"

"Nope," his dad replied. "I'm done. Here, honey, mix the next batch."

"So, Mom, how's your gift comin' along?" Jay asked.

"Miss Cora and I meet once a week, and she's teaching me tons of stuff," Diane said. "I have a gig in Pine Ridge once a month at the library. The ladies there love it when I come in. They promote me, and we are always booked up."

"That's great, Mom," Jay said. "Dad, you keepin' busy?"

"You know I am," his dad replied. "My work keeps me out of mischief."

Diane looked at Hank, then said, "We miss you terribly. These little visits help a lot, and I thank The Divine for each and every one of them. "

"Me, too, Mom," Jay said, kissing her on the cheek.

"Diane, I do believe that pie is ready for samplin'," Hank said

"I'll get the ice cream and whipped cream," Jay said.

"All right, you two, let's sample this pie," Diane said as she put pie on their plates and brought them to the table.

Ice cream and whipped cream were added, and they enjoyed Diane's creations for a while.

"This is heavenly," Jay said, scooping more ice cream onto his spoon. "Just what I needed."

"After all those cookies at Katelyn's, I'm surprised you have room for pie," Diane said.

"I always have room for more," Jay said, pointing to his dad. "And so does Dad."

"He's right," Hank said, rubbing his belly.

The shadows began to show just a little, and Diane broke their silence as she said, "Well, it's time to pack up and get to The Store."

"Mom, Dad, this has been great," Jay said as he hugged them both. "It's time for me to go back to being a ghost. I'll check in with you all evenin'."

They hugged for a minute more; then Jay dissolved back into his energy form. He waved and then disappeared as usual.

"Well, Hank, let's clean up and get on to The Store. Folks will be arrivin' in a bit," Diane said with tears flowing down her cheeks.

Hank pulled his wife into a big hug, saying, "I know. I miss him, too."

They held each other for a long while, comforting each other with their shared love.

Ted and Michael had everything ready at The Store. Tables and chairs were set up on the porch since it was a warmer-than-usual fall evening. A few pop-up tents had been placed next to the porch with tables and chairs as well. Chairs had been set around the inside, too. Chairs were everywhere. Folks began arriving, parking along the road and across the way at Kendra's places.

"Hey, Ted," Hal said as he walked into The Store. "I put my frames at one of the tables under a tent just like you suggested. Anything I can help with?"

"Hey, Hal," Michael replied faster than Ted. "I could use your help for sure. Would you take this basket of plasticware and napkins out to the tables set up along the wall?"

"Sure," Hal said as he picked up the baskets. "I love all the tables under the windows thing. It works so well."

"Thanks, Hal," Ted said. "You can help me get the salads out next."

"Sure thing," Hal said, walking outside.

Sami, Katelyn, and Kendra arrived, carrying their specialty dishes, and were instructed to place them on the tables under the windows.

"This looks great," Sami said. "I like bein' the reason we all get together."

"So do we," Lanie and Mo said as they walked over.

Hugs were shared as more and more people arrived. It didn't take long before most of The Creek was gathered around The Store, hugging and sharing news and telling a tall tale or two.

The chiefs arrived together as if they were twins. Offerings of thanks were given, and the festivities got underway.

"Miss Cora, your cornbread is scrumptious as always," Mo said.

"Thanks, Mo, my pleasure," Miss Cora replied.

"The chicken barbeque is to die for," Ian said.

"Thanks, Ian. You know how I love to barbeque," Chief Charlie replied.

"And we love when you do," Hal added.

A while later, when most folks had finished eating, Sami deemed it the perfect time to share her news.

"Hey, Sami, it's great to have ya' back in The Creek," Miss Cora said. She was sitting right next to Sami and Katelyn.

"Thanks, Miss Cora. I appreciate that," Sami said.

Sami looked at Katelyn, and they winked at each other.

"Folks," Sami began as she stood up, "Y'all know how much I love each and every one of you. I love bein' here with my Katelyn."

"We love you bein' here, too," Bubba hollered out.

Folks laughed at this as Bubba and Earl weren't known for sayin' much.

"Thanks, Bubba. I appreciate the sentiment," Sami said, nodding at Bubba and Earl.

"She tried some of the shine," Earl said. "She's a keeper."

"Sure is," Bubba added.

"I think Katie told some of you that I'm here for a long week, compliments of my bosses. They said I needed a vacation. I agreed with 'em. Katelyn and I have been talkin' a lot, as we always do, and I have decided to make The Creek my permanent home from now on."

A moment of silence erupted into hoots and hollers for the longest time.

"Hot damn! Best news we've heard in a while," Hal said, running over to hug Sami.

Sami was smothered in hugs and love from everyone for quite some time. Folks talked about this great news and started planning all kinds of things to help Sami move home. Eventually, things calmed down some, and questions were asked.

"Where ya' gonna live, girl?" Scott asked.

"I've already been told I am livin' on the other side of Kendra," Sami replied.

"Good idea," Miss Cora said. "Our Katie has been missin' you somethin' fierce."

"How soon do you think you'll be here for good?" Ted asked.

"I have to arrange things back in Montgomery. I spoke with my bosses this afternoon, and they're thrilled for me. I told my landlady, and she's just as happy. So, after my vacation here at home, I'll go back to the current project for a few days, then head to Montgomery. Kendra is helping with the packers and movers and all," Sami explained.

"I like the sound of that," Ethan said. "I suspect we'll have to tether Katelyn to the ground just to keep her focused on her work."

Everyone laughed at this, and the ideas and suggestions kept coming.

"While we're all helpin' Sami plan the rest of her life with us, the deserts are ready," Ted said. "Help yourselves."

The dessert table was magnificent, as always. Moans and groans of pure delight were heard all around.

"Oh, Sami, should you need any crystals for your new place, I know where you can find some. Just ask Ted and Michael," Jordan offered.

"Cute, Jordan," Michael said, shaking his finger at Jordan.

"Oh, yeah, speaking of crystals," Katelyn said. "Miss Cora, while Ethan and our crew were walkin' the Bancroft's land the other day, we came upon a magnificent white quartz crystal in the woods just over their northern boundary line. It was the size of one of these small tables anyway. Ethan mentioned he remembered hearin' somethin' about The Crystal Caves north of there, and I was wonderin' if you knew anything about them."

"Oh, Miss Cora, I remember the Bancroft name but haven't been able to place them. Could you help out with this, too?" Ian asked.

The place became quiet, waiting for Miss Cora to begin.

"Well, the first thing I want to talk about is the Bancroft family," Miss Cora began. "Ted, could ya fetch me a cup of tea, please?"

"Of course, Miss Cora," Ted replied.

"Now, about the Bancroft's. Their old family home is a ways north and east of here on the land they originally settled on. I heard about Gina and Terry, hey, there, inheriting Terry's grandparent's parcel. Sorry to hear about Miss Rose. She was a splendid lady. She was nearly one hundred years old if I remember right."

"Thanks so much, Miss Cora," Terry said. "She was one hundred and two and still lived in her home. My cousins moved in quite some time back to care for her and the place. I loved her more than the moon and stars. She was so special to me. I want to honor her with the farm we're buildin'."

"Terry, you are doin' just that, and I'm right proud of ya'," Miss Cora said. "You stop by any time you want. Now, the Bancroft's first settled here in the mid-1800s. They came from England up near Scotland. They arrived just like the rest of us. They were looking for a new life and brought just a few things with 'em. They settled about two hundred acres and began plantin' and settin' up a paddock for their horses. They got here in early spring. They built the first house with six rooms and two fireplaces, with one at each end of the cabin. They had three children, two dogs, and a bunch of cats who found their way to their farm over the summer. I do believe the foundation of that first cabin is still there for all to see. After about five years, they moved their house to the southern end of the property. There were bigger fields with a couple of creeks running through. Made it easier to get water to the farmhouse. This is the farmhouse that is in use today. It's been rebuilt and upgraded over time as needed.

"Now, as most of you know, the one thing that made the Bancroft place really special is the honey they produce. Terry, you tell everyone how that whole thing got started."

"Yes, Ma'am," Terry said as he stood up, touching his hat to Miss Cora.

"I sure do like it when you boys show respect," Miss Cora said.

"Always, Miss Cora," Terry replied. "Well, as I remember it, seems the second year the first Bancroft's settled here, they had a bit of a problem with honey bees. Seems they invaded one specific meadow like nobody's business from the first hint of a warm spring day to the last bit of warmth before old man winter came a-callin'. My ancestors wanted that meadow for the horses, but the bees ruled the place. I don't mean a few bees. There must have been thousands of them. Story goes that my greats-grandfather decided to follow those bees one evening to find out where their hives were. So he followed them for a few minutes into the woods. And the surprise that was waiting for him could have never been dreamed up.

"He came to a dead stop when he saw where those bees were goin'. There were a couple of big old dead oak trees covered with bees. They were flyin' into the center of the trunks one at a time. The sound was amazin'. Legend says it took near an hour for all the bees to get inside the tree trunks. Then, my greats-grandfather happened to look up at the upper branches, and he saw honeycombs all over those trees. He said it was a sight to behold with the last of the sun's rays shining through them. It made the grove look like it was made of gold.

"He hurried back home and told the family what he had found, and they worked out a plan to harvest some of that honey. It was made from the pollen of wildflowers. Y'all know how sweet that kind of honey is. I can see you do. Well, over time, they created a way to harvest honey from the branch combs without disturbin' the main trunks. Those bees were very industrious as they created a whole other hive near the southern border where the current farmhouse was built. My relatives harvested so much honey the first year that they began to sell it and have continued sellin' it to this day. It's called Golden Wildflower Honey from the Bancroft hives. To this day, we keep three meadows for the bees."

Folks applauded and called out for a few minutes.

"Thanks, Terry. That was told real well," Miss Cora said. "Now about The Crystal Caves and all. I'll tell ya the legend as it was told to me. When I finish, I'll need more tea and a piece of Katelyn's mayonnaise cake."

"Anythin' you want, Miss Cora," Katelyn said.

"I'm obliged," Miss Cora said. "Way back at the beginnin' of time, it seems The Magic needed a place to hide. So when the earth was ripped apart after Pangea, The Magic came to live in these here mountains. They're now called The Appalachian. Our part is the Blue Ridge, as you know. The Creek is one of the special places The Magic lives and is protected from the outside world. We protect The Magic with our lives."

There was a quiet agreeing from everyone present.

"Now, The Magic couldn't just live on the land. It needed a safe place and the powers that be made The Crystal Caves just for that purpose. We've all heard about the caves north of here, now north of where the next generation of Bancroft farms is gonna be. Katelyn told me that when Ethan and everyone was up there the other day, they found a big, huge white quartz crystal setting between trees. I feel that crystal is a guardian crystal, there to protect those caves.

"When I was a youngster, my friends and I tried all one summer to find those caves. We never did. As I grew older, I came to know that those caves aren't there for just anyone to find. They are well hidden in The Magic and are only shown to those who need to see them. I suspect it's to protect The Magic that lives in these here mountains.

"Legend says there's a fierce creature that protects those caves in the north. It sits at the entrance to keep people and The Dark Forces away. No one has ever been able to describe that creature. One man from a long time ago says he saw a great shadowy thing with wings and a long tail pacing out in front of that side of the mountain as if it were ready for a fight. He never did see the actual creature. But, then, he never went back to that spot either. He didn't relish comin' face-to-face with whatever that creature was.

"Most of us have seen the cave paintings over on the Tennessee side of the mountain. It shows a creature sittin' in front of a cave entrance. Above the creature and the entrance is what looks like a spaceship. There are lines that look like beams of light surroundin' the whole drawin'. Then there's the etchin' on that huge boulder over by the dig site. It's been photographed and analyzed all over the place without any final say as to what it is. It looks like a creature of some kind. Maybe a dinosaur. Maybe somethin' else. It's a mystery, for sure.

"There are a few other crystal caves around here. One of them is just up from the hot spring behind The Store. Most of us have walked around inside it. It sure is a beautiful sight to behold. I believe we all have a crystal or two from that cave. Seems Mother Earth is happy to share her gifts with us. Then there are those small crystals that showed up after that big storm a few weeks ago. Some of them are on the window sills inside.

"We know how precious crystals are and how they have energy that protects and heals us. Some of us here are Gifted with special powers that allow us to see spirits. Some of us are warriors sworn to protect The Magic. Most of us are regular folks with a knowing about The Magic. I deeply believe The Crystal Caves of the legend are here. I will protect them and The Special Powers and The Magic that lives in them for all my days."

There was a quiet silence for a bit as folks thought about what Miss Cora had told them. Then, they all heard the sound of tiny windchimes ringing through the place. They looked at the windchimes hangin' from the porch. They weren't moving. There wasn't any breeze to move them. The sound lasted just a few seconds, then was gone.

Jordan looked at Katelyn and winked. Sami looked at Kendra and smiled. Miss Cora saw all of it.

"Well, I'd say The Magic is happy with Miss Cora's recollection of the legend," Finn offered.

Folks agreed, and tea and a piece of mayonnaise cake were brought to Miss Cora.

"Folks, help yourselves to more desserts and coffee and tea or whatever makes ya' happy," Ted said.

A minute later, Ethan stood up and said, "Folks, I'd like to propose a toast to our Sami." Folks got on their feet and raised their glasses. "To our Sami. We love ya' to pieces and are beyond happy that you've come home to stay. May The Magic of The Creek bless you all your days."

"Here, here," was heard from everyone, and Sami showed her appreciation, throwing back a bit of shine from Bubba and Earl.

"Well done," Finn whispered in her ear.

"This stuff will rip the rust off a truck," Sami said, laughing.

Katelyn and Finn laughed along with her.

"Bless all your little ol' pea-pickin' hearts," Sami said to everyone.

"Miss Sami, that was real nice of ya' to do," Bubba said.

"You're ours forever," Earl added. "We'll be sure to leave a little some-thin' for ya' in a day or two."

"I appreciate your showin' me the love, fellas," Sami said, shaking hands with the boys.

They touched their hats and moved along.

"How anyone can drink this stuff and survive is beyond me," Sami said, wiping sweat off her forehead.

As usual, the desserts disappeared as folks enjoyed more of their favorites.

Jordan texted Katelyn, asking if they could meet the next day—just the two of them. Katelyn looked over at Jordan and nodded her head in response.

Things began to wind down, and folks took their leave. Some stayed to help the guys get ready for the morning.

Katelyn, Sami, and Kendra were the last to leave.

"This has been a great day," Sami said, looking at the others. "I'm so ex-cited to settle down here and have y'all as my family."

"Same here, our Sami," Ted said.

"Thanks for helpin' out," Michael said as he turned off the rest of the lights. "You know we appreciate it."

"We know," Kendra said as the girls walked out the side door. "See ya tomorrow."

"This air feels good," Katelyn said. "And look at that sky. There are the usual millions of stars shinin' bright."

"Get some sleep," Kendra said as they went to their front doors.

"I'll come by tomorrow to sign papers and all," Sami said. "Just let me know when."

Kendra waved as they went inside.

"I feel like a whole week has happened in just a few hours," Sami said, yawning as she walked to her room.

"Sweet dreams, my Sami," Katelyn said.

"Sweet dreams, my Katelyn, Sami said.

The Creek slept peacefully that night. The breeze was whispering secrets to The Crystal Caves about changes to come.

CHAPTER 3

Fall was in full swing on Sunday, and The Creek was lovin' it. The leaves put on quite the show with the changing colors, and smoke rose from chimneys all over the mountains. Katelyn and Sami slept in a bit and laughed when they saw the time.

"Guess we needed that sleep," Katelyn said after her shower. "And I didn't even have any shine."

"That shine gives ya' crazy dreams," Sami said, laughing. "And, no, I don't have a hangover."

"I figured as much," Katelyn said as they made their breakfast and settled at the kitchen table. "I think it was all our excitement for you movin' here and all."

"I agree," Sami said. "I'm goin' over to Kendra's in a bit to sign papers and whatever else she needs me to do."

"Okay," Katelyn said. "I've got a couple of boring errands to run, so I'll do that when you're over there."

"Sounds good," Sami was saying when they heard loud voices outside.

The girls stepped onto the front porch and laughed at what they saw. Seems someone had a sense of humor and had set up a mini football field in the meadow next to Katelyn's house. Folks were looking it over and laughing.

"Hey, Ted, how about we get some kids over here to play on this field later?" Scott said.

"Great idea," Ted replied from The Store's front porch. "I'll send an email out in a few."

"Wonder who did that?" Sami said.

"I don't know, but I have a few guesses," Katelyn said.

"Like what?" Sami asked.

"Jay, for starters," Katelyn said. "He loved football like no one you know."

"No fair figurin' that out so fast," Jay said, standing next to Katelyn and laughing. "Hey, Sami."

"Hey, Jay," Sami replied. "Wondered when you'd be making another appearance."

"That field looks great," Jay said. "I heard Ted say he would get the kids together this afternoon."

"Yup," Katelyn said. "The Creeks gonna love this."

"I'll be back," Jay said. "Love ya. Later." And Jay vanished as usual.

"Now, that's wicked awesome to be able to appear as a ghost whenever," Sami said.

"It is. We miss him somethin' fierce," Katelyn said. "We all appreciate The Divine's gifts of Jay both in spirit and as a real person." Katelyn bowed ever so slightly.

Sami bowed as well, then said, "I still find myself thinkin' about The Battle on The Rise. That's when Jay comes to mind. Makes me smile and feel at peace."

"Me, too," Katelyn said. "I think I'm gonna be processin' that whole thing for a long, long time. Seems Jordan will be, too."

"Absolutely," Sami said.

They stood on the porch for another minute or two, then went back inside.

"Guess we did sleep in," Katelyn said as they cleaned up the kitchen. "It's already past ten."

Sami's text alert sounded. She looked at it and said, "Kendra says to come over any time. I texted her in about twenty minutes. I've got a few emails to answer."

"Okay," Katelyn said. "I'll go run those errands in a few, too."

Katelyn texted Jordan to see if she could meet him soon, and he replied anytime.

"Later," Katelyn said to Sami, sitting at the kitchen table answering emails.

"Later," Sami replied without looking up.

"Hey, Jordan," Katelyn said as she walked through the back door. "George greeted me with a fly-by."

"He's such a show-off," Jordan said, laughing. "I've got your favorite hot chocolate ready to go. Just say the word."

"Have at it," Katelyn replied, sitting at the island.

Jordan brought their mugs to the island and sat across from Katelyn.

"Tastes great. Thanks," Katelyn said, sipping away.

"You're always welcome," Jordan said.

"I think I know why you want to talk," Katelyn said. "I got the same adrenaline rush when I heard Miss Cora mention The Crystal Caves. Right?"

"Yes," Jordan said, looking anxious.

"Talk, Jordan," Katelyn said.

"Okay. You know how I want The Magic to leave me alone so I can try to get a grip on all that's happened. Yeah, you know. So, when I heard Miss Cora mention The Crystal Caves and my heart skipped a beat, I was ready to get pissed off again. But then, something different happened. That's why I want us to talk. I'm not sure what it was. Maybe a deep sense of knowing about those caves or something. Somehow, I knew I was supposed to hear about them last night. And, it's not necessarily The Magic at work. Whatever IT is, it's bigger than The Magic. I mean, The Magic as I know it. Does this make any sense?"

"Yes, it does, Jordan," Katelyn said. "I got a sense of familiarity about them when I was walking the Bancroft's land the other day. Kind of like a hint of a distant, deep memory. Thing is, I've never been up there before. Ever. Even as a kid and all. Never had a reason to be that deep in the forest. And that crystal. Holy God, it's magnificent. All white and glowing like a laser was inside of it. Just sitting there between two old oaks like it's been there forever."

"Yeah, that's it," Jordan said. "As if I've known all about those caves from a long time ago. More than de ja vu even. It almost makes The Magic I know seem small. Not that it is. It's amazing and overwhelming at the same time. But those caves seem inviting and familiar. Almost as if there's nothing to worry about."

"Exactly," Katelyn said. "Don't worry about how much you have experienced about The Magic around here. Ya can't compare any one event to another. They're all incredible, whether small like all those little crystals that showed up after the storm or The Battle. They all have power in them. Let's sit quietly for a few minutes and think about The Crystal Caves and see what we come up with. Oh, I think George wants in."

"He does," Jordan said as he opened the back door, and George walked right in. "I see you've figured out how to knock on the door, wise guy."

"Squawk," George replied, whacking his wing on Jordan's leg.

"Hi, George," Katelyn said. "Thanks for the special greetin' today."

George raised his wing at Katelyn and winked.

"He just winked at me," Katelyn said. "Nice goin', George. Now you've learned how to flirt. Why not? A flirtin' eagle now lives in The Creek. Perfect."

They laughed, and George hopped around a bit to show his fun side. George finally settled down, and they got back to talking about The Crystal Caves.

"Okay. Ready?" Katelyn said.

"Yup," Jordan said and they each took a deep cleansing breath, blowing out through their mouths, and settled into silence with their eyes closed and hands resting on the island with their palms open, holding their twin crystals.

It was a short while later when Katelyn and Jordan opened their eyes at the same time.

"Well, what happened?" Jordan asked.

"It was amazing," Katelyn replied. "At first, I saw your cave and all the rooms in it. By the way, there are a lot more rooms than what we've seen so far. It would seem that they appear as needed depending on the task we are working on."

"I got the same thing," Jordan said. "That cave is beyond beautiful."

"Have you been out there since The Battle?" Katelyn asked quietly.

"No. I don't want to experience any more Magic. I'm on overload right now," Jordan replied.

"Thought so," Katelyn said. "No worries here. You'll go there when you feel the need. I saw that huge crystal in the forest, and it shot a beam of energy behind it as if it were pointing to a specific place. I couldn't make out just what it was tryin' to show me."

"I saw a deep forest with a cave set into the side of a mountain. It had a small opening but widened after walking a few steps into it. It was full of crystals, too. It had a place along one of the walls that looked like some kind of sleeping thing. Maybe a pallet of straw and grasses. It was quiet and comfortin', and the crystals glowed softly. It all felt familiar, just like when I heard Miss Cora talkin' about them. Not sure what's goin' on here."

"Me, either," Katelyn said. "It does feel like I've been there before—that I know for sure. Everythin' else is a mystery."

"What should we do now?" Jordan asked.

"Well, I do have one idea, but I'm not sure you're ready for it," Katelyn said.

"We need to go there, right?" Jordan said.

"Yup. You got it," Katelyn said. "Even though you don't want to be actively involved with The Magic, you're still pickin' up on some of the signals The White Light gives us. Don't be angry. There's a reason why all of this is happenin'. Just don't have the foggiest idea what it is."

"Okay. I can accept this for now," Jordan said. "Don't add anythin' else y'all."

"Oh, they hear you loud and clear," Katelyn said when a sunbeam shot through the kitchen.

"Good to know," Jordan said, laughing.

"I do love the way they keep us in the loop," Katelyn said, laughing as well. "I didn't get anythin' about the petroglyphs Miss Cora mentioned."

"Me, either," Jordan said. "Although I do think they're interestin', especially since they show some kind of huge creature in those caves. I love the speculation of it bein' an alien or dinosaur or whatever."

"Me, too," Katelyn said. "Gets the imagination goin'."

"Thanks for comin' by. This has made me feel okay," Jordan said.

"I'm glad we talked, too," Katelyn said. "There isn't anyone else I can talk to about those caves."

"I know," Jordan said as they walked outside.

George took off flying around the barn and then out over the field.

"He sure loves to fly," Katelyn said as they watched him for a minute.

"He sure does. Sometimes, I just stand in the field and watch him ride the thermals. So calmin' and soothin'," Jordan said.

"Oh, hey. I was just rememberin' to ask you somethin'. You remember that weird vision we had of us in old clothes in a cave mixin' potions or somethin'?"

"Oh, yeah, I do," Jordan replied. "I remembered it just this mornin'."

"I remembered it right after we left the field with Ethan and everyone the other day. It was a quick memory, then gone."

"Wonderin' why we're both rememberin' it now,? Jordan said.

"Don't know. It was a powerful vision in every detail," Katelyn said.

"I know," Jordan said, smilin'. "I remember that dress thing you were wearin'."

"Wiseass," Katelyn said.

"Guilty," Jordan said. "I'm sure Finn would love to see you in somethin' like that."

"Don't even think of mentionin' it to him," Katelyn said. "Did you get the email about the mini-football field next to my place?"

"I did, and I'll be there," Jordan replied. "Ted said around two. Can't wait to see it."

"Okay, then," Katelyn said as she walked over to her SUV. "I'm on my way. By George, wherever you are."

"I know he heard you," Jordan said. "Later."

Katelyn took care of her errands and was home a short while later.

"How were all your emails?" Katelyn said as she walked into the house.

"Most of them were simple. One was a bit detailed about a floor plan for the bridal suite at the Charleston property. It's all good now. We're combinin' the old south with current-day themes. It's been a little tricky, but I think we're finally there. The hotel owner will look it over and get back to me later this week. He knows I'm on vacation, so he's tryin' not to bother me too much," Sami explained.

"He shouldn't be botherin' you at all. You're on vacation," Katelyn said.

"I agree. That's why I reminded him of that exact fact," Sami replied. "He apologized profusely."

"Good. So, don't answer his emails until a week from tomorrow," Katelyn suggested.

"That's exactly what I plan on doin'," Sami said. "I'm hungry. Let's eat."

"Did you get everythin' sorted out with Kendra?"

"Yup. Just like you. No forms, just a verbal agreement between friends," Sami replied.

"I figured as much," Katelyn said. "I bake her goodies from time to time to show my love for her."

"I was thinking' of doin' a sketch of her houses as if lookin' from the porch of The Store," Sami said.

"Great idea," Katelyn replied. "I know she'll love it. She says she can't draw anythin' more than a short line."

"I know," Sami said as she brought their lunch to the table. "That's what gave me the idea. Dig in."

The girls enjoyed themselves, rememberin' some of their more colorful antics from the past.

The Creek was having a lovely Sunday afternoon as well. Folks began gathering on the field around two, and the kid's football game got underway. It was flag football, and all the kids were invited to play. Moms and dads were referees, and it was a blast watching them as well as the kids. Cheer groups were formed and took to rooting for their favorite team.

Half-time was called, and refreshments were shared. Everyone was having a grand time.

The game ended without any injuries, and it was deemed a tie. The kids were thrilled and asked if they could do this again next week. Folks said they'd think about it, and that seemed to satisfy the kids. Everyone went on home to supper and showers and getting ready for school and work the next day.

"Nice goin', Jay," Finn said quietly as folks cleaned the field.

"I thought so," Jay replied, walking next to Finn.

"It was a blast for The Creek," Finn said, looking at Jay. "What's goin' on, Jay?"

"There's gonna be a shift of energy soon. All good. Just want you to know it's comin'," Jay said.

"Okay," Finn replied. "As long as it's not another battle. The last one took all I had."

"They said I could give you a heads-up. I think Miss Cora and Emily have felt it already," Jay said.

"I wouldn't be surprised," Finn said as he walked over to Katelyn and Sami.

"Later," Jay said as he vanished.

"That was a blast," Sami said. "Those cheer kids worked really hard. I think their folks are takin' them to Hank's Diner for a reward."

"Great idea," Finn said. "I'm headed home. Dad has a project for the two of us. I think he said somethin' about getting ready for the cold."

"We're headed home, too," Katelyn said. "I've got crock-pot stew ready."

"Kendra said I could move in now if I wanted to. So I think I'll set up one of the bedrooms as an office. That way, I can spread stuff out and not bother Katie," Sami said.

"After dinner," Katelyn said.

Exactly," Sami replied. Then, Sami walked over to the house to give Katelyn and Finn a moment for themselves.

Finn wrapped his arms around Katelyn, and they shared a long kiss.

"I do like this," Katelyn said as they parted.

"Me, too," Finn replied. "I'm glad I stayed over the other night. And now, Sami has her own place. This is so awesome."

"In lots of ways," Katelyn said, running her hand down Finn's chest.

"Oh, Katie girl, don't get me started," Finn moaned as he kissed her again.

They finally parted with promises of spending some time together soon. The girls enjoyed their stew and then took Sami's office stuff over to her new house.

"I am so lovin' this," Sami said as they set up her office. "I see I'm going to need a few things. I'll order them and have them delivered here. Will you keep an eye out for them?"

"Of course," Katelyn said. "Kendra and I will take care of everything. You need a real computer desk and chair. The stuff back in Montgomery worked well for a while, but I remember you sayin' this past spring that you needed real office furniture."

"You're right about that," Sami said. "I'll order it this week after I have time to measure things and look through the business's online supply catalog."

"Sami, I seem to remember a desk and drawing table combo. Oh, my God, Sami! You should come to the shop with me tomorrow and look at all the stuff I have. It's the coolest stuff. The desk and drawing table morph into whatever you need. I'm sure Ethan and Ian have all the orderin' details. I love it."

"That's a fantastic idea," Sami said. "Do I have to get up early on my vacation and follow you?"

"Oh, God, no. Just come over when you're ready. I'll be in the office all day tomorrow. I'll be working on the plans for Gina and Terry's house. You can help out."

"I like the sound of that," Sami said. "Let's finish up here and set on the porch and watch the sunset."

"Deal," Katelyn said, and a little while later, that's where Kendra found them.

"Hi, y'all," Kendra said as she sat down. "I see you're settin' up house-keepin'."

"I am," Sami said. "I thought it would be a good idea to work from my new home so I wouldn't be botherin' Katie."

"And I appreciate that," Katelyn said.

"Good idea," Kendra said. "Let me know if you need any supplies. I have a ton of office stuff."

"I'll come by tomorrow and raid your stash," Sami said.

"The kids had a blast this afternoon," Kendra said as the sun began to sink below the treetops.

"They did," Katelyn replied. "I love this exact moment when the sun starts to throw beams through the trees just before it hides behind the mountains."

"My granny used to call it in the gloaming," Sami said.

"Your granny? Really?" Katelyn said.

"My ancestors lived on the earth a long time ago. We've always protected the planet," Sami said.

"Well, I learn somethin' new every day," Katelyn said.

"We all do," Kendra said.

"Look at that color," Sami said. "The sky is all shades of purple, pink, and a little gold."

Ted and Michael had just come outside to watch the sunset, too.

"That's incredible," Ted said, grabbing hold of Michael's hand.

A sunbeam shot through The Creek just as the sun disappeared below the mountains.

"I'll take that as some love from The Other Side," Michael said.

The sun was gone in just a few moments, and the night sky began to share its secrets.

"There must be a bazillion stars up there tonight," Ted said. "They look so perfect."

"They do, Ted," Katelyn said from across the road. "Makes a body wonder if there's life on any of them."

"I would think so," Sami said, winking at Katelyn and Kendra.

"I would hope so," Michael added. "I wouldn't want us to be the only life forms around. That would be sad."

"It would, indeed," Kendra agreed.

"Well," Ted said with a sigh, "Time to get back inside and close up. Sleep well, girls. Love ya'."

"We love you guys, too," Katelyn said as the girls waved them back into The Store.

Just as deep night fell on The Creek, Kendra saw a huge shadow fly across the treetops behind The Store.

"Look at that," she said, pointing to the sky.

"That's huge," Sami said.

"What the hell is that?" Katelyn asked as they watched it circle back and fly over The Store and then over them.

"It was huge," Sami said. They walked around the houses but didn't see it again. "It looked to be flying east of here," Sami said as they came back to the front yard.

"I've never seen anything that big flyin' around here before," Katelyn said. "Have you, Kendra?"

Kendra looked at them for just a second before replying, "Yes, I have. It was back in the winter or early spring. I felt restless, wrapped up in a blanket, and stepped out onto the porch. I saw that thing fly over The Store, then over the house, just like tonight. I have no idea what it is."

"It's way too big to be an owl or eagle," Sami said.

"I agree," Katelyn said. "I'll be sure to write this all down in my journal."

"Crazy place we live in," Kendra said. "Time for me to get on home. Thanks for the company. Sleep well."

"Sweet dreams," Sami said as she and Katelyn went inside and settled for the night.

Katelyn sat quietly in her room for a bit. She was getting that crazy sensation that she knew what that huge flying shadow was. It was just a tiny bit of a distant memory, but it was familiar to her. It seemed The Magic was beginning something again. It was not a bad feeling like something evil was afoot. It was more of a knowing that whatever was about to happen, she had some past with it.

CHAPTER 4

Monday morning found Jordan in the barn talking with George.

"George," Jordan said. "I know this may sound crazy, but I want to walk out to My Cave before I start my work."

"Not crazy at all, Jordan," George replied. "That place has healing energy."

"It does, George. Please join me," Jordan said as he walked out of the barn and headed over the field to The Cave.

Jordan held the bushes aside for George, and they walked into the big room. The crystals were softly glowing, emitting a soft musical sound.

Jordan stood at the edge of the room for a long while with his eyes closed, taking in the healing energy.

He sighed and said, "Just what I needed. I feel more grounded and peaceful than I have since The Battle. How ya doin' George?"

"Same here," George said, looking into the middle of the room.

Jordan looked all around the room, and the crystals began to glow more brightly.

"Thanks, y'all, for sharin' your energy with me," Jordan said, bowing.

The crystals flashed at Jordan, and this made him laugh.

"George, these crystals are wise guys just like you," Jordan said.

"Indeed they are, and we're proud of it," George said as he morphed into a human.

"You're lookin' good, George," Jordan said.

"Thanks. I thought so," George said, smiling.

"Your modesty needs work," Jordan said as he began to walk around the perimeter of the room. "These are beautiful as always. I will never grow tired of seein' them."

"Me, either," George said as he followed Jordan.

They looked at the crystals as they walked, pointing out the ones shaped like flowers and animals, enjoying themselves for a while. Then, as they returned to where they had begun, Jordan felt the need to walk into the middle of the room. George remained silent. He knew what was about to happen and hoped Jordan was ready for it.

Jordan stopped and looked at the floor covered in crystals of all colors, shapes, and sizes. He was drawn to a purple one. It was deep purple, and its shape reminded him of something. He spent a few minutes looking at it; then, it increased in size until it was as big as a small lamp. He kept looking at it and then suddenly realized what the shape was.

"That's a dragon crystal," Jordan said, looking back at George.

George walked over and looked at the crystal. "It does resemble one."

"George?" Jordan said. "What the hell is going on here?"

"Now, Jordan, don't get all crazy on me," George said. "Just look at it, and when you're ready, pick it up if you want to."

"Why?" Jordan asked.

"It has special healing powers within it. We think you are in need of these extra-strong powers right now," Geroge explained.

"Why does it look like a dragon?" Jordan asked.

"You figure that one out," George said.

"I swear, George, if I wasn't such a gentleman, I'd deck you right now," Jordan said.

"Thanks for the consideration," George said, taking a step back.

"I'm getting' the feelin' that this is a good thing," Jordan said a minute later. "Okay, I'll pick up the crystal."

As soon as The Crystal Dragon was in Jordan's hands, he began seeing things from a long time ago. It was as if a movie was being played on the back wall of the room. He saw a man dressed in robes with a long beard working at a bench with plants and water and such. He was mixing things in a small bowl. He suddenly knew this was part of the vision he and Katelyn had shared when they touched their twin crystals together last summer.

As he watched, the young woman walked into the room, carrying flowers and green plants, and began to set them in clay jars and vases. It was the same young woman from the shared vision. He knew these two people, although he had never met them. He really knew them. He continued to watch for a few more minutes. The vision moved as if it were walking outside into the forest. As he looked at the setting, he saw a large shadow just in his peripheral vision to his left. It was huge and reminded him of a dinosaur. Then, he knew exactly what it was. It was a dragon—a deep purple-colored dragon in all its glory. The vision faded, and he stood there for a minute.

"George, what the hell was that all about?" Jordan asked as he walked back to the edge of the room.

"What did you see, Jordan?" George asked.

"I saw the same vision Katelyn and I saw last summer when we touched out twin crystals together. But, this time, the vision went outside, and I saw a purple dragon. What the hell is that all about?"

"What do you think it was about?" George asked.

"No double-talk, George," Jordan said, sending the look of death at George.

"Really, Jordan, what are your thoughts on the whole thing?" George answered quietly.

"I don't have the foggiest idea," Jordan said. "The only thing I know is that this here crystal looks like a dragon. A purple one. And dragons aren't real."

"Then why did you see a dragon in the vision?" George asked.

"The Magic can make anything happen whenever it wants to," Jordan replied. "This crystal is warm, and I can feel its energy throughout my body. It feels great."

"The Magic can make anything happen whenever it wants to," George said. "You just said that. Now, think about it."

"If that is really true, then The Magic can make dragons come to life. That's what you're telling me?"

"You said it," George replied.

"So, the dragon I saw in the vision is real in the vision," Jordan continued.

"Yes, since the vision came from The Magic," George said.

"Okay. I accept that," Jordan said. "But, what does it have to do with me?"

"That's for you to figure out if and when you want to," George said.

"Oh, brother. Things are gettin' complicated here," Jordan said

"They are," George replied. "Just hold onto The Crystal Dragon, and its energy will help steady you."

"It is doing just that," Jordan said. "I love the energy of this crystal."

"I love the energy of crystals, too," George said as he picked one up and held it close. "So soothing and calming."

"Okay, y'all over there, I accept this Crystal Dragon. Its energy is keeping me calm, and I am grateful for that," Jordan said.

The Crystal Dragon covered Jordan in purple light to show it heard him.

"And this is exactly why I love My Cave," Jordan said. "Time to get on back home and get to work."

"It is," George said as he morphed back into this eagle self.

"Thanks for being with me, George," Jordan said as they left The Cave and returned home.

"Always, Jordan," George replied. "Time to fly."

Jordan set The Crystal Dragon on the desk next to him as he got busy with his research, and the morning flew by. That crystal glowed softly all day long.

Katelyn was busy, too. She was drawing up preliminary floor plans when Sami walked in around ten.

"Hey, girl," Finn said. "Katelyn said you'd be stoppin' by."

"Hey, Sami," Ian and Ethan said.

"Hey," Katelyn said as she walked over to Sammi and hugged her. "Let's put your stuff in my office."

"You know I love this place," Sami said. "This drawin' table is perfect."

"Watch," Katelyn said as she grabbed a remote, and the drawing table folded itself against the wall.

"That's sick!" Sami said.

"You love our toys, huh?" Ethan said, laughing along with the others. "Come out here and watch this."

Ethan had Sami stand in the middle of the room, facing a blank wall.

"Nice paint job, Ethan," Sami sassed.

With the click of a button, the wall became a huge screen, showing an aerial view of Gina and Terry's land.

"Whoa!" Sami said, walking over to the wall and running her hand all over the landscape. "I don't know what to say. This is amazin'."

"We love it," Ian said. "Our clients are thrilled with seein' their land from the air. It really helps them decide just where they want to build. It gives us all the things we need to know."

"You mean like rivers, creeks, rock outcroppings, and caves?" Sami said.

"Exactly," Ethan replied.

"It's important for me to find the water sources for geothermal use," Finn added.

"Yea. That would be important, and it must cut way back on the time needed to walk the land," Sami said.

"That, too," Ian replied.

"So, I'll take one of every toy y'all have in here," Sami said, laughing.

"We get it," Katelyn said. "Ethan, do you have the info for my drawing table for Sami?"

"I do," Ethan said. "Don't faint. It's a very pricey toy."

Sami looked at the info and whistled. "I'll say it is. But it's got everything I need. I just can't afford it now. I'll stick with the one I have."

"Sami," Ian said, walking over to her. "I do believe it is customary to give newcomers to The Creek a housewarmin' gift."

"It is, indeed," Ethan replied.

"My momma wouldn't have it any other way," Finn said.

"What?" Sami said.

"Sami, we've already ordered one for you to show how much we love you and that we're beyond happy that you're makin' The Creek your home," Ethan said.

Sami looked at them all as tears rolled down her cheeks. "I, I don't even know how to begin to say thanks."

"Hugs are always accepted," Katelyn said.

"It should be here tomorrow, and Kendra and I already got a few things in place in your new office," Ethan said.

"You guys do work fast," Sami said. "I think I'll donate my old table to the local youth center for the arts program. I'll bet they could use one."

"That's a great idea, Sami," Katelyn said. "We used to go there once a month and help out. The kids are amazin'. Some of their work is so advanced. The center put on a show for them a couple of months before I came home."

"Wait!" Sami said. "I have an even better idea. How about we give the table to the local school right here?"

"Already gave them mine," Katelyn said, laughing. "You give yours to the center."

"Well, aren't you special," Sami sassed.

"You know I am," Katelyn replied, taking a bow.

"The Bancroft's are here," Ian said, laughing at the girls. "Let's see if we can make some magic for them."

And that's exactly what they did. It was past lunchtime when they finally called it quits.

"I can't believe the amount of stuff we did today," Terry said.

"This is way beyond my wildest dreams," Gina said. "I especially love the idea of a mural of crystals on the big wall in the open space downstairs across from the wall of windows."

"That idea is all Finn's," Ian said.

"I thought since we were gonna make the basement a walk-out on account of the small rise the house will be built on, a wall of French doors and windows would bring natural light in.

"And the wall opposite the windows would be the perfect place for Katelyn and Sammi to design a mural. I like the idea of asking Jenna to be a part of this, too." Finn said.

"I love the idea," Sami said. "She showed me a bunch of the murals she's been designin' ever since she came back to The Creek. They're amazin'."

"Did you see the one of the faeries and faerie circles?" Katelyn asked.

"Not yet," Sami replied.

"Look here," Katelyn said as she sent the picture from her phone to the wall screen.

"These faeries look so cute and real," Gina said. "Was this for a child's room?"

"It was for the kid's playroom," Katelyn said. "Jenna gets texts and emails from their parents showing her the kid's drawings of faeries. So cute."

"This has been amazin'," Terry said. "Well, time to get goin'. It's way past lunchtime."

"And still so much more to do," Gina said as they walked outside. "I'm gonna love every minute of it. Thanks, everyone."

As Gina and Terry drove away, Finn said, "I'm so hungry. Time to attack the frig."

The group ate lunch and got back to work, and Sami went back to the house. It was quitting time when Katelyn got a call from Jordan.

"Hey, Jordan," Katelyn said as she got ready to leave.

"Hey, Katelyn," Jordan said. "Do ya have a few minutes to stop by on your way home?"

"Sure," Katelyn replied. "What's up?"

"Oh, stuff," Jordan said hesitantly.

"Okay, be there in a few," Katelyn replied.

"Thanks," Jordan said as they ended the call.

Ethan and Ian were staying for a few more minutes, and Finn walked out with Katelyn. Katelyn put her stuff in her SUV and then turned to Finn. He pulled her into him and kissed her deeply. He ran his fingers across her breasts, and she moaned. She ran her hand across his hard cock, and he moaned.

"Katie, we need some alone time," Finn said as the kiss ended.

"We do," Katelyn said breathlessly.

"My folks are away for the night. Come stay with me," Finn said.

"I will," Katelyn replied. "Sami gets us."

"I know she does, and I love her for it," Finn said.

They shared a few more intimate moments before separating.

"Later, my Katie girl," Finn said.

"Later, my Finn," Katelyn said as she got into her SUV.

"Be careful," Finn said as he got into his truck.

Katelyn waved at him as she drove off. She was at Jordan's a couple of minutes later.

"Hey, George," Katelyn said as George flew over and landed at her feet.

"Squawk," George replied, raising a wing at her.

"I see you've been properly greeted," Jordan said as they hugged.

"Indeed I have," Katelyn said as they walked up onto the back porch and sat down.

"That's for you," Jordan said, pointing to a sweet tea beside Katelyn's chair.

"Much obliged," Katelyn said, taking a long drink. "I love sweet tea. So, what's up?"

"I went out to My Cave the other day. Felt like I needed to. No crazy Magic going on. Just the usual glowing and humming of the crystals. I felt the need to walk into the center of the big room, and when I looked down, I found this."

Jordan set The Crystal Dragon on the table between them. It was glowing and humming as usual.

Katelyn stared at it for a few minutes before saying, "It's magnificent. It's purple."

"Yes, it is," Jordan said, watching Katelyn.

"It was just sitting on the floor in the center of the room?" Katelyn said.

"Yes," Jordan said.

George was watching them both to see if either one of them mentioned its shape.

"It's a dragon. Plain as day," Katelyn finally said.

"It is," Jordan replied.

"What the hell is a dragon crystal doin' in your cave?" Katelyn asked, looking up at Jordan.

"Hell, if I know," Jordan replied.

"Oh, my God!" Katelyn said softly.

George knew she had made the connection between seeing the huge shadowy flying thing and the crystal.

"Jordan, for what it's worth, and you know how coincidences don't happen, Kendra, Sami, and I saw a huge shape flyin' over The Store and then over us just last night or the night before."

"And," Jordan said.

"When I looked at The Dragon Crystal just now, I know what that thing was," Katelyn said. "Don't get crazy on me, Jordan."

"I thinkin' I already know what you're gonna say. Say it anyway," Jordan said.

"It was a dragon that flew over us," Katelyn said, looking right at Jordan.

"I believe you're right about that," Jordan whispered.

"What? You know it was a dragon? You know there's a dragon in The Creek. What the fuck, Jordan! Spill," Katelyn said, standing up and pacing back and forth.

"Well, it goes somethin' like this," Jordan replied, looking at George. George nodded his head at Jordan, letting him know it was okay to tell Katelyn about the dragon. "I've seen that shape flyin' around the farm a couple of times this summer at nightfall. I couldn't make it out, so I figured it was just an owl of somethin'."

Katelyn sat back down, nodding her head in agreement. "That's what we figured, too."

"It was the day after The Battle on The Rise and the discovery of our tattoos that I could really see what it was. It was just as evening melds into the night. I was standing out at the edge of the field, and it flew over me and the barn, then came back and got really close. It was a dragon. I saw a dragon. It winked at me, then flew off over the field."

Katelyn just stared at Jordan for the longest time, then said, "Fuck!"

"Exactly!" Jordan replied. "Fuck!"

"What the fuck is all this about?" Katelyn said. "A dragon? A real dragon? Here? In The Creek? Where does it live? Why is it here? A dragon? For real?"

Jordan laughed, saying, "I have all the same questions. Why do you think I can't take any more of The Magic? That dragon is for real."

"Is it full of bad energy?" Katelyn asked no one in particular.

"I think it's all good," Jordan replied. "At least that's the first impression I get from it."

"How many times have you seen it since?" Katelyn asked.

"None. Just that one time," Jordan replied.

"And now The Crystal Dragon," Katelyn said. "It looks like there's a strong connection here."

"I agree," Jordan said. "Look!"

The Crystal Dragon was flashing a brilliant dark purple energy all over the place. George was squawking like crazy and hopping all over the porch.

"I'll take that as a big yes," Katelyn said. "George agrees."

"He sure does," Jordan said. "The purple light feels great."

"It does," Katelyn said, sitting back in her rocker and enjoying the energy.

"That energy is why I agreed to keep the crystal and bring it home. It sits on my desk with me when I'm working and next to my bed at night," Jordan said. "It keeps me off the edge of madness for sure."

"I'll say it does," Katelyn replied. "Its energy is very calmin' and soothin'. It's almost as good as some of Lainie and Mo's special blends."

"Oh, I never thought of that," Jordan said. "You're right."

Jordan and Katelyn just sat there absorbing the purple energy from The Crystal Dragon for a few more minutes. Then, the crystal calmed down, and the energy dissipated.

"Thanks for the energy bath," Katelyn said. "However, that doesn't explain why there's a dragon in The Creek. We need answers."

There was a brilliant flash of white light in response to Katelyn's statement, but nothing else.

"Well, I guess that's all we get right now," Jordan said.

"Guess so," Katelyn agreed.

"Now what?" What do we do next?" Jordan asked.

"I have no idea," Katelyn said. "Do you know where that dragon lives? Is it in The Creek, or does it just appear and disappear when The Magic deems it necessary?"

"I don't have any answers to those questions," Jordan replied. "I have the same questions myself. Why do you think I'm going nuts over here?"

"I agree with you," Katelyn said. "I do know that we are not to say anything about the dragon to anyone. We can talk together about it, but no one else is to know."

"I'm getting that same feeling," Jordan said. "I won't tell anyone."

"Me, either," Katelyn said, starting to laugh. "Can you imagine what folks would think if we told them there's a dragon in The Creek? They'd think we were hallucinating."

"Or, we were finally going over the deep end," Jordan added.

"Or, they might get really scared and start a panic," Katelyn said.

"Oh, yeah. That, too," Jordan agreed.

"So, we keep quiet," Katelyn said.

"Yup," Jordan said. "This is crazy for sure."

"Time for me to get on home. Sami will be wonderin' about me," Katelyn said, standing up and stretching.

"So glad you came by," Jordan said as they walked over to Katelyn's SUV. "Never a dull moment in The Creek."

"Never," Katelyn said as George took to the sky. "Later, George." George squawked as he flew off over the field.

"An eagle with attitude," Katelyn said as she got into her SUV.

"That's for sure. Oh, one other thing," Jordan said. "I'd like us to take a look at those caves over the Northridge Footbridge. We can get to them from the Bancroft's land, right?"

"Yes, we can," Katelyn replied. "When do ya want to go over there?"

"Sami and I are meetin' again in the mornin' to go over our supply list. So I'm free in the afternoon if you are," Jordan said.

"I do believe I am free tomorrow afternoon," Katelyn replied. "I told Ethan I needed to walk the area again to look at how the sun hits the place in the afternoon. I need pictures for Lainie and Mo's solar panel setup. After that, we'll have plenty of time to find those caves. Ethan left the gator and a full gas can there for our use."

"Great. That guy thinks of everythin'," Jordan said. "I'll meet you at your house around one."

"Sounds good. I get the feelin' you and I are supposed to find those caves together," Katelyn said.

"I agree," Jordan said.

Katelyn waved and drove off and was home a few minutes later. Lights were on in Sami's house, so she walked over to take a look. She found Sami in her office organizing things.

"This looks great," Katelyn said.

"Thanks. It's getting there," Sami replied. "It'll really come together after the table gets here. I still can't believe those guys would give me my artist's table."

"That's how we take care of each other around here," Katelyn said as she squeezed Sami's shoulder.

"I'll be workin' on a bit of sharin' after I get moved in and all," Sami said.

"I came over to tell ya I'm headed to Finn's for the night. His folks are away, so we're gonna spend some time together," Katelyn said.

"Good for you," Sami said. "I can take care of myself."

"I know you can," Katelyn said. "I'll see ya tomorrow."

"Enjoy yourselves," Sami said as Katelyn left.

Finn heard Katelyn as she drove down the driveway and went to greet her.

"Hey, Katie girl," Finn said, taking her stuff from her.

"Hey, Finn," Katelyn said as they walked into the house.

Finn dropped Katelyn's stuff on a chair and pulled her close.

"I've been thinking about us all afternoon," Finn said as he ran his hands over her breasts.

"Me, too," Katelyn replied as she pulled his jammie pants off. "I do like the way you greet me."

Finn walked them into the living room. He had started a fire and had pillows ready for them. Katelyn slowly removed her blouse and jammie pants, standing in her tiny bra and thong. Finn removed his shirt and took her breast in one hand while caressing her hot spot with the other. Katelyn closed her eyes and enjoyed every sensation.

Finn laid them down on the pile of pillows in front of the fireplace. He opened Katelyn's bra and took her breast into his mouth. She moaned and reached for his hard dick.

"Take it all off," Katelyn said.

"You, too," Finn replied as they removed the rest of their clothes. "God, you're beautiful."

"I love your hard dick," Katelyn said as she ran a finger up and down his shaft.

Finn shuttered at her touch and had to pull away so he wouldn't explode. He leaned down, took her breast into his mouth again, and began to suck and tease the nipple. Katelyn tried to move closer, but Finn gently blocked her so he could use his other hand to stroke her hot spot. He found her clit and began to flick it fast and hard. Katelyn exploded into her first orgasm quickly. He let her calm down for just a minute before he began to stroke her again.

Katelyn rolled on top of him and began to take his hard, hot dick into her wet, pulsing pussy. He moaned as she slowly and rhythmically took him deeper and deeper into her. Finn stroked her breasts as she brought him closer and closer to exploding.

Finn couldn't take this much longer. He wanted to make her cum before he did. He rolled them over and slid down Katelyn's belly until his tongue found her clit. He licked and licked her until he felt her about to cum. Then, he slid up and began to push his hard, hot shaft into her.

"Oh, God, Finn. Push harder and faster," Katelyn cried out.

"I do as I'm told," Finn said as he pushed harder and faster into her.

She came hard a minute later, bucking and writhing as the organism took control. She grabbed his ass, pulling him into her. Finn joined her in her organism, and they flew together into that dimension of pure ecstasy. Then, they came back to the here and now and slept.

"Hey, you," Finn whispered in Katelyn's ear.

"Hmmm," Katelyn replied as she reached for Finn and found him ready to go again.

Katelyn brought Finn close again as she stroked him before he pulled her on top of him. She pushed onto his hard shaft and began to ride him. He rubbed her clit until she started to cum, then pushed harder and harder as she came. He joined her again, and they collapsed in a heap on the pillows.

"Holy shit!" Katelyn said. "We are so good at all this."

"We sure are," Finn said as he gently kissed Katelyn.

"I do love our time together," Katelyn said, stretching like a feline.

"Only one thing about it, though," Finn said.

"What's that?" Katelyn asked.

"All this physical activity gets me hungry," Finn said.

"Me, too. Let's raid the frig," Katelyn said.

They found their clothes and found leftovers in the frig. They warmed them up and then sat at the kitchen table.

"I love your mama's cookin'," Katelyn said.

"Me, too," Finn replied. "I gotta say, though, everyone in The Creek is really excellent at cookin' and bakin'. When I was away at school, I couldn't believe how bland some of the food was, especially in the dorms. So when Jay and I moved into our own place, we had our mom send us her recipes, and we started cookin'. We learned a lot, and our cookin' is rather good, according to our folks."

"I agree with you," Katelyn said. "You do cook rather well."

"Thanks, Katie girl," Finn said as he cleared the table. "How about a movie?"

"Great. Which one?" Katelyn replied as they settled in the living room.

"You pick," Finn said. They looked through the list online and finally chose Spider-Man, No Way Home.

They enjoyed the movie pretending to throw webs and fly around just like Spidey did.

Katelyn and Finn yawned at the same time when the movie was over.

"Time for some sleep, Katie girl," Finn said.

"Same for you, handsome," Katelyn replied as they settled the house and walked into Finn's room.

"That bed is just too small," Fin said. "Let's camp out in the living room. It's all ready for us."

"Great idea," Katelyn said. "Your bed needs an upgrade."

"That's a great idea," Finn said. "I'll have you help me pick out a mattress and frame tomorrow at the shop. I want a memory foam mattress, but I'm not paying that outrageous price the name-brand folks want."

"Agreed. I have one I found online. I love it," Katelyn replied as they settled down. "This is heaven."

"I agree," Finn replied as they snuggled close and fell asleep.

It was around three in the morning when Katlyn got up for a minute. She found Finn ready for her when she got back. They made slow, delicious love again, taking their time exploring each other before finally rocketing into oblivion as they came together. They slept deeply.

Katelyn's phone alarm woke them hours later. She had set This Girl's on Fire as her ringtone.

Finn opened his eyes, laughing at her. "Really? That's your ringtone?"

"Damn straight it is, mister. You'd better get used to it," Katelyn said as she ran off to the shower.

Katelyn was fixing breakfast when Finn came in already for the day.

"I love your omelets, Katie girl," Finn said.

"Make some toast, will ya?" Katelyn asked as she poured the omelet mix into the sauté pan.

"Yes, Ma'am," Finn said as he got busy.

"All ready," Katelyn said as she set their breakfast on the table.

"This tastes great," Finn said with his mouth full.

"Thanks. I agree," Katelyn replied.

"Katie girl, I enjoyed last night with you," Finn said as he finished.

"I did, too," Katelyn said. "I always enjoy our time together."

"We'll have to spend a lot more of it this way," Finn said, taking Katelyn's hand in his.

"We will. Sami's leaving on Sunday morning. So let's plan on Sunday night at my place," Katelyn said, stroking Finn's hand with her thumb.

"I could sit here for hours letting you touch me like this," Finn said, closing his eyes and enjoying Katelyn's touch.

"I know. But it's time to clean up and get to the shop," Katelyn said, letting go of Finn's hand. "We have homes to design."

"Yes, we do," Finn said. "I'll be in the office all day, working on geothermal plans for two of our builds over the Tennessee line. How about you?"

"In the office all morning, then in the field for the rest of the day. Ethan wants me to get some sun readings on Gina and Terry's build site for Lainie and Mo's solar panel needs. Gina and Terry are going to use solar energy on all their buildings. So I'll be busy for a while. You know how much I love being outside."

"I do," Finn said as they gathered their things, closed the house, and walked out to their vehicles. "Be sure to text me a couple of times when you're out there. I want to make sure you're safe and all."

"You guys all think the same way," Katelyn said, laughing at Finn.

"What do ya mean?" Finn asked.

"Ethan and Ian already made me promise to do the same thing," Katelyn said.

"Of course they did," Finn said, walking over and kissing Katelyn.

"See you at the shop," Katelyn said.

"In a few, my Finn," Katelyn said.

"In a few, my Katie girl," Finn replied.

The morning flew by for everyone in The Creek. Lunch came and went. It was just one o'clock when Jordan pulled into Katelyn's driveway. Katelyn walked out to Jordan's truck and got in.

"You look like you're ready for a hike," Jordan said as they got underway.

"So do you, my friend," Katelyn said as a shadow flew over the truck and then in front of them. "I see we have an escort."

"We do. He won't let me go anywhere without him," Jordan said.

"He's a loyal eagle," Katelyn replied as they drove along.

They arrived at the small entry road to Gina and Terry's property. Karl had cleared a single tract a few days before so Ethan and his crew could get started on surveys and such.

"I see Karl's been here," Katelyn said as they parked in the field.

"I like Karl. He's always on top of things and never clears more than is absolutely necessary. We got to know each other when he was working on my build," Jordan said.

"I agree," Katelyn replied as they got out and put their things in the gator. "I've gotten to know him well, too, with all the work he does for us. Nice guy, for sure."

"Whose drivin'?" Jordan asked

"I am. I know the lay of the land," Katelyn replied as she got in the driver's seat.

George flew in just then, landed, and squawked.

"Hey, George," Katelyn said. "Thanks for the escort."

George bobbed his head in response, then took to the air, circling the field, waiting for them to get moving.

"I guess we know who's in charge today," Jordan said, laughing as they set out for the field where the house would be built. They drove through the woods and emerged into the open a few minutes later.

"Katelyn, are y'all going to have to take down all those trees to get to this spot?" Jordan asked as they stopped, and Katelyn gathered her gear.

"That's what Ian and Ethan are working on right now. They're planning on a drive that runs next to the first field we were in. The Bancroft's are going to raise horses, and that field is one of the ones they'll be using. They're building stables just where the woods begin. Ian doesn't think we'll have to take down a lot of trees. He said he thinks we can save most of them. The driveway will go through the woods to reach the house. Ian's working with Scott and the MacKinnon's to create a replanting plan for the area once the heavy machinery is gone."

"This is a big project," Jordan said, following Katelyn to the stakes set to show the house's four corners.

"It sure is," Katelyn said as she set up portable solar panels along the staked line for the front of the house.

"How does that work?" Jordan asked as George flew in and landed next to Katelyn.

"Finn and Mo came up with this idea," Katelyn said as she stepped aside so the panels could absorb the sun's rays. "These portable panels will collect energy for one hour. That tells Finn how much energy can be produced during the sun's highest trajectory of the day. So we'll leave them here for most of the afternoon. I set their timer for four hours from right now," Katelyn explained as she set the re-mote timer.

"That's really cool," Jordan said. "So, let me get this straight. Once Finn has these readings, he can look at the cloud cover, if any, and calculate how much energy the solar panels will produce. That will give him an idea of the amount of usable energy for the house and other buildings. Then, coupled with the available geothermal energy, this property should be completely off the grid. Right?"

"Exactly," Katelyn said. "You get it. Maybe we'll hire you to work with Finn sometimes."

"I'll help if I can, although I'm wicked busy with the URR," Jordan said.

"Yes, you are, and you love it," Katelyn said.

"We ready to go cave huntin'?" Jordan asked.

"We are," Katelyn said. "We'll start at the northern edge of the property where we found that crystal that lies between the two old oak trees. Hop in."

As they approached the edge of the woods, they saw an eerie glow through the trees.

"It's the crystal between the trees. Follow me," Katelyn said as they walked into the trees.

"This is incredible!" Jordan said as they approached the crystal.

"It sure is," Katelyn said as they stood there absorbing the energy. Then, the crystal began to dim until the glow was gone.

"I'd say that was a welcome sign," Katelyn said.

"Agreed. Now what?" Jordan asked.

Katelyn walked around the tree, and crystal then said, "I found an animal path back here. Let's see where it takes us."

As they set out on the path, the air seemed to change, and the animals became quiet.

"This is weird," Jordan said as they rounded a bend in the path and came to a wall of solid rock.

"Whoa!" Katelyn replied. "I don't remember seein' this rock wall from the meadow. It's big enough to see for miles around."

"I know," Jordan said. "How could anyone miss this thing? It's as big as some of the smaller mountains around here."

"It goes on and on in both directions," Katelyn said as she stepped closer. "Look. There's a drawing here of some kind."

"It's called a petroglyph. Miss Cora was talkin' about them at supper on Saturday," Jordan said.

"I remember. It looks like an animal or somethin'. And there's more along the way. These look like people and some kinds of small animals."

"This looks like an eagle or somethin'. It's really big. Maybe it's from the dinosaur age."

"Good thinkin', Jordan. Let's look in both directions for a bit," Katelyn suggested.

They spent some time first going to the east, then back to the west past where they had started.

"Look here," Jordan said, pointing to a specific drawing. "It looks like an openin' or somethin'. And there are three spirals set around it. What do ya think?"

"I agree with you," Katelyn replied. "I remember seein' these spirals on the TV show about aliens."

"You mean the Ancient Aliens series?" Jordan asked.

"Yup. They seem to think it's a symbol for the universe and a possible portal," Katelyn replied.

"Look closer. That area in the middle that looks like an entrance to some-thin' is a different color than the rock wall itself. It's almost as if someone or some-thin' painted it so it would be noticed," Jordan said as he ran his hand over the drawing.

The spirals began to glow, and before Katelyn and Jordan could even take a breath, the wall opened into a cave.

"Holy shit!" Jordan exclaimed.

"What the hell did you do, and what the hell is this?" Katelyn asked as she stared at Jordan and the opening in the rock wall.

"I, I don't know," Jordan said, staring at everything as well. "This is un-believable."

"Now what?" Katelyn said. "What do we do now?"

"Hell, if I know," Jordan replied. "But I do believe everythin' happens as it's supposed to. So, it would seem we were guided here to do everythin' we've done, including openin' this secret door into that cave."

"Just what is it with you and caves anyway?" Katelyn said, laughing. "You have your own gorgeous cave on your farm, and now this."

Just then, George swooped in and landed next to Jordan.

"I wondered where you were," Jordan said as he touched George on the top of his head. George replied with a quiet squawk.

"Hey, George, glad you're with us," Katelyn said. George raised a wing in response.

"Did you notice the change in the air as we started into the woods?" Jordan asked.

"I did. I figure it's because we're in an old-growth forest," Katelyn replied.

"I'm not sure about that," Jordan said, looking around. "The bird song has stopped, and there seems to be a hush all over the place."

Katelyn listened for a minute, then said, "I agree with you. It does seem different. Not sure about the whole thing, though."

"Me, either," Jordan agreed. "I do get the feelin' we're supposed to go into this cave."

"Okay," Katelyn said as they cautiously took a few steps into the cave.

Katelyn and Jordan shivered at the same time.

"That was creepy," Katelyn said.

Jordon nodded his head as he looked around.

The cave had a small, short entryway, then opened into a very large main room. The walls were covered in millions of crystals, all glowing softly. The floor was covered in sand. The ceiling looked like it was a screen of some kind. It was shades of blue that kept changing.

"This is wild," Jordan said, pointing to the ceiling.

"I know. It's like we're watchin' the real night sky," Katelyn said. "Look there. That star formation looks like a dragon."

Jordan just stood there. He knew deep within his soul that he had seen a dragon fly over him after The Battle on The Rise.

"George?" Jordan said, looking at his eagle.

George did not respond in any way.

Katelyn looked at Jordan and George. They were acting rather oddly.

"You two have a secret or somethin?" she asked.

"Now, how could we have a secret? He's a bird, and I don't speak eagle," Jordan said, trying to calm down.

"You both look guilty of somethin'," Katelyn said.

George squawked and flapped his wings a bit.

"I swear that bird knows exactly what we're sayin'," Katelyn said, laughing at George.

"I agree with ya there," Jordan said, giving George a stern look.

Jordan looked at Katelyn and was taken back to a time from long ago. She was standing beside a rough table in the same cave they were standing in now. But it was a different time. She was dressed in a dress that went to the floor. It looked similar to the way she had been dressed in the shared vision from a few months ago. It looked like she was putting something into clay bowls. George was nowhere in the cave.

As Jordan continued looking around the cave, he saw a hawk perched on the back of a chair. It was huge, even bigger than George. Its talons were long and curved, and its beak was hooked. It had red and silver wing feathers, and its head was covered in iridescent blue feathers. It had a ring around its neck the color of gold. Its eyes were gold-colored, too. The hawk was looking at someone else in the cave. Jordan followed the hawk's gaze and saw a man. He was similar to the man in the vision that Katelyn had been in. But, this time, Jordan could tell he wasn't as old as the man from the first vision. He was dressed in trousers of some kind with a long tunic and had a robe that covered his clothes. The robe had a hood hanging from it. The robe was a dark gray, almost black. It had symbols of some kind across the back. It looked like the man had just come into the cave. He was giving small pouches of plants to the woman. That's what she was putting into the clay bowls.

Jordan looked up at the ceiling and saw the same star patterns he and Katelyn had just seen. One was of a dragon. It was intimately detailed right down to the scales along the dragon's back. He watched as the dragon stars began to glow and shine, as if someone had flipped a switch and made them shine.

Katelyn looked over at Jordan at the same time he turned to look at her. She was surprised to see that she was again dressed in a long dress like those worn from a time long ago. She was putting some plants into clay bowls on a rough kind of table. She looked around and saw the man she had seen in her shared vision with Jordan a few months back. He was not as old-looking as that vision. He looked to be in his mid-twenties. He had a full beard and dark hair and was dressed in some kind of trousers with a long tunic covering them. He had a dark gray robe over his clothes with the hood hanging down that back as if he had just pushed it off his head. There were symbols of some kind all along the back of the robe.

As Katelyn looked just past the man, she saw a magnificent creature. It was perched on the back of a chair. It looked like a hawk but was much bigger. It had red and silver feathers along its wings, with iridescent blue feathers surrounding its head. It had a gold band of feathers around its neck and golden eyes. Its talons were huge and curved. Its beak was curved as well.

Katelyn suddenly realized she was in a cave. It looked exactly like the one she and Jordan were exploring. She thought for only an instant as she looked up at the ceiling. It was there. The dragon pattern just like in the current cave. This one had more detail. You could easily see the scales along the back of the dragon right down to its split tail. That tail looked familiar to Katelyn. As she continued to look at the dragon on the ceiling, the light changed in the cave, and the dragon pattern began to glow and shine as if a switch had been flipped, bringing electricity to the ceiling. Only thing was there wasn't any electricity in this old place. It was from a time so very long ago. But, somehow, it all looked and felt familiar to her.

Jordan was thinking the same thing. This place looked and felt very familiar to him. He had a flash of memory as if he'd been here before. That was absurd. This place was from an ancient time.

Then, just as it had taken them back to this ancient place, they looked at each other and were returned to the here and now.

They looked at each other for a few minutes, trying to figure out what had happened.

"What the hell was that all about?" Jordan hollered, looking right at George.

George gave a loud squawk and hopped all over the place.

"I agree, George," Katelyn said. "What the hell WAS that all about?"

"Beats me," Jordan said, shaking his head. "I told Them no more Magic. They aren't listenin'."

"I know that feelin'," Katelyn replied.

"What the fuck!" Jordan hollered out.

"I see you're using my favorite word again," Katelyn said, smiling at Jordan.

"I am," Jordan declared. "And, what was that dragon thing on the ceiling of the old cave? Oh, sorry, I forgot you weren't there. I mean, in the vision, you were there, just not the you from now."

"I was there," Katelyn said. "I saw that dragon with all the scales down its back ending in a split tail. That tail reminds me of something."

"Yes, it does," Jordan said. "It's a distinctive pattern, for sure. Oh, my God! I know where we've seen that before. Our marc from after The Battle on The Rise."

Jordan lowered his shirt so Katelyn could see his marc.

"That's it, exactly. Look," Katelyn said as she lowered her shirt so Jordan could see the marc across the back of her neck ending on her shoulder.

"Yes, it is," Jordan looking at the marc.

"This whole thing is going beyond strange," Katelyn said. "It would seem there's a dragon involved in The Magic. That I accept. The Magic is everything and more than we can ever imagine. But what the hell is a dragon doin' around here? And are dragons really real? I know they are in The Magic."

"That's a given," Jordan said, pacing around the cave. "But in real life, the real-life we know? Dragons? Really?"

"Look," Katelyn hollered, pointing to the ceiling. "That dragon is glowing just like in the old cave vision."

"You saw that, too?" Jordan asked, looking at the ceiling.

"Sure did," Katelyn replied. "Let's take a minute and sit down and compare visions. Somethin' weird is happenin' around here, and I think we should share the vision just like before."

"Agreed," Jordan said as they found a place to sit down.

They had a long drink of their cold water and then started talking.

"It was like the other vision we had. We were in a cave of sorts. I think the man was you. Not too sure, though. Both of them had on clothes that looked like they were from the Middle Ages or the time of King Arthur," Katelyn began.

"Yup," Jordan replied. "You still looked beautiful."

"Wiseass," Katelyn said, laughing. "I just can't see how a person could do anythin' in a long dress like that. Anyway, I was puttin' plants into clay pots, and there was a magnificent bird perched on the back of a chair."

"It was magnificent. Kind of like a hawk but much bigger and more color-ful," Jordan said. "The man was lookin' at the bird and all around the space. It did remind me of a cave, but it could have been a thatched hut or something. Did you see the dragon etched on the roof?"

"I did," Katelyn said, getting all excited. "It showed great detail down to the split tail."

"Same here," Jordan said. "You might think I'm crazy or somethin', but I got the feelin' that I knew that place. It seemed really familiar to me, and at the same time, I have no idea what it is or where it was located."

"I got the same feelin'," Katelyn said.

"So, now what?" Jordan asked.

"I don't have the foggiest," Katelyn replied, staring off into space.

They sat quietly for a minute until George nudged Katelyn.

"Hey, George. What can I do for you?" Katelyn asked.

George squawked and pointed to the ceiling. The dragon's tail was glow-ing.

"Holy shit! Look, Jordan," Katelyn exclaimed as they both looked up at the ceiling.

"Oh, oh," Jordan said. "I think The Magic is alive and well in this cave, too."

"Great deduction," Katelyn said, giving Jordan a soft punch in the arm.

"That's the same tail that's on our shoulders and was in the vision we just had," Katelyn said.

"It's the same tail," Jordan and Katelyn said at the same time.

"Right here on the ceilin'," Katelyn said.

"What's it doin' on our shoulders?" Jordan said.

"And on Sami's shoulder, too," Katelyn added. "We all have the marc of the dragon."

"Why do you call it that?" Jordan asked.

"I don't know. It just came out of me," Katelyn said, looking a bit sur-prised.

"That's exactly what it is," Jordan said. "The Marc of The Dragon. I like that. It's a statement like The Knights of The Round Table."

"Yeah, it does sound like that," Katelyn said. "The Marc of The Dragon. Sounds like a warrior thing."

"Well, that's appropriate after The Battle on The Rise and all," Jordan said.

"Truth," Katelyn said, nodding her head.

"Now what?" Jordan asked as he looked around the cave. "The crystals seem to like this conversation. They're glowing beautifully."

Katelyn looked around and then laughed. "George is enjoyin' them for sure."

Jordan saw George and laughed along with Katelyn. "He knows how to have a great time. It's almost like the feelin' you get from a good soak in a hot tub."

George opened his eyes and gave a soft squawk as he stood up and walked over to them. He laid his head against Katelyn's leg for a minute.

"I know the feelin' George. Glad you could have a rest with the crystals." Katelyn said as she patted his head.

"I enjoy the energy of the crystals, too, buddy," Jordan said as he looked at George, and George winked at him.

"It's time to leave this magical place. I wonder if this cave is part of the caves Miss Cora was talkin' about. The ones you have to cross the Northridge Footbridge to get to. It's nowhere near the footbridge, though," Katelyn said, thinking out loud.

"Good thinkin', Katelyn. We'll have to take a hike over that way in a couple of days. How about Saturday mornin'?" Jordan said.

"Not gonna work," Katelyn said. "Sami and I have lots to do before she leaves on Sunday. Plans to solidify for her move and all. And, some fun time, too."

"That's right," Jordan said. "Maybe Sunday afternoon after she leaves, then."

"Now, that's a good idea. Let's plan on it if nothin' else happens," Katelyn said.

"Deal," Jordan said as he turned to walk back into the forest.

The three of them walked back to the entrance of the cave. As they turned around to look again at the room, they were met with an amazing sight. The crystals were throwing rainbows of light all over the place, including onto them.

"Wow!" Katelyn said.

"Incredible!" Jordan said.

George squawked rather loudly.

The light show began to fade, and they walked out of the cave back into the forest.

"Look at that!" Jordan exclaimed as they turned around to look at the cave entrance. It was gone along with the wall of rock. Only trees and other forest plants could be seen all around them.

"Well, The Magic is large and in charge for sure," Katelyn said, looking at Jordan. "You okay with all this?"

"Well, Katie, at first I wasn't. But the more we stood in that cave and then saw the dragon on the ceiling, I got okay with it. The discovery of the split tail of the ceiling dragon in the cave and our shared vision kind of cemented it. Then, realizing that exact tail was on our shoulders, well, it has to be The Magic. Whom am I to deny that?"

"You are a courageous and kind soul, my friend," Katelyn said, squeezing Jordan's shoulder. " I think I'd have gone totally bonkers with all this if I were in your place."

"I was about to but then felt calm. It's as if the crystals were helping me accept everythin'. I guess this means there's more Magic about to happen around here."

"I get the same feelin', too. Nothing bad, but lots of The Magic is about to take place," Katelyn said.

"Let's get back. It's getting' late in the day," Jordan said as he looked towards the west.

The sun was shining through the tops of the trees, and it wouldn't be long before it was suppertime.

"Let's eat our snacks as we walk back to the meadow," Katelyn suggested.

George took to the air, circled the forest, and greeted them as they walked into the meadow. They finally got back to Jordan's truck and put their things in the back.

"The Magic has done it again," Katelyn said as she looked at her phone. "It seems like we've been gone forever, but it's only been a couple of hours."

"This is my first time thing in The Magic. I guess there may be more comin' my way," Jordan said as they drove down the track back onto the road.

"I agree," Katelyn said. "Let's keep today to ourselves. Seems the right thing to do."

"I will, "Jordan replied as they turned into Katelyn's driveway. "See ya' in a couple of days. Thanks for today. I'm gonna take some time to think about everythin'."

"Thanks for comin' with me. We'll talk later," Katelyn said.

Jordan pulled out onto the road as Katelyn went inside and got settled for the night. She sent the measurements and photos to Ian and Finn and then got supper started.

Jordan walked into his kitchen with George right behind him. George morphed into his human self and raided the fridge. Jordan watched him and laughed.

"It was a busy afternoon," George said as he warmed up a piece of apple pie and put a scoop of ice cream on it.

"Me, too," Jordan said as he did the same thing.

"You seem okay with this afternoon," George said between bites.

"I am. It seems those crystals were workin' hard to keep me calm and collected," Jordan replied.

"And your curious nature helps to move things along," George said, smiling.

"Funny, George," Jordan replied sarcastically. "So, I guess all this stuff means somethin' is about to start up again around here."

"Good perception," George said.

"You're not going to tell me," Jordan said. "I know, only what The Magic needs me to know."

"That's right, Jordan," George replied. "Don't worry. You know we'll take good care of you through it all."

"I do know that," Jordan said. "I do have one question for you if they'll let you tell me. In our shared vision, we saw a magnificent bird with vivid colors. It reminded me of a hawk, but it was huge. Was that bird a friend to the man in the vision like you are to me?"

George took a minute before answering. "I asked them if I could tell you, and they said I could. Yes, it is a magical friend to the man in the vision. It's beautiful."

"Yes, it is. And thanks to everyone over there. I appreciate the info," Jordan said, bowing his head.

"Time for me to go back to my eagle self. Lots of patrolling to do," George said as he put his dishes in the sink. Then, he walked through the kitchen and was his eagle self in a flash.

Jordan watched him soar for a few minutes, then cleaned up his stuff and got busy making supper. He liked the whole dessert thing before the meal. He could get used to it for sure, especially when the pies were gifts from his friends in The Creek.

Evening came along, suppers were cleaned up, and The Creek settled into the night. That cave in the north was busy. The dragon lights were flashing something fierce as The Magic came alive again.

CHAPTER 5

By the end of the week, Ethan had obtained all the necessary permits to start excavation on Gina and Terry's new home. Finn had been on their land all week with Karl, setting stakes to mark the areas for the geothermal pipes to be run from the hot springs just north of the property. A couple of the springs were underground, which called for special planning and placing of the pipes.

Ian and Katelyn had been busy with Gina and Terry. They finally agreed on the shape of their house, and the plan was prepared and sent to the building inspector for approval. The approval came through late Thursday. So, Ethan and his team were on the property at first light Friday morning. Finn and Karl beat them there.

"I see we're not the only early birds this mornin'," Ethan said, shaking hands with Karl.

"We beat ya here, boss," Finn said. "And we've got breakfast sandwiches from Michael and Ted. You know how fast news travels through The Creek. They heard we'd be here early and texted me to pick things up. Everythin's in the thermal bag on the seat of my truck. Help yourselves."

"There's coffee there, too," Karl added as he bit into his sandwich. "Those two really know how to take care of us."

"Yes, they do," Katelyn said as she grabbed a sandwich with her name on it. "They even labeled them for us."

This brought laughter all around as they enjoyed their treats from The Store.

"This makes getting up before the crack of dawn so worth it," Finn said as they finished and gathered around Ethan's truck.

"So, the plan for today is to mark, stake and set the lines for the foundations of the house, stables, and barn. The gator is ready to go. Finn and Karl will be doing the same for the geothermal lines. We'll be here all day. The porta-potties should be arriving any minute. I ordered two of them. They'll be set just beyond the two-track, off to the side, out of the way of the trucks and all. Karl, when will you start diggin'?"

"I plan on Monday mornin' first thing. The crew will be bringing the heavy equipment over this afternoon. We chose to park them on the southern edge of the meadow. That way, they'll be out of sight of the road and out of the way of every-thing else," Karl explained.

"I see great minds are workin' together again," Ian said. "Ethan and I chose that area to store the building supplies in. Closer to the actual foundations, though. So you can have all the space you need."

"Let's stake that area first with the orange tape," Ethan suggested.

The area was set in a matter of minutes.

"That tall sign looks great," Ethan said as Karl drove it into the ground. "Karl, you keep comin' up with awesome ideas. That's why we love you, ya know."

"Much obliged, fellas," Karl said as he finished securing the sign in the ground. "I wondered why I hadn't thought of this before. I've got signs for the three buildings as well."

The sign read 'Park Your Big Equipment Here.'

"It's those little things that usually make such a big difference," Ethan said. "So you and Finn carry on with the pipelines, and the rest of us will get busy on the building outlines."

"Sure thing," Finn said as he and Karl set out for the woods and the hot springs. "I decided not to use the hot spring near the house. That's just for their use."

"Good idea," Karl said as they entered the woods and found the first hot spring. They were using LIDAR to map the course of the pipes. They set stakes with blue tops along the designated route.

It was around eleven when Ethan sent a text to come back to the meadow for a break. Finn and Karl had just entered the northern meadow and waived at Ethan. This was the meadow that would be the paddock. The pipeline was set to run along the edge of the meadow up to the house. The second hot spring line would feed hot water to the stables and barn.

"You two are makin' great progress. Run into any problems along the way?" Ian asked as they sat down on the meadow.

"We did," Karl said. "We ran into a length of solid rock, probably granite, where we wanted to run the line. So we had to remap a bit to the west. It all looks good now."

"Funny thing, though," Finn added. "That solid rock showed some form of crystal in it. It was white on the LIDAR."

"Probably quartz," Katelyn said.

Ian and Ethan stared at her.

"Since when did you become a geologist?" Ethan asked.

"Well, most granite has some amount of quartz in it. With all the crystals around here, I suspect those white spots were quarts. Quartz has an electrical charge of its own."

"That's all true," Karl said. "I hope you're gonna give her a raise for sharin' all this excellent knowledge?"

"I like the way you think, Karl," Katelyn said, laughing at the looks on Ian and Ethan's faces.

"You do keep surprisin' us, Katie girl," Ethan said. "Let's get back to work."

Katelyn knew exactly what that length of solid rock was all about. It had to be part of the rock wall she and Jordan had found. Yes, indeed. The Magic was alive and strong out here on the Bancroft's land.

Early afternoon found the water lines marked and the house foundation outlined, ready for Karl and his crew.

Lunch was fun as usual, and it was just a few minutes later when Gina and Terry arrived.

"Hey, guys," Terry said as they walked across the meadow, looking at everything.

"Looks like you mean business out here," Gina said.

"We do," Ethan said as they walked over to the stable area. "Where did ya park?"

"At the end of the track just behind you," Terry said.

"Okay," Ethan said. "We're expecting the heavy equipment in a bit, and I want to make sure you're SUVs out of the way."

"Oh, okay," Terry said. "Seems like there's a lot to do before you start pounding nails."

"There is," Ethan said. "Let's walk over to the house foundation for a minute."

"This looks huge," Gina said.

"It does. That's because it is a big house," Ethan explained. "We need to dig about four feet further out than the plan calls for so we can get all the rough plumbing and foundation supports in place."

"That makes perfect sense," Terry said, walking around the stakes.

"I love your curiosity about all that's being done out here," Ethan said. "But, I do need to ask you not to drop by on a whim. I need to know that the place will be safe for you to walk around. For the rest of the afternoon and next week, I'm gonna have to ask you not to come by. We're expectin' the heavy earth movin' equipment in about a half hour, and I don't want anyone here that doesn't have to be here. Safety is my first concern."

"Wow! I never thought of that," Terry said. "We will stay away for sure."

"Thanks for understandin'. I'll let you know when you can come by and watch the first nail go into the house foundation. It's quite a site to see," Ethan replied.

"I definitely want to be here for that," Gina said.

"Just ask Emily about her experience with that. She was in tears," Ethan said.

"We'll do just that. She said to come by this afternoon for a visit," Gina said.

"I can't wait to see her covered bridge," Terry said as they started to walk back across the meadow.

"That was Karl's idea," Ethan said as Karl walked up to them.

"You're quite the creative type, Karl," Terry said as they shook hands.

'Thanks. I love that bridge as well," Karl replied. "Ethan, the crew is on its way with the equipment. They should be here in about a half hour."

"Great. We'll make sure everything is ready for them," Ethan said.

"Time for us to get out of here and let y'all do your thing," Terry said as he and Gina got into their SUV.

"Thanks so much for understandin'. I'll send some pictures later," Ethan said.

Gina and Terry drove off and passed Karl's crew as they drove past The Store. They were headed to Pine Ridge to pick up a few things before going to Emily's Meadow.

"Terry, our new house will be perfect for us," Gina said.

"Yes, it will," Terry agreed. "It's close to our real home, so we can keep an eye on things. That's why we're back here. We have a very important job ahead of us. You ready for the challenge?"

"I am. We've been informed that our main target isn't quite ready for all that's about to happen. Seems this particular person is a little leery of the future. Everyone is doin' their best to get things in place for the main event to happen," Gina said.

"I know. We just need to be aware of everythin' happening around us and The Creek. I hear these folks are very protective of their own. I like that," Terry said as they drove down the Pine Ridge Road and on to get their errands done.

Hardhats went on when the heavy equipment arrived and was driven across the meadow, then parked along the edge as planned. It took about two hours to unload, park the heavy machinery, and then place the trailers along the top of the two-track. Everyone had moved their vehicles to the northern edge of the meadow to clear the way. It looked like a well-planned dance of the machines.

Karl and his crew left as soon as everything was in place. Ethan, Ian, Katelyn, and Finn spent a few more hours placing and outlining the stables and barn. It was just getting to that time of the day when afternoon morphs into early evening when they finished.

"What a day," Katelyn said as they put their equipment in their vehicles.

"It sure has been," Ethan said, yawning.

"I don't know what I need first. A nap or food," Finn said.

"I say food first," Ian said, looking at something Katelyn was holding. "What cha' got there, Katelyn?"

Katelyn showed them the crystal she had found when they were parking their vehicles on the northern edge of the meadow. It was an opalescent black and somewhat shaped like a rounded triangle.

"That's beautiful," Ian said.

"It reminds me of a giant fish scale," Ethan said. "Or a dragon scale like the ones down the back of a dragon."

"Where did that come from?" Finn asked, looking at the crystal.

"I have no idea," Ethan replied. "Just look at it, though."

"It does look like a dragon scale for sure," Katelyn said. " A little rounded on the edges as if it's been washed over by dirt and water for a long time. Really cool."

"It is," Finn said. "Hold it up to the sunlight for a minute."

Katelyn did just that, and when the sun hit it, the crystal threw rays of every color of the rainbow all over the place. It lasted just a few seconds.

"That was great," Ian said. "It reminds me of Jordan's crystal on his front porch."

"Sure does," Ethan said. "So, I propose we go to The Store for supper. On the business, of course."

Everyone agreed, and a short while later, they were gathered around the table in The Store.

Gina and Terry spent a little while before supper visiting with Emily.

"That bridge is incredible," Terry said as they settled on the porch after their tour of the place. "We met Karl at our site a little while ago. He said we'd enjoy that bridge."

"It is great," Emily said. "I usually walk down there at sunset to stand inside and watch the pond. That way, the critters don't know I'm there, and they come and go into the night as usual."

"I never thought of that whole thing. That's great," Gina said, looking out over the mountains. "This porch, this place, is special."

"Yes, it is," Emily said, whispering as they watched the sun begin its slow descent toward the trees.

They talked about how special The Creek was to them, and Emily listened with a smile on her face the whole time.

"How did you get here anyway?" Terry asked. "I don't remember you livin' here and all."

"That's true, Terry," Emily said. "I decided a new life was in order and chose this place. It was as if the mountains were callin' me home."

Emily was very careful in giving the details of her relocation story. Even though that horrible danger that had put her here was gone, the U.S. Marshalls were still in full protection mode. She gave the story they had decided on to anyone who asked.

"I know what you mean," Gina said. "When we found out about the inheritance, we instinctively knew we had to come home. Make this our forever home."

"That's it exactly, honey. Our forever home," Terry said.

"I like the way you say that. It fits you well," Emily said.

"Emily, I'd like to ask you somethin'. Feel free to say no," Gina said.

"Go ahead," Emily said, knowing what Gina would ask her.

"Are you gifted like Miss Cora by any chance?" Gina asked.

"Yes, by every chance, I am.' Emily said. "Not with all the powers she has, but a lot of them. I'm a psychic medium and healer."

"I just knew it," Gina said.

"There are quite a few special ones in The Creek," Terry added. "It seems as if this place was made especially for them. It's here to protect them and nurture them."

"I feel the same way," Emily said. "I didn't even know this place existed until I decided to step into my gifts full force. I love The Creek and everyone in it," Emily said quietly.

"So do we," Terry said. "That was probably the biggest deciding factor that brought us home."

"So, have you decided on anything extra special for your build?" Emily asked.

"Not yet. You've already got the covered bridge, and we don't have a pond to cross to get to our house. We keep talkin' with Ian and everyone, and I'm sure that an idea will pop into our heads when least expected," Terry replied

"Isn't that the way things usually happen?" Gina said.

They talked for a while more then Gina and Terry decided it was time to move along.

"Thanks for havin' us. Your farm is wonderful," Gina said as they got into their SUV.

"You are welcome to stop by whenever you want to. Trouble will let us know you're here."

"He's a great pooch," Terry said. "So long."

Gina and Terry left, stopping for a few minutes on the covered bridge and getting out of their SUV to look through the walls at the pond. They were greeted by the usual array of ducks, swans, and little critters that had made the pond their central watering hole. They moved on a few minutes later.

Emily had just received a text from Ethan to join him and the group at The Store for supper. She texted back a big smiley face, washed up, and was on her way in short time. Sami had received a similar text from Katelyn and arrived at the same time as Emily.

Emily and Sami walked into The Store together and joined everyone at the table just as Katelyn was showing them her dragon scale crystal.

"Where did you find that one?" Hal asked as he gave his order to Ted.

"Before you answer that, let me get Emily and Sami's orders," Ted said.

They gave Ted their orders, gathered napkins and all, and sat across from Katelyn.

"We've been up at the Bancroft's land all day setting stakes and outlinin' everythin'. We had to park our cars and trucks up on the northern border of the paddock meadow so Karl could get his heavy equipment in for Monday. I was closest to the forest, and when I opened my door, I happened to look down and saw this shiny black thing just past my door. I picked it up and saw that it was a crystal. I've never seen one like this before. I mean the color and shape. It's like an opalescent black color, and it glows all the time. Finn suggested I put it in the direct sunlight, and it sent rainbows all over the place," Katelyn explained.

"It reminded us of Jordan's crystal on his front porch," Ian added. "Just a really small version."

"Ethan said it looked more like a big fish scale than a dragon scale," Finn said. "We asked him why he thought of a dragon scale, and he said it just came to him like that."

"Really? You thought of a dragon scale?" Hal said.

"Our Ethan has quite the imagination," Sami added.

"Guilty as charged," Ethan said as Ted came through the kitchen door with a tray full of food.

"Supper is served," Ted said as he handed around their plates.

"This looks great," Katelyn said. "I think I could eat two suppers tonight. Bein' outdoors all day makes me wicked hungry."

"I know that feelin'," Emily said. "Takin' care of the farm has the same effect on me. Some nights, I'm just too tired to do a lot of cookin'. Glad Ted's here for us."

"Sure is one of the best benefits of movin' to The Creek as far as I'm concerned," Sami said.

"Hey, Ted, that reminds me to say thanks for the fantastic breakfast this morning," Finn said. "We all appreciate the love you sent our way."

"You are very welcome, as always," Ted said as he went back into the kitchen.

"This crystal is amazin' for sure," Hal said as he gazed at it.

Jordan walked into the dining area just then and saw the crystal.

"Would ya look at that?"! Jordan said as he picked up the crystal. "I've never seen a black one before."

"None of us have," Finn said.

"Does it really look like what I think it looks like?" Jordan asked, looking at everyone.

"And what would that be?" Ian asked.

"Well, here goes. It looks like a dragon scale from the back of a dragon," Jordan.

"Sure does," Ethan replied. "We all think it does."

"Ya just never know what's gonna happen next around here," Jordan said, looking at Katelyn for only a second.

"Ain't that the truth," Michael said as he joined the group for a minute. "Just when we think things are getting back to normal, one more thing happens."

They all agreed with Michael.

"Desert, anyone?" Ted asked.

"Not for me," Finn and Katelyn said at the same time.

"You've stuffed me well again," Sami said.

"I'll have a piece of your sinfully wonderful chocolate cake," Hal said.

"Ice cream with that?" Ted asked.

"Sure. Why not?" Hal replied.

"Anyone else?" Ted asked.

The others said no, and Ted went to get Hal's cake and ice cream.

"Who found it?" Jordan asked.

"I did at the northern edge of the paddock meadow," Katelyn replied.

"Have Gina and Terry seen it yet?" Hal asked.

"Nope," Ethan replied.

"Miss Cora know about this?" Michael asked.

"I sent her a picture and texted her about how I found it," Katelyn replied. "She said she's never seen anythin' like this. Wants to come by tomorrow evenin to have a look."

"I'm sure she's thinkin' on it right now," Emily said.

They talked for a few more minutes before folks started to leave.

"Has anyone seen Matthews and Jenna lately? Seems they haven't been around much since the football game," Hal asked.

"Jenna has a commission creating some artwork for a wall at the Boone library. So she's spendin' a lot of time there. Matthews is at a conference at Quantico. Andrews is here keepin' an eye on things. You remember him, Emily? He joined the group right after your battle thing," Michael explained.

"I do remember him. He stopped by the day Matthews left. Said Mathews will be back Sunday afternoon. Nice guy," Emily answered. "Ethan, you look like you're about to fall asleep. Come on home. I'll tuck you in."

"How can I say no to this?" Ethan said as the others laughed at him.

"Ya can't," Ted replied. "Get goin' now."

Ethan and Emily headed to Emily's Meadow, and the others went on home as well.

Sami and Katelyn were settling down for the night.

"Katie, can't tell ya how thrilled I am to come live here with ya," Sami said, plopping down on Katelyn's bed.

"I'm still tryin' to believe it's for real," Katelyn replied. "When I left to come home, I was wicked sad about us not bein' together anymore and just as thrilled about comin' home. We promised to visit a lot, and we have. But it just hasn't been the same. Even knowin' just where you are hasn't changed how much I love ya'. And, now, all this stuff happenin' around here with the best part bein' we're back together again. I'm beyond words."

"Me, too," Sami said as tears of joy rolled down their cheeks. "No matter what happens, I'm never movin' away from you again. I love my new job. But missin' you has been agony."

"Ditto," Katelyn said, yawning all the way down to her toes. "Time to crash. Love ya' forever and always, my Sami."

"Love ya' forever and always, my Katie," Sami said as she went to her room.

They were both asleep even before their heads hit their pillows.

Jordan took care of things and then walked out into his field as evening gave way to a million stars in the night sky. George flew over and landed next to Jordan.

"Pure magic," George said, looking up into the sky.

"Sure is," Jordan replied.

They stood there quietly for a while, just watching the sky. A shooting star flew overhead, and they smiled.

In an instant, the world changed for Jordan. That huge shadow he had seen after the Battle on The Rise not only flew overhead, but it landed a ways from Jordan and George. George immediately morphed into his human self as Jordan watched the shadow take form.

"What the hell is happenin'?!" Jordan yelled, looking at George. "Oh no. If you're human, then Magic is about to go nuts around here."

"Yup," George said. "Try to remain calm."

"Seriously?" Jordan said.

"Watch there," George said as the form became solid.

"What the fuck? That's a real dragon. A real dragon in my field," Jordan yelled out. "What the hell is a dragon doin' in my field? Dragons are real? What the fuck?"

"Well said, Jordan," George replied, laughing at Jordan. "I couldn't have said it better."

"Shut the fuck up, George," Jordan replied, giving the death look to George. "Don't even try to talk right now. Is that thing for real?"

The dragon nodded its head at Jordan.

"It understands me?" How can it understand me?" Jordan said. "Talk to me now, George."

"The dragon is real. It's pure magic," George said as he walked over to the dragon and touched its wing. "Hi there, Penny. Great to see you again."

"It's wonderful to be together again, George," Penny replied.

Jordan sat down on the ground quite suddenly, in total shock. "Not only does it look real, you seem to know this dragon, George. Details now!" Jordan demanded.

"Well, Jordan, I do know this dragon. You know that I am a magical creature, and you seem to accept that as real," George said.

"I do accept you as a magical creature," Jordan replied. "Not sure how all this really works, but I do like your friendship and protection. Thanks to everyone on The Other Side."

A quick flash of light was the response from The Magic.

"This is gonna take a while," George was saying when the dragon interrupted him.

"Now, George, let me take over here," the dragon said. "Hi, Jordan. I'm Penelope. George and a few other special ones are allowed to call me Penny. You can call me Penny."

Jordan just stared at her.

"Well, that wasn't too well received," Penny said. "Jordan, I'm going to move closer to you. Is that okay with you?"

Jordan looked over at George, then looked back at Penny and nodded his head. Penny took a few steps closer to Jordan, but not too close. She didn't want him going totally nuts.

"This is much better," Penny said as she settled down. "Jordan, dragons are real. You've been shown some amazing magic these past few months, and I know you're on overload. I know Katelyn is helping tremendously as well."

"She is," Jordan said, agreeing with Penny.

"She is special indeed," Penny said. "I know the two of you were in the caves to the north of here, and you felt a calming, soothing, healing energy there. You needed that healing, for sure. So glad you picked up on the idea of going there with Katelyn."

"Katie has a way of making sense of all this magical stuff. So does George," Jordan said, looking right at Penny. "They help me stay focused."

"You have been exposed to so much magic, and you've accepted the challenge every time. We thank you for that. I have to say that the crystal sword is magnificent even if it did come from my home," Penny said.

"Your home? My cave is your home?" Jordan asked.

"Yes, it is, Jordan. I'm so glad you felt pulled to this land and decided to buy it and settle here. Ethan and Ian have built you a beautiful home and barn. I know George is thrilled with the barn," Penny said.

"I am. I love my home in the barn," George replied.

"Glad to hear it, George. You're very welcome," Jordan said.

"I'm glad you accepted the gifts of crystals I left for you. They're very important in The Realm of The Magic."

"You left those for me? Thanks," Jordan said. "That one on the front porch is amazin' the way the sun hits it and throws beams of color everywhere."

"I agree," Penny said. "Anything created by The Magic is incredible. Now, back to this minute and you seeing me for the first time. I am really real. What color am I?"

"You're purple, like the dark purple of royal robes," Jordan answered.

"Perfect description," Penny replied.

"It was you I saw in that tunnel down the hall that day, wasn't it?" Jordan asked.

"It was," Penny replied. "I was checking in on you."

"So, Miss Penny, why are you here now, and why am I talkin' with you?" Jordan asked as he stood up. "You still look huge when I stand up."

"I am huge. I'm a full-grown dragon. And, yes, before you even ask, I can breathe fire if needed," Penny said.

"Oh, great! Another potential problem. I'll try hard not to piss you off," Jordan said sarcastically.

"He's taking this rather well, don't you think, George?" Penny said.

"He's in total shock, Penny. He's gonna flip out in a few more minutes. So let's save the fire breathing for another time," George cautioned.

"Rightly so, George," Penny agreed. "Jordan, I will never breathe fire on you ever. I'm here to protect you."

"From what?" Jordan asked, still looking bewildered.

"That's another subject for another conversation," George said before Penny could answer Jordan.

"Somethin' is gonna happen in The Creek again, isn't it?" Jordan asked.

"Not anything like the battles. The Dark Force is being held captive for a long while. We're all safe here from that horrible reality," George replied.

"Then what?" Jordan asked.

Neither the dragon nor George said a word.

"I see. It's like that. I don't need to know the details. Okay. That's probably a good thing 'cause I'm gonna need a lot of time to decide if this whole evening is reality or I'm hallucinating," Jordan said.

"Rightly so, again," Penny replied. "Jordan, please walk over to me and touch my wing. I'm very real.."

Jordan looked over at George, and George walked with Jordan to stand in front of Penny. It took Jordan a few minutes to finally reach out and touch Penny's wing.

"It's really warm," Jordan said.

"You have a lovely touch, Jordan," Penny replied, sighing. "And, why wouldn't I be warm?"

"I don't know. I guess I figured if dragons were real, they'd be cold like reptiles. Sorry about that. I now know that dragons are very real, and you are wonderfully warm," Jordan explained.

"Well said," George replied as he stroked Penny's wing.

"Is she purring?" Jordan asked George.

"I do believe she is. She's quite content at the moment," George explained.

Jordan laughed as he said, "I guess I have a lot to learn about dragons then, don't I."

"You do," Penny replied. "Jordan, you found The Crystal Dragon I left for you. Any time you need me for anything, all you have to do is raise it up, and I'll feel its energy and be here in an instant."

"You left that for me? Thanks," Jordan said. "I'll remember to do just that."

"Penny, I think Jordan's had all he can take this evening," George said.

"I agree. Time to return to my cave for a rest. I'll talk with you later, Jordan. Oh, and don't worry about me showing up whenever I feel like it. We need to keep me a secret from The Creek. I'm your dragon, Jordan. Always have been and always will be. Later," Penny said and took to the air, flying over the field toward Jordan's Cave.

"What did she mean by always have been and always will be?" Jordan asked George.

"Dragon speak, I guess," George said, looking away from Jordan.

"Oh, brother! More secrets," Jordan sighed.

"Always more secrets in The Magic. Time for me to go back to my eagle self. Later, Jordan. You'll be all right with all this dragon stuff. Follow me back to the barn. Time for some sleep," George said.

Jordan walked back to the barn with George flying around him. George settled in for the night as Jordan closed the big barn door.

"Sleep well, Jordan," George said.

"You, too," Jordan replied.

Jordan walked into his kitchen and yelled, "What the hell? More incredible Magic? I need some help here so I won't go completely nuts. And, whatever happened to no more magic?"

A voice came out of the air, answering Jordan. "You took that well. We thank you. Now rest. We'll send healing energy all night as you sleep. We are grateful for your acceptance of Penny."

"How can I not believe in dragons? I just touched one and talked with one for a while. I need some food and sleep," Jordan said. "Later."

Jordan knew he had eaten something but couldn't remember what it was a minute after he finished. He took a quick, hot shower and flopped down onto his bed. He didn't remember falling asleep. He did remember his last thought was of a dragon named Penny he had talked to.

Gina and Terry decided to go out to their land after supper. They had something they needed to do out there. It was close to dark when they parked at the end of the two-track. All the big, heavy earth-moving equipment was in place, just like Ethan said it would be. They headed to the northern edge of the paddock meadow and stepped into the woods. If you didn't know better, you'd have said they knew exactly where they were going.

The instant they stepped into those woods, that crystal between the two old oak trees began to glow.

"Nice to be welcomed home," Terry said as they passed the crystal and headed north.

Just as they were in about the same place Katelyn and Jordan had been when they saw the solid rock wall, the entrance to that same cave materialized right in front of them. They entered the cave, and the dragon drawing on the ceiling came to life.

"We are home again," Gina said, looking all around. "It feels perfect."

"Yes, it does," Terry said as he walked over to a ledge on the far wall and ran his hand over it. Food and drink appeared, along with a table and chairs.

Gina and Terry sat and ate, not talking for a bit.

"Katelyn and Jordan have been here," Terry said as they finished eating. "I can feel their residual energy."

"Me, too," Gina said. "It feels so right and proper. Just like it always has and always will."

"I know they haven't been shown everythin' yet. We still have some time before they're gonna be needed in this place, though."

"You're right," Gina agreed. "We just need to stay focused on the build. It must be completed as scheduled."

"Ethan and Ian are excellent," Terry said excitedly. "I would have never thought up that geothermal thing. And Ian and Katelyn. Aren't they incredible with their ideas and all?"

"Oh, they all are the best," Gina said. "It's gonna be fun driving that first nail into the foundation in a couple of weeks. I love the wrap-around porch idea, too."

"Me, too," Terry said as he stood up and stretched.

"Not now, Terry," Gina said. "We need to be patient."

"I know," Terry said. "I was just thinkin' about it. That's all. I guess I'm tired. Let's get back to the old home place."

"We should before anyone begins to miss us," Gina said.

Gina and Terry waved their hands across the air in the room, and the table and chairs disappeared.

"I love doin' that," Gina said, giggling.

As they left the cave, the entrance disappeared as before. They walked through the paddock meadow and were in their car in no time. It was a good thing that Ethan hadn't installed the security cameras yet. But they already knew that. They were back home and settled for the night just as Penny took to the air. She was flying her usual route, making sure The Creek was safe and sound. It was. For now.

CHAPTER 6

Sami had breakfast all ready when Katelyn finally woke up.

"Lazy bones," Sami said as she set a cup of hot chocolate in front of Katelyn.

"Much obliged," Katelyn said, taking a sip. "I guess bein' out-side all day yesterday made me really tired. It was great fun and all, though."

"How much did you get done?" Sami said as they ate their breakfast.

"We got all the buildings staked and outlined. We worked right up until the sun began to set. About supper time."

"It must look great," Sami said. "Did Karl get his equipment delivered?"

"Sure did," Katelyn said. "The place looks like it's ready to go. And, it is."

"I'll bet Gina and Terry are all excited," Sami said. "Did they stop by?"

"Yup. And Ethan had to explain to them that they really shouldn't do just that on account of safety and all. He said we'd be sending pictures and texts while all the excavation was goin' on. Then, he asked them if they wanted to be there to pound the first nail into the foundation of their new home."

"OMG, they must have been thrilled," Sami said, laughing.

"They were and promised to follow Ethan's rules and all," Katelyn said. "Ethan's security guys will be setting up security cameras and all today. That guy really knows how to organize things."

"I agree with you there," Sami said. "Just like Jordan. Whenever I give him a task, he has a plan in place a few minutes later. And he can organize things faster and more completely than I ever could. So, you had a great idea in suggesting I hire him."

"I did, didn't I?" Katelyn said.

"How'd you know he could do all this stuff?" Sami asked as they cleared the breakfast dishes.

"It was a hunch. Remember when we were in grad school, and you'd say somethin', and I'd have an idea for it? That was the hunch thing," Katelyn replied.

"Oh, God, yes, I do remember," Sami said. "And, now, we can do just that hunch thing again."

"Forever and always," Katelyn replied.

The two of them went about their morning, doing laundry and packing Sami's few things to take with her when she left.

"Leave all your other stuff here. I'll take it over after you leave tomorrow," Katelyn suggested.

"Great idea," Sami said. "More time for us to get into trouble. Speaking of trouble, can't wait to see your brothers and the progress on their houses."

"That's right," Katelyn said. "You haven't seen the mess in the fields yet. The foundations were poured about two weeks ago, and Ethan says the framing will start on Wednesday. Those two are so excited ya' can hardly keep them still long enough to talk with them."

"I can just see them runnin' all over the place," Sami said, laughing. "Hope they'll sit long enough to enjoy supper tonight."

" Oh, they will. They love to eat. Mom and Dad are thrilled for them, too. They keep givin' them ideas about how to decorate their places that the boys had to finally ask them to stop. They all laughed, and Mom promised to slow down and only give advice when they asked her for some."

"I've been workin' on a little somethin' for them. Come look," Sami said as they ran over to Sami's house.

Katelyn burst out laughing when she saw Sami's sketches. One was of a strawberry house, and the other was of a blueberry house.

"These are great! I can't wait to see their faces when you give them the finished work," Katelyn said, laughing with Sami.

"They'll be ready for their housewarming party down the road," Sami said.

Sami and Katelyn talked about those sketches as they went back to Katelyn's house to bake for the family supper that night.

Jenna had gotten home late Friday night and was having a bit of a sleep-in. She got up around nine, made breakfast, and got showered and ready for a slow and easy Saturday. She had been working long hours all week on the mural for the library in Boone and needed a break. The mural was all sketched and ready to be painted into place. She incorporated photos from the City of Boone's long history and the library's history throughout the mural. They were being framed by a master wood craftsman she met just after returning home. Hal had supplied the wood for the frames from the downed trees from all the craziness from the summer.

As Jenna sat out on the barn's back deck with a cup of hot coffee, she suddenly had a vision of a dragon. It came to her out of nowhere, and she smiled.

"Nice try, guys," she said, looking out over the field toward the faerie house. "Really cute."

The faerie house twinkled lights at her comment.

"Love y'all, too," Jenna said, bowing her head to show respect. "I guess this means dragons are gonna be my next theme. I love dragons, as you well know."

This time, the whole field flashed colored lights at her. Jenna laughed and continued to sit quietly, watching the morning take over the land.

It was near ten thirty when she finally got up to return to the house. Just as she walked down the few steps to the ground, a shadow flew over the barn. She looked up as it returned to fly directly over her. It was a huge flying thing. It was a ways up and flying in a sunny sky. For just an instant, Jenna could have sworn it was the shape of a dragon.

She stood there for a minute more, then said, "Okay. I get it. Dragons. Nice trick having that shape fly over me. I really wish dragons were real. I'd love to befriend one. They are majestic and beautiful."

Jenna went back into the house and got busy with her slow-day stuff. Matthews was coming home today, and she could hardly wait. That dragon shadow was on her mind all day.

Hal and a couple of his childhood friends were sitting on the porch at The Store that same Saturday morning, talking about whatever came to mind.

"So, Hal, I see you've been busy with those frames and tables," Bob said.

"Sure have been," Hal replied. "That frame just inside the store with the picture of all of us at the Grandaddy Mimm's sign is one of them."

"That whole sign thing is still crazy," Ned said. "Every time I think of it, I start laughin' all over again."

"Me, too," Hal said, smiling. "It does look real good over there. Y'all did a great job resettin' in a ways off the road."

"I appreciate that," Bob replied. "Ethan was real kind in askin' for our help."

"That's the truth," Ned said. "Hal, I was just thinkin' about what Miss Cora was sayin' about those Crystal Caves. Seein' all these little crystals out here made me think about that. Do ya' really think they're up there somewheres?"

"Now, Ned, I do believe they are up there way past Emily's meadow. I was thinkin' about takin' a look for them. Ya' know, just wanderin' around up there for a while," Hal said.

Kendra came across the road just then, and the boys stood up and said their good mornings.

"Hey, Miss Kendra," Ned said, removing his hat with the others.

"Good mornin', boys," Kendra replied. "Havin' a sit this mornin'?"

"Yes, Ma'am, we are," Bob replied. "It's such a great day we thought we'd just sit out here for a spell."

"Great idea. I'm headed in for a breakfast bagel. See y'all later; enjoy the day," Kendra said as she went into the store.

A couple more folks came and went for a bit before the boys got back to their talking about the caves.

And then, a different kind of visitor came by. It was a pig. A full-grown pig. It walked right up the steps and sat down next to Hal.

"Hey, there, Wanda Sue. How ya been?" Hal asked as he gave her a pat on the head.

Wanda Sue gave a soft grunt, and it looked like a smile came across her face.

"I swear that pig's smilin'," Bob said.

"Sure looks like it to me, too," Ned said.

"She probably is," Hal replied, laughing with the guys.

Michael came out onto the porch just then, saw Wanda Sue, and said, "Looks like Wanda Sue decided to take a bit of a road trip this mornin'."

Michael grabbed one of the water bowls he and Ted kept full on the porch and placed it in front of the pig. Wanda Sue had a long drink and then laid down and settled into a nap.

"Must have been a long walk over here," Hal said.

"She's from the Harrington's farm down past Ethan's place on the Pine Ridge Road. Don't mean she set off from there. She has a lust for wanderin' about," Bob said.

"That's true, Bob," Ned said. "I hear tell she goes along for days before someone takes her back home. Miss Cora's even got some special food for her when she visits."

This made everyone laugh.

"Pete usually gets a phone call and comes by to fetch her from time to time," Ned explained. "He told me he's tried all kinds of pens to keep her in, but she manages to escape anyways."

"He locks her up at night in the barn. She seems to like that. I hear tell it's in the morning when he lets the cows out into the pasture that she makes her move," Hal added.

"Maybe her name should be Houdini instead of Wanda Sue," Ben was sayin' when some folks came by The Store.

"Looks like Wanda Sue's out wanderin' again," Valerie said.

"She sure is," Bob replied.

"She was at our place a couple of weeks ago. She set a spell. We gave her water and food. She took a nap and then went on her way," JJ added.

"Well, we'll be seein' ya," Valerie said as she and JJ went into The Store.

The guys got back to talking about those Crystal Caves.

"About those caves," Bob said. "I've been thinkin' about them, too. I think we'd have to go up to the stream and cross the NorthRidge Footbridge to get to them,"

"I agree," Hal said, sitting forward in his rocker. "I was thinkin' that exact same thing. It seems to me that they'd have to be that far into the forest. I remember bein' up there with you guys. We were just hikin' around, not lookin' for anythin' special. Remember?"

"We do," Bob replied, nodding his head along with Ned. "We musta' spent about three hours hikin' around up there. We didn't find the bridge until late in the day, so we didn't go too far into the forest before we had to turn around and get home."

"That's right," Ned said. "That footbridge is so old. It's all made of stones and rocks. Looks like a real master craftsman made that thing by hand. I would think it's gotta be at least three hundred years old or so."

"I agree," Hal said. "It surely is a work of art. That's The Crystal Creek flowin' under it, right?"

"It most definitely is," Bob replied. "I should now bein' a forest ranger and all."

"Has it ever been washed over in a flood?" Ned asked.

"Not that I know of. We keep detailed records of that stuff, and I've never come across a report of flooding near the footbridge," Bob answered.

"I've got an idea," Hal said with a big smile on his face. "You up for a hike?"

Ned and Bob began to smile as Bob said, "Are you thinkin' what I think you're thinkin'?"

"I believe he is," Ned replied. "We're gonna go look for those caves."

"Indeed, we are," Hal said. "How about we meet here at ten tomorrow mornin', ready to go? We can get sandwiches from Ted and take off."

"It's supposed to be a beautiful fall mountain day tomorrow," Ned said. "Count me in."

"Same here," Bob replied. "Be sure to pack the right gear and all. I think we've learned a great deal about wanderin' through the forest since we were kids."

Hal and Ned laughed along with Bob. The guys spent a bit of time planning their hike before they went inside to place their lunch order with Ted.

"Oh, Ted," Hal said as they walked up into the dining area.

"You guys hungry already?" Ted said, teasing them.

"Never can get enough of your cookin', Ted," Ned replied.

"Ted, we're gonna go hikin' tomorrow and want to place our lunch requests with you today," Bob said.

"That sounds like a good idea," Ted replied as he served a few folks their breakfasts. "Decide what ya' want, and I'll be back in a minute."

The guys took a minute to say hey to the folks at the table.

"You're right about Ted's food," Hazel said. "It really is addictive."

They talked for a bit before Ted returned.

"So, what can I get ready for y'all?" Ted asked.

The guys gave him their lunch orders and asked for them to be ready at ten.

"It's a deal," Ted said. "Where do y'all plan on goin' tomorrow?"

"We're gonna go lookin' for those Crystal Caves Miss Cora was talkin' about. Maybe we'll find them," Hal answered.

"Could be," Ted said. "Be sure to charge your phones. I'll let Matthews know where you'll be just in case you don't get back before dark."

"That's a great idea, Ted. Thanks for thinkin' of it," Bob said.

"As a pilot, I learned ya' should always leave a flight plan; for you guys, it would be a hikin' plan with someone in case something strange happens," Ted said.

"So glad you thought of that," Hal replied. "We'll be sure to do just that every time we set out on an adventure into the great outdoors."

"You can text it to me, and I'll post it at the register, just in case," Ted said. "I'll send an email around lettin' folks know what we're doin'. We all gotta take care of each other."

Folks talked for a few minutes more before the guys took their leave.

"See ya in the morning," Ned said as they all went their separate way.

Jordan was busy in the barn getting things ready for the winter. He took his gator and rakes and set out for the front of the house to clean up the downed branches and such from the latest wind storm. George flew alongside and settled on the porch to watch.

"At least you could help me out here," Jordan said.

"Not this time, my friend. I'm gonna stay right here and supervise," George replied, laughing.

"Like hell you are," Jordan replied, throwing a handful of leaves at George.

"Real cute, Jordan," George replied, pushing them off the porch with his wing.

"At least you cleared them off the porch," Jordan sassed back.

"It seems I do clean up after you a bit," George said, hopping off the porch and walking over to Jordan.

"I do believe that's part of your destiny," Jordan said, throwing sticks into the back of the gator.

"Jordan, watch out," George hollered as he pushed Jordan aside.

A large branch from an old oak tree came crashing down just where Jordan had been standing. As it was, the smaller branches brushed over Jordan before they settled down onto the ground.

"George, where are you?" Jordan said, trying to find the eagle.

"I'm over here under the small branch to your left," George replied.

Jordan walked over and lifted the branch, and George walked out from under it.

"You hurt anywhere?" Jordan asked as he watched George fluff his feathers and spread his wings.

"Nope. I'm in good shape," George answered.

"Except for the leaf sticking out of the back of your neck. Kinda looks like a crazy necklace or somethin'," Jordan said as he removed the leaf. He checked George's neck and back to make sure nothing else was caught and nothing was hurt.

"Ya look okay," Jordan said. "Everythin' in workin' order?"

"Yes, it is, Jordan. I'm all okay. Thanks for the help," George said. "This is a rather large branch."

"It is," Jordan replied, walking the length of the branch. "I've been watching it all summer. I thought it was cracked and wondered when it would fall. Well, it has. It's bigger than I realized. I'm gonna go get the chainsaw to cut it up. Keep an eye on things. I'll be right back."

Jordan hopped into the gator, drove into the barn, and put more tools in it. He was back in the front yard a few minutes later.

"Nothing else has fallen," George said. "I'm gonna do a flyover while you cut up that branch. You going to keep it for firewood?"

"That's what I was thinkin', George," Joran said. "Have a nice flight."

George took to the sky, and Jordan spent the rest of the morning cutting, loading, and stacking the pieces of the branch in the barn for use later in the winter.

Jenna was in the kitchen when she heard the back door close. She ran and threw herself at Matthews as he stepped into the kitchen.

"Why, Miss Jenna. I do like the way you greet me after bein' gone a while," Matthews said as he kissed her long and deeply.

"I do like the way you show me how much you've missed me, Mr. Matthews," Jenna replied, running her finger along his belly to his hard dick.

Mathews ripped Jenna's clothes off as she did the same to him. Then, he set her up on the butcher block island, spread her legs, and began sucking her breast and stroking her clit.

Jenna moaned as she neared her first climax. Matthews slid his fingers into her, and she came.

"Matthews, take me with your hard dick," Jenna hollered out.

They fell to the floor on the pile of clothes, and Matthews moved between her legs.

"Anything you want, Ma'am," Matthews said as Jenna grabbed his hard shaft and pushed it into her wet place.

"More! More!" Jenna screamed as Matthews began to push into her hard and fast.

Jenna grabbed Matthews's ass and pushed against him as he pushed against her. In a flash, she began to climax. Matthews felt this and pushed harder and faster, finally meeting her moment of ecstasy with his own. They flew off into the universe and then slept a bit right there on the kitchen floor.

Jenna felt Matthews stroking her sides as she began to wake up.

"I do believe I approve of your welcome home surprise," Matthews said.

"Ditto," Jenna replied, stroking Matthews as well.

"Shall we take this upstairs?" Matthews asked.

"Indeed," Jenna replied as they got up, locked the house, and resumed their lovemaking for quite some time.

It was mid-afternoon when they both said, "God! I'm starvin'."

They laughed and showered and ran downstairs to raid the frig. Jenna had made a few of Matthews's favorites the day before, and he let her know how much he appreciated her efforts. They spent the rest of the day and evening getting caught up on their worlds and The Creek.

Sami and Katelyn arrived at the family farm right on time. They were greeted with big hugs from Nate and Jeremy.

"Welcome home, Sami," Nate said.

"God! I love y'all," Sami said as Katelyn's mom and dad shared hugs with the girls.

"I do love havin' two daughters for sure," Joe said.

"And I do love bein' a part of this great family," Sami said as she wiped a few tears from her cheeks.

"Come on in. Supper's ready," Jackie said as she wrapped an arm around Sami's shoulders.

"I suggested Katie and I bake some stuff, but she said you had told her not to," Sami said as they gathered around the kitchen table.

"That's right," Jackie replied. "I need to show you how to make my famous pies first. We have plenty of frozen berries to use throughout the whole winter."

"I am lookin' forward to that for sure," Sami said.

"So are we. We love Mom's cookin'," Jeremy said. "So, you come over a lot to practice makin' pies and all."

"Nice, boys," Joe said, laughing with everyone else. "It would appear that you're only happy about Sami joinin' our family for her culinary skills."

"Oh, no, sir," Nate replied. "We love her for her. The fact that she wants to learn to bake like mom is a bonus."

Katelyn threw her napkin at her brother, saying, "Nice try, bro. Didn't work."

"Thanks for stickin' up for me, Katie. But, as you are quite aware, I can handle these two just fine. Who said you'd get to eat my pies?"

"Nice touch, Sami," Jackie said. "I do believe I don't have much to teach you at all. I may learn a thing or two from you."

"Great! More girl stuff to deal with," Jeremy said.

"You got that right, boy," Katelyn replied.

"Let's settle for a minute and give thanks for this family and supper," Joe said, saying a few words in recognition of all the Divine had done for them.

The evening carried on with lots of laughter and fun as they brought their desserts to the living room to settle and watch the fire. A bit later, Katie and Sami stood up at the same time.

"What are the two of you up to?" Jackie asked.

"We're goin' to The Rise to have a look around. Haven't been there since The Battle," Katelyn replied.

"Have a nice visit," her dad said.

A few minutes later, the girls were at the bottom of The Rise. The staircase showed itself, and they climbed to the top. The view was amazing, as always. They stood in a world of their own silent thoughts as they looked out over the land in all directions. Night descended over the Blue Ridge, and those magnificent heavenly bodies glowed like diamonds in the sunlight.

Katelyn and Sami sighed at the same time, then looked at each other with that look ya get when you intuitively know what the other person is thinking.

"Yup," Katelyn said as she scrunched shoulders with Sami

"Yup," Sami replied, returning the shoulder hug. "This place is beyond words. The Magic here is so strong. All ya' need to do is stand here, and it'll bring balance to your soul."

"Truth," Katelyn said as she looked around the top of The Rise. "These crystals are glowin' like always. They look like tiny rainbows on steroids."

Sami laughed at this. "Yes, they do," she said. "Look at this bunch over here. What does that remind you of?"

Katelyn followed Sami to the southern area of The Rise and looked at the crystal formation.

"Good grief! It looks like a dragon," Katelyn said as she squatted down to get a closer look.

"It most certainly does," Sami said, joining her.

"A teeny, tiny dragon of all colors," Katelyn said. "These are really warm. Put your hand over here."

"Wow! They are really warm and seem to be humming like all the other ones," Sami said.

As they watched the crystals, a shadow covered The Rise for a second or two.

"What the hell was that? It was really close," Sami said, standing up and looking up into the night sky.

"Beats the hell out of me," Katelyn replied. "It sure was close. Too big to be an owl."

"I agree," Sami said as she kept looking around.

"You think it'll come back?" Katelyn said, looking for the shadow.

"Don't know," Sami replied. "But if this thing is connected to The Magic around here, I think it will come by. Look!"

As Katelyn looked over toward where Sami was pointing, they saw a small shape begin to fly toward them. The closer it got, the bigger it became.

Just as it approached The Rise, Katelyn saw what it was.

"Oh, my God! That's a dragon!" Katelyn yelled. "A for real dragon."

"It's huge!" Sami said as it flew over them, circled to the north, and came back.

"What the hell is a dragon doin' in The Creek?" Katelyn yelled out.

"How the hell should I know?" Sami replied as the dragon flew over them again.

"Hey! It just raised a wing at us like it was sayin' hi," Katelyn said as the two of them turned to watch the dragon fly away to the south.

"I saw that!" Sami said, jumping all over the place.

Katelyn looked at Sami, and Sami looked at Katelyn in silence for just a moment. Then, they began to talk at the same time.

"A real dragon?" Sami said.

"It was huge," Katelyn said.

"And it waved at us as if it knew us," Sami added.

"Yeah! What the fuck was that all about? I would know if I had met a dragon in my lifetime," Katelyn exclaimed.

"For sure," Sami said, agreeing with Katelyn. "I have definitely never met a dragon before ever that I can remember."

"In all your travels here and around the universes?" Katelyn said, looking right into Sami's eyes.

"Yes! Definitely! I'm not holdin' anythin' back," Sami said. "I always hoped dragons were real and that, maybe, one day, I'd meet one. But, holy shit! Now? Here? Oh, oh. What's goin' on, Katie girl?"

"Me? How the fuck am I supposed to know?" Katelyn said, plopping down onto the rise next to the dragon crystals. "Hey, these things are glowin' more brightly since the dragon flew by."

Sami looked at Katelyn and said, "Gee. I wonder why?" sarcastically.

"I swear, Sami, I don't know what's happenin'," Katie said.

Suddenly, she jumped up and ran over to Sami.

"What the hell are you doin'?" Sami said as Katelyn pulled Sami's shirt down from her left shoulder.

"I knew it," Katelyn said. "The tattoos are glowin'!"

Sami pulled Katelyn's shirt away from her shoulder and just stared at the tattoo.

"Oh, my God! Yours is glowin', too!" Sami hollered out.

Both of them just sat on The Rise in silence again. This time, all they could think about was the dragon that had flown overhead and the tattoos on their shoulders.

"Jordan has one, too," Katelyn said.

"Yes, he does," Sami replied. "Those tattoos showed up right after the battle here. The Rise must be part of The Dragon Magic."

"Dragon Magic?" Katelyn said.

"Yeah. What else should it be called?" Sami replied.

"That sounds about right, then. Dragon Magic. Holy fuck!" Katelyn said in a hushed tone.

"Dragon Magic," Sami repeated. "Here in The Creek. Well, I can truthfully say I am not surprised by it all. After all, this is The Creek."

"Agreed," Katelyn replied. "Now what?"

"I'm not even gonna try to figure this out. Just gonna go with the flow," Sami said as she made her hands look like waves in motion.

"I like that plan," Katelyn said. "Me, too. Whatever is gonna happen is gonna happen no matter what we do right now anyway. So, let's just keep goin on with our everyday stuff."

"Plus one dragon," Sami said. "Wonder where it lives?"

"Oh, cripes," Katelyn said as she pulled Sami to her feet. "Wherever it wants to."

The girls laughed as they walked to the center of The Rise. They quietly offered thanks for the dragon and all and set off down the stairs to the field.

"We keep the dragon secret," Katelyn said in a firm voice.

"Agreed," Sami said.

As soon as they got back to the farmhouse, Sami and Katelyn both said, "I'm starvin'!"

"We figured as much," Jackie said. "Raid the frig."

The girls put together leftovers, microwaved them, and then joined the rest of the family back in the living room.

"Why is it that leftovers taste so good?" Sami said with her mouth full.

"Don't know. They just do," Nathen replied.

"Need some more pie," Katelyn said as she finished her snack and headed to the kitchen.

"Now, that's an idea I can agree with," her dad said.

"How was The Rise?" Jack asked as they enjoyed their pie.

"It was magnificent as always," Sami answered.

"Everything looks so different from up there," Katelyn said.

"The sky looks amazin', too," Jeremy added.

"Sure does," Sami said. "You can almost touch the stars."

"It's like a different place when you're up there," Joe said.

"I agree," Nathan said. "I feel all my worries disappear when I'm up there. It's so peaceful and calm."

Sami and Katelyn exchanged that look that said 'not always.'

"Have you arranged for the movers and all yet?" Jackie asked.

"Yes, Ma'am, we have. Katie and I moved my stuff into my new house today. I'll meet the movers in Alabama on Wednesday morning. They're gonna pack everything for me. My bosses insisted on it—all except my clothes and such. I'll pack my art supplies and bring them with me back here," Sami replied.

"When do you think you'll be back?" Jeremy asked.

"Well, kinda hard to pinpoint that, bro," Sami answered. "I'm goin' straight to my job site when I leave Alabama. My bosses are gonna throw a party Wednesday night, and they've arranged for me to stay at one of the company's suites at a local hotel. I'll check on my place again Thursday morning, then the movers and I will head out. The movers said they'll be here Saturday afternoon."

"I'll come by and help get everything set up," Jackie said.

"That would be wonderful," Katelyn said. "I kinda know where Sami wants things, and I could use all the help I can get. Kendra's gonna help, too. And Ted and Michael said they'd take care of supper."

"This sounds well thought out," Joe said. "Your brothers and I will be busy here with everything. Pumpkins, cornstalks, and stuff."

"It's a busy time for the farm," Nathan said.

"It's always busy around here. Especially now with our houses being built," Jeremy said.

"How are they comin' along?" Sami asked.

"Well, the foundations were held back a couple of weeks on account of all the rain in September. Karl was finally able to dig them out, and the forms were set two weeks ago. The concrete was poured about ten days back, and Ethan says he plans on starting the framing on Wednesday if the weather behaves," Nathan explained.

"Will Ethan be able to get them weather-tight before the really cold weather and snow come in?" Sami asked.

"I'll take this one," Katelyn said. "We were just talking about that very thing yesterday. Ethan has hired on six new guys for the two builds. He's quite sure we can get them tight before the end of November. That's when the really cold weather hits. We're hopin' to have the geothermal lines in place and heating the house by then. It makes it a lot better for the inside work to have some heat."

"Will Finn be wicked busy as well?" Joe asked.

"Yes, he will, Dad," Katelyn answered. "We have Gina and Terry's build to work on, too. Ethan has a separate crew for them. Karl will be digging out the foundations starting Monday. The weather looks good for only light rain in the evening this week, so the forms should be placed on time. We're hopin' to pour the foundations for all the buildings a week from Monday."

"And that's only two of Ethan's builds," Jackie said. "He's got a few others as well. Busy guy, for sure."

"No kidding. Ian and I are straight out with our customers and their plans," Katelyn said, laughing. "I'll be workin' late every day this comin' week. Good thing you'll be busy as well 'cause I don't think we'd see much of each other even if you were here."

"Thank God for the digital world," Sami added. "At least we'll get to see each other for a few minutes whenever."

"Did you see the Instagram post Ted sent around the other day? Seems Wanda Sue's out and about again," Joe added.

"Yup. It was quite amusing," Sami said. "Seems that pig is a social butterfly for sure."

"Looks like she's on a tour of The Creek for a while. Most folks have her special food ready for her. I'm sure there will be pictures all over the place, too," Jeremy added.

"Speaking of the digital world, keep us updated with your stuff, too, Sami," Nathan said.

"Oh, I will," Sami said as she began to yawn.

"And with that yawn, I do believe it's time for the two of you to get on home," Joe said as they walked the girls out to Katelyn's SUV.

Hugs were shared, and promises were made to keep everyone in the loop about Sami's move and the new builds. A short time later, the girls were back home and sound asleep in the blink of an eye.

Sunday morning found Hal, Bob, and Ned meeting at The Store.

"Mornin' men," Michael called out as they went back to the kitchen table.

"Mornin' Michael," they all replied.

"Time for some breakfast before we head out," Ned said as Ted came into the room.

They placed their breakfast orders with Ted and settled at the table. Miss Cora arrived a few minutes later and headed straight back to the table. The three men stood up and removed their hats while bidding Miss Cora good morning.

"Always good to see some men with manners," Miss Cora said as Ted placed her cup of tea on the table. "You, too, Ted. Thanks much."

"You're always welcome, Miss Cora. What are ya thinkin' for breakfast this beautiful mornin'?" Ted asked.

"A good old-fashioned country breakfast, Ted," Miss Cora replied.

"Yes, Ma'am. Comin' right up," Ted said as he went back into the kitchen to prepare everyone's breakfast.

"I see Wanda Sue's takin' a shine to ya, Hal," Miss Cora said, laughing.

"It would appear so," Hal replied.

"She stayed for a while, then moseyed on after I gave her some treats," Ted said, handing out everyone's orders.

"She keeps us on our toes," Ned said.

"Where you boys headed this mornin'?" Miss Cora asked.

"We're headed out to look for those Crystal Caves over the NorthRidge Footbridge," Bob replied.

"Have a nice hike. Ya know they only show themselves to those that need to see 'em," Miss Cora added.

"We know," Ned said. "We're just hopin' we're three of those folks."

"Here ya go, boys," Ted said as he brought their lunches out. "Stay safe."

"Thanks, Ted. We will as soon as we finish breakfast," Hal replied.

A short time later, the boys headed out on their hike, and Miss Cora stayed for another cup of tea. That's where Emily found her when she walked into The Store.

"Hey, Miss Cora," Emily said, kissing her cheek.

"Mornin' sweet Emily," Miss Cora replied with a hug for Emily.

"Hey, Emily," Ted said, stopping at the table. "Would ya like anything this mornin'?"

"I'll grab a juice," Emily said. "I fixed a big breakfast for Ethan and me a while back. Michael texted me that my order of herbs was here."

"It sure is, Emily," Michael said as he set the package on the table.

"Thanks, Michael," Emily said. "I see Wanda Sue's been around lately."

"She has. She seems to be takin' a shine to our Hal," Ted said.

"I can see why. He's a sweet soul and loves animals," Emily replied.

"She was so content after her long drink of water, she lay right down next to him and was snoring in no time," Ted said.

"She must know my Trouble. He does the same thing," Emily said, laughing with everyone.

"What's Ethan up to this mornin'?" Miss Cora asked.

"He's taking care of a few things in the stables. He decided to add some shelves to the area just next to the last stall. He said it would hold the stuff we keep walking back to the tack room for. I love the way that man thinks," Emily explained.

"Sounds like a right smart idea to me," Miss Cora replied. "Emily, Hal, Ned, and Bob are hikin' up near where they think The Crystal Caves are. What are your thoughts on that."

Emily answered very quietly, "Miss Cora, I know they won't find them. They hold very Special Magic, and only a few of us are to be shown where they are. I know I'm not one of the chosen."

"I know that, too," Miss Cora replied.

"Do you know where they are?" Emily asked.

Miss Cora was quiet for a minute, then replied, "I do. No one is to know that I do except you and two others."

"Katelyn and Jordan, I suspect," Emily said.

"Why them?" Miss Cora asked.

"I don't know where that came from," Emily said, rather surprised. "It just came out like that."

"The Magic knows what to do," Miss Cora said.

"I do know that," Emily agreed. "I won't say a word to anyone about this."

"Just you and me," Miss Cora replied.

Ted came through the kitchen door just then with a tray full of small dishes.

"I need taste testers," Ted said, setting the tray on the table. "Oh, Michael."

"I smell something divine," Michael said as he stepped up into the dining area.

"The first one is my version of beef burgundy. The second sample is my version of chicken marsala. The next set is a new dessert with cherries, raspberries, cream, and a dark chocolate drizzle. There's a thin filo crust on the bottom. Enjoy, and let me know your thoughts," Ted explained.

The only thing anyone heard in The Store for the next few minutes were moans of joy.

"This is pure joy," Emily said as she finished her dessert. "It's a keeper."

"So are both of the other dishes," Miss Cora said. "I'd like to take some of all three home with me for Sunday dinner if that's possible, Ted."

"Of course it is, Miss Cora. I already packed up a basket for you whenever you're ready to leave. I love the fact that you have a microwave now."

"Me, too, Ted," Miss Cora replied. "I know I was mighty stubborn about not havin' one for the longest time. But the more I saw how y'all use them, the more I thought about it and decided to get one. Kendra helped me out, and she set it up, too. She knows a lot about all this fancy stuff."

"She does," Emily replied. "We have one in the house and one in the stable office, too. Coffee cools quickly out there."

"Good thinkin'," Miss Cora said. "I'll let ya know when I'm ready to leave. Thanks so much, Ted. Ya gonna offer them on the menu today?"

"Yes, Ma'am. I'm about to add them to the digital menu board. You just watch," Ted said as he grabbed his tablet and changed the menu board to show the new dishes.

"I love the whole color thing, Ted. Makes everything pop out and easy to read," Emily said.

"Thanks, Emily," Ted said. "This was Jenna's idea. Love the way that girl thinks."

"She's a special artist for sure," Emily replied. "Have you seen her sketch of the dragon mural for the kid's room she's workin' on?"

"Not yet. She said she'd come by and show us soon," Michael said from the front of The Store.

"It's amazin'. She said she loves dragons and would love to meet one, one day," Emily said.

"If they only existed," Ted said. "I'd love to meet one, too."

"Ya never know with The Magic around here," Miss Cora said. "Just when I think I've learned and seen everythin', somethin' else comes along."

"Oh, boy, am I learnin that for sure," Emily said. "Always more to experience around here."

"Always more to discover," Miss Cora said. "It's time for me to get along. Ya' got my package there, Ted?"

"Here it is, Miss Cora," Ted said as he brought her basket of food to the table. "Remember, you never pay for anythin' here, Ever."

"I remember Ted," Miss Cora said as she hugged him. "We'll talk again soon, Emily."

"You enjoy those goodies this afternoon, Miss Cora," Emily said as they shared a hug.

"Michael, thanks for takin' care of us all," Miss Cora said as she left The Store.

"I do love that lady," Michael said as he watched her get into her truck and drive off.

"We all do, Michael," Emily said. "Time for me to get back to the meadow."

"Have you thought of a name for your place yet?" Michael asked as he walked her to the door.

"I was thinkin' about just that yesterday," Emily replied. "Nothin' seems to fit yet. I know it will one day."

"Sure will," Ted said as he joined them. "See ya' soon."

"Later, boys," Emily said as Michael held the door for her.

Emily and Ethan carried on with their day, as did most folks in The Creek. Jordan was outside taking care of some chores with George's help.

"You supervisin' again, George?" Joran asked as he stopped what he was doing.

"Yes, indeed, Jordan. And, I will say you are doing a splendid job with the place," George replied.

"Wiseass!" Jordan replied, ruffling George's feathers.

"Always," George replied as he flew around Jordan's head.

"Looks who's comin' up the drive," Jordan said as he brushed George away from his head.

George flew down the drive to greet their visitor.

"I do believe this is Wanda Sue," Jordan said as Wanda Sue and George joined him. "Hey, there, Wanda Sue. Welcome to the farm."

Wanda Sue grunted, walked around the barn, and returned to the porch to join Jordan and George. Jordan had a bowl of water ready for her. She drank all of it, and Jordan filled it again.

"I do believe she likes it here," George said.

Wanda Sue gave a loud grunt, looking right at Jordan.

"You're welcome any time, Wanda Sue. I've got some treats for you inside," Jordan said as he went into the kitchen and returned with a couple of bags of pig treats. Ted had sold a few to others in The Creek in case Wanda Sue showed up. He gave her a handful, and she thoroughly enjoyed them. She grunted her pleasure and found a cozy spot on the porch to lie down. She was asleep in no time.

"Just like the Instagram post said. She falls asleep in an instant, and her snoring is rather loud," Jordan said.

"It is. I do believe it's even louder than yours," George sassed.

Jordan stuck his tongue out at George in reply.

"Cute, Jordan," George said, laughing at Jordan's sassiness.

"I'm goin' back to work," Jordan said as he went out into the area behind the barn to clear the mowed weeds and all.

George flew over and settled on a perch off the barn.

"George, I've decided to plant this area in wildflowers next week. Hal's bringing his rototiller over to help get the ground ready. I ordered a couple of big bags of wildflower seeds, and they should be here in a few days," Jordan explained to George.

"That's a great idea, Jordan. I love wildflowers, and so do the bees and other creatures. Did you get sunflower seeds in the mix?" George asked.

"I did. Two different kinds. Hal said they usually grow well around here," Jordan replied. "I'm gonna stake the area now," Jordan said as he started pounding a stake into the ground.

"How far away from the barn are you going?" George asked.

"All the way to the edge of the planted field. I'm leaving a path for the tractor to turn around without damaging either field. The wheat will be harvested this comin' week, too," Jordan said.

"I'm glad you're allowing some of the area framers to use your field," George said.

"It only seemed like the right thing to do," Jordan replied as he walked over to the second stakepoint and set the stake.

"These bright orange stakes are a great idea. You can see them from any-where," George said.

"That was Ethan's idea. He gave me four of them to try out. I'll send him a picture when we're done. Take a look from the air and tell me if this is in line with the first one, please," Jordan asked of George.

"Will do," George said as he took to the air and flew over the area.

"You've got a good eye. Well placed," George said. "I'll fly over to the next spot."

"Good idea," Jordan said as he walked over. "This look okay?"

"About three more steps to the east," George said.

Jordan set the stake, and they both went to the last spot.

"How's this line up with the others?" Jordan asked as a shadow flew over them.

"Incoming," George said as Penny landed outside of the grid.

"Penny. Nice to see you. But, aren't you supposed to only show up at night so no one will see you?" Jordan said.

"Hi, Jordan, George," Penny said. "I see you're taking my existence rather well, Jordan."

"I'm still in shock, so I figured I'd just go along with whatever we're do-ing," Jordan explained.

"That's a good way to handle all of this," Penny replied. "I see Wanda Sue is visiting," Penny said.

"You know Wanda Sue?" Jordan asked as he gave the stake one last hit.

"I do. She's a sweet soul and loves being a pig. She's still asleep on the back porch," Penny replied.

"I'm sure she is. It's a long way for a pig to travel around The Creek," George added.

"So, why are you here in the daytime?" Jordan asked.

"I need to tell you a little something new," Penny said.

"Oh, brother! More magic stuff," Jordan said as he walked back to the barn.

"Could you stay here for a few minutes, Jordan?" Penny asked.

"I'll be right back as soon as I put my tools away," Jordan replied as he went into the barn.

"Is he taking all this okay, George?" Penny asked.

"He hasn't said anything to me about it yet. I do believe he was talking with Katelyn about this, though. He seemed to be more settled when he came home after being with her," George explained.

"Good. I knew she'd be able to help him with all this," Penny explained. "I showed myself to her and Sami last night.

"Really? How'd that go?" George asked, laughing.

"Better than we thought it would. They saw the tiny dragon crystal form on The Rise just before I showed myself to them. They were amazed and thrilled. They both wished that dragons were real and, now, know we are. That seemed to make them happy. They've decided not to tell anyone about me, though," Penny explained.

"I wouldn't think they would tell anyone," George was saying as Jordan walked out of the barn towards them.

"Okay, you two. What gives?" Jordan said as he stood in front of Penny. "I still can't believe I'm havin' a conversation with a real dragon."

"Keep breathing along, Jordan," Penny said. "So, I need to give you some information about my being here."

"Good. I'm ready," Jordan said as he sat down on the field. "Not that it's going to make much sense or anything."

"You are taking all of this rather well. Thank you," Penny said. "Now, my home, your Crystal Cave, has been here since the earth was first formed. The crys-tals were formed from volcanic eruptions, earthquakes, and the millions of years of movement until the current formation was set into place."

"I get that," Jordan said.

"Once the earth was set, those crystals began to grow from tiny, tiny pieces of quartz into the magnificent shapes and colors you now see. The Magic was placed in this cave to be protected both in and by the crystals."

"I do believe and understand that," Jordan said.

"I know you do," George added.

"How did you feel the first time you entered the cave besides seeing all that magnificent beauty?" Penny asked.

Jordan stood up and walked around for a few minutes. He walked over to stand in front of Penny as he said, "I'll be totally honest with you both," Jordan stated. "I felt like I'd seen that cave before or something like it. I know that sounds crazy 'cause I'd never been on this property before I bought it. But, it really felt like I had a very distant memory of the cave."

Penny and George looked at each other before Penny said, "I believe you humans call that Deja vu."

"We do," Jordan said. "Why?"

"Think about it for a minute," George said as he morphed into a man.

"Oh, no way, dude. No more crazy Magic," Jordan said

"No more, Jordan, for real," George said. "Answer me this: Have you ever dreamed of the cave before you moved here that you can remember?"

"Now that you put it that way, yes," Jordan said. "I have dreamed of a cave with shiny rocks in it. That's probably why I got that Deja vu feelin' when I first found My Cave."

"Exactly," Penny said. "Anything you remember feeling when you were there for the first time?"

"I remember wonderin' about all how all those crystals came to be in My Cave," Jordan said. "I still do. I mean, I know The Magic is at work in there, and you're part of The Magic. I just keep wonderin' why you're here."

"I like that train of thought," Penny said as she stood up.

"Spill, Penny," Jordan said.

"Jordan, you've probably figured out that The Magic is about to happen again. It is. Something in The Magic is always happening. We just want you to be aware of this new thing. That's all. And, you knowing me is a part of the new thing."

"Okay. This I can understand," Jordan said. "But, no more. This is more than enough."

"We understand," George said. "You remember to raise The Crystal Dragon into the air if anything happens that's more than you can handle."

"Oh, George, I do get that for sure," Jordan said. "And, thanks for the warning, Penny. I'm much obliged."

"You are a true gentleman, Jordan. Time for me to get back to our cave for a rest. Later," Penny said as she took to the air, circled the farm, and headed out to The Cave.

"Ya know, George. Even with all this craziness of The Rise and finding out a real dragon lives in My Cave and talking with her, the sight of her lifting into the as if she were a feather and flying out into the afternoon sky is truly a miracle. Magnificent!" Jordan said as Penny flew out of sight.

"I agree," George said. "I think I'll stay around for a while. What's in the frig?"

"Now that you brought that up, I am wicked hungry," Jordan said. "Let's get some supper goin'."

Jordan and George raided the leftovers and enjoyed a fun Sunday supper. It was close to sunset when George stood and said, "This had been fantastic. We'll do it again soon. Time to fly."

"Thanks for the human company, George. Enjoy the sky," Jordan said as they walked out onto the yard behind the house. George became his eagle self, and he was airborne in no time. Jordan watched as he caught a thermal and enjoyed the ride.

Hal, Ned, and Bob were standing on the NorthRidge Footbridge by late morning.

"This truly is a magnificent piece of craftsmanship," Ned said.

"Sure is," Bob said. "Now, which path do we take? There are three of them here. One goes due north, and one goes kind of northwest; the third one goes south."

"I choose the second one that goes northwest. We've followed the south one a few times and know there aren't any caves along it," Hal said.

"True," Ned said. "Bob?"

"I agree with Hal," Bob said.

"Let's get movin' then," Hal said as they set out down the northwest path.

The path was really an animal path. It was narrow in some places, but you could still see it ahead.

The path brought them into a meadow filled with critters. The guys stood stock still as they watched a family of deer crossing at the far end. A hawk flew overhead on the thermals, and they saw a fox sitting just inside the woods to the east. The tall growth moved a bit as something small walked through the middle. The deer went on their way into the woods, and the guys proceeded to cross the meadow. They found two animal paths and chose the larger one.

"I can see a hillside or something' up ahead," Hal said as they walked on.

"I see it, too," Bob said. "It looks more like the side of a mountain."

As they rounded a bend in the path, they saw the mountain a short distance ahead.

"How about we take a short break here in the woods?" Hal said. "We've been walkin' for quite some time."

"I'll say we have," Ned exclaimed. "It's already one thirty."

"Really? Doesn't seem like we've been out here for almost three hours," Bob said.

"Ya' now how we get lost in time when we're in the woods," Hal offered.

It only took a few minutes to walk to the bottom of the mountainside.

"Let's walk along the path here," Ned said. "It follows the curve of the mountain. Maybe we'll find a cave or something."

"Good idea," Hal said.

They walked about a half-mile and found an opening in the mountainside.

"Hey, look here," Ned said. "It looks like a cave or something."

"Be careful," Hal said. "We don't know if a family of bears lives in there."

As they walked under the roof of the opening, they were in for a surprise. The cave was not a cave. The arched entryway opened into a small valley. It looked like someone had scooped the mountainside away and left the little rounded valley below.

"This is incredible," Bob said as they walked into the valley.

"Looks to be a bit bigger than a football field," Hal offered.

"Is that what I think it is?" Ned said as he walked over to something shining in the afternoon sun.

Ned bent down and tried to pick up a shiny stone. Turns out it was a lot bigger than he thought. It was a quartz crystal, the color of the meadow. The yellow streak had caught the sun's rays and made it glow.

"Would ya look at that?" Bob said as he and Hal walked up to Ned.

"How big is it?" Hal asked.

"I think it's really big," Ned said. "It looks to be covered in dirt and overgrowth."

"Do ya think we should clear around it?" Bob asked.

A flash of light was the answer.

"I'm takin that as a yes," Hal said. "Let's be careful and go slowly."

They put on their work gloves and started to brush away the loose dirt. The overgrowth was easy to pull away. About a half-hour later, the crystal was completely uncovered. It was massive.

"That thing is huge!" Bob hollered out as they stepped back and looked at it.

"It's about the size of my small closet floor. It looks like it goes down into the earth a ways, too," Hal said.

"Look at all the colors. It's got green, brown, gold, yellow, orange, and even some pink in it," Ned said. "And it's glowing like that crystal on Jordan's front porch."

"That's what it reminds me of," Hal said. "Good thing we've got our sunglasses on. It's about as bright as Jordans, too."

"Let's clean up around it a bit more so the overgrowth doesn't take over too soon," Bob suggested.

A few minutes later, there was a small cleared area around the meadow crystal.

"Well, I'm gonna say the obvious," Bob said. "I do believe we're really close to those Crystal Caves."

"Let's walk along the edge of the valley floor. Maybe we'll find those caves," Ned offered.

The guys spent a couple of hours looking for a cave but didn't find any.

"We'll, we looked, and we did find a bunch of crystals," Bob said as they set them on a flat rock.

"I think we better ask if we can keep these," Hal said. "Y'all remember how Miss Cora says not to take anything from the earth without permission."

"That's right," Ned said. "Let's pick three each and ask if we can keep them."

"Okay. Good idea," Hal said.

They each picked three of the crystals they had found, and Bob asked if they could keep them. A quick flash of light from the crystals was their answer.

"That's wicked amazin'," Hal said. "Thanks, Mother Earth."

"It's getting late in the day," Bob said. "Look at how the shadows are beginning to grow long across the valley."

"It's time to go," Hal said as they put their crystals in their backpacks. "Let's leave these other ones right here. They can glow in the mornin' sun."

"It's gonna take us about two hours to get back to the bridge," Bob said. "Let's eat lunch just outside the archway first."

"Another good idea," Ned said as they left the valley and settled on some rocks near the archway.

"I took a few pictures of the valley and sent them to Emily and Miss Cora," Hal said as they ate. "Miss Cora just sent back a text sayin she never knew there was a little valley up here. She loves the picture of the meadow crystal and our crystals, too."

"There's so much to be discovered up in these Blue Ridge Mountains. I'm not surprised that even our Miss Cora doesn't know about the valley," Ned said.

"Time to get movin'," Hal said.

They set out and looked back at the Crystal Meadow just as the sun's rays lit up that magnificent crystal.

"Just like Jordan's," Bob said.

They entered the forest and were back on the NorthRidge Footbridge just as the sun was settling behind the trees.

"This has been a great day," Ned said. "I just texted Ted and told him we're back at Hal's truck."

"Good idea," Bob said. "I sent him pictures of the valley. He said it was beautiful."

"This is such a peaceful place," Hal said. "I could stand here for a long while."

"I could, too, except not today. I need a hot shower, some food, and my recliner chair," Ned said, laughing.

"I am feelin this hike in my bones already," Hal said. "But I'm glad we went. That valley is so cool."

"Homeward, men," Bob said as they left the bridge and got into Hal's truck. He dropped them off at their homes and was settlin' in just like the rest of The Creek as evening gave way to the night.

Katelyn and Sami were saying goodbye next to Sami's SUV.

"Hey, no tears this time," Katelyn said.

"I know," Sami replied. "I'm so excited about movin' here. I just can't be sad as I leave this time."

"Same here," Katelyn replied. "It's about one, so you should be able to get back to the hotel before the dark of night sets in."

"As long as there's no crazy traffic out there," Sami said, getting into the driver's seat.

"Wait a minute," Ted hollered as he hurried across the road. "Ya' can't leave without some goodies. Michael and I want to make sure you are well-fed for a few days. I'll put the cooler on the floor in the front."

"Good heavens, Ted," Sami said. "There's enough food here for a week."

"That's the idea," Ted replied. "We can't have our Sami girl wastin' away out there."

"You guys are amazin'," Sami said as she got back out and hugged Ted. "Share that hug with Michael."

"Oh, he will," Michael said from the porch of The Store.

"You be safe out there," Ted said as he crossed back over the road.

"I will," Sami said. "I've got the whole of The Creek makin' sure I am."

Katelyn and Sami hugged, and Sami settled into the driver's seat again.

"See you sometime next week," Katelyn said.

"I love you forever and always, my Katie," Sami said.

"I love you forever and always, my Sami," Katelyn said.

Michael, Ted, and others on the porch at The Store waved to Sami as she left The Creek.

The afternoon flew by with chores and such. It seemed like only a few minutes after Sami left that Katelyn heard Finn's truck pulling into the driveway. The sun was just going behind the trees on the ridge behind The Store.

Katelyn stepped out onto the porch, saying, "Hey there, handsome."

Finn walked right over to Katelyn and kissed her soundly.

"Now, that's what I call a solid hello," Katelyn replied. "Let's sit out here for a while and watch the sunset."

"I like that idea," Finn said.

"I'll grab us a cold one," Katelyn said, returning with two ice-cold beers.

"Just what I was thinkin' about," Finn said as he took a long pull of his beer. "Did Sami get off okay?"

"She sure did," Katelyn replied. "Best thing was neither of us shed a tear 'cause we know she's comin' home soon."

"I was just thinkin' about that, too," Finn said. "Seems the two of you are supposed to be together."

"That's what we think," Katelyn replied. "How's the thermal stuff on Gina and Terry's land comin' along? I haven't had a minute to ask about it these last few days."

"I noticed how busy you've been," Finn replied, waving at a couple of kids walking by. "The two geothermal resources will work perfectly. I met with Karl and the energy expert on Friday, and the path we set out is a go. There's a granite shelf about thirty feet below the surface. We won't bother it a bit; it will help keep the water hot. Thomas, the energy guy, said we couldn't have picked a more perfect place. Karl is gonna use LIDAR to set the stakes for the excavation of the pipes. He said they'll dig the trench on Tuesday, and the pipes will be ready to be placed on Wednesday. Crazy busy place this is."

"You said it," Katelyn said. "Monday, Ian and I are meeting with five clients alone. Gina and Terry have decided on the shape of their house, barn, and stables. Now we need to think about color schemes."

"You should show them the sketches Sami made of your brother's houses," Finn said, laughing. "She sure has a great imagination."

"Sure does," Katelyn said, laughing along with Finn.

"I gotta be there when she gives them to your brothers. I'll record the whole thing," Finn said.

"It's a deal," Katelyn replied. "I want to record their reactions so we can always tease them about it."

"Hey, you two," Hal said as he walked over from The Store.

"Hey, Hal," Finn replied, standing up and shaking hands with Hal. "What are y'all up to on this fine evenin'?"

"Just grabbing a few things for supper," Hal replied. "I wanted to tell ya' about our hike up near the NorthRidge Footbridge."

"Enjoy yourselves?" Katelyn asked.

"We sure did," Hal replied, leaning on the porch railing. "We never did find those Crystal Caves. I guess Miss Cora was right tellin' us that The Magic only lets those that are special find 'em. We did find a small valley, though. Did ya' take a look at the pictures I sent?"

"They are amazin," Katelyn replied. "I never knew that valley was there. I'm gonna have to plan a hike up to see it. Be sure to create a map for me before I go so I won't get lost."

"I sure will," Hal said. "How's Gina and Terry's build comin' along, Finn?"

"Right on time. Thanks for askin'," Finn replied. "Lots of things goin' on right now. The foundation excavations are about to start, and we'll be diggin' the trench for the geothermal pipes right after that."

"Sounds wicked busy," Hal replied. "Well, I guess I'll get on home to my supper. Yours smells fantastic."

"Crockpot chicken stew. Thanks for stoppin' by," Katelyn said as Hal got into his truck and drove away.

Finn and Katelyn watched as the sun settled through the trees and finally dipped below the mountain ridge.

"Time to get some supper of our own," Katelyn said. " I'm gonna put some homemade buttermilk biscuits in the oven right now."

"Sounds great," Finn said, wrapping Katelyn up into a big hug as they walked into the kitchen.

Finn preceded to kiss Katelyn thoroughly, and she showed her appreciation by running her hands all over his ass.

"Supper first," Katelyn said. "I need a lot of energy if we're gonna take this into the bedroom."

"Oh, we are," Finn said as Katelyn put the biscuits in the oven. "I do need to taste test this stew first, of course. Gotta make sure it's just right for my Katie girl."

"Go ahead," Katelyn said, laughing at Finn. "It's not like I could stop you even if I tried."

Supper was a fun time, talking about some of Finn and Jay's crazy stunts and Katelyn and Sami's adventures during their college days. As soon as the kitchen was cleaned up, Finn took Katelyn by the hand, locked all the doors, turned off all the lights, and walked them into the bedroom. He gently removed every stitch of her clothes, and she did the same for him. They lay on the bed and began to explore each other.

"I love the way you touch me," Katelyn said, signing.

"I love to touch you and make you happy," Finn said as he began licking her nipples.

Katelyn moaned as she tried to get her hands on Finn's hard shaft. He finally moved so she could stroke him, making him harder and harder.

"Oh, God, Katie. Not yet," Finn said as he slid down her belly and found her wet mound with his mouth.

Katelyn was lifted off the bed with the power of her organism. Finn slid his hand into her as she cried out. She finally calmed down and looked at Finn. He was looking at her.

"Jesus Christ, Finn! That was incredible," Katelyn said.

"Seems it was," Finn replied as he gently kissed her.

Katelyn slid down to take Finn's hard shaft into her mouth. She began flicking his shaft, and he began to moan. The more she flicked and licked him, the harder and hotter he got. He grabbed her, laid her on her back, and began to rub her mound as he sucked her breasts. He didn't know if he could hold on for very long.

Katelyn moaned and moved as she felt another organism begin. Finn felt it, too, and brought her to the edge.

"God, Finn, fuck me hard!" Katelyn cried out.

"Yes, Ma'am. Whatever you say," Finn said as he began pushing into her.

She grabbed his ass and wrapped her legs around him, pushing against his thrusts until she felt a wave of pure pleasure moving through her. She pushed harder and faster, and Finn did the same until he couldn't hold on another second.

Katelyn cried out as she hit the pinnacle of her organism as Finn kept pushing into her. She felt him cum at the same time she did. They pushed and thrust until they were spent and then drifted into that place of pure ecstasy somewhere in another realm of existence.

It was full-on dark when they finally woke up. They sighed at the same time.

"I don't know what was in that chicken stew, but be sure to keep makin' it exactly like that from now on," Finn said as he stretched and rolled over to look at Katelyn.

"Anythin' you want, Mr. Finn," Katelyn said, smiling at him. "Must be past midnight."

"Nope, only nine-thirty," Finn said, laughing with Katelyn. "I know bein' in The Magic makes time stand still. I guess our love makin' does the same thing."

"That's because it's pure Magic," Katelyn replied, smilin' slyly at Finn.

"Well said," Finn said. "Now, speakin' of chicken stew, what's for dessert besides you?"

"Fresh apple pie I made right after Sami left," Katelyn said as she got up and put some clothes on.

"Hot damn!" Finn said as he did the same, following Katelyn down the hall to the kitchen.

Katelyn set two plates of warm apple pie with vanilla ice cream on the table with the whipped cream next to Finn.

"You know me so well," Finn said as he covered his pie with whipped cream.

"I do believe I do," Katelyn said.

They enjoyed the pie as the night carried on.

"Time for me to get along home," Finn said. "We have a great deal to do tomorrow, and if I spend the night, neither of us will get much sleep."

"Truth in that," Katelyn said as she set the dishes in the sink. "We can go on and on with no regard for the time."

They spent a few minutes saying goodbye without speaking a word.

"Love you, my Katie girl," Finn said.

"Love you, my Finn," Katelyn said.

Katelyn waved as Finn drove away and went back inside. She tidied the kitchen before flopping down on her bed and falling sound asleep for the entire night.

The Creek slept peacefully that night. Penny flew over The Creek to make sure everything was ready for The Magic to take hold again.

CHAPTER 7

n early Monday morning text from Sami told Katelyn she was safe and sound at her hotel project location and would leave for Alabama later that day. She sent a bunch of emojis and signed off.

Katelyn and Finn arrived at the shop just a minute behind Ethan and Ian.

"Y'all ready for a whirlwind week?" Ethan asked as they gathered around the table.

"Yes, indeed," Katelyn replied.

"Ready and willing," Finn replied.

"We have five clients coming in today to meet with Katie and Ian. Finn, you and I are headed to Gina and Terry's to get the excavation started for the foundations. We should be gone all morning anyway," Ethan explained.

"I'm hoping we can settle on the colors for the buildings today," Ian said. "They've chosen all the windows and exterior doors, too."

"Let's see if we can choose interior doors and cabinets for the kitchen, stables, and barn as well," Katelyn offered.

"That's my plan," Ian replied.

"All right. Don't wait for us for lunch," Ethan said. "We'll probably grab something from The Store."

"Lucky ducks," Ian said as Ethan and Finn gathered their stuff and headed out.

"I brought leftover chicken stew and buttermilk biscuits for us, Ian. No worries," Katelyn said.

"I do love your cookin', Katie. Thanks," Ian replied as the first clients parked outside.

"Here we go," Katelyn said as they greeted their clients at the door.

The morning flew by. The excavation was well underway at Gina and Terry's. Ethan sent pictures to them, and their response was great. They sent emojis of shovels and dump trucks back to Ethan and Finn. Ethan grabbed lunch for himself, Finn, and Karl from The Store. They ate, sitting on the tailgate of Karl's truck. They ended up spending the entire day at the site, and by the end of the afternoon, the excavation for the foundation of the house was completed.

Ian and Katelyn enjoyed the chicken stew for lunch and got right back to work as well. Gina and Terry were the last clients for the day, and when they were finished, they had chosen cabinets for all the buildings and interior doors as well.

Jordan was busy all day with extensive research for the hotel projects. Throughout the day, he talked with Sami, choosing specific parts of the research articles to include in the final write-ups that would appear on the walls of the current hotel and one in the Atlanta area. George came by a few times to check on Jordan. He saw that Jordan was busy with his work and not thinking about The Magic. That was a good thing.

Miss Cora kept feeling the slightest energy shifts throughout the day. Nothing bad. They were just there as if to say something was on its way to The Creek. She smiled and thanked The Magic for the update.

Gina and Terry felt those energy waves as well. As soon as they left Ethan's shop, they talked about it.

"It's almost time," Gina said as they drove back to their farmhouse.

"I know. I can feel it," Terry said as they passed their build site. "They're still workin' in there."

"Sure are," Gina said. "I just got a text from Ethan. He says the excavation for the house is complete. They'll be workin' on the barn tomorrow."

"They work fast," Terry said. "Can't wait to drive that first nail into our house."

"Me, either," Gina replied. "How about we visit our cave soon? I'm feelin' the need to stretch out a bit."

"Deal," Terry said as they drove on.

Matthews and Jenna had been crazy busy, just like everyone in The Creek that Monday.

"How's the dragon mural comin' along?" Matthews asked as they got supper ready.

"Take a look," Jenna said as she showed him the pictures. "I started paintin' it today."

"This is gonna be spectacular," Matthews said. "Can't wait for the family to see the finished mural."

"The parents are keepin' the door locked so the kids can't see it until it's done," Jenna said, setting dinner on the table.

"That's gonna be great," Matthews said as he brought drinks over. "Have you been down to the creek and Faerie House lately?"

"No. But I did see the Faerie Lights twinkle the other mornin' before you came home. I saw a huge shadow fly over while I was on the deck with my mornin' coffee. I swear it was a dragon shadow. When I said this out loud, the Faerie Lights flashed like crazy. I laughed and thanked them, of course."

"I love how they let us know we're doin' the right thing," Matthews said. "Let's take a walk down there after supper. I feel the need to take a look."

"Okay. Sounds good to me," Jenna said as they spent the next while eating and chatting about stuff.

Matthews and Jenna walked down to the creek just a few seconds before the sun started its slow descent through the trees. The creek was moving along at a leisurely pace. The big purple crystal on the bank looked beautiful as the sun's rays splashed across it.

Jenna pointed to the Faerie House just as the sun sent a blast of light onto it. The whole thing lit up like a Christmas tree.

"Would you look at that? Beautiful," Jenna said.

Matthews nodded in agreement as they continued to watch the colors change as the sun set lower and lower. The light began to fade as the sun sank below the ridge. It shot rays back up into the sky as if to show how magnificent it could be.

As they watched, that large shadow flew right over them at tree top level.

"Whoa! What the hell was that?" Matthews said as it watched it fly out of sight.

"That's exactly what I saw the other day," Jenna said. "It's the shape of a dragon."

"Oh my God, Jenna! You're absolutely right. It is," Matthews said as he continued to watch the sky after that dragon shadow thing was gone.

"I guess The Magic is havin' a great time with us tonight," Jenna said.

I agree," Matthews added. "Look at our field."

The field was aglow in faerie lights of every color imaginable.

"We thank you for this fantastic light show and the dragon shadow thing," Jenna said, bowing her head towards the field.

"Same here," Matthews said as he did likewise.

They watched the field for a few minutes, and the lights continued to flash and glow.

"Let's walk back slowly," Matthews suggested.

"Good idea," Jenna said as they started out.

The faerie lights moved aside as they walked through the meadow. By the time they had reached the barn, the faerie lights were still glowing.

"Thanks, everyone, for this magnificent gift of love," Jenna said. "I think I'm gonna add some faerie lights to the mural."

The faerie lights flashed brilliantly, then faded away. Jenna and Matthews stood silent for a few minutes, then went into the house and settled for the night.

It was around three in the morning when Jordan was suddenly awakened from a deep sleep. He sat up in bed and looked around. He was alone. He couldn't figure out why he was awake.

He thought for a minute, then said, "If this has somethin' to do with The Magic, you are in deep trouble. Wakin' me up in the middle of the night is not acceptable."

Jordan sat there for a few more minutes, then felt wicked sleepy, fell back against his pillows, and fell asleep in a second. He dreamt that he was walking over the NorthRidge Footbridge with someone but couldn't figure out who it was. He slept deeply until it was time for him to get up Tuesday morning.

Katelyn was awakened at three in the morning as well. She stood up and looked around. She'd been deeply asleep, and the suddenness of being woken up startled her. She went to the kitchen for a drink of cold water and leaned against the counter for a minute. She tried to clear her head and figure out why she'd been awakened.

She saw a vision of herself and someone else standing on the NorthRidge Footbridge. It was late day. She couldn't figure out why they were there. She must have zoned out for a minute because all of a sudden, she knew what she had to do and with whom. She wrote this down on her tablet beside her bed and fell sound asleep.

Tuesday found The Creek busy as usual. Jordan was at his desk when he had a vision of him and Katelyn back in the cave, just like the visions before. Except this time, there was the shadow of a dragon on the wall. The vision was only there for a few seconds. Jordan was stunned. He didn't know what to think, so he went back to work, telling himself he'd call Katelyn later for a chat.

Katelyn was in her office when she had the exact same quick vision of the dragon shadow on the wall in the cave, just like Jordan. She made a note on her phone to call Joran later that day. They really needed to talk.

Jordan needed a break. He went outside and found George sitting on the back porch.

"Hey, George," Jordan said, looking out over the barn.

"Hey, Jordan," George replied.

"Let's take a walk over to My Cave," Jordan suggested and set out with George flying around the farm.

Jordan held the bushes aside for George, and then he entered his cave. He walked to the center of the big room and called out for Penny.

"Oh, Penny. Would you please make yourself appear?" Jordan said sarcastically.

"Oh, oh," George mumbled to himself as he transformed into his human form.

"That's right, George. You need to be human for this," Jordan said as he saw Penny take shape next to him. The cave grew larger as she became solid.

"Hello, Jordan," Penny said rather pleasantly.

"Hi, Penny. You know why I called for you," Jordan said.

"Tell me, anyway," Penny said, sitting down.

"Really? Fuck! Okay. Why was there a dragon shadow in my vision this mornin'? And, what the fuck is The Magic doin' messin' with me when I specifically told them "NO!" Jordan hollered.

"Right to the point," George said.

"Don't even try," Jordan said.

"And, what was that thing that woke me from a dead sleep last night? I know y'all did that. Why? What does standing on the NorthRidge Footbridge have to do with me?" Jordan added.

"Now, Jordan, please try to remain calm," Penny said sincerely. "We in The Magic need your help for a bit."

"NO!" Jordan hollered out all over the room.

No one said a word.

"I cannot believe the nerve of some people," Jordan said. "I'm barely hangin' on here, thanks to Katelyn. And, now, y'all want me to come to your rescue? No!' Jordan hollered out, staring right at Penny.

Jordan saw Penny's eye change from her usual deep purple to brilliant green.

"So, you do understand me," Jordan said.

"Why do you say that?" Penny asked.

"Your eye color just changed from purple to green. Bright green. Not happy with me, huh?" Jordan said.

George laughed out loud as he said, "Penny, old girl, he's catching on quickly. Better be careful around him."

"Yes, he is a quick study," Penny replied. "You are an observant one."

"Enough with the compliments," Jordan said. "What the hell is goin' on now?"

"At least you didn't throw a crystal at me," Penny said.

"I'd never do that. These are special, and I wouldn't harm a lady," Jordan explained.

"Your mama raised you right," Penny said. "Thanks for that. These crystals can leave quite a dent in my scales."

"Why can't y'all in The Magic just leave me alone? Find someone else to help you," Jordan pleaded, sounding defeated.

"Oh, Jordan, you're the one we need," George said as he walked over and stood next to Jordan. "This is not about a battle like the one on The Rise. We just need you to go to that cave you and Katelyn found one more time. Everything else will fall into place. Really."

"That's it? Nothin' else?" Jordan said, looking from Penny to George.

"That's all, Jordan. I swear on my scales that's all we'd like the two of you to do," Penny said, agreeing with George.

"Well, that doesn't seem too wild and crazy," Jordan replied. "I'll speak with Katelyn, and I'm sure you'll know her answer as soon as she speaks it."

"That we will," Penny said. "Now, Jordan, come over here and lean on my wing. I want to share some energy with you."

"Why, thanks, Penny," Jordan said as Penny raised her wing and Jordan stepped under it. She settled it back down so that it partially covered Jordan.

"This feels great," Jordan said quietly.

They stayed in that place for quite some time. George had joined Penny and was sharing in the energy bath as well. It was some time later when Jordan took a deep breath and stepped away from Penny.

"Penny, that was splendid. I thank you very much," Jordan said as he stroked her wing tip.

"That feels the same for me," Penny said as she purred a bit.

"I see your eyes are purple again. That's a good thing," Jordan said as he stepped in front of her.

"It is," George said. "I've seen them other colors, and you don't want to be on the wrong side of Penny when that happens."

"Understood," Jordan said, smiling at Penny.

"Now, on with your day. Thanks for coming along," Penny said. "And remember to take The Crystal Dragon with you everywhere from now on."

"Oh, I will," Jordan said. "And you're welcome."

"Later, George," Penny said as she vanished from sight.

"George, time to get on home," Jordan said. "I'm starving, and I need to get a hold of Katelyn."

"Yes, you do," George said as he morphed back into his eagle self. "I'm off to the skies."

Jordan held the bushes as they left his cave, and George took to the air.

Jordan had something to eat and called Katelyn.

"Hey, Jordan," Katelyn said as she answered his call. "I was just gonna call you."

"Have anything to do with the NorthRidge Footbridge and the cave we found?" Jordan asked.

"Exactly," Katelyn answered. "I know we're supposed to go back to that cave we found."

"I agree," Jordan said. "After supper. Tonight."

"Now I agree," Katelyn said. "Thing is, we can't go through Gina and Terry's build with all the security cameras."

"I know. Don't ask me how, but we need to get there over the NorthRidge Footbridge," Jordan said.

"I know you're right about that," Katelyn replied. "Not sure how I know, but I do."

"I'll pick you up right after supper," Jordan said.

"Deal," Katelyn replied. "Later."

They both went back to their busy day.

Gina and Terry had taken things into their own hands. As soon as night fell Monday evening, they set out for the NorthRidge Footbridge themselves. No one else was around, and they got to the cave from a secret front entrance.

As soon as they entered it, they sighed and settled against one of the walls full of crystals.

"I really need to stretch out here," Terry said.

"Not yet," Gina said. "Tomorrow night, just as has been planned. Be patient. It will all start to make sense for them tomorrow night."

"I know," Terry said. "This is the longest I can remember of us being in this form. I just want to get back to our other original selves."

"Me, too," Gina said as she stroked Terry's cheek. "We will soon. These crystals are helping us calm down."

"I love these crystals," Terry was saying when a large shadow appeared across the back wall.

"He's here," Gina whispered as the shadow became real and walked into the room.

"Thanks for being so patient," he said. "We really are thankful for the two of you and your families and all going back to the first epoch. We have a great deal of work to do this time. Continue on as Gina and Terry. Come to The Crystal Caves every night if need be. We'll be here for you."

"Thank You, Q," Terry said, bowing toward the voice.

"Thanks so much, Q," Gina said, bowing just like Terry.

"Your family is waiting to see you again as soon as those two are in place," Q informed them. "They are all just fine as always."

"Thanks for letting us know. Tell them we love them like always," Gina said.

"I will. Time for you to get back home. Lots to do tomorrow," Q said as he began to walk toward the back of the cave. "By the way, your new home layout is fantastic. I can't wait to visit it when it's done."

"We can't wait to drive the first nail into place," Terry said. "Take care, and thanks again."

Q waved at them as he rounded the bend in the room and was gone.

"I do feel more settled," Terry said as he and Gina left The Crystal Caves and headed back to the NorthRidge Footbridge.

"Let's get some sleep," Gina said as they walked through the front door of the old farmhouse. "I'm wiped out."

"Me, too," Terry said as they went up to their bedroom and fell into bed.

Jordan pulled into Katelyn's driveway just past suppertime Tuesday late afternoon. She hopped into his truck, and they headed for the NorthRidge Footbridge. Not a soul was around when they got there. They stood on the arch of the bridge, watching and listening to The Crystal Creek as it flowed by.

"Well, time to get movin'," Jordan said as he stepped off the bridge and headed north along one of the animal paths. "Don't know how I know this, but this is the right path to follow."

"I agree," Katelyn said as they set out at a brisk pace.

Just a few minutes later, Katelyn hollered out, "Jordan, look over there to your left. See that glow? That's where we need to be."

"I love how The Magic sends us guidin' lights," Jordan said, laughing as they turned toward the glowing woods. "Not much of a path here, but it looks clear enough."

The glowing light brought them to the arched entry of the little valley Hal and his buddies had found on Sunday afternoon.

"This must be the valley the guys found," Katelyn said as they walked under the stone archway and into the valley.

"It's beautiful," Jordan said. "Look there."

"I see it," Katelyn said. "It looks like a door or somethin'."

They walked over to the west to a place in the rock wall that did, indeed, look like it was a door.

Katelyn put her hand on the rock face, and the door slowly swung open to reveal the entrance to a cave.

"Wicked awesome!" Jordan said as they entered the cave.

The cave entrance was short and opened into a room covered in crystals from the ceiling to the floor and every other space that could hold a crystal.

"Oh my God!" Katelyn said in a whispered tone. "This must be the entrance to The Crystal Caves Miss Cora told us about."

"It's magnificent!' Jordan said, looking all around. "Look there. It looks like a miniature of the crystal sword I flew to you in the Battle of The Rise."

"It most definitely does," Katelyn said. "I just love the way The Magic connects with us."

"Some sense of humor," Jordan said as they began to walk around the room. Just like in his cave, the crystals cleared a path for them as they walked.

"Jordan, don't get crazy on me, but I think we're about to experience more of The Magic around The Creek. Why else would the two of us be here?" Katelyn offered.

"I know. I'm just so worn out from all that's happened, I don't think I have the energy to be a part of anything more," Jordan said.

"I feel the same way," Katelyn replied.

"You, too? I thought you were used to all this stuff," Jordan said as he reached out and touched a bright orange crystal. "This crystal is pulsing and humming."

"Jordan, I'm just as new to most of this stuff as you are," Katelyn said. "Remember how I told you nothin' really started happenin' until I got home on the July 4th weekend? Then, it all happened really fast. I haven't had time to wrap my head around all this stuff, either. I figured I'd just go with it and see what happens next. Worryin' about it only made me lose sleep and get crazy."

"I do remember that, but I thought it was just The Rise Battle. I figured you'd been with The Magic a lot longer. Sorry about that," Jordan said, still holding on to the orange crystal.

"I guess things happened so fast we all haven't had time to talk about everything," Katelyn said as she walked over to Jordan. "Let's take some time over the next few days and weeks and make sure we talk about all this stuff. That orange crystal is awesome."

"It sure is. It's keepin' me calm," Jordan said. "And, I like the idea of talkin' things out on a regular basis. Maybe both of us will figure out how to better cope with all this Magic stuff. Look over there."

Jordan pointed to an area at the back of the room.

"It looks like another room or hallway or something," Katelyn said. "Let's go have a look. Maybe we'll figure out why we're supposed to be here."

They walked across the room and found a hallway leading further into the mountain. They started walking along the hallway and found a few other rooms leading off on each side. Some were little, and some were bigger ones.

They stopped when the hallway split into two other paths.

"Ya' notice how very quiet it is in here?" Katelyn said. "Almost as if somethin' was about to happen."

"I noticed," Jordan replied. "Which path?"

"You choose," Katelyn replied.

"The one on the right," Jordan said, and they set off down the path. The walls were lined with crystals, and the ceiling looked like the night sky with thousands of glowing stars in it.

"This is wicked cool," Katelyn said as they rounded a bend in the path and came to a sudden stop. "Oh, my God! It's the cave we found. It's part of The Crystal Caves."

"The dragon constellation is all lit up on the ceiling just like before," Jordan said, pointing to the ceiling.

"This is unbelievable for sure," Katelyn said as she looked around. "Jordan, have you been havin' strange dreams that have you in a place out of time?"

"Yup," Jordan replied. "You, too?"

"Yup," Katelyn said. "I feel like I've been in those places before. They're real to me as if I was rememberin' my past."

"That's exactly it," Jordan said. "It really looks like a Middle-Earth kind of place with the cave and all, the fire, and all the plants you keep bringin home."

"We've been havin' the same dreams," Katelyn said. "That's not a coincidence. That's The Magic at work."

"Oh, shit! Jordan exclaimed. "I was hopin' it wasn't. Now what?"

"I have no idea," Katelyn was saying when she saw a shadow on the wall near the other entrance. "Look. There's somethin' there."

"What the hell is that?" Jordan said. "It's huge!"

The shadow kept getting bigger and bigger as it came closer to the room. Jordan reached into his backpack and pulled out The Crystal Dragon. He raised it toward the ceiling, and the light of the crystals in the room made it glow brightly.

"What's that?" Katelyn asked.

"Just wait. You're about to meet a new friend of mine. I've got a few questions for her," Jordan said as he held The Crystal Dragon high.

A moment later, the room began to get really big, and a form began to take shape.

"Don't be worried, Katelyn. She won't hurt you," Jordan said as the form became solid.

"That's a dragon!" Katelyn said in a stunned tone.

"Yes, she is," Jordan said. "Thank you, Penny, for getting here so quickly. I have a few questions for you."

"Hello, Jordan and Katelyn," Penny said as she sat on the floor. "I'm sure you do."

"What the hell is goin' on here? Why did The Magic wake both of us from a sound sleep and give us the idea that we should come here? She can talk?" Katelyn said, staring at Penny. "And her name is Penny?"

"Oh my God, Katelyn. I'm so sorry," Jordan said, taking hold of Katelyn's arm. "This is a real dragon. Her name is Penelope. She said I could call her Penny as only a few are allowed to. She's really deep purple and has long eyelashes. She's a real-life dragon."

"That about sums it up, Jordan," Penny said, laughing a bit. "Katelyn, keep breathing. I am a real dragon. We live in The Magic. That same Magic you know so well. I am here to protect Jordan and The Magic in The Creek. He's having a very difficult time with all this information, so we've been taking baby steps into The Magic. I am for real, Katelyn. Come on over and touch my wing if you'd like."

"Okay. I'll try most things at least once," Katelyn said as she approached Penny.

Katelyn stood in front of Penny and reached forward to touch her wing. It was warm and soft.

"You are a very pleasant dragon to touch," Katelyn said as she stroked Penny's wing.

"And you have a lovely touch," Penny replied as she closed her eyes and purred.

"She's purring, Jordan," Katelyn said. "Did you know dragons could pure?"

"Only after I met her the first time," Jordan said. "This is all new to me, too."

Katelyn stood there stroking Penny's wing for quick some time. She eventually stopped and stepped back.

"Katelyn, that was wonderful," Penny said. "You and Jordan have a healing touch."

"Thanks, I guess," Katelyn said as she looked over Penny. "You do have lovely eyelashes."

"Thank you," Penny said. "Now, how about the two of you sit at the table, eat, and drink while we talk."

A table and chairs appeared, and the table was immediately set with food and drink. Jordan and Katelyn sat down and looked at each other.

"This is probably the weirdest thing that's happened to me in The Magic, and there's been a lot of stuff that's happened," Katelyn said.

"I hear ya' for sure," Jordan said.

"Eat and drink and ask anything you want," Penny said.

"Katelyn, Penny is here to protect me, as I said," Jordan explained. "Other than that, I have no idea about what's goin' on."

"So, Penny, what is goin' on around here? Why have I been shown Dragon Magic?" Katelyn asked.

"That's a good way to put it," Jordan said. "By the way, Penny, this food is delicious."

"Sure is," Katelyn said. "Thanks to The Magic for this treat."

"You are both entirely welcome," Penny said, bowing her head slightly.

"I know that somethin's about to happen in The Creek with me meeting you and all," Katelyn began. "So, can you tell us anything about it?"

"Katelyn, that's good deducing," Penny said. "I can't give you any details other than it's not going to be anywhere as intense as the Battle on The Rise. You sent that evil Dark Force into oblivion. It's going to be there for a very long eternity."

"Good to know," Katelyn replied. "But why a dragon now?"

"Good question, Katie," Jordan said, looking at Penny.

"That I cannot tell you," Penny said. "The Magic will show itself over time."

"As usual," Jordan said. "I know I can't take any more surprises. Good thing I have George to keep me somewhat sane."

"He is a character the way he squawks at you as if he knows exactly what you're sayin," Katelyn said, laughing. "I love that eagle."

"George is a special friend for sure," Penny said, looking directly at Jordan. Jordan nodded his head just a bit to show Penny that George's Magic was safe.

"George is probably of The Magic, too. I wouldn't be surprised," Katelyn said.

"Everything is connected with The Magic," Penny added.

"So, will I see you around The Creek?" Katelyn asked.

"No. I need to stay hidden from everyone," Penny said. "I live in Jordan's cave. When he needs me, he holds The Crystal Dragon up. It signals to me that I am needed. Just like he did today."

"That's wicked cool," Katelyn said as she sat back in her chair. "This has been a wonderful meal. I'm stuffed."

"Me, too," Jordan said.

"Oh, Penny, can we get something for you to eat?" Katelyn asked.

"That is very kind of you to think of me. I'm all set," Penny said, smiling.

"Now what?" Jordan asked.

"Yup," Katelyn said. "Now what?"

"I cannot tell you," Penny replied. "Everything will take place as it should. You'll understand as things move along. Don't be alarmed by any of it. Just keep steady in The Magic."

"Jordan, looks like we're in for a crazy ride," Katelyn said.

"Penny, really, I can't take any more of The Magic. I'm at my breakin' point," Jordan said, sounding scared.

"Jordan, take this and hold onto it," Penny said, handing the orange crystal to Jordan. "Just breathe."

Jordan took the crystal and immediately felt calmer. "I love how the crystals calm me."

"You will have that with you always," Penny said. "It's time for us to leave this place. Katelyn, you and Jordan will remember all of this when the right time comes. I will be close by."

"Thank you, Penny," Katelyn said. "Jordan, let's get along now. We'll leave the way we came. Ethan has security cameras everywhere on Gina and Terry's property. If we leave through there, we'll be seen."

"Oh, good thinkin'," Jordan said as he stood up to join Katelyn.

The chairs and table disappeared.

"I'll see you later," Penny said as she stepped back into the hallway from which she had come.

Jordan and Katelyn stood there in the silence for just a moment.

"Let's go," Jordan said as he led the way back to the cave entrance.

"Of course, it looks like we've been gone for only a few minutes," Katelyn said as they stepped back into the meadow.

The rock door softly closed and looked just like the rest of the mountain.

"This place is beyond beautiful," Jordan said as they returned to the archway at the entrance to the valley. "We can't tell anyone we found The Crystal Caves."

"Agreed," Katelyn said as they walked back through the forest.

It seemed like just a few minutes had passed when they saw the NorthRidge Footbridge.

"That was quick," Jordan said as they stepped onto the bridge.

"Let's just look at The Crystal Creek for a few minutes. The sound is quite soothing," Katelyn said as they walked onto the highest point of the arched bridge.

They didn't know how long they stood there. It was quite some time, though. It was the changing air that brought Jordan back to current time.

"Katelyn," Jordan said quietly.

"I feel it, too," Katelyn replied as they watched the air begin to change colors and gently swirl around the bridge.

And as the air began to change colors and swirl around them, they vanished.

CHAPTER 8

I t had been a long and dangerous journey this time. They needed a safe place to live and work with The Magic. The man felt himself beginning to wake up. He was cold. As he looked around, he found himself in a cave of sorts. He remembered that he and his assistant had found the cave late the night before and settled in it. As he looked around, he saw that the space was large and airy. He got up and looked at the tunnel that was letting sunlight in. He found the tunnel and stepped outside. He saw a lake a short walk from the cave. The place was heavily wooded, and as he turned to look back at the cave entrance, he saw that it was set on a small rise and was completely covered with shrubs and such. You wouldn't know there was a cave there just by looking around the place. He instinctively knew that The Magic had shown it to him. This was the place they would live for a very long time, serving The Magic.

He spent a few minutes gathering firewood. He spotted some bushes with berries. That was good. They would have some food to start the day. He also found some mint plants next to the cave entrance. He picked some of the leaves and entered the cave. He saw a place with a small opening in the roof. He chose this for his fire. He made the fire, then went outside to look for the smoke. He had to walk around the small hill to find the place where the smoke came out. It looked like it was a hut of some kind. Nice way to disguise the cave. He went to the lake, got a gourd full of water, and returned to the cave. He set about boiling the water for tea.

As the space began to warm, his assistant woke up. She sat up and looked around. She saw the fire and smiled. Jandor was thoughtful like that. He always made sure there was water and food for them. They had traveled together for a few years now. He was twenty-five, and she was twenty-three years old. They had met while looking for vegetables in a local farming area in the mountain region known as the Place of The Giants. He knew she was to be with him to learn and to share in the knowledge of The Magic.

Jandor of Myrgannia was born to his mother and father under a full moon in the land of the Lowsantha. His father was killed by raiders when he was just a few days old. His mother hid the two of them in a secret cave until the evil men were gone. She left and traveled northeast to a small village and settled there. She became known as a healer and offered herbal remedies in trade for food and other things she needed. Her son, Jandor, was raised in this small village that was next to a crystal blue lake. He learned about the earth and water from a local wizard and about medicinal plants from his mother. One night, as he gathered herbs by the full moon, he was visited by an ancient man who told him he would be a great wizard one day. The Ancients told him it was his destiny to go forward and find an assistant and learn all he could from the earth, water, and sky. He left the small village when he was eighteen, holding his mother close for the longest time. He suddenly knew he would never see her again.

On Jandor's first night of his journey, he was visited by three ethereal beings. He was told this was real and that he was now a part of The Magic that existed in all the universes. He stood in awe.

"Jandor, you have been chosen to become one with The Magic. You now possess special powers that will allow you to travel to the past and the future as needed and to mold the future of this island to benefit The Magic. Do you accept this life?"

Jandor stood tall and bowed as he replied, "Oh great, and Ancient Ones, I accept this journey and these powers from you. I will work hard to bring about the changes that you foresee."

"We will send you an assistant in a few days. You will know who she is. Take good care of her; she is as important to The Magic as you. Do not tell her your true identity until we say so. She needs to learn many things first."

"I will obey your wishes," Jandor said.

In an instant, Jandor was charged with a brilliant light energy that lifted him off the ground. As the light faded, he was returned to the ground. He saw something flying at him. It stopped before running into him and perched on a nearby tree branch. It was a hawk. It was a magnificent hawk. It had red tail feathers, a blue streak down its back from the base of its head to the tip of the longest tail feather, and the wings looked like they had been dipped in gold. Jandor bowed to the ancients as they vanished and looked over at the hawk. It flew down to stand in front of Jandor and gave a squawk. Jandor bowed to the hawk, and the hawk returned the bow.

"Hawk, thank you for being with me. It's time we slept," Jandor said as he lay down on his palate of straw and animal skins. The hawk flew back to the branch and settled in as well.

Jandor traveled southwestward for a few days, coming upon the farm stand where he met Feyanna. He knew she was the one to be his assistant. He had learned how to listen to the energy of the air. They came to stand next to each looking over the food. She picked apples, and he chose blueberries. He chose a variety of gourds, root vegetables, and red berries.

They turned and looked at each other at the same moment.

"I am known as Jandor," Jandor said.

"I am known as Feyanna," Feyanna replied.

"Are you from around here?" Jandor asked as they paid for their food.

"No. I am from the village of Tessandria in the region of Cadenmoore," she replied. "And you?"

"I am from the region known as Myrgannia," Jandor replied. "Shall we sit and talk?"

"Let's sit over there, away from the others," Feyanna said as she walked away from the villagers.

They sat in a quiet meadow where no one would hear them.

"These berries are quite sweet," Jandor said. "Would you like to try a few?"

"Yes, thank you," Feyanna replied, taking them from Jandor's outstretched hand.

As soon as their fingers touched, a strong bolt of energy went through them.

"What was that? It almost hurt," Feyanna said as she ate the berries.

"I don't know," Jandor replied. "It was very strong but not painful. I suspect there's a bit of Magic going on here."

"Magic? We'd better be very quiet about that. We could be hanged if we even mention the word out loud," Feyanna said. "The King said Magic is evil, and only he can control it."

"I know, but I'm sure that's what's going on here," Jandor replied. "Magic is everywhere. It's as normal as these red berries. It's crazy for someone to think they can control The Magic. No one can. So, let's call it something else then."

"Good idea," Feyanna said. She thought for a moment, then said, "How about wheat?"

"Too common," Jandor said. "How about mud?"

"That's just plain silly," Feyanna replied, laughing. "Especially if we talk about mud and everything is dry."

"Oh, yeah. Good thinking," Jandor said.

"How about the word home?" Feyanna said. "Everyone talks about their home so it wouldn't be out of place. Oh, wait, I've got it. Bridge. It's common enough not to raise suspicion."

"Good choice," Jandor said. "Bridge it is."

They shook hands, and another energy bolt was sent through them.

"That's some bridge," Feyanna said as they laughed. "By the way, these berries are delicious. I think I'll get some more."

"Feyanna, wait," Jandor said. "That energy we felt tells me that there's bridges between us. I sense that you feel the same way. Tell me about it."

Feyanna looked out over the land for a bit, then said, "I have always known about bridges. My family were bridge builders. I knew I had the ability to understand bridges and all from the time I was a little child. My mother taught me about the earth, water, and air. My father taught me how to protect myself from bad bridge builders. My family is all gone now from the sickness that recently swept through this land. My mother gave me herbs and sent me to a small cave to live in while the sickness was about. I never got the sickness. When I went back home, I found them all gone. Not just dead, but gone. An old village lady showed me where they had been buried. I spent some time there talking with them. Then, I returned to the family home and grabbed my things, food, and a pouch of coins my father had hidden. I left five days ago and was told to head south. And, here I am."

"Oh, Feyanna. I am so sorry about your family," Jandor said, looking at the ground. "A wizard in my village taught me about the earth, air, and water. He taught me how to follow the stars, moon, and planets. My mother taught me about the plants and medicinal herbs. She also taught me how to make potions for every reason you can think of. I left our village just a month ago when I turned eighteen. I was told I would have an assistant to help me with my work on the bridges. I was told I would know who that was when the time came. I believe you are that person."

"Me? Why me?" Feyanna asked.

"You know about the bridges," Jandor explained. " We met here under a beautiful sky, and we both felt the energy of the earth and air. That's all I need to know."

Feyanna stood up and walked away from Jandor. She needed to connect with The Others to make sure this was the right thing to do. She quietly called to them in a whisper. She saw some people looking at her and smiled back and picked a few wildflowers for her basket. The people smiled back and then went about their business. Feyanna continued to collect wildflowers while awaiting an answer from The Magic. The answer came as a soft whisper on the air. She was told this was her destiny. She was told Jandor was a good and honest soul. She would be protected by The Magic always. The decision to join Jandor was hers to make. She returned to Jandor, put the flowers in her basket, and sat down.

"I will join you," Feyanna said quietly. "The Others have informed me that it is my destiny."

"Thank you for your decision," Jandor said. "I feel the need to buy more food and get away from here as quickly as possible. Trouble is close at hand."

"I feel the same," Feyanna said as she and Jandor purchased more food from the vendors.

They headed along a dirt track toward the west. A while later, they felt the earth tremble and ran deep into the woods so they wouldn't be seen by whoever was coming along the track. They saw the King's brigade ride by. There must have been about twenty knights on horseback with many weapons by their sides.

Jandor and Feyanna slowly made their way back to the edge of the track once the earth stopped trembling. They looked in both directions, then set out again. They kept silent for the better part of an hour.

"I don't like what I heard," Feyanna whispered.

"I agree," Jandor whispered in return. "They are looking for witches and wizards. The king has ordered all people who practice Magic to be hanged. We need to get far away from here. I know of a place where the Magic does rule. It will be a long and hard journey."

" I agree and like your plan. We will need to gather herbs and food along the way to be able to survive. I just asked my Guides to help us. See that glowing bush over there? It has those sweet red berries we like. Let's gather them and be gone."

Jandor and Feyanna took all the ripe berries from the bush. Pouches appeared under the bush, and within a short time, they had gathered ten pouches of berries and set out on their way westward. They made good progress by the time the sun began its descent towards the mountain ridges ahead.

"We need to find a place to hide for the night," Jandor said. "These woods are used for nighttime hunting."

"It looks like there might be an opening in the hillside up there," Feyanna said, pointing to a dip in the outline of a hill. "Let's take a look."

They found an old kind of cave-like room under an overhang on the hill. It looked like no one had been in there in years.

"Let's clean a few things up, make a kind of door from the downed trees outside, and eat," Jandor said.

"Agreed," Feyanna said as they cleared some space on the floor.

They found a table and two stools and set them in the middle of the room. Next, they dragged some of the downed tree branches to the opening in the hill, trying to make it look like they had always been there.

"That looks good," Feyanna said as they stood a little ways from the opening.

"It does," Jandor said. "Now, let's get inside. It's almost nightfall, and the hills will be full of Dark Forces for sure. We will not light a fire of any kind. Too risky."

"I agree," Feyanna said as they stepped through the side of the branches and entered the cave. "I have an idea. Listen. Oh, Great Ones that watch over us, would you please provide a soft light that cannot be seen outside this space you provided for us? We thank you for this space and all your gifts."

In an instant, there was a soft glow coming from the walls. It was enough to see everything.

"Thank you, benevolent beings and Feyanna, for asking for this. It's perfect," Jordan said. "Let's eat."

As they set about putting food on the table, a platter appeared. It was a roast chicken and potatoes.

"I love how The Magic takes care of us," Feyanna said.

"I do, too," Jandor replied as they sat for a while and ate their meal.

"It's full-on night out there. Time for us to sleep," Jandor said.

And two pallets of straw with blankets appeared.

"I guess we're doing the right things here," Feyanna said as she bowed, facing the north. "We really appreciate the ways you take care of us."

Jandor bowed as well as he said, "Many thanks and gratitude for these gifts."

Jandor and Feyanna settled down on their pallets and were asleep in an instant. They had walked a long distance that day. Jandor knew the evil that lurked in these woods and wanted to get to the vast meadows near the ocean as soon as possible. They would turn north and follow the coast for a few days before arriving at a small crystal blue lake. The lake held a lot of Magic, and it would transport them to a safe place where they could learn the ways of The Magic without fear of being attacked and murdered. Getting to that lake would be one of the hardest things the two of them would have to face on this journey.

Jandor awoke at sunrise and got a pot of water boiling for tea. Feyanna awoke a few minutes later. They ate and set out on their journey.

"I slept so deeply and peacefully last night," Feyanna said. "You?"

"Yes," Jandor replied. "I can't remember when I've slept so well. Be cautious now. We are entering the most dangerous part of this forest. The Dark Forces are strong here. We should be able to make it through in about four hours. Then, the forest thins until we reach the meadows.

"I call upon The White Light to surround and protect us this day as we travel," Feyanna said, standing with her hands held open in front of her.

"I've not heard that incantation before," Jandor said. "Who taught you this?"

"My mother," Feyanna said. "She was strong in The Magic and The White Light. We started each day with this prayer, and we were always safe. I say it every morning when I wake up."

"And, now, so shall I," Jandor said as he opened his arms and hands and recited the incantation.

They proceeded carefully. It was about an hour later when the first hint of trouble got their attention. The air seemed to be still, and the light faded to a dusky gray. As they walked on, Feyanna thought she saw some of the tree branches moving like someone's arms.

"Jordan," Feyanna said, pointing to the trees in front of them.

The trees had moved their branches in such a manner to block the path.

"Stand behind me," Jandor said as he took something out of one of his pouches.

It was a black powdered substance. Jordan held it up in front of the trees and said, "I demand that you allow us to pass."

A deep, growling voice responded, "You cannot pass. This forest is for those who walk in the Dark Force. You are weak and disgusting with your puny powers."

"I call upon the Guardians of the life force of these trees. I banish the Dark Forces from these trees," Jordan said as he blew some of the black powder at the trees.

The trees screamed as if in pain.

"You are no match for our master," the trees said in unison.

One of the trees close to Feyanna reached out and wrapped its branches around her, pinning her in place. Then, it lifted her high into the air, ready to throw her back onto the earth, killing her.

"I call upon The White Light to protect me," Feyanna said.

This made the tree scream as if it had been pierced with electricity.

"You have no power here," The biggest of the trees said. "We will kill you and all your kind for eternity."

"I call upon the power of the earth, the air, the water, and the light to assist us here and now," Jandor chanted as he continued to blow the black powder at the trees that blocked the path.

A deer ran onto the path, and the Dark Forces ripped it to shreds, throwing the pieces of its body all around the forest. A rabbit bolted across the path, but not fast enough. The smaller trees along the side of the path proceeded to pierce the rabbit's body with their claw-like branches for what seemed a long time before the rabbit finally died. Then, one of the claw-like branches threw it high into the air, and the older trees shredded it into a million pieces, all the while laughing and howling in triumph.

Jandor had managed to get closer to the trees that blocked the path while the animals were being killed without being noticed by the trees. He took another powder out of his pouches and mixed it with the black one. He took a deep breath and blew this mixture onto the trees that blocked the path.

The trees began to scream and howl in pain. Jandor blew the mixture onto the trees again. The sound was horrible this time, as if a person was being torn apart while still alive.

The oldest tree screamed at Jandor. "You will die now."

Feyanna started to chant a protection chant her mother had taught her. She called on The White Light to wrap her and Jandor in a cloud of silver energy. As the silver cloud enshrouded them, the whole forest screamed out in agony. The trees in front of them began to smolder and erupted into flames from the ground to the top of each tree. The branches that had blocked the path were instantly incinerated and turned to ashes. As soon as the ashes touched the earth, they were taken by the Spirit of The Wind into a holding place between the universes.

The oldest tree took the longest to turn to ashes. As it burned, the flames turned from red and orange to pure black. It hollered out just before it was incinerated.

"You have not won this round. There are many others who will kill you along this path."

"The Dark Forces have lost this time. Mother Earth, I return this part of the forest to you," Jandor said as he sprinkled a white powder while turning around.

When the white powder hit the earth and plants, they all turned green, and the light was returned to the forest. With one last howl, the oldest tree became ashes, which were taken into the space between the universes like the others.

The air became soft, and you could hear birdsong once again. Feyanna found herself lying on the path without remembering how she got there. She was unharmed. Jandor fell to the ground as the oldest tree was taken. Feyanna crawled over to him and noticed he was pale and sweaty. She grabbed the red berries and put some into his mouth. She grabbed the water pouch and set it against his lips. He drank and ate more red and blueberries for a short time. His color returned, and he stood up.

"Thank you for taking such great care of me," Jandor said. Then he chanted something in a language Feyanna did not know. Whatever it was, it seemed to strengthen Jandor.

"It's time we moved on," Jandor said. "We still have a ways to go to get to the meadows."

"This has been horrible," Feyanna said as they set out once again. "I'm glad my mother taught me so much about calling on The Magic to help us. But I feel I have a great deal to learn."

"Your mother is to be praised for all she taught you. She has done a great job," Jandor said. "And, yes, you have a great deal to learn, as do I. That is why we need to get to the lake and a safe place as soon as we can."

They walked for a while without stopping to eat. The forest seemed to be thinning out, and the air seemed brighter because of this.

"We're almost to the meadows," Jandor was saying when he felt something against his ankle.

He looked down and saw a poisonous snake wrapping itself around his foot and leg.

"Jandor," Feyanna said, pointing to Jandor's leg.

"I know," Jandor said. "Here, take this pouch and sprinkle some of the crystalline powder on the snake. It should kill it."

Feyanna did just that, and the snake sizzled and died, falling to the ground.

Jandor looked around and saw an ugly sight.

"Look," Jandor said.

"They're everywhere," Feyanna said. "Now what?"

A growl came from the air and said, "You were warned by the trees. Now you die a slow and painful death."

In an instant, snakes were wrapping themselves around Feyanna's legs and slithering up her torso. Jandor leaned over and threw some of the crystalline powder on her, and some of the snakes died and fell away. There was a bright yellow and orange one that wasn't affected. He kept slithering up her torso until he was at her neck.

The snake reared back and spoke, looking directly into Feyanna's eyes.

"You are the one that killed my lineage in the village of Tessandria in the region of Cadenmoore. Now, I will have my revenge."

"I do not know what you speak of," Feyanna said.

"How could you forget that day when you killed all my kin that were hiding in the kiln?" the snake said.

"The kiln? I must have been no more than ten or eleven years old," Feyanna said. "My father showed me how to light the fire in the kiln so we could harden the pots we had just made. I lit the fire. I did not know there were snakes in the bottom of the kiln."

"They weren't in the kiln but in the depression below the kiln where the fire raged. You killed them on purpose. You are an evil soul," the snake hissed.

"Snake, I did not know there was anything below the kiln. You have my deepest sympathy and apologies," Feyanna said, trying not to tremble from the tight grip the snake had on her body.

"You killed them. Now, I will kill you," the snake screamed. "And, you, Jandor of Myrgania, you have no potions in those poches that can kill me. You are powerless here."

Jandor started to chant in that other language he had used before. The snake's head seemed to grow bigger in front of Feyanna. The more Jandor chanted, the more restless the snake became. Jandor changed chants, trying not to move because snakes had encircled him, too. He still had some of the crystalline powder in his hands and tossed some on the snakes closest to his hands. Those snakes sizzled and died. This gave Jandor more room to maneuver. He grabbed a pure white quartz crystal from his pocket, dipped it in some kind of liquid in one of the pouches, and then held it toward Feyanna. He started chanting again, and the snake that held Feyanna prisoner began to grow weak.

"Your crystal has no power over me," the snake hissed as it began to lose its grip on Feyanna. "I will have my revenge!"

The snake lurched forward and bit Feyanna on the chest as it lost its hold and slithered onto the ground. Jandor sprinkled some of the liquid from the crystal onto the snake, and it exploded into a million pieces, which vanished into thin air.

Feyanna fell to the ground. Jandor threw more crystalline powder all around them, and the snakes that were hit sizzled and died. He could see the edge of the meadows. He picked up Feyanna and ran to the meadows. He fell to the ground and laid Feyanna down. She was unconscious, and her breathing was shallow and labored. The poison was getting a hold of her, and Jandor needed help to stop the poison from killing her.

Jandor raised his hands toward the sky and called out, "I need your help. I do not have the medicine to cure Feyanna. I beg of the gods and goddesses to save her life. She walks in The White Light and is a good soul."

Plants underneath Feyanna began to cover her, and a brilliant light from the clouds shone upon her. It was lavender and yellow. Jandor knelt in awe of what he was seeing. As he looked at Feyanna, the plants sounded like they were absorbing fluid from her body. They grew huge and turned black as more and more fluid was drawn from her. The beams of light caressed the black plants, returning them to their green and blue colors. This played on for quite some time. Feyanna began to moan and toss and turn. The light beams turned white and shown directly on her, wrapping her all around in their power like a blanket.

It seemed like hours had passed when Jandor heard his name whispered.

"Jandor," Feyanna whispered.

"Feyanna, you're alive. Praise the gods and goddesses and all The Magic around us," Jandor said.

Feyanna saw tears flowing across Jandor's cheeks.

"I am alive and healing quickly," Feyanna said. "I thank The White Light and all The Magic for saving my life. I will serve you through the end of my days."

"You look so much better," Jandor said as he crawled over to her. "You want to try to sit up?"

"Yes, please," Feyanna said. The white light and plants were still on her. Feyanna sat up with Jandor's help.

"I think some of the poison is still in me," Feyanna said. "I feel light-headed and unsteady."

"Lean back on me while the light and plants finish their healing," Jandor said.

Feyanna did just that, and it was into the evening when the heavenly light ascended back into the sky, and the plants left her side.

"I thank you, healing light and plants, for your medicine," Feyanna said as she bowed to the sky and earth.

There was a flash of sunlight, and the plants in the meadow swayed for a second in response.

"Jandor, thank you for all you did to save me," Feyanna said, laying her hand on his. "I am eternally grateful for your assistance."

"You are welcome," Jandor replied, squeezing Feyanna's hand in response. "How about you stay right here, and I'll fashion us some supper?"

"I like your plan," Feyanna was saying when The Magic once again provided them with their evening meal and fresh water. "And, I thank The Magic for your supper assistance."

"This has never happened to me before. You might just be handy to have around," Jandor said, winking at Feyanna.

"Any time, my friend," Feyanna replied.

They ate their supper in a lighter mood than they'd been in since they left the village food vendors. It was late evening when they finished, and their supper was cleared by The Magic as well.

"Well, we need to find shelter for the night," Jandor said.

"I agree," Feyanna replied.

"Let's stand here and look around and see if we find anything," Jandor suggested.

They did just that and saw at the same time a kind of hut not too far to the west.

"Just there," Jandor said.

"I see it," Feyanna said. "Let's go."

"You feel strong enough to walk that far?" Jandor asked.

"I am still a little weak, but I do have the strength to make it to that hut," Feyanna said with great conviction.

"Okay. Let's go," Jandor said.

They stopped a couple of times so Feyanna could rest a bit. They finally arrived as the night took over, and a million stars glowed overhead.

"This is perfect," Feyanna said. "Look, Jandor, two beds with straw and blankets for us. I'm going to sleep now. I'm very tired."

"You do just that," Jandor said as he tucked Feyanna in.

Feyanna was asleep in a heartbeat. Jandor secured the hut for the night. He knew he was in friendly territory and wasn't too concerned about robbers and thieves. He fell asleep right away, too, as he thanked the powers that be for their safety.

They woke up with the sun the next morning.

"How are you feeling this beautiful morning?" Jandor asked as he started a small fire.

"Great!" Feyanna replied as she put their things in order. "I feel as if I was never poisoned by that horrible snake."

"Good to hear," Jordan said. "I'm making tea. How about you set some food out for breakfast?"

"All set," Feyanna said as they sat down to fruit, tea, and a few biscuits. "So, are we headed north today?"

"Not yet. We need to continue in a westward and somewhat northerly direction until we see the shores of the Seas of Hidden Secrets. Should take us all of today and part of tomorrow."

"This meadow is beautiful," Feyanna said. "I only saw a glimpse of it yesterday, but that glimpse was amazing."

"It is a beautiful and peaceful place," Jandor said. "We can gather herbs for medicinal purposes and cooking as we go."

"That's a great idea," Feyanna said. "I do need more lavender and sage."

"And I need more milk thistle, calendula, and a variety of greens," Jandor added.

"I have room in my basket for a lot of plants and a few empty pouches as well," Feyanna said.

"I have a few empty pouches, too," Jandor said. "I think we have room for everything we'll gather along the way. You about ready?"

"Just need to take care of one more thing," Feyanna said as she left the hut. She returned a few minutes later, saying, "All set."

They set out and had a pleasant journey. They found most of the herbs and plants they were looking for.

The afternoon was just beginning to fade into evening when Feyanna stopped and pointed to something a little ways ahead of them.

"Look," she whispered to Jandor.

It was a family of deer. There were two females and three fawns. A buck stood apart, watching over them.

"Beautiful," Jandor whispered.

The two of them stood and watched until the deer caught the scent of an animal and ran off.

"That's what makes life so worth living for," Feyanna said as they continued their journey.

"And, worth fighting for," Jandor said.

Feyanna turned and looked at Jandor. He was staring off into the unknown and looked like someone who'd had to fight for their life. Feyanna did not speak until Jandor returned to the here and now.

"Sorry about that," Jandor said, taking a deep breath and standing tall.

Feyanna placed her hand on his arm for a second in response.

"Let's find a place for the night. I'm hungry," Jandor said.

"Me, too," Feyanna replied as they walked on a bit before finding a hill with a hollow tucked in the side.

"This will do," Jandor said. "I'll start a fire if you set things up for the night."

"I'll get the firewood," Feyanna said. "I saw some just a few feet from this hollow."

"Good," Jandor said as he prepared a space for the fire.

Feyanna was right back with a big pile of firewood in her arms. She could hardly see over the top.

"I guess when you set out to do something, you really give it your all," Jandor said, laughing as he took the firewood from her.

"I tend to get quite involved with the task at hand," Feyanna replied, letting the rest of the firewood fall to the ground.

Supper was ready and thoroughly enjoyed, with stories told of some of the funnier pranks of their youths.

"Feyanna, follow me," Jandor said as he stepped away from their camp.

An incredible sight awaited them.

Feyanna was speechless at what she saw. The sky was ablaze with oranges, reds, yellows, and gold, with sunbeams shining through it all. As they watched, the colors began to change as the sun set lower in the sky. Purples, blues, and hints of pint took over for a few minutes until the sun disappeared below the horizon. A splash of sunbeams was sent throughout the sky as the stars began to show themselves.

"Amazing," Feyanna whispered.

"Yes," Jandor whispered back.

They stood there until the sky was dressed for the night. It was a clear night, and the stars peppered the sky as far as one could see.

"Well, that was a great way to end our day," Jordan said as they returned to their camp.

"I am always amazed and awed at what the universe shows me," Feyanna said.

"Me, too," Jandor replied as they settled on their pallets. "Tomorrow, we should arrive at The Seas of Hidden Secrets. Then, we begin to travel northward. Sleep well, Feyanna."

"Same to you, Jandor," Feyanna replied.

As they slept, a magical creature began to awaken. It would be needed before long.

They set out early the next day and arrived near the shore around noon. The Seas of Hidden Secrets had a few whitecaps on it as if there had been a storm out at sea.

"This is beyond anything I could have imagined," Feyanna said as they stood on a rise looking out over the Seas.

"That's right," Jandor said. "You've never seen an ocean before."

"It seems to go on and on forever," Feyanna said. "I can smell salt in the air. Is that from the ocean?"

"It is," Jandor replied, pointing to something a ways off the shore. "Look there. Whales."

"Oh my!" Feyanna said in amazement. "My father told us about them from when he was at sea as a fisherman. He said they were huge and graceful. I never thought I'd see one."

"They seem to be a bit closer to the shore than usual," Jandor said as he watched them.

"Why would that be? Isn't it too shallow for them this close?" Feyanna asked.

"It could be," Jandor replied. "Sometimes there are deep waters just a few feet from the shoreline. That's what must be going on here. And I'll bet the food they eat is swimming close by. They follow the food."

"Do they ever get stuck in shallow water?" Feyanna asked.

"Not usually," Jandor said. "If there is a massive storm at sea, they might get confused and swim close to the shore. I figure they might be sick or old and end up on the beach, too."

"That makes sense," Feyanna replied.

"This is magnificent," Feyanna was saying when two whales breached, splashing the water with their arms, and they fell back into the water.

"It looks like they're having a bit of fun," Feyanna said, laughing.

"Look there," Jandor said as he pointed at a whale. It had come so far out of the water that it showed its massive tail as if dove back down.

"I am speechless," Feyanna said as they watched the whales for a while more.

"Time to move on," Jandor said. "I do believe this would be a great spot for lunch."

Jandor pointed to a tree not far from the cliff's edge.

"Great!" Feyanna replied. "We can watch the ocean while we eat."

They enjoyed watching the whale show. A few dolphins joined, too. Feyanna and Jordan finally got back to their journey. They followed a path that kept them going northward and meandered around the meadow, leaving the shoreline from time to time. It was going onto dusk when Jandor felt a change in the air.

"Feyanna, I feel a storm is coming along," Jandor said. "We need to find strong shelter for the night. Maybe there's a hut farther inland. Let's take a look."

"How can you tell a storm is coming?" Feyanna asked as they left the ocean and looked for shelter. They were on the top of a tall hillside, and as they walked downhill, they could no longer see the ocean. They were following an animal trail when Feyanna saw a dark area on the hillside.

"Jandor, it looks like it might be a cave," Feyanna said.

"Let's take a look," Jandor replied. "Be careful. There might be animals that live inside."

When they got to the cave, a family of sheep came out.

"Guess this isn't the place," Jandor said. "Let's keep looking along this side of the cliffs. It'll be dark soon, so we need to hurry along."

A short while later, they found an old hut set against the cliffside. It was falling apart, and the roof was gone.

"Not this one, either," Feyanna said.

They walked a few feet further and came upon another cave entrance.

"I'll go in first," Jandor said. "I'll light this torch to help me see if anyone's home."

He entered the cave, and a minute later, a flock of bats emerged. They were on their nightly quest for food.

"That's the only sign of life in here," Jandor said. "They were quite a ways back in the cave. We don't need to go that far back, though. Come on in."

Feyanna entered the cave and saw a small entryway that opened into a good-sized room.

"This looks good," Feyanna said. "Is your torch smoke going through the roof?"

"Yes, it is," Jandor replied. "There seems to be a natural opening somewhere up there. We can start a fire for warmth. It is a little damp in here."

"Probably because it's part of the ocean," Feyanna offered.

"I believe you're right about that. You can hear the wind as well," Jandor said. "It sounds like the rain has begun."

Feyanna walked back to the entrance and saw that it was raining. A steady rain it was.

"It is," Feyanna said. "Nothing fierce. It reminds me of the summer rains back home. They would come on along sundown and stay throughout the night. They ended at sunrise. Everything looked freshly washed in the morning."

"Time for supper," Jandor said as he passed a mug of tea to Feyanna. "It looks like someone uses this from time to time. There's a slight breeze coming in from the entryway. So, I made up our pallets out of the way over there."

"Thanks," Feyanna said as they ate their supper.

A rumble of thunder was heard.

"Sounds like a good thunderstorm out there," Jandor said.

"So glad we found this place. Lightening frightens me," Feyanna said.

"It can be dangerous, although I've never seen it hurt anything or anyone," Jandor replied.

"It's amazing to see when it streaks across the sky, though," Feyanna added.

"It is. Let's get some sleep. We have a long way to go tomorrow," Jandor said.

"I love listening to the rain as I fall asleep," Feyanna said as she settled on her pallet. "It's almost like a lullaby."

"Sleep well," Jandor said as Feyanna closed her eyes and fell into a deep sleep.

Jandor's sleep was something different. He saw Feyanna and himself walking northward a ways inland from the Seas of Hidden Secrets. The ocean was close by, just not within sight. As they walked along, Feyanna pointed to the sky. Jandor looked and saw that the sky was beginning to fill with black clouds, and the wind had picked up. The wind became so strong you could taste salt in the air from the ocean.

"We need to find shelter,' Jandor heard himself say.

"I don't see anything in sight that would work as a shelter,' Feyanna replied.

Jandor looked all around and nodded his head in agreement. They kept walking towards the north, and the sky became filled with black clouds. Lighting was seen flashing across the skies, and loud, crashing thunder was heard.

Just as the rain crashed down from the heavens, Feyanna pointed to a shape ahead of them. They walked through the downpour to find an old animal hut. The roof was in good shape but was open to the east, away from the ocean. Jandor held up his arms and chanted something, and a covering appeared across the opening. He bowed and thanked whomever he had chanted for.

"That was amazing," Feyanna said, dripping wet.

"I'll start a fire, and you set these tree stumps in front of it. We can spread our clothes across them to get dry," Jandor said.

"These weren't here a minute ago," Feyanna said. "Thanks for all the gifts today."

A quick shimmer of the cloth wall told her she had been heard.

The fire was going strong, and they set their cloaks and boots on the stumps. The floor was covered in straw and had not gotten wet from the rain. The storm raged on for a long time. They had supper and set up their pallets for the night.

"I don't think this storm is going to give up any time soon," Feyanna said as lightning streaked through the sky and loud thunder was heard and felt. "I'm glad I can't see most of the lighting."

"This is quite the storm," Jandor replied. "It seems to have come from the ocean. I hope it's gone by morning."

"Me, too," Feyanna said, yawning. "Sleep well, Jandor. Thanks for taking such good care of us."

"You, too," Jandor said. "I thank all those that have taught me and continue to assist me on my journey."

They fell asleep while the storm raged on. His dream seemed so real. He didn't realize it was a dream until he woke up the next morning.

It was a little bit before sunrise when the storm finally left the area. Feyanna was awakened by the silence. She got up, pulled the cloth wall aside, and was greeted with a beautiful sunrise.

Jandor joined her, and they pulled the cloth all the way aside so they could see the sun ascending into a gold and purple sky.

"That was beautiful," Feyanna said as they prepared breakfast.

They set out walking toward the north again and spent the day gathering more herbs and flowers and enjoying the meadow and the sea. They stopped for supper on a cliff that overlooked the Seas of Hidden Secrets. The sky was clear, and there was a slight breeze blowing in from the ocean.

"I've always wondered why this ocean is called the Seas of Hidden Secrets," Feyanna said. "I asked my father, and he said a lot of things have happened in the ocean, and no one knows why."

"He was right," Jandor replied.

"Like what?" Feyanna asked.

"Well, there have been lives lost in these waters without an explanation. No storms, no other ships around. A number of vessels have just disappeared. All souls lost."

"My father did say some men were lost during the storms. That makes sense to me," Feyanna said.

"There are stories of great sea creatures that pluck men off vessels and fly away with them. Some fly high into the sky, and other creatures dive straight down into the waters, never to be seen again," Jandor said.

"That's horrifying," Feyanna replied.

"It is," Jandor said. "Then, there's a tale that's been told for centuries about a beautiful woman creature that lures men to their deaths. She is supposedly seen off in the distance, and her beauty is beyond anything one could imagine. The ship's captain set a course for her, and before they knew it, they crashed upon a wall of rocks. The ship was torn apart, and all perished in the deep. Not one piece of any vessel has ever been found."

"That's just crazy," Feyanna said as she looked out over the ocean.

"Other sailors have told of seeing gold and silver in the shallows," Jandor continued. "They row ashore and wade out to where they see these gems, and just as they're reaching for them, a giant creature with two heads and many arms grabs them and takes them underwater, never to be seen again."

"I guess it has earned its name, then," Feyanna said.

"Makes sense to me," Jandor replied. "Time to move on. We need shelter for the night. Let's walk inland a little bit so we're on the other side of those dunes. We may find a cave or hollow or something. Look far out to sea. See those clouds on the horizon?"

"I do," Feyanna replied. "They look a bit odd to me."

"Good eye," Jandor said. "I think the Seas are trying to get our attention. They may not want us to get to our destination."

"Really? The earth and water can try to block us?" Feyanna asked as they walked a bit northeastward.

"It's not the earth and water," Jandor explained. "It's the Dark Forces manipulating the earth and water to bring chaos to the universe."

"I understand that," Feyanna said as they turned to walk along the back of the dunes.

It was close to sunset when dark clouds once again filled the skies. They had just found a cave and were walking into it when a blast of wind threw them to the ground.

"What was that?" Jandor said, gasping for breath.

Feyanna just lay there without speaking.

Jandor crawled over to her. "Feyanna, can you hear me?" Jandor said.

Feyanna moved to sit up. "What the hell was that?" she said, coughing a bit.

"I do believe the Dark Forces are trying to impress upon us that we shouldn't keep going," Jandor replied as he sat on the ground beside her.

"Not gonna happen," Feyanna said. "I got this. I call upon the White Light to build a shell of protection around us as we travel to our destination. We walk in The White Light. You say that, too."

"I walk in The White Light," Jandor said.

A tremendous white flash filled the little cave, and they were able to breathe once again.

"I hear a humming sound," Jandor said.

"It's the energy of the earth protecting us," Feyanna replied. "The earth prefers The White Light to the Dark Forces."

"Great. Thanks to everyone over there," Jandor said as he stood up and held a hand out for Feyanna to grasp.

"Look at the opening of the cave," Feyanna said. "That's the power of the good guys."

Jandor looked over and saw the air shimmering gold as it covered the opening.

"That's amazing," he said. "Let's get settled."

They got a fire going, heated some food, ate, and finally placed their pallets on the ground.

A sudden roaring sound was heard and felt throughout the cave.

"It's just the Dark Force screaming because they can't get to us," Feyanna said.

"Bad form," Jandor said, laughing.

"It's meant to scare us," Feyanna said, laughing as well. "Didn't work."

"Time to rest," Jandor said.

"Indeed," Feyanna replied as she fell asleep.

They set out just before sunrise the next day. There was an ominous feeling in the air. The day looked beautiful, but the energy was off. It was mid-afternoon when Jandor pointed something out to Feyanna.

"Look," Jandor said. "The meadow melds into that copse of trees. Let's head there for the night."

They hadn't even taken a step when the skies opened, and torrential rain and hail assaulted them. They tried to walk, but it was as if a solid wall of stone was in front of them.

Jandor grabbed Feyanna's hand and pulled them to the ground. They hunkered down without any shelter. The hail became bigger and bigger and began to cause injury to them.

Feyanna cried out as a large rock-sized piece of hail hit her head. She fell forward, dazed. Lightning struck the ground close to Jandor, and he was knocked down. Unconscious.

Feyanna couldn't move. She felt like something had her pinned to the ground.

Hail and rain beat down on them for the longest time. Just as Feyanna was about to lose consciousness, she felt something standing over them. She no longer felt the rain and hail. She couldn't see what it was because she was so weak she couldn't lift her head. She felt a gentle warmth come over her and let herself slip into a deep, deep sleep.

Jandor was the first to wake up. He looked around and saw something covering them. It was big and curved. He didn't really know what it was. Nonetheless, he offered thanks for the protection.

He crawled over to Feyanna and saw the blood on her head. He reached into his cloak and grabbed a pouch. He sprinkled some of the powder on her cut, and it healed right before his eyes. She began to move and finally opened her eyes. She saw the great curved thing covering them, too, and gave thanks for its protection.

"Feyanna," Jandor whispered.

"I'm alive," Feyanna answered. "You look terrible."

"I was struck by lightning that hit the ground," Jandor said. "The Dark Forces really want us dead."

"Why?" Feyanna asked. "I don't know what's covering us, but I'm sure glad it's here. Maybe we could ask it to move a bit so we can sit up."

"Good idea," Jandor was saying when the thing suddenly disappeared.

"It's gone," Feyanna said as they stood up.

They looked all over the place and couldn't see anything anywhere that was like the thing that had covered them.

"Well, we'd better get to those trees right away. I don't think the trouble is over yet," Jandor said.

They hurried toward the trees and only had to deal with a swarm of moths along the way. It didn't cause any problems, and as soon as they stepped into the copse, the moths vanished. It was beautiful here. The sun shone through the leaves on the trees, and birds and bees buzzed among the plants.

"We need to rest here," Jandor said.

"I agree," Feyanna said.

They ate and slept and didn't realize they had slept all night until the sun woke them the next morning, shining on their faces.

"Good Morning, Jandor," Feyanna said as she prepared the tea.

"You're up before me," Jandor said as he left and returned a few minutes later. "I found some more red berries for us."

"Thanks. They'll be a part of our breakfast," Feyanna said as she poured water over the tea leaves.

"This tea is delicious," Jandor offered.

"Thanks. My mother taught me all about herbs and teas. I love to make tea," Feyanna said.

"Then, you now have morning tea duty," Jandor said.

"I accept," Feyanna said, giving a little bow.

"We should reach our stopping place this evening," Jandor said. "I don't think it's going to be an easy journey. As a matter of fact, I think it will be a difficult journey. You ready?"

"I am," Feyanna replied. "I get the feeling that it will be difficult, too. Don't know why or how, though."

"Me, either," Jandor said as he led the way northward again.

When they left the copse of trees, they entered a grassland with rocks and some trees. It was a bit rough, but nothing that would hold them back.

All of a sudden, the temperature dropped to freezing cold. Frost covered the grasslands, and the sun became hazy with no warmth.

"Let's put on warmer clothes," Jandor said.

They added clothes to their bodies and closed their cloaks up to their chins.

"This is much better," Feyanna said.

"We still have a long ways to go," Jandor said as snow began to fall.

"So glad we have our boots on," Feyanna said.

The wind began to blow the snow all around, and they had to bend their heads to be able to see where they were. The sky darkened as they walked on, and it looked like night, even though Jandor knew it was mid-afternoon.

"The Dark Forces are trying to mess with us," Feyanna said.

"They are, but we are prepared," Jandor replied. "See there?"

Feyanna looked skyward, and a milky sun showed through the darkness.

"Love when this happens," Feyanna said.

"We need to be careful. It's getting colder, and the grasslands are beginning to freeze over," Jandor said.

"I noticed when I slipped a minute ago," Feyanna said.

They kept going until it was pitch black outside, and about a foot of snow was on the ground.

"I'm so very tired, Jandor," Feyanna said as she stumbled into Jandor.

He held her close for a moment.

"I can see an opening in the hillside across the rest of the grasslands," Jandor said. "Do you think you can make it?"

"I'll try my best," Feyanna replied.

It seemed like forever when they finally stumbled into the cave.

They managed to eat something, then fell deep asleep, exhausted from their journey.

CHAPTER 9

And that's how Jandor and Feyanna came to be in the cave by the lake.

They were preparing breakfast when a great shadow appeared on the back wall of the cave.

"Jandor, do you see that shadow there?" Feyanna asked as she poured the tea.

"I do now," Jandor replied, looking toward the shadow. "Wonder what it is?"

"I don't get a bad feeling about it," Feyanna replied. "Do you?"

"Nope," Jandor answered just as the shadow grew bigger.

They watched as the shadow fell away from the wall, and a creature, a huge creature, appeared. Huge wasn't the right word to describe the thing. It was gargantuan. And it was deep purple.

"No way," Jandor said as it began to approach them

The cave grew bigger to accommodate the size of the creature.

"Is it really what I think it is?" Feyanna said as she and Jandor stood up.

"I do believe it is," Jandor replied.

"But it's purple," Feyanna said.

"I know," Jandor said. "I didn't know they came in purple."

"Me, either," Feyanna said. "They're usually black or dark gray."

The creature was close by now and sat down, looking at the two of them.

"It is what we think it is," Jandor replied.

"A real purple dragon," Feyanna said in awe. "I'm dumbstruck!"

"Me, too," Jandor said as they continued to stare at the dragon.

"I think this is its home," Feyanna said after a bit.

They just stared at the creature for the longest time. Then, it spoke.

149

"Hello, Jandor and Feyanna," it said.

"It talks," Jandor said in a surprised tone.

"Of course I do," it said. "How else am I going to communicate with the two of you?"

"Are you really what we think you are?" Feyanna asked.

"I am," it replied. "And my name is Penelope. You both may call me Penny. Only those I cherish are allowed to call me Penny."

"And she has a name," Jandor said.

"Only those you cherish can call you Penny?" Feyanna asked. "We've never met you before. So, how can you cherish us?"

"I've known you both since you were born into the human world. I've been watching over you all this time," Penny replied, settling her huge wings back against herself.

"She's a purple dragon," Jandor said in awe.

"Yes, she is a purple dragon," Feyanna said. "You're beautiful!"

"Why, thank you, Feyanna. That's very kind of you to notice," Penny replied.

"I'm still trying to get past the fact that a dragon is talking with us," Jandor said.

This made Penny laugh. "You take all the time you need as long as it's just a few more minutes. We need to be somewhere else soon."

"Do we have time to finish breakfast?" Jandor asked.

"Of course," Penny replied.

"Thanks," Feyanna said as she and Jandor ate.

Not a word was said all through the meal and as they packed their things, preparing to leave the cave.

"We're ready to go," Jandor said to Penny.

"Good. Now, head north until you reach the edge of the lake. You know which one I speak of, Jandor."

"Yes, I do. I've been seeing it in my dream visions for quite some time now," Jandor replied.

"I'll meet you there," Penny said as the three of them walked out onto the meadow. There wasn't any trace of snow. It was a warm, sunny day. "I will be keeping you safe from the Dark Forces as you approach the lake. No worries."

"This must be some special place," Feyanna said.

"It is," Penny replied. "You'll see just how special in a bit. Now, get going."

"Yes, Ma'am," they both replied as Penny took to the air.

Feyanna and Jandor looked at each other for a second, then started talking at the same time.

"A dragon?" Jandor said.

"Our own dragon?" Feyanna said.

"A talking dragon," Jandor said.

"She's purple," Feyanna.

"That, too," Jandor said, following Penny's flight up into the sky.

"Oh my God! Jandor, we have our own dragon," Feyanna said, jumping all over the place and laughing.

Jandor laughed as he watched Feyanna. "This is unbelievable," he said.

Feyanna stopped all of a sudden and said, "Oh, oh. You thinking what I'm thinking? If we need protection, that must mean we're about to learn a whole bunch of stuff centered around The Magic that the Dark Forces don't want us to know about."

"Exactly what I was about to say," Jandor said as they started walking along. "Our own dragon. We have our own dragon. And she's purple and can talk with us. This is gonna take some getting used to."

"I agree," Feyanna said. "Look!"

Feyanna pointed to a dark cloud that was forming into a vortex.

"Looks like the Dark Forces aren't wasting any time," Jandor said.

They watched as a twister touched the ground up ahead. Penny flew smack dab into the middle of it, and it was gone in an instant.

"Thanks, Penny," Feyanna called out.

Penny flew overhead to show them she had heard Feyanna, then headed north.

"That was incredible," Jandor said, bowing to the north.

"Indeed," Feyanna said as she sent off a prayer of thanks.

They continued north without any further mishaps, then stopped to eat mid-afternoon. Penny showed up and sat with them for a bit.

"Well, this has been a pleasant time," Penny said as she stood and stretched. "We need to move on. We should reach the lake just before sunset."

"Okay with us," Feyanna said as she and Jandor headed north again.

It was close to dusk when they reached the top of a small hill covered with trees and looked down on the lake. It was a shade of blue hard to describe and so clear it reflected the sun's rays like a mirror.

"This is beautiful," Feyanna said as they descended the hill.

"Even more than in my dream visions," Jandor added. "That shade of blue is like nothing I've ever seen before."

"Me, either," Feyanna said.

As they walked down the hill, the trees seemed to come alive and grow vines. The vines reached out for Feyanna and Jandor to trap them and keep them from reaching the lake. The sky darkened, and the ground trembled.

"This is not good," Jandor said as vines began to wrap all around his legs.

The vines had wrapped Feyanna around her waist and were reaching for her arms.

"I call upon The White Light to protect us," Feyanna shouted out as one vine reached her throat.

"I call upon The Magic to help us," Jandor screamed as vines pinned his arms to his body and wrapped all around him.

"These really stink," Jandor said as a vine wrapped itself across his fore-head.

Just as the vines were about to fully cover Jandor, a great shadow flew overhead. Penny. She dipped toward the two of them, saying, "Don't move!"

As she came very close to Jandor, she reached out with her wing tip and cut the vines down one side of his body. The wind screamed. Penny swooped down again and cut the vines off Feyanna as well. The vines fell to the earth, bleeding bright yellow fluid.

"Jandor, grab your lavender and sprinkle it around the two of you," Penny said.

Jandor did just that, and the vines that were sprinkled with the lavender shriveled up and vanished in a dark smoke.

The ground trembled again, and Penny blew fire at the trees with the vines. A great cloud of fire and black smoke arose from the trees, and everything vanished into thin air.

Feyanna sat down, amazed at all that had happened.

"I think I'll join you," Jandor said as he sat beside Feyanna. "What the hell was that?"

Penny flew in and settled in front of the two of them.

"My dear Jandor, that was The Dark trying to keep you from the lake," Penny said.

"It stank," Feyanna said. "I thought I was going to throw up."

"It was a foul odor by all means," Penny added.

"Thanks for taking care of us," Jandor said, bowing his head toward Penny.

"That's one of the things I'm here for," Penny said.

"I gotta' say, seeing you blow fire at the trees was incredible," Feyanna said. "I'd heard dragons could do that, but I've never seen it until just now. Does it hurt your throat?"

"Why, Feyanna, thanks for being concerned about me. No, it doesn't hurt any part of me to do that," Penny replied. Then, with a wink and a smile, she added, "I can blow ice, too."

"Now that's just plain amazing," Jandor said, laughing along with Feyanna and Penny.

"Penny, will those trees grow again, or did The Dark put them here just for today?"

"Great question, Feyanna," Penny replied. "Look there."

As they watched, the trees reappeared just as they had been before The Dark attacked them.

"They're just as magnificent as before the whole stinky thing," Feyanna said.

"Mother Earth takes care of her children quite well," Penny replied. "Now, are you two ready to get to the lake's edge?" Penny asked as she stood tall and spread her wings to their fullest width. She did make a frightening sight for sure.

"I am," Feyanna said as she stood up. "I really feel small when you are at your best, Miss Penny."

"Good to know, just in case either of you take a notion to be mischievous," Penny replied, winking at them.

"Ready here," Jandor replied as he gathered his things.

"Let's go," Penny said, and they walked the rest of the way down the hill to the lake.

It seemed like just a few minutes later when they arrived at the lake's edge.

"This place is beautiful," Feyanna said.

"Yes, it is," Penny said. "Let's sit under this tree here. I have some things to tell you."

Once settled, Penny began to speak.

"Well, now, let's get busy with the business at hand," Penny said. "The two of you are going to learn many things in The Magic. You have been taught well. Feyanna, your mother, was a gifted healer. Jandor, your teachers have blessed you with their knowledge. Now, it's time to move on from worldly things. Follow me."

Penny stood up to her fullest height and walked to the edge of the lake. Jandor was awed by the water and all the reflections he saw. Feyanna was hushed by the energy of all the life forms around the lake.

"Now what, Penny?" Jandor asked as he continued to stare at the lake.

"What do you see?" Penny asked him.

"So much," Jandor replied. "I see a castle surrounded by people, both commoners and knights. I see a baby being born that is covered in a golden glow. I see a fierce black dragon circling around the land. I see a cave with a caldron and herbs, metals, and plants. Feyanna, you're in this cave. I see a great hawk like the one that visited me when I started my journey. This place I see is not of this world, is it, Penny?"

"You are correct, Jandor," Penny replied, looking at Feyanna,

"How can it not be of this world? What else is there?" Feyanna asked, puzzled and a bit afraid.

"No need to be afraid, young one," Penny said. "You will be well protected."

Penny stepped onto the lake and stood above it. "Come to me."

Jandor and Feyanna walked over to Penny and did not fall into the lake.

"Touch my wings," Penny said.

As Feyanna and Jandor touched Penny's wings, the air began to move in a swirl of blue and white mists. The mist covered the lake, and they felt themselves lifted into the air.

"Do not fear," Penny said as they began to move forward. "You can let go of my wings. You will be safe."

Feyanna and Jandor let go and found themselves moving through the mists as if they were flying. Penny flew in front of them, and it was only a few minutes later that the mists began to clear, and they landed in a circle of stones. The circle of stones was very tall, and the stones looked like they had electricity running through them in sparkling blue waves.

Feyanna and Jandor stood there looking all around as the mists cleared. A great forest surrounded the circle of stones. The trees were bigger than either of them had ever seen before. There was a soft breeze blowing through the circle of stones from the forest. It was dusk, and there was an orange kind of glow to everything.

"Welcome to the Great Forest of Garanthowen. This is where you'll live as you begin to learn all that you will need to live your lives in The Magic," Penny said quietly.

"This is amazing," Jandor said as he pointed to the stones.

"It is, indeed," Penny replied, smiling. "These stones are full of The Magic, and the energy from them gives life to the forest and all the creatures that live here."

"It sounds like they're humming," Feyanna said. "Listen, Jandor."

"It does," Jandor said. "A soft, sweet sound, for sure."

"Why is the air orange?" Feyanna asked.

"The sun is just setting, and if you look over there, you'll see the two moons that surround this place just peaking over the tops of the trees," Penny explained.

"Two moons?" Feyanna questioned.

"Yes, my dear Feyanna, two moons," Penny replied.

"We don't have two moons in the sky back home," Feyanna said, beginning to feel uneasy.

"You are not back home now," Penny said. "You and Jandor are in a special place. Only those blessed with The Gifts of The Magic from The White Light are allowed to enter."

"Is this place another planet? I have seen many starts and such in the night skies," Jandor offered.

"No, Jandor. Not another planet," Penny replied. "You will learn about this place as you learn about The Magic. You agreed to this before you were born as a human."

"Really?" Feyanna said, feeling a little more at ease.

"Indeed," Penny said. "There is so much for the two of you to learn. Let's go into the Great Forest and find your dwelling," Penny said as she led the way.

They walked for only a few minutes before they saw the dwelling ahead of them.

"It looks like it's set into a small hill," Jandor said.

"It is," Penny replied. "It's a house in the front which opens into the hill for work and such."

"It is charming," Feyanna said. "Whoever built it had some great ideas about how it should look."

"I do like the colors on the outside," Penny added. "Go inside. A meal awaits you. Sleep. I'll see you in the morning. You are safe here."

"Thanks, Penny," Jandor said. "We do appreciate all that has been done for us in The Magic."

Feyanna bowed and offered a quiet thanks as well.

"Good night," Penny said as she took to the sky.

"I think I'm about to be on overload," Feyanna said as she sat down rather abruptly.

"Me, too," Jandor said as he walked around the room, looking at everything. "A lot of this is familiar. There are herbs and plants here and even some dried fruit. At least that is the same as home."

"I guess this is home from now on, wherever we are," Feyanna said as a tear rolled down her cheek.

Jandor hurried over to her and knelt by her side. He put his arms around her and said, "No need for tears. This is all so much to take in right now. The energy is all good," Jandor said soothingly.

Feyanna stayed with her head resting on Jandor's shoulder for quite some time. The quiet was soothing and peaceful.

She finally sat up and said, "Thanks for the shoulder. It felt good," Feyanna said as she gave Jandor's arm a squeeze. "This place is cozy, and I do recognize those plants and such. All of a sudden, I'm starving. Let's eat."

"I agree," Jandor said as he sat across from Feyanna. "There's roast pheasant, lots of vegetables, and even some bread. It smells heavenly."

"And it's still hot," Feyanna said as they began eating. "I thank The Magic for all of this."

They spent the evening looking around their new home, discovering the entrance to the work area deep in the hillside. It was well past dark when they found their own rooms. Everything they needed was in plain sight. There were clothes, a closet of sorts, a bed with plenty of linens and furs, and a chair and table. The best thing was a fireplace against the wall opposite the bed. A small fire was going even though it was summer. The fire kept the damp out of the space.

"This is great," Feyanna said as they looked through both rooms. "Everything we need is here. Well, I guess it is time to get some rest."

"Good night, Feyanna," Jandor said. "Sleep well."

"You, too," Feyanna replied as they went into their rooms. There was a cloth hanging across the entryway. It had a pattern of the night sky on it. And, if you looked at it closely, you could see the shape of a dragon in the upper left corner, flying past the full moon. The Magic had a great sense of humor.

Jandor woke with the rising sun and put water on to boil for tea. He made a hot grain porridge for their breakfast. Feyanna woke up because she smelled the porridge's aroma with all of its herbs floating across the air.

"Good morning, Jandor. This smells wonderful," Feyanna said as she stepped over to the cooking fire and inhaled deeply. "Ah, cinnamon and nutmeg. Smells delicious."

"Thanks," Jandor replied as he brought the pot to the table. "There's honey there as well. I found a hive just a short walk away. The bees were very generous."

"How many stings did you get?" Feyanna said, laughing.

"Only one in my arm," Jandor said as he showed the spot to Feyanna. "I put some herbs on it, and it's almost gone already."

"Good job there," Feyanna said as she tasted her porridge. "This tastes heavenly. We haven't had a hot breakfast for a long while. Thanks."

"You're very welcome," Jandor replied. "That's just what I was thinking. I could have made the porridge using Magic, but I chose to leave The Magic alone. I know we're going to need it down the road."

"I do, too," Feyanna said. "That's why I've decided to enjoy this time of peace and calm."

Just then, there was a knock on the door.

"Who could that be? No one knows we're here," Jandor said as he went to the door. As he looked outside, he added, "Except Penny. Good morning, Penny."

"Good morning, Jandor and Feyanna. Enjoying breakfast, I see," Penny replied as she stuck her face inside the door. "I'll wait out here, of course."

Feyanna laughed as she replied, "I would think that would be a great idea, as you don't fit in here."

"Take your time," Penny replied as she backed away from the door. "I'm going to nap right here in the sunshine."

"Okay, Penny," Jandor replied, smiling at Feyanna. "We'll take care of things in here and wake you when we're done."

The only response they got from Penny was a quiet snoring.

A short while later, they stepped outside and saw Penny all curled up, sleeping peacefully.

Jandor walked over to her and whispered," Oh, Miss Penny. Time to rise and shine."

Feyanna laughed at this as Penny opened one eye and looked at Jandor.

"It's a good thing I like the two of you," Penny said as she sat up and stretched. "I usually greet those I don't like with a bit of fire."

"Now, Miss Penny," Jandor replied. "Isn't that being a bit unsociable?"

"It gets the point across," Penny said as Feyanna laughed at the two of them.

Penny stood tall and, after looking around the forest, said, "Please follow me. We have a great deal to get done today."

Feyanna and Jandor followed Penny along a path through the forest away from their home.

"It's beautiful here," Feyanna said as they walked through a patch of flowering plants. "I recognize a lot of these herbs."

"Good for you," Penny said. "You'll need to harvest some of them this afternoon. Jandor, look ahead and tell me what you see," Penny said.

Jandor took a minute, then replied, "I see Hawthorne trees. Their berries are good for the heart. Their thorns make good weapons as well. I see the mighty oak. The wood of the oak makes excellent posts and supports for building huts and such. I see the Ash, Alder, and Hazel trees whose trunks make great spears and arrows. I see the willow tree whose bark makes good medicine to lower fevers. And, I see the sacred Holly Tree. Wands made from this tree hold The Magic and are used to banish The Dark Forces. Sprites and Faeries live in the Sacred Holy Tree in the winter months, and therefore, it should be protected."

"That is superb, Jandor," Penny said. "Take this branch of the curly birch and fashion a walking stick from it. It will come in handy as we go along."

"Thank you, Penny," Jandor said as he picked up the branch and looked at it. "Thank you, curly birch tree, for this gift."

They walked on and soon entered a meadow. There were birds flying all over the place. It looked like they were carrying straw in their beaks. As the three of them watched, the birds banded together and carried something over to them.

It was a basket, and it was placed at Feyanna's feet. The birds landed in the meadow in front of the three of them, and all was quiet.

"This is beautiful," Feyanna said as she picked up the basket. "I appreciate all the hard work you all did to fashion this basket for me."

The birds chirped their reply, then took to the sky and flew away.

"This is exactly what I need to gather the plants and such," Feyanna said as she showed the basket to Jandor.

"I'm getting the idea that we are going to be very busy making potions and remedies and lots more very soon," Jandor said.

"Exactly," Penny said. "Now, I have one more thing to show you before you two begin to gather the things you will need to make all those potions and things. Follow me."

They walked across the meadow and back into the forest. This time, the air was moving. The trees seemed to move around a lot more than the wind would make them, and the creatures of the forest appeared along the trail as if watching Feyanna and Jandor.

Penny stopped when they came to a circle with a stone altar in the middle. The sun sent a beam of light onto the altar.

As Penny stepped back, an eagle appeared, circling the altar. It landed in the middle and morphed into a kind of creature. It had long black hair, blue eyes and wasn't quite human looking. It wasn't scary-looking, either. Just different.

"Penny, we thank you for bringing Feyanna and Jandor to this place," the tall creature said. "Step forward, Feyanna and Jandor."

Feyanna and Jandor took a step toward the altar.

"Step right up to the altar, please," the tall creature instructed them.

Feyanna and Jandor stepped up to the altar. The tall creature placed a flower on the altar. As they watched, it morphed into a small child-like creature.

"I am the keeper of the flowers," it said. "I am called Nadalyna."

"We are honored to meet you," Feyanna replied.

"I will help you learn all you need to know about the flowers in The Magic," Nadalyna said, then vanished.

The tall creature next set a stone on the altar. It morphed into a full-sized bear. The bear stepped off the altar and stood at the tall creature's side.

"I am called Zecushna," the bear said. "I will teach you the ways of the animals."

"We are honored to be in your presence, Zecushna," Jandor said.

Zecushna vanished.

The tall one placed a piece of winding ivy on the altar, and it morphed into a dragonfly.

"I am known as Lyla. I will teach you the ways of the tiny things in the forest," Lyla said, then vanished.

The tall one spoke. "You have much to learn. Go now with Penelope. Call upon these creatures when you need their knowledge and wisdom." The tall creature morphed back into the eagle it had been, and flew high into the sky.

Feyanna and Jandor stood still and quiet for some time. It was Penny who broke the silence.

"Well, now," Penny said softly, bringing Feyanna and Jandor out of their thoughts.

"This was amazing," Feyanna said. "It's as if I already knew this and just needed to be reminded of it."

"That's it, exactly," Jandor said.

"Well done," Penny said, smiling at them.

"You mean we have met these creatures and all before?" Feyanna asked.

"Yes, and this was a way for you to remember them," Penny replied.

"We have so much to catch up on and learn,' Jandor said. "I get the sense that we are being prepared for something more to take place."

Feyanna looked at Jandor and replied, "Same here. Something really big."

"Follow your instincts," Penny said. "They're usually spot on."

"That's it? You're not going to tell us anything more?" Jandor said.

"Nope," Penny replied. "Now, back to the meadow so Feyanna can gather flowers, berries, and such. You, too, Jandor. Here's a basket for you."

And a basket appeared at Jandor's feet.

"Funny, Penny," Jandor said as they all laughed and turned around to go back to the meadow.

Feyanna and Jandor picked flowers, fruit, and vegetables until their baskets were full.

"Thanks for the harvest," Feyanna said.

"Same here," Jandor added. "I love these red berries. Now, we have some wheat to make flour with. I might be able to fashion some bread and scones with the berries."

"That sounds delicious," Feyanna said. "I'll grind the wheat when we get back home."

They returned to their house in the late afternoon. Penny took her leave, and Feyanna and Jandor set about sorting through the plants they had gathered. Feyanna ground the wheat into flour, and Jandor made redberry bread. The house smelled wonderful all evening long. Feyanna made a vegetable stew for supper, and they talked about their day.

"Jandor, do you get the feeling that something really big is going to take place?" Feyanna asked as they ate.

"I do," he replied. "Not for a while, though. I know we need to learn a lot of new skills that will take a very long time."

"Like years long?" Feyanna asked.

"In human time, yes. In The Magic, it may only take a few months," Jandor said.

"Very true, Jandor. Very true. And, since we're in a Magical place, I suspect it will be months. Very busy months," Feyanna said.

They settled for the night, and sleep came swiftly. Penny slept close by. She knew what was about to happen and wanted to keep them safe.

CHAPTER 10

enny was waiting for them the next morning.

"It's time you learned about this great forest," Penny said. "Follow me, and I will introduce you to the trees."

"This sounds interesting," Feyanna said as they walked along a well-worn path.

The path adjusted its shape to accommodate Penny. It looked like the trees were waving at her as they walked along. A short while later, Penny stopped next to a grove of trees. They had bright yellow bark and orange flowers hanging from the branches. The flowers looked like little bells and as they swayed in the breeze, Jordan could have sworn he heard them ringing.

"You hear them?" Penny asked.

"Yes, I do," Jandor replied.

"I do not. They are beautiful, though," Feyanna said.

"No worries," Penny said. "You'll hear them when the time is right."

The trees gave a little shake, and all the bell flowers rang at the same time.

"Now that I can hear," Feyanna said with a laugh.

"We all can," Penny said. "Thank you, lovely trees. We have enjoyed your concert."

Penny took to the path again, and it was just a short walk before she stopped again.

"These trees are huge!" Feyanna said as she looked at the ones closest to the path.

"They most certainly are," Jandor agreed. "They look to be ancient."

161

"They are," Penny said as she walked over to one and touched it with the tip of her wings. She looked like she was hugging it. "These trees are the oldest life forms in Middle Earth."

Jandor and Feyanna looked at each other in surprise.

"Middle Earth?" Feyanna said. "My mother used to tell me stories of Middle Earth, but I thought they were just that, stories."

"I've heard of Middle Earth as well," Jandor added. "I've heard villagers across the land talk about The Magic that can only be found in Middle Earth. Some I believed, and other stories I thought were just made out of wishes and dreams."

"I am familiar with those stories as well," Penny replied, stepping back from the tree. "Middle Earth is very real but only for those that are of The Magic. You two are of The Magic, and it is here where you will learn all you need to know to go forward and live in The Magic. You will protect The Special Ones and The Special Places one day. You have lots to learn now before any of that takes place. Step over here, Jandor. I would like to introduce you to this beautiful tree."

Jandor walked over to Penny and bowed towards the tree.

"Great One, this is Jandor of the Earth dimension. He is here to learn our ways and all the things you can teach him about," Penny said. "Jandor, this is the Great One, known as Dytonaidium."

"It is an honor to meet you, Great One," Jandor said, bowing low toward the tree.

"It is an honor to finally meet you," The Great One replied. "Your Magic is known far and wide."

"Feyanna, step over here, please," Penny said.

Feyanna walked over to Penny and stood next to her.

"Dytonaidium, this is Feyanna of the Earth dimension. She is here to learn all you can teach her as well. Feyanna, this is The Great One," Penny said.

Feyanna bowed low to The Great One and said, "I am honored and humbled to meet you and learn all I can from you and these beautiful plants and critters here in The Great Forest."

"We are honored to meet you as well," Great One replied. "Thank you, Penny, for getting them here safely."

Penny bowed, saying, "Let us return to the path."

Jandor and Feyanna bowed to the tree and returned to the path with Penny. They walked for quite a while before entering a forest of trees with very crooked trunks and branches.

"These are amazing," Feyanna said. "May I touch them?"

"Yes, you may," a voice was heard to say.

"Was that one of the trees?" Jandor asked as he and Feyanna walked over to a tree and ran their hands along the trunk.

"Yes, it was us," a number of voices replied.

"This is wonderful," Feyanna replied. "I mean that you can talk with us about the beauty of yourselves."

"Why thank you, Feyanna," the tree she was touching replied.

Feyanna laughed out loud in response. "These trees make me want to laugh and shout with joy."

"I feel the same thing," Jandor replied.

"They do have that effect on us," Penny said, laughing with everyone, including the trees.

"What are these trees called?" Jandor asked.

"They are appropriately called the laughing trees," Penny answered.

"Good name for them," Feyanna said.

"I dare say they are here for their incredible shape and to help us feel lighter as needed," Jandor said.

"That is it, exactly," Penny replied.

"Any time you are in need of joy, come to us," the trees said in unison. "We will lift your burden and may even help you solve a problem or two."

"We accept," Jandor and Feyanna said at the same time.

"Good day, and thank you for your beautiful energy," Penny said as the three of them returned to the path.

A few steps later, they stopped at a group of six black-trunked trees. They were taller than anything Feyanna and Jandor had ever seen, and you couldn't even see the tops of them.

"I can feel the great power of these trees," Jandor whispered.

"Indeed," Feyanna added.

"Yes," Penny replied in a quiet voice. "These are the Warrior Trees of Garanthowen. Their Magic is powerful. Jandor, you will learn how to communicate with these trees here in person and from a distance. They protect The Special Ones in all dimensions. Their Magic can be poisonous or healing as needed. Be very careful when you use the bark from these trees. They will give you the bark when it is needed. Feyanna, you will learn how to use the bark, leaves, and sap from these Warrior Trees for many situations."

"I am humbled and honored to be allowed to be in your presence," Feyanna said as she bowed.

"As am I," Jandor added, bowing.

The forest became very still and quiet. A moment later, a faerie appeared from behind one of the Warrior Trees.

"You are welcome here to learn from these great Warrior Trees," the faerie said. "You will know when to come and learn."

"We accept this privilege," Jandor replied.

The faerie vanished right in front of them.

"This is truly Magical," Feyanna said.

"Middle Earth?" Jandor whispered. "Really? This is unbelievable."

"And that, too," Feyanna added.

"Yes. Middle Earth," Penny said as food appeared on a small table before them. "Eat and rest for a bit before we move on."

"Thanks for the food," Jandor and Feyanna said at the same time.

"I'll be napping right here," Penny said as she settled down and closed her eyes. She was snoring in no time.

"I'm so overwhelmed with all of this, I'm just going to go along and take it all in," Feyanna said. "I'll try to make sense of it another time. This food is delicious."

"Same here," Jandor said. "And, yes, the food is quite yummy."

Penny woke up a while later and said, "We have one more set of trees to meet. Follow me."

As they walked around a bend in the path, Feyanna saw the trees and knew just what they were.

"These are Tulip Trees," Feyanna said as they stopped among them.

"Yes, they are," Penny said. "I wondered if you would recognize them."

"I do recognize them, but I can't recall where I've seen them before," Feyanna replied.

"You will in time," Penny said with a little smile on her face.

"You're not going to tell me, are you?" Feyanna said, laughing.

"You got that right," Penny replied.

"She's catching on quickly," Jandor said, laughing with them.

"The flowers are beautiful," Feyanna said. "The yellow and white flowers are soft and fragrant. I see lavender flowers, too. Wonderful."

"What are the healing properties of this tree?" Jandor asked.

"A poultice can be made from the tea of the roots and or seeds and applied to wounds and boils. The tea can take care of coughs, aches, and pains and even reduce fevers," Feyanna answered.

"That is correct, Feyanna. Your mother taught you well," Penny replied. "You may take from these trees as your needs dictate. Be sure to ask for the bark, and the tree will let some fall to the ground for you."

"I most certainly will," Feyanna replied.

"The flowers are quite fragrant," Jandor said. "The scent has a calming effect."

Just then, one of the trees released a small branch of flowers and set them at Jandor's feet.

"Thank you for this precious gift," Jandor said as he picked up the branch.

"Time for us to return home," Penny said. "I give thanks to The Great Forest of Garanthowen for your information and gifts this day."

They all bowed and then set out back along the path until they reached the meadow next to their house. The sun was beginning to drop among the treetops.

"I didn't know we had been out for such a long while," Jandor said as they walked across the meadow.

"It surely didn't seem like the whole day," Feyanna added.

"That's how it is in The Magic," Penny said. "Dinner is ready for you. Sleep well. I'll see you in the morning."

"Thanks, Penny. Rest easy yourself," Feyanna replied as Penny took to the air.

Just as she flew out of sight, a great hawk set down on the roof of the cottage house.

"I take it The Magic sent you, Great Hawk," Jandor said.

The hawk replied with a quick squawk.

"Will you be staying?" Feyanna asked, smiling at the hawk.

"What do you know that I don't know?" Jandor asked as the hawk flew down and settled next to Jandor.

"So very much," Feyanna replied, laughing.

"Very funny," Jandor said.

"I know that many of us in The Magic are given animals to protect and assist us in our Magical Duties," Feyanna replied. "I'd say this hawk is your special one."

The hawk replied with a few squawks.

"I'll take that as a yes," Jandor said. "Welcome, hawk. You are beautiful, and I am honored that you will be with me on this journey. Let's go inside."

Dinner was waiting for them, just as Penny said. They ate, sharing with the hawk. The hawk decided the back of a chair near the fire was an excellent place to settle. Jandor banked the fire, and they settled in for the night. Sleep came swiftly and the hawk watched over them as they slept.

It must have been in the middle of the night when Feyanna began to realize someone was touching her. She liked it and stretched and rolled over onto her back. Someone was caressing her breasts through her sleeping shirt. She let it go on for a while, then suddenly realized what was happening. She was a virgin and knew this would lead to lovemaking. But, damn, it felt so good. As she became fully aware of what was happening, she tried to figure out if this was all a dream. She tried to open her eyes and look around, but they just would not open. So she figured it was a dream. And, since it was just a dream, no harm in letting it go on.

Feyanna sighed and let the dream continue. She felt her sleeping shirt being removed, which left her naked.

It wasn't just a hand touching her breasts. She felt a tongue on her skin. It licked her nipple, and this made her moan. Then, whoever it was took her breast into their mouth and began to suck it.

Feyanna thought she was going to explode. The sensation was beyond anything she'd ever felt before.

As her breast was being sucked, someone, or something, moved her legs apart. That's when she heard a voice speak to her.

"Feyanna, do not be alarmed," the voice said. "You have served The Magic well, and this is a reward for you. Enjoy."

Feyanna couldn't tell if it was a man or a woman speaking to her.

"I'm not sure about all this," Feyanna said, trying to open her eyes again. This time, she succeeded and saw an unbelievable sight in her room.

There were creatures that kind of looked like faeries but were human-sized. Male and female. All naked. Some were touching each other and moaning like she had. As she watched, a female-like creature bent down and started licking the hard shaft of a male-like creature. The woman took the shaft into her mouth and sucked on it while pumping the shaft with her hand. The man was enjoying this so much that he pulled away from the woman and laid her down on the floor. He then spread her legs apart and moved between them.

As Feyanna watched, the man pushed his hard shaft into the woman again and again until they both hollered out in ecstasy and collapsed. Feyanna knew how animals bred. No one had told her it could feel so good. She realized that someone was rubbing their fingers on her private parts, and she really liked this. Her mother had told her that when a man and a woman loved each other very much, they would physically enjoy each other. If this is what her mother had meant, Feyanna was all for it.

Feyanna began to feel something building in her. The woman who had been sucking her breasts moved away, and Feyanna saw a man between her legs, rubbing her mound with his finger. As she watched, he began to lick her mound while pushing his fingers into her wet place. This felt amazing, and she began to tighten her body to increase the feeling. She knew something was about to happen because she couldn't control how she felt. The man knew it, too. He raised himself up and pushed his hard shaft between Feyanna's legs. She opened her legs for him and grabbed his shaft to guide it into her wet place. The man began to push into her faster and faster. His hard shaft seemed to get bigger and bigger as he pushed faster and faster. Feyanna began to meet his thrusts with her own and felt the beginnings of a pulse of energy go through her.

The man felt her begin to climax and thrust harder and faster as she hollered out. She pushed harder, too, and they came at the same time. Feyanna felt like she was soaring through the universe. The pulsing in her groin seemed to go on for a long time before it slowed and then quieted. She fell asleep and didn't wake up until morning.

Feyanna was the first to wake up, and she got the water for tea going. She was remembering the dream vision and how real it had felt. She was smiling when Jandor joined her a few minutes later.

"You seem quite happy this morning," Jandor said as he set the table.

Feyanna thought quickly as she said, "It's beautiful here. I still can't really believe we're in such a special place. Middle Earth is for real. It's gonna take a bit for me to think of all of this as normal."

Feyanna would have to be careful not to tell him about the dream vision. It was very special for her alone.

"I know what you mean," Jandor said. "I keep thinking about how we got here and all. I think I'll blame all this on the red berries."

"And here they are," Feyanna said as Jandor set a bowl of them on the table.

"I think this is going to be another busy day," Feyanna said.

"We have so much to learn," Jandor said as they ate breakfast.

"Yes, we do. I think we're going to add to our knowledge of plant life today," Feyanna said.

"Yes, you are," Penny replied from outside.

"Good morning, Miss Penny," Jandor said.

"Hi, Penny," Feyanna said.

"Good morning to the both of you," Penny said, peeking through the window. "Did you sleep well last night?"

"I most certainly did," Jandor replied.

"Same here," Feyanna added.

Penny smiled and knew what had happened to Feyanna. She was glad she had been blessed by The Magic. Feyanna needed to understand about the physical attractions between people so she would be able to prepare herbal remedies for them. Feyanna would have a lover or two down the road. Right now, she needed to learn many things as she moved forward in The Magic.

Jandor and Feyanna stepped out of their cottage home and joined Penny. She was watching something in the sky.

"What are you looking at?" Jandor asked.

"Look there," Penny said, pointing to a small dark shape flying in the far-off distance.

"It's a long way off," Jandor said. "It must be big if we can see its shape from here."

"There are a few unruly creatures in Garanthowen. We will need to be aware of them," Penny said.

"Are you going to tell us about them?" Feyanna asked.

"You will learn in time," Penny replied. "Now, let's get going. We have a bit of a walk ahead of us to get to the special meadow."

They headed out in a different direction than the day before. They crossed the meadow next to their cottage home and headed north.

"This is the most beautiful blue lake I've ever seen," Jandor said as the lake came into view.

"I agree with you," Feyanna said. "It holds a great deal of Magic."

"How do you know that?" Jandor asked.

"I just do," Feyanna replied. "I don't know how, but I do. It's as if I've always known."

"Must be The Magic," Jandor said.

"Most definitely," Penny replied as they stopped along the lake's shore. "Now, close your eyes and listen."

Feyanna and Jandor did as they were told.

"I hear so many things," Feyanna said. "Birds singing, leaves rustling in the forest, and splashing in the lake."

"I hear that, too," Jandor said. "I hear what sounds like the crying of a small animal and the beating of birds' wings. They must be flying close by."

"Very good," Penny said. "Now, keeping your eyes closed, tune in even more."

It took a short while before Feyanna and Jando heard other sounds.

"I hear a heartbeat," Jandor said. "It's slow and steady as if the creature were resting."

"I hear the hatching of an egg," Feyanna said. "It's far away, but I do believe another chicken is about to be born."

"Excellently done," Penny said. "You will need this skill from now on."

It was around noon when they came to the edge of a vast meadow. It was alive with blossoms, bugs, and critters.

"This is magnificent," Jandor said.

"There are colors here I've never seen before," Feyanna added.

"There are many things here that neither of you has ever experienced before," Penny said. "Let's rest and eat under that big oak tree. Then, we'll get busy with today's lessons."

"Penny, how long have you been in Middle Earth?" Feyanna asked.

"I come and go as needed," Penny replied.

"How do you know when you're needed?" Jandor asked.

"Just like you, I get asked to help out," Penny replied, smiling.

"I'm so new at all this Magic stuff; I don't even know how it all works," Feyanna said.

"I began getting hunches when I was around seven years old," Jandor said.

"Like what kind of hunches?" Feyanna asked.

"I remember the first time I knew something was very different for me. I had a vision that a terrible storm was coming," Jandor told them. "I was playing outside, and my mother was in our little garden. I looked up at the sky and for just an moment I saw a huge storm raining down on our village. Lightning struck a couple of the cottages, and the river rose over its banks and overflowed, racing down the road through our village. Trees, carts, and even a few people were swept away.

"My mother looked over at me. She had been calling my name and I didn't answer her. She walked over to me and saw I was in some kind of trance. She gently touched my arm, and I came back to her. She asked what I had seen, and I told her. She hugged me and said we needed to talk after we got inside and made sure everything was safe before the storm came.

"My mother explained to me about my abilities to see things in the future and began teaching me how to use them that very day. The storm came in the night, and everything I had been shown happened. I was scared crazy. Thank the gods and goddesses for my mother. She was patient and loving as I learned about my connection with The White Light and The Special Magic. She walked in The White, too."

"You remember well, Jandor," Penny said.

"I'm not surprised you know about that," Jandor said. "After all, you are a Magical creature, and you're here to protect us as we learn and grow into our powers."

"Our powers?" Feyanna asked.

"Yes, your powers," Penny said. "You're already using some of them with the remedies you prepare. It's time to learn about a few special plants that only grow where they are needed. Follow me."

They walked over to a group of purple plants. The plants stood about six feet tall and had small stem branches along the main stem. The main stem was dark purple and as each stem branch grew out from the main stem, it was different shades of purple. At the very tip of these small stem branches, bright yellow and orange flowers opened. They looked like something between a rose and a bell. The small leaves at the base of the flower were brilliant green.

"These are called the bell-rose plant," Penny said. "All parts of the plant are medicinal. The roots are used as a stimulant for the growth of other plants. The main stem is used to draw poisons from the body. You steam the stem and use it in a tea or as a paste. The stem branches are used to draw fever from the body as a tea. The flowers can be dried and used in food and to make teas.

"The small brilliant green leaves at the base of the flower are toxic. They can be used as a poison to kill all living things. There are tiny thorns at the edge of each leaf. If you are pricked with a thorn, you will die within a few minutes. There is no cure for the poison."

"Wow! I would think harvesting this plant would be very difficult," Jandor said.

"It is," Penny replied. "As you can see, these plants are in various stages of growth. If you harvest the plant before the stem branches begin to bud, you should be safe. The poisonous tiny leaves don't begin to grow until a few days after the flower bud first appears as it branches out from the stem."

"Willow bark is a good remedy for drawing fever from the body and not so difficult to harvest," Feyanna said.

"Exactly so," Penny replied. "You will keep a list of all plants and how they can be used as remedies. You will find writing tools in the workspace in the cave at the back of your cottage home."

"I guess I know what I'll be doing for a long while," Feyanna said, laughing.

"Look over here," Penny said as she walked a few steps beyond the bell-rose plants.

"These are beautiful," Feyanna said, looking at the bright pink flowers.

"These are known for their ability to smooth the lines on one's face," Penny said.

"I know there are a lot of people that use the paste from this plant, hoping to remain young as they grow old," Jandor said.

"Exactly so," Penny said. "The oil is used for its pleasing scent. It is added to candles to make the space smell nice."

"Does it have a name?" Jandor asked.

"It is simply called the sweet pink flower," Penny replied.

"And you look lovely standing next to them," Feyanna said, smiling.

"Yes, I do," Penny said, winking at them.

"And the dragon has a sense of humor," Jandor said, laughing with everyone.

"Look over there at the green-gray plants with small lavender flowers," Penny said.

"This is skullcap," Feyanna said.

"Tell me about it," Penny said.

"It is used as a sedative and to quiet the nerves," Feyanna replied. "It can be used on people and animals alike."

"That is correct," Penny said.

"It is also used to quiet skin irritations in the paste form," Jandor added.

"Yes, indeed," Penny said. "The two of you know this plant well. Harvest it in quantity as people will be asking for it."

"Will do," Feyanna said. "Penny, if it has sedative effects, can a large dose kill someone?"

"Yes, Feyanna, it can. So, use caution. It has to be prepared by someone knowledgeable in herbal remedies. Some people try to make tea from it and get very sick from drinking it," Penny replied.

"Understood," Jandor said.

Penny showed them a few more plants that were to be used as remedies. They came upon a fallen tree as they headed back across the meadow toward home.

"Miss Penny, may I have a branch of this tree?" Jandor asked.

"Ask the tree," Penny replied.

"Tree, may I take a branch or two from you? I would like to fashion a mandolin," Jandor asked.

The tree replied by breaking three pieces of wood off from its main branch.

"I thank you," Jandor said as he gathered the wood and put it in his carry sack.

"You know how to make a mandolin?" Feyanna asked.

"I do," Jandor replied. "There was an old man in my village who played many instruments. He taught me how to play the mandolin and had me make a few of them. He said the wood from the apple tree makes the best sound for a mandolin."

"That is true," Feyanna said. "Our village musician said the same thing. He made wood flutes from them. They sounded beautiful."

"Did you learn to play the flute?" Jandor asked.

"I did. And I was rather good at it," Feyanna replied.

"Well, then, tree, may I take another few branches to make some flutes for Feyanna to play?" Jandor asked of the tree.

The Tree released another five smaller branches from its trunk.

"Thank you, sweet tree," Feyanna replied as she gathered the branches and placed them in her basket.

"Well, this had been a wonderful day with the addition of the branches to be made into musical instruments," Penny said. "Even I didn't know this would happen. Now, let's talk insects."

"There are quite a few here," Jandor said.

"You both know about the common ones. Here, there are a few special ones. That red and green one over there, hovering above the bluebells, is called the invisible bug. It can become invisible when it's about to sting its dinner or anything that threatens it.."

"How big is its dinner?" Jandor asked.

"Anything from another insect to birds and mice, moles, and such," Penny replied.

"Has it ever stung a human or bigger animal?" Feyanna asked.

"It has, and you get quite sick from it. Headache, bellyache, and muscle weakness," Penny replied.

"What causes it to attack people?" Jandor asked.

"The one thing that would make the invisible bug attack a person if its home is threatened," Penny replied. "They live in decaying trees and leaves. Walking on the decayed leaves will threaten them for sure. You need to ask the land if you want to move anything for any reason. Watch."

Penny approached the invisible bugs hovering above the bluebells and said, "Dear creatures of Middle Earth, may I speak with you?"

The insects formed into a cone shape and flew over to Penny, hovering in front of her.

"Thank you for allowing me to speak with you. These are the Special Ones that have come here to learn. I would appreciate it if you did not attack them. They are just learning the ways of The Magic and Middle Earth."

The invisible bugs swirled in a circle and then flew around Jandor and Feyanna, humming pleasantly.

"Thank you, invisible bugs," Jandor said.

"We appreciate your patience on our behalf," Feyanna added.

"Thank you, my little friends," Penny added. "You may return to the bluebells."

The bugs went back to the flowers, and Penny, Jandor, and Feyanna set out for home. Just as they reached the edge of the Great Meadow, a gray shape appeared in front of them.

"You are not welcome here," a sinister-sounding voice said. "Go back to where you came from."

Before Feyanna or Jandor could reply, Penny stood up to her full height and spread her wings wide and tall.

"Your dragon cannot protect you," the voice said.

Penny inhaled deeply and blew smoke out to cover the apparition. The apparition flew apart into the air and was gone.

"So much for that nuisance," Penny said, settling back down to her usual shape.

"What the fuck was that?" Jandor hollered.

"That, my dear wizard, was The Dark Forces trying to scare you from learning anything more," Penny replied.

"Thanks for protecting us," Feyanna said.

172

"My pleasure," Penny replied. "Besides, it's been quite some time since I vaporized anything. It was great fun. I may need to do it again."

A quick flash of light told her to behave.

"I get the message, Great Ones," Penny replied, bowing her head ever so slightly.

"With all due respect to The Other Side, it was totally wonderful. I'm glad we know you can do that to protect the Special Ones," Jandor said, winking at Penny.

Penny returned the wink, and they all laughed as they left the Great Meadow and headed down the path. They talked about the plants, animals, and insects as they walked home, thoroughly enjoying themselves.

They had a guest waiting for them when they returned to their cottage home.

"Well, it looks like we have company," Jandor said as he walked over to the porcupine.

"It's a porcupine," Feyanna said.

The porcupine looked right at Feyanna and smiled.

"Looks like she knows we live here," Jandor said.

The porcupine squeaked in response.

"I do believe we just got the answer," Feyanna said. "Welcome to our home."

Just then, the hawk flew over from the nearby tree and perched on the roof of the cottage home.

"I do believe we have two new family members. The hawk last night and now the porcupine," Jandor said. "What shall we call them?"

"Ask, and they'll tell you," Penny replied.

"Okay, Penny. What is your name, hawk?" Jandor asked the hawk.

"George," was heard on the wind.

"Definitely Magic at work here," Feyanna said. "Hi, George."

The hawk squawked a reply.

"And, you, porcupine, what are you to be called?" Feyanna asked.

The porcupine looked at Penny, and Penny nodded approval of the silent question asked.

"I am Goldie," the porcupine answered.

"And it talks," Jandor said, staring at Goldie.

"Of course I do," Goldie said. "Why are you surprised?"

"I honestly don't know," Jandor replied. "I'm still getting used to being in such a Magical place."

"I'll accept that for now," Goldie said. "Now, where do I sleep?"

"Where would you like to sleep?" Feyanna asked.

"I love to be warm, so by the hearth would be acceptable," Goldie replied.

"Then that's where you'll sleep from now on," Feyanna said. "You have such beautiful eyes, Goldie. Is that how you got your name?"

"You are brilliant and kind," Goldie replied. "Thank you for noticing, and yes, that is how I got my name."

"I thank The Magic for everything we've been given," Feyanna said, bowing her head to show respect.

A quick flash of light was seen in response.

"You have done well today, Feyanna and Jandor," Penny said. "George and Goldie are given to you to help you learn as you move forward in The Magic. Time for me to call it quits. It's been a long day, and I need my rest."

"We hear you, Penny," Jandor said. "Sleep well."

Penny took to the sky in one silent move and flew off.

"I'll start supper," Feyanna said. I'll set the fire, warm some red berry bread, and make a salad for us. What about Goldie? What do we feed you?"

"No worries," Goldie replied. "I've had my food for today."

The four of them went inside.

"Geroge, you gonna sleep in here?" Feyanna asked.

Geroge gave a squawk and settled on the back of one of the chairs just like last evening.

"I guess you got your answer," Jandor said.

Goldie sat beside the hearth, and Feyanna placed a blanket on the floor. Goldie made herself right at home.

"This is lovely," Goldie said. "Thank you."

Feyanna and Jandor ate supper and decided to go to bed. They were both very tired.

"Sleep well, Jandor," Feyanna said.

"You, too," Jandor replied.

The night came on, and the four of them fell asleep with the Great Forest keeping watch over them.

Feyanna's real work began the next morning, right after breakfast. She began to organize her plants according to use, with cooking herbs in one place and medicinal herbs on their own shelves.

Jandor was setting up his working space as well. He knew he would need journals to keep track of his work. He also required quills and ink. Just as he was thinking about how to get supplies, Goldie walked over to him.

"Hi, Jandor," Goldie said. "I do believe I have a solution for your quill problem. Here."

Goldie popped three quills from her back onto the floor.

"Goldie, thank you so much. This is very kind of you," Jandor said as he retrieved the quills and set them on his workbench.

"As for the journals, I believe you will find five of them on the lower shelf just waiting for you," Goldie said.

Jandor looked at the lower workbench shelf and found the five journals.

"Thanks to whoever gave these to me," Jandor said. "I know how to make the ink. I just need to find the right plants."

"I can help with that," Feyanna said as she walked over to Jandor and Goldie. "I saw some red peonies, safflowers, roses, lavender, and hyacinths in the meadow next to us. I also have tomatoes and turmeric, which can be used. We can use the oil from the olives we gathered yesterday. Jandor, I'll need a small press made to collect the oil, please."

"I will get the things to make you your press. I ask the Great Forest to provide us with the materials we need, and I thank you," Jandor said.

"Well done, Jandor," Penny said.

"Hi, Penny," Feyanna said. "Didn't hear you come up."

"I can be very quiet when need be," Penny said, laughing. "I didn't see you in the main house and thought you might be here in the workspace in the hill. I can make my voice be heard anywhere."

"We're coming right out," Jandor said as the four of them walked through the house and stepped outside.

George took to the sky, and Goldie wandered about, looking for berries and bugs to eat.

"Feyanna is right about the plants," Penny said. "I see you found the journals, Jandor."

"With Goldie's assistance," Jandor replied.

As they watched, a mist began to form and swirl around a spot in front of them. A moment later, all the things Jandor needed to make the olive oil press were there.

"This is wonderful," Jandor said. "I love how The Magic takes care of us."

"It's a beautiful day out here," Feyanna said. "I'll gather the flowers for you, Jandor. I need a few herbs as well."

"I'll go with you, Feyanna," Penny said as they set out across the meadow.

Feyanna had all the flowers and herbs she needed in short time.

"These are so beautiful," Feyanna said as she gathered another bunch of red, pink, and yellow peonies. "I'll set these on the table for all of us to enjoy."

"You'll find just the right vase for them there, too," Penny said.

"Penny, may I ask you about something?" Feyanna said as they walked back across the meadow toward the cottage house.

"Of course," Penny said, sitting down.

"I've been feeling a bit uneasy," Feyanna said. "It's not really a strong thing, just a hint that something not pleasant is about to happen."

"You are right," Penny replied. "You are becoming stronger in your intuitive powers. Keep tuned in to those powers. The unsettled feeling you've been having is usually a warning that The Dark Force is about to try to bother you. Always ask The White Light to surround and protect you each day and whenever you have that feeling of unease or danger around you."

"That's exactly what I do," Feyanna said. "My mother taught me to do that when I was very little."

They arrived back at the cottage house a few minutes later to find Jandor cutting pieces for the press. George was watching, and Goldie was giving advice.

"Jandor, the other small saw will work better for you," Goldie said.

"Goldie, I appreciate your thoughts. But, since you've never built a food press as a porcupine, I do believe I know best," Jandor said.

Penny laughed at this. "He's got you there, Goldie," Penny said.

"Just because I'm not a human right now doesn't mean I don't know what I'm talking about," Goldie sassed back.

"True," Jandor said. "Have you ever made a food press in any living form before?"

Goldie remained silent.

"Well, have you?" Penny asked.

"You know very well I have not," Goldie said, turning all red.

"No, Goldie, don't get all upset," Penny said. "You know you shoot your quills out in all directions when you get angry."

Goldie walked around, trying to calm down. It worked. A few minutes later, she returned to her gray/brown coloring once again.

"That's much better," Penny said.

Goldie and Penny shared a silent thought for a minute.

"What are you two up to?" Feyanna said. "I saw the look you shared."

"She caught us," Penny said.

"She's good," Goldie added.

Jandor looked at the three of them, then stood up and said, "Magic everywhere. I have all the pieces cut for the press. I just need to put them together, so I'll be at my workbench for a bit."

"Jandor and Feyanna, Let's take a walk to the back of the workspace. There's something you need to see," Goldie said.

"Okay," Jandor said as they walked into the workspace and up to the back wall.

"Looks like the inside of a mountain to me," Jandor said.

"Yup," Feyanna added. "Dirt, roots, and such."

"Now watch," Goldie said.

Jandor and Feyanna concentrated on the wall. It began to look blurry and fuzzy. Then, everything changed. The wall opened up, and there was a path into the mountain. At the end of the short path was an amazing sight. It looked like the path ended at a wall of crystals of every shape and color one could imagine. They were all glowing and throwing rainbows everywhere.

"Walk down the path to the crystals," Goldie instructed them.

As Feyanna and Jandor reached what looked like a wall of crystals, the path opened into a large room. Crystals covered everything. They stood there in awe for the longest time. Every shape, size and colors no one had ever seen were in this space.

"This is amazing," Feyanna whispered.

"Absolutely amazing," Jandor added.

"It is magnificent," Goldie said. "And even though I've seen it many times, it still takes my breath away. Walk into the room. The crystals will make a space for you."

Feyanna and Jandor walked into the center of the room.

"That was great," Jandor said. "I liked how the crystals moved around so we didn't walk on them."

"Listen, Jandor," Feyanna said. "It sounds like they're humming."

They stayed quiet for a few minutes. The crystals were humming and flashed light in a rhythmic pattern.

"This is mesmerizing," Jandor said with his eyes closed. "I could stay here all day and be at peace."

"Crystals hold a great deal of energy and power," Goldie said. "Those of us in The Magic know about them, but few of us have been taught how to use them. Both of you are to be taught how to use the crystals and their power."

"Why?" Jandor asked.

"I am not privy to that matter," Goldie replied. "I just do what is needed."

"How will we know what to do with them?" Feyanna asked.

"You will be told when the time is right," Goldie said.

"Goldie, it looks like there are more rooms down this hallway," Jandor said as he looked around the main room.

"There are," Goldie said. "Let's take a walk."

The crystals moved around again as they crossed the room to the hallway and started walking along.

"Look," Feyanna said. "Another room."

"There are many rooms and hallways in The Crystal Caves," Goldie said.

"The Crystal Caves? Is that what this place is called?" Jandor asked.

"Yes, it is," Goldie said. "It's pure Magic."

"I can believe that," Feyanna said as they came to a little space in the hallway. It had three tunnels leading from it, and each tunnel was a different color. The one on the right was deep purple.

"I take it this is where Penny lives?" Jandor asked.

"It is," Goldie replied. "It is when she's not needed anywhere else."

"What a beautiful place to live," Feyanna said as she looked into the purple tunnel.

"Look down at your feet," Goldie said. "I do believe the crystals have placed a gift there for you."

They looked down and saw identical crystals at their feet. They picked them up and held them next to each other.

"They're humming," Feyanna said.

"And glowing," Jandor added.

"These were made especially for you," Goldie said. "Make sure you have them with you at all times. Keep them in a pouch so no one can see them. They hold powerful Magic."

"Yes, Goldie," Feyanna said. "Jandor, look. They're changing colors at the same time, too."

The three of them watched the twin crystals for a moment. They kept humming and changing colors the whole time.

"It's time for us to go back to the main room," Goldie said, leading the way.

Feyanna looked down the purple tunnel again and saw the shadow of a great creature on the wall. She knew it was Penny. This made her smile.

As they entered the main room, Goldie said, "Jandor, look to your right. There is a special crystal for you."

Jandor turned and looked and saw an incredible sight. It was a crystal shaped like a dragon. He picked it up and held it close. It was the size of an eagle.

"This is beyond anything I could ever imagine," Jandor said softly. "The energy from this crystal dragon is strong and soft at the same time."

"It is for you," Goldie said. "One day, you will use it to call Penny to you. You will know when that day is."

"I accept the gifts and thank The Crystal Caves," Jandor said, looking all around the room.

"Time to return to the workspace," Goldie said as she began walking down the path away from The Crystal Caves.

"Thank you for all of this," Feyanna said as she stepped away from The Crystal Caves.

"I am honored and humbled to be chosen to be here," Jandor said as he stepped away.

As they walked into the workspace, Feyanna and Jandor turned to look back down the path, but it was gone. The mountain wall was back in place.

The quiet only lasted a minute before they all started talking at once.

"That was beyond incredible," Jandor said.

"Those crystals were magnificent," Feyanna said.

"I love visiting The Crystal Caves," Goldie said.

"I need to make pouches for our twin crystals right away," Feyanna said as she looked around for the right material to use. "I think this will work just fine."

Jandor looked over at her and said, "It looks sturdy enough but not too heavy."

"I'll use this bit to make the drawstrings with," Feyanna was saying as she gathered all that she would need.

"Feyanna, look at The Crystal Dragon," Jandor said.

He had placed it on the bench on a piece of parchment. It was softly glowing, sending light beams all around the workshop.

Feyanna stepped over to Jandor, laid a hand on his shoulder, and sighed. They stood there for a quiet moment, watching The Crystal Dragon as it hummed and changed colors.

Jandor was the first to speak.

"This has been quite the afternoon," Jandor said.

"Is it even afternoon yet?" Feyanna asked. "I've lost all track of time."

"Same here," Jandor said. "Where's Goldie?"

They looked around the workshop and then went into the house. They found her sound asleep, softly snoring, on her blanket by the hearth.

"Hey, George," Jandor said. "Thanks for keeping an eye on Goldie. She must be really tired after everything we just went through."

George raised a wing at Jandor and winked his eye.

"Got it," Jandor said, winking at George.

Seems the hawk knew a lot more than you would think. But, of course, he did. After all, he was a part of The Magic of Middle Earth.

Feyanna stepped outside and saw that it was indeed mid-day.

"Time to eat. I'm starved," Feyanna said as she put food on the table.

"These peonies are beautiful," Jandor said. "I'm glad you thought of bringing some home to enjoy."

"'I am, too," Feyanna said. "It seems like we were gone for hours. Turns out it was really only about a half-hour. Crazy how spending time in The Magic gets everything off schedule."

"I know," Jandor said. "I think it's gonna take a long while for me to get used to it."

"Learning about Middle Earth and how things work here, now that is going to take me a long, long time," Feyanna said.

"Agreed," Jandor said as they cleaned up their lunch things.

"I'm going to put the food press together. It shouldn't take more than an hour or so—a real hour, that is," Jandor said, laughing.

Jandor spent the next while putting the food press together, and then he got busy making ink. It took the rest of the day. When he was finished, he had three small jars of ink ready to be used. Feyanna had finally organized her workspace and was ready to write down her herbal remedy recipes, but it was late, and they both needed to eat and get some rest.

Supper was quick. George went out for a fly-around, and Goldie wandered around, finding a few last yummy morsels before she went to sleep. They both came inside at the same time.

Jandor looked at George and said, "George, I do believe your feathers are changing color. I've never seen that before."

"Jandor, George looks like he's getting bigger, too," Feyanna said.

George gave a firm squawk to confirm their thoughts.

"This is going to be interesting," Jandor said. "Good night, everyone."

Jandor and Feyanna went off to their rooms for the night.

Goldie looked at George and said, "They have no clue as to how much you are going to change, my friend."

Geroge raised a wing to Goldie then they both settled in for the night. Feyanna and Jandor needed their rest. They could never have imagined what was about to happen to them.

.

CHAPTER 11

J andor and Feyanna were jolted awake in the dead of the night by a rumbling of the earth and an all-consuming thunderous noise. They tried to stand up and couldn't. They crawled to the door of their cottage home and had to hold onto the frame to stand up. They opened the door and saw a horrible sight. Everything was swirling around the meadow in a black cloud. Twigs and such flew right into the house, and they slammed the door shut.

"What the hell is going on?" Jandor hollered above the roar of the wind.

"I don't have the faintest idea," Feyanna said. "Whatever it is, it's horrible."

Goldie walked over, and her eyes were glowing brightly.

"This is bad," Goldie said as she looked at the two of them. "It seems The Dark Forces have become aware of your powers and are very angry."

"Why?" Jandor asked.

"I'll let Penny explain," Goldie said as she turned and began walking into the workshop space. "Follow me."

Jandor and Feyanna had some trouble walking through the house. They continued to hold onto anything that could support them. They finally arrived at the wall in the back of the workspace. It opened into The Crystal Caves. Penny was waiting for them in the main room. All of the crystals were glowing brightly and pulsating in a shared rhythm.

"This is truly amazing," Feyanna said as she and Jandor entered the room.

"Hi there," Penny said, motioning them to sit in the chairs that suddenly appeared. "We have a great problem and need the two of you to help send The Dark Forces away from Middle Earth."

Feyanna and Jandor looked at each other for a second, and then both replied, "Okay."

"You agreed rather quickly," Penny said as they sat down.

"The way I figure this," Jandor said, "Is that whatever is happening is worse than fighting for The White Light."

"I don't know what to think," Feyanna said. "I know I'm supposed to be here, so I'll do whatever it takes to stay here."

"Thank you," Penny said. "Let's talk about the fight we're about to be in, and then we'll get busy fighting for your souls."

"That sounds ominous," Feyanna replied.

"It is," Penny said. "First, gather all the herbs you have in the workspace and put them in this basket. Jandor set a pot of water to boil. Use one of Goldie's quills to stir in clay and sand. I will tell you the exact instance to drop this tiny crystal into the pot. It won't be easy. The potion you create will send The Dark Forces far away from Middle Earth for a long while. They will return in the future. But, for now, they need to be pushed away to keep you safe as you learn how to harness and use your powers."

They left The Crystal Caves and were back in the workshop. It was very difficult to stand and walk, but they figured out a way to do both by holding onto the roots that grew from the earthen walls and then the workbench. Feyanna gathered one of every herb and flower she had, and Jandor set a pot of water over a small fire to start concocting the potion Penny had told him to make.

As soon as Feyanna placed her plants in the special basket, the wind grew stronger, and the earth quaked and got stronger, too. As soon as Jandor added the clay and sand to the boiling water, a fierce howl was heard that shook all creatures to their very souls. Feyanna fell to the floor and raised her hand to show Jandor she was not hurt. Jandor grabbed onto the workbench to keep from falling. Goldie was scurrying around, keeping things that fell from the shelves out of Feyanna and Jandor's way.

"Thanks, Goldie," Jandor said. "We appreciate you keeping things cleared away.

Feyanna looked at Goldie and saw that her eyes were glowing like starlight.

"Jandor, look at Goldie's eyes," Feyanna whispered to Jandor.

Jandor looked at Goldie and then nodded at Feyanna.

"Something Magical is going on," Jandor whispered back.

"Oh my God, Jandor! Look!" Feyanna said

Snakes were coming out of the earthen wall. Black snakes with bright white eyes.

"This is not good," Jandor said.

A bowl of tiny black crystals appeared in front of Feyanna.

"Jandor," Feyanna said as she threw a tiny black crystal at one of the snakes. The snake disintegrated into nothing.

"Here, use these," Feyanna said as she placed the bowl between them.

They threw tiny crystals at the snakes that kept crawling out of the earthen wall. They were down to the last crystal.

"Now what?" Jandor asked as he threw that last tiny crystal at another black snake.

"Let me help," Goldie said as she stood before the earthen wall. A giant black snake came out of the wall and went for Jandor. Goldie focused her eyes on the snake, and as Feyanna watched, she shot bright gold rays from her eyes and evaporated the snake into nothingness. She did this three more times, and then the snakes stopped appearing.

"Goldie, that was amazing," Jandor said.

"Are you alright?" Feyanna asked.

"Most certainly," Goldie answered. "Thanks for asking."

The earth quaked so severely that the three of them were thrown to the ground. Even Goldie, who was close to the ground anyway. She rolled over into the workbench leg then just lay there for a minute.

"I guess The Dark Forces are getting really angry," Jandor said as they got up off the floor.

"It would appear so," Goldie said as she tried to walk over to the hearth.

Black shadows began to appear in the workshop.

"Go outside and throw the gray-green plants into the wind," they heard Penny say.

It took a few minutes to get to the door and open it. As soon as Feyanna stepped outside, she was blasted with a gust of wind so strong, it tried to take her basket from her. She grabbed one of the gray-green plants and threw it into the wind. The wind immediately stopped blowing. This made The Dark Force even more angry.

"I will crush all of you and own Middle Earth for all eternity," a deep, growling voice screamed into the air.

"I know what to do," Jandor said as he held onto his pot of water, clay, and sand. "White Light, surround and protect us."

Lightning bolts shot from the black swirling cloud, hitting the ground next to Feyanna, Jandor, and Goldie. The earth was blown up and taken into the black shadow. The black shadow began to swirl, and a vortex was created. It began to suck the meadow and forest into its folds.

"Your powers are weak and no match for my forces," the growling, screaming voice said. "Your White Light cannot help you. You are mine for eternity."

"It already has," Feyanna said as she threw lavender and sage into the black shadow tornado that had fully formed.

The energy of the lavender and sage weakened the black shadow tornado down to that of a dust devil. A weak dust devil. The Dark Force sent ten more black shadow tornados to Middle Earth. Orange lightning shrieked through the sky in all directions, and the earth began to break apart, first in the meadow, then in the forest next to the cottage home. Water rushed in from the blue lake and surrounded the cottage home, making it a small island. Giant flying creatures began to dive at Feyanna and Jandor, trying to claw them. The creatures sprayed a sizzling green liquid at Feyanna and Jandor, but The White Light kept this off from them.

Goldie screeched out as one of the giant flying creatures grabbed her and flew off with her. Goldie turned to look at the creature, then sent her laser rays into the beast. The creature gave a high-pitched scream and then exploded into a million black pieces that vanished into one of the black shadow tornadoes. As Goldie began to fall to the earth, a huge black creature grabbed her and set her down every so gently next to Feyanna and Jandor. It was hard to make out what that specific creature was because of the tornadoes that consumed every bit of the cottage home island. The sky remained black as the battle raged on.

The Dark Force sent evil red insects with huge pink eyes that shot razor-sharp shards of glass at Feyanna, Jandor, and Goldie. Feyanna placed a circle of salt around them, and the shards of glass hit an invisible wall and turned into water. The Dark Forces conjured up small creatures in the waters surrounding the cottage home. They had antennae that sent beams of fire at the three of them and the cottage home.

Much to the surprise of The Dark Force, the blue lake water showered down on those fire-throwing creatures. They burst into harmless pieces of sand that were swept away by one of the black shadow tornadoes. The Dark Force grew the tornadoes into huge wind monsters with bright green eyes and the power to destroy everything in Middle Earth by blowing hot, searing flames over everything. Feyanna and Jandor felt as if they were dying.

"I now own you," The Dark Force said as the cottage home turned into an ice cave.

"Now, Jandor," Penny said.

Jandor had to think for an instant because the heat was draining his strength. He placed his hand over the now boiling concoction he had made and dropped the tiny crystal into it, just like Penny had told him to.

There was a second of absolute silence, and then the world in front of Feyanna and Jandor went nuts. The fire wind was quenched with what looked like water creatures that appeared high above the wind monster. Every time another wind monster and its evil flame throwers were destroyed, The Dark Forces howled. Again and again, The White Light destroyed the wind monsters until only one was left. It had grown even bigger as the others were destroyed.

Feyanna nudged Jandor and pointed to the sky. The great black flying creature that had rescued Goldie was flying toward the wind monster. Just as the wind monster threw flames at it, it sent a blast of ice into the wind monster's flames. The flames were extinguished. The great flying creature sent three more rounds of ice into the wind monster as it shrank in size.

"Feyanna, throw the remaining plants into the wind," Penny said.

Feyanna threw the basket with the plants into the wind. A moment later, the wind monster exploded into a shower of yellow, orange, and black particles. They were taken by The White Light and placed in the meadow, the forest, and the lakebed. A moment later, plants grew and bloomed where the earth had been destroyed. The blue lake waters receded into their lakebed, and the cottage home was once again on dry land. The plants that fell where the forest had been immediately grew all the trees and plants that had been destroyed. And the wind was silent. The creatures of Middle Earth were once again in all their places.

Middle Earth was back to the way it had been before the attack by The Dark Forces. Feyanna fell to the ground and sat there in shock. Jandor joined her and Goldie walked over to them and sat on the other side of Jandor.

It was quite some time before anyone spoke.

"What the hell was that?" Jandor hollered.

"Ditto," Feyanna said.

"Not sure about the huge black flying creature that saved Goldie," Jandor said.

"Sure glad it did," Feyanna added. "Thanks, whoever you are."

"Ditto," Goldie said, smiling.

"What are you smiling about?' Jandor asked.

"It's nice to know that someone cares about me," Goldie said.

"I am beyond exhausted," Feyanna was saying when Penny flew in. "I don't even have the energy to go inside and eat then crawl into bed.

"You all were magnificent," Penny said as she sat in front of them. "True warriors of The White Light. The Dark Force has been banished from Middle Eart for a long, long time."

Food and drink appeared before them, even some stuff for Goldie.

"Thanks for this," Feyanna said as she ate.

"Ditto," Jandor added.

"Why is it still dark out? It must be the next day," Feyanna said. "I feel like I haven't slept in days."

"That can happen in The Magic," Penny replied.

"What does that mean?" Jandor asked. "And, keep it short. I need to get to bed."

"The battle you were all just a part of took place in The Magic," Penny said. "Time doesn't exist in The Magic. When you're in the realm of The Magic, it can feel like a few minutes or a few days. It all depends on what you need to do."

"It makes sense to me," Feyanna said. "How long were we gone in real time?"

"About ten minutes," Penny said.

"Oh, this is going to take some time to get used to," Jandor said, winking at Penny.

"Cute, Jandor," Penny replied, laughing.

"I'm going to bed," Goldie said as she got up and walked into the cottage house.

"Me, too," Jandor said as he went inside.

"We'll talk more tomorrow," Penny said. "Sleep now."

"We will," Feyanna said as she walked inside, and Penny flew off.

Feyanna closed the door and saw that Goldie was sound asleep on her bed by the hearth. A fire had been set, and the cottage home was warm. Feyanna was asleep before her head hit the pillow. Middle Earth was content, and all was good. For now.

"Good Morning, everyone," Penny said as she stood outside the cottage home.

"Good morning, Penny," Jandor said, yawning. "Why are you waking us up so early?"

"Jandor, the sun's been up for two hours," Penny said, smiling as Jandor opened the door.

"Really?" Jandor replied as he shielded his eyes from the bright sunlight.

Goldie walked past Jandor and stepped outside. "It really is way past sunrise," Goldie said. "Time for some food."

"Hello, Goldie," Penny said.

"Hello, Penny," Goldie said as she walked past Penny. "Wicked hungry this morning. Must be because of all the work we did last night."

"Oh, yes. The battle in the night," Jandor said as he yawned again. "Time for some tea."

"Good morning, Penny," Feyanna said as she entered the room. "Is it really well into the morning?"

"Indeed, it is," Penny said. "You needed extra sleep last night. You both fought well to save yourselves and The Magic here in Middle Earth."

"So, that was all real?" Feyanna said as she put fruits and bread on the table. "I was hoping it had been a horrible nightmare."

"I'm so sorry," Penny said as she lay on the ground so her face was in the doorway. "It was very real. You'll both need a day of rest today."

"I agree," Jandor said, yawning again. "I can't remember ever being this tired before."

"Me, either," Feyanna agreed.

"A few of the farmers will be stopping by today," Penny said. "They heard about you battling The Dark Force and want to show their appreciation. Please accept their gifts of gratitude."

"Oh, my. That's very kind of them," Feyanna said. "Of course, we'll accept their gifts. I'll let them know I'm here should they need healing and such."

"That's a great idea," Jandor said. "I'd be happy to assist them in any way I can as well."

"Now, that is very kind of you both," Penny said. "Enjoy their visits. Tomorrow, we will learn about spiritual beliefs centered around The Magic in Middle Earth and your homeland. You need this knowledge to survive."

"Okay. Thanks, Penny," Jandor said.

"Same here," Feyanna said.

"Time for me to fly. I have work elsewhere today," Penny said as she backed away from the door and flew up into the air.

"Would you look at George," Feyanna said. "He's doubled his size, and his feathers are so many different colors. George, you are beautiful."

George squawked in reply, flapping his wings.

"I do believe Feyanna is right, George," Jandor said as he walked over to George. "Your eyes are pure gold like Goldies."

George bopped his head in reply.

"Feyanna, I do believe something is about to change around here," Jandor said as he returned to the table.

"I feel it, too," Feyanna said. "Not just this minute, but soon for sure."

Goldie walked in as Feyanna was speaking.

"You are perceptive, Feyanna," Goldie said as she settled on her rug by the hearth. "Always trust your intuition. It will serve you well. Not just yet, but indeed, changes are close by. Time for a nap."

Goldie was snoring softly in no time. Jandor and Feyanna gave a little laugh at her antics and cleared the breakfast table.

"What do you think Penny meant about us surviving?" Feyanna asked.

187

"I'm not sure, but I think a great many things are about to change, just as Goldie hinted at before she fell asleep," Jordan said.

"Kind of scares me," Feyanna said.

"Me, too," Jandor said. "I wonder just how crazy things could get for us."

"I think I'll go for a walk in the meadow," Feyanna was saying when they heard a knock on their door.

Jandor opened it and found a farmer and family there.

"Good day, sir," Jandor said as Feyanna joined him.

"Good day to you," the farmer replied, taking off his cap. "My family and I would like you to have this butter, eggs, and cheese. We are grateful for the way in which you kept our home safe last night."

"This is very generous of you," Jandor said. "We gratefully accept your gifts."

Feyanna was looking at one of the children. She noticed his eyes were cloudy.

"May I take a look at you, son? I see his eyes are sick," Feyanna said.

"We would appreciate that," the farmer said. "Simon, this lady is going to look at your eyes. Don't be afraid. She is a gentle healer."

"Hi, Simon," Feyanna said as she touched his hand. "You cannot see anything, can you?"

"No, Ma'am, I cannot see a thing," Simon replied.

"How old are you, Simon?" Jandor asked.

"I am ten years old, sir," Simon answered.

"Simon, I am going to walk you into our workshop," Feyanna said. "Your family may join us. Come this way."

"You have a porcupine sleeping by the hearth," the mother said. "Isn't that dangerous?"

"No. Goldie is gentle and kind," Jandor replied as he settled the family on a bench across from the workbench.

Feyanna set Simon on a stool and asked his mother, "Would you please sit here, Ma'am?"

The mother sat next to Simon and held his hand.

"Simon, I am going to put drops in your eyes," Feyanna said. "I have steamed them from the Bilberry plant. This will not hurt you. Are you ready?"

"Yes," Simon said.

Feyanna put three drops in each eye and then covered them with a warm compress steeped in green tea.

"This compress is saturated in green tea," Feyanna said. "Simon, I am going to take you to a cot so you can lie down for a bit. We need to let the herbs do their work."

Feyanna walked Simon, with his mother's help, over to a cot and laid down.

"Farmer, how many animals do you have?" Jandor asked.

"We have three milk cows and a bull. One of the milk cows will birth soon. We have six goats, several chickens and cats, and two dogs," the farmer replied.

"How delightful," Jandor said. "You are blessed with the Gifts from Mother Earth."

"We are, indeed," the farm replied.

"How would you two children like to learn how to make a wreath from grasses and flowers?" Feyanna asked.

"I would," the girl said.

"Me, too," the other boy said.

"Come on over, and I'll show you how to do just that," Feyanna said.

Feyanna spent a little while with the younger children, and soon, they showed their work to their parents.

"These are beautiful," their mother replied. "We'll hang them above your beds."

"They are quite colorful," Simon said as he sat up.

Simon had removed the green tea cloth from his eyes, and his eyes were clear and bright.

"I can see," Simon said. "Just like I used to when I was younger."

"Praise the Gods and Goddess," his parent said.

"This is truly a miracle," his father said, hugging Simon.

"How did you know to do this?" his mother asked, crying with joy.

"I noticed a film covering his eyes," Feyanna said, "Simon, were you bitten by a big orange bug right before you lost your sight?"

"Yes, Ma'am, I was," Simon replied. " It really hurt, and my leg got sick, too."

"I thought that might be how it happened," Feyanna said. "Simon didn't do anything wrong. The big orange bug is called the sight-stealing insect. It lives in muddy places. Simon must have been digging along a stream and opened the nest. Next time you want to dig in the mud, stay away from mud that looks bluish-green. That is a nest of these horrible things."

"I most certainly will," Simon said. "Can I make a wreath now, too?"

"Of course, you can," Feyanna said as he and his mother went to her work-space.

"Farmer, may I ask your name?" Jandor said.

"I am known as Aaron," the farmer replied.

"I am known as Jandor, and she is Feyanna," Jandor replied.

"I have made a potion for your pregnant cow. Mix about a spoonful into her feed two times a day until she gives birth. She is carrying two calves. That is a great blessing."

"It most certainly is," Aaron replied. "I suspect you might be a wizard, sir."

"No, not really," Jandor replied. "I learned about plants and animals as I grew up."

"Look here," the mother said as she and Simon showed everyone their wreaths.

"These are beautiful, too," Aaron said. "We are thankful for the healing and will keep you supplied with butter, cheese, and eggs from now on."

"We appreciate that," Feyanna said. "Let us know if you need help with anything else."

"Take care," Jandor said as the family walked away across the meadow.

"I'm starving," Feyanna said. "I'll fix us egg and cheese sandwiches."

"That sounds most excellent," Jandor said as they went into the main room and prepared their meal.

Jandor and Feyanna spent the rest of the day gathering plants and flowers in the meadow next to their cottage home and resting, just as Penny told them to.

Right after breakfast the next morning, Penny was at the door.

"Good morning, Jandor and Feyanna," Penny said as they walked outside.

"Good morning, Penny," Feyanna replied. "This is another beautiful day we have."

"It is, indeed," Penny said. "Let's sit under that Purple Berry tree. We have much to talk about."

The Purple Berry tree was just a few steps from the cottage home. It was in full bloom and looked beautiful.

"I'll begin by asking each of you a question," Penny said. "Feyanna, what do you know about the history of your village? The deep past?"

"My mother told me that our village has been there since the beginning of time," Feyanna said. " No one really knows when it first appeared, but the stories told throughout the generations have always said this. My mother said she was told by her grandmother that there were special visitors who told the villagers about the plants and their healing powers from ancient times. These visitors only stayed a short time, then left and never came again.

"My mother was shown a cave close to the village that has drawings of animals, people, and some kind of creatures on the walls. My mother and a few of the villagers showed me this cave when I was about ten years old. There are spiral circles of all sizes every few feet, and some kind of strange shapes next to the spirals. All of the spirals were made with red dye. Some of the strange creatures had what looked like a chest plate covering the upper part of their body. I recognized the people and the animals, but not the strange-looking creatures and those strange shapes. I can still see them in my mind as if I were standing in that cave right this minute.

"There are star constellations on the walls and ceilings as well. I was learning the constellations from the local wizard, so I recognized a lot of them. My mother thought that the strange creatures had something to do with the creation of the first villagers. She said she could never prove this but knew in her soul it was true.

"As I grew older, I began to wonder if the religious practices of the village had something to do with the cave drawings. Those pictures tell a story. And, you may think I'm a bit crazy, but I do believe those strange creatures may be from the stars."

"I agree about the creatures being from the stars," Jandor replied. "I was taught that the beliefs and practices of my village were similar to yours, Feyanna. We had a kind of manager of the village. He was our religious leader. He handled any disputes and led the villagers in the religion of the times. I've come to realize he was an evil man. My mother told me never to question him, even when I didn't agree with him. She said I could be put to death if I disagreed with his beliefs. That was great advice at the young age of about twelve years. I disagreed with him for forcing a young girl to marry an old man because the young girl had fallen in love with a peasant boy. The priest said the young boy was stupid and poor and not a good enough person to marry such a beautiful young girl. The old man was the priest, and he treated her poorly. He blamed her when she didn't become pregnant, and after a couple of years, he cast her out of his house. She and the young boy, now a man, ran off and built a cottage of their own. They chose to live a great distance from their village in fear of retribution from the priest.

"I heard many stories about the creation of our village. Some said star people came to this planet and taught the first people how to build, farm, and heal using the gifts of the forest. The priest said it was blasphemy and anyone heard talking about this would be burned alive. We had secret meetings in the deep dark of the night. Many believed that we were brought here from another place in the heavens to create a civilization on this planet. We had a few carvings and drawings on the rocks near our village.

" I truly believe that the priest was from one of those planets, and he was sent here to destroy what the first star people created. You know about my leaving the village and how we met. I do believe with all my heart and soul that you and I, Feyanna, are supposed to be together as caretakers of The Magic."

"Well told, both of you," Penny said, stretching a bit. "Now, what about the laws and rulers of the land? How did all of that come about?"

"I believe that the star people were seen as gods of some kind, and the first peoples revered them and wanted to please them," Feyanna replied.

"I agree, Feyanna," Jandor said. "I think those early beliefs evolved and morphed into today's current religious beliefs and laws."

"That is exactly what I was hoping you would say," Penny said. "There are many who know about The Magic but feel it is evil and must not be spoken of. The Magic was given to the planet and the first peoples as a Gift from The Divine. It was a normal part of life for millennia. Then, there was a battle between The White Light and The Dark forces. The Dark Forces are, and were at that time, always looking for The White Light. The Dark Forces work hard at destroying The White Light to take control and rule in chaos and evil. They travel the universes and dimensions, trying to find The White Light to destroy it.

"That's what happened on this planet in ancient times. Battles occurred between the good star people and the evil star people. The people of this planet watched the horrific battles in the sky and became terrified of what they saw. Some of the Magic of the Star People destroyed parts of this planet. Cities were blown completely off the planet. There came a time when the people of the planet disobeyed the Star People and began destroying all that they had been gifted. The people were warned, but they continued to disobey. The Star People were greatly saddened and angry and decided to destroy all the peoples of the planet in hopes of starting with new peoples that would better follow the rules. A great catastrophe engulfed the planet. Volcanic eruptions, floods, fires, and earthquakes wiped out all life on the planet. The Star People recreated the life on this planet, bringing life forms called humans here to begin anew. Animals, fishes, insects, birds, and all the creatures that are here now were placed here in the ancient times after the great catastrophe."

"Penny, were dragons and other magical creatures here as well?" Jandor asked.

"Yes, indeed, they were, Jandor," Penny said. "All the magical creatures were here. The Star People creators chose who would be able to see them and learn from them. The Magic was guarded by all the Star People creators and the magical creatures living on this planet from that time forward, right to today."

They all sat quietly, thinking about what Penny had told them.

"Did the humans know about the Star People?" Jandor asked.

"At the very beginning of the first measure of the new time, the Star People came to this planet and instructed the people on how to build the structures the Star People needed as an energy source for their flying machines. The Star People had the power to float large boulders and stone pieces into place to build the great walls and pyramids we are aware of now. Wise men postulate that the pyramids are burial places for great kings from ancient times, but no burial mounds have ever been found in them. The early humans believed the Star People to be gods and began worshiping them and holding them in high regard. The humans built temples to honor them, and the priests and rulers created religions and laws that demanded obedience be paid to the rulers so the gods would be happy."

"I do believe that obedience was in the form of food, money, and manual labor in exchange for staying alive," Jandor said.

"You are correct, Jandor," Penny replied.

"That's just what it's like today, too," Feyanna said. "The farmers have to give a portion of their crops to the rulers of their areas. Some have to pay taille. If they don't, the rulers sometimes take their children and make them into slaves. Horrible."

"It is, indeed," Penny said. "Here, in Middle Earth, we have mayors of the villages who oversee arguments about everything. No one is required to pay taille or give their crops to the mayor, though. Most folks barter their crops and services for things they need."

"That's what it was like in my village," Feyanna said. "We were so small, I don't think the regional overlord bothered with us."

"Not in my village," Jandor said. "We had an overlord who was full of himself and ordered everyone to bow to him when they passed by. He also took any food he wanted and made even the poorest villager pay him in crops or services."

"Your world does need an overseer," Penny said. "Someone to make sure things are done fairly. Someone to protect the good people from harm. Someone to guide the people on their journey. You know them as kings. Some are greedy and harsh. Some are more benevolent, although the greedy kings try to take over the benevolent king's lands and people. The Great Spirit has allowed The Magic to be alive in your world. As you know, it helps with healing and protecting the innocent ones. That brings me to the reason why you're in Middle Earth."

Feyanna and Jandor looked right into Penny's dark purple eyes, waiting for her to explain herself.

"Your world was destroyed in ancient times because the people became greedy and ruthless. They did not follow the rules their kings had created. What's even more horrible is this: The Star People mated with the humans, and the Divine Spirit was outraged. It decided to put an end to the negative world and start over. It sent volcanic eruptions, earthquakes, and floods. When these had ended, an ice sheet was sent over the whole planet for many years. Once The Dive was satisfied with the results, it allowed the ice sheet to begin to melt and move back towards the poles. The land was reconfigured, and the land, lakes, and mountains we know now were created. New humanoid creatures were brought to this place and began to populate the planet again. This time, The Divine forbade The Star People to be known to the humans for fear of another frightful occurrence like before. "

193

"I've seen The Star People," Feyanna said.

"When?" Jandor asked.

"It was about ten years ago. I was in my fifteenth year and walking along the banks of a stream near our home. It was late into the night. I hadn't been able to sleep, so I decided to go for a walk. I was sitting on the edge of the water when I noticed that the water was beginning to shine brightly. It was first white, then blue and green. A shadow came over the place where I sat, and I looked up. I saw a round shape hovering in the night sky a ways above the treetops. It flashed a yellow light, and then a creature was standing next to me.

"I wasn't scared. I was curious. It didn't look like anything or anyone I'd ever seen before. It was shorter than me and had a bluish-gray skin tone with lots of wrinkles. It had large black almond eyes and no hair on its head. I saw three fingers on its hands. It wasn't wearing clothes. I stood up and walked closer, and it extended its hand to me. I took its hand, and it was warm. The creature smiled and told me not to be afraid. But not with a voice. I heard the words in my head. I smiled and nodded my head. We stood there for a few minutes, just holding hands. A sack appeared next to me, and the creature said it was gifts from The Others.

"I asked who these Others were, and the creature pointed to the thing in the sky. The yellow light flashed again, and the creature was gone. I looked in the sack and found pots of herbs and plants I had never seen before."

"Those are the ones you have now, aren't they?" Jandor asked.

"Yes, Jandor, they are. I take special care of them," Feyanna answered. "I looked up into the sky and the ship slowly rose into the stars and was gone. I haven't seen the creature since that night."

"The Star People do visit the planet quite often," Penny said. "They check on us to see if we need any special help. They do not want another catastrophe to occur and only intervene if absolutely necessary. The Divine has sent special creatures to this period of existence to help with everything. But, only The Special Ones are allowed to know about The Magic."

"You and your kind are some of those special creatures," Jandor said. "I've seen the dragon shadows appear in the full moon sky from time to time. I know The Magic is here because I've been blessed with the Gift of healing as Feyanna has been blessed. I know that The Magic is real because of the things I've experienced as a small child and this place, Middle Earth."

"Very well," Penny said as she stood and stretched to her full height. She was a magnificent creature to behold.

"You are very tall, Miss Penny," Feyanna said.

"Thank you for noticing," Penny replied, bowing toward Feyanna with a wink of her beautiful purple eye.

"I suspect we have a great deal to learn here, in Middle Earth," Jandor said as Penny settled again.

"Yes, Jandor, you do," Penny replied. "We are approaching a time of change. The change could be good or bad. It all depends on the choices humans make. If the wrong choices are made and continue to be made, this planet is headed for another great catastrophe. If better choices prevail, there is hope that this existence will continue. Feyanna and Jandor, you have been chosen to be a part of The Magic that could guide this existence to remain.

"You must know that if you choose this challenge, it will be long and hard at times. There will be good times, of course. I will be right beside you throughout this journey. Take some time to think about this before you make your decision. I will return later today."

Penny stood tall, and in one great whoosh, she was airborne.

Jandor and Feyanna looked at each other for the longest time before they said a word.

"Well, " Feyanna said. "I guess we have some choices to make."

"Seems so," Jandor said. "I can't even begin to imagine how all of this will take place."

"Me, too," Feyanna said. "I know that I was meant to meet you and was brought here for a purpose greater than the one I was working on."

"I, too, know this," Jandor said as he stood up. "I know deep within my soul that I am to accept this challenge. It is my destiny."

"I, too, accept this challenge," Feyanna said. "This, too, is my destiny."

Feyanna stood with Jandor as he called out to Penny. "Penny, please come back to us."

Penny flew right over and landed in front of them.

"Miss Penny, I accept this life and am honored to have been chosen by The Great Magic," Jandor said as he bowed toward her.

"Miss Penny, I accept this life and am honored to have been chosen by The Great Magic.," Feyanna said, bowing as well.

"We are pleased and thrilled with your decisions," Penny replied.

"It feels so right to be doing this," Feyanna said. "It's as if I've been guided to be here."

"Same here," Jandor said. "I do believe it's time for lunch. Will you join us, Miss Penny?"

"I'd love to," Penny replied. "And, both of you, lose the Miss. I'm Penny."

"Okay, Penny," Feyanna said as she and Jandor went inside to grab some food.

They found Penny sitting under the great oak tree, munching on something she had found. Lunch was a pleasant time for the three of them. They told stories of their childhoods, and Pennys were quite amusing.

"When I was about three months old, my color started changing," Penny explained. "We are born with a lot of colors and as we grow, our true color takes place and covers us completely. Well, as soon as my mother and father saw the purple appear, they were worried that something was wrong with me. They tried to cover me with mud and leaves. It didn't work. The more they tried to cover me up, the stronger the purple became until I was six months old. That's when a dragon's true color is permanently in place.

"There had been stories told that the purple dragon was a special creature. No one really believed this story until I started becoming purple. My little friends made fun of me. I made fun of me, too. We played lots of games about how a purple dragon would behave. We decided I would probably blow purple fire and smoke. And when I blew out ice crystals, they would be all shades of purple. We laughed and worked hard at trying to blow smoke. We were told that it wouldn't happen for a few more months. We tried all the time and even fell over when we blew too hard. We laughed and played, and my purple color became a normal thing for all the dragons in the area.

"There was one dragon who knew that the story about the purple dragon being a highly magical creature was true. He watched me as I grew, and when the time came for me to learn about my destiny, he began teaching me about the magical powers I possessed. My parents were told all of this, too. The first time I tried to use one of my special powers, it turned out rather funny. I tried to move a rather large boulder with my mind, and I made the thing roll across the field and land in a pond with a big splash. We all laughed about it, of course."

"Penny, those are precious memories for sure," Jandor said, laughing along with everyone.

"Does your color ever change?" Feyanna asked.

"It does," Penny replied. "It all depends on my mood. You'll see. My eye color changes as well. Especially if I'm in battle or trying to protect someone. Red is a color you don't want to provoke in me. If you see my eyes turn red, you know I'm about to become fierce and powerful. Usually protecting you both and the innocent ones."

"Thanks for the warning," Jandor said, smiling along with Feyanna.

"What do you know of your Earth-centered practice of honoring the gods and goddesses?" Penny asked.

Feyanna and Jandor both said the same things. There wasn't any structured religious practice in any sense. The four seasons were a time of special celebrations.. People honored the Earth, the sky, the wind, and the sun as they chose to. Each person chose to believe in whatever powerful entities they chose. They called them gods and goddesses. Most people were aware of The Magic in their world and had reverence for this. The Magic was used by rulers to tell them about the future, or so they thought.

"You both have a good understanding of your world," Penny said. "The Divine decided, when this world was re-created, that The Magic would not rule the world. The Star People would be able to watch but not directly interfere. The Star People would show themselves to a chosen few to assist in the evolution of the earthlings. As you have both experienced, The Star People fly around the planet quite often. You have seen their flying ships a number of times."

"Like that one right there?" Feyanna said, pointing to a flying ship over Penny's head.

Penny stepped a few feet back and looked along with Jandor.

"That's exactly right," Penny said. She spread both wings to show the Star People that they had been acknowledged.

The spaceship did a loop-de-loop in response and then shot straight up into the universe.

"That was great," Jandor said. "Penny, do the people in Middle Earth know about you?"

"They know about some of us dragons," Penny replied. "Most do not know about the other special creatures."

"Goldie?" Feyanna asked.

"Exactly," Penny replied. "The Magic knows what it's doing. It's up to the earthlings to decide if they want to be aware of The Magic, then walk in The Light and do the work of The Magic."

"We understand," Jandor said quietly.

"Well, now what?" Feyanna asked.

"It's time to learn a great many things," Penny said. "Jandor, you will work in your workshop for the next while, learning about metallurgy and alchemy. Feyanna, although you have a solid foundation of knowledge with the plants, you still need to learn a great many things. You will both learn how to blend the gifts of Mother Earth to be used to protect the innocent ones. Time to go inside and begin the next part of your journey."

Jandor went into the workshop and found many new things. There were pouches of ore with silver, gold, and magnetite, different types of sand, volcanic rock known as obsidian, andesite, and many others. Two fires had been created in the back wall, with chimneys going straight up through the hill.

Feyanna followed Jandor and saw that a lot of pouches of new plants had been placed on her workbench. Some were dried and labeled, and some were in pots, alive and growing. There was some kind of light source for the plants that neither of them had ever seen before. Using this light source meant the plants didn't need to go outside to grow.

Feyanna and Jandor spent the rest of the afternoon becoming familiar with their new supplies and finding storage spaces for them. It was going on to evening when they realized they hadn't taken time to eat.

"Feyanna, follow me," Jandor said as he grabbed her hand and walked her out into the main room of their cottage home. "Time to eat and rest."

"Oh, my," Feyanna replied, looking out the window. "I do believe it is. I'll get something started."

"I'll take care of supper tonight," Jandor said. "You go sit down and get cozy."

"Why thank you," Feyanna said as she sat beside the hearth.

"He is a gentleman," Goldie said without even opening her eyes.

"Indeed, he is," Feyanna said, laughing. "You comfy, Goldie?"

"Yes, I am. Thanks for asking," Goldie replied. "I just came in before you and Jandor. I love my fluffy blanket and this hearth."

"The fire is so warm and soothing," Feyanna said as she yawned.

"Good thing supper is ready," Jandor said as he walked into the room with their supper on a tray.

Jandor handed Feyanna her supper and settled on the other side of her.

"This is delicious, Jandor," Feyanna said. "I'm so glad we met Aaron and his family. The eggs, cheese, and butter have greatly improved our kitchen supplies."

"I agree," Jandor replied. "And the herbs you grow really add a great deal of flavor."

A short while later, they were headed to bed.

"Good night, Jandor. Sleep well," Feyanna said.

"You as well," Jandor replied.

Sleep came swiftly to Feyanna and Jandor. Penny was busy working with The Magic. Feyanna and Jandor were about to embark on a fantastic journey that would change their lives forever.

CHAPTER 12

O ver the next few months, Jandor was taught how to create precious metals by the Wizards of The Magic. He was taught how to make bronze, a mixture of copper, tin, nickel, zinc, and a few other metals. The Magic gave him a conjuring spell to create gold from regular raw metals, sand, water, and sunlight. Jandor was cautioned about using this conjuring spell. It was only for a few special events that he would be shown as time moved along.

Jandor had a great time learning a great many conjuring spells for everyday use. One he thoroughly enjoyed was creating meadows. Some were all one type of plant, such as sunflowers. The bees and butterflies loved sunflowers. The farmers that kept beehives loved the new sunflower meadows because the bees would produce a lot of honey which was used to barter goods and services.

Jandor knew Feyanna was learning a great deal about plants and their medicinal properties so he would create small meadows of the plants she needed. One afternoon, about six months after Jandor and Feyanna arrived in Middle Earth, Jandor had a quick vision of trees dying. He asked The Magic if his help was needed, and an immediate brilliant flash of white light was the answer.

Feyanna," Jandor called out. "Come here, please."

Feyanna was outside planting some flowers around the base of their cottage home.

"Yes, Jandor," Feyanna answered as she walked into the workshop. "Hi, George. You look magnificent."

George bobbed his head in response.

"Feyanna, our help is needed in the Great Forest," Jandor said. "I was just shown a vision of some of the older trees losing branches and bark for no apparent reason. I asked The Magic if I was needed. I am. We are. Let's tune in and connect with The Magic to see what we can do."

Feyanna and Jandor stood silent as they called out to The Magic. The Magic answered them by sending an ethereal being to guide them.

As the air began to shimmer, Feyanna and Jandor stepped back and watched. An apparition began to take shape. A figure draped in a dark purple robe appeared, hovering above the floor.

Feyanna and Jandor bowed.

"Thank you for listening to our call," the figure said. "A dark poison has been placed at the base of twelve old oak trees and is slowly killing them. This poison will spread throughout the Great Forest of Garanthowen. It is quickly moving toward Dyantonadium, The Great One. If it kills this tree, all Magic in Middle Earth will be lost to the Dark Forces. The Dark doesn't know we are aware of the poison yet, so we have a little bit of time to destroy the poison. We need both of you to stop the poison."

"Of course," Jandor said. "Tell us what we need to do."

"This won't be easy," the apparition said. "It will be the most dangerous and deadly thing you've ever done. The battle will be grueling."

"We must save the forest," Feyanna said.

"You may lose your lives fighting The Dark Forces," the apparition informed them.

Feyanna and Jandor looked at each other for just a second.

"We accept the call," Jandor said as Feyanna nodded in response.

"Thank you," the apparition said. "We are sending someone to work with you as you prepare special potions. He will arrive as soon as I leave. Ask him his name. He is known as Ryganmorak."

"We will listen well," Jandor said.

The apparition quickly faded away and there was a knock at the door.

Feyanna and Jordan answered the door together.

"Hello," Jandor said.

The stranger tried to walk into the house, but they blocked him.

"What name do you go by?" Jandor asked.

Goldie was standing next to the wall, where the stranger could not see her. Her gold eyes were glowing brightly. Jandor gave Goldie a hand signal the stranger did not see.

"Why do you ask my name?" The stranger asked.

"It is good to call each other by your given name," Feyanna said, instinctively knowing this was not Ryganmorak.

"I am known as Darmon," the stranger answered. "I am here to help with the sickness in the trees."

Before anyone knew what had happened, Goldie turned from the wall and killed the stranger with her laser eyes. He dissolved into a million black shards that vanished into the air.

"Goldie, that was amazing!" Feyanna said.

"You are truly of The Magic," Jandor said. "We thank you for protecting us just now."

"You are very welcome," Goldie said. "He was pure evil."

"I felt the same thing a second before you vaporized him," Feyanna said.

"Same here," Jandor said. "Now, how about a yummy treat, Miss Goldie?" I happen to have a collection of bugs just outside the door in that jar covered with a piece of bark. All for you."

"I accept," Goldie said as she walked outside. "Protecting The Magic always makes me hungry.

Feyanna and Jandor laughed as she devoured the jar of bugs and then belched.

"Time for a nap," Goldie said as she settled on her blanket. "Love this place."

Goldie fell into a sound sleep just as another knock was heard at the door.

"Must be okay if Goldie is asleep," Jandor was saying when George flew past the two of them and blocked the door.

"I take it it's the Dark Force again?" Jandor said.

George bobbed his head and pointed a wing at a pouch of powders Feyanna had been blending.

"You want me to throw the powder on the stranger?" Feyanna asked.

George bobbed his head and pointed his other wing at the window.

"I understand," Feyanna said.

Feyanna stepped onto a small stool and leaned out of the window next to the door. With a nod from George, she threw the powders at the stranger, and before he could even scream, he vaporized just like the last one.

"I hope that's all for now," Feyanna said. "I need to make more of this powder."

"Look in the pouch," Goldie said without opening her eyes.

"It's full," Feyanna said, showing the pouch to Jandor. "Thanks to The Magic."

"Indeed, yes," Jandor said. "Thanks for protecting us, George."

George gave a squawk and settled on the back of one of the chairs.

"George, you have grown quite a bit," Feyanna said. "You won't fit on the chair before long."

"I guess I'll have to make a special perch for you, George. After we take care of the forest," Jandor said.

George and Goldie agreed with Jandor.

A third knocking was heard, and Jandor and Feyanna looked at each other. Both Goldie and George were asleep, so this might be a good energy.

Feyanna opened the door and found the farmer Aaron and one of his children standing there.

"Good day, Miss Feyanna," the child said. "We have brought you some eggs, butter, cheese, and a special bread my mother makes."

"Why thank you," Feyanna said as she handed the food to Jandor. "How is everyone at the farm?

"We are all well, thanks to you," Aaron said. "The two young calves are growing like crazy, just like our children. My wife wanted to celebrate our great fortune and made this bread for you. We have some at home, too."

"We are very grateful for this treat and happy to hear that all is well with you," Jandor said. "Let us know if you need anything at any time."

"We will," Aaron said. "Come along. We have chores to do."

"Take care," Feyanna said as a stranger appeared from the forest.

"Good day to you both," the stranger said. "I am Rygamorak, and I have been sent by The White Light and The Special Magic to assist you in helping the trees."

A soft blue light covered Rygamorak then Jandor and Feyanna.

"Welcome," Jandor said. "Please come inside. I believe we have a great deal of work to do."

"Indeed we do," Rygamorak replied as they walked into the workshop.

"Saving The Great Tree is our goal," Rygamorak said. "I see you have all the things we need. Feyanna, here is a list of potions that need to be prepared. Please do so."

Feyanna took the list and got busy.

"Jandor, please set three pots to boiling with plain water," Rygamorak said.

Jandor did as he was instructed to do. As soon as the first pot began to boil, Rygamorak gave further instructions.

"Feyanna, please bring the first blend of herbs here," Rygamorak said. "You will need to add them to this pot of boiling water."

Jandor hollered out, "No! This will make a poisonous gas and kill all of us."

"Very well done, Jandor," the apparition from earlier appeared. "You know your potions well. Rygamorak, I see you've tested them as instructed."

"Yes, I have," Rygamorak said, bowing to the apparition.

"So, you felt the need to test our loyalties," Jandor said angrily.

"We have always followed The White Light," Feyanna said. "Why did you think you needed to test us?"

Rygamorak and the apparition looked at each other for a moment.

"You are right in that you have never questioned your Gifts and how they are used," the apparition said. "There are a great many things that need to be done. The Special Magic wanted to be sure you were ready."

"Well, this was a terrible way to find out," Feyanna said. "We could have been killed just to show you our loyalty."

"Oh, my. We never thought of it that way," the apparition said, looking past them as if it were talking with someone else.

The room became hushed for a bit as they all thought about what had just happened.

"Well," Jandor was saying when a brilliant white light filled the cottage home.

An eagle flew through the door and landed on the floor in front of the fireplace. Goldie awoke and bowed to the eagle. George flew onto the floor next to Goldie and bowed to the eagle.

The eagle morphed into a solid person. He wore dark blue robes and looked ageless. His hair was long and dark, and his eyes were the color of the sky. He smiled at Jandor, Feyanna, Rygamorak, and the apparition.

"Indeed, you have always followed the path of The White Light," the man said. "We are grateful for that. Yes, this was a test of your loyalty and your intelligence. Jandor, you have done well in disagreeing with Rygamorak's instructions. That shows great knowledge and the ability to stay true to what you know to be right."

"Well," Jandor said. "I guess that's okay then. You, sir, are a great wizard, aren't you?"

"Yes, Jandor, I am," he answered. "I am known as Hokyne."

"Why do this to us?" Feyanna asked.

"We need to know you will follow your instincts even if a knowledgeable person says otherwise. Wisdom is knowing the difference between what some tell you and knowing the truth about the situation. You both have followed your instincts well here," Hokyne replied.

"What's this about?" Jandor asked.

"You will only be told that which is necessary at any given time," Rygamorak said. "Right now, the trees need you and your special powers."

"Yes, indeed," Feyanna replied. "You told us they are under attack by being poisoned by The Dark Forces. What do we need to do next?"

"Thank you for being so gracious, Jandor and Feyanna," Hokyne said. "I have a special powder here that needs to be sprinkled at the base of The Great Tree to stop the poison from killing it. Rygamorak has other things and instructions for you to follow. Time to prepare these things, eat a good meal, including the bread that was given to you by Aaron's wife, and then sleep well. Tomorrow morning, you begin your journey to save the forest."

"Something tells me we're in for a fight," Feyanna said.

"I agree," Jandor added.

"Thank you for appearing today," Rygamorak said to Hokyne.

"You are very welcome," Hokyne replied. "We will meet again."

Feyanna and Jandor bowed to Hokyne as he vanished. The apparition was still with them.

"Time for me to leave as well," the apparition said. "We will be watching as always."

"Thank you," Jandor said as the apparition faded away.

"Time to learn and prepare for tomorrow," Rygamorak said.

Feyanna, Jandor, and Rygamorak spent the rest of the day learning about the new things Rygamorak had brought with him. Jandor learned how to conjure potions needed specifically for tomorrow's battle, and Feyanna was shown how to prepare special powders for the battle as well.

"Oh my," Feyanna said as shadows began to grow dark in the workshop. "It's long past supper time. I'll get something started."

"It sure is," Rygamorak said. "Let's put these into their pots and get some supper."

A short time later, the three of them were gathered around the table near the hearth, enjoying the soup Feyanna had made and the special bread from Aaron's wife.

"This is just what I needed. Tastes delicious," Jandor said.

"This bread is excellent," Rygamorak said. "I taste cinnamon and lavender."

"I heated it up, and the aroma is just as delicious as the bread," Feyanna said.

"It smells heavenly," Goldie added.

"You always were a porcupine of great taste," Rygamorak said, laughing.

"You know our Goldie?" Jandor asked.

"Indeed I do," Rygamorak replied. "We've worked together before."

"He can be a bit pushy sometimes," Goldie said.

This made everyone laugh. Even George gave a squawk.

"I swear that hawk knows exactly what we're saying," Jandor said.

Rygamorak laughed with the others and winked at George as if they had a secret between them.

"Well, it's time to get some sleep," Feyanna said as she cleared the table.

"We'll help with cleaning up," Jandor said.

A short time later, the kitchen was settled, the fire was banked, and Ryga-morak settled near the hearth with Goldie. Feyanna and Jandor fell asleep as soon as their heads hit their pillows, and the cottage home was quiet as deep night fell in Middle Earth.

Feyanna awoke at sunrise to screaming.

"Jandor, do you hear that?" Feyanna said as she hurriedly dressed and stepped into the main room.

"It woke me up, too," Jandor said as they heard another scream.

"It's the trees," Rygamorak said as he stood up. "It's so horrible."

"It is," Goldie said as she went outside.

George followed her and they saw him take to the sky.

"Let's eat and get out there," Jandor said.

That's exactly what they did. They followed Rygamorak's instructions about how to stack the pouches in their bags and set out for the forest next to their cottage home.

The screams were constant now as they walked through the forest.

"Dyantonadium is a long walk from here," Rygamorak said. "The Dark Forces still don't know you are here to save it."

"That's good," Feyanna said. "Should I keep sprinkling this yellow powder along the path?"

"Yes," Rygamorak answered. "It will filter through the earth and go into the trees. It will shield the trees from the poison. It doesn't look like any of these have been affected by the poison yet. We should begin to see the damage quite soon."

A few minutes later, they saw their first tree that had been poisoned. The bark was falling off, and the branches looked like they were being pulled off. The tree screamed every time a branch fell.

"Feyanna, sprinkle the pink powder at the base of this tree," Rygamorak said. "Just a tiny bit and watch what happens.

Feyanna sprinkled a tiny bit of the pink powder as instructed and stood back. The tree stopped screaming, and the bark began to be replaced along with the branches that had been killed. The tree was back to its beautiful self in just a few minutes.

"That's amazing," Jandor said. "Will that happen to all the trees we use the pink powder on?"

"Yes," Rygamorak replied. "However, some of the older and bigger trees need more than the pink powder. That's where your conjuring powers come into play."

"Okay. Just tell me where and when," Jandor replied.

Feyanna kept sprinkling the pink powder as they walked along. It was well past mid-day when Rygamorak suggested they stop for a rest and food.

"I didn't bring anything," Feyanna said.

"No need, " Rygamorak. "Watch. I humbly ask the forest to feed us."

In an instant, fruit, vegetables, bread, and water appeared. They ate and drank and rested for a little bit.

"Thanks, everyone," Feyanna said. "Look. My pink powder pouch has been replenished."

"Always," Rygamorak replied. "It is time for me to leave. This battle is for the two of you to fight."

And Rygamorak was gone in a flash of soft blue light.

"Well," Jandor said, "Looks like we need to get moving. Be ready for anything."

A minute later, they came to an older tree that was almost dead. The bark was gone, and most of the branches had fallen to the ground.

"I know what to do," Jandor said as he reached into his bag. He brought out a pouch with a dark blue powder inside. "Dear tree, I hear your whisper to end the pain. Be at peace."

Jandor sprinkled a little of the dark blue powder at the base of the tree. The tree gave a sigh and then fell to the earth. The trunk crumbled into dust, and the stump withered to nothing. As they watched, a shoot rose from the withered stump. Leaves appeared, and more branches grew upward. In no time, a fully grown tree appeared, healthy and strong.

The tree bent a branch towards Jandor and said, "Thank you, great wizard, for giving me new life. I am strong, and the poison that killed me cannot ever harm me again."

The tree touched Jandor's head and then stood tall.

"That was inspiring," Feyanna said with tears in her eyes.

"I am overwhelmed," Jandor said. "I love the way The Magic takes care of the innocents."

"Me too," Feyanna said.

A great scream was heard that shook the earth.

"It's The Great Tree," Jandor said. "The Dark Force poison has reached it. We must hurry."

A great wind came along and stopped them in their tracks.

"I can't move," Feyanna said.

"Take the black stone from your pouch and touch the earth with it like this," Jandor said as he did just that.

As their black stones touched the earth, a type of tunnel appeared and they were able to move along the path. Feyanna was now sprinkling the green powder on the base of most of the trees they passed while Jandor dropped two drops of a potion he had conjured. This killed the poison and turned it into water to nourish the trees.

"It's getting very dark in here," Feyanna said as they heard another horrible scream that shook the earth so hard that they almost fell down.

"The poison is destroying the roots of The Great Tree," Jandor said.

"Look!" Feyanna said as they rounded a bend in the path.

They could see The Great Tree a ways ahead of them. As they tried to get closer, huge ugly red and orange flying insects attacked them as the wind came roaring in. Their razor-sharp claws tried to pierce Feyanna and Jandor's heads and arms time and time again.

"White Light, surround and protect us," Feyanna whispered into the roaring wind. She didn't have much energy to keep fighting the ugly bugs.

Jandor tried to get to his bag of potions, but the wind kept pulling his bag away from him. Jandor finally figured that if he turned away from the wind for just a second, he might be able to grab the pouch he wanted. So, just as the wind came after him, he turned away and was able to grab a gray pouch with a white powder with pieces of pink stones in it. He grabbed a handful and turned back into the wind just as a bunch of ugly bugs were at his face. He threw the powder on them, and they sizzled and burst into tiny pieces of dead bugs. The wind drew them away from Jandor and Feyanna and was very angry.

They placed more powders at the base of the dying trees, and the trees were reborn. The Dark Force finally saw this and was very angry. It sent vortices of black clouds with lightning throughout the forest, trying to kill Feyanna and Jandor. The White Light protected them as they bent into the wind, trying to keep walking.

It seemed like forever as they continued to fight the Dark Force winds and lightning as they saved more trees. Just as they caught sight of The Great Tree, Feyanna felt something on her foot.

"Jandor, look," Feyanna shouted, pointing to her foot.

It looked like the roots of a plant were trying to wrap themselves around her and keep her in one place. The root was moving up her leg when Jandor threw something from one of his pouches onto Feyanna. The root screamed, turned into a serpent, and withered into nothing.

"Thanks, Jandor," Feyanna was saying when a great wing grabbed him and lifted him from the ground. The wing belonged to a hideous beast. It had two heads with five eyes in each head. It had two mouths in each head, and they were drooling some disgusting-smelling liquid that burst into flames when it hit the ground. The beast was trying to fly away with Jordan, but the trees kept getting in its way.

Jandor was trying not to fall as the beast flew higher into the sky.

"I call upon The Special Powers to save Jandor," Feyanna screamed into the black winds. She wasn't sure if anyone or anything had heard her. She was trying to get to The Great Tree and watch Jandor at the same time. She was terrified as whirling silver creatures with sword blades for arms came toward her. She felt a searing pain in her left shoulder and saw that she had been cut open. She grabbed some powders from her pouch and rubbed them over the cut. The bleeding stopped, and the wound began to close. This made The Dark Forces even angrier.

The beast carrying Jandor seemed to be moving higher into the sky. It was hard to see him as the day turned into night. Just as Feyanna tried again to move forward, she saw something in the sky. She looked again and saw a great creature flying after the beast that had Jandor in its grip. She heard a fierce roar, and then the black sky lit up as if a thousand candles had been lit at the same time. She saw the beast drop Jandor from its grip as fire surrounded its head. Jandor was in a free fall. Feyanna screamed at seeing this and didn't know what to do.

Just as Jandor was about to hit the top of one of the old trees, the tree gathered its branches and caught Jandor. Next thing Feyanna knew, a flying creature had taken Jandor from the tree cradle and was bringing him to the earth next to her. It was Penny.

"Penny!" Feyanna hollered out as soon as she recognized her.

Penny set Jandor down as gently as a mother tends her newborn babe. Jandro was a bit shaken.

"Jandor, here. Drink this," Feyanna said. She had mixed some powders with her water and handed it to Jandor.

He drank all of it and felt better right away.

"Thanks, Penny, for saving me," Jandor said. "And, you, Feyanna, for mixing this water for me. That was one crazy ride."

"You are entirely welcome," Penny said. "Now, I do believe you have some work to do."

"We do," Jandor said as he stood up. "Let's go, Feyanna. Later Penny."

As Penny flew off into the darkness, Feyanna and Jandor worked at getting to The Great Tree. The Dark Forces kept trying to stop them. It had almost succeeded with Jandor being taken away. But the two of them kept going. Just as they neared The Great Tree, The Dark Forces sent another terrifying bunch of creatures at them. These were little creatures with big heads and many rows of razor-sharp teeth. The creatures worked at biting Feyanna and Jandor's feet and legs time and again. Jandor threw red powder on the creatures, and they burst into flames, only to be replaced by more little creatures.

Feyanna had a thought. She saw a green plant with cup-shaped flowers. Inside the cup was a liquid. She didn't know how she knew to do this, but she grabbed some of the flowers and threw them at the little creatures. The little creatures looked surprised and then disintegrated into nothing. She grabbed more flowers as she and Jandor took a few more steps toward the Great Tree. They were almost there as the more of the little creatures tried to bite them. Feyanna kept throwing the flowers on them. The flowers appeared next to her the whole way to The Great Tree. The wind was howling, and those sword-bladed things were still flying all around them.

Jandor was one step away from The Great Tree when his arm was pinned to his side by a weird-looking vine.

"I don't think so," Feyanna said as she threw a flower at the vine. The vine withered, and Jandor's arm was free.

Jandor grabbed a pouch Feyanna had never seen before and took a ball of something from it. He worked the ball into a long piece of rope and threw it at The Great Tree. It landed at the base and wrapped itself around the base. The Dark Forces howled something fierce and sent an earthquake to loosen the rope. It didn't work, but Feyanna and Jandor were thrown to the ground. Jandor managed to stand up, rocking back and forth as the earth shook. He needed one more potion to save The Great Tree.

The Dark Forces knew he had that potion and did everything it could to kill him. Saw blades came flying through the air. Jandor moved all around to avoid them. Lightning was sent to kill Jandor, but he managed to move away at the last minute. Feyanna was throwing a bright orange powder into the air around them, and it seemed to lessen the wind and quaking earth.

Jandor felt the earth quiet some and knew this was his only chance to set the powder at the base of The Great Tree. He was standing right next to the tree as he bent down to lay the brilliant purple powder on the earth. The Dark Forces sent a more fierce quake that threw Jandor to the ground. Jandor rolled over to the tree as The Dark Forces sent a serpent to grab his hand. He placed the dark purple powder at the base of The Great Tree just as the serpent bit into his arm. He felt the pain and nothing else.

Feyanna looked over at Jandor just as he placed the purple powder at the base of The Great Tree, and the serpent bit into his arm.

"No!" Feyanna cried out as she tried to stand and run to Jandor.

There was a moment of absolute silence, and then all craziness happened. The sky became clear as a tremendous howling scream filled the air throughout Middle Earth. As Feyanna watched, Dyantomadium was healed and returned to its magnificent self. The Special Magic destroyed and ripped the tree poison from the earth. All the trees that had been poisoned and died were restored. The earth stopped quaking and Feyanna was able to run to Jandor.

Jandor lay on the earth, not moving. Feyanna took some of her special herbal blend she had hidden in her pocket and rubbed it on Jandor's chest. It took a minute, but he finally took a deep breath and began to move. His color changed from gray to pink, and he opened his eyes and looked right at Feyanna.

"What'd I miss?" he asked as he tried to sit up.

"Let me help you," Feyanna was saying when The Great Tree bent down and helped Jandor to sit up.

"Thank you, Great Tree," Jandor said. "I think I'm going to need to stay here for a while."

"I think we both need to sit here for a while," Feyanna said as she sat down next to Jandor.

The air had cleared, and the sun showed throughout The Great Forest.

"Here. Eat this," Feyanna said as she gave Jandor some of the bread from Aaron's wife.

"You, too," Jandor said as he took a bite.

They ate and drank and rested for quite some time.

Then Dyantonadium spoke.

"I am forever grateful for your bravery in saving me and my forest," The Great Tree said.

Feyanna and Jandor stood up and faced the tree.

"We are honored and humbled to have been able to help all of you," Jandor said.

"It is because of your Gifts of The Special Magic that we are alive and well," Dyantonadium responded.

"We are grateful to be alive," Feyanna said. "Your forest is beyond magical."

As she looked around, a flock of birds brought a bouquet of flowers to her. They gave Jandor a gold and silver sword.

"I am honored to receive this," Jandor said. "I will cherish it always and use it to protect the innocent ones and The Magic."

"You will be taught how to use it soon," Dyantonadium said. "Feyanna, enjoy the beauty of the flowers."

"I will," Feyanna said. "Thanks to all of you for these beauties."

"It is time for you to return home," Diynotonadium said. "Close your eyes, and you will be there in an instant."

Feyanna and Jandor closed their eyes, and in less than an instant, they found themselves back in their cottage home, sitting near the hearth. Goldie and George were waiting for them.

George squawked and flapped his wings as Goldie whistled for them.

"Thanks for the warm welcome," Jandor said.

"Goldie, I didn't know you could whistle. Very nice," Feyanna said as Jandor and Feyanna nodded at her and George.

"George, I see you have your new perch," Jandor said. "Thanks be to The Special Magic for making that for you."

George bobbed his head in response.

"So glad you won the battle," Goldie said. "I am getting quite fond of the two of you."

"Thanks, Goldie," Feyanna said as she and Jandor laughed. "We are quite fond of you and George, too."

"It was a crazy battle," Jandor said, yawning. "I need some sleep. I'll see you in the morning."

"Does he know you've only been gone about an hour?" Goldie asked Feyanna.

"No. He's really worn out. I don't think he remembers how time changes when we're in The Magic. He'll probably sleep the rest of the day all the way through to the morning. Time for some tea and a little something to eat," Feyanna said.

Feyanna made tea and a light supper. It was late in the afternoon, after all. Goldie came in at dusk and settled in her favorite place. George flew in and settled on his new perch. It even had three branches for him to spread out on. She smiled at them both, gave them a wink, and closed the cottage home for the night. She was soon asleep, needing her rest as well. The trees in The Greta Forest of Garanthowen were celebrating their new lives. Penny slept close to the cottage home that night. And the great flying creature that had sent fire to kill the beast that held Jandor in the battle was close by as well. He would be needed soon. Middle Earth slept.

The next day found everyone going about their work as usual. Feyanna was making new herbal remedies given to her by her Guardian Mentor. Jandor was trying his hand at creating new potions. Some worked well. Some were a mess.

"Jandor!" Feyanna said, coughing. "What in the name of all that is good is that? It stinks. I need to go outside."

"I'm right with you," Jandor said as he grabbed the potion bowl and stepped outside.

"Walk far away from here," Feyanna said, laughing. "I don't need to smell that again."

Jandor walked quite a ways from Feyanna and dumped the bowl of goo on the earth. The earth sent up a bit of green smoke as the goo was burned away.

"Well, that didn't work," Jandor said.

"Ya think?" Feyanna said, still laughing at Jandor.

"Yup. Total disaster," Jandor agreed, laughing as well. "I guess I'll give it a rest and try again later."

"You mean after that smell clears out of the workspace and all," Feyanna said.

"Exactly," Jandor replied. "Maybe some of these wildflowers will make the place smell better."

"That's a great idea," Feyanna said. "Dear Earth, may I take some of these home to clear the air?"

Flowers were set at her feet in an instant.

"Thanks so much," Feyanna said as she gathered the flowers. "I'll go put these in some water. You coming?"

Feyanna looked over at Jandor. He was looking at something in the sky.

"What is it?" Feyanna said as she looked skyward.

"There," Jandor said, pointing to something small and black. "See it?"

"Yes," Feyanna said as she spotted the object. "It looks like it's getting closer."

They watched the black object as it flew closer to the meadow.

"I can't make out its shape," Feyanna said.

"Me, either," Jandor agreed. "It looks to be getting bigger."

Just then, Penny flew over.

"Hi, Miss Penny," Jandor said.

"What are the two of you looking at?" Penny asked, with a small smile on her face.

"That thing," Feyanna said, pointing to the black object getting closer as they spoke.

"Oh, I see it, too," Penny said.

"I can't make out its shape yet," Jandor said.

"Maybe you're not supposed to," Penny replied, looking at Jandor.

"Oh. I see," Jandor said. "It's one of those Magic things for now."

"There seems to be a lot of that going around, Miss Penny," Feyanna said, looking at Penny. "And why are you smiling like that?"

"You'll find out soon enough," Penny replied. "Jandor, I can smell that horrible potion you made. Glad you threw it away. Not one of your best ones."

Jandor laughed with everyone. "I agree. Some things work out, and some things don't. I'll keep working at it."

"Good idea," Penny said. "I came to tell you that it's almost time for more lessons."

"I thought it might be," Jandor replied.

Feyanna looked out into the meadow and seemed to lose all accounting of place and time.

"Feyanna," Jandor called out to her.

Feyanna did not reply. She was lost in a vision. She saw a castle among the hills and valleys of a place she was not familiar with. Small hamlets dotted the landscape. The fields were freshly planted. Smithies were busing at their fires. Women and children planted new seeds and took care of the home. Men took to riding throughout the countryside. Some hunted, some were carpenters and brick-layers, while others were on some kind of business for the realm. There were even a couple of younger men repairing a wagon wheel. Kids were having fun running around and being called out by their mothers to come and help with the chores.

A bit of a ways from the hamlet proper, Feyanna noticed a good-sized cot-tage home set way back into the woods. It wasn't easily seen from the road. The path to it was more like an old animal trail that had become overgrown with under-brush. It was as if the person who built it didn't want to be easily seen or found. It was built into the side of a small hill. It reminded Feyanna of the cottage home she and Jandor were living in right now. Smoke rose through a chimney from a fire inside the cottage home. There were a couple of benches and tables along the sides of the building, and there was what looked like a shelter for animals. A good many chickens roamed around the place and a wagon was set against the side of the shel-ter. The beginnings of a large garden were seen a ways from the cottage home. The ground had been turned over and staked in rows for planting.

As Feyanna continued to look at the forest around the hamlet, she saw many birds flying around, making nests in the eaves of the houses and buildings. Rabbits were seen hopping through the forest. And then, she saw something that looked familiar. She knew the shape for sure. It was the shape of a dragon. It flew along the wind over the forest. People in the hamlet saw the dragon, and a few screamed at each other to get inside. The dragon circled the hamlet once, then flew north. It was all black and huge. It was even bigger than Penny. It seemed to be checking on the hamlet to make sure everything was okay. Most folks stayed out-side and watched the dragon. They didn't seem to be alarmed or afraid of it.

The vision began to fade and Feyanna found herself back in her meadow by her cottage home.

"Feyanna? Oh, Feyanna?" Jandor was saying as she returned from wher-ever she had been.

"Feyanna?" Jandor said as he walked over to her.

"Don't touch her, Jandor," Penny advised. "She's been having a vision, and we don't want to startle her."

"Okay. I understand," Jandor replied.

Feyanna became aware of her surroundings and heard some of what Penny had said.

"Oh. Hi there," Feyanna said, looking at Jandor and Penny.

"I see you've returned to us," Penny said as she walked over to Feyanna. "Lean on my wing. It will help you steady yourself."

Feyanna did just that and, a few minutes later, stepped back, placed her hand on Penny's wing, and said, "Thanks so much for sharing your energy. I am fully returned now."

"You are entirely welcome," Penny replied. "I'll always be here to take care of the both of you."

"You look much better," Jandor said. "What happened to you?"

"I don't really know," Feyanna said. "One minute, I was here in the meadow, thanking the Dear Earth for the gift of the flowers to help clear the air from your disastrous potion thing, and in the blink of an eye, I was in a small hamlet in a place I've never seen before."

What did you see?" Jandor asked as they walked back to the cottage and sat down outside.

"Well," Feyanna began. "I was looking at this hamlet like I just said. It was a spring day. People were busy working. Some were planting gardens. Some were working in their smithies. Some were riding through the forest hunting and a few looked like they were part of a royal guard. I saw a castle in the distance, so maybe they were part of the king's troops or something like that.

"There was a cottage home like ours but much bigger. It was in the forest, and you wouldn't have known it was there because it was well hidden from most. Then, I saw a dragon fly over the hamlet. It was bigger than you, Penny. And it was all black. Some people ran inside, but most stayed outside looking at it. They didn't seem to be afraid of it. It flew over the hamlet once, then turned and flew north. Then, the vision faded, and here I am. I guess."

"That was some vision, Feyanna," Jandor said. "Wonder what it means?"

"Well, I get the feeling that it might be a glimpse into our future," Feyanna offered quietly.

"Why do you say that?" Penny asked.

"It just felt familiar to me," Feyanna replied. "I know I've never been in that place before, but it feels like I'm connected to it somehow. A distant memory or something."

"Maybe from a past life," Jandor offered as he looked at Penny. "I know that look, Penny. It's tied to The Magic."

Feyanna and Jandor stared at Penny for the longest time until she finally said, "Yes, it's tied to The Magic."

"Feyanna, I do believe you had a vision of our future," Jandor stated.

"Jandor, I do believe you may be correct about that," Feyanna replied.

Penny didn't say a thing. She wouldn't even look at the two of them.

"Well, since Penny won't say boo about any of this and still won't look at us, I am sure it's true. It's where we're going next," Jandor said.

"All right," Penny finally said. "It is about something like that. I just can't give you anything more. Rules are rules."

"Understood," Feyanna replied.

"I guess that means we may be moving soon," Jandor offered. "We'd better get busy learning everything we can about potions, alchemy, and such. We may be moving along sooner than we think."

"I agree," Feyanna said as she got up and headed to the door, sending a look back at Penny.

"You will find a few new things on your workbenches," Penny said as she spread her wings, preparing to take flight. "You're going to need them and everything you've learned and created before long."

With that said Penny rose into the sky and flew out of sight as Jandor and Feyanna returned to their workshop.

"Oh my god, Jandor," Feyanna said all of a sudden. "That black dragon I saw in my vision. It looked familiar, and now I know why. It was the black thing we saw when we were fighting for the trees. I know it was."

"I believe you," Jandor said, looking over at Feyanna. "I feel a change coming along soon. I can feel it in the very depths of my soul."

"Same here," Feyanna said as she began blending herbs in a new recipe to help alleviate headaches.

Jandor began mixing and heating new potions that worked this time. It was late in the evening when Jandor looked across the workshop at Feyanna. The shadows had deepened.

"Feyanna, it looks like the night is upon us," Jandor said as he quenched the flame under his mixing bowl stand. "We missed supper, and I'm very hungry."

"You're right," Feyanna said, laughing. "I'm famished. I'll fix us some eggs and such. Let's go."

"This is delicious," Jandor said a short time later. "You can make this stuff anytime you want to."

"Thanks, Jandor," Feyanna said. "Eggs with veggies, cheese, and seasonings are one of my specialties. Your bread is a great addition, too."

"That's my specialty," Jandor said. "One of the villagers taught me how to make it when I was a kid. So glad she did. I've added a few things over the years like the berries and such. This all tastes fantastic."

They finished their meal in silence and cleared things away.

"Do you two ever sleep?" Goldie asked as she settled for the night.

George squawked at them, too.

They laughed at Goldie and George.

215

"Of course we do," Feyanna said as she closed the cottage doors and windows for the night. "That's exactly what we're doing right now."

"We get so wrapped up in all the things we're learning we sometimes forget what time it is," Jandor said. "That is until we are reminded that we need food."

"It's a good thing you pay attention to something other than your work," Goldie said, yawning. "Get some rest."

"Yes, Ma'am," Jandor replied, blowing out the candle above the hearth and banking the fire.

"Good night, George," Feyanna said as the cottage became dark, and she and Jandor walked into their rooms.

"Sleep well, Jandor," Feyanna said.

"You, too," Jandor replied.

Penny stood outside, listening to them all. She lay down to sleep there for the night. Jandor and Feyanna were about to be thrust into a new adventure, and Penny wanted to make sure they got all the sleep they could. The Special Magic was about to take over their lives.

CHAPTER 13

It happened so fast that Jandor and Feyanna didn't have time to think about it. The morning after Penny hinted at their lives changing in the near future, things changed at the speed of a lightning strike.

It happened right after breakfast. Goldie went outside looking for her breakfast, and George took off into the sky for his morning flight. Jandor and Feyanna had just walked into the workshop, and the back wall began to shimmer.

"Jandor," Feyanna said, pointing to the wall.

"I see it," Jandor said as the wall opened into the same entryway they had experienced before with Goldie.

"Come to the center of the main room," a voice instructed them.

They walked along the path and entered the main room. It was alive with crystals glowing and casting rays of every color all over the place.

"This is so beautiful," Feyanna said as they looked around the room.

"This place is bigger than it was when we were here before," Jandor was saying when the center of the room cleared.

"Please walk into the center of the room," the voice instructed them.

They did as they were told. They found themselves standing on a circle. It was glowing a dark purple.

"This color reminds me of Penny," Feyanna said.

"As it should," Penny said as she joined them.

"What's this all about?" Jandor asked.

"Listen," Penny replied.

As they watched, a mist began to rise from the walls and ceilings, changing colors and swirling around them. A form began to take shape in front of Feyanna and Jandor. In an instant, there was an ethereal being standing before them. It had long, flowing silver hair and brilliant gold eyes, just like Godlie's. It wore an opalescent kind of garment that swirled around with the mist. Then it spoke.

"Jandor. Feyanna," the ethereal creature said. "I am known as the Mist of The Universes. I come before you to thank you for all that you have done and learned here in Middle Earth. Especially for following your hunches and using your Gifts for the good of all."

Feyanna and Jandor bowed their heads in response.

"Penny, you have done a great job getting these two here. We thank you," the Mist of The Universes said.

"Always," Penny replied, bowing as well.

"You may call me Lyana," Lyana said. "We will be seeing each other a bit going forward."

Lyana walked over to Feyanna and placed her hand on Feyanna's arm.

"You are a sweet and determined soul with great intelligence and wisdom," Lyana said.

Lyana walked over to Jandor and placed her hand on his arm.

"You are of a strong body and dedicated spirit with great resilience," Lyana said.

Lyana stepped back and looked at both of them.

"Are they ready, Penny?" Lyana asked.

"They are," Penny replied.

Feyanna and Jandor, we are asking you to take on a challenge," Lyana said. "It involves so many things that you already know and a great many things you will be learning and experiencing. The humans of this planet are in need of The Special Magic that will help them learn and move forward from a dark place. Many of them have cried out to their Gods for help. As you know, we, the beings from a different time, place, and universe, brought your race here to grow and flourish. You know that the first group was destroyed for many reasons. It is this second group that we populated the Earth with that has developed a great deal throughout your time. Many of them have respected the Earth and taken care of her. Some have not, and that will be dealt with on its own. A council of elders was held, and they have decided to help your kind in this dark time and place. Will you help them as well?"

"Of course," Jandor replied.

"Yes," Feyanna replied.

"You did not hesitate," Lyana said.

"We are grateful for the Gifts the White Light and Special Magic have bestowed upon us," Jandor said. "We will always help when asked."

"It is our honor to answer the call," Feyanna added.

"We all thank you," Lyana said. "Are you ready, Penny?"

"Yes, as you wish it to be," Penny replied.

"You will be sent to a place in your time known as the village of The Meadows. It is a pleasant hamlet on the shores of the lake known as Avalon. The lake holds great Magic. The people are poor and need help with everything. Your herbal remedies, Feyanna, are in great demand, and Jandor, your potions will help immensely. Goldie and George are waiting there for you now," Lyana informed them.

Lyana stepped away from the circle and said, "Step into the blue light with Penny, and you will be in the cottage home Feyanna saw in her vision. All of your things will be there and many new tools and such. We will be in touch once you get settled. We thank you for your acceptance of this undertaking."

With the wave of her hand, Lyana was gone, and Penny stepped into the blue light.

"Here we go," Penny said as the mists enveloped them, and they were instantaneously transported to the cottage home Feyanna had seen in her vision.

As soon as the mists cleared, Feyanna said, "It's the cottage home I saw in my vision. Exactly just like it."

"This is amazing," Jandor said as he walked around and looked at everything. "We are secluded. I can't even see the smoke from a fire in the hamlet."

"The hamlet is about a ten-minute walk northeast of here," Penny said. "Avalon is about a five-minute walk to the northwest. We'll find those places later. Time now for some food and rest," Penny said. "I'll fly over the hamlet at a distance so they don't see me. Dragons have a bad reputation in this place. It is understandable, as some of my kind kill for the fun of it. Bad group they are."

Penny took to the air on her mission to have a look around the place.

Feyanna and Jandor looked at each other for a minute before Jandor said, "Good to know about the bad dragons."

"Well, let's take a look inside. I'm hungry," Feyanna said as they walked into their new cottage home.

"The shelves are fully stocked with food and spices and such," Feyanna said as she looked into every cupboard and on every shelf.

"I'll set the table," Jandor said. "Seems you've got an idea about what we're going to eat."

"I do," Feyanna said as she set a fire in the cooking stove. "I'm going to poach these salmon, add herbs for flavor, and make a rice dish from these lovely kinds of rice."

"It already smells wonderful," Jandor said as he stood near Feyanna as she added more herbs to the salmon and rice to a pot of boiling water.

"Will you check the rice? It should be ready in about five minutes," Feyanna asked Jandor.

"Sure," Jandor replied as Goldie walked into the cottage home. "Hi, Goldie. I see you've found your special place near the hearth."

"I most certainly have," Goldie replied. "Traveling in The Special Magic always makes me hungry and tired. Time for a nap."

Goldie was sound asleep in an instant, as her snoring proved.

"Time for us to eat, Jandor," Feyanna said as she set their plates on the table.

"This is delicious, Feyanna," Jandor said.

"Thank you," Feyanna replied.

They enjoyed their meal while looking around the place.

"Let's go into the workshop and look around," Jandor suggested as they cleared the table. "I'm curious about what's been added in there."

"Me, too," Feyanna said as she set the dishes in the wash bucket. "I'll clean these later. To the workshop!"

As they walked into the much bigger space, the back wall began to shimmer, just like in the cottage in Middle Earth.

Feyanna and Jandor walked along the entryway into the main room. It looked exactly like the one they had just been in. All was the same except for one thing: the ceiling had the outline of a dragon in white crystals on it. And they were glowing something fierce!

"Would you look at that?" Jandor said as they both stared at the ceiling.

"That's amazing," Feyanna said in a hushed voice. "It reminds me of the constellation Draco, the dragon."

"You would know that, of course," Jandor said, laughing at Feyanna.

"Cute, Jandor," Feyanna replied. "If I didn't know better, I'd say there's something going on here with the whole dragon thing. We met Penny. We saw a dark dragon shadow over the forest in Middle Earth, and, just now, Penny told us about some of her fellow dragons that like to breathe fire into villages just because they can."

"Good point," Jandor said, still looking at the ceiling. "This place is still amazing."

"It is," Penny said as she walked into the room from a long hallway to the right of the main room.

"You're back," Jandor said.

"Yes. I just needed to take a quick look around the place," Penny replied, sitting down. "Everything looks calm for now."

"So, the village known as The Meadows is close by?" Feyanna asked.

"Yes, it is. The Lake of Avalon is close by as well," Penny said. "The village is to the left once you reach the dirt track, and the lake is to the right. They are both about five minutes away."

"Will the villagers be surprised about our being here?" Jandor asked.

"They might be," Penny replied. "Just answer their questions with facts. Jandor, you can help them with their crops and animals. Feyanna, you are a healer."

"Well, that's exactly what we are," Feyanna said.

"True. Penny, why are we here, in this exact place?" Jandor asked.

"You do get to the point rather quickly, Jandor," Penny replied. "I have to ask permission to give you more information."

Penny looked off into the room and seemed to be far away. It was a while later when she finally returned to the present.

"Are you okay?" Feyanna asked.

"Yes, I am now," Penny replied. "Thanks for noticing. It takes a lot of my energy to communicate with The Other Side. They always make sure I'm rested and ready to go after our chats."

"Good," Feyanna replied. "What can you tell us?"

"I am told to tell you to get settled here and let the locals become used to you. They need healing right away. So, Feyanna, how about you take that basket of herbal remedies over there and walk into the village? Tell everyone you meet that you are a healer and am ready to help anyone who needs it. Jandor, you go with her and let the villagers know that you can help with their animals and the spring planting."

"And?" Jandor asked.

"That's all for now," Penny said. "You both need to be accepted here before anything else can occur. That's all I can tell you for now."

Penny just looked at them and said no more.

"Okay," Feyanna said as she took the basket that had been put there for her and walked back into the workshop.

"We're on our way," Jandor said. "You coming along or watching from a distance?"

"I'll be high in the sky keeping an eye on you two," Penny said.

"There's something about this crystal cave," Feyanna said as she paused near the entrance. "It reminds me of something, but I just can't figure it out."

"I get the same feeling," Jandor said as they both looked up at the dragon crystals on the ceiling. They blinked twice and then dimmed.

The wall closed as they walked through the workshop and into the main room.

"You coming with us, Goldie and George?" Jandor asked.

"Not this time," Goldie replied. "We were told to stay here."

"See you later," Feyanna said as she and Jandor left the cottage home.

Feyanna and Jandor followed the path to the dirt track and turned left. They found themselves at the edge of the village a few minutes later.

"Here we go," Jandor said.

They walked to the center of the village, where a few people had set up tables with items to sell.

Feyanna found a spot under one of the trees and set her basket on a rather large boulder. Jandor set his things next to hers, and they smiled at the folks close to them. One of the village men stepped over and introduced himself.

"Good day, strangers. I am John of The Meadows," John said. "This is our village known as The Meadows. My ancestors started it many generations ago."

"Good day, kind sir," Feyanna said. "I am Feyanna, the healer."

"I am Jandor," Jandor said, offering a hand to John. "I am known for helping with the animals and supplying potions for the health of your crops."

"Welcome," John said, clasping hands with Jandor. "We are in need of both of your talents."

"We are happy to assist," Feyanna said.

John called out to the villagers close by, and they walked over to meet Feyanna and Jandor. The day seemed to fly by, and it wasn't until late in the day that a rather rude man questioned them.

"Where are you from? Who sent you here? How do you know of this place?" the rude man asked.

"Samuel!" John shouted at the rude man. "You are disrespectful and rude. Do not shout at our new neighbors."

"I think they are spies sent here to see how our crops grow so the king can take them from us," Samuel replied.

"Please do not be bothered by Samuel. He is always suspicious of things he cannot control, including the weather and new people," John explained.

"We are not worried about Samuel," Jandor said so only John could hear him.

Feyanna was watching Samuel. He seemed to be having a problem standing on his left foot.

"Samuel, I am Feyanna, the healer," Feyanna said. "I see you are having some discomfort with your left foot. May I offer my services?"

"How do you know about my foot? You're a witch!" Samuel said as he lost his balance and fell to the ground. "See, she put a spell on me and made me fall."

Some of the villagers laughed at Samuel.

"Samuel, you are a stupid man," a woman said. "You lost your balance because of the big sore spot on your left foot. Let Feyanna have a look. She may be able to help you. Don't be so nasty and rude."

Others agreed with the village woman and encouraged Samuel to let Feyanna help him.

"All right," Samuel said, trying to stand up.

"You may stay sitting on the ground, Samuel," Feyanna said as she knelt down. "Please remove your boot."

As Samuel removed his boot and the filthy rag he had wrapped around his foot, Feyanna could smell the rotted skin.

"How long has this bothered you, Samuel?" Feyanna asked as she threw the filthy rag to the side. "Burn this rag right away."

John picked the filthy rag up with a long stick and set it in the fire at the Smithy's shop. It smelled horrible as it burned red hot.

"I've had it for about a fortnight," Samuel replied as Feyanna ran water over the open wound. "That stings."

"Yes, I'm sure it does," Feyanna replied. "I must clean away the rotted skin so I can have a good look at what caused this wound."

Feyanna sprinkled yellow powder with red bits over the wound, and the rotted skin fell off Samuel's foot. The wound was now fully open, and Feyanna could see what had caused the problem.

"You have a thorn in your foot," Feyanna said. "Didn't you notice the pain from the thorn when it went into your foot?"

"Sure I did, but I didn't think anything of it," Samuel said. "My boots are old, and lots of things get inside. I just dump the stuff outside and wear them again."

"This is going to hurt for a few minutes," Feyanna said. "This green powder will draw the poison from the thorn from your foot. Try not to move. John, if you and a couple of the men would hold Samuel still while I put the powder on his foot, I would greatly appreciate it."

Two more men knelt down and held Samuel still for Feyanna.

"Here we go, Samuel. This is going to be very painful," Feyanna said as she poured a good amount of the green powder over Samuel's foot.

Samuel hollered out and tried to move around, but the men held him still. The powder began changing color as the herbs started to make the poison drain from his foot. The liquid that flowed from the wound smelled horrible.

"That stinks," Samuel hollered. "Let me go!"

"No!,' John and the men replied as they tightened their hold on him.

Feyanna had mixed a red powder with some water into a paste and poured it into the wound. It sizzled as it made contact with the poison.

"This pain is horrible," Samuel yelled.

"Do you think you can save his foot?" the village woman asked.

"Oh, yes, but the next powder will probably make him pass out," Feyanna said as she sprinkled a brown powder over the wound.

Samuel gave a loud scream and then passed out.

"Now, I can get to work removing the thorn," Feyanna said. "It has moved deep within his foot, and I need to pull it out. Good thing he can't feel this."

Feyanna took a pair of pinchers from her bag, sprinkled a white powder on them, and then pushed their thin teeth into Samuel's foot. She felt the thorn, pinched the teeth of the tool together, and pulled it out with a mighty jerk. The thorn was all black and stank something horrible. She poured some of the paste over it, and it dissolved.

"It's out," Feyanna said as Samuel came to.

"Are you done? I don't think I can take anything more," Samuel said. "I know you are a black witch because a good witch wouldn't have caused so much pain. She needs to be hanged."

"Shut up, Samuel," the village woman said. "She just saved your foot from needing to be cut off."

"What?" Samuel said as he looked at his foot.

Samuel's foot was bleeding some, but the stink was gone, and it had almost returned to its normal size.

"It doesn't hurt like it did, and it doesn't stink anymore," Samuel said.

"You will need to stay off your foot for about ten days. You can use the outhouse only. You will need to stay sitting down and lying down so the medicine can heal the wound," Feyanna said as she placed a bandage with a white paste on it around Samuel's foot. "Swallow this."

Feyanna handed a mug of medicine to Samuel.

Samuel held the mug for a minute then decided to drink it. "It's bitter."

"Drink all of it, you old man," the village woman said. "All of it."

Samuel finished the liquid and handed the mug back to Feyanna.

"Is there anyone here who can take care of Samuel for the next ten days? I'll come by twice a day to change his bandages and give him more medicine," Feyanna explained.

"I'll see to him. I'm his sister, Claricia," Claricia said. "He can stay with me. And, you will not be rude and grumpy, old man."

"Very well, and thank you, Claricia," Feyanna said as she packed her things back into the basket and stood up. "Men, will you please take Samuel to Claricia's cottage? Be sure to come get me if anything changes and if anyone else needs me. I am here to care for everyone."

The village men took Samuel to his sister's cottage and she got him settled.

"That was amazing," John said. "We are fortunate to have you here. Jandor, I have a cow that is getting ready to calf. Would you take a look at her? She seems a bit off her feed."

"Of course. Lead the way," Jandor replied. "I'll get home later, Feyanna."

"Miss Feyanna," a quiet voice was heard to say. "Could you take a look at my girl? She seems to be having trouble hearing me?"

Of course," Feyanna said as the woman stepped over to her with her child. "How old are you?" Feyanna asked the girl.

The girl looked at her and didn't say a word.

"Can you hear me?" Feyanna asked.

The girl still didn't say a word.

Feyanna had an idea.

"You are her mother?" Feyanna asked.

"No. I am her sister. Our mother is away working in the fields planting crops for the season," the young woman replied. "I am Lisell."

"Lisell, would you please walk across the road?" Feyanna asked.

"I need to tell my sister what you're saying," Lisell replied.

"Please, do as I ask," Feyanna said.

Lisell walked across the road, and Feyanna turned the girl so her back was to her sister.

"You can hear everything just fine, can't you?" Feyanna asked.

"I most certainly can," the girl replied.

"Why don't you answer your sister?" Feyanna asked.

"I don't like her. She's mean and yells a lot at us," the girl replied.

"What is your name?" Feyanna asked.

"I am Sylvianna," the girl said.

"Are you older than your sister?" Feyanna asked.

"Yes, I am. Two years older," Sylvianna said. "Why do you ask?"

"Tell me the name of the seven sisters?" Feyanna asked.

"They are known as the Pleiades," Sylvianna replied.

"How often do you see the flying discs in the sky?'

"All the time," Sylvianna said. "You see them too?"

"I do," Feyanna said. "Tell me what else you see."

"I see Spirits all the time," Sylvianna replied. "They just won't leave me alone. That's why I don't say anything. I want them to leave me alone."

"Hold my hand, and I'll ask for help right now," Feyanna said as she reached out for Sylvianna's hands.

Sylvianna held hands with Feyanna as Feyanna said, "White Light, I ask that you surround and protect this beautiful child who has been gifted with The White Light from the Divine. Keep her safe from harm as she learns of your ways."

Sylvianna looked at Feyanna and smiled. "I feel so much better. Thank you."

"Come to my cottage in the forest tomorrow, and I will begin to teach you the ways of The White Light. You are safe for now. How old are you?"

"I am sixteen years old," Sylvianna said as her sister walked over.

"What is going on over here?" Liseell asked.

"Your older sister, Sylvianna, is going to come to me to learn the ways of healing. Be kind to her," Feyanna said rather sternly. "She does not have a hearing problem. She has heard every word you've said to her."

"You have been mean and hateful to me," Sylvianna said. "Stop it."

Lisell looked at her sister and didn't know what to say.

"Well, are you going to stop being so mean to all of us?" Sylvianna asked.

"I, ah, why, yes, I will stop being so hateful," Lisell said. "I thought you couldn't hear anything."

"I can hear quite well. I just don't like being yelled at and called such horrible names," Sylvianna replied.

"I will try to be kinder towards everyone," Lisell said. "Let's go get our little brother and sister and get supper started. Our mother will be home soon, and she will need food and rest."

Sylvianna turned to Feyanna and said, "Thank you so much for everything. I will come by soon."

The girls left, and Feyanna set out for her cottage home. Jandor wasn't home yet, so Feyanna started to make a stew from the chicken she had been paid for taking care of Samuel's foot. She cleaned the chicken and put it in a separate pot, set to simmer. She cleaned and placed potatoes, turnips, carrots, garlic, and onions in another pot to simmer. She took her healing basket into the workshop and replaced the herbs she had used.

It was full onto night when Jandor came through the door. Goldie and George were already settled for the night. Feyanna had just put the chicken meat into the vegetable pot and was adding herbs.

"That smells fantastic," Jandor said as he walked into the workshop and set his things on the workbench.

"How was the cow?" Feyanna asked as she worked at the cook stove. She was making biscuits.

"That cow decided to give birth to twins, just like Aaron's did," Jandor replied. "The farmer was so surprised he fell to the floor in shock. It was a bull and a cow. The family was thrilled, and the mama cow seemed happy to be rid of the calves."

"You seem to have a way with the twin thing," Feyanna said as she placed the biscuits in the space below the cook stove. "These should be ready in about ten minutes."

"As always, everything smells great," Jandor replied. "I cleaned up at the farmer's place. I'll get some water from the well for the cottage. Be right back."

The stew and biscuits were on the table as soon as Jandor finished replenishing the cottage water buckets.

"Where'd the chicken come from?" Jandor asked.

"It was from Samuel's flock," Feyanna said. "His sister said it was in thanks for taking care of her brother's foot."

"I like the way folks think around here," Jandor said. "The farmer said his children would be by tomorrow with milk, butter, and eggs."

"I do like the sound of that," Feyanna said. "Let's eat."

Feyanna and Jandor finished supper and settled in for the night. The dragons left the village alone that night. Penny kept watch over everyone. The night was quiet.

Just as the sun rose the next morning, Jandor was awakened by a voice calling his name. He looked around, didn't see anyone, and tried to fall asleep.

A minute later, he heard his name again. This time, Jandor got out of bed, put his robe on and walked into the main room of the cottage home. Goldie was just waking up, and George was staring at Jandor.

"George, why are you staring at me?" Jandor asked as he walked over to George.

George raised a wing in greeting.

"Who keeps calling my name?" Jandor asked as he looked around.

All was silent. Goldie was awake now and walked over to the door. "Would you please open the door, Jandor?"

Jandor opened the door, and Goldie walked outside.

"You're free to go fly about, George," Jandor said as he opened the door.

George flew out the door with a squawk of thanks.

"You're welcome, both of you," Jandor said as he closed the door. "I guess I'll get the cookfire going. Looks like I'm not going to get any more sleep."

"Jandor," the voice said.

"Who are you, and why are you calling out to me?" Jandor said.

Penny appeared in the window, and Jandor walked outside. "What's going on?"

"Do not answer them. They are evil," Penny warned.

"That voice woke me up this morning. What the hell is going on?" Jandor hollered.

"The Dark Forces are now aware of you and Feyanna and the powers you hold," Penny said. "The Divine has sent me to teach you how to add a stronger level of protection to yourselves. Here's Feyanna now."

"Holy cow, Jandor," Feyanna said as she yawned. "What's all the hollering about?"

"Penny here has been telling me that the voice that woke me up this morning is of The Dark Forces. They know about us now."

"I'd be hollering, too," Feyanna said.

"Penny is going to teach us how to add a stronger layer of protection to keep us safe," Jandor explained.

"Can we do it after breakfast?" Feyanna asked. "I'm starving."

"Me, too," Jandor said. "Can we eat first, Penny?"

"Yes, indeed," Penny replied. "I'll be right out here keeping you safe. Enjoy your breakfast."

"Thanks," Jandor said as he and Feyanna went back inside and prepared breakfast.

"Never a quiet moment for us," Feyanna said as they ate.

"I agree," Jandor said. "I get the feeling that a whole lot more is about to happen to us."

"I just had that feeling, too," Feyanna said. "We've barely settled in here, and now, more Magic and all."

"I think we'll always have more of The Magic happening to us," Jandor said as he drank his tea. "This tea is delicious. Have you been creating new recipes?"

"Why, yes, I have," Feyanna said as she raised her mug to Jandor. "Thanks for noticing."

"Let's tidy things and get back to Penny," Jandor suggested.

A short time later, Feyanna and Jandor joined Penny under the big oak tree near the meadow.

"We are ready for your instructions," Feyanna said.

"Good. Let's get started," Penny replied. "Know that The White Light will always protect your spirit."

"What you're trying to tell us is that we may die," Jandor said.

"That is correct," Penny said. "But only your physical body. Your spirit is always protected by The Divine."

"Great to know," Feyanna said, looking at Jandor. "I really don't want my physical body to die any time soon."

"Same here," Jandor said as they looked at Penny.

"That's why I'm here," Penny replied. "First, you've already chosen to walk in The White Light and protect yourself every day as you first learned. You've called out for help as well. Good work. Now, The Divine has asked us, my fellow dragons, to assist you in staying alive."

"Your fellow dragons?" Jandor asked.

"Dragons are going to help protect us?" Feyanna asked.

"Yes, in a word," Penny replied, smiling at them.

"You are glowing dark purple, Miss Penny," Jandor said as he watched her.

"Must mean she's quite happy,' Feyanna said.

"It does, indeed," Penny replied. "Good observation, Jandor. You don't want to see me turn red. Red means I'm furious. Red usually signals a wrath of fire is about to be seen."

"Now, that's good to know," Feyanna said, laughing with Jandor.

Penny smiled and winked at them with her long purple eyelashes. This made everyone laugh.

"Cute, Miss Penny," Jandor said.

"I try," Penny said. "Now, please stand next to each other and repeat after me: I call upon the White Light Paladins to help me at this time."

"I call upon The White Light Paladins to help me at this time," Feyanna and Jandor said.

A bright white flash took over the meadow, and six warriors appeared in full silver and white garb. Each one of them had a bright blue crystalline sword hanging at their side. They bowed to Penny and walked over to Jandor and Feyanna.

"Oh, my," Feyanna said in a hushed voice.

"Thank you all for appearing," Penny said as she bowed her head.

Jandor and Feyanna bowed as well.

"You look splendid," Penny said.

"We are here as you requested," one of them replied. "I am known as Cryton. Miss Penny asked us to show ourselves to you and explain how we can be of assistance."

"Feyanna and I appreciate you answering the call," Jandor said.

"All you have to do is call out for us," Cryton said. "Just as you did. There are as many of us as needed for any particular battle. We will work hard to help you vanquish whatever The Dark Forces attack you with."

"That sounds like very bad trouble," Jandor replied.

"If you're calling upon us, it usually is very deep trouble," Cryton said.

"I hope we never have to call upon your help," Feyanna said, looking a bit scared.

"Feyanna, do not be frightened," Penny said. "There will always be the struggle between good and evil. You and Jandor have chosen to walk in the good energy. We protect our own."

"And we thank you all for this," Jandor said, putting an arm around Feyanna. "We will be alright."

"All these changes since we met have left me a bit rattled," Feyanna said to Jandor. "So much in such a little bit of time. We battled evil forces just to get to the edge of the lake, where we met a dragon. Penny led us to Middle Earth, which is beautiful. But the poisoning of the great trees in The Forest of Garanthowen was horrible. I'm glad we had Penny to help save the forest and Dyantonadium."

"Feyanna, you and Jandor have experienced a great deal in a very short amount of time," Cryton said. "We have been watching you, and you both have done quite well. Now, The Divine wants you to know that you have more helpers to keep you safe."

"We do have Miss Penny," Feyanna said. "She is wonderful."

"She is indeed," Cryton said, smiling at Penny.

"And, now, we have The White Light Paladin to add to our troops," Penny said.

"I like the way you said that," Jandor replied. "It feels right."

"Yes, it does," Feyanna said. "It does make me feel better protected."

"Good," Penny said.

"If I may," Feyanna said, "Your swords are magnificent. Just like all of the crystals in The Crystals Caves."

Cryton walked over to Feyanna and handed her his sword. "Please, hold onto it for a minute."

Feyanna took the sword from Cryton, and as soon as she touched it, the crystals began to pulse and hum.

"That is amazing," Feyanna said. "Jandor, look at this."

"I am," Jandor said. "It looks incredible."

"Please, Jandor, hold my sword for a minute," a second White Light Paladin said. "I am known as Brakendor."

"Thank you, Brakendor," Jandor said as he accepted the sword. "It does feel incredible."

They stood there for what seemed a long while before the swords quieted, and Jandor and Feyanna gave them back to their owners.

"Absolutely fantastic," Penny said. "I can feel their energy as well. Thank you for sharing the Magic of your swords with Feyanna and Jandor."

"Many thanks, indeed," Feyanna said. "I feel much better about all this good versus evil stuff."

"Same here," Jandor said.

"It's time for us to leave," Cryton said. "Call upon us anytime you are in need. We will be here in an instant."

"Call upon us if you have any questions as well," Brakenfor added. "We'll know if your call is for help or information."

"Thanks so much for all of this," Jandor said. "We greatly appreciate you and The White Light Paladins for being here for us. Thanks to The Divine for this gift."

The White Light Paladins vanished instantly. Feyanna, Jandor, and Penny were silent for a bit.

"Well, that was amazing for sure," Feyanna said as they walked back toward the cottage home.

"There's more I need to tell you," Penny said. "You both have been working hard at learning about your Gifts and how to use them. It's now time for a change. You are staying right here. No more moving for many years. However, The Divine needs one more thing from you both. You will be made aware of this in short time. No worries. You will still be you. All good changes are coming along. Now, I do believe Feyanna has a new student to begin teaching about herbal remedies. Then, you need to visit Samuel. Jandor will be going into the village for a while. So, off to work, both of you."

"I guess we know who's in charge around here," Jandor said.

"Indeed we do," Penny replied as she took to the air. "More about the dragons later."

Feyanna and Jandor looked at each other, then just nodded their heads. Dragons, indeed!

"Well, here comes Sylvianna for her first lesson," Feyanna said as she waved to the girl.

"I'll go into the village and offer my services should anyone need them," Jandor said as he went inside to gather his things.

Feyanna spent a couple of hours with Sylvianna, and Jandor helped a couple of folks in the village. Sylvianna was leaving as Jandor returned home.

"I'm off to Samuel's to change his bandages. I'll be home for lunch in just a bit," Feyanna said. "How was the village?"

"I'll fix lunch for us," Jandor said. "The villagers are eager for our help. More after you get back."

Feyanna was at Samuel's cottage in just a few minutes.

"Good day, Miss Feyanna," Claricia greeted Feyanna as she arrived.

"Good day to you, Miss Claricia. How's Samuel?" Feyanna said as she stepped into the cottage. "This is a very pleasant home you have."

"Thank you," Claricia said. "Samuel, Miss Feyanna is here to change your bandages."

"Good day, Miss Feyanna," Samuel said. "My foot is feeling so much better. I'm truly sorry for the way I behaved yesterday."

"Thank you for the apology. I accept it," Feyanna said as she uncovered Samuel's foot and looked at the bandage. "It hasn't bled much."

"I changed the bandage last night," Claricia said. "It was quite messy. I put the salve on it just like you showed me."

"You have done a good job," Feyanna said as she removed the soiled bandage. "The swelling is almost completely gone. Can you feel my touch, Samuel?"

"Yes, I can. It tickles," Samuel said as he laughed.

"That is an excellent sign," Feyanna said as she put a different type of salve on his wound. "It means your foot should heal completely as long as you follow my instructions."

"Oh, I will," Samuel said. "I have asked the bootmaker to make me a new pair of boots that are sturdy and strong."

"And he said he will come by next week to measure your feet," Claricia added. "I will be doing some sewing for his family to pay for the boots."

"That is a good barter," Feyanna said as she stood up and gathered her things. "Samuel, keep following my rules, and you should be back walking tall and pain-free in a couple of weeks."

"Oh, he will," Claricia said. "I'll make sure of that."

"You old hag," Samuel said, winking at Feyanna.

"You old coot," Claricia replied. "Miss Feyanna, I'll change Samuel's bandages if you want me to."

"I like that idea," Feyanna said. "I'll come by for the next three days, and if it looks like it's closing up, I'll show you what to do. I'll bring extra bandages and salves with me then. Thank you for the offer. I do appreciate it. I'll see you after supper."

"Thank you," Samuel said as Feyanna left the cottage.

"Well, how was Samuel?" Jandor asked a few minutes later when Feyanna walked into the cottage home.

"He is in a much better place," Feyanna said as she walked through to the workshop and put her basket on the bench. "Pain can make you angry."

"I hear that," Jandor said. "Lunch is ready."

"This looks really good," Feyanna said. "Leftover stew and you made some bread. Red berries?

"Yes, indeed," Jandor replied as they ate. "One of the village children gave them to me for fixing her small cart. The wheel had fallen off. I fashioned a new screw to hold it in place. She was very happy."

Feyanna and Jandor spent the afternoon in the workshop. Jandor made some potions one of the villagers had asked for, and Feyanna blended herbal remedies to replenish the ones that were low in supply. A knock on the door brought them back to the day.

"Well, hello there," Jandor said when he found two children at the door. "How are the baby calves?"

"Oh, they're very happy," the boy said. "My father keeps their stall filled with sweet grass and a bucket of water for the mother."

"Those babies drink her milk all the time," the girl said. "I don't think they'll ever get enough."

"Oh, they will," Jandor said, smiling. "What have you here?"

"My mother sent you some eggs, milk, and butter to say thank you for helping our father with the calves."

"That is quite generous of your mother," Jandor said as he handed the food to Feyanna. "This here is Feyanna. She's my friend and a healer."

"Thank you for these beautiful things," Feyanna said as she went across to the kitchen area and put them away.

"Oh," the boy said. "My father wanted you to know that there is a special place by the shores of Avalon that has ice on it all year long. Our mother said to tell you that if you keep the ice on a bed of straw and put the food on it, the food will last a long while. Father said to show you where it is."

"I like the sound of that," Jandor said. "Feyanna, are you coming with us?"

"I most certainly am," Feyanna said as they walked into the forest.

The lake was nearby, and the children showed Feyanna and Jandor the ice lagoon. It was well hidden in a small depression in the ground. Jandor had brought two buckets with him to hold the ice.

"This place is beautiful, and you can see Avalon from here," Feyanna said.

"I love the Lake of Avalon. It is so beautiful and fun to play in on a hot day," the girl said.

"Our mother says the ice lagoon is made of magic," the boy said.

"I agree with your mother," Feyanna said. "We thank The Magic and Avalon for these gifts."

"Why do you say that?" the girl asked.

"We should always say thank you to The Magic and the Earth for the things that we are given. It is a sign of respect," Feyanna explained.

"Let's get back to the cottage home," Jandor said. "I'm sure your father will be looking for you."

They walked back to Feyanna and Jandor's cottage home. Jandor gave the boy a potion to help the mother cow stay strong and produce lots of milk for the twin calves. They said goodbye and were quickly on their way.

"I have the perfect place for the ice," Jandor and Feyanna said at the same time. Then laughed.

"Let's set this up," Jandor said. "I have some rocks to line the space."

"I'll gather some straw I saw in the meadow," Feyanna said. "I'll be right back.

When Feyanna returned, Jandor had fashioned a wood cabinet lined with rocks that sat back into a depression in the earthen wall in the workshop. They put the straw around the rocks and then placed the chunks of ice on the straw.

"This looks great," Jandor said.

Feyanna put the butter, milk, eggs, and leftover stew inside. Then, she removed the food and put more straw on the ice, placing the food on the straw.

"Great idea," Jandor said, watching her. "This way, the food won't freeze."

"That's what I was thinking," Feyanna said. "We'll have to figure out how often we need to replace the ice. I don't mind walking to the ice lagoon. It's a beautiful and peaceful walk."

"I guess we'll have to take turns then," Jandor said. "How about I make stew pastries for supper? You can make a fruit dessert."

"I like that idea," Feyanna said as they got busy preparing their evening meal.

"This was a great idea," Feyanna said as they sat back after finishing their meal.

"I know this probably sounds silly, but I'm really tired," Jandor said, yawning.

"We were rudely woken up at sunrise," Feyanna said as she cleared the table.

"I'm gonna go to bed," Jandor said, yawning again.

"I am, too," Feyanna said. "As soon as I finish cleaning up. Sleep well. White Light, I ask that you protect us from The Dark Forces as we sleep and for always,"

"Thanks be to The White Light," Jandor said as he walked back to his room.

"I see you two are ready for the night," Feyanna said as she closed the cottage home. "Sleep well, my friends."

Goldie winked at her, and George raised a wing. Feyanna took her candle to her room, changed into her nightshirt, blew out the candle, and fell asleep as soon as she lay down. It had been a very busy day.

It was somewhere in the middle of the night that Jandor and Feyanna were awakened.

"Jandor. Feyanna," Penny said. "It's me, Penny. We need you to wake up and go into the workshop."

Jandor woke up first. He looked around and said, "White Light surround and protect me."

As Feyanna woke up, she said the same thing.

"Jandor, it feels safe to do what the voice said," Feyanna said.

"I get the same feeling, too," Jandor said as they walked into the workshop.

The back wall was shimmering, and the entryway to The Crystal Cave appeared. Feyanna and Jandor looked at each other and then walked down the entryway together.

As they walked into The Crystal Cave, every crystal was humming and glowing like crazy.

"Something tells me there's a lot of Magic about to happen," Jandor said, looking all around.

"I think so," Feyanna said. "Look over there; that crystal looks like a tree."

"It does. And it's even green," Jandor said.

They spent a few minutes finding other crystals shaped in familiar forms. They even found one that looked like their cottage home in miniature.

The hallway to the right began to expand, and Penny appeared.

"Thanks for waking up so quickly," Penny said as she stepped into the room. "Good job calling for protection. You are fast learners."

"Miss Penny, it must be the middle of the night," Jandor said. "What's so important that it couldn't wait until morning?"

"You do look quite tired, Jandor," Penny replied. "I must say that I do what The Special Magic commands. And, they commanded that I awaken both of you and meet you here."

"We understand," Feyanna said. "What can we do for The Special Magic?"

Penny winked at both of them. "Watch."

Penny pointed to the middle of the room, and a mist began to swirl, just as it had before.

"Where are we going this time?" Jandor asked.

"Nowhere," Penny replied. "Just watch."

Three forms began to take shape. They finally materialized as ethereal forms: two men and a woman draped in deep blue, purple, and dark red robes. The mist faded away, and the room became quiet. Even the crystals hummed more quietly.

Penny turned and bowed at the robed ones.

"Penny, thank you for waking Feyanna and Jandor and directing them to The Crystal Caves," the figure in the dark red robe said.

"Caves? You mean there are more of these?" Jandor asked.

"Indeed," Penny replied. "The Special Magic creates as many as needed at any given time and place."

"That's truly Magic," Feyanna said.

"You have been called here by The Divine," the figure in the dark blue robe explained.

"We are in great need of your help," the figure in the purple robe said. "Please come and sit here."

Feyanna and Jandor walked into the middle of the room and sat in chairs made of crystals.

"These are magnificent," Feyanna said. "We thank the crystals for making these chairs for us."

The crystals flashed in a quick response.

The figure in the dark red robe floated over to them and became a solid being.

"Allow me to explain why we need your assistance," the being said. "We know Penny has told you about the creation of this time and place. Well done, Penny."

Penny nodded her head in response.

"You are aware that The Divine allowed humans to come to this planet a second time to learn and grow. For the most part, this is an ongoing lesson. However, in this place and time, in your home country as it were, the people are losing hope for the possibility of a safe place to live. There has been much turmoil among the rulers and much bloodshed. We expect bloodshed at some point, but it is getting out of control right now. The common folks are having a hard time growing crops, hunting, and supplying their families with the bare essentials. The ruling class keeps taking their harvest and animals and enslaving their women and children for their own greed.

"The Divine has agreed to keep the humans on the planet. However, The Divine is going to step in to make things a lot better. This is where you two come in."

"Step in?" Jandor asked. "Do you mean that The Divine, in all respect, is going to manipulate humankind to allow it to remain alive?"

The three figures looked at each other for a minute before responding.

"Yes," the figure in the purple robe answered.

"That's a direct answer," Feyanna said. "Has this ever happened before? Has The Divine, with great respect, ever intervened before to keep humankind alive?"

"Yes," the figure in the purple robe replied.

"Oh, I see. Thank you," Feyanna said.

"A great leader, or king as you call it, needs to come to rule here and lead the people into better times. The Divine is going to send a boy to your village to be cared for and nurtured into his young adult years to prepare him to become the king that is needed."

"Who will be his family?" Feyanna asked.

"The family known as the cart makers will accept the boy as their own should he arrive," the figure in the dark red robe explained.

"What do you mean, should he arrive?" Jandor said.

"That's where you come in, Jandor," the figure in the dark blue robe said.

Feyanna and Jandor looked at each other and then nodded at the figure.

"Please explain," Jandor asked.

"The Special Magic needs a teacher who knows the ways of The Special Magic to guide the boy. The Divine is asking you, Jandor, to be that guardian teacher," the figure in the purple robe explained.

"Me? Why me? I don't know that kind of Magic," Jandor said.

"We are aware of that," the figure in the purple robe replied. "You have been learning many things since you were born. You accepted your path and were taken to Middle Earth to continue learning. You have done well."

"Thank you, I guess," Jandor said a bit hesitantly.

"Jandor, The Divine has never left us on our own," Feyanna said. "The Special Magic brought us Miss Penny and gave us this splendid cottage home. And, this place. Jandor, this place is beyond words."

"All true," Jandor said. After some thought, Jandor replied, "I will be your guardian teacher for the boy, as asked. And I will need Feyanna with me."

"Of course, Feyanna will be with you always," the figure in the dark green robe replied.

"Thank you," Feyanna said.

"Jandor, arise and step into the purple circle," the figure in the purple robe said.

Jandor stepped into the purple circle as instructed. The crystals began to hum and pulse. Jandor was bathed in purple light for quite a long spell.

As the light faded, the figure in the purple robe said," Jandor, from this instant forward, you will be known as Merlin The Wizard."

Particles of shining silvery light covered Merlin for an instant, then vanished. Merlin's black hair now had silver streaks.

"Jandor! I mean Merlin, look at yourself," Feyanna said as a mirror appeared before him.

"Oh my god," Merlin said. "I am taller, and my hair is jet black with a silver streak going all the way to the back of my head. It's wavy, too."

"You do look different," Feyanna said in astonishment.

"What will the villagers say? They know me as Jandor," Merlin said.

"They will accept you as you are now. They will think it was Merlin who has helped them all the while," the figure in the dark green robe replied.

"Oh. Okay then," Merlin said. "Now what? What about Feyanna?"

"Feyanna will remain as she is," the figure in the dark green robe replied. "Feyanna, you will continue to be a healer. We will assist you from time to time. We thank you for accepting your Gift when you were just a wee child."

"I am honored to have been chosen," Feyanna said.

"This is splendid," Penny said. "Absolutely splendid."

The three figures smiled at Penny as the figure who had become human returned to the ethereal form.

"Penny, please give your gift to Merlin," the figure in the purple robe said.

"Indeed," Penny said as she reached down into the crystals on the floor and picked up a particular one.

Penny stood in front of Merlin and stretched her wing out to him.

"Merlin, please take this purple crystal dragon," Penny said. "It is a Gift from The Divine. Any time you need me, for anything, all you have to do is hold The Crystal Dragon up into the air. I will know you require my assistance and come to you immediately."

Merlin accepted The Crystal Dragon from Penny and said, "This is magnificent. Thank you to The Dive for this beautiful gift."

"It's purple just like you, Miss Penny," Feyanna said as Merlin handed it to her. "And, it's humming, too. The energy is wonderful."

Feyanna handed it back to Merlin.

"It is humming," Merlin said.

"The Divine thanks you both for accepting this request," the figure in the purple robe said. "It is time for us to move on."

Penny, Merlin, and Feyanna bowed to the three figures as they vanished in a swirl of purple mist.

The Crystal Cave was in utter silence for a while. Penny was the first to speak.

"Well, that was amazing," Penny said in a hushed voice.

"I agree," Feyanna whispered in response.

Merlin just nodded his head.

"It's time to go back to work," Penny said as she turned to walk back down the hall to her place.

"Penny?" Merlin said.

"Yes, Merlin," Penny said, smiling.

"Just what is my work now?" Merlin asked.

"Keep doing all that you usually do," Penny replied. "You will be given new information and skills as needed."

"Okay," Merlin replied.

"What is it, Jandor?" Feyanna asked as she placed her hand on his arm.

"Well," Merlin replied, "I'm a bit worried about being responsible for changing people's minds and all."

"I get it," Feyanna said. "I have that same worry myself. What I do know is that The Special Magic is with us, and Penny will guide us so we don't do too much harm."

"Is she right, Penny?" Merlin asked.

"She is to a point," Penny replied. "You own your actions and decisions. The Divine has sent special energies to assist you in making those decisions. However, the final actions are your own."

"I understand," Merlin replied. "I will take great care in making decisions that affect others."

"That's a good start," Penny added. "Sometimes, you will have to make split-second decisions. Sometimes, horrible things will happen if a decision is not made at that specific moment. You'll figure this out."

"I'll do my best," Merlin replied. "Oh, and Feyanna, it's Merlin now."

"I realized I called you Jandor right after I said it," Feyanna said. "I'll try to be more attentive to your new name."

"Thanks," Merlin replied. "I'll try to remember that Merlin is my new name."

"Time for sleep. Go back to your beds," Penny said. "I'll see you in the morning."

"Thanks, Penny," Feyanna said.

"Good night, Miss Penny," Merlin said as Penny disappeared around the bend in her hallway.

Feyanna and Merlin left The Crystal Cave without speaking. As soon as they emerged back into the workshop, the back wall returned to its earthen self. They walked through their cottage home and were in bed asleep in no time. Goldie and George had watched the whole thing and couldn't wait until sunrise. The village slept quietly that night. No dragons dared to fly near the place.

As Feyanna and Merlin walked into the main room the next morning, Merlin said, "Feyanna, I slept so well last night."

"Me, too," Feyanna said as she went into the workshop to gather breakfast things from the cold box.

"We must have been gone for hours," Merlin said as he started the cookfire.

"Now, Merlin, try to remember that when we are in The Magic, time here stands still," Feyanna reminded Merlin, laughing. "You seem to have a bit of trouble remembering that."

"I have you to remind me," Merlin said as Feyanna nudged him away from the cookfire so she could get their breakfast made. "That looks so yummy."

"I gathered the vegetables from the garden late yesterday and decided to make an egg and cheese pie with them. Put some of the red berry bread in a towel and place it here to warm up."

A short while later, Feyanna and Merlin were enjoying themselves as they ate breakfast.

"It's so wonderful to have butter, eggs, and cheese," Feyanna said.

"Oh, it is," Merlin replied. "I'll accept them in a barter any time."

"Well, I wonder if anything will happen today since you became Merlin last night," Feyanna was saying when they heard a knock on the door.

"I guess so," Merlin said as he walked over and opened the door.

A man about his age was standing there.

"Good day, sir," Merlin said.

"Good day, Merlin," the man replied. "I am Hamlen, the cart maker from the village. I noticed that you and Feyanna have to carry many things as you go about. I made this small hand cart for you for taking care of my little girl's cart yesterday."

"Oh, my," Feyanna said as she walked past the man and looked at the hand cart. "This is lovely."

"Why, Hamlen, that was very generous of you," Merlin said as they all looked at the cart.

"My little girl's cart gives her so much joy that when I learned it had broken and you fixed it, I decided you needed one, too. I was away fixing a wagon for a farmer north of the village yesterday," Hamlen explained.

"It was a pleasure to repair the cart for her," Merlin said, shaking hands with Hamlen. "She was so happy; she gave me a big hug as a thank you."

"Sarah is a sweetheart," Hamlen said. "She is a bright child and loves to help me with my work. She has learned a lot about cart making already, and she is only eight years old. She is going to work with me as I fashion a new kind of cart. I want to make one that is easy to hitch animals to so they can pull the carts. It has to be kind to the animal as well."

"I like that idea," Merlin said. "Maybe we should work on this together. I already have a few ideas about it."

"I would surely appreciate that," Hamlen replied. "I'll be home all day. Our home is the first one you see when you approach the village. It is a ways away from the others as we have a big garden and a few farm animals."

"I know the place," Feyanna said. "The flower gardens are beautiful."

"I'll pass that along to my wife," Hamlen said. "She and our two children are the gardeners. I do not know how to keep plants alive. Carts, I know."

"I hear you," Feyanna said, laughing. "Merlin is the man to help you with your idea. He's always thinking things up."

"She's got that right," Merlin said. "I'll stop by soon."

"I can't wait to use our little cart," Feyanna said. "I need to gather a bunch of things from the meadow today, and this beautiful gift will come in handy."

"Well, then, I'm glad I made it for you," Hamlen said. "I'll see you later, Merlin. Good day, Miss Feyanna."

"Good day to you and your family," Feyanna replied as Hamlen walked back down the path to the road.

Merlin looked at Feyanna for a minute.

"What are you thinking, Merlin?" Feyanna asked as they walked around with the cart.

"Did you ever get that feeling that you knew someone the first time you met, and you know you've never seen them before?" Merlin said.

"I know what you mean," Feyanna said as she watched Merlin. "Only one time, though."

"I swear I've met Hamlen before," Merlin said. "It seemed as if we've had that conversation before. I just can't quite make it out."

"Well, with all The Special Magic happening around here, I'm not surprised. And, as Miss Penny reminds us, we'll know about things as we need to."

"I know you're right about that," Merlin said. "Well, it's time for me to get to the workshop. Breakfast was delicious. Thanks."

"You are very welcome," Feyanna said as they walked back into their cottage home. "I need to tidy up around here and take our new little cart to gather flowers and plants. I have a lot of remedies to make."

"And I have a lot of new potions to fashion," Merlin replied.

They went about their day busy as always. As the evening settled in, Feyanna and Merlin sat outside, watching their world get ready to settle into night. George was flying low over the meadow, watching Goldie look for bugs. She was always ready to eat.

"I thoroughly enjoy watching those two," Feyanna said as George buzzed Goldie and Goldie chattered back at him.

"They are entertaining," Merlin said. "Look at the color of the sky. Must be close to sunset with all those gold and orange clouds."

"My mother used to say that the sun shined at its best with all the colors it made as it set," Feyanna said.

"I agree with that," Merlin said as he noticed something in the sky. "You see that?"

"What? Where?" Feyanna said as she looked for the object Merlin was pointing out to her.

"It's right above that patch of red flowers," Merlin said. "It looks quite large."

"I see it now," Feyanna said. "It looks like it's flying closer to us."

"It does," Merlin said as he stood up. "Look! Here it comes."

Feyanna stood up and watched with Merlin as the object flew right at them.

"Oh my god!" Merlin said. "It's a dragon. A huge dragon."

"Here it comes," Feyanna said as the dragon flew right at them.

It landed in the meadow and walked over to them.

"You are enormous," Feyanna said.

"And you're a black dragon," Merlin said.

"You are both correct," the dragon replied. "No worries. I won't kill you. Quite the opposite. I'm here to protect you."

"We have a dragon protector," Feyanna said. "And here she is."

Penny flew in and settled next to the black dragon.

"Did I not tell you to wait for me, Q? You're scaring these wonderful humans," Penny said, giving Q quite the look.

"You did," Q replied. "I didn't feel like waiting."

"Your name is Q?" Merlin asked.

"It is," Q said. "You are Merlin, and this lovely creature is Feyanna, the healer."

"I am," Feyanna said. "Nice to meet you, I think. Is Q okay, Penny?"

"Yes, he is," Penny replied. "Feyanna and Merlin, this is Q. He is a warrior dragon and has agreed to watch over you and the villagers."

"Nice to meet you," Merlin replied. "Do you ever kill people?"

"Good question," Q replied. "Only when my humans are in danger. Then, I go into full dragon mode."

"Do the villagers know about you?" Feyanna asked.

"They do," Q replied. "Most of them know I only fly overhead once in a while."

"Now, Q, you know perfectly well that the people of this place and those abroad are terribly afraid of dragons. Some of them hunt our kind to try to kill us. They've only succeeded a couple of times."

"What did you and your fellow dragons do about that?" Feyanna asked.

"We killed the ones who killed our kind," Q replied. "Most humans leave us alone. But, there's still a few who would rather kill us than leave us to ourselves."

"That's crazy," Feyanna said. "Dragons are of The Special Magic and are sent to places they are needed to make sure humankind carries on. I love dragons. I was rather thrilled when I met Miss Penny for the first time. And she's purple. Beautiful"

"Thank you, Feyanna," Penny replied.

"Q, you are as black as the night," Merlin said. "Is that so you can't be seen?"

"Yes, it is. Partly," Q replied. "The Warrior Dragons are all deep black. Our color doesn't change like Miss Penny's does. Have you seen her when her color changes?"

"No, not yet," Merlin said. "We would rather not see the red color ever."

"Miss Penny warned us about that color," Feyanna added.

"Good idea," Q said. "I've only seen her change into that bright red a few times. But I'm here to tell you the result was incredible. She completely destroyed a village of murderers once. Gone. Not a pebble to be found. She is a mighty dragon."

"We've gotten a hint of that," Merlin said, smiling at Penny.

"So, Q, where do you live?" Feyanna asked.

"I exist as Penny does in The Crystal Caves," Q replied. "When needed, I emerge through a tunnel into the forest and take flight. That's what I just did. I love to fly."

All of a sudden, Penny stood tall.

"Q," Penny said.

"I hear it," Q replied.

"What's wrong?" Merlin asked.

"There is a band of ruthless thieves coming along the road from the north. They'll be in the village in about an hour. Q, I do believe I may be changing color right now," Penny replied.

And she did. In a few minutes, Penny was bright red, and her eyes turned red as well.

"You are very angry," Q said. "Now, keep your fire under control until we get close to those thieves. Once we're at treetop level, we'll blast them."

"Oh, my," Feyanna said. "Do be careful."

"Why, thank you, Feyanna," Q replied.

"They won't have a second to wonder what hit them," Penny said. "They have been terrorizing the villages all along the north road, and it's time they were stopped."

"Do they have any innocents with them?" Feyanna asked.

Q and Penny were silent for a minute, then Q said, "They have a young boy they kidnapped a few weeks ago from a village. The villagers would not give them their crops, so the thieves killed the boy's family and took him with them to work as a slave. We'll make sure he doesn't get harmed."

Feyanna and Merlin looked at each other as Merlin said, "Bring the boy here when you are finished. I know just the family for him to grow and be safe in."

"We will," Penny said as she walked away from them and took flight.

"Nice meeting you both. Later," Q said as he followed Penny, and they banked north to meet up with the band of thieves.

"Well, how do you like that? We have another dragon protecting us," Feyanna said as they walked back into their cottage home and through to the workshop.

"I shouldn't be surprised, but I am," Merlin said. "I guess the more, the merrier. I am just getting used to Penny. And, now we have Q."

"I know how you feel," Feyanna said.

"Oh, Feyanna, I had a thought this afternoon while working with a candle. I was staring at the flame from the candle and suddenly had this idea," Merlin said.

"Well, what is it?" Feyanna asked as she stood next to Merlin by the workbench.

"As I watched the flame, I noticed one of the quartz crystals that was close to the candle was shining something fierce," Merlin explained. "I quenched the flame, and the crystal continued to glow for hours. So, I thought, what if we try a little experiment? We could set a bunch of the larger quartz crystals out in the sunlight all day to capture the sun's energy, then use them instead of candles for the evening. I'm not sure how long they would glow, but we can try different settings and times."

"I love the idea," Feyanna said. "We can use different types of crystals, too. I know that quartz has its own energy and all. We could charge different colored ones and see what happens. Then, we could use some of the other crystals that have some quartz and see how that works."

"Great ideas," Merlin said. "I'd feel safer using the crystals as light sources than the candles."

"I agree," Feyanna said. "And there wouldn't be so much soot on the ceiling and walls."

"That, too," Merlin said as he looked around the workspace. "I still can't figure out how I got that idea, though. One minute, I was working with a potion, and the next, I caught myself staring at the flame."

"I suspect it was The Special Magic," Feyanna was saying when she got all excited. "Oh my god, Merlin! If this works, we can tell the villagers about it. It will save them money, time, and worry. No more making candles for light. No more fires from the spilled flames and hot wax. This is great!"

Merlin laughed at Feyanna as she jumped around the place, all excited.

"You do get excited about your ideas for sure," Merlin said, laughing.

Feyanna stopped moving around and replied, "I guess I do."

They laughed for a bit as they gathered the quartz crystals and set them by the door.

"We'll put these outside first light," Merlin said. "I'll make a stand or something that holds them a few feet above the ground and place it in the meadow so the shade from the forest doesn't cover them."

"I have a dark-colored cloth to place them on. Darker colors absorb the sun's energy and may help the crystals absorb the energy as well," Feyanna said.

"Good thinking, Feyanna," Merlin said as he yawned. "I do believe it is past time to get some sleep. It's been an eventful day. We already have a busy day planned for tomorrow."

"I agree," Feyanna said. "You two ready for some rest?"

"I am for sure," Goldie said as she snuggled into her blanket.

"Me, too," George said as he winked at Feyanna and Merlin.

Feyanna and Merlin stared at George.

"Did he just talk to us?" Feyanna asked.

"I believe he did," Merlin said as he walked over to George. "Out with it, George. You can talk, can't you?"

"Why, yes, I can, Merlin," George said, laughing at Feyanna and Merlin.

"You've always been able to talk, haven't you," Feyanna said as she touched George's wing.

"Indeed, my Feyanna," George replied. "Your touch is so soothing and warm."

"So, you've understood everything from the instant you came into our lives back in Middle Earth," Merlin said.

"Guilty as charged," George said, making Goldie laugh.

"And you knew it," Feyanna said as she looked over at Goldie.

"Yup," Goldie replied, smiling.

"I, I don't have words for this," Feyanna said. "I shouldn't be surprised being in the Special Magic like we are, but I am."

"Holy shit!" Merlin said, just staring at George and Goldie for the longest time.

"It was a great surprise finding out that Goldie could talk," Feyanna said.

"I'm not even used to her yet," Merlin said. "And, now, George."

"Ah, Jandor, I mean Merlin, I'm getting the feeling that something rather spectacular is about to happen around here," Feyanna said.

Goldie and George nodded their heads.

"Good call, Feyanna," George said. "Good call."

"Okay, so let's think about this for a minute," Merlin said as he began to pace around the room. "We met Q. Magnificent Dragon for sure. Penny and Q told us about a plan of attack they have for right about now. Okay, with that. I met Hamlen, the cart maker, today. I felt like I already knew him even though I'd never met him as far as I know. The Magic is at work, for sure. And Penny and Q said an innocent boy would be protected from their attack on the band of thieves. They are bringing him here to us. I instantly knew that he would live with the cart maker's family when the dragons told me about him. It all felt right. Gotta be The Special Magic at work again. Now, George can talk. Holy shit!"

"Oh my god, Merlin," Feyanna said. "You two know about The Special Magic and everything, right?"

"Evey bit of it," Goldie and George replied.

"Merlin, I do believe this all has something to do with the visit we had by The Special Ones from The Divine. Remember what they said about a mission of sorts for us? About how The Divine, with all due respect, was giving humankind a second chance at existence? Well, I do believe that little boy is the one they were hinting at."

Merlin was silent for quite some time before he said, "I know you're right about this. All of it. Now what?"

"Well, how about the two of you get to bed," George suggested.

"Good idea, George," Merlin said. "Let's go Feyanna. I get the feeling tomorrow is going to be another incredible day."

"I do, too, "Feyanna replied.

"Time to sleep," George said as he settled on his perch. "I see Goldie is comfy."

Feyanna and Merlin laughed as they heard Goldie's gentle snoring.

"She does know how to get cozy," Merlin said.

Feyanna and Merlin walked down the hallway and into their rooms. They were sound asleep in an instant as The Special Magic wrapped them in soothing pink light. The village was safe thanks to Penny and Q. They had the little boy safe and sound in The Crystal Caves, sleeping in peace for the first time in a long, long time. Tomorrow, he would begin his new life.

It was shortly after sunrise, as Merlin and Feyanna were putting the crystals on the stand in the meadow, that Penny flew in. She settled close to them. As she bent her head down, the little bot slid down her neck and landed on the ground with a soft thud. He laughed and hugged Penny, then looked around and saw Feyanna and Merlin.

"Good Morning, Miss Penny," Merlin said. "And, you, young one."

"Good morning, Miss Penny," Feyanna said. "We see you have a passenger this morning."

"Good morning to you both," Penny replied. "I do indeed have a passenger. He's as light as a feather and has a great laugh."

"What might your name be?" Merlin asked as he held a hand out to the boy.

The boy shook hands with Merlin and replied," I am known as Quintan. My father named me after his father."

"A fine, strong name for sure," Feyanna said.

Quintan laughed as he looked over at Penny. She was winking at him. "I've never met a dragon before yesterday. The black one and Miss Penny were fierce fighters when they attacked the bad men. I was lifted off the ground and placed in a pile of hay away from them by a magical force. I watched as the dragons blew fire on the bad men, and they were instantly gone. It was scary and amazing. Miss Penny flew over to me and winked at me just like she is doing now. She has the longest eyelashes I've ever seen. And they're purple now. They were red last night."

"They are beautiful," Feyanna said as she winked at Penny. "Quintan, are you hungry?"

"No, thank you," Quintan replied. "Miss Penny had breakfast for me this morning. She said we were going on a short flight and would meet you both. And we have."

"You are well-spoken, Quintan," Merlin said. "Did your mother teach you these things?"

"She did," Quintan said as tears rolled down her cheeks. "The bad men killed my mother, father, and two sisters. They were bad, bad men. Then, they grabbed me and made me take care of them."

"I am so sorry," Feyanna said as she wrapped her arms around Quintan. He fell into her hug, and they stayed that way for a while.

Quintan eventually stepped back a bit and said," Thanks so much for the hug. I miss my mother."

"I understand," Merlin said. "Our mothers sure knew how to take care of us."

"Yes, they did," Quintan replied. "Miss Penny and the black dragon said I will be living with a new family close to you. When will I meet them?"

"Very soon, young one," Miss Penny replied. "The black dragon's name is Q."

"Well, that sounds just right for him," Quintan said. "It's a strong name, just like he is."

"I'll be sure to tell him you said that," Penny replied. "Now, let me introduce you to these two people. This here is Master Merlin, and this is Miss Feyanna."

"Nice to meet you," Quintan said.

"It's a pleasure to meet you," Merlin replied. "We were just setting these crystals out to collect the energy of the sun. I noticed one of them glowing in my workshop last night after it had been near a candle. I got the idea from a special source that they might be used to replace candles. So, Feyanna and I are trying this experiment to see if they can hold the sun's energy for a long while."

"You are really smart," Quintan said as he walked over and looked at the crystals. "This one looks like a fish."

Feyanna joined him and looked at the fish-shaped crystal. "It sure does," she replied. "And, it's blue like the water. It's already glowing brightly."

"Do you like to be on the water?" Merlin asked before he knew what he was saying.

"I do," Quintan replied. "My father took me fishing many times, and we had great fun. Mother was very happy when we came home with a lot of fish. We usually got soaking wet and dried some by the time we got home. Mother just laughed at us and made us clean up before coming into the house. She said she didn't want everything smelling like old fish."

This made everyone laugh.

"Well, it's time for me to get along," Penny said. "Now, Quintan, you can talk to Feyanna and Merlin about Q and I, but no one else. Remember, most people are afraid of dragons. You know the truth about that, too."

"I remember, Miss Penny," Quintan said. "Thanks for taking such great care of me. And Q, too. I will see you again, right?"

"Oh, yes, you will," Penny replied. "Merlin will teach you many things, including how to call for us. You are safe now, young one. Enjoy your childhood."

"I will," Quintan said as Penny began to take to the air. "Thanks again."

Penny was gone in a minute, and Quintan turned and looked at Merlin and Feyanna and asked, "Now what?"

"Well, I do believe we should go to the cart maker's home. They are going to be your new family. They are a fine family, and you will be safe there," Merlin replied.

"Is Miss Feyanna coming with us?" Quintan asked.

"If you want me to," Feyanna replied.

"I do, please," Quintan said, looking a bit afraid.

"There is nothing to be afraid of," Merlin said as they set out. "Hamlen is a good man, and his family is well respected and liked here. Hamlen made the cart Feyanna is using as a token of his respect for me when I fixed his little girl's cart. Hamlen was away, and she was not happy. Her name is Sarah, and she's eight years old. She has a sister, Margaret, who is ten years old."

"I'm eight years old, too," Quintan said.

"They have a farm with animals and a big garden," Feyanna added. "I'm sure you'll find lots to learn and have lots of fun with them. Merlin and I wouldn't let you join a family unless we knew you'd be well taken care of."

"Thanks for that," Quintan said. "This is a beautiful place. My home didn't have a lot of trees. And it was very cold in the winter. Is it cold here?"

"Well, I don't really know," Feyanna replied. "We're just getting settled here, too. The three of us are new here. I have met some of the villagers, and they are nice and kind."

"Good," Quintan said. "Some of the people that lived near us were mean and nasty. They took our apples and stole some of our chickens, too."

"That was not nice," Merlin said. "I don't think that will happen here. We can always ask Hamlen about that. There's their farm, now."

Merlin pointed to the big fence that surrounded the garden and home. Hamlen looked up from his work and saw the three of them approaching. He hollered out to his family, and they came along the fence to meet Merlin, Feyanna, and Quintan.

"Good day, Merlin," Hamlen said as he and Merlin shook hands. "This is my wife, Glendianna. You know Sarah. This is her older sister Margaret."

"Nice to meet all of you," Merlin said. "How's your cart working, Sarah?"

"On, wonderfully, thank you for fixing it," Sarah said.

"This is my partner, Feyanna. I think you know of her from the village," Merlin said.

"Yes, I know about the whole foot thing," Glendianna said, laughing. "You really put that old man in his place. I hear his foot is healing well."

"Thank you," Feyanna said, laughing with everyone. "He was a feisty one for sure. His sister says he is doing everything I told him to. She is a force to be reckoned with."

"And, who is this fine-looking young man?" Hamlen asked

"This here is Quintan," Merlin said. "He has come to us from a place far north of here. His family was killed in a raid by thieves. The thieves have been taken care of. He is in need of a loving home, and Feyanna and I thought of you straight away."

Hamlen looked over at Glendianna, who smiled at him.

"Quintan, it is a pleasure meeting you," Hamlen said as he placed his hand on Quintan's shoulder. "Would you like to take a look around and see if we might be a good fit for you?"

"I would, indeed," Quintan said. "Thank you."

Quintan was lifted over the garden fence and set down next to Sarah.

"Quintan, let's go look at the cows and chickens," Sarah said. "They can be quite funny sometimes."

"We can pick some vegetables after that," Margaret said as she joined them.

As they ran through the garden, Merlin said, "Looks like Quintan has found a new family."

"Did he see everything?" Glendianna asked.

"Yes, unfortunately, he did," Feyanna said. "I've started him on some herbal remedies to help with the nightmares I know he'll have. Here they are. I wrote down when to give them to him. I suspect he's going to need a lot of hugs and love for quite a while. The remedies will not make him forget; just calm him when he remembers."

"I agree," Hamlen said as he put his arm around his wife. "We lost our son a few weeks after he was born. He was frail and got sick. He's with the angels now. Quintan's coming here is an answer to our prayers. My wife has not been able to bear children since Sarah was born. This is truly a blessing."

"We thank the gods and goddesses," Glendianna said, bowing her head.

"Indeed," Feyanna said, doing the same thing.

"It looks like Sarah has a twin brother now," Merlin said, laughing with everyone as the kids came running back to the garden, laughing and carrying on.

"You're right. It seems so," Glendianna said.

"Well, did you take a look at the farm animals?" Feyanna asked.

"We did," Quintan replied. "The chickens can be very noisy, and the cows just kind of stand there."

"Well, Quintan, what do you think about this farm and everyone here? Do you think you could feel happy and safe here?" Merlin asked.

Quintan took his time looking over the farm and then looking at each member of Hamlen's family.

Quintan had tears in his eyes as he spoke. "I know I could be safe and happy here. Thing is, do they want me to be a part of your family?"

"Well, girls, what do you say?" Hamlen asked his daughters.

"YES!!!" they both yelled and grabbed onto Quintan and hugged him for a long while.

"I guess that answers that question," Feyanna said.

"Come on down to the house, and we'll have something cold to drink," Hamlen said.

They settled around a table outside the home and talked and made plans for Quintan's future.

"Oh, Merlin, here are the plans for that wagon I was telling you about," Hamlen said.

Merlin looked at the plans and then asked for a writing tool. He spent a few minutes adding things to the diagram before showing it to Hamlen.

"What do you think?" Merlin asked.

Hamlen spent a minute looking at what Merlin had done, then said, "This is exactly what it was missing. That extra harness and support for the yoke will ease the strain on the ox and horses," Hamlen said.

"Glad it looks like it will work," Merlin said.

"Men and their toys," Glendianna said. "Always thinking up one thing or another."

"Well, it's about time I returned to my cottage home and my chores," Feyanna said. "I need some ice from the lagoon, too."

"What lagoon?" Hamlen said.

"You mean you don't know about the ice lagoon on Avalon?" Merlin replied.

"No," Hamlen and Glendianna answered.

Feyanna looked at Merlin and then was quiet for a minute.

"It's okay, Merlin," Feyanna said. "They can keep the secret as well as the kids. Just got the okay from Them."

"There is a small ice lagoon back in the forest just off the shore of the Lake of Avalon," Merlin said. "The ice is there year-round. I'll show you how to build a cold box while Feyanna and the kids get the ice."

Feyanna gathered the three children and took her hand cart to the lagoon.

"Now, you three, you are not to tell anyone about this place," Feyanna said.

"The Magic put it here," Sarah said.

"How do you know that?" Feyanna asked as they broke off chunks of ice and put them in the hand cart.

"I've always known about The Magic," Sarah said. "I talk with the faeries and spirits all the time."

There was a soft flash of yellow light to confirm what Sarah had said.

"She thinks she can see faeries," Margaret said.

"She can," Feyanna replied, pointing to three little faeries that were watching them. "And, so can you if you'd just let yourself believe."

Margaret thought about this for a minute, then decided to believe in The Magic.

"Oh my god!" she yelled. "There are three faeries watching us. They're beautiful and so tiny. I always thought I was just daydreaming when I saw them. They're really real?"

"Yes, they are," Sarah said as she waved to them. "I told you so. Now, do you believe me?"

"I do believe you," Margaret said. "I'm sorry I was mean to you about them."

Quintan was waving at them, too.

"Quintan, can you see them, too?" Margaret asked.

"Yes, I can," Quintan replied. "Their wings are so shiny."

"Faeries are extraordinary creatures," Feyanna said as she bowed to them. "They protect the entrances between the earth and the world of The Magic. Always respect them."

"We will," the three children said all together.

They finished gathering ice chunks and went back to the farm. Hamlen and Merlin were just finishing the cold box, and Glendianna had gathered rocks and straw for it.

"We're here," Sarah said as she ran ahead of Feyanna. "We got a bunch of ice."

"We made a box for the ice," Hamlen said. "Now, what would be the best place to keep it?"

"I would think against the earth," Glendianna said. "Our home sets into a little rise, so maybe the wall between the back door and the kitchen would work."

"Let's take a look," Merlin said. "I'll bring the tools."

Margaret took a long look and said," Father, I do believe the box will fit right here. The space just needs to be dug out a little."

Glendianna laughed as she said, "Margaret, you never cease to surprise me. One would think you've had years of learning about building and all."

"She is perfectly right," Merlin said. "Good eye, Margaret. Keep thinking like that, and you'll do well in life."

It took Hamlen and Merlin about ten minutes to create the perfect space for the cold box. It fit perfectly. The children brought the cart with the ice chunks, and the straw was layered with the ice. Glendianna brought the food over and placed it into the box.

"This is splendid," Glendianna said. "Now, the food won't spoil so fast."

"We just put ours together a couple of days ago," Feyanna said. "We're still figuring out how long the ice will last and how to make sure the food doesn't freeze."

"We'll have to compare notes," Glendianna said.

"Well, it really is time I got going," Feyanna said. "I'll go check on Samuel while I here. Then home to make more remedies."

Me, too," Merlin said. "Always lots to do in the workshop. Quintan, you okay with staying here?"

"Of course," Quintan replied. "It's home now."

Hugs were shared, and Feyanna went into the village, and Merlin went back to their cottage home. Penny and Q had watched everything and were very pleased with the results.

"That poor boy," Penny said. "He's been through so much at such a young age."

"I know, Penny," Q said. "It's those hard things that will help him be a compassionate man. The Divine needs a compassionate human to handle what's ahead for that little boy as he grows into manhood."

"I suppose so," Penny said. "Now, Q, about those rouge dragons. What are we going to do about them?"

"I fear a battle with them may be on the near horizon," Q replied, his black scales beginning to shine ever so brightly.

"Now, Q, calm down," Penny said as she reached out a wing and touched his wing. "You know how this topic gets you all riled up. Save your energy for when it's needed."

"Yes, Miss Penny," Q replied. "You know me so well.

"We have been together quite a long while," Penny said.

"This is going to be a long adventure with Quintan, isn't it?" Q asked, looking off into space.

"I fear it is," Penny replied. "And the life of this planet will hinge on that outcome."

"Well, at least we have some time before it all comes to a head," Q replied. "Time for some food and rest."

"Yes, indeed," Penny said.

It was going to be quite the adventure for all of them, humans and dragons alike.

CHAPTER 14

Quintan blended into his new family over the rest of the summer and fall as if he had always been there. He started calling the farm the Cart Farm and soon, the whole village was calling it that. Feyanna was learning about new plants and creating new remedies. Merlin was busy with potions that helped the villagers and their animals and crops. The crops looked to be the biggest harvest ever known in these parts.

Hamlen and Merlin had become fast friends, and a day didn't go by that they didn't at least talk with each other, even if only to greet each other in passing.

Samuel's foot healed splendidly, and he told everyone he knew that Feyanna was a miracle healer. He even brought a chicken over every few weeks just to say thanks. Feyanna asked if he could bring a live one over one time, and he showed up with four. Merlin, Hamlen, and Samuel fashioned a chicken coop with sturdy fencing that went deep into the ground. Merlin surprised Feyanna and made it look like a little barn. She was tickled, and all the villagers came by to have a look.

Q and Penny were always close by. They stopped in after sunset most days to check up on Merlin, Feyanna, and Quintan, of course.

Merlin's crystal idea had worked out after a bit more experimenting. Feyanna and Merlin asked Penny if they could visit The Crystal Caves to gather crystals for this use. And, right in front of them, a whole pile of different colored crystals appeared. It was a huge pile, and they thanked The Divine and Mother Earth for this gift. Merlin made more stands for the new crystals. They tried the new crystal lights for a few weeks, then decided to show the villagers how they worked.

So, one late afternoon in mid-autumn, Feyanna asked the villagers to stop by as she wanted to show them something special. They had been charging the crystals in the meadow with the sun's energy for a couple of days. The meadow glowed like a rainbow most nights.

It was just after the evening meal when the villagers came by. The sun was just beginning to touch the treetops and sunset would be soon. The villagers were surprised by all the glowing crystals.

"These are amazing!"

"How did you make them glow?"

"The colors are like nothing I've ever seen before."

"I like the pink ones," a child was heard to say.

"Please, walk among them," Merlin said. "They are magnificent."

The villagers spent quite some time wandering through the glowing crystals, amazed at the light they gave off.

As the sun finally set, everyone stopped walking and talking. The crystals were sending light into the sky in every color imaginable.

"This is so beautiful," Sylvianna said. "How do they do that?"

Well," Merlin replied, "The crystals are made of a special kind of stone called quartz. The quartz has an energy charge of its own. When the sun shines on the crystals, the quartz is charged with the sun's energy, and they can keep shining for hours."

"Wow!" a small boy said.

"The main reason we asked you all here is this," Feyanna said, smiling at Merlin. "We would like to give everyone a few of these crystals so you can use them to light your homes instead of using candles."

The villagers hollered out in amazement. They talked with each other for quite some time before quieting down.

"Please, come by and pick out three crystals for yourselves, including the children. Everyone gets three crystals."

"This is very generous of you," Samuel said. "I'll be sure to bring you another chicken in thanks."

"We'll bring eggs and butter," some of the farmers said.

"I'll stop by, and we can talk about adding a room to your cottage home," one of the villagers said. "I do believe you're going to need it."

"That's a splendid idea," Feyanna replied. "We are very happy to accept your kindness."

"The women of the village have decided to come by and show you how to make some of our favorite recipes," Glendianna said. "We'll have the men over for supper, and we'll celebrate these amazing gifts from the gods and goddesses."

Everyone agreed with this idea, and plans were made for a day the next week. The villagers finally began to leave, carrying their glowing crystals with them. Penny and Q watched the trail of the crystals as the villagers carried them home. It truly was a Magical sight.

As promised, the next week, the women and children gathered at the cottage home and cooked up everything they could imagine. The men showed up around supper time, and everyone had a grand time. It was the first time Feyanna and Merlin celebrated with the villagers.

It was just after sundown when Quintan saw something fly over the meadow. He thought he could make out a dragon but didn't want to scare anyone. He hoped it was Penny or Q. Everyone went home happy with the day.

The fall harvest took place, and everyone shared it with their neighbors. The new room on Feyanna and Merlin's cottage home was finished. It was just what they needed. The village welcomed a new young woman. She turned out to be a teacher, and all the children, except the very young ones, were required to spend the mornings learning to read, write, add and subtract, and even learn about the earth. The afternoons were spent learning a trade whether it be carpentry, farming, sewing, cooking, and anything else that was deemed important. A separate cottage was built for the young woman. It had a room for the schooling to take place. The children seemed to like the teacher. She was known as Miss Kerianita. Folks shortened her name to Miss Kerry.

And so the fall turned into the winter. Snow fell several times, as was the norm. The road was rather quiet due to the frozen earth. The villagers were left alone most of the winter. The dragons kept close watch over Quintan. They knew his destiny and needed to make sure nothing threatened his life.

The seasons came and went by rather quickly, or so it seemed. It was the third year after Quintan arrived that the quiet began to be broken. It was well into the spring. Quintan was now eleven years old and was growing quite tall. He had made friends with most of the village children and they all enjoyed their childhoods. There had been a few close calls with thieves coming into the village, but the men had banded together and created an army of sorts. The men took turns scouting the road north and south of their village around the clock during the warmer months. If they heard about or saw trouble coming, they would ring a bell they carried with them. The men blocked the road, and the thieves or whatever they were had to retreat. It was a good system.

There was one time when the band of thieves was larger than the village army. The scouts rang their bells and ran into the village, where the villagers rang theirs as well. This was a signal that something very bad was about to happen. The women and children ran inside and hid. Unbeknownst to the villagers, Penny, Q, and a group of dragons were always watching their village. The dragons let the villagers take care of themselves most of the time. This time, however, The Dragon Brigade intervened.

The band of thieves raced into the village on their horses and stopped short. The village was empty. There wasn't any smoke rising from the chimneys, no clothes hanging on the line, and no animals outside. It was a strange sight. The leader gave the signal to raid the place anyway.

Just as the men started to break down the cottage doors, a great shadow covered the village. As the thieves looked up, they couldn't believe their eyes. They saw dragons flying overhead. The thieves took their weapons and arrows from their quivers and prepared to shoot the dragons. They never got the chance.

The Dragon Brigade attacked. Q was in the lead. There had to be more than a dozen dragons of all sizes and colors. Each dragon pinpointed a thief and attacked.

First, they blew smoke at the thieves, hoping they would move on. The thieves stayed in the village. The dragons signaled each other and began their attack. Q was the first one to send a stream of orange fire at the leader of the thieves. The leader was incinerated in an instant.

The other thieves became frightened and tried to ride through the village along the south road. The other dragons attacked their chosen targets—fire flames of red, orange, and bright yellow shot out from the dragons. Screams could be heard all the way to Avalon as the flames hit them, and one by one, the thieves were killed. Black smoke rose into the sky for quite some time. They died a horrific death, along with all the horses. Miss Penny asked if the horses could be reborn as they were innocents. The Divine granted her wish, and the horses were alive once again. The horses had all the things they had had when they were owned by the thieves.

The villagers came out of their hiding places as soon as the noise quieted. They were stunned to see about a dozen pack horses just standing in the middle of the village. Hamlen looked through the horses and said, "These horses need food and water right away. Come help me."

Villagers took the horses home, gave them water and feed, and settled them in a shady place.

Hamlen and some of the villagers began talking about the horses.

"I suspect these belonged to the thieves," Hamlen said.

"I agree," Samuel said. "And I don't see any one of those bad boys around here. It does smell like something was burned, though."

"I agree," Jameson said. "I'm not sure, and don't yell at me for what I'm about to say. I think something took place here that involved dragons."

"Dragons are bad creatures," one of the villagers said.

"Not so," Horacio replied. "I've been told by travelers that there are some good dragons that don't burn everything down, including killing people."

"I heard that, too," young Portia said. "My mother used to tell us that there are good and bad dragons. Now that I have grown some, I really believe her. I've seen huge shadowy shapes flying through the night. I believe we may have some good dragons around us."

"Now, young Portia," Samuel said. "Your mother was a wise and well-respected lady; may she rest with the gods and goddesses. She knew things that no one else knew. So, I will agree with you that there are good and bad dragons. I suspect you are right about our village being protected by good ones."

"Thank you, Samuel," young Portia replied.

"Let's get about our business," Samuel suggested.

The villagers went back to what they were doing before the dragons attacked the thieves. All except Quintan. He set off down the south road to the path in the woods. He was headed to Merlin and Feyanna's cottage home. He had a few questions for them.

Penny and Q flew straight over to Merlin and Feyanna's cottage home.

Feyanna saw them land and called out to Merlin to join her outside.

"Penny. Q," Feyanna said as she looked them over. "You are wounded. Let me help you."

"We accept," Q said as Feyanna ran into the workshop for her basket of herbal remedies and a bucket of water. Merlin followed with potions of his own.

"It's nothing much," Penny said as Feyanna looked over her wings. "Just a few scratches is all."

"That's all I see," Feyana said as Merlin spread one of his potions on the scratches.

"Oh, that feels so much better," Penny said as she lay down and got comfy.

"Q, your tail has a rather nasty scratch here," Merlin said as he gently touched Q's tail near the wound.

"I got it as one of the thieves tried to throw a rock at me," Q replied. "I had to swerve to avoid the rock, and my tail hit a large branch of one of the trees. I apologized to the tree, of course."

"Let's put both my salve and your potion over the wound, Merlin," Feyanna said as they went to work to dress the wound.

"That feels warm," Q said as they finished.

"As it should," Merlin said. "It's a combination of herbs and grasses I was given by The White Light. They said I'd know when to use it."

"Thanks be to The White Light," Q said as he joined Penny on the meadow.

"Here's some water for you," Feyanna said as she poured water from the bucket she had brought with her into two gourds next to the dragons. They both drank deeply and sighed.

"Just what I needed," Penny said. "We're going to take a nap for a bit."

"But, before we do, Quintan will be here shortly," Q informed them. "You both have been made aware of the battle between the band of thieves and the Dragon Brigade. The other dragons were not harmed. They've returned to The Crystal Caves to rest. We were told to come to you for these healing potions and to give you a message."

"We are honored by your presence, as always," Feyanna replied.

"As we are honored by your gift of healing," Penny replied.

"We were told to inform you that it's time Quintan began learning about The Magic. Not the specifics that you two know about and practice. Start with the basics. He is growing strong and will be ready to accept his destiny in a few short years."

"We are happy and honored to teach Quintan about The Magic," Feyanna replied.

"I've been feeling that it was time he began to learn the ancient ways," Merlin said.

"Tell him about the ancient religion," Q said. "He will need to know about that right away. He has begun to question some of the religious ways around here, and we need him to accept the ancient ways so we can carry on."

"Understood," Merlin said.

"Sleep and heal now," Feyanna said as Q and Penny closed their eyes. They became invisible as dragons do in an instant.

"It looks like we have some work to do," Merlin said as he and Feyanna returned to their cottage home. "I'm getting the feeling that this is one of the main reasons we're here. To guide Quintan along his journey."

"More like prepare him for his destiny," Feyanna added.

"Indeed," Merlin said. "Let's replenish our herbal remedies before he arrives."

It was a short time later when Merlin turned to Feyanna and said, "We're about to have company."

They walked out to the front door of the cottage home just as Quantin was approaching.

"Good day, Quintan," Merlin said as Quintan came to the door.

"Good day, Miss Feyanna and Master Merlin," Quintan replied. "It looks like you were expecting me."

"We were," Merlin replied as he stood aside for Quintan to enter.

"Quintan, may I offer you some refreshments?" Feyanna asked.

"That's very kind of you," Quintan replied. "I accept."

"Let's sit here, and we can talk," Merlin suggested as he walked them to the table.

Feyanna brought muffins and tea to the table.

"These are quite lovely," Quintan said as he bit into a muffin. "I taste cinnamon, lavender, and butter."

"You are correct," Feyanna said, smiling.

They chatted about the day as they ate until Quintan changed the subject.

"Master Merlin, you are aware of the battle in the village," Quintan stated.

"I am," Merlin replied.

"Even though you were not there," Quintan continued.

"That is correct," Merlin replied, looking over at Feyanna.

"Miss Feyanna, you, too?" Quintan asked.

"Yes, Quintan," Feyanna replied.

Quintan took a moment and said, "I know that The Magic is alive and well here."

Feyanna and Merlin looked at each other. They knew it was time to tell Quintan about The Magic and begin teaching him about the ancient ways.

"You are correct," Merlin replied.

"I know those dragons are from The Magic, too, "Quintan added.

"You are correct," Feyanna replied.

"All of the dragons," Quintan said.

"You are correct," Merlin said.

"Why here? Why now?" Quintan asked.

"Quintan, I must say you are so much more than eleven years old," Merlin said.

"What do you mean by that?"

"You know about things even old men never understand," Merlin answered.

"Oh," Quintan. "I just all of a sudden know things," Quintan said.

"I get that same thing from time to time," Feyanna said. "It's kind of scary and wonderful all at the same time."

"Exactly," Quintan said. "Sometimes, I just like being a kid, and other times, it seems I know a lot more than my friends. Even Miss Kerrianita said so."

"So you like her, Quintan?" Merlin asked, smiling.

"Most of the time," Quintan replied. "But not when she makes us work with the numbers. You know, adding and stuff like that."

"Why don't you like that stuff?" Feyanna asked, laughing.

"It takes a long time to get the answer," Quintan replied. "I want the answers right away."

"You are, indeed, eleven years young," Merlin said, laughing with Feyanna.

"And a boy," Feyanna added. "Boys always want stuff right away and don't want to take the time to learn about them and make them."

"That's right," Quintan said, sitting up straighter.

This made all of them laugh and tease each other for a minute.

"Sometimes, Quintan, taking the time to learn about something is a good thing," Merlin said. "You might miss a critical piece of information that doesn't help you find a solution to a problem."

"I can see that," Quintan said. "Like when Father is making a cart. I asked him why he measured everything at least two times, and he said it's better to measure twice to make sure you have the correct measurements rather than cutting a piece of wood and having it be too short or too long. He said then you have wasted precious time and need to redo everything."

"Hamlen is a wise man," Merlin replied. "It's best to listen to him and learn from him. Those lessons may serve you well as you become a man."

Quintan was quiet for a minute, then replied, "I understand what you're saying and what my father is saying. I'll try to slow down and learn."

"That is a very wise decision," Feyanna said. "It makes me think you are much older than eleven."

"Sometimes I feel all grown up, and it makes me feel weird," Quintan said, looking a bit sad.

"Don't be sad or afraid of those feelings," Feyanna said. "They mean that you're growing up, away from childhood into the first part of becoming a grown man."

"That's what mother says, too," Quintan said, looking relieved.

"Your mother is a loving and wise woman," Merlin said, ruffling Quintan's hair.

"Okay, now back to the dragons," Quintan said, taking control of the conversation like a man with many years of life behind him. "I know Penny and Q. Where did the others come from? And I'm quite sure Penny and Q were hurt. Are they okay?"

"Let's take a look," Merlin said as they walked outside and looked at the meadow.

"I don't see them," Quintan said, looking all around.

"Just keep watching the meadow," Feyanna said.

"The air is beginning to shimmer," Quintan said as Penny and Q became visible.

"They've been here the whole time?" Quintan said as he walked over to them. "Are you okay? I saw you get hurt."

Penny yawned, and this made Quintan laugh.

"You have a huge yawn, Miss Penny," Quintan said.

"I do, indeed," Penny replied, staying on the ground.

"Hi, Quintan," Q said as he yawned, too.

261

"Are you okay?" Quintan asked.

"We are healing nicely, thanks to Feyana and Merlin," Q replied. "Take a look at my tail for yourself."

"And my wing," Penny added as she spread her wing a bit so Quintan could see the wound.

Quintan spent a few minutes looking at both of them.

"The wounds look almost healed," Quintan said. "Is it because of The Magic?"

"Yes, Quintan, partly," Penny replied.

"And the herbal potions and salves Feyanna and Merlin used on them," Q added.

"The gifts of Mother Earth always have The Magic in them," Feyanna told Quintan.

"I truly believe that," Quintan said as he joined Feyanna and Merlin. "You both look okay to me. Almost okay."

"We are going to stay here for the rest of the day and sleep and heal," Penny said.

"Good idea," Merlin replied. "We'll bring you water and food later."

"Thank you," Q said as he closed his eyes.

"We appreciate you," Penny said as she fell back to sleep.

In an instant, they vanished from sight.

"That is really amazing," Quintan said. "I guess they do that to protect themselves."

"Exactly right," Merlin said. "Let's go back inside. We have a lot to tell you."

"And don't worry about your parents," Feyanna added as they settled around the table again. "They know you are with us."

"As you have shown us, you are aware of The Magic," Merlin began. "It is strong in our world. Those of us Gifted with The Magic have to choose between working in The Light or working in The Dark Forces. It is time for you to make that choice."

"Merlin and I have chosen to work in The Light," Feyanna added.

"I know about The Dark Forces. The thieves that killed my family and kidnapped me were in The Dark Forces. They always had dark shadows around them. It was as if those shadows were telling them what to do."

"You are right about that," Feyanna said, placing her hand on Quintan's hand.

"I miss my family," Quintan said as he began to cry.

Feyanna went over to him and held him for a long time while he sobbed for the loss of his family. Merlin and Feyanna cried as well. They could feel the deep sorrow in Quintan's soul.

"Thank you for holding me," Quintan said as he sat up. "I feel better now. You have been crying, both of you."

"Yes, Quintan," Merlin said. "We feel your deepest sorrow, and it saddens us to know that humankind can be so evil and cause such sorrow in you."

"Will I feel all that, too?" Quintan asked.

"You will," Feyanna said.

Quintan was quiet for a minute, then said, "I choose to walk in the White Light. How do I do that?"

Feyanna and Merlin instructed Quintan on how to choose The White Light. As soon as he had completed Merlin's instructions, he sat quietly with a smile on his face.

"I feel like I'm flying," Quintan said, laughing that wonderful laugh of a happy child.

"It does make you feel that way," Feyanna said as she made tea for them.

"Drink this," Feyanna said as he placed a mug in front of Quintan. "It will ground your newly found energy."

"Okay," Quintan said as he took a sip of the tea. "It tastes delicious."

"Thank you," Feyanna said. "It has juniper berries in it with other herbs."

"Delicious," Quintan said as he finished the tea. "I do feel more steady."

"The energy of The Divie is indescribable," Merlin said. "Welcome to The White Light, Quintan."

"Thank you," Quintan said as he held his hand out to Merlin.

"I prefer hugs," Merlin said as he wrapped Quintan into a big one.

Feyanna joined them, and they laughed and hugged for a minute.

"I feel so much happier now," Quintan said as he and Merlin sat back down.

"I'll fix us some lunch," Feyanna said.

"We'll help," Merlin said as he motioned Quintan to join him.

The three of them made lunch, laughing and telling stories, and continued with the laughter through their meal.

"Time to learn a few new things," Feyanna said after they finished. "Let's sit outside under the big tree."

"Quintan, I know you are aware of the religious beliefs in the village," Merlin said. "Hamlen and Glendianna have taught you well. Hamlen and I talk a lot about the children in the village and how they are raised to respect the gods and goddesses. What you may not know is how our religious beliefs came to be. It was when the Earth was just being formed that The Divine decided to allow people to live here. It took millions of years for the Earth to take shape as we know it today. The Divine populated the Earth with beings from another universe. Those people are the same as we are today. They lived all over the Earth and began to do things The Divine disapproved of. He sent warnings, but they kept misbehaving. So, The Divine sent fire, floods, and disease and shook the earth so hard that the people all died, and the Earth's oceans and lands changed shape. He cleaned things up and then decided to give mankind another chance.

"He brought more people to this Earth. He decided they needed guidance this time, so he created the religion we have now. The people were instructed by wise ethereal beings to follow the rules set forth by The Divine. The people called The Divine God and promised to behave. They also created the legend of other gods and goddesses and taught their children for millennia about respecting the Gods and Goddesses as were the rules set forth by the Sacred Ones."

"I've been taught all of this by my new mother and father," Quintan said. "I just have one question: Who created us, and why are we here? I guess that's two questions."

"Those are the two most important questions anyone could ask," Feyanna said. "We were created by a benevolent energy, and our ancestors were placed here as a mighty gift from that benevolent energy we call The Divine. We lived, and still do, on a very distant star world millions of years from here. We have been tasked with the job of learning to live in harmony with all living creatures, including Mother Earth. The first group of our ancestors did not follow the rules, just like Merlin told you. But we, the current group of beings, are doing a better job of living in harmony."

"However," Merlin said, "We are not doing so well right now. The Divine has decided to give us the gift of The Magic to help all of mankind to learn to live a better life."

"What about the bad guys like those thieves?" Quintan asked.

"Good point," Merlin said. "One of the things The Divine gave us was freedom of choice. That means we can choose how we live. There will always be a conflict between good and evil. We know it as the ongoing battle between The White Light and The Dark Forces. The Divine gave our ancestors and us the ability to choose how we live. The three of us have chosen to walk in The White Light because we know about The Special Magic. Many people do not know about The Magic, so they live their lives making choices that aren't always good ones. Some choose to walk in The Dark Forces. Bad group they are. We are tasked with trying to keep The Dark Forces away from the innocents."

"I understand that," Quintan said. "Where do I fit in?"

Feyanna and Merlin looked at each other for a minute.

"They are not allowed to discuss that with you just now," Penny said from the meadow.

"Leave it at that," Q added.

Quintan felt a powerful energy wrapping around them and replied, "I accept that answer. For now."

"Good choice," Penny said. "Carry on, Merlin."

"Quintan here is one more thing you need to understand," Merlin said. "Being in The White Light doesn't mean you do no harm. You should try not to harm a thing. But, if those you love, if the innocents around you are being harmed or in danger of any kind, then you will need to step in and protect them. Do you understand?"

"I think I do," Quintan said. "But how do I do that? I don't even know how to hold a sword or shoot a bow with arrows. I don't even know how to protect myself from that bully in the village."

"Oh, you mean the boy called Lutey," Feyanna said.

"Yes. He punched me yesterday, and I ran away from him," Quintan replied. "I run faster than he does. I got home before he could catch up to me."

"Good choice to run away," Merlin said. "I am going to teach you how to defend yourself from such bullies. I will teach you how to use a sword. Hamlen will teach you how to use a bow and arrows. You are learning how to ride your horse now. That is excellent."

"Yes, my mother is teaching all of us how to ride," Quintan said. "I love my horse. Her name is Buttercup because she likes to eat the flowers with that name."

"I saw you all the other day," Q said. "You are learning well."

"Thank you, Q." Quintan said. "You feeling better now?"

"We are," Penny replied.

They were still invisible.

"Quintan, look at your feet," Q said. "This is a gift from The White Light and Mother Earth for you."

Quintan looked down and was surprised at what he saw. He had just looked at his feet, and it wasn't there a minute ago. Now, he saw a deep red crystal shining brightly in the sunlight. It was the shape of a small dragon.

"This is magnificent!" Quintan said as he picked it up. "It's vibrating and glowing."

"I guess it likes you," Penny said.

"Quintan, all you have to do is hold this crystal out in front of you, and we'll be right here. It's been given to you to help you stay safe," Q explained.

"It's so small," Quintan said, looking at the crystal.

"Size is not important here," Penny said. "It's the energy in the crystal that makes it special. The Divine made that crystal just for you. If anyone holds it, it won't vibrate and shine like it's doing now. Only when you're holding it. Always keep it with you in a pocket or something."

"I'll have my mother show me how to sew a pouch and wear it around my neck," Quintan said.

"That's a splendid idea," Feyanna said. "If she's too busy, I'll help you."

"Thank you, Feyanna," Quintan said." I'll let you know. And thanks to everyone for this wonderful gift."

"Your father is coming to fetch you home, so we'll stay invisible for now," Q said.

"Good idea," Quintan said as Hamlen came through the path into the meadow.

Quintan put his Crystal Dragon in his pants pocket. He felt that no one else should know about it just yet.

"Hello, everyone," Hamlen said as he shook hands with Merlin. "I've come to relay some news and fetch Quintan home."

"What is the news?" Feyanna asked.

"The horses are all being taken care of and resting well. The thieves have disappeared. We all know dragons helped us stay safe from them, and we thank the Gods and Goddesses for sending them to us."

"We are very thankful to The Magic as well," Feyanna said.

"Indeed we are," Merlin said, winking at Quintan.

"Father, Feyanna, and Merlin have been teaching me about The Magic," Quintan said. "It is very interesting for sure."

"It most certainly is," Hamlen said. "We all thank you for sharing your knowledge with our Quintan. Merlin, I have completed one of the wagons we designed and wondered if you'd like to come by tomorrow to have a look?"

"I most certainly would," Merlin replied. "I'd love to see it in action."

"That is wonderful, father," Quintan said. "Does the horse like pulling it?"

"We'll find out tomorrow morning while you're in school," Hamlen said.

"Ah, father, can't I miss school to see it?" Quintan asked.

"No, you cannot," Hamlen replied. "But if you show improvement with your numbers, I might just let you take a ride with me after school."

"I will do just that," Quintan said.

"It's a deal," Hamlen said, shaking hands with the young Quintan.

"You'll have to tell me how it all turns out," Feyanna said.

"I promise I will," Quintan said.

"Time for us to get along, son," Hamlen said, taking Quintan by the hand.

"Thank you all for today," Quintan said as he winked toward the meadow.

"You are always welcome here, Quintan," Merlin said. "We'll have another lesson soon."

"Off we go," Hamlen said as they walked down the path to the road.

Penny and Q appeared and sat up, stretching and moving about.

"That was wonderful," Penny said. "He is going to be the perfect one for the job ahead."

"I agree," Q said. "My tail feels much better, thanks to Feyanna and Merlin."

"My wing, too," Penny said.

"You are both very welcome," Merlin said. "You look much better. How about some food and water?"

"Splendid idea, Merlin," Penny said. "I see the faeries have supplied us with both just there in the woods."

They all walked over to the edge of the forest and saw exactly that—a mound of fruits and vegetables and large gourds of water for Penny and Q.

"Thank you, sweet faeries, for this feast," Penny and Q said.

There was a quick flash of blue light throughout the area in response.

"Enjoy your meal," Feyanna said. "I appreciate seeing the faerie's light. Beautiful."

They flashed a yellow light over Feyanna and Merlin that made them laugh.

"You faeries are delightful," Merlin said. "We thank you."

"We'll let you and Q eat now," Feyanna said. "Will you be returning to The Crystal Caves after you eat?"

"We will," Penny said with a moth full of winter berries. "We need the energy of the crystals to complete the healing of our wounds."

"Do you have the strength to get there?" Merlin asked.

"Of course, Merlin," Q answered. "The Crystal Caves are where we need them to be. The entrance is just over there near that large oak tree. See it?"

"I do," Merlin answered. "I've just learned that The Special Magic can create anything anywhere it's needed."

"That is correct," Penny replied. "These winterberries are my favorite."

"Rest and heal well," Feyanna said as she and Merlin went back to their cottage home.

Penny and Q finished their meal and entered The Crystal Caves. They were greeted by thousands of crystals of every color imaginable flashing all over them as they went to their separate caves and settled for the sleep they needed. The crystals healed them all the while they were there.

The next day, Hamlen and Merlin took the new wagon for a trial ride. It worked perfectly. The ox pulling the wagon was not overly stressed at all. They hooked up the workhorse next, and he didn't seem to be bothered either. They deemed it a great success and got the word out to the rest of the villagers to come see the new wagon. The villagers were thrilled with it, and two of the farmers asked Hamlen to make them each a wagon. Hamlen was quite happy with the new prospects for his family from the work he and Merlin had done. Sarah was sent to get Feyanna and bring her to the farm for a celebratory supper. The evening was great fun, and everyone enjoyed themselves.

The children complained when it was time for bed but went off happy. Feyanna and Merlin left soon afterward and talked about the wagon all the way back to their cottage home.

The next day was the last day of April, and the Festival of Beltane was ready to be celebrated as the sun set. May first marked the first day of summer. Preparations had been made all week by the villagers. Doors and windows were decorated with bouquets and garlands of hawthorn, gorse, and marsh marigold blossoms. These flowers were used because they had a special connection with fire. It was believed that the Beltane fires evoked special purification energy and kept people, livestock, and crops healthy and strong.

All household fires were doused in the late afternoon and would be relit from the flames of the Beltane bonfires. This was done to bring positive energy into the house and all you lived there.

As soon as the sun went down, the huge bonfires were lit all over the land. The villagers had set two bonfires to life in the field of one of the farmers. Cattle from all the farms were driven between the fires to purify them before they were taken to the summer pastures. The villagers danced around the fires all night in hopes of finding a life mate.

It was well into the night, and many of the village children lay asleep on blankets a ways from the fires. Quintan and a couple of his closest friends were still awake. They were watching everything. Flutes could be heard along with drums as some folks danced around the bonfires. Many of the younger children had made wreaths for the faeries. It was believed that the faeries were especially active during the Beltane celebrations. Miss Kerrianita had encouraged the young ones to make wreathes and place them at the edge of the meadow near the trees. It was widely believed that faeries could go between the worlds, and the edge of the woods and meadows were suspected places of entry.

So, the young ones placed their wreaths and garlands along the edge of the woods. Quintan waved at his friends that he was going to walk over by the woods. His friends motioned that they would stay closer to the fires. Quintan walked through the meadow and noticed the wildflowers in bloom. Some looked like the sun, while others resembled bells and looked to be ringing in the night air. Some were closed for the night.

Just as he reached the edge of the meadow, where it became a forest, he thought he saw something moving. He figured it was a night creature and looked all around. As he stepped into the woods, he was greeted by several little creatures. They had wings and Quintan knew without a doubt that they were faeries.

"Hello, beautiful faeries," Quintan said softly.

He heard what sounded like whispers and a tinkling sound.

"You have such lovely voices," Quintan said. "I'm going to stay right here because I don't want to damage your homes."

A bright blue faerie flew up to him and hovered before his face.

"Thank you for being respectful," the blue faerie said. "I am known as Blue Bell."

"Hello, Blue Bell," Quintan replied. "I am known as Quintan."

"We know," was heard all around Quintan.

"Let me guess," Quintan said, laughing. "Penny told you about me."

"Yes, she did," Blue Bell replied. "She told us to watch out for you tonight. She said you'd wander over here, and here you are."

"I am curious about you faeries," Quintan said. "I would like to know more about you and your ways."

"Okay," Blue Bell said. "Let me land on this branch, and I'll tell you a few things."

Blue Bell settled on the branch, saying, "We live in the forest where the trees rise from the ground. There are magical doors or entryways for us to go through when we feel like it. Mostly to watch over this place and keep the innocents safe as best we can."

"I wondered about all of that," Quintan said. "May I sit here?"

"Yes, indeed," Blue Bell said. "You won't be harming anything."

"I've seen you on my window ledge at night after everyone has gone to bed," Quintan said. "Why are you watching me?"

The faeries looked at each other and then encircled Quintan where he sat.

"You are one of the Special Ones," a pink faerie said.

"Special Ones?" Quintan asked.

"Yes. I am Enetia," Enetia said. "I am one of the older ones."

"Nice to meet you, Enetia," Quintan said. "Great to meet all of you. But, what do you mean that I am one of the Special Ones?"

"Not every child can see and hear the faeries," Enetia explained. "You can, and that makes you special."

"Okay, I understand that," Quintan said. "But why me? Why can I see and hear you?"

"You are a kind soul and have always been aware of things that can't be explained by everyday people. Remember when you were standing by the stream last year, and that frog hopped onto your foot?"

"I do," Quintan said, laughing. "I was quite surprised."

"That frog wasn't scared of you because it could tell you knew about The Magic in this world," Enetia said.

"It stayed on my foot for a few minutes before it finally hopped into the stream," Quintan said.

"That's because it could tell you would not harm it," Enetia said. "You are aware of The Magic."

"Yes, I am aware of magical things that can happen," Quintan said. "I never told my mother and father about that. The king that ruled our village hated The Magic and said if anyone talked about it, he would have them killed."

"There are many rulers who don't understand The Magic and think it's evil because they cannot control it," Blue Bell said. "You were brave to keep quiet as such a young child."

"Now, I have a new family," Quintan said. "They believe and know about The Magic a little bit. That is a good thing."

"It is, indeed," Enetia replied. "We faeries have been instructed to keep you and your family as safe as possible."

"That is very kind of you," Quintan said.

"Thank you," Enetia said, looking to the others so as not to say anything further. "We love the wagon Hamlen and Merlin fashioned. It is very kind to the animals."

"It is, indeed," Quintan said. "I worked hard at learning my numbers, and father let me take a ride in it with him in our meadow. It is very sturdy."

"You looked quite happy riding in it," Blue Bell said.

"I was very happy riding in it," Quintan said.

Just then, he heard his mother calling for him.

"I'm just here in the woods," Quintan replied. "I'll be right over. Time for me to leave. Thank you all for this magical visit. I hope I see you again soon."

"You will," Enetia said. "Enjoy the fires."

"I will," Quintan said as he ran back across the meadow to join his family.

"What did you find in the forest?" his mother asked as he sat down next to her.

"All the usual things," Quintan replied. "I wonder if the faeries are happy about tonight?"

"Tradition says they are," his mother replied. "The livestock have been driven between the fires and returned home by your father. All the villagers have done this. Now, we are going to watch the fires until sunrise, then take a branch

270

home to light our hearths with the special energy of the Beltane fires on this eve of the beginning of summer."

"The fires look magnificent," Hamlen said as he joined them. "Your sisters are asleep. They'll have a good night's rest out here next to the fires."

Quintan stayed awake well into the wee hours of the morning, falling asleep just before sunrise. He found himself in his own bed when he woke up later that morning. He didn't remember getting there but was happy nonetheless. As he became fully awake, he remembered his visit with the faeries. They had been beautiful and so sweet.

The day after the Beltane celebration, the village was rather quiet. It was a tradition that the villagers rested and took care of the essentials but did not do more. They were all very tired and the afternoon found many of them taking a nap. Prayers to the gods and goddesses had been said at sunrise as the hearth fires were lit with the Beltane flames. These prayers were in thanksgiving for all they had received since the last Beltane fires and offered love and thanks for the coming summer growing time and fall harvest.

The next few weeks found the villagers taking care of everyday things. Crops were planted and watched. The children were taught to read and work with numbers. Their learning days would be over in another week at the end of May. They were all excited and wanted to do something to celebrate.

Quintan was riding around the meadow on the last day of learning and suddenly had an idea. He thought about it for a bit, then acted on it. He took care of his horse, making sure it had fresh hay and water, then walked down the south road to Feyanna and Merlin's cottage home.

"Well, hello, Quintan," Feyanna said when she looked up from drying a batch of flowers and saw Quintan as he approached.

"Hi, Miss Feyanna," Quintan said as he walked up to her. "Making more remedies, I see."

"Yes, indeed, I am, young Quintan," Feyanna said, rather amused by his choice of words. "You certainly don't sound like a young child today."

"Thank you," Quintan replied. "I feel grown up sometimes, and other times I still feel like a child. I am about to be twelve years old, too."

"That's right," Feyanna said. "That is usually when we celebrate a child becoming an adult. We will have the ceremony for you soon. Your mother told us about it."

"I'm glad you'll both be with us," Quintan said. "Is Merlin about?"

"He should be back in a few minutes," Feyanna answered. "He went to the ice lagoon. We both love to go there, so we take turns. Today was his turn."

"It is a beautiful and peaceful place. I like to go there, too," Quintan said. "Here's Merlin now."

Merlin was just coming through the path from the woods and called out to Quintan when he saw him.

"Greetings, Quintan," Merlin said as he brought the little handcart to the front door. "Help me with the ice, please."

"Of course," Quintan replied.

Merlin and Quintan spent a few minutes getting the ice to the ice cupboard in the workshop.

"This really works well in here," Quintan said. "How long does the ice last?"

"Usually four to five days," Merlin replied. "I suspect it may be a day shorter as the weather warms up."

"Good thinking," Quintan said. "I'll remember to check our ice cupboard more frequently."

"So, what brings you our way?" Feyanna asked as she entered the cottage home.

"We children are all excited about this morning being the last day of lessons and want to celebrate somehow. Everyone is trying to come up with a good idea. I came up with one and would like your help with it."

"Well, what's your idea?" Merlin asked as they all stood around the workbench.

"I was thinking that a parade with the light crystals from one end of the village to the other would be a good start," Quintan said.

"That's a wonderful idea," Feyanna said. "The children could charge their crystals all day and gather on the bend in the north road at sundown, then walk through the village."

"That's just what I was thinking," Quintan said. "And, then, we could all gather on the village green, and the children could make shapes with their crystals for all to see. The younger ones could make the simple shapes, and us older ones could make more complicated designs."

"That's a splendid idea," Merlin said. "I'm already thinking about how everyone could see them. They would have to be up off the ground because the grasses would hide some of them. You and I could fashion some risers that are about three feet off the ground, and the crystals could be placed there."

"That's a great idea as well," Quintan said.

"We'd need to know the shape of the risers," Feyanna said. "Let's have some tea and think about this more."

Tea was prepared, and sweet bread was served. The three of them created the risers according to the size of the children. They devised a plan to accommodate all the patterns and designs.

"This is going to be so much fun," Quintan said when they finished with the designs. "When can I come by and help you make the risers and platforms?"

"Well, how about the day after tomorrow?" Merlin said. "I have some things to do for a few of the farmers north of the village tomorrow so that the next day will work. That would make it Sunday."

"I have to do my chores first, so how about after that? I'll tell the other children, and we'll keep it a secret," Quintan said.

"When do you want to have this parade?" Feyanna asked.

"Well, it looks like rain for the first couple of days next week, so let's plan on Wednesday," Merlin replied.

"Okay. I'll tell all the kids about this idea and see if they want to do it," Quintan said. "I don't see why they wouldn't. And, I'll tell them to keep it a secret."

"Let me know tomorrow," Feyanna said. "I'll be here making remedies most of the day. You can use some of our bigger crystals if you wish."

I will," Quintan said. "Thanks for helping me with the idea. I'd better get back home. Always more chores to do. Father finished one of the carts and wants to deliver it to the farmer. He said I could go with him."

"That sounds like it might be a delightful ride," Merlin said as they walked outside.

"That's what father said, too," Quintan said. "Thanks again."

Quintan went off down the path home and Merlin and Feyanna went back to their work. Quintan got the word to the village children, who loved the idea. Feyanna said she would let them use some of her bigger crystals for the display, and Quintan was thrilled. The children made plans on how to walk in the parade, and by suppertime, everything was in place. Penny and Q were delighted with how Quintan took charge and was kind and thoughtful with all the ideas the children came up with. He truly was older than his almost twelve years.

The next few days flew by. Quintan and the children met a few times to create their parade. Merlin and Quintan made the risers on Sunday. They decided to bring them to the village green early Wednesday morning. It rained on Monday and Tuesday, just as Merlin had predicted.

Merlin and Hamlen loaded the risers just before sunrise and, with Quintan's help, had them in place in no time. The children told their parents they had a surprise for them at sunset that night. Everyone put their crystals out in the sunshine and made sure they stayed in the sunshine all day long. The village was abuzz with curiosity at what the children were up to. The day seemed to take forever to go along as far as the children were concerned. But, it was finally suppertime, and the children were very excited.

The days were getting longer as summer moved toward the solstice. Evening chores were finished in a hurry that night. The children gathered on the north road just as the sun set below the treetops.

"Now?" one of the younger boys asked.

"Not yet," Quintan replied. "We need to wait for the sun to shoot sunbeams all over the sky as it settles below the horizon. Just watch."

The children sat down and watched as the sky put on a show for them.

Penny, Q, and a few of their dragon friends were also watching the sky. There had been a rumbling of trouble in the dragon world. Penny and Q were on the watch for any problems that might occur during the children's celebration.

The sun finally dipped below the horizon, sending a few purple and pink beams through the sky. Quintan signaled to the children to take their places. One of the older girls began playing the flute as the children started their parade. The crystals glowed brightly as they walked along the north road, through the village, and down the south road to the stopping point. They turned around and walked back to the village commons to begin making their shapes on Merlin's risers.

The young ones were first. They placed their crystals in circles, squares, triangles, and diamonds just as they had practiced. The parents cheered them on as each new shape was made. Penny and Q were circling high above, enjoying the festivities.

The crystals glowed brightly, sending rainbows everywhere. The older children took their places at the risers and began to create more intricate shapes. Some were with the same-colored crystals, and others were all different colors. The finale brought all the children to the center of the village green. Everyone became very quiet. Then, Quintan gave the signal, and they raised their crystals to the heavens. The sky was alive with every color you could imagine and then some. The villagers were thrilled and cheered and cheered for the longest time. The children finally lowered their crystals and joined their parents.

Samuel stepped forward to say, "Children, that was amazing. I know I thoroughly enjoyed this celebration. Your parents should be very proud of you for all you have learned. Master Quintan, you have shown great leadership skills when working with your friends. Your parents should be proud of you as well. Good job, everyone."

More cheering was heard throughout the village. A short time later, the villagers began to make their way home with very happy children. It wasn't long before the village was settled for the night. Well, most of them. Merlin and Feyanna had felt something in the air. Penny, Q, and the Dragon Brigade flew north to investigate that energy shift.

Merlin and Feyanna set their crystals around the cottage home, waiting for Penny and Q to return and report on what they found.

It was well after midnight when Penny and Q landed in the meadow. Feyanna and Merlin joined them.

"Sorry to have to wake you in the middle of the night. We have some disturbing news," Q began. "The current king, King Owen of Kelwyn, is on a rampage. He thinks some of his subjects, the villagers, including our villagers, are cheating him out of his portions of their crops and creations. He has sent his knights to collect that which he has ordered to be paid. If the person questions the order or doesn't pay the price, they are to be beheaded in front of their family. The knights will leave at first light."

"This is outrageous," Feyanna said. "This is just wrong."

"Oh, we agree," Penny said. "We have a plan we want to share with you."

"Great! Go ahead," Merlin said.

"The Dragon Brigade is on alert. We have already found two of the rogue dragons that are terrorizing the countryside. First, we're going to stop them. You don't want to know how."

"Okay," Feyanna said. "We trust you."

"Good," Penny replied.

"Once we have neutralized them, we're going to hunt down the king's knights and deal with them before they can kill anyone," Q explained.

"Even in broad daylight?" Feyanna asked.

"If we need to," Q replied. "We don't want to be seen, but if it means we can save the innocents, then so be it."

"This is quite serious," Merlin said. "Do you need our help in any way?"

"Yes," Q answered. "Please alert the village about this threat. It has already begun. The king's castle isn't far from here, so this will be their first stop. They are setting out at first light. We need to leave to hunt down those rogue dragons. We should be here before the knights arrive. If not, instruct the villagers to give them whatever they want. The Magic will make sure they have just what the knights are demanding. We have called on The Special Magic to help us at this time. Go. Alert the villagers. We will be close by."

Merlin and Feyanna ran back to their cottage home as Penny and Q took to the sky. It was going to be a long and dangerous night.

Merlin began knocking on doors to gather the men at Hamlen's farm. Feyanna helped organize the women and children, sending them into the forest caves to be safe. Merlin told them about the king's knights and what was about to take place. He didn't mention The Dragon Brigade, hoping all would be taken care of before dawn.

"What if we don't have what the knights demand?" Thomas asked.

"You will," Merlin said quietly. "Whether you believe in this or not, The Magic is taking care of us this night."

"How do you know that?" Thomas asked. He was the skeptical one in the village. He never believed in anything he couldn't witness for himself.

Merlin was silent for a minute as he listened to The Special Magic, giving him instructions that only he could hear.

"Thomas, I know about this, just as I know you took three eggs from Samuel's coop this morning without paying for them."

"What? You stole from me, Thomas?" Samuel said. "That's dishonest."

"Yes, it is," Hamlen said. "How are you going to remedy this, Thomas?"

Thomas looked around for a minute, then said, "Merlin, who told you I took those three eggs this morning?"

"I was informed of your dishonesty by The Magic just now," Merlin replied. "And, before you say I saw you do this, I was home in my workshop, as Feyanna will tell you. Now, how are you going to remedy this action?"

"All right," Thomas growled. "I did take those eggs. I didn't have any and was hungry. Since I am the leather craftsman here, what can I fashion for you to pay for the eggs, Samuel?"

"That's a right nice idea," Samuel said. "I'll think of something as soon as this emergency is over. Maybe we can barter some more."

"I agree with that," Thomas said. "So, The Magic is real? I'm not convinced."

Merlin began to smile as The Special Magic told him what was about to happen.

"Thomas, look up there," Merlin said as he pointed to the full moon. "Now, be patient and watch."

Just a moment later, Penny and Q flew across that bright moon, and their shapes were not to be mistaken for anything else except for what they were.

"Those were two dragons," Thomas said. "I don't believe in them, but I just saw them. You made that happen with some trickery."

"I saw them, too," Samuel said. "For the love of Pete, Thomas, why don't you just believe in them for a change? You need them to land here and touch you?"

"Well, if they were real, they most certainly would," Thomas said in a nasty reply.

And just like that, Q landed beside them in Hamlen's meadow. Most of the villagers were thrilled to see a real dragon up close. Some were scared. Thomas was in shock.

"Ask, and you shall receive," Merlin said. "Go up to the dragon Thomas and touch him so you'll know he is real. He's not just some quirk of your imagination."

"How did you do that?" Thomas said as he stepped back away from everyone. "This isn't real. Dragons are just stories made up to scare people."

Two of the villagers grabbed Thomas and carried him right up to Q.

"This real enough for you?" Padrick asked as he pulled Thomas's arm forward and made his hand touch Q.

"Thank you, sir dragon, for your patience with this one," Samuel offered.

Q bowed in return.

Thomas passed out. Q looked over at Merlin and smiled.

"I do believe that dragon just smiled," Hamlen said.

"I agree with you," Merlin said, winking at Hamlen.

"He is magnificent," Samuel said.

"May I ask the dragon a question?" Horatio asked Merlin.

"Yes, of course," Merlin said, bowing toward Q.

"Mr. Dragon, are you a friend or a mean dragon," Horatio asked.

Everyone looked at Q, waiting for an answer.

Q smiled at Merlin and nodded his head.

"He is a friendly dragon," Merlin said.

"How can you tell?" Samuel asked.

"If he were a bad dragon, we'd all be dead already," Merlin replied.

"Oh, yeah, good thinking," some of the villagers replied.

"This dragon needs to leave," Merlin said. "He has work to do."

"Thanks for coming here," the villagers said.

"Stay safe, Mr. Dragon," Horatio added.

Q lifted off and was high in the sky in an instant.

Thomas was finally waking up. He saw Q lift off.

"That was a real dragon," Thomas said as he stood up. "I believe in them now."

"Good thinking, Thomas," Samuel said as they all laughed with him.

"Now, back to what's about to happen," Merlin said. "Feyanna has sent the women and children into the caves in the forest. They'll be safe there. I truly believe that the king and his court do not know about those caves."

"I agree," Samuel said.

"We need to go back to our homes and farms and wait for the knights to arrive," Merlin said. "It'll be dawn soon, and that's when the attack will begin. Remember, think before you speak. The Magic will have just what they ask for at your fingertips."

"I trust you, my friend," Samuel said as the others joined in.

Merlin joined Hamlen in his farm home.

"This is going to be bad, isn't it?" Hamlen said as he listened at one of the windows that looked out on the road.

"Not necessarily," Merlin answered, looking directly at Hamlen.

"You know something," Hamlen said.

"I do," Merlin replied.

"You were sent to us by The Magic," Hamlen stated. "You and Feyanna. You're here so Quintan could come here and be with my family. You are a Wizard of the highest level."

Merlin paused a moment, then replied. "All true," Merlin said as he bowed to Hamlen.

"I knew it," Hamlen replied. "From the minute I first saw the two of you, I knew The Magic was at work here. And, now, meeting a dragon. I don't know what to say."

"I know how you feel," Merlin said, laughing. "I remember when I realized dragons were real, and Feyanna and I had been saved by one. We were trying to get here, and the evil out there was trying to kill us. It may look like we've always been around dragons, but this is all new to us, too."

"It's Quintan," Hamlen said. "There's something special about him."

"I can't say much, but I can tell you that that is true," Merlin said. "You are raising him well. The Special Magic appreciates that."

"It is an honor to have him with us," Hamlen said. "We all love him dearly."

"As do Feyanna and I," Merlin was saying when he heard horses approaching. "I do believe we have visitors. The sun is just peaking over the horizon. Stand strong. Give them what they want."

"I will," Hamlen said as someone began pounding on his door.

Hamlen opened the door, and a knight of the king ordered him to kneel down in front of him. The knight could not see Merlin as Merlin nodded at Hamlen.

Hamlen knelt down, and the knight said, "You have not paid your share of grain to the king. I demand it now."

"Yes, sire," Hamlen said, staying on the ground. "May I rise and take you to it?"

"You may," the knight said.

Hamlen walked outside and turned to walk down the track to the barn when Merlon yelled out to him.

"Hamlen, fall to the ground!" Merlin hollered just as a dragon flew overhead.

Hamlen fell to the ground, and the dragon breathed fire onto the knight and his two aides. They were incinerated in an instant.

Hamlen quickly rolled away from the burning carcasses as Merlin ran over to him.

"Are you okay?" Merlin asked as he helped Hamlen to his feet.

"That really stinks," Hamlen said, walking away from what was left of the three men.

"It sure does," Merlin said as they walked back into the house.

Just then, Hamlen and Merlin heard a lot of yelling and loud noises.

They hurried into the village and saw an incredible sight. There must have been at least six dragons in the air. Each one was targeting a knight. One of the knights was trying to kill Samuel, but Samuel wouldn't hold still.

"You are the reason King Owen is so angry," the knight said as he swung his sword at Samuel. "You refuse to pay your portion; we must take it from you. Now, where is your gold?"

"Gold? You think I have gold?" Samuel said as he dunked from another attempt from the knight's sword.

"Yes," the knight replied. "I want all of it. Now!"

"I don't have any gold," Samuel yelled as the knight's aid knocked him over.

"Don't lie," the knight said, poised to swing his sword at Samule's throat. "Our scouts heard you talking about your precious gold a few days ago."

Samuel started laughing. The knight didn't like this. He placed the tip of his sword at Samuel's throat, drawing a bit of blood.

"The only gold I have are my golden hens. My chickens. They have feathers the color of gold," Samuel said, laughing at the knight and his aide.

Just as the knight began to swing his sword, he went airborne. As everyone watched, they saw a dragon the color of green fields fly high with him in his mouth. A minute later, the dragon let go of the knight, and he fell and splattered the earth with his guts. The knight's aide tried to mount his horse, but another dragon grabbed him and flung him high and wide. He, too, splattered the earth with his guts.

One by one, the other four knights were incinerated by the dragons before they could get back to their horses. The villagers were stunned. They stood there for the longest time without saying a word.

Finally, Samuel spoke. "That was horrible."

"Yes, it was," Padrick said. "That king has got to be dealt with. Thank the gods and goddesses that we were blessed with The Magic of The Dragons."

"What happened to you, Merlin?" Thomas asked.

"The knight and his two aides came to my door demanding more grain," Hamlen said. "I told them I had it ready for them and to follow me outside. As soon as we cleared the house, Merlin yelled at me to fall to the ground. A dragon flew low over me and burned the three king's men to death. It was horrible."

"We're glad you and Merlin are okay," Padrick said.

"Is this all of the knights?" Merlin asked. "I count six of them."

"It looks like it is," Samuel replied. "Liam, are there any more knights in the area?"

"No, Samuel," Liam replied. "Our scouts informed me that these six were the only ones coming our way. We should be safe for a while until King Owen wonders where his knights are."

"That's true," Hamlen said. "His anger will increase as soon as he finds out that his knights are nowhere to be seen. He'll think they abandoned him. We'll have to be vigilant about strangers passing through here from now on. Don't answer any questions."

"That's a good idea, Hamlen," Merlin said as he looked skyward. "Look there."

Everyone looked into the sky and saw three dragons flying overhead. They circled the village and then flew on.

"Looks like we're being taken care of here," Padrick said.

"It does," Thomas replied.

"Here are our families," Hamlen said as the women and children came along the road.

Everyone was very happy to see that no one had been killed or hurt. They talked for a few minutes and then went on home. Merlin and Feyanna waved at the villagers as they walked down the south road.

"What happened, Merlin?" Feyanna asked.

"The knights showed up demanding things, and The Dragon Brigade dealt with each and every one of them. It was gruesome. There are only a few tiny patches of ash left to be seen. And, look, they're disappearing, too," Merlin explained.

The patches of ash were gone in a minute. You couldn't tell that a battle of sorts had taken place just a short while ago.

"I thank The Special Magic and our dragons for protecting us," Feyanna said as she bowed her head.

"I do, too," Merlin said. "Thanks be to The Dragon Brigade and The Special Magic."

Merlin bowed to the earth, the sky and the air in thanks.

"Merlin, my sweet friend, I know it's only morning, but I'm wicked tired," Feyanna said as she walked down the hallway to her room. "I'm going to sleep for a while."

"Me, too," Merlin said as he lay his head on the pillow.

They were both asleep in a minute. The faeries hovered near their windows, making sure they were safe. Penny and Q flew over, waved at the faeries, and then flew off. The villagers were napping, too. It had been a long night. Quintan looked out his window just as he fell to sleep. He saw Blue Bell and Enetia and smiled at them. They sent twinkling lights over him, and he slept peacefully.

CHAPTER 15

Merlin knew it was finally time to begin to prepare Quintan for his final destiny. The attack by the king's knights was a warning sign. Merlin could feel the change in the peace of the countryside. It was a soft and quiet change of energy. Feyanna had mentioned it that morning when they were gathering plants in the meadow.

"Merlin, I feel a change in the energy here," Feyanna said quietly.

"I know," Merlin said. "I've been aware of it since yesterday."

"About mid-day," Feyanna said.

"Yes," Merlin agreed. "Tell me what you're thinking."

Feyanna stood up and said, "I feel it's time for Quintan to learn serious Magic."

"I agree," Merlin said, facing her. "Feyanna, it's time we started to prepare Quintan for his final destiny."

"He showed good leadership skills with the children's parade," Feyanna said.

"He did, indeed," Merlin said. "Have you noticed the way he's begun to speak? As if he were already an adult."

"Yes," Feyanna said as she gathered red poppies. "I mentioned just that to him the day he came by to talk to you about the parade. He said that he sometimes feels like a kid. Then, a minute later, he feels like a man."

"I remember those times," Merlin said, smiling. "Rather confusing."

"Will you begin now? Today?" Feyanna asked as they walked back to their cottage home.

"Yes," Merlin said. "I'm off to get him now."

Merlin made short work of getting to Hamlen's farm. Quintan was riding his horse. He was working on making sudden directional changes, and his horse responded well to his demands.

"Good day, Hamlen," Merlin said as he walked over to the barn.

"Good day, Merlin," Hamlen replied as they grasped hands. "I know why you're here. It's time for Quintan to learn a few things from you."

"It is, indeed," Merlin said as he watched Quintan. "He has learned how to handle his horse well."

"That is all his mother's doing," Hamlen said. "She is an excellent horsewoman. The village children are taking lessons from her every day. They love riding."

"That is most excellent," Merlin said.

Quintan came riding over to the two men.

"Good day, Master Merlin," Quintan said as he got off his horse.

"Good day, Quintan," Merlin said. "You ride quite well."

"Thank you," Quintan said as he walked his horse into the barn. "My mother is an excellent teacher. I need to take care of Buttercup before we can talk, though."

"I understand," Merlin replied. "I'll be right outside with your father. We have a new wagon design to talk about."

"I'd like to hear about it later," Quintan said as he removed the saddle and blanket from Buttercup.

Merlin and Hamlen went outside and talked about the new design. They were going to figure out how to add a canopy to the wagon. It was Sarah's idea. She said having a top on the wagon would be better to keep the rain and hot sun off the people.

A while later, Quintan left the barn and joined the men.

"All set?" Hamlen asked

"Yes, Father," Quintan said, smiling. "Buttercup is quite happy with the brushing I gave him. And the apple and carrots, too."

"You take good care of him," Hamlen said. "Merlin is here to speak with you."

"Quintan, now that you are about to be twelve years old, it's time for you to spend a great deal of time with me, learning the science of the elements."

"You mean The Magic," Quintan said.

"I do," Merlin replied. "Your father is aware of The Magic and knows how important it is that you begin your training now."

"You mean this minute? Today?" Quintan said.

"Yes. Now," Merlin replied in a serious voice.

"Okay," Quintan said. "I am ready."

"My son, I know you are," Hamlen said as he hugged Quintan. "Go and learn from Master Wizard Merlin."

"I suspected you were a wizard, Master Merlin," Quintan said. "I am ready to learn everything you can teach me. Father, please tell Mother I'll be away all afternoon."

"I will, my son," Hamlen said.

"Thank you, Hamlen," Merlin said. "We're off."

Hamlen watched them go down the south road until they could not be seen anymore. He was sad and happy at the same time. His son was growing into a man.

The shadows were growing long when Merlin called a stop to the day.

"Already?" Quintan said.

"Yes, Quintan," Merlin said. "Didn't you hear Feyanna call us in for supper?"

"No," Quintan replied. "I guess I've been fully focused on all that you've told me."

"You're an excellent listener," Merlin said as he quenched the fire on his workbench. "Let's go outside and wash up."

Merlin and Quintan quickly returned to the main room just as Feyanna set a stew on the table.

"This smells wonderful," Quintan said.

"Thank you, Quintan," Feyanna said. "I created a new bread recipe with garlic and onion. Let me know if you like it."

The three of them enjoyed the meal. Quintan told Feyanna he especially liked the bread and asked if he could have her recipe to tell his mother. He knew she would like the bread as well. She told him the recipe as they were cleaning up.

"Feyanna, thanks for a great supper," Quintan said.

"Quintan, it's time we walked you home," Merlin said. "You'll come by every day from now on. Be here after breakfast and your morning chores."

"I will," Quintan promised. "See you tomorrow, Miss Feyanna."

"Sleep well, Quintan," Feyanna replied.

Sarah was watching for Quintan. The minute she saw him, she called out to her family that he was almost home.

Sarah ran up to Quintan and hugged him.

"Hey, there, Sarah," Quintan said, hugging her in return.

"I missed you," Sarah said. "Where have you been all day?"

"I've been with Master Merlin. He's teaching me all about the earth," Quintan replied, winking at Merlin.

"Tell me something new," Sarah said as he put her on the ground.

"Let's see," Quintan said. "I know. I learned there are more rain storms in the spring than any other time of the year."

"Well, now I know that, too," Sarah said as they arrived at the house.

"I see Sarah has been bothering you, son," Hamlen said as he hurried Sarah over to her mother. "Time to get ready for bed, children."

"Good night, Master Merlin," they all said as they walked down the hall.

"Good night, young ones," Merlin replied. "Sleep well."

"How was your afternoon, Quintan?" his father asked.

"It was amazing," Quintan replied, yawning. "I've already learned a lot of things."

"So I heard," Hamlen said, laughing. "You know Sarah is going to ask you about something new every day."

"I know," Quintan replied. "I'll have something ready for her for sure."

"Off to bed with you," Hamlen said as he hugged his son. "Sleep well."

"Thank you, Father. Good night, Master Merlin," Quintan said as he yawned his way to his room.

"Well, Merlin?" Hamlen asked.

"He has done well today," Merlin replied as he walked to the door. "He is wise beyond his years already. Make sure he does his chores and rides Buttercup before he comes to me every day. I told him to come by after breakfast and chores. Should be mid-morning, please."

"I will make it so," Hamlen replied. "Thank you, my friend. I am grateful."

Merlin waved as he started down the south road. He was home a few minutes later and found Penny and Q waiting for him. There were two other dragons as well. One was a yellow-green blend, and the other was blue.

"Penny. Q. Great to see you," Merlin said, touching hand-to-wing with them. "I see Feyanna has been having a great visit with you."

"Of course she has," Penny replied. "We are lovely dragons to have as friends."

This made the two new dragons laugh, and Q just shook his head at Penny.

"So, my dragon friends, who are these two lovely new dragons?" Merlin asked.

"Oh, he is a kind talker," the yellow-green dragon said.

"I got that," the blue dragon said.

"And, of course, they have quite the sense of humor as well," Feyanna said, laughing with Merlin.

"Of course," Merlin replied.

"Merlin and Feyanna, I would like to introduce Clarice and Roman. They are to be Quintan's protectors," Penny explained.

"I understand," Merlin said. "He will not know about them for a few more years, correct?"

"Yes, that is correct," Penny said. "However, they are on duty as of right this minute."

"They will remain invisible around Quintan and all the others," Q added. "We need to keep them a secret."

"I do understand," Feyanna said. "It has to do with his destiny."

"Yes, Feyanna," Penny said. "That is correct. You are wise beyond your years, too."

"Why, thank you, Penny," Feyanna said, running her hand along Peny's wing.

"That feels so wonderful," Penny said, closing her eyes. "You can do that any time you like."

"Merlin, we see that you've started Quintan's lessons with you," Q said. "They will go on for the next few years. We know you will prepare him well."

"I will do my best," Merlin said. "I was thinking of asking Hamlen to fashion a practice sword out of oak for Quintan. I feel he needs to start learning some defensive moves."

"We agree," Q said as all the dragons agreed.

"Why oak?" Penny asked. "Shouldn't it be metal?"

"Not to start, Penny," Merlin answered. "He needs to build the muscles in his arms, back, and legs first. Oak is a heavy wood and will do well in preparing him for the metal swords he will use later."

"That's a brilliant idea," Clarice, the yellow-green dragon, said.

"It most certainly is," Roman said. He was the blue one.

"I appreciate your support," Merlin said, yawning. "Sorry, dragons, I have had a most busy day."

"Yes, you have," Penny said. "Time for some sleep. I ask the faeries to cover you with sleep dust to give you a good rest."

"I thank the faeries for their gift," Merlin replied.

"Time to fly," Penny said. "We'll always be close by."

"We thank you for that always," Feyanna said as she and Merlin watched them take flight. They were soon away into the night sky.

"Merlin, look," Feyanna said as they walked into their cottage home.

"Thanks for the gifts," Merlin called out quietly.

There were three oak swords leaning against the table. Two were shorter ones for Quintan, and the other one was for Merlin.

Feyanna gathered the crystals and set them in the windows after closing the shutters.

"Good night, sweet friend," Feyanna said as she passed Merlin's room. He was already asleep. "Thank you, sweet faeries. We love you."

There was a soft flash of faerie light in response.

Feyanna was asleep a few minutes later.

"Well, Goldie," George said as he settled his feathers. "I do believe the time of The Special Magic is upon us just as it was foretold."

"I agree, my friend," Goldie said. "It looks like this is the time to begin preparing Quintan for his destiny."

"It is," George said. "We both know it will happen in a flash. Are you ready?"

"I am," Goldie replied. "I hope Feyanna and Merlin are ready. So very much is going to be demanded of them. I know the Special Magic will help them."

"It will," George said. "Sleep well."

"You, too," Goldie said as she closed her eyes.

Goldie and George were asleep as quickly as Merlin and Feyanna. The faeries made sure they all slept well that night.

Quintan's time with Merlin was intense. As the summer moved on, Quintan spent his mornings learning about the elements: the earth, air, water, and sun. The afternoons included sword practice. This was hard work. Quintan learned right away that you need a strong body to handle a sword. Feyanna and Merlin showed him some basic fencing moves in the first few weeks. Quintan thought he could learn these quickly. He soon realized that what looks easy is not always easy to do. Merlin started Quintan on strength training, which involved lifting weights. Granite rocks were the weights. Merlin included distance running and swimming as well.

Quintan loved the swimming part. He had been drawn to water since he could walk. If his mother couldn't find him nearby, she would walk down to the pond near their home and find him wading in the water. He had unlimited questions about the water: how did it get there? What lived in it? Why didn't it dry up under the hot summer sun? His mother answered every question he had, and if she didn't know the answer, she would take him to the local herbalist to get the answers.

Merlin, Feyanna and Quintan would go to Avalon at the end of the day. Quintan would swim from one part of the shore to another several times. Then they all played in the water. The village children soon figured this out and would run down to the lake for some fun of their own when Quintan was there. They cheered him on while he was swimming laps. It was hard work and fun.

The work of The Dragon Brigade increased as soon as Quintan began his lessons with Merlin. Seems The Dark Forces had an idea about what was happening. The Dark Forces didn't know about the whole plan for Quintan, but they knew something in The White Light was happening. So, they increased the chaos on the earth. This included recruiting more dragons as harbingers of the chaos.

Word reached the village one late summer evening about a dragon attack on a camp near the king's castle in Kerwyn. It seems two dragons decided to destroy the whole camp. That's precisely what they did—they burned it to the ground. It was a camp that had tradesmen and farmers in it. They gathered there every day to sell their goods and take jobs fixing things in the castle grounds. It was on the outskirts of the city of Kerwyn. Not a soul survived.

The king ordered his knights and the men throughout his kingdom to kill every last dragon they could find. They were to bring the heads to the castle, and they would be greatly rewarded. After the six were killed in the village raid for grain and gold, more knights were hooded. The king sent these new knights on patrol. They gathered the local men and instructed them to ride with the knights. There were six patrols: one knight and four countrymen. Every knight had an aide to take care of his gear and his horse.

Word got around about this order, and Merlin and Feyanna called Penny and Q to meet them in the meadow.

It was after dark on a cloudy, new moon night when they gathered.

"King Owen is crazy," Feyanna said. She was visibly upset.

"We agree," Penny said as she touched Feyanna's arm to soothe her.

"Your touch is gentle and warm," Feyanna said. "Thank you for this."

"It is my honor to help you be calm," Penny replied.

"Merlin, I am to teach you a spell that will cloak all the good dragons. as they fly through the night," Q said.

"I thought all dragons could become invisible," Merlin said.

"They can," Q replied. "It takes a great deal of energy to stay cloaked while in flight. So we need to have you cast this spell every night at sundown until this mess is over."

"Indeed I will," Merlin said. "What do I need."

"First, go to Avalon and get a full bucket of water," Q said. "Bring it here when you have it."

"I'm away," Merlin said as he ran to the cottage home and grabbed a bucket.

"What can I do?" Feyanna asked.

"We need you to prepare many potions for healing wounded dragons," Penny said. "You gathered some nettle the other day. You will need a lot more. It grows just past us. Bring a crystal and your biggest basket and gather it now."

Feyanna ran to the cottage home and grabbed two large crystals and her biggest basket. The basket had been a gift from one of the framer's wives on the north road for helping heal her goat. She used her handcart to bring these things to Penny.

"Look behind us, and you'll find the nettle," Penny told her. "Be sure to wear your gloves. Those thorns can be nasty."

"I know," Feyanna said, smiling. "I found that out when I was a little girl."

"I remember," Penny said, laughing with Q. "Your mother used the exact potion you are going to make now, then, to get the thorns out and heal your cuts."

"You've been watching me since I was little?" Feyanna asked as she walked past Penny and Q.

"Since you were in your mother's womb," Q replied. "The Special Ones are dear to us."

"We all are grateful and honored that you have always watched over us," Feyanna said as she began to gather the nettle.

Feyanna finished with the nettle just as Merlin returned with the bucket of water.

"I was going to ask why water from Avalon, but then I instantly knew," Merlin said.

"And you are right about that," Penny replied. "Keep the secret."

"Feyanna and I will," Merlin said. "Now, what should I do with the water?"

"Feyanna, take some of those red rose petals and put them in the water," Penny said.

Feyanna did just that.

"Merlin cut a piece of that hawthorn branch with the berries on it and put it in the bucket," Q said.

Merlin did just that.

"Ah, just what we need next," Q said as he saw a few faeries fly over from the forest.

"We have brought the eight elements for the potion," the pink faerie said.

"We are grateful," Q replied. "Please place them in the bucket one at a time."

The faeries placed their special elements into the bucket and flew back a bit to watch.

"There is one more thing we need," Q said. "It is a hair from your head, Merlin. Please."

"Of course," Merlin said as he pulled a hair from his head. It was long and gray.

"Now, Feyanna and Penny, stand back as Merlin places the hair in the potion. Merlin, you will be protected," Q told them.

Penny began to chant in a language Feyanna and Merlin were not familiar with.

As soon as she finished, Q said, "Now, Merlin."

Merlin leaned forward and dropped his hair into the bucket. A bright blue flash enveloped the countryside for a minute. It was so powerful that Merlin was thrown backward onto the ground. The others shielded their eyes until the light faded. Then, the bucket began to boil, and an orange steam rose from it. The steam turned deep red, then deep purple, and spilled over onto the meadow. A ring of purple liquid encircled all of them. It kept bubbling for a bit.

"Merlin, are you okay?" Feyanna asked without moving.

"I am perfectly okay," Merlin said, lying still. "This is all incredible."

"It most certainly is," Feyanna said.

"Look," Penny said, pointing to the purple ring of liquid.

The purple liquid began to solidify into crystals with many points. Light flew off those points into the night sky as far as you could see. Stars became super bright whenever that purple crystal light hit them. It looked like the night sky was on fire. It lasted for only a moment, then all was quiet. The bucker stopped boiling, and the crystals lowered their light energy so that only the four of them could see it.

"The potion in the bucket is charged with a great deal of positive energy. Take it to your workshop and place it in a safe place. You will know when it is needed. When that happens, take a crystal from the bucket and put it in the meadow. The energy from the crystal will cloak the good dragons for hours so they can pursue the rogue ones and end them," Q instructed Merlin.

"I understand," Merlin replied as he got up and walked over to the bucket. The bucket looked like it had when he grabbed it from the workshop. The difference was that it was filled with small purple crystals that were glowing and humming.

"They're humming, Feyanna," Merlin said as he walked over to her. "Listen."

"Yes, they are," Feyanna said as she listened. "They sound beautiful."

"Most crystals do sound wonderful when they are humming," Penny said. "It usually means they are charged and ready to help The Special Ones."

"The dragons are certainly Special Ones," Feyanna said.

"Indeed," Merlin added.

"It's time for you to get some sleep," Q said. "The Dragon Brigade is on patrol. Place one of the crystals in the meadow now so we will be protected."

Merlin set a small purple crystal in the meadow and felt the energy it sent out into the night.

"Whoa! I felt that," Merlin said.

"We all did," Penny said as she spread her wings.

"Thanks for helping us," Q said as those rose into the night sky.

"Always," Feyanna said.

"Always," Merlin said quietly.

The next day, Hamlen stopped by to talk with Merlin and Feyanna.

"Good day, Miss Feyanna," Hamlen said as he walked over to the cottage home.

"Good day to you, Master Hamlen," Feyanna replied. "Please sit and have a cool dipper of water from Avalon."

Hamlen took a long drink and said, "Ah, that was refreshing. Always is from Avalon."

"Hamlen," Merlin said as he stepped outside.

"Merlin," Hamlen said as he stood and shook hands with Merlin.

"What brings you to our place in the meadow this fine morning?" Merlin asked as they both sat down.

"This meadow is lovely," Hamlen said. "Well, Glendianna and I were talking about the children the other day. We realized we didn't know when Quintan was born. We've celebrated the girl's birthdays, but not his. He hasn't said anything about it, but I wonder if he feels left out."

"I can see how that might be a concern," Merlin said. "What can we do about it?"

"We thought we might pick a day before the fall sets in and celebrate it then," Hamlen said.

"That's a lovely idea," Feyanna said.

"What day did you have in mind?" Merlin asked.

"Well, the children go back to learning right after the harvest, which begins in about two weeks. You know it can last well into six weeks with all the different crops we have. So, we thought maybe before the harvesting begins," Hamlen said.

"That sounds like a good idea," Merlin said. "Quintan has been working very hard this summer with me, and I think a celebration is exactly what he needs."

"Have you noticed that the children have all learned to swim watching Quintan during his time in Avalon?" Feyanna said.

"Indeed they have, and it's a good thing, too," Hamlen said. "Last winter, one of the younger ones fell through the ice and almost drowned. His father got to him in time, but he spent a couple of weeks recovering from a chest ailment he got from the ice-cold water. If he knew how to swim, he could have gotten to shore and spent less time in the water. Maybe he wouldn't have gotten sick."

"Then I'm happy to have Quintan swimming laps if it means the other children have learned to swim," Merlin said.

"I have an idea," Feyanna said. "Let's have the celebration at Avalon. That way, the children can show us how well they swim. We could have a few races for fun."

"Great idea, Feyanna," Hamlen said. "I'll tell my wife; she can plan everything with the other mothers. When should we have it, Merlin? Any bad weather coming our way?"

"We should be getting a day of rain tomorrow, so anytime after that is good," Merlin said.

"So be it," Hamlen said. "The day after tomorrow. I finished the third wagon with the canopy. The village women love them. Sarah thinks we should make them different colors. I told her she should talk with her mother and you, Feyanna, because you both know what plants to use to color things."

"I'd be happy to help her," Feyanna said. "I can't wait to see a colored canopy. What fun!"

"Sounds like we all have a few new projects to work on," Merlin said.

"We do," Hamlen said as he stood up. "Time to get back to the carts. I have five orders to fill before the winter sets in. Everyone loves the new harness we designed, and that's all anyone wants now. And I have an idea about making a cart with skids to go over the snow and ice. I could use your thoughts, Merlin."

"That's an excellent idea," Merlin said as he and Feyanna walked Hamlen to the road. "Let's work on that after the celebration."

They parted ways, and each went back to their work. Hamlen shared the news with Glendianna, and she got busy making plans and telling the rest of the village about Quintan's birthday celebration. Hamlen told Quintan about his special day at supper that night.

"Quintan," Hamlen said as they finished their supper. "Your mother and I have a surprise for you. We have decided that the day after tomorrow will be your very own birthday celebration."

"For me?" Quintan said. "Really?"

"Yes, son, just for you," Glendianna said.

Quintan looked around the table, and tears rolled down his cheeks.

"You are very special to us, just like our girls," Glendianna said. "Of course, we will celebrate your birthday."

"But I don't know when it really is," Quintan said softly.

"We know, son," Hamlen said as he lay a hand on Quintan's arm. "So, we decided it would be the day after tomorrow. You have been working very hard with Merlin. He suggested we celebrate all your hard work along with your new birthday. You tell him our plans, Mother."

"We are going to have a celebration at Avalon with the whole village. Feyanna suggested we have a few swimming races since all your hard work in the water made the children want to learn how to swim. And they have learned well. What do you think?"

"I think this sounds wonderful," Quintan said, smiling.

"Can we help get things ready?' Sarah and Margaret said at the same time.

"Of course, you can," Glendianna said. "I will need a lot of help all day tomorrow."

"Yay!" both girls replied.

"Thank you, both," Quintan said. "This is very special to me."

"You mean the world to us, son," Hamlen said. "Never question that ever."

"As you do to me and always will," Quintan said. "I am so honored that you took me in. I will be your son always."

Hamlen and Glendianna couldn't speak for a minute. They were overwhelmed by Quintan's love for them.

"Well," Hamlen said, clearing his throat, "I have a few things to settle for the night. How about you help with the animals, Quintan?"

"Yes, sir," Quintan said.

The village settled down later than usual, as everyone was busy making plans for Quintan's birthday celebration. Handmade presents were being created by the children.

Penny and Q were busy hunting down rogue evil dragons. Another village had been terrorized the night before. The evil dragons had burned down a barn with three horses trapped inside. Then, word reached them about the latest news concerning the knights and countrymen.

The knights and countrymen were having a hard time finding any dragons to kill. Just when they heard about a dragon attack, they rode to the site, and the dragons were long gone. The king had declared that all dragons were evil and must be killed. The knights and countrymen had camped well to the north of the kingdom as they heard that that's where a lot of dragons lived. They searched the caves but didn't find any. This made them angry, so they raided a village, raped the women, killed a few men, and took all their food.

Penny and Q were informed of this and decided to take matters under their own wings, so to speak. They gathered The Dragon Brigade and told them about the barn and village attack the same night Quintan's celebration was being planned.

"It's time we attacked the rogue dragons. We know there are four of them, and they have hit three villages in the far north. I think we should send a patrol to the far north, and one should stay closer to the castle and these villages around here," Q said.

"Roman and I will stay here," Clarice said.

"Yes. Understood," Penny said. "I would rather have you not be involved in any battles. We need you to protect your innocent one."

"We understand," Roman replied.

"Let's put four of us in each group," Q told them. "The rest of you can stay close by in case we need help."

"We will need the cloaking magic," Fesoldan said. "Is he ready with it?"

"He is," Q replied. "I'll send a signal now."

They all watched as Q sent an energy wave towards the cottage home.

"Did you feel that?" Merlin asked.

"I did," Feyanna replied. "I'll go with you to the meadow."

Merlin went into the workshop and took a small purple crystal from the potion bucket. It had many little spikes shooting out from it. He joined Feyanna, and they walked into the meadow.

"Here we go," Merlin said as he set the crystal down.

Spikes of purple energy quickly shot into the sky and then disappeared.

"That was amazing," Feyanna said. "Look at the crystal. It's all white now."

"So it is," Merlin said as he picked it up. "I'll put it back into the potion. Let's go."

"I pray the dragons are safe tonight," Feyanna said quietly as they settled in their cottage home.

"As do I," Merlin said as he entered the workshop and placed the now-white crystal into the potion. "Feyanna, come quickly."

"What is it, Merlin?" Feyanna asked as she walked over to him.

"Look," Merlin said.

The bucket of potion was beginning to bubble, and the white crystal began to change its colors. As they watched, it finally settled on purple, and the potion calmed down.

"Now, isn't that a wonder?" Feyanna said.

"It sure is," Merlin said.

"I do believe The Magic has everything under control in here," Feyanna said.

"I believe it does," Merlin said as they went back into the main room.

The dragons felt the energy wave as the purple crystal sent it out.

"We are safe," Q said. "Time to get going."

Penny stayed with the group near the village and castle. Q went with the group to the north country. It was in the north country that they found what they were looking for.

"There they are," Q said, turning to the east. He had the dragons settle in a glen not far from the two evil dragons they had found. It was almost dark, and they would attack soon.

"As soon as those two take to the air, we attack. Each of us will go to the sides of the dragons. Two apiece. When I give the signal, the dragons with the evil one on the right will attack him, making him fall. The others will set fire to the one on the left. This should make both of the evil dragons fall to the ground, where we will incinerate them. Make sure you don't burn each other," Merlin instructed them.

The evil dragons took to the air, and Q and the brigade encircled them as planned. The invisible dragons bombarded the dragon on the right, making him lose control and fall to the ground. The two that had attacked him mid-air now dove at him and sent streams of fire onto him. The evil dragon screamed so loudly that the villagers in the next village, some five miles away, heard him and were terrified.

The evil dragon tried to get up, but the flames were killing him. The two attackers each sent another stream of fire at him, making the evil dragon blow up. Millions of dragon bits flew into the night sky, then back to the earth as ash.

The evil dragon left in the sky became frightened and tried to fly away. Q sent a stream of fire at him, and it hit him in the head. This made the evil dragon lose control and crash into the earth. The two dragons following him sent streams of fire at him, and he was instantly incinerated. He did manage to send a scream of terror into the sky just before he died. This, too, was heard by people near and far.

The king's knights and countrymen heard these horrible screams and rode toward the sounds. What they saw when they got there made them sick. They fell off their horses and threw up for a long while. They were scared beyond life as they watched the second evil dragon burn to death. As they watched, the ashes of the dead dragon disappeared into thin air. This added more horror to those watching. They mounted their horses and rode south as fast as they could. One of the knights knew about a cave they could hide out in. They all stayed there until sunrise the next morning. They didn't say a word all night long.

Q, Penny, and the Dragon Brigade met up near Merlin and Feyanna's cottage in the wee hours of the morning. They slept there until sunrise woke them. That's what Feyanna and Merlin found when they walked out of their cottage home: a meadow full of sleeping dragons.

"Would you look at that?" Feyanna whispered to Merlin.

"They deserve this rest," Merlin whispered back. "They worked hard last night."

"Yes, we did," Q said, opening his eyes. "We can hear for miles. Thanks for whispering, though. It was a soft way to wake up."

"So sorry to wake you," Feyanna said as she walked up to Q.

"No worries," Penny said. "It's time to feed this dragon."

"I agree," Fesoldan said. "We are all quite hungry."

The dragons began waking up and agreeing with him. And, in an instant, the faeries brought mounds of food and water for the dragons. They were very happy and appreciative.

"I don't think I could have imagined this picture," Feyanna said. "A meadow full of dragons of every color and size."

"None of you are still young ones, right?" Merlin said.

"That is correct, Merlin," Q replied. "The young ones are well hidden and guarded. They have many years of learning to do before they will be ready for battle."

"Just like we humans," Merlin said.

"Indeed," Penny replied. "This food is delicious. Thank you, dear faeries, for always taking such great care of us."

"You are always welcome," Enetia said. "We love taking care of you."

"And we are grateful," Clarice said as she and Roman joined the group.

"The young one is safe," Roman said before Merlin could ask.

"I figured as much," Merlin said. "Thank you."

"We appreciate you figuring out the energy signal I sent," Q said. "I didn't have time to tell you about it."

"The Magic has taught me well," Merlin replied. "I try to stay aware of energy from them."

"You have done superbly this time," Penny said. "We appreciate your quick response."

"I enjoyed watching the white crystal turn to purple as soon as Merlin placed it back in the potion," Feyanna said. "Truly magical."

"Now, if everyone is content, we should be on our way," Penny said. "The rain is about to start, and I'd like to be in my cave before that happens."

"We hear you," the rest of the dragons said.

One by one, the mighty dragons lifted into the sky and flew away. A moment later, the clap of thunder could be heard from far off.

"Time for us to go inside," Merlin said when a flash of lightning was seen, followed by a loud crash of thunder.

"The rain is here," Feyanna said as she stepped into their cottage home, and the sky opened up.

A steady rain kept everyone inside for most of the day, finally ending around sunset.

"Merlin, would you look at that?" Feyanna said as she opened the door.

They were greeted by a huge rainbow arching across the full expanse of the meadow and forest.

"Beautiful," Merlin said as they watched it for quite some time.

The sun eventually set, and the rainbow dissipated, leaving sunbeams flashing through the sky. Night fell upon the village as millions of stars flashed. The dragons kept watch all through the night. The other two evil dragons were still at large. Q and Penny knew they would lay low for a few days after discovering what had happened to their rogue friends. The knights and countrymen stayed sheltered for a few days, too, trying to come up with a new plan to find and kill every dragon in the realm. They had no idea that The Magic wasn't going to let them harm one dragon. Ever.

Quintan's birthday dawned clear and warm. Everyone got busy with their morning chores. Glendianna and some of the other women were baking special treats for the birthday celebration. The children were working on a song to sing for

Quintan. One of them had a wood flute and played along. Feyanna and Glendianna spent a bit of time talking about the colors for the new canopies.

"It's very hard to dye leather," Glendianna said. "Do you have any ideas for some other kind of cloth we could use?"

"Indeed I do," Feyanna said. "We could weave material from the strands of some of the plants we harvest: hemp, cotton, and sunflower stalks. I think the hemp would take the dye exceptionally well."

"I like that idea," Glendianna said. "I have a piece of hemp cloth here. Let's take some of the red berry die we made and try it."

Glendianna placed the hemp cloth in a wooden bowl on the table. She then poured water on it until it was soaking wet and covered by the water. Next, Feyanna put a few spoons of the red dye in the bowl.

"Look there," Glendianna said as she touched a piece of the cloth with her wooden spoon. "It 's turning pink."

"It sure is," Feyanna said. "Let's move it around and see if any of it turns darker pink or red."

They stirred the cloth and dye mixture for about ten minutes and watched as the pink cloth began to turn light red.

"It's been about ten minutes," Glendianna said. "We have light red. Maybe we should put another few spoons of the dye in."

"Good idea," Feyanna said.

Feyanna had just spooned the extra dye into the bowl when Sarah and Margaret came in.

"What are you doing?" Sarah asked as she watched Feyanna stir the bowl.

"We are trying a red dye I made from red berries on this hemp cloth," Feyanna explained.

"It's turning red!" Margaret said.

"It most certainly is," Glendianna said. "It's a lovely shade of red, too. Should we remove it from the dye now?"

"I think so,' Feyanna said as she lifted the cloth from the bowl of dye and placed it in another bowl. "Let's put it on the fence rail so it can dry. We should be able to see if the red color stays red or fades some."

The girls walked outside with the women and watched as they placed the cloth on the fence rail. Red dye dripped from the cloth onto the lower rails, turning them reddish-brown.

"Even the wood turns colors from the red dye," Feyanna said. "I wonder if it will stay that way after it rains?"

"We'll take a look after the next rain," Glendianna said.

"This is a lovely red," Sarah said. "Some of the cloth is different shades of red, though."

"That has to do with the way the hemp was grown," Feyanna explained. "The plant may all look the same, but there are always differences along the leaves and stem. Even the flowers are different from each other. Just like you girls are different."

"I never thought of that before," Glendianna said. "It makes perfect sense when I think of it. I always see different shades of color in plants, especially the stems and stalks. That alone will make the cloth we weave take the dye differently. I can't wait to make the other dyes and try them on the cotton cloth and sunflower stalk cloth."

"Especially the sunflower stalks," Margaret said. "I was looking at them a few days ago and noticed that some looked striped instead of all one color."

"I'll bet those will make amazing clothes," Sarah said. "We are going to have the most beautiful canopy wagons anywhere."

"Yes, we are, thanks to your idea and Feyanna's knowledge about dyes. It's far more advanced than mine. I thank you, Feyanna," Glendianna said.

"You are all very welcome," Feyanna replied. "Time for me to get back home. I have a few things to do before we gather at Avalon."

"Bye, Miss Feyanna," Sarah and Margaret said at the same time.

Suppertime drew near, and the village gathered along the shores of Avalon. The sky was crystal blue and there were only ripples on the lake. The meal was shared among everyone and all had a great time.

"May I have your attention, please?" Hamlen said.

Folks quieted down and looked over at Hamlen.

"Today, my family celebrates an extraordinary birthday. Quintan is twelve years old today," Hamlen said.

People jumped to their feet, clapping, hollering, and whistling in response to the news. Hamlen pulled Quintan next to him.

"It is the tradition of our world that we recognize the special meaning of this twelfth birthday. Today, my son, you have become a man."

The village men grabbed Quintan, raised him high onto their shoulders, and paraded around the place for some time.

Once Quintan was set back down next to his father, he said, "I am truly honored and blessed to be a part of this village family. I love each and every one of you. My family is extraordinary. They took me in and made me a part of them. I thank the gods and goddesses every day for their kindness and love. Even my sisters aren't so bad."

This made everyone laugh and cry.

"I have made the special cake for Quintan's celebration," Glendianna said. "Quintan, please take a bite. It is filled with special herbs to help you walk a good life. This will signify you're moving from your boyhood days into becoming a man."

"I thank you, dear mother, for making this for me," Quintan said. He took a bite and smiled. "It tastes heavenly."

Quintan kissed his mother on the cheek, and everyone hollered and clapped for this auspicious moment.

"Let the fun begin," Samuel called out, and the children lined up on the shore of Avalon for the swimming races.

The children participated in many races and were rewarded with ribbons for their efforts. Quintan helped some of the young ones as they tried to swim. He lifted them up to the waterline and held them as they moved their arms and legs in a swimming fashion, which brought cheers from the folks on the shore.

The older children performed acrobatics in the water, to everyone's joy. Once everyone was dried and dressed, gifts were given. A bonfire had been built on the sand, and everyone gathered around it.

The first gift was the children's song they wrote for Quintan. It was funny and beautiful.

"I thank you all for this beautiful gift of song," Quintan said. "It has made my heart very happy."

Other gifts were given and received with heartfelt thanks. Merlin's was the last gift to be presented.

"Quintan, you have been working very hard this summer, learning about our world and learning new skills. Fencing seems to be made for you. You handle the oak swords with ease now," Merlin said.

"All due to your excellent guidance. I was very sloppy for quite some time. Feyanna, I thank you for being my sparring partner. You are quite excellent with the sword yourself," Quintan replied.

"I enjoy our matches, Quintan, and look forward to many more," Feyanna said.

"As do I," Quintan said, bowing to Feyanna.

Merlin reached behind his back and brought forth a sword of extraordinary design. The villagers gasped when they saw it, and the whole place became silent. Merlin placed the sword in Quintan's outstretched hands. Quintan stood there in awe for the longest while.

"Well, I don't really know what to say," Quintan began. "This is magnificent. Beyond my wildest dreams of any sword I could imagine. Merlin, you fashioned this for me. I can tell."

"Yes, Quintan. A man needs his own sword to go forth and protect what is sacred and special to him," Merlin answered. "This is that sword."

Quintan looked into Merlin's eyes and saw them change to gold and back to blue. He knew The Magic was at work here.

"I thank you, Master Merlin, for such a special gift, and I will use it accordingly," Quintan said, bowing before Merlin.

"You are very welcome," Merlin said as he placed his hand on Quintan's head.

The sun broke through the trees at that exact moment and sent a sunbeam right onto Quintan's head, where Merlin had placed his hand. There was a golden glow that encompassed them both for a moment. Then, the sunbeam lifted back into the sky, and the glow disappeared.

"I am forever honored," Quintan said as he lifted the sword high above his head, pointing into the sky.

The villagers cheered and ran over to examine the sword. They suddenly knew they should not touch it.

"The hilt is made of bronze," Quintan said. "The blade is pure silver. Merlin just told me he fired it for twelve nights to make it strong. It is a thing of great beauty. The design on the hilt is new to me. I'm sure I'll know what it's all about when I'm supposed to."

Only Quintan, Feyanna, Merlin, and The Dragon Brigade could see the dragon design on the hilt. Everyone else saw a pattern of flowers and animals.

"I fashioned this scabbard for your sword to protect it when it isn't needed," Feyanna said, handing it to Quintan.

"It is beautiful," Quintan said. "I especially love the design you made with your sketching knife and dyes. It is one of a kind."

Thank you," Feyanna said. "It was great fun making it and keeping it a secret."

"Even I didn't know she was making it," Merlin said, laughing. "You most certainly can keep a secret, Feyanna."

"You have no idea how true that statement is, Merlin," Feyanna replied, laughing.

"We women keep all kinds of secrets from you men," one of the village women said.

This made everyone laugh and share stories about times gone by. The children spent a long time looking at Quintan's sword, being careful not to touch it. They grabbed sticks and played at sword fighting. The fire finally began to die down, and the families began to pack their things. Quintan went to each and every one of them to thank them for his special celebration.

It was well into the night when Hamlen's family, Merlin, and Feyanna, were ready to leave.

"Father, I'd like to stay for a minute more with Merlin and Feyanna, please," Quintan asked.

"Of course," Hamlen replied. "We'll see you at home."

"What is it, Quintan?" Merlin asked with a questioning look on his face.

"Watch," Quintan said as he stepped into the water a bit.

Quintan set the tip of the sword on the lake. A mist appeared, and a boat with a woman standing in it approached the shore.

"Sir Quintan," the woman said. She wore a light blue robe with a silver hood on her head and shoulders.

"Lady of The Lake," Quintan said as he knelt before her and bowed his head.

"You have been given a magical sword now that you are a man," the Lady of The Lake said. "Use it wisely. Never foolishly. If you are in danger or injured, place the tip in Avalon, and I will come get you. There is a safe place for healing and hiding in The Mists."

"I am forever grateful, Lady," Quintan said. "I am honored by The Magic."

"Rise, now," the Lady of The Lake said. "You have much to learn in a very short time. The time of your final destiny fast approaches. Learn well. Serve your parents well. The Magic deeply loves them. I will be watching."

"Thank you, my Lady of The Lake," Quintan said as he stood. "I shall do all that you have asked."

"Merlin," the Lady said. "You are our special one as well. As is Feyanna. You will be Quintan's advisor soon. Feyanna, you will be Merlin's assistant as always. You both will know when the time is right for all of this to take place. Until then, enjoy this place and these people. We, in The White Light, are delighted with Sarah's covered wagon idea. She makes us smile."

"I'll be sure to tell her that her canopy wagon is now called a covered wagon," Merlin said. "She will love the new name, I'm sure. I will take good care of our Quintan as The White Light has instructed me. And Feyanna. We will always be ready to serve The Divine."

"I am honored as well," Feyanna said.

"It is time for me to go back into The Mists," the Lady of The Lake said as The Mists began to swirl around her. "Blessed be all."

"Blessed be you as well," Quintan said as the Lady moved out of view and The Mists disappeared.

The three of them just stared at the water and each other for a moment.

"How did you know to touch the tip of your sword to the water?" Merlin asked quietly.

"I just knew all of a sudden," Quintan said. "It must be The Magic."

"Indeed," Feyanna said. "We do not tell anyone about this. Understood? This is a high secret in The Magic, and we must keep it."

"Understood," both Merlin and Quintan said.

"Let's move along and get you home, Quintan," Merlin said as they began walking. "We have a great deal to do from here on."

"Today changed my life in ways I couldn't fathom," Quintan said.

"Today changed our lives as well," Feyanna said. "We are forever connected with each other."

Hamlen was waiting by the fence when they arrived at the farm.

"Father, this has been a most amazing day, and I thank you," Quintan said as he hugged his father tightly.

"Your mother and I feel the same way," Hamlen said. "I do believe you've grown a couple of inches just today, son."

"I think so, too," Quintan said. "Good night, Master Merlin and Miss Feyanna. Thanks so much for everything."

"You are so very welcome," Feyanna said. "Time to leave. See you tomorrow morning."

"Yes, I will be there," Quintan said.

"Good night, my friends," Hamlen said as he and Quintan walked over to the door.

"Rest easy," Merlin said as he and Feyanna walked down the south road to the path.

Merlin and Feyanna were quiet as they walked home.

As Feyanna closed their cottage home and Merlin gathered the crystals to place in the windows, Feyanna said, "This has been an extraordinary day in The Magic."

"Yes, it has been," Merlin said. "Things are beginning to move rather quickly. I have many things to teach Quintan by his fourteenth birthday."

"As do I," Feyanna said. "Right now, we need some sleep. Good night, my dear Merlin. Good night, all you dragons."

"Good night, you two," Penny replied.

"She never misses a thing," Merlin said, laughing.

"Neither do we," George said. "We loved watching the celebration."

"Especially when Quintan's friend dropped him into the lake," Goldie said, laughing.

"That was very funny," George said. "The look of surprise on Quintan's face was priceless."

"It most certainly was," Merlin said as they all laughed, remembering the big splash that followed.

"Sleep well," Goldie said a second before she started her snoring.

"Good night, my friends," George said.

"Good night. Sleep well yourselves," Feyanna said as she and Merlin walked down the hall to their rooms.

Quintan lay awake for quite some time after the rest of his family and the village fell asleep. He felt a change from within. His time as a boy was waning quickly. He now faced new responsibilities and had much to learn. He finally fell asleep with his sword at his side.

The harvest began a few days later and lasted an unheard-of eight weeks. Everyone helped with the harvest in some way. Wheat and other grains were cut and thrashed. Their seeds were divided among the village for use as food for people and animals alike. Seeds for planting had been harvested throughout the late summer and stored in earthen jars. Hay and straw were cut and rolled into wheels for storage. Everyone's vegetable gardens were picked and used right away or canned or dried for use during the winter. Fruits were harvested as they became ready. Apple picking was always fun. The younger kids got to gather all the apples that fell to the ground, and the older ones climbed the trees and picked the ripe fruit. Peaches, pears, and lots of berries were gathered, too.

A fall harvest festival was held in late October, and people from other villages came and sold their foods and wares for three days. The countryside was full of people, and everyone got to hear the latest news from far and wide. All three days were filled with sunshine and cooling temperatures. The trees were changing color, and the days were getting much shorter.

The festival was deemed a hit, and Hamlen's covered wagons, as Sarah now called them, thanks to Merlin's suggestion, were a big hit. Hamlen had ten orders and would be working on them all winter long to have them ready for the spring. He even had a few orders for the sled wagon he and Merlin had designed. The winter snows were closing in.

Merlin began teaching Quintan about how The Magic and religion were related. Merlin first explained about The Magic and how The Divine had brought humans to the planet.

"That makes perfect sense," Quintin said. "I always thought that something had to be in charge of everything. That the earth didn't just make itself appear and make all the living creatures on it. The Magic makes perfect sense."

"Good," Merlin said. "Allow Feyanna and I to tell you how religion got started."

Merlin and Feyanna spent three days explaining about religion. Quintan had lots of questions along the way.

On the third day, he said, "I see that religion is different in other places. It seems that each area or region created a way to explain why things happened as they did. We here in this area chose to honor gods and goddesses for everything that man can't make happen. Like a good harvest, rain when needed, and cures for sickness. However, the herbalist does take care of a great deal of the sick and injured. I believe the gods and goddesses gave that information to those like you and Feyanna so others could be well.

"I also believe that people need gods and goddesses to connect with so they don't feel alone. And it's a way to keep humankind in check. I do have this one question, though."

"What is it?" Merlin asked on this cold day.

"What about people who break the laws and rules? If mankind doesn't punish them, how do they get caught?" Quintan asked.

"Excellent question," Feyanna said. "Allow me this one. Quintan, some of the bad people, as we label them, have come to this earth to be bad people. They come here to learn what it's like to be a bad person, allowing others to choose how they respond to them. Do they ignore them? Do they learn from them so they don't make the same mistakes? Do they pursue them to be brought to justice? This is a very wise thing that The Divine has set amongst mankind."

"I never thought of it that way," Quintan said, leaning forward as if to hear more.

"And, then, there's the ones who come to the earth to live a certain way of life and decide they want to do something different. If it's a good choice, not much happens. But, if it's to walk away from the promise they made to The Divine in a negative way that harms others, then they have to answer for this when they go back into The Light."

"That would be when the body dies, and the soul goes back into The Light," Quintan said.

"Exactly," Feyanna replied. "You are learning so much so quickly. And you have a strong grasp of some of the complexities associated with these aspects of being in The Light and being in a body. Good for you!"

"Thank you, Miss Feyanna," Quintan said. "I spend a lot of time thinking about these things. And Merlin keeps me busy with sword, bow, and arrow practice and all the other things. I do enjoy learning about making potions."

"I know," Feyanna said, laughing. "That last one yesterday really stank. Did you use Hogwart in it?"

"We did," Merlin said.

"A bit too much," Quintan added, laughing with them. "When Merlin said a small pinch, I grabbed more than that. I have learned from that mistake to always double-check how much of something I have in my hand before I use it."

"It only took me once, too," Feyanna said. "Our cottage stank so badly that my mother and I slept outside for four days."

"What did you use?" Quintan asked.

"Too much dried black toad's foot. It was awful," Feyanna replied.

"That I can understand," Quintan said. "It stinks before you use it."

"Indeed it does," Merlin said. "But it does keep those pesky mosquitoes and flies away."

"I can see why," Quintan said, laughing with everyone.

"Time for supper," Feyanna said. "I have meat pies in the outdoor oven and a berry pie for dessert."

"It smells wonderful as always," Merlin said. "Let's go wash up, Quintan."

Supper was fun as they told more stories about their not-so-good herbal concoctions and potions. It was dark when supper was cleared, and Merlin got Quintan ready to go home.

"Thanks, Miss Feyanna," Quintan said. "You are still a clever swordwoman. I need to work harder."

"You'll get there, my friend," Feyanna said. "Give my love to your family."

"I will," Quintan replied as he and Merlin walked outside.

"It's getting colder these days," Merlin said.

"The first of the snows will arrive very soon," Quintan said as they set off down the path to the south road.

"It will be fun to see how your father's sled wagon works in the snow," Merlin was saying when a huge shadow flew over them.

Merlin and Quintan turned and ran back to the cottage home just as the first line of fire was sent toward them.

Feyanna was at the door with the purple crystal. "I called out to Penny and Q. They should be here now."

"Stay here," Merlin said when Quintan tried to go outside.

"He'll be okay," Feyanna said.

As Merlin crossed the meadow, he saw Q come zooming in and then disappear as he dropped the crystal on the ground. He felt the energy wave and knew the dragons would be safe.

"What in the name of the gods and goddesses was that?" Quintan asked as Merlin came through the door.

"That was a rogue dragon," Merlin said. "I suspect they've come to kill you."

"What?" Quintan said as a great noise was heard.

The ground shook a moment later as if something huge had fallen on it

"They're here," Feyanna said. "We're safe."

"Who's safe, and who's here?" Quintan asked.

"You'll be told when it's your time to know," Merlin said in a stern voice.

Quintan knew better than to ask further questions. A brilliant orange light filled the sky outside for a moment, then the darkness returned.

"Should we look outside?" Quintan asked.

Feyanna and Merlin thought silently for a moment.

"We can now," Merlin said as he opened the door and walked outside.

Penny and Q were waiting for them in the meadow.

"Miss Penny and Master Q," Quintan said as he hurried over to them. "It's been a long while since we saw each other."

"Quintan," Penny said, reaching out a wing to touch him. "You have grown a great deal these few days."

"I have," Quintan said. "Mother said it's crazy trying to keep up with my growth. My trousers fit well one day, and a few days later, they're too short."

"I can see that," Q said. "That happens with growing dragons, too. One day, they're a few different colors, and the next day, they've settled into their adult color and grown a few feet."

"A few feet in a few days? Wow!" Quintan said. "Must take a lot of food to keep them happy."

"Oh, it does," Penny said, laughing. "It seemed Q couldn't never get enough Winterberries when he was growing like that."

"It's the truth," Q replied. "I love Winterberries to this day just as much."

"Q, are you and Penny safe from whatever just happened?" Quintan asked.

"We are, Quintan," Q replied. "We took care of this whole thing. That rogue dragon is no more."

"Thank you for that," Quintan said. "I've heard talk in the village about a couple of bad dragons that are burning villages and killing people and animals. The king's knights have been through here a couple of times lately looking for them. They said there's a big reward for turning in a dragon's head."

"We can tell him," Q said to Penny.

"Tell me what?" Quintan asked.

"Quintan, when a dragon dies, his physical body and essence are taken by The Divine before anyone can touch them. They are of The Special Magic and are returned to it as such," Penny explained.

"So, no matter what, the king's knights and countrymen will never retrieve a dragon's head. I like that," Quintan said.

"We hoped you would," Q said. "I see Merlin and Feyanna have been teaching you well."

"Yes, they have. Indeed well," Quintan said.

"Time for us to go along," Q said. "There's one more rogue dragon causing havoc just north of your village."

"I hope you find him before he does any damage," Feyanna said.

"Stay safe," Merlin said as Penny and Q became airborne and banked to the north.

"I love those dragons," Quintan said to no one in particular.

"We do, too," Feyanna said.

"Time to get you home," Merlin said as he and Quintan set off again.

"Sleep well," Feyanna said. "See you tomorrow."

Quintan waved his hand over his head at Feyanna as they turned in the path.

Merlin was back at the cottage home a short time later, and he and Feyanna settled for the night. Quintan slept easily that night. He didn't even dream of dragons. The Magic needed him well-rested as he continued the journey toward his destiny.

CHAPTER 16

Three years seemed to go by in a flash. One minute, Quintan was just turning twelve, and the next, he was soon to be fifteen. The winter of his twelfth year saw Hamlen's wagon sled design come to life. It worked well, and the villagers loved it. He had orders for two more that winter. His cart-making business had developed so rapidly that he had to hire two assistants to help him. They were young men from a farm just north of the village. Their father bought a covered wagon from Hamlen, and his sons used it to go about the countryside. Hamlen was pleased with their progress in learning how to make carts.

The winters found the village children enjoying the snow. Quintan loved sledding, and he and the other children could be found on a nearby hill every chance they got. Quintan had grown close to one of his boyhood friends. Hugho and Quintan were always together when time allowed. They learned to hunt with Hugho's father. They learned to repair wagon wheels with Hamlen. They learned to sew ripped clothes, which they always seemed to come home with after one of their adventures. Their mothers got so frustrated with them that both women told their sons to repair their own clothes. So, Glendianna set both boys down one summer afternoon and taught them how to thread a needle and make simple repairs on their clothes. Hugho's mom was so thrilled with this that she began teaching all the village children how to sew and make simple pieces of clothing.

One of the themes that Merlin and Quintan continually discussed was how The Magic had shaped religion. Merlin had covered the basics in Quintan's early time with him. As Quintan grew up, Merlin threw in twists and turns about this concept. One winter night, when Merlin was visiting Hamlen, Quintan asked him a question.

"Master Merlin, may I ask you a question concerning religion?" Quintan asked.

"If it is okay with your father and mother, then yes," Merlin replied.

Glendianna and Hamlen nodded their approval. The girls were already in bed.

"If The Magic helped shape religion, has religion shaped the laws the king makes?" Quintan asked.

"That is a profound question, son," Hamlen said.

"Share with us what you are thinking," Merlin said.

"For instance, we know that there are dragons here about. Many believe that The Magic created the dragons. There were those four rogue ones that destroyed villages and killed people and animals a while back. The king created a new law that all dragons must be killed. I suspect that's because he couldn't control the dragons like he controls the people. He declared that all dragons were to be killed because they were evil. I think he said that because he was afraid one of them might kill him. Only the gods and goddesses know what goes on in that king's head and heart. So, I suspect that the king may be using religion to make his laws."

"You have done a great deal of thinking on this," Hamlen said.

"I have," Quintan replied. "So, my question is this: Does the king use religion and Magic to control the people so he can have anything he wants? And, so he can kill anyone that doesn't do what he wants?"

"You are surely no longer a boy," Glendianna said. "You have the mind of a full-grown man."

"Yes, he does," Merlin said. "Yes, Quintan, to answer your question. Kings use religion and Magic to rule their kingdoms. Some of it is good. Religion has some positive sides to it. It can be used as a guide for people to live benevolently. It can also be used to do evil things against those that do not follow the king's rules and laws."

"I know that just from listening to everyone," Quintan said.

"I'm glad we do not live close to the castle," Hamlen said. "Life would be very different. We would always be under the eyes of the knights and have to give our food and wagons to the king. Give them. Not receive a penny for our work. There is much underhandedness that goes on around the castle."

"Indeed there is," Merlin said, agreeing with Hamlen. "Any other questions, Quintan?"

"No. Not right now," Quintan answered. "Thanks for answering my question."

"It's time for me to get home," Merlin said, wrapping his cloak around his body. "It's mighty cold out there."

"It is," Glendianna said. "Put this against your chest. It will stay warm all the way home."

Merlin took the cloth from her and placed it in his cloak.

"How did you make this?" Merlin asked.

"I heat small crystals, then place them in this flannel I made," Glendianna said. "We use them to stay warm all winter long."

"This is splendid," Merlin said. "I thank you and will be sure to tell Feyanna about this. I may have a warmer bed soon."

"That's one way we use them at night," Hamlen said.

"Sleep well, my friends," Merlin said.

"Good night, Master Merlin," Quintan replied as he closed and locked the door.

"Sleep well, my son," Glendianna said as she handed Quintan his hot crystal cloth.

"I will. Thanks for this," Quintan said as he went off to bed.

The cart maker's family settled for the night along with the village. Snow fell quietly for a while, and the earth slept deeply.

As time moved on, other things were happening in the Kingdom of Kerwyn.

The king's knights were still on the hunt for dragons. They hadn't found any yet, but the attacks on the king's villages had greatly decreased. So, the king wasn't too concerned with this problem.

Merlin and Feyanna continued to learn from The White Light about special potions and new herbal remedies. It was in the spring of Quintan's thirteenth year that they learned how to cast a spell. They were cautioned to do no harm to the innocents when casting spells if at all possible. There was growing unrest in the kingdom, and The White Light was a bit concerned about the increase in chaos. A well-placed spell could ease the chaos if need be.

It was in the spring of Quintan's thirteenth year that things did, indeed, begin to change in the kingdom. King Owen began to act strangely once in a while. It was as if he wasn't aware of what was around him. His court figured it was his old age that caused this problem. It wasn't.

Hamlen had been given an order for three covered wagons for the court. It was on this fine spring day that Quintan got his first look at the King's castle and the city of Kerwyn.

Hamlen and Quintan left early on a Wednesday morning. Their horses had been tied to the back of the wagon for the ride home. They were delivering two of the three wagons that day and the third one the next day. It took about two hours to ride south to the castle and a little less to ride home.

"It is a fine day, father," Quintan said as they prepared to leave.

"It is, indeed," Hamlen said as he checked his wagon and horse one more time.

"Here you go, my two fine men," Glendianna said as she handed them a sack of food and water. "Be safe."

"We will," Quintan replied. "Thanks for the provisions."

"Do you have your sword?" his mother asked.

"Right here," Quintan said as he pointed to his waste. "And my bow and quiver as well."

"Good thinking," his father said. "I have my bow and quiver, too."

"Let's hope you don't have to use either," Glendianna said.

"We're away," Hamlen said as he led them out of the pasture and onto the south road toward Kerwyn.

Merlin felt their energy as they left the farm.

"Hamlen and Quintan are on their way," Merlin said.

"I feel it, too," Feyanna said. "I've surrounded them in The White Light for their journey."

"As have I," Merlin said. "They should be well protected. We both know this is Quintans's first look at the castle and the world surrounding it. He will be full of thoughts and questions when he returns."

Just then, Penny and Q landed in the meadow.

"We have company," Feyanna said as they walked outside.

"Good morning," Penny said as she and Q settled.

"Good morning to you both," Merlin replied. "I suspect you're here about Hamlen and Quintan's journey today."

"We are," Penny replied. "Here come Clarice and Roman."

They settled next to Penny and Q.

"Good morning, everyone," Roman said. "We are here to inform you that we will be following Quintan and his father the whole time they are gone."

"I thought you might do that," Feyanna said.

"I brought a purple crystal with that in mind," Merlin said as he showed them the crystal he had in his shirt pocket.

"I told you he already knew what we were going to ask of him," Clarice said.

"You did," Roman replied. "You are very keen about these things."

"She is," Q replied. "Always has been. Are you ready to leave?"

"We are," Clarice replied. "We wanted to stop by to talk with Merlin and Feyanna first, though."

"You know we love it when you visit," Merlin said.

"As do we," Clarice replied. "Here's the thing. It seems something is happening near the castle. Something bad. The Dragon Brigade has become aware of a shift in the energy balance there. Something dark is beginning to grow."

"You mean The Dark Forces are causing chaos again?" Merlin asked.

"We do," Q replied. "Clarice, you need to speed things up here."

"Yes, Q. Thanks for reminding me," Clarice said. "The king has had a few instances of forgetfulness. Some say it's his old age. He's not that old yet—only forty years. His knights are concerned. They've had a few private meetings to discuss this. They are cautiously watching him for now."

"What do you think, Penny?" Q asked.

"I don't have an opinion now," Penny said. "I'll keep an eye on him and let you know."

"Okay. Thanks," Q said. "Now, be on your way."

Merlin set the purple crystal on the meadow, and all the dragons became invisible.

"This is kind of fun," Roman said. "We can watch everyone and maybe help someone if they need it."

"That's true," Penny said. "Keep our Quintan safe."

"And his father," Feyanna added.

"We will," Clarice said. "Here we go."

Merlin and Feyanna felt a rush of wind as the dragons took off. Penny and Q became visible again.

"Those two really are characters," Penny said.

"I got that same impression," Feyanna added.

"They may seem a bit silly, but don't let that fool you. They are two of the most dedicated and incredible warriors we have," Q said.

"Well, time to get going," Penny said. "Lots for this dragon to do. You, too, Q."

"Yes, Ma'am," Q said, waving his wing at Penny.

"Later, you two," Merlin said, laughing with Feyanna.

Feyanna and Merlin got back to work. Hamlen and Quintan reached the city's outer edge, which surrounded the castle by late morning. They were greeted warmly by the people there.

"Father, there are a great many people out here," Quintan said, watching everything.

"There needs to be," Hamlen said. "The court needs everything we have at home. We grow our food on the land and with the animals. We make cloth, preserve our food, have water wells, and make or barter for the other things we need. The court does the same but on a much bigger level. That's why there are all these people here. They sell and barter their wares and goods to those in need. That's what a city is all about."

"Do you see the girls over there?" Quintan asked.

"I do," Hamlen said. "You remember what I told you about bedding a woman, son. Some of those girls look a lot older than girls your age. They are selling themselves to anyone who will pay the price."

"I remember Father," Quintan said. "But a few of those girls are my age and quite pretty."

"Indeed they are," Hamlen said. "Look as much as you'd like."

"Oh, I am for sure," Quintan said as he acknowledged the girls.

They were surprised, giggled, and turned away.

Hamlen had been told to go to the east castle gates. When he arrived, he and Quintan were allowed to pass. They were met by a guard just inside the wall.

"Greetings, cartmaker," the guard said. "We have been expecting you. Please put the wagons over by the smithy's shop. You'll find water and food for your horses just past there. The king's man will be here shortly."

"Thank you, fine sir," Hamlen said, bowing his head. Quintan did the same.

Hamlen and Quintan drove the wagons over to the spot the guard had pointed out to them. They got down, untied their horses, and took them to the food and water place.

The inner castle grounds were bustling. There were guards everywhere. Women were carrying food from the outdoor vendors, men were working in the Smithy's shop or building a great many things, and sword practice was taking place among the older boys. Guards were patrolling everywhere.

Hamlen and Quintan ate some fruit while waiting for the king's man. Quintan had worn his sword and looked like he belonged there. A few of the guards looked at him when they passed.

"Why are the guards looking at me?" Quintan asked.

"Because you are tall and wear your sword," Hamlen answered.

"Oh," Quintan replied.

"Hamlen, the cartmaker?" A man dressed in the king's colors asked.

"Yes, sire. I am," Hamlen replied, bowing.

"These are fine wagons," the man said. "I've never seen one with a cover before. One of our knights passed through your village last fall and saw one. He mentioned it to the king and queen one evening. Her Majesty loved the idea, so the king asked to have them made."

"My family is humbled to be asked to make these for His Majesty," Hamlen said.

"Here is the coin you requested," the man said as he handed a pouch to Hamlen. "It is all there."

"I trust the king in this business transaction," Hamlen said, putting the pouch in his inner vest pocket.

"A wise decision," the man said. "Is this your son?"

"It is," Hamlen replied. "Quintan is almost fifteen and a good scholar and swordsman."

"I see you have a sword, Quintan," the man said. "Will you show it to me, please?"

Quintan looked at his father for approval, which Hamlen gave. Quintan drew his sword from the scabbard and held it sideways for the man to examine.

"This is a beautiful sword," the man said. "It has been made by a master craftsman. May I ask his name?"

"He is known as Merlin," Hamlen replied. "He resides to the south of our village."

"I have never seen such detailed work. Is this Merlin teaching you how to use your sword, Quintan?" the man asked.

"Yes, sir, he is," Quintan replied. "He is a taskmaster when it comes to my training."

"That is a good thing," the man replied. "Thank you for allowing me to have a look."

"You are most welcome," Hamlen replied. "Is there anything His Majesty wishes from me?"

"Not at this time, cartmaker," the man replied. "We will be in touch should we need anything else. We have been thinking about the wintertime. Is there any kind of cart you make that can ride easily over the ice and snow?"

"There is, indeed," Hamlen replied. "Merlin and I designed a sled wagon just for that purpose last year. It has been a great success for the villagers and far and wide."

"Do you have a drawing of one of these sled wagons, Hamlen?" the man asked.

"I do," Hamlen said as he took a folded paper from his pocket and handed it to the man.

The king's man looked it over for a few minutes, then smiled. "This is exactly what we have been talking about. I will show this to the stable master and the king and get back to you should we decide to order one."

"I would be honored to make a sled wagon for the court," Hamlen replied.

"Time to return to my post," the man said. "Thanks for bringing the wagons. I know there is one more."

"We will deliver it tomorrow," Hamlen said.

"I look forward to it," the man said. "Use the same gate, and the guard will let you in. Take care now."

Hamlen and Quintan watched the king's man walk away.

"Let's get out of here," Hamlen whispered.

They mounted their horses and rode them to the gate.

"I'll be here tomorrow when you arrive," the guard said.

"Thank you, kind sir," Hamlen said.

The guard signaled for the gates to open so Hamlen and Quintan could leave. As soon as they were clear of the castle walls and the city, Hamlen signaled Quintan to follow him. He was headed in a slightly different direction than the one they arrived from. They rode for the better part of an hour before Hamlen reigned in his horse and stopped.

"Do you expect trouble, Father?" Quintan asked.

"Always, son. No matter how nice someone seems to be, trouble is always at hand. The king's man was especially interested in your sword. It is made of precious metals, and I doubt that there is anyone with such a fine sword as yours," Hamlen said as he dismounted. "Let's eat."

They walked the horses to a nearby stream and settled on the ground next to them to eat their lunch. It was a quiet place, and they enjoyed the few minutes they spent there.

"Something is off," Quintan said all of a sudden.

"It is, indeed," Hamlen said. "Time to go."

They grabbed their horses, swung up into the saddle, and took off at a gallop.

"There are two king's men in pursuit," Hamlen said.

"I see them," Quintan replied.

Just as the two king's men seemed to catch up to Hamlen and Quintan, a very large tree fell across the road, blocking them from going any further.

Hamlen and Quintan slowed to a walk, looking back at the tree.

"I believe we have protectors with us today," Hamlen said.

"We do," Quintan replied.

"How do you know this?" Hamlen asked.

"I can feel it," Quintan replied. "Besides, that tree was alive and very strong. It didn't just fall because it was dead."

"True, son," Hamlen said. "I believe The Magic is keeping us safe."

"As do I," Quintan said. "Thanks be to the gods and goddesses."

"Thanks be," Hamlen added.

"Those men were not from the court, Father," Quintan said.

"How do you know that?" Hamlen asked.

"Their clothes were worn, and the colors were not quite the right red, green, and gold."

"You have excellent eyesight," Hamlen said. "Let's get home."

About an hour later, they rode into the farm. Glendianna had food, a hot bath, and clean clothes waiting for them. Quintan fell asleep as soon as he was dressed and slept through the night. Hamlen and Glendianna smiled as they watched him sleep.

"My love," Hamlen whispered. "It won't be long before our Quintan leaves us."

"I know," Glendianna said. "I will cherish every minute with him up until that day."

While Hamlen and Quintan were riding home in the afternoon, there was a bit of uneasy energy moving around the woods just past the outer castle walls.

A middle-aged woman lived there alone. She was known as a witch because it was believed that she could cast spells to make anything happen. The king's knights had been seen visiting her. She was an herbalist, and many of the area people went to her for healing remedies and potions. She had been near the castle when Hamlen and Quintan rode through with the wagons. She didn't think much of them as many people rode to and from the castle.

It was when they left on horseback that she picked up on an energy surrounding them. She felt a strong protective energy go through the place when Quintan rode past. Hamlen and Quintan were nowhere near her cottage. Quite the opposite. They were on the far side of the field, a long way from the witch. She returned to her cottage and set a pot of water to boil. She added several herbs, and when the steam began to rise from the pot, she poured some of the liquid into an earthen bowl set above a flame.

The witch began to chant, invoking Spirits to answer her questions. She didn't get anything at first, but finally, she saw a symbol in the air—the Pentagram.

"Who is the pentagram for? Me or the boy?" she asked the Spirits.

They answered immediately by placing one of her Spirit cards in front of her. It was that of a young man holding a sword.

"It's for the boy?" she snarled. "I am the powerful one here and you insult me with this card?"

A flash of bright white light momentarily blinded the witch. She became frightened and bowed down on her knees.

"I apologize for my insolence," she said. "I am greatly surprised by this news. I thought my wishes were being granted. I shall remain patient."

Her sight returned immediately. She threw the potion out the door. It bubbled and burned the grass, then was gone.

"There is much work to do now," she said to herself as she walked around the cottage. "I need to think about this. That boy is well protected by The White Light. I feel he will have some influence with the court before long. He must be stopped. How can I get rid of him without being found out? I will have to think about this for a few days and be very careful with my plans."

The next day, Hamlen delivered the third covered wagon in the morning, just like the day before. The same guard was at the gate and let him in.

"Good day, cart maker," the guard said. "I see you are alone."

"Good day, sir," Hamlen replied. "I am. No need for both of us to make the journey."

"Take the wagon to the same place as yesterday. The king's man will be here shortly."

"Thank you," Hamlen said as he drove the wagon next to the smithy's shop. He untied his horse and took him to get food and water. That's where the king's man found him.

"Good day, cart maker," the man said.

"Good day to you, sir," Hamlen said.

"I must tell you that Her Royal Highness, the queen, loves her covered wagon. She took a ride about the countryside yesterday and was very happy when she returned."

"I am happy to hear the news," Hamlen said.

"Here is your payment as promised," the man said. "I showed your drawings to the king and his council, and they like the sled wagon idea. The king has asked me to request one from you before the winter comes along."

"I am honored to be asked to make one," Hamlen said.

They talked about the details and the payment needed. All was agreed on in a few minutes.

"Cart maker, how will you get it here?" the man asked.

"I will make the chassis on a regular wagon I have made. It's longer than the sled wagon and makes it quite easy to transport," Hamlen answered. "I use a ramp to remove it from the wagon."

"That is brilliant, cart maker," the man said. "May I ask your name again?"

"Of course. I am Hamlen," Hamlen said.

"Ah, yes, that is right," the man said. "I am known as Rory."

"Nice to make your acquaintance, Rory," Hamlen said as they shook hands.

"Send a messenger when the sled wagon is almost ready, and I'll make sure things here will be ready as well."

"I will, Rory. Thank you kindly," Hamlen said. "Is there anything I can do for the court?"

"Give my regards to your son Quintan," Rory said.

"I shall," Hamlen replied as he swung up into the saddle. "Good day."

"Good day," Rory said as Hamlen approached the gate. The guard waved as he opened the gate, and Hamlen left the castle grounds. He set out straight for home, asking for protection from the gods and goddesses. The witch watched as he rode away. The boy was not with him as before. She was forming a plan and needed a bit more time.

Penny and Q were flying just over his head the whole way. Just before he left the edge of the outer castle fields, he felt a cold wave pass over him. Then he watched as a stream of fire from an invisible source was sent down to the two men who had tried to overtake him and Quintan the day before. They were incinerated instantly. Only ashes were left where they had hidden. No one knew they were there, so no one saw what had happened. The witch saw the flame but not the dragon. She knew White Light Magic was responsible for this. This made her even angrier than before. She must cast a spell right away to kill these people.

Goldie and George were also close by. They watched as Penny and Q took care of the bad men. Goldie chattered with George as he took to the air.

"You look magnificent as an hawk," Goldie said.

"Thanks, Goldie," George replied as he circled overhead to make sure Hamlen was safe. "I'll follow him all the way home."

"Good," Goldie said. "I'll be on my way. It's a long way back."

"Goldie," Penny said. "I'll give you a ride. I'm next to that oak tree to your right. On the left side."

"Thanks so much, Penny," Goldie said as Penny became visible.

Goldie walked up to Penny's wing and settled herself on her back near her neck. "I'm ready."

"Here we go," Penny said as they became invisible.

"This is great fun," Goldie said as George flew close by.

"It sure is," George said as he went back to flying above Hamlen.

"Thanks to the gods and goddesses for protecting me," Hamlen said as he picked up his pace. He was home a while later. Once the horse was settled, he asked about Quintan.

"Hamlen, he's with Merlin, of course," Glendianna said, looking at her husband.

"Oh, yes. I was thinking it was closer to evening," Hamlen said. "I have a great deal on my mind, including an order for a sled wagon for the king."

"That is great news," Glendianna said as she kissed her husband.

"Not as good as this," Hamlen said as he untied her gown and ran his hands across her breasts.

"No news is ever as good as this," Glendianna said as she untied his trousers and ran her hand across his hard shaft.

Hamlen led Glendianna to their bed chamber, and they undressed each other completely. He took her breast into his mouth and began to suck her. Glendianna moaned with pleasure. She moved them onto the bed, where Hamlen ran his hand across her wet mound and began flicking her with his finger.

Glendianna grabbed at his hard shaft and played with it until Hamlen called out for her to stop. He moved over her and kissed her breasts. He slid down her belly and found her clit. He licked her until she cried out.

"Fuck me now!" she cried.

"With pleasure," he replied as he slid up until his hard dick touched her wet pussy.

Hamlen then pushed hard into his love, and she met his thrusts with her own. They set a rhythm they knew well. She felt him get harder, and he felt her push against him. He quickened his thrusts, and she cried out as she climaxed. This made him hit his peak, and they flew together into that place of indescribable pleasure. They soared for a long, long time before finally coming back to reality. They slept for a while.

"That was perfect," Glendianna said as she felt Hamlen move.

"It was," Hamlen said. "You are all I could ever want in this life."

"Same here, my husband," Glendianna said. "Time to dress. The girls will be home soon."

They dressed and were making tea as the girls ran into the house. The afternoon chores and lessons were completed just as Quintan came home.

"Hello, my son," Hamlen said.

"What's this?" Glendianna said as she looked at the small bandage on Quintain's forearm.

"Feyanna is swift with her sword," Quintan said, laughing. "It's nothing more than a scratch. Feyanna bandaged it so we could finish my fencing lesson. She said to tell you not to worry a bit."

"Then I won't," Glendianna said. "You and your father take care of the animals while the girls and I set the table."

"Yes, Ma'am," Hamlen and Quintan said as they left.

The evening gave way to night, and the village settled down for a rest. The spring was turning out to be well on its way.

A couple of weeks later, Samuel came running to Feyanna and Merlin.

"We need your help," Samuel said. "There's a sickness in the village, and my sister sent me for you. Bring all your medicines and come quickly. Please."

The three of them hurried down the path onto the south road. They arrived first at Hamlen's house.

"I'm so glad you're here," Hamlen said. "Glendianna is sick. She can't stay awake for more than a few minutes. She hasn't eaten much in a couple of days. I tried to get her to drink tea, but she fell asleep. Kerrianita is sick, too. All the children are at home."

"I'll take a look at Glendianna. You go with Samuel and find the others who are sick," Feyanna said.

Feyanna looked over at Glendianna. She didn't have a fever. There were no sores on her skin. She just couldn't stay awake for more than a minute or two. Feyanna made her a tea to help her stay awake. It took a little while, but Glendianna finally finished all of it.

"What's happening?" Glendianna said as she finished the tea. "I can't seem to stay awake."

"When did this first start?" Feyanna asked.

"About two days ago. Some of the women in the village are sick like this, too. Even some of the men," Glendianna replied.

"Did you all eat the same food or drink from the same bucket?" Feyanna asked.

"No. Not at all," Glendianna said. "I am so sleepy."

"Are the girls affected?" Feyanna asked.

"No. Hamlen says they're okay," Glendianna replied. "I need to close my eyes."

And that's exactly what Glendianna did. She was sound asleep in no time. Hamlen came into the house and asked about her.

"Hamlen, Glendianna says she just got sleepy a couple of days ago," Feyanna said. "She said no one shared food and drink. Do you know if she was bitten by an animal or insect?"

"I don't know," Hamlen said. "Let's take a look. You two stay out here."

Hamlen helped Feyanna remove Glendianna's clothes. Feyanna looked at every inch of her body and found no bites, scratches, or sores. They dressed her into a clean nightgown while she slept.

"I gave her a potion to keep her awake for a while. It only lasted about ten minutes," Feyanna said as she packed her things. "She did drink a large mug of tea, so she's had some nourishment. Try to get her to drink more every half hour. I'm going into the village and check on the others."

"Thank you, Feyanna," Hamlen said. "I will. Quintan, make some supper for your sisters."

"Yes, sir," Quintan said. "Sarah and Margaret, come help me, please."

The girls joined Quintan in the kitchen, making supper.

Feyanna found Merlin on the village green, talking with Samuel.

"Good. You're here," Merlin said. "Half of the village adults are affected by this sleeping sickness. Men and women alike. I asked if any of them ate from the same plates and drinking water, and they all said no."

"I'll have to look over their skin for any bites, scratches, or sores next," Feyanna said. "Let's get started. Merlin, you can help me with the men. I'll ask one of the women to assist me with the sick women. I don't think this is a contagious illness because not everyone is sick."

Feyanna and Merlin spent the next three hours looking at the sick villagers. None of them had a bite, scratch, or sore on their bodies. They didn't have fevers or a cough. This was truly a mystery for Feyanna and Merlin.

When they finished, it was nighttime. They met with the unaffected villagers on the village commons.

"I don't know what this is, but I am sure it is not contagious," Feyanna said.

"Is it a plague?" Samuel asked.

"No, Samuel, I am quite sure it is not a plague," Feyanna replied.

The villagers sighed in relief.

"Merlin and I are going back to our cottage home to try to figure out what this is," Feyanna said.

"If anyone else becomes ill like this or in any other way, send one of the children for us," Merlin said.

"It doesn't seem like the children are affected," Horatio said.

"That's what I was thinking, too," Feyanna replied. "It is a mystery right now. Merlin and I will do our best to figure it out."

"We know you will," Horatio said.

"I know you will because you fixed my foot," Samuel said.

"Thanks for that, Samuel," Feyanna said. "We're on our way."

Feyanna and Merlin got home in a quick fashion.

"Merlin, there is something evil afoot here, I'm thinking," Feyanna said as they walked into their workshop.

"I was thinking the same thing," Merlin said. "But why now? Why here?"

"I'm quite sure it has to do with Quintan," Feyanna said. "He is quickly coming into his own self. And we know what his destiny is after all."

"All true, and I agree," Merlin said, pacing about.

"I do believe I'm starving," Feyanna said as she left the workshop and started pulling things together for supper.

"Oh my god, we haven't eaten yet," Merlin said as he helped. "No wonder I can't think straight."

"Yup," Feyanna said as she chewed on a carrot. "These have stayed quite fresh throughout the winter in their root cellar. Try one."

"Thanks," Merlin said as he bit off a piece. "They are very fresh and sweet."

"I'm making a salad from some of the veggies in the root cellar. How about you heat some of that leftover soup? There's bread in the breadbox."

Feyanna and Merlin made quick work out of making supper and ate every last bite.

"That was delicious and just what I needed," Merlin said as he yawned.

I agree," Feyanna said as she yawned. "I'm not getting sick. I'm just exhausted from this afternoon. I've already asked for extra special protection so we don't become ill."

"I asked for it, too," Merlin said.

They both looked at each other and said, "The dragons need a crystal."

Merlin grabbed a crystal from the bucket, and they ran out into the meadow. Penny and Q were waiting for them. Merlin set the crystal down, and the energy wave rippled across the space.

"Thanks for that," Q said. "We've just been informed that a very mean rogue dragon is headed this way on his way to the castle. The Dragon Brigade is already in flight."

"Be safe," Feyanna said.

Penny and Q lifted quickly into the air and were gone.

"The sickness and now this," Feyanna said as they closed their cottage home for the night.

"It would seem that The Dark Fores are striking wherever they can," Merlin said. "No matter what, it will not deter us from preparing Quintan for his final destiny."

"Agreed," Feyanna said. "Sleep well."

"You, too," Merlin said.

The Special Magic made sure they slept well. They had a great deal of work to do for the next couple of days.

Feyanna and Merlin were up with the sun and in the village a short time later. Most of the adults were ill with the sleeping sickness. Feyanna gathered the children and gave them chores to complete throughout the day. The older ones gathered vegetables and fruits from the gardens, washed and hung clothes to dry, and took care of the animals. The younger ones helped the older ones as needed. Feyanna had some of them bring everyone's crystals out into the sun to gather energy for the night. Hugho and Quintan were in charge of making sure the children did their chores and had the help they needed. Katherine and Molly, two of the teenagers, were in charge of the meals for the children as they were the only ones not affected by the sickness. Feyanna made sure the few adults still well had the food and drink they needed.

Feyanna dreamed in the night about an herbal blend that would block the sickness from affecting the children. She made it first thing that morning and set about making a tea for all the children to drink. They all drank their tea by midday. Feyanna would watch them for a couple of days to see if anything strange happened to them.

Merlin was making a potion he hoped would help those who were sick. He tried it out on Samuel. It was a drink that was rather nasty tasting. But Merlin made Samuel drink it anyway. Samuel fell back to sleep. Merlin would keep an eye on him to see if it made a difference.

Meanwhile, Penny and Q were kept busy making sure the mean rogue dragon caused no harm. They chased it all through the night wherever it went and stopped it from killing anyone and anything. The rogue dragon was furious that he was being blocked by an invisible force. This had been going on for weeks when the villagers became ill.

Penny and Q met with Merlin and Feyanna in the meadow after dark on the fifth night of the sickness.

"You look exhausted," Penny said when she saw the two of them.

"We are," Merlin said, sitting on the ground. "This sickness has illuded every one of our potions and remedies."

"I don't know what to do next," Feyanna said as she joined Merlin on the ground. "I'm beginning to think it must be a curse of some kind."

"Oh my god," Merlin said, jumping up. "I'm certain you're right."

"I am?" Feyanna said, looking up at Merlin. "Does that make sense to you two?"

"It most certainly does," Merlin replied.

"Then, I guess that means a spell was cast to kill our villagers," Feyanna said.

"I know for certain now that it was a spell," Merlin said.

"But why?" Feyanna said. "Why would someone want our villagers dead?"

"I know why," Merlin said quietly. "Quintan."

"He's still so young," Feyanna said. "Do you mean someone else knows about his destiny?"

"No," Penny said. "No one else does. It means that the energy change around Quintan is beginning to be felt."

"Does that put him in any danger?" Feyanna asked.

"It very well could," Q replied. "I think that's what has happened here. I think we are dealing with a witch. An herbalist who is using the Magic of the earth for her own plans."

"How did this person feel Quintan's energy?" Feyanna asked.

"It was when he and Hamlen delivered their carts to the castle. The city of Kerwyn is very big, and there are lots of people gathered there. I'll bet the witch lives close to the city, probably in the woods. She is an herbalist, as most witches are, and she most likely heals the sick and wounded."

"That's why she hasn't been found yet," Feyanna said.

"What do you mean by that?" Penny asked.

"She knows enough Magic to heal," Feyanna said. "She most likely casts spells that will benefit her. So, no one has probably connected the two things together. For instance, when a man dies suddenly. The witch was probably paid to cast a spell on him because he was seeing another woman. Not necessarily true, but that's an idea of something."

"And a good one," Penny said. "It happens a lot around here."

"Now, Miss Penny," Q said, smiling at her. "I think Feyanna is exactly right."

"Can we protect Quintan from her?" Feyanna asked.

"It's already been done," Penny replied. "The Special Magic has surrounded him with strong protective energy. He'll not get the sleeping sickness."

"Okay then," Feyanna said, standing up. "Who is the witch, and how do we reverse it?"

"I think reversing or blocking it will be the easier of those two questions to answer," Penny suggested.

"She's right," Merlin said. "We'll have to make a potion that blocks evil curses. I think I may have just the recipe."

"How's that?" Feyanna asked.

"I was in that place between dreams and awake this morning, and I kept seeing red poppies and the ash from freshly burned green corn stalks. Not sure how it all goes together, but I know we need it."

"Who has corn stalks? It's just the beginning of summer," Feyanna said.

As they watched, a pile of fresh green corn stalks appeared before them.

"Well, how do you like that?" Merlin said. "Thanks to all of you."

"I have the dried red poppy flowers in the workshop," Feyanna said.

"There is one more thing you will need and a lot of it," Q said.

Merlin looked at Feyanna and instantly knew what that was.

"Water from Avalon," Merlin said quietly. "I'll get it at first light. All of a sudden, I'm so sleepy I don't think I can keep my eyes open to walk inside."

"He's not sick, just wicked tired," Penny said. "Off with both of you. Sleep. We'll wake you at sunrise."

"Thanks," Feyanna said as she and Merlin walked into their cottage home and fell onto their beds. They were instantly asleep. Penny and Q asked The Special Magic to give them great rest and protection. They knew the evil witch was about to figure out that Merlin and Feyanna had a spell that would block hers completely. When that happened, there was going to be hell to pay.

Merlin kept hearing his name being called ever so softly. He rolled over to sleep more when he heard his name a bit more loudly. Penny! He was wide awake now. He laughed as he got up and got ready for the day.

Feyanna was preparing breakfast when he came in smiling.

"How long did it take you to wake up?" Feyanna asked, laughing with Merlin.

"Probably a minute or two. Penny was calling my name quite softly at first. Since I didn't wake up with that, she decided to call my name a bit more loudly. I woke up straight away," Merlin said as he drank his tea.

"It only took two times to get me awake," Feyanna said as she brought fruit and bread to the table. "The egg and cheese pie will be ready in a minute."

"Did you add bacon to it this time?" Merlin asked.

"I did," Feyanna said. "Horatio slaughtered one of his hogs and bartered meat for other things. He said he would bring us this bacon for helping everyone when the sleeping sickness first appeared. He wants us to stay healthy and strong."

"My thanks to him, and I agree with him," Merlin said as Feyanna brought the pie to the table.

As they ate, they talked about their plans for the day.

"I will take your hand cart to Avalon and fill as many buckets as I can right after we finish this lovely pie," Merlin said with his mouth full.

"It did come out quite yummy," Feyanna added as she put another forkful in her mouth. "I wonder how Horatio smokes his meat. This had a hint of hickory in it."

"And maple, too," Merlin said.

"It does smell delicious," Penny said as she settled in the meadow with Q.

"Thanks for the wake-up call, Miss Penny," Merlin said, laughing.

"You are quite welcome, Merlin," Penny replied.

"Thanks for my gentle wake-up call, Q," Feyanna said.

"You are welcome, Feyanna," Q replied.

"Feyanna, I guess it's time we cleaned up here and talked with our company," Merlin said.

They cleaned up the main room and walked outside to find Penny and Q sitting tall in the meadow.

"I'm off to get the water," Merlin said as he filled the handcart with as many buckets as it would hold.

"Good," Penny said as Merlin walked into the woods toward Avalon.

"Feyanna," Q said. "Please bring the herbs we talked about last night out here."

Feyanna gathered the dried red poppy flowers, lavender, and the green corn stalks and returned to the meadow.

"Feyanna, pile the corn stalks over there," Q instructed her. "I've cleared a place for them to be burned without damaging the meadow."

Feyanna placed the green corn stalks in the dirt circle that Q had made. She sprinkled lavender over the corn stalks, thanking The Divine for the gift and energy of the lavender. Next, she sprinkled sage over the corn stalks, thanking The Divine for the wisdom and protection of the sage. Lastly, she sprinkled periwinkle, thanking The Divine for the beauty of the flower. Then, she stepped back from the circle.

"That was beautiful," Penny said. "Allow me."

Penny blew a small stream of fire on the circle, and the green corn stalks began to burn. It only took a few minutes until they were burned down to ash. Merlin arrived at that same moment.

"I saw the smoke and figured you were taking care of the green corn stalks," Merlin said.

Merlin left the water by the cottage home.

"Merlin, that is just the right amount of water," Q said. "Sit and rest for a few minutes. That was a heavy task to complete."

"It was," Merlin said as he sat on a stool by the door.

Feyanna ran inside and brought a mug of tea to Merlin.

"Here. Drink this. It will restore your strength," Feyanna said as she handed the mug to Merlin.

Merlin drank all of it, saying, "It does taste rather sweet,"

"Yes, it does," Feyanna replied. "I put a bit of homey in it to take away the bitter taste."

"Well done," Merlin said.

"Let's get this potion started," Penny said. "Merlin, have you the recipe for this potion?"

Merlin looked out across the meadow for a while. He looked like he was talking with someone. Penny, Q, and Feyanna watched him. He nodded and turned to them.

"I do now," Merlin replied. "Feyanna and I need to get busy. This potion is going to take a full day and night to complete. The energy of the rising sun is the last ingredient needed."

"That is correct," Q said. "We'll stop by later and see how you are doing. Feyanna, as soon as Merlin doesn't need you, please go into the village and check on the people there. Quintan and the older boys are taking care of the animals and chores. The older girls are taking great care of the children and meals."

"I will," Feyanna said. "Thanks for helping us."

"Always," Penny said. "We're off."

Q and Penny took to the sky, and Merlin and Feyanna got busy preparing the potion to block the spell.

"We need an open-air workspace," Merlin said. "Let's bring a couple of the benches out here and place them away from the cottage."

They set up two of the workbenches on some of the risers Merlin had made for the children's parade.

"This looks good," Feyanna said. "It's not too high for me."

"And it's not too low for me," Merlin said.

They next brought out the herbs they would need. Merlin set up a fire and placed his pot holder over it. He added some of the water from Avalon to get it hot.

"Merlin, is there any way to shade this space?' Feyanna asked. "The sun is high and bright today."

"You have the answer to that," Merlin said, smiling.

"Oh my god," Feyanna said, laughing. "I most certainly do."

Feyanna ran into the cottage home and came out with her arms full of colorful material.

"You have been very busy," Merlin said. "I'll make a frame for the top of the workspace, and we can drape some of this material over it. Come help me."

Merlin and Feyanna had the frame made and draped in about an hour.

"This looks great," Feyanna said as she stood under the covering. "It works well."

"Yes, it does," Merlin said as he stepped underneath the canopy. "The water is quite hot now. Let's add the first ingredient."

"It's the lavender," Feyanna said.

She added the full bowl of dried lavender seeds, and a mist arose from the pot.

"It smells wonderful," Feyanna said. "How long does it need to simmer?"

"One full hour," Merlin said. "I've turned the sands of time. Let's gather the ashes from the corn stalks next."

Feyanna and Merlin walked over to the now-cool ashes and put them in a pouch. As soon as the ashes were gathered, the dirt circle grew back into the meadow. It didn't even look like something had ever been there.

"I love it when The Magic happens," Feyanna said.

"Me, too," Merlin said, bowing toward where the circle had been.

Feyanna set some new lavender flowers on the spot, and a new lavender plant grew and bloomed instantly.

"Now, that's amazing," Merlin said.

"Time for me to prepare the dried poppy flowers," Feyanna said.

"How will you do that?" Merlin asked as they stepped up to the workspace.

"I need to separate the seeds from the petals," Feyanna said. "It takes some time because the seeds are tiny."

"Use this," Merlin said as he handed Feyanna a small sieve. "The wholes are big enough for the seeds to fall through but too small for the petals to go through."

"Merlin, you are a genius," Feyanna said, taking the sieve from him. "When did you dream this up?"

"A while back," Merlin replied. "I've watched you use the one in the cooking area, so I thought I could use a small one for my potions and such."

"It's always the simple things that make the biggest difference," Feyanna said as she worked at separating the seeds from the petals.

"I agree with that," Merlin said as he got busy writing the potion recipe down for later use.

A few minutes later, Feyanna said, "I'm all set here. I'll go check on the villagers if you don't need me for anything else right now."

"Good idea," Merlin said. "The lavender mixture will need to cool some, so I won't need you for about an hour or so."

"Okay," Feyanna said as she went inside to grab her bag of remedies. "I'll send one of the children along if I'm going to be longer."

"Be safe," Merlin said as Feyanna set off down the path to the south road.

Sarah and Margaret saw Feyanna coming along the south road as she approached the village.

"Miss Feyanna," Sarah called out.

"Hello, girls," Feyanna said as she walked into the pasture. "How is your mother?"

"She still sleeps, as is father," Margaret replied. "We are washing the clothes and linens today. It's hard work."

"It is indeed, and you have been doing a great job," Feyanna said as she looked at the clothesline.

"When will mother and father wake up?" Sarah asked.

"Merlin and I are working on a cure right this minute," Feyanna said. "I'm checking on everyone to see if you need anything."

"No, we don't," Margaret replied. "Quintan and Hugho are busy with everyone's animals. He recruited the older girls to milk the cows."

"Good thinking," Feyanna said. "I'll go check on your family now."

Feyanna spent a few minutes making sure Hamlen and Glendianna were clean and safe. They were.

"You have been taking excellent care of your parents," Feyanna said. "Keep it up."

"We will," the girls replied as Feyanna went on into the village.

Feyanna checked every house and found the adult villagers in good shape and soundly asleep. She found Quintan and Hugho as she left the last house near the north road.

"Quintan, you and Hugho are taking excellent care of the animals," Feyanna said.

"Thank you, Miss Feyanna," Hugho replied.

"It is hard work," Quintan added. "But it must be done."

"That is right, Quintan," Feyanna replied.

"How is Master Merlin? Has he found a cure yet?" Quintan asked.

"We are working on one right now," Feyanna said. "We should have it ready by morning. Make sure you eat and rest with the other children."

"Margaret has taken control of the house," Quintan said, laughing. "She's a force to be reconned with already."

"I saw her in action a few minutes ago," Feyanna replied, laughing with the boys. "It's time for me to get back to Merlin. Send one of the children if you need anything."

"We will," Quintan and Hugo said.

"How are the villagers?" Merlin said as Feyanna walked into the meadow.

"The same," Feyanna replied. "The children are doing a great job taking care of their parents and villagers and the whole village."

"That is good to hear," Merlin said. "The mixture has cooled as instructed. Time to add the hawthorn berries."

"I have them here," Feyanna said as Merlin hung the cooled cauldron back over the fire.

"Go ahead and put them in the cauldron," Merlin said.

Feyanna poured a small amount of hawthorn berries into the cauldron. The cauldron began to swing back and forth. They took a few steps back from the cauldron.

"That is an interesting reaction," Merlin said. "I've never seen that happen before."

"I suspect the water has something to do with it," Feyanna said, thinking out loud.

"Yes, I believe you are correct," Merlin replied.

"What next?" Feyanna asked.

"It's time for the dried poppy flowers," Merlin said.

Feyanna walked over to the workspace and picked up the bowl of dried poppy flowers.

"Here they are," Feyanna said. "It's the exact amount you requested."

Merlin began chanting as he placed the petals, a little bit at a time, into the cauldron. A great cloud of red smoke arose from the cauldron straight up into the heavens. Merlin kept chanting until all the dried poppy flowers were in the cauldron. As the last ones became saturated with the mixture, the red smoke ceased.

"Wow!" Feyanna whispered.

Merlin nodded his head, agreeing with Feyanna. "The mixture needs to simmer for twenty hours. I'll be adding the water every hour until it is all in the cauldron."

"I'll keep track of the time," Feyanna said. "This means we'll be up most of the night."

"It does," Merlin said. "Let's fix something to eat. I'm starved."

"You're always ready to eat," Feyanna said, laughing as they went into their cottage home. "I'll start a venison stew that will take care of us for the next couple of days."

"Good idea," Merlin said as they prepared and ate their meal.

When they were finished, Merlin said, "Time to add more water."

"I'll take care of things in here," Feyanna said. "Then, I'll join you outside. We still have to add the poppy seeds as the sun rises."

"Make sure our crystals are all outside for the afternoon," Merlin said. "We'll need them to light out workspace throughout the night."

"I hadn't even thought about that," Feyanna said. "I'll take care of them shortly."

Feyanna and Merlin went about their chores for the rest of the day. It was at sundown that they noticed a change in the potion. It was when Merlin added the next measure of water that it happened.

"Feyanna, look!" Merlin said as he stirred the potion.

Whoa!" Feyanna said.

The potion was changing colors and bubbling, not really boiling. A vapor rose from the cauldron. It circled the meadow, circled the two of them, then drifted off into the woods. It was a soft green color, and it smelled like a field of wildflowers after a soft summer rain.

"Now what?" Merlin asked, shaking his head.

"I don't have the faintest idea," Feyanna said. "This is some potion."

"This is going to be a memorable night," Merlin said.

"You take a nap," Feyanna said. "I'll wake you up when it's time for more water."

"Thanks," Merlin said as he settled on a pile of skins and cloth.

He was asleep in no time. Feyanna cleaned things up in their makeshift workspace. She set the poppy seeds near a small crystal that was softly glowing.

She must have dosed off because she suddenly became aware of a soft buzzing near her ear. Looking around, she saw a faerie flying near the sands of time, which were almost empty.

Feyanna went over to Merlin to wake him.

"Oh, Merlin," Feyanna said whispering. "Time to get up and add water to the cauldron."

Merlin opened one and said, "I'm going to remember this. I was dreaming of a warm fire and a beautiful woman sitting next to me."

Feyanna laughed as Merlin got up and went to get the water. He poured it into the cauldron, waiting to see if anything would happen. It didn't. The cauldron continued simmering. Merlin added wood to the outer ring of the fire circle to keep the fire burning at just the right temperature.

Feyanna felt a swoosh of air and looked up into the sky. She didn't see anything. She turned and instinctively knew the dragons were in the meadow.

"I can sense your presence," Feyanna said as she walked toward them.

"I told you we couldn't fool her," Penny said as they became visible.

"Good evening, Feyanna," Q said, ignoring Penny. "How is everything going?"

"Quite well, Q," Feyanna answered, laughing at their antics.

"Hello there, Q and Penny," Merlin said as he walked over to them. "How goes the battle with the rogue dragon?"

"We caught up to him and did some damage," Penny said, pointing to Q.

"We told him to go away. He didn't. We warned him again. He ignored us. So, we sent a fiery message his way. He didn't like that."

"The fire burned his left wing," Penny explained. "He had a hard time flying away, but he managed to fly north. We followed him until he landed and went into a cave. I suspect he will be quiet for quite some time. His wing will need at least a couple of weeks to heal."

"He knows who we are," Q said. "I think he might want a bit of revenge down the road."

"Is that going to be a problem for you?" Merlin asked.

"It might be," Penny replied. "We're on our way to meet with The Dragon Brigade in The Crystal Caves to inform them of all that's happened. We'll come up with a plan for whatever that rogue dragon may do."

"At least he won't be bothering the countryside for a while," Feyanna said.

"Do you need a crystal placed here?" Merlin asked.

"No, we don't. Thank you for asking," Penny said. "We have been sent here to keep watch over you for the night. A group of men from Kerwyn have decided to go hunting just south of here. We, Q and I, think they're really on a spying mission."

"What's there to spy on around here?" Feyanna asked.

"That's what we were asking," Q said. "I'm quite sure they're looking for Quintan. He was noticed by some of the countrymen when he delivered those wagons with Hamlen. His sword was seen by many, and they wanted to know how he got such a magnificent sword. He's the son of a lowly cart maker. That's their way of thinking."

"What a nuisance," Feyanna said. "Merlin, time to add the corn stalk ashes."

"That's right," Merlin said as they carried the pouch of ashes to the cauldron. "They are to be added in the middle of the hour, which is right now."

Penny and Q watched from where they were sitting. Merlin emptied the pouch into the cauldron, and Feyanna stirred the potion.

"Now that's just plain silly,' Feyanna said, laughing at what she saw.

The potion had turned a bright pink color and was glowing like crazy.

"That's something I would have never guessed. A bright pink potion," Penny said.

"The Magic always surprises us," Q said.

"That's for sure," Penny replied.

A few minutes later, the potion changed its color to a light brown. Merlin and Feyanna walked back to the dragons.

"So, you think the men will show up around here tonight?" Merlin asked.

"We do," Q said. "We're going to keep them away from the village and you."

"How are you going to do that?" Feyanna asked.

"We are going to be our most magnificent dragons for them," Penny replied, laughing.

"How's that?" Merlin asked.

"People think dragons fly through the night and bother people. So, that's exactly what we're going to do," Penny replied, laughing.

"We'll have help from George and Goldie as well," Q said.

"Oh, this is going to be great," Merlin said, laughing. "I can just imagine Goldie shooting her needles at the men and George flying close to them."

"I can see that for sure," Feyanna said, laughing with everyone. "Then, the two of you flying high and low over them. Will you breathe any fire at them?"

"We talked about that and have decided to use smoke first," Q answered. "We're hoping that will be enough to make them turn around and run for home."

"If they stay, then we'll be forced to use fire to scare them," Penny said. "If they still choose to stay, then we'll blast them with fire."

"Let's hope it doesn't come to that," Merlin said. "I'd hate to draw attention to our village."

"Agreed," Q said. "But then, if they die, who will know where they died? Their bodies will be all ash, and the ash will be blown all over the place."

"That's true, and a great way to hide the event," Feyanna said.

"How's the potion coming along?" Q asked.

"It's coming along," Merlin said. "I need to add more water now. Excuse me."

Merlin took the small bucket of water to the cauldron and poured it in. Nothing happened.

"Well, that was quiet," Merlin said.

"It's time for us to fly," Penny said. "We'll be back to tell you how this goes."

"Thanks, you two," Feyanna said as the dragons lifted into the sky.

The dragons circled the meadow twice and then headed south.

Merlin and Feyanna took turns taking naps throughout the night. It was just before sunrise when there was a flash of orange and red light not far from the meadow.

"Merlin, wake up," Feyanna said rather loudly.

"What?" Merlin replied.

"There was a flash of orange and red light south of here a little ways," Feyanna said. "I think Penny and Q are battling with the men from Kerwyn."

Merlin jumped up, saying, "That means things are going well."

Another flash of red light was seen south of the meadow again.

"I guess not," Feyanna said. "That was the second flash. I'm thinking they had to kill the men."

"I agree," Merlin said. "It's almost sunrise. Let's take the last of the water and the poppy seeds over to the cauldron."

Merlin and Feyanna stood on the west side of the cauldron, watching the first rays of the sun appear in the eastern sky.

"We only have a moment to go," Feyanna said.

Just as the sun appeared, Penny and Q landed close by. Merlin poured the last of the water from Avalon into the cauldron, and Feyanna placed the poppy seeds in. The cauldron began to shake, and the potion started to boil. The potion became a deep blue, then dark green, and then bright red. As the sun cleared the trees, sun rays poured into the cauldron, and the cauldron became airborne. It rose along the sun's rays up into the sky until it was just a tiny drop.

As they watched, it began to descend back to the meadow. It landed on the ground next to the fire in perfect condition. No one said a word for a long time.

As the sun rose higher and higher in the sky, Feyanna finally spoke.

"Um, I'm, um, amazed," Feyanna whispered.

"Me, too," Merlin whispered. "Dragons?"

"Never saw anything like this before," Q said.

"Me, too," Penny whispered.

"Merlin, look at the potion," Feyanna said as she looked into the cauldron.

They all looked into the cauldron, and what they saw was like nothing they'd ever witnessed before.

"The potion is now a bunch of tiny biscuits," Merlin said. "Really tiny like dots."

"And they're pink," Feyanna said.

"Of course," Penny replied, laughing softly.

"There's one more thing that needs to take place before you can give these to the ones who are ill," Q said. "Go ahead, Merlin."

Merlin began to chant in the same language the dragons had used a while back. The tiny biscuits started to glow bright pink for a moment. As soon as Merlin finished the chant, the tiny biscuits toned down a bit. They were still pink.

"Now, you may give them to the villagers," Penny said. "You chanted a spell to block the evil magic of the witch. That was the last ingredient needed for the biscuits to work. Go now and make them all eat one. Only one, though."

"What if it doesn't work for some of them?" Feyanna asked. "I'm not doubting that they won't. I just want to be prepared."

"Good thinking, but no need," Penny replied. "They will work for every-one. Some may take a minute or two longer, but they will work."

"All right," Merlin said. "Let's go. Oh, Penny and Q, before we leave, how did the encounter go?"

"We say the two flashes of flames," Feyanna said.

"Those men were stubborn," Q said. "They said dragons weren't real and that someone must have drugged them. We gave them many chances to see that we were real."

"In the end," Penny said, "We had to incinerate them. They drew their crossbows on us, and we were very close. We sent the smoke. They just waited for it to clear. They aimed again, and we both sent the first round of fire at them. A couple of them died right away. This made the rest of the men angry and scared. They drew their crossbows again, and we incinerated the rest of them."

"Their ashes have already been blown away by the morning breeze," Q added.

"No one will ever be able to find them," Penny said. "When we undertake a job, we do it well."

"This will probably make the witch and the king angry. We need to be cautious," Merlin said.

"As soon as she sees that her spell is blocked, she will be furious," Feyanna said. "How were George and Goldie?"

Penny and Q laughed for a minute.

"Well, when the group started for the south road, she blocked them while George flew around their heads. They grabbed their bows, and Goldie let loose with her needles," Penny explained. "I'm surprised you didn't hear the screams here."

"Those two are quite the pair," Merlin said. "Thanks for keeping us all safe."

"We're headed to The Crystal Caves for food and rest," Penny said. "We'll stop by later."

The dragons flew off, and Merlin and Feyanna grabbed the cauldron, poured the tiny pink biscuits into a bucket, and headed into the village. They started at Hamlen's house, and as soon as the biscuit was swallowed, Hamlen and Glendianna woke right up.

Quintan said he would explain what had happened to his parents so Merlin and Feyanna could explain it to the rest of the villagers.

It didn't take very long to give the tiny pink biscuits to all the sleeping villagers. They all woke up rather quickly, and their children and friends explained what had happened. Merlin and Feyanna left as the village came back to life.

"I'm going right to bed after we eat something," Feyanna said as they walked down the path to their cottage home.

"That smells wonderful," Merlin said as they walked through the door.

Breakfast was ready for them. Eggs, bacon, fruit, and tea were set on the table.

"Who did this for us?" Merlin said as they sat down.

There was a flash of light, and a big group of faeries appeared right there in the main room.

"We did it," Enetia said. "You worked hard to block that evil spell, and we're grateful. Enjoy!"

"As are we for this feast," Feyanna said.

The fairies were gone in a little flash of soft pink light.

"And they have a sense of humor," Merlin said, laughing with Feyanna.

Merlin and Feyanna finished their breakfast, went to their rooms, and fell into their beds. They slept well into the afternoon, waking refreshed and hungry. Again.

Feyanna found Merlin preparing tea when she got up.

"Thank you, Merlin," Feyanna said. "I am quite famished."

"Me, too," Merlin said as he brought tea, bread, fruit, and cheese to the table.

"This looks quite lovely,' Feyanna said as she poured the tea for them.

"This has been a crazy week," Merlin said. "I'm glad it's over."

"For now," Feyanna said.

"For now?" Merlin replied.

"Yes. Now that Quintan has been noticed by the people of Kerwyn and the king's guard and manservant, things are going to change here rather quickly. Quintan is now six feet tall. That alone sets him apart from most men. His swordsmanship is excellent. He is quick with his crossbow. And his knife skills are coming along well."

"That's all true," Merlin said. "His friendship with Hugho is strong. A man needs a great companion by his side."

"Indeed, he does as does a woman," Feyanna said.

"Exactly," Merlin said. "Speaking of such a friend, do you have one yet?"

"I'd say yes to that," Feyanna answered. "Glendianna and I have become quite close."

"As have Hamlen and I," Merlin replied.

"This is good for both of us," Feyanna said. "Merlin, how will we protect Quintan and the rest of us from the evil witch?"

"I was just thinking about that," Merlin said.

They were silent for just a few seconds.

"A protection grid!" They both hollered out, then laughed.

They sat back in their chairs and looked at each other.

"That would take care of things quite well," Merlin said.

"I agree," Feyanna said.

"Quintan!" they both said at the same time.

"This is so weird," Feyanna said.

"Not really," Merlin said. "We have been gifted with The Special Magic. Thinking the same thing at the same time is probably a good part of our Gifts."

"I agree," Feyanna said. "Speaking of our Gifts, I do believe Quintan is about to knock on the door."

That's just what happened a second later.

"Come in," they both said, laughing.

"Good afternoon to both of you," Quintan said. "You seemed to be having a pleasant afternoon."

"Good day, Quintan," Feyanna said. "Join us for tea."

"I will. Thank you," Quintan said as he sat down, and Feyanna poured the tea.

"How is everyone in the village?" Merlin asked as he bit into an apple.

"Everyone is quite well again. They are all going about their day as if nothing has happened."

"Do any of them remember sleeping for a week?" Feyanna asked.

"No, not really," Quintan replied. "My mother asked why all the laundry was hanging to dry. She said she hadn't even started it yet. I told both of them about the sleeping sickness and all that had happened. They were surprised and shocked. The whole village is thankful that you found a way to stop it."

"So are we," Feyanna said.

"It was The Magic that helped. I know this for sure," Quintan said, looking at both of them.

"It was, indeed," Merlin answered as he looked at Feyanna for a moment.

They both remained quiet for a bit. It seemed that they were having a conversation with an unseen entity.

"Quintan, we have been given permission to tell you about the cause of the sleeping sickness," Feyanna said.

"It was brought on by an evil witch that lives in the forest west of Kerwyn," Merlin said.

"Why?" Quintan asked. "Why us?"

"We were just talking about that," Merlin replied. "It's because of you."

"Me?" Quintan said.

"Yes, you," Merlin replied. "You have been noticed by the people of Kerwyn and the court guards. You are taller than most. Your sword is magnificent. That alone draws attention to you. Even the finest swordsmiths could not have fashioned your sword. Your energy was felt by the evil witch, and she is now threatened by that."

"My energy? How's that?" Quintan asked. "I have a lot of questions, don't I?"

"As you should," Feyanna replied. "You live in The Magic. That alone is a threat to The Dark Forces. The Dark Forces enjoy causing trouble and chaos. They were having a great time until you were born. Your energy was kept quiet until you turned twelve and became a man. That's when your energy begins to become strong and become noticeable. It has been felt throughout the area by many. Mostly those that walk in The White Light. But, just as they have felt your White Light energy, The Dark Forces have also become aware of it. That evil witch wants to stay in control of the people around Kerwyn, and your energy is threatening her."

"How can my energy threaten her?" Quintan asked, smiling and shrugging his shoulders.

"Because you are using it to protect the innocent ones," Feyanna replied.

"That is true," Quintan said. "I do try to make sure everyone has what they need and remain safe."

"Yes, you do," Merlin said. "Your friend Hugho is a good companion for you in those endeavors."

"He is," Quintan said. "We have a great time together."

"Including using those two donkeys from the farm north of here for a fun nighttime ride a few weeks ago?"

"How did you know about that?" Quintan asked, surprised he had been found out.

"The farmer and I were talking just before you delivered those wagons. He heard a bit of noise outside his house in the middle of the night. He looked out and saw the two of you returning with the donkeys. He said you took great care of them and fed and watered them well. He told me he laughed himself to sleep thinking about how you thought you had not been caught."

"Is that why he asked Hugho and me to help him on his farm?" Quintan said.

"It is," Feyanna said, laughing as well. "He said he paid you by offering you the use of those two donkeys should you need them for anything."

"I wondered why he made that offer," Quintan said, laughing. "It all makes sense now. "I'll be sure to grab Hugho, and we'll talk with the Farmer. Barnebus is a good man and deserves our apologies and respect."

"That is exactly what you should do," Merlin said. "Tomorrow would be a good morning for that."

"I was thinking of going over there this evening," Quintan said. "Why tomorrow, Master Merlin?"

"We have something we need you to take care of with us," Feyanna said quietly.

Penny, Q, Clarice, and Roman had just landed in the meadow and walked over close to the cottage home.

"I do believe our favorite dragons are here," Quintan said. "Let's take a look."

"Here they are," Merlin said as they walked outside.

"Hello, lovely dragons," Quintan said, bowing.

"Hello, dear Quintain," they said.

"As much as I would love this to be a social call, I do believe we have some work to do in The Magic," Quintan said.

"He is coming along faster than expected," Penny said, smiling at Quintan.

"I'm not even going to ask," Quintan said.

"Good idea," Feyanna said, smiling at Quintan.

"Quintan, I told you a few days ago it was time for you to learn some of The White Light Magic. Today is one of those days," Merlin said.

"I am ready, Master Merlin," Quintan said in a serious voice.

"Quintan, we have concluded that the evil witch that cast the sleeping sickness spell will be wicked angry when she finds out it was blocked. This will, most likely, make her want to kill everyone in the village and us," Merlin said. "Feyanna, go ahead."

"Merlin and I came up with a way to protect all of us at the same time," Feyanna explained. "We are going to set a protection grid around the village and this meadow. No Dark Forces will ever be able to penetrate the grid. Every living thing will be protected under the grid."

"That sounds wonderful," Quintan said. "I suspect it will take a great deal of time and energy to do this."

"You are correct," Merlin said. "Once we start the grid, The Dark Forces will know what we are doing and will try to stop us from finishing the grid. It will be dangerous out there."

"We will keep the three of you protected," Penny said.

"The Special Magic will, too," Q added. "I was just informed of this."

"Know this, Quintan," Merlin said. "It is your soul that The Special Magic and The White Light Paladins will protect. Your physical human body may die, but your soul will live on in The White Light."

"That's serious stuff," Quintan said. "So, I guess learning about The Magic is vital to my existence."

"It is, along with your fighting skills," Q said. "Keep working with Merlin. I suggest that Hugo begin training with Merlin as well. Teach him the fighting skills and how understanding knowledge about these skills will help him be an excellent fighter. Not The Magic. Not now."

"I was thinking the same thing, Q," Merlin said. "Thanks for the validation."

"When should I bring Hugo here?" Quintan asked.

"The day after tomorrow," Merlin said. "We are going to be very busy for the rest of the day into the night. You will need to rest tomorrow. And visit Barnebus. Go and tell your father that you will be training with me through the night."

"I'm off," Quintan said. "I thank you all."

"We are staying close to Quintan from here on," Roman said.

Clarice and Roman took flight to catch up with Quintan.

"Hi, you two," Quintan said as he stepped onto the south road. "Why are you following me?"

"Quintan, we are your protectors," Clarice said.

"Wow! That's amazing," Quintan said. "I'm not even going to ask why. I know it has to do with me learning the ways of The Special Magic."

"It does," Roman replied.

"Shouldn't you be invisible?" Quintan asked

"We are about to be," Clarice said. "Watch."

In the blink of an eye, they disappeared.

"Now, that's awesome Magic," Quintan said, laughing.

"Just remember not to talk with us when people are around," Roman said. "They may think you've gone crazy."

"Good idea," Quintan said as they approached the farm. "Like right now."

"Yup," Clarice said. "The animals will see us and know we are good."

"Okay," Quintan said as he jumped over the fence and ran to meet his father as he was going into the barn.

"Quintan, done at Merlin's already?" Hamlen asked as Quintan helped him spread some hay.

"No, father. That's why I'm here," Quintan said. "I will need to spend the rest of the afternoon and night with Merlin and Feyanna. I just wanted you to know so you wouldn't worry."

"Thanks for letting me know," Hamlen said. "I'll be sure to tell your mother."

"Thank you, Father," Quintan said. "I'm heading back there right now."

"Be safe, my son," Hamlen said as a cool breeze blew through the barn. "That breeze feels good."

"Yes, it does," Quintan said as he ran back across the meadow and set out for Merlin's cottage.

"My horse saw you," Quintan said. "That's why I gave him a hug and a carrot. He gave me a nod and a soft whinny to let me know he knew I knew about you."

"Yes, he did," Roman said. "Buttercup is a sweet soul."

"And a protective soul," Clarice added. "He will stay by your side for a very long time."

"I do love my horse," Quintan said as they turned down the path. "Here we are."

"I'm back," Quintan said. "My father is okay with me being here for the night."

"That is good," Merlin said.

"We need to gather the things for the energy grid, eat a sturdy meal, then set out."

"I'm glad you made the venison stew. It will taste wonderful," Merlin said.

"And some of the garlic and onion bread, I hope?" Quintan added.

"Yes, Quintan. I made some a little while ago," Feyanna said.

They gathered a shovel, a pouch of white quartz crystals, a bucket of salt, and sage and lavender.

"Time to eat," Feyanna said as they settled around the table.

They enjoyed the food and told more stories from their youths. It was an enjoyable time. They would need to remember all those wonderful times they'd had growing up to be able to face what was about to happen.

Just as evening was giving way to nightfall, Feyanna explained what they were about to do.

"Quintan, we are going to place an energy grid around the village and our meadow to protect us from The Dark Forces. We will need to invoke The Magic of Mother Earth and Father Sky to set the grid. We will be walking a great distance as well. We have all the things we need to set the grid. Merlin has prepared the water pouches for us, and I have some dried fruit to sustain us. Be sure you bring your sword. It will be needed tonight."

"I have it with me always," Quintan said. "May I carry anything?"

"Yes, please," Feyanna said. "Take the fruit and the pouch with the sage and lavender. Thank you."

"We will set the first point to the west," Merlin said. "The woodland animals will show us the path to that place."

"We are setting elements in the four directions, aren't we?" Quintan asked.

"How do you know that?" Merlin asked.

"I just know it all of a sudden," Quintan said.

"The Special Magic is strong with him," Q said.

"As prophesized," Penny said.

"We need to get started," Merlin said. "I feel an energy shift coming from the south. Most likely from the witch."

Merlin, Feyanna, and Quintan set out along a path in the forest, heading west. The animals helped them find the furthest western point of the village and the meadow.

"We start here," Feyanna said.

"Quintan, please dig a narrow, deep hole," Merlin said.

Quintan dug the hole without incident.

"To you, Mother Earth, we set this crystal back into your loving embrace," Feyanna said. "We offer this lavender and its sweet essence as a gift of love."

Feyanna sprinkled some lavender into the hole.

"We offer this gift of the sage, asking for protection and wisdom as we set this protection grid," Feyanna said.

Merlin sprinkled some sage into the hole. Nothing happened.

"Quintan, please set the first crystal into the hole," Merlin said.

Feyanna took one of the crystals from her pouch and gave it to Quintan. He dropped it into the hole. A stiff breeze blew through the woods.

Merlin covered the hole, and there was a flash of lightning straight above them.

"The Dark Forces know what we're up to," Merlin said as they gathered their things.

"Time to walk to the northernmost point," Feyanna said.

"You mean The Dark Forces sent the breeze and the lightning?" Quintan asked.

"It did," Merlin answered. "It will be sending stronger forces the closer we get to each point."

"The last one, the southernmost point, will be the most dangerous," Feyanna said. "Once the grid is in place, an invisible rope of energy will connect all the points and make everything in it safe from The Dark Forces. The Dark Forces will be able to destroy anything outside of the grid, but not inside it."

"That's some powerful Magic," Quintan said.

Feyanna started a trail of salt from the western point as they walked along.

"Why the salt?" Quintan asked.

"The energy of salt protects those in need. It also purifies the area where it is used," Feyanna. "It has been known to keep evil away from those that step into a circle of salt."

"Thank you. I understand now," Quintan said as Feyanna continued to leave a trail of salt behind them.

As they approached the northernmost point, the wind began to pick up.

"Quintan, dig the same kind of hole right here," Merlin said.

As Quintan began to dig, the wind increased. It was not strong enough to push him away.

Feyanna repeated the offering of the herbs.

"To you, Mother Earth, we set this crystal back into your loving embrace," Feyanna said. "We offer this lavender and its sweet essence as a gift of love."

Feyanna sprinkled some lavender into the hole.

"We offer this gift of the sage, asking for protection and wisdom as we set this protection grid," Feyanna said.

Merlin sprinkled some sage into the hole. Nothing happened.

"Quintan, please set the second crystal into the hole," Merlin said.

Feyanna took a second crystal from her pouch and gave it to Quintan. He dropped it into the hole. A flash of lightning hit the ground close by just as the westernmost and northernmost points were connected by a brilliant blue energy line.

"Whoa!" Quintan said as he was pushed back away from the hole.

"Quintan, repeat after me," Merlin said. "White Light, surround and protect me."

"White Light surround and protect me," Quintan said loudly.

A flash of white light surrounded the three of them as Quintan regained his balance.

The brilliant blue energy rope connected the westernmost point with the northernmost point.

"The Dark Forces really don't want us to do this, do they?" Quintan said.

"No, they do not," Merlin said. "Things are going to get difficult from here on."

As they began their walk to the easternmost point and Feyanna continued the trail of salt, the wind became very strong, and lightning flashed all over the skies. The roar of the wind was loud, and the night animals were silent. The trail was difficult to see at times, so Merlin asked for help from the night creatures.

"Dear night creatures, please show us the way," Merlin asked.

A raccoon appeared and led them part of the way. A tree was hit by lightning and blocked the path.

"Now what?" Quintan asked.

"It's our turn to help," Penny and Q said. "Wrap this rope around the trunk of the tree. Tie a tight knot and give us the rope. We'll do the rest."

Quintan and Merlin did as the dragons told them and gave both ends of the rope to Penny and Q.

"Stand clear," Q said as he and Penny began to fly upwards.

The tree began to move, and a moment later, it was well off the ground.

"Quickly now," Merlin said as he led Feyanna and Quintan under the tree to the other side of the path.

Penny and Q set the tree back on the path and released the rope.

"Take the rope with you," Q said. "You may need it another day."

"Thank you both," Feyanna said.

"Let's go," Merlin said as they continued the walk to the easternmost point.

This took them above the village, crossing the north road. That was the easy part. Once they entered the forest on the east side of the north road, the wind became gale force. They had to bend forward to keep from being blown down. The lightning increased and was constant. The noise was deafening. It took them a couple of hours walking through this to get to the easternmost point.

When they arrived, Quintan took the shovel to dig the hole. He was knocked down. He got up and tried again. He was thrown down this time. Merlin gave him a hand up and they both worked at digging the hole. It took a while, as the wind was relentlessly striking them, but they completed this task.

Feyanna began the herbal ritual, but every time she tried to place the herbs in the hole, the wind blew them away.

"I have an idea," Feyanna said.

She sat on the ground close to the hole and tried again. This time, it worked.

"To you, Mother Earth, we set this crystal back into your loving embrace," Feyanna said. "We offer this lavender and its sweet essence as a gift of love."

Feyanna sprinkled some lavender into the hole.

"We offer this gift of the sage, asking for protection and wisdom as we set this protection grid," Feyanna said.

Merlin sprinkled some sage into the hole. The wind began to scream.

"Quintan, please set the third crystal into the hole," Merlin said.

Feyanna took the crystal from her pouch and gave it to Quintan. As he went to drop the crystal into the hole, it looked like someone or something grabbed his arm and threw it backward. Quintan stumbled and fell. He got up and tried a different way. He sat next to the hole just like Feyanna had done. He let his hand trail across the ground and slipped the crystal into the hole. It worked. They all saw the brilliant blue energy line connect the northernmost point with the easternmost point.

The Dark Forces howled something fierce.

"I guess we must be doing something right," Merlin yelled. "Stay close as we walk to the southernmost point. It's at the southern tip of the meadow. This will take quite some time."

The wind increased to hurricane force, and there were times when the three of them had to sit down to avoid being blown away. The lightning was relentless and so bright it hurt their eyes. They could hardly open them to see where they were going.

"We need some help here, White Light," Merlin cried out.

They found their faces covered with a dark cloth. They could see through it and it dulled the lightning so much that they were able to see where they were going. This made The Dark Force scream.

"I can feel that in my bones," Quintan said.

Feyanna shook her head as she continued to leave the trail of salt. It was a bit ragged, but she was to keep it connected.

"We're almost there," Merlin said.

As soon as they arrived at the southernmost point, The Dark increased everything. He sent a tornado to destroy the whole place for miles around. The Special Magic blew it apart before it could harm anyone or anything. The wind was so strong that Quintan, Feyanna, and Merlin had to crawl the last few feet to the place where the hole needed to be dug.

Quintan got on his knees and began to dig the hole. He was knocked down by a branch from a nearby tree. His face was cut and bleeding. Feyanna made a bandage for him and put it in place with a paste she had just made that day. The bandage stayed in place. Quintan wrapped the black cloth around his head and tried again.

Merlin and Feyanna got on their knees and helped dig the hole. It took some time, but they got it in place. The Dark Forces sent lightning bolts to the earth near them. The air buzzed with energy, as did their heads. They couldn't talk, so they made hand gestures to signal each other.

Merlin and Quintan held Feyanna while she lay next to the hole to drop the herbs in.

"To you, Mother Earth, we set this crystal back into your loving embrace," Feyanna said. "We offer this lavender and its sweet essence as a gift of love."

Feyanna sprinkled some lavender into the hole.

The Dark forces howled.

"We offer this gift of the sage, asking for protection and wisdom as we set this protection grid," Feyanna said.

Merlin sprinkled some sage into the hole. Nothing happened.

The Dark Forces made the earth shake.

Merlin signaled Quintan to set the last crystal in the hole.

Feyanna took the last crystal from her pouch and tried to give it to Quintan. A hoard of snakes appeared and grabbed at Feyanna's hand.

Merlin reached into this cloak and grabbed a yellow powder from a pouch. He scooched over to Feyanna and let the wind blow the powder onto the snakes. They sizzled and blew up into a million pieces.

The Dark Forces saw this and became extremely angry. It sent a lightning bolt at them, but it was blocked by The Special Magic. Feyanna was able to give Quintan the last crystal.

All of a sudden, Quintan felt like he was pinned to the ground. He couldn't move, and it was getting hard to breathe. Merlin saw this and motioned to Feyanna to look at Quintan. Feyanna nodded her head as she reached into her cloak and drew out a piece of wood. It looked like an ordinary piece of wood. It was more like a small branch. Merlin saw her mouth moving as she waved the wand toward Quintan. She was casting a spell.

Feyanna took a couple of minutes to send the spell to Quintan. The wind tried to take the wand from her, but it wouldn't budge from her hand. As she finished, The Dark Forces sent a lightning bolt so brilliant that the three of them were blinded. Quintan could now move, and he felt for the hole. He found it and began to crawl on his stomach toward the edge. He kept the crystal tucked in his hand. The Dark Forces sent roots to wrap around his legs to keep him from moving. It didn't work. Every time a root began to wrap itself around Quintan's leg, Mother Earth cut it off, and it withered and died. It wasn't one of her children. It was concocted by The Dark Forces to look like one of her children, so she had no problem killing it.

Quintan was at the edge of the hole. Just as he reached out to drop the crystal into it, the earth quaked so hard that nearby trees fell to the ground with a loud thunder. The earthquake kept building and the earth began to collapse in on itself.

Quintan was beyond exhausted. He didn't think he had any energy left. He called out to The White Light for more protection as he lay there in a daze. He felt something wrapping around him. It gave him energy and quieted the noise of The Dark Forces. He took a deep breath just as The Dark Forces sent twin tornados at the three of them. Feyanna and Merlin felt themselves being lifted from the ground and swirled into the tornados.

Quintan reached out his hand with the crystal in it one more time and opened his hand. The crystal fell into the hole just as he was pulled from the ground by one of the tornados. He found himself being swirled around in a dark cloud of noise.

As soon as the crystal touched the earth at the bottom of the hole, everything went silent. Penny, Q, and Roman grabbed Feyanna, Merlin, and Quintan and set them gently down on the ground. They sat there in utter shock for the longest time.

"It's not noisy anymore," Feyanna whispered as she opened her eyes and looked around.

"Then why are you whispering?" Merlin asked.

Feyanna shrugged her shoulders and looked for Quintan. She found him right next to the hole. He was looking at the brilliant blue energy rope. It had connected the four directions and caused the Dark Forces to be blown away. There was a gentle humming in the air.

"I can feel that," Quintan said as he sat up. "Whoa! I'm a bit dizzy."

"Just sit there and breathe deeply for a minute," Feyanna said as she tried to stand up.

She sat right back down, saying, "Me, too."

"We've been through an energy storm the likes of which I've never even imagined," Merlin said. "We'll need a few minutes to regain our balance."

"You will, indeed," Q said as he landed with Penny and Roman close to them.

"Hey, this place doesn't look like it was damaged at all," Quintan said. "I saw the earth being swallowed up into itself and the forest destroyed by the wind storms and lightning."

"Yes, you did," Feyanna replied. "Thing is, The White Light restored the damage."

"Now, I'm officially overwhelmed," Quintan said.

"So are we," Feyanna said, trying to stand up again. "Okay, I can stand up now. I still feel very weak and exhausted."

"All of you are weak and exhausted," Penny said. "Take the drink from the faeries, please."

They drank the drink from the faeries, thanked them, and felt immediately better. Food and drink appeared on a blanket next to them, and they ate and rested as the sun rose.

"Now, that's a beautiful sunrise," Merlin said.

"It most certainly is," Quintan said as they watched the sun rise up from the earth and begin its climb into the sky. "I have never seen so many colors all at once in my life."

"Me, either," Feyanna said. "These are beautiful."

"I thank The Divine for keeping us alive during this protection grid ceremony," Merlin said quietly as tears flowed down his cheeks.

"I am grateful as well," Quintan said.

"I am thankful, too," Feyanna said.

The three of them sat there quietly as they ate and rested for quite some time. The dragons were being cared for by the faeries as well. The sun was well up in the sky when they all stood up at the same time.

"I guess we're all thinking the same thing," Merlin said.

"Time for us to return to The Crystal Caves for some rest," Penny said. "Clarice is here to watch over Quintan while Roman gets some rest, too."

"I appreciate you both," Quintan said. "All of you."

George came zooming in, "Are you all okay?" George asked. "That was an incredible storm."

Goldie came running across the field at the same time. Her eyes were gold, and she was ready to fight.

"Are you all okay? Dragons, too? I see you are all standing. That's a good sign. Are you hurt at all? Dragons, do you need help?" Goldie said as she walked around to make sure everyone was alive.

"We are all okay, Miss Goldie and George," Penny said. "The White Light has made sure of that."

"I know The White Light takes great care of us," Goldie said as she sat beside Merlin. "It was such a horrible attack; I was scared for everyone."

"We appreciate the love, Goldie," Quintan said as he lay his hand on her head.

"You have such a soothing touch, Quintan," Goldie said as her eyes returned to their usual green color.

"Well, we now know that Quintan can calm Goldie," Feyanna said. "Good to know."

"Wise ass," Merlin said.

This made everyone laugh.

"The protection grid is in place for eternity," Merlin said. "All those who are within its shield are safe from The Dark Forces. Not necessarily from natural storms and such. Just anything The Dark Forces try to throw at us."

"I will sleep so much better now that I don't have to worry about the evil witch," Quintan said.

"And anyone she sends to hurt us," Feyanna said.

"That, too," Merlin said, yawning. "I need some sleep. Come along, Feyanna and Quintan."

"Me, too?" Quintan asked.

"Indeed," Merlin replied. "You won't get any sleep at your house with the girls being busy and all."

"That's true," Quintan said.

"We're away," Penny said.

"Merlin, will you please place a crystal in the meadow? I need to be invisible in case someone comes along," Clarice said.

"Of course," Merlin said, taking a purple crystal from his shirt. "Here you go."

Merlin placed the crystal in the meadow, and all the dragons disappeared. The dragons flew off, and the others walked back to their cottage home.

"Sleep well," George said. "Goldie and I will keep watch."

"Thanks very much, you two," Feyanna said as she pointed to a bed for Quintan near the hearth. "If Goldie snores too loudly, just throw something soft at her."

"Cute, Feyanna," Goldie replied.

A few minutes later, Quintan, Feyanna, and Merlin were sound asleep. The protection grid was in place keeping the whole village safe. The witch had just learned that her sleeping sickness had not worked. She was pissed! She was so angry that she threw one of her potion mugs through her window. It hit a rock and shattered. And this made her even more furious, so she cast a spell to blow up any frogs that got close to her cottage for the rest of the day. Every once and again, you could hear a pop as a frog hopped too close to her cottage and was blown up.

Merlin had Hugho join Quintan a couple of days later.

"Hello, Hugho," Merlin said, shaking hands with him. "Do you know why I've asked Quintan to bring you here?"

"Good Morning, Master Merlin," Hugho replied. "Quintan said he needed a sparing partner closer to his age."

"That is mostly correct," Merlin replied. "We, Feyanna and I, and perhaps Quintan, too, are going to teach you the art of fencing: how to use a sword."

"I see," Hugho said. "I really don't know much about it. I'm quite ready to learn."

"Splendid," Merlin said. "Quintan, show Hugho the warm-up exercises you do. I'll be along in a bit."

"Yes, sir," Quintan said as he motioned Hugho to follow him into the meadow.

"What exercises? Sword fighting isn't all that hard, is it?" Hugho said.

It was only a few minutes later that Hugho called it quits.

"This is really hard," Hugho said as he tried to catch his breath. "This sword is super heavy. May I hold yours for a minute?"

"No, Hugho," Quintan replied. "A man's sword is made especially for him. No one else should ever touch it."

"Oh. I didn't know that," Hugho said. "Did you have to use these oak swords to learn, too?"

"I did. And they are heavy," Quintan said, laughing with Hugho. "Merlin has me do these warm-up exercises every day before we start. I also do a lot of physical conditioning."

"Is that why you make it look so easy?" Hugho asked.

"Partly," Quintan replied. "Some of it's because you aren't a challenge for me yet. You will be, though. Merlin will see to that. Now, for the exercises."

Quintan showed Hugho the warm-up exercises, and they went through them together.

"Even these are hard to do," Hugho said. "I thought I was in pretty good shape. I'm not. So glad Merlin asked for me to join you. Maybe I'll get to be as strong as you."

"I truly believe you will," Quintan said as they finished the exercises.

Merlin joined then just then.

"Well, Hugho?" Merlin said.

"Master Merlin, I have a great deal to learn, and I thank you for the opportunity to do so," Hugho said, bowing to Merlin.

"Well done, Hugho," Merlin said. "You show respect and sincerity in your words. Now, let's see how you do with the instructions. Feyanna will be your partner after you watch Quintan and I go through our paces."

"Yes, sir and Ma'am," Hugho replied.

Feyanna and Hugho watched Quintan and Merlin as they went through their usual practice mode. Merlin added a few new moves, to Quintan's surprise. He was able to counter one of them. The second one, he didn't handle so well. All part of learning.

Hugho spent another hour with Feyanna, learning the basic fencing moves, while Quintan honed his knife skills with Merlin.

Mid-day arrived before anyone realized the morning had flown by. The four of them shared the meal and conversation.

"Hugho, you have done well this first day," Merlin said. "Return home now and help with the chores. Your father has approved of you practicing after supper for an hour each day."

"Thank you so very much, Master Merlin and Miss Feyanna," Hugho said. "I will be working on those strength-building exercises each morning before I start my day and join you. I am a wimp!"

They all laughed at Hugho's antics.

"I'll see you this evening, my friend," Quintan said as Hugho set out for home.

"He is learning quickly," Feyanna said. "He will be a good challenge for you as you go."

"Yes, he will," Quintan said. "I know just how he feels. I was a wimp for a while, too."

"We all were," Merlin said, smiling. "Time to get to your lessons about the earth's Magic."

"Yes, sir," Quintin said, winking at Feyanna. "I'll see you later."

"Charmer," Feyanna said, laughing as the men went into the workshop. She walked into the meadow to gather flowers and herbs.

The evil witch had just learned that none of the villagers were sick. They were all healthy. This made her angry. She couldn't imagine how anything could interfere with her dark magic. She grabbed her crystal ball and asked to see who had caused her spell to be broken.

The crystal ball was cloudy for quite some time. When it eventually cleared, all the evil witch could see were healthy villagers. Then, the vision changed. She saw a brilliant White Light shining over the village.

"Damn!" she hollered. "The White Light healed them."

She asked the crystal ball to show her the person responsible for this. It remained cloudy. She asked the crystal ball if any other protection was in place. The crystal ball immediately showed her the protection grid. She suddenly realized that there was more here than she could control. She sat angry and scared for a long time until there was a knock on her door. She took a deep breath and opened the door to find a village woman standing there.

"Good day, Miss Helena," the woman said.

"Good day," Helena replied. "How can I help you today?"

"I am in need of some herbs to lessen the effect of the pollen in me," the woman said.

"I have just the thing for you," Helena said as she took a small earthen jar from her shelves. "Make a tea from this herb twice a day as long as the flowers are in bloom. It will lessen the effect."

"I am grateful, Miss Helena," the woman said. "Please accept these few pence for your work."

"I accept," Helena replied.

The woman left and Helena went back to trying to figure out who was using The White Light Magic. She knew most of the people in Kerwyn and the castle. It had to be someone farther away. She did not have the power to see those at a long distance. Now, she was furious.

"Ah," she suddenly said. "I may not have the power to stop The White Light Magic, but I do have the power to get that lame King Owen off the throne and have my King Gorham crowned. This I will speed up right now."

Helena conjured a more potent spell than the one in place. The current one made King Owen look like he was losing his concentration and staring into space. Helena would double the potion for the spell, and the King would have to be replaced right away.

This happened in just two weeks. The king couldn't remember the names of his knights and court. The knights gathered with the high chancellor and decided the king needed to be removed from the throne. The high chancellor suggested Lord Gorham of the northern regions as the next king. The chancellor explained that Lord Gorham had been loyal to King Owen and had controlled his region with a firm hand. He was swift to punish those that were disobedient.

The knights and the high chancellor voted unanimously to bring Lord Gorham to the castle for a round of conversations about how he might rule the kingdom. They also invited two other lords from the southern and eastern regions for meetings. They didn't want it to look like they had already made their choice with Lord Gorham.

The Dark Forces were in charge of getting King Owen replaced. The Dark Forces let the humans think they were in control because it was great fun to see how evil the humans would be.

Lord Gorham had made a deal with The Dark Forces. He called them the devil. He sold his soul to become king. And so it was about to happen.

While King Owen's knights and the high chancellor were preparing to send messengers around the region, Lord Gorham had one of his well-known temper tantrums.

"That cow hasn't produced a calf yet," Lord Gorham yelled to his keeper of the livestock. "Kill it and get me a new one. No, wait. I'll go to the farmer who sold me the cow and make him pay with his life. Prepare my horse and tell my knights to follow me."

A short while later, Lord Gorham rode onto the farm of the man who had sold him his cow.

"You there, farmer," Lord Gorham hollered at the man. "The cow you sold me is defective. It hasn't produced a calf yet. You will pay for this."

Lord Gorham's temper was well-known in the region.

"Sire, I'm so sorry about this problem," the farmer said. "How old is the cow now?"

"She's one year old," Lord Gorham replied.

"That explains it then," the farmer replied. "Cows have to be at least one year old before they can get pregnant."

"That's not good enough for me," Lord Gorham said as he dismounted and drew his sword. "You will pay for this defective animal with your life."

"Sire, please, I beg of you to give me another chance," the farmer said as he knelt before Lord Gorham.

"Why should I?" Lord Gorham asked. He liked to see his subjects beg for their lives.

"I have a pregnant cow ready to give birth. I will give her to you with any bull you choose," the farmer said. "I'll take back the young cow, or you may keep her as you wish."

Lord Gorham thought about this for a moment. He would get a cow ready to give birth and a bull and keep the one that wasn't quite ready to conceive or give it back. That was a good deal. He needed to make the farmer stay in fear of him, though. He spotted a young maiden in the barn.

"Farmer, I accept your peace offering," Lord Gorham said. "Make it so," he ordered his knights. The knights went with the farmer to get the pregnant cow and pick a young bull from the herd in the pasture.

Lord Gorham went into the barn to find the young maiden. She had huge breasts that were tight against her apron, and he wanted to fuck her hard. He found her taking care of the milking pails.

"Young maiden," Lord Gorham said as he walked up behind her. "I am your lord and master and demand that you please me."

The young maiden was terrified of Lord Gorham. She had heard about the ways he raped the women around the region.

"What may I get for you, sire?" the young maiden asked in a whisper.

Lord Gorham turned the young maiden around. She was about sixteen years old and beautiful. He untied her apron and let it all fall to the floor. He untied her dress and dropped it to the floor. He ran his hands across her breasts, grabbing them and playing with them through her corset.

The young maiden was trembling with fright.

"This is in the way," Lord Gorham said as he ripped her corset and under-clothing off so she was naked.

He pushed her down in the hay and dropped his trousers. He knelt over her, grabbed her breasts, and played with them. The young maiden was crying uncontrollably with fear.

"I like it when you are scared of me," Lord Gorham said as he pulled her breast into his mouth and roughly sucked it.

His dick was hard and red, and he thought he'd burst. He spread her legs apart and mounted her. He began to enter her, and she cried out in pain.

"A virgin," Lord Gorham cried out with glee. "That's even better."

He pushed harder and harder, trying to get into her, but she had pulled her legs closer together as a reaction to the rape. He struck her across the face, yelling, "You will not resist me, or you will die."

He pushed one of her legs aside as he pushed into her again. This time, he got further inside and kept pushing. The young maiden was hysterically crying now. The pain was beyond belief. She passed out, but he slapped her back into consciousness.

"You will stay awake for this," Lord Gorham said as he began pushing harder and faster.

The young maiden made herself stay conscious, and he at last gave one very hard push, yelling out in ecstasy. He collapsed onto her, breathing heavily. She lay still, looking away from him. He finally got up, pulled his trousers up, and walked out of the barn.

Lord Gorham paused at the door and said, "You are a whore now, and you belong to me."

The young maiden lay there, not moving a muscle until she heard the sound of horse hoofs leaving the farm. The farmer ran in and cried when he saw her. He hollered for his wife, and she took care of the young maiden.

"You will be taken to the far north to hide with good people," the farmer's wife said. "Take this tea. It will flush out any disease he gave you. It will also cause a miscarriage if he caused you to conceive. Drink it all."

The young maiden sat on the milking stool, shaking and crying as she drank all the tea.

"Come with me," the farmer's wife said. "I will feed you and clean you up. The men will be here soon to take you north."

"He said I was his whore from now on," the young maiden said. "He will look for me and be angry when he can't find me."

"We will take care of that," the farmer was saying when a soft white light encircled them.

It stayed for a few minutes, then faded away.

"What was that?" the young maid asked. "It was wonderful."

"That, my dear girl, is the power of good Magic," the farmer's wife said. "No worries. All of us on this farm walk in The White Light. You will be taught about that when you are settled."

"We will dig a grave and show it to Lord Gorham if he returns. We'll tell him you became quite ill a few days after his visit, and we buried you to make sure no one else got the sickness. We'll tell him you got the pox. He will be glad you are dead and he didn't get sick."

The young maiden laughed at this. "That is a great idea."

A short while later, two men rode in with a third horse. The young maiden was dressed as a young man to disguise her so they wouldn't be stopped along the way. It would take two days to get to the farm in the far north, nestled into the foothills of the Great Northern Mountains. This territory was not a part of Lord Gorham's territory.

"Be safe," the farmer said.

"May the gods and goddesses ride with you," the farmer's wife said.

"Thanks be to the gods and goddesses for all of you," the young maiden said as tears gently rolled down her cheeks.

The three of them rode away into the northern forest to hide another victim of Lord Gorham's obsessive behavior, taking any woman he wanted. He was convinced every woman in his region was his property. Many women and young girls had been swiftly taken to the north for safety.

King Owen's knight rode out at first light the next day to request Lord Gorham's presence at the castle.

The king's knight rode up to the front of Lord Gorham's manor house. He dismounted and handed the reigns to the servant. The door was opened as he approached, and he entered into the front vestibule. The manservant awaited him and asked the knight to follow him to Lord Gorham's business chamber.

"Greetings, sir knight," Lord Gorham said.

"Greetings, Lord Gorham," the knight replied.

"What business do you have for me from King Owen this day?" Lord Gorham asked as he sat down. The knight remained standing.

"I have a message from the king, sire," the knight replied as he handed the parchment to Lord Gorham.

Lord Gorham read the message and smiled.

"I am honored to accept this invitation from King Owen," Lord Gorham said. "I will arrange for travel and leave within the next few days."

"The king requests you arrive in one week's time, sire," the knight said, making sure Lord Gorham understood the timetable.

"I understand and will arrive exactly one week from today if it pleases the king," Lord Gorham said.

"That will be excellent," the knight replied. "Should I wait for you to pen a response, sire?" the knight asked.

"Yes," Lord Gorham said. "Go to the kitchen and have the cook feed you. I will send my manservant when I am ready."

"As you wish, sire," the knight said as he bowed and walked out of the room.

He saw the manservant pointing in the direction of the kitchen. He smiled and walked along the hallway until he could smell something delicious cooking.

"Good day, Madam cook," the knight said as he entered the kitchen.

"Good day to you, sir knight," the cook replied, smiling.

"It's been a long while since we talked, Aunt Beatrice," the knight said as he hugged her.

"It has been," Beatrice replied, kissing his cheek. "How is the castle? We're hearing that the king is not so well."

"That's true," the knight whispered. "He is getting along in his old age, I suspect."

"He's younger than me, and I'm all good," Beatrice replied, taking a roasted chicken from the fire.

"All true," the knight replied. "It does seem odd that he's acting like an old man already."

"I suspect there is some foul play at hand," Beatrice whispered as she passed him.

"We think so, too," the knight whispered. "No way to prove it, though. How is Lord Gorham?"

"His usual nasty self," Beatrice whispered even more quietly. She didn't want the helpers to hear them. "Word is he raped a young maiden yesterday. Told her she was his whore from now on. That man is pure evil. He was so angry the other day; he shopped the heads off two barn cats."

"That's the general thought around the kingdom," the knight said as she set a plate of food in front of him. "This is delicious, Aunt Beatrice. I love ya."

"Same here, dear boy," she said. "Lord Gorham still doesn't know we are related. He would have you killed if he knew. He doesn't like family working to-gether. He's afraid they will conspire against him."

"He can't order me dead," the knight replied. "I am under the command of King Owen. At least for a little while longer."

"So that's why you're here," Beatrice said. "Picking a new king?"

The knight nodded ever so slightly as one of the helpers brought him a mug of grog.

"Thank you, miss," the knight said as he took a long drink. "This is excel-lent.

"Thank you, sir knight," the helper replied. "My father makes it here in the lower level. He said the grog needs to be kept cool. I will tell him you enjoyed it."

The lord's manservant entered just then.

"Lord Gorham is ready for you, sir knight," the manservant said.

"Thank you, kind sir," the knight said as he stood up. "I thank the cook for this delicious meal. I hope you get some of it as well."

"I'll see that he does," Beatrice said, smiling at the two of them.

The manservant brought the knight to Lord Gorham's business chamber as instructed.

"Here is my reply," Lord Gorham said, handing the parchment with a wax seal on it to the knight. "Make sure it is kept safe."

"Indeed, sire, I will," the knight said as he wrapped the parchment in a piece of cloth and placed it in his saddle bag. "I thank you for your hospitality, Lord Gorham. I am away."

The knight left the chamber and followed the manservant to the front door.

"Thank you for your service, kind man," the knight said as he left.

"You are always welcome, sir knight," the manservant replied.

The knight took the reigns from the servant and swung up into the saddle.

"May the gods and goddesses keep you safe," the servant whispered.

"You as well," the knight replied as he road away.

The knight returned to the castle in mid-afternoon. He gave his horse to the stable boy and found the other knights gathered in an empty stall at the far end of the stable.

"Lord Gorham has accepted King Owen's request for an audience," the knight reported. "He will be here by midday one week from today. King Owen will be ill, and Lord Gorham will meet with all of us and the high chancellor instead. We will carry out the meeting as planned. The other two Lords will be here tomorrow and the next day for a short visit with us. Do you have any questions?"

"None," they all replied.

"I fear we won't have to dose King Owen," Knight Harold said. "He took to his bed this morning after collapsing during a meeting with us. He is talking out of his head as we speak."

"This is progressing faster than the court healer expected," Knight Jameson said. "Be sure to keep each other posted on all news and changes with King Owen. We'll hold court sessions with the high chancellor. Godfrey can handle all the complaints. He usually tells the king what the outcomes should be, anyway."

They all agreed and went about their daily business. Court was held, and High Chancellor Godfrey did a great job handling the complaints. No one was held in the dungeon, as most complaints were minor. King Owen stayed in his bed for the rest of the week. The two lords were interviewed and sent on their way. Lord Gorham was due the next day.

The witch Helena was thrilled with the king's downward spiral. She knew her spell was working well. The Dark Forces wanted her to think that for now. They would take care of her soon.

The day of Lord Gorham's arrival dawned clear. He had brought three of his knights with him for the meeting, which took place as soon as he arrived, even though it was midday. No meal was served before the meeting.

They were gathered in the outer court chamber.

"Why aren't we in the throne room?" Lord Gorham said in a rather loud voice.

"Lord Gorham, King Owen is ill and is in his bedchamber," Knight Jameson replied. "High Chancellor Godfrey and we knights will be meeting with you."

"That is unacceptable," Lord Gorham replied. "I demand to see the king."

"That is not advised, Lord Gorham," Godfrey replied. "We are unsure of the cause of his sickness and would not want you to become infected."

"I understand and apologize for my outburst," Lord Gorham said. "I wish the king a speedy recovery."

"We'll relay your message," Godfrey replied. "On that note, Lord Gorham, the healer, doesn't think the king will recover. Therefore, this council has been meeting with possible candidates to replace him. We want to ask you some questions."

"I am sorry to hear this news," Lord Gorham said as he puffed out his chest, sure that he would be the new king. "Ask any questions you may have."

"Thank you for accepting our meeting," Godfrey replied. "This first question involves the religion that is in place here in Kerwyn. What are your thoughts on this?"

Lord Gorham knew he had to be careful answering this question. He hated the magic used in religious ceremonies and healing rituals. He would abolish it as soon as he became king, but for now, he needed to give an acceptable answer.

"High Chancellor Godfrey and you knights of the king," Lord Gorham began. "The religion that is in place here in Kerwyn is a vital part of life for all. It is important to have a set of rules that govern our souls. I would leave things as they are, as this seems to work well."

"What about the dragons, Lord Gorham?" one of the knights asked. "How would you deal with them?"

"I know King Owen has ordered them hunted and killed," Lord Gorham replied. "I agree with this edit."

"How would you handle disobedient subjects? The ones that disobey minor laws," High Chancellor Godfrey asked.

"I will fit the punishment to the infraction," Lord Gorham replied. "If a man stole a pig from his neighbor, I would require the man return the pig or a similar animal and work for his neighbor for three days."

The council liked that response. Knight Jameson wasn't so accepting of Lord Gorham's answers. He knew deep in his gut that Lord Gorham was lying. It seemed a powerful force was in charge of the way Lord Gorham answered their questions. He suddenly knew if they voted Lord Gorham as king, he and some of his fellow knights would have to run and hide. Lord Gorham would surely order their execution as soon as he was crowned king. That wouldn't happen until after King Owen's funeral.

Other questions were asked and answered.

"Thank you for your time here today," Godfrey said. 'A meal will be served if you wish to stay for it. Or, you may leave now if you wish."

Lord Gorham found this to be a strange event. He thought he'd be staying for a few days. Right then and there, he decided that he would have Godfrey beheaded first thing when he became king and all the knights beheaded as well. Godfrey and the knights had plans in place to flee the kingdom as soon as possible. They knew Gorham was fond of beheading the people who disagreed with him.

"A meal would be greatly appreciated," Lord Gorham replied.

Godfrey signaled the servants to bring in the food. There was plenty for everyone. Lord Gorham expected a fest that would last for hours. Instead, he got a midday meal of usual means. The council sat and ate. No one talked much. A few thoughts about the hunting and fishing in the area were discussed. The meal soon ended, and the council stood to signal the end of the visit.

"We thank you for your prompt visit, Lord Gorham," Godfrey said as he walked over to Lord Gorham to signal that he should stand. He did. "We will send a messenger if we have further news."

"I am honored to have been considered for such a serious duty," Lord Gorham replied as his knights left the room ahead of him.

"Safe journey, Lord Gorham," the council said in one voice.

Lord Gorham found himself outside the castle walls. His horses were ready for him and his knights. They mounted their steeds and left the castle grounds. Lord Gorham was furious. He wanted to kill something. Then, a thought came to him. He felt that he should be calm so the council wouldn't suspect anything amiss. He knew he would be crowned king because he had made that deal with The Dark Forces. Why bother wasting his energy on something when he already knew the answer? His knights watched his fury disappear and were glad. They hated seeing him kill innocent animals.

The villagers had been told about the king's sickness and were worried. They had heard that three of the lords were being invited to the castle for talks. The two lords from the outer areas were kind and strong rulers. The villagers didn't think they'd be seriously considered. Word was that Lord Gorham was the favored candidate. They knew about Lord Gorham's reputation for raping women and young girls and killing anyone he didn't like. Merlin and Feyanna knew instantly that Gorham was in with The Dark Forces. This was going to be a dark time for the kingdom if he were to be crowned king. It was a good thing the protection shield was in place. It wouldn't allow any negative energy through the shield. This was good for the villagers. They still kept watch along the north and south roads. Just in case something odd might happen. It was when any one of them needed to leave the protection of the grid that worried Merlin and Feyanna. They would have to work with The Special Magic to learn ways to protect Quintan. His destiny was already in play.

It was in the wee hours just before dawn at the time of the summer solstice when the mid-summer eve celebration was happening that King Owen died in his sleep. The castle sent black smoke up the central chimney, signaling his death. The funeral preparations started immediately. All the lords and mayors throughout the kingdom were required to attend. They all arrived three days later and were assigned rooms throughout the castle. The castle gates were draped in the king's colors with a black band over them. Thousands of the people flocked to Kerwyn and set up camp all around the castle and city wherever they could find space.

The villagers stayed home, and Merlin and Feyanna stayed home. They all knew that wicked things happened at times like this and wanted nothing to do with it.

King Owen's funeral service lasted four hours. It started in the castle chapel, where his soul was given to the gods and goddesses. Only their immediate family, his knights, and the high chancellor were allowed to attend. The ancient prayers were said in the ancient language. Offerings of incense, flowers, and herbs were made. His body had been prepared with herbs before the casket was sealed.

At the conclusion of the service, his body was carried by his knights to a waiting carriage, and a procession began in the inner castle grounds. It then went through the main gates, where the lords, mayors, and castle servants followed it. The common people fell in line and walked to the burial ground three miles away to the south. This took four hours as thousands of people joined the procession. It was late afternoon when the carriage carrying the king's body came to rest next to his crypt.

The body was placed inside the crypt, the doors were sealed, and the prayers for the dead began. These chants lasted another hour. At the end of the chants, the king's family climbed inside the royal carriage and were taken to their new home in the southern region, outside the boundaries of Kerwyn. Trumpets sounded a while later, and everyone was called to the grounds outside the castle.

Lord Gorham was inside with the other lords, waiting to hear who the new king would be.

High Chancellor Godfrey entered the council room alone. He stepped up onto the platform at the front of the room.

"Gentlemen, a decision has been made by the high council," Godfrey announced. "Lord Gorham is to be our new king. The coronation will take place in one hour. Lord Gorham, please remain here with your knights. The high council thanks the rest of you. Please follow the court aide and await the coronation ceremony."

The cheer sent up from those in the room was less than robust. Lord Gorham noted this and bowed before the high chancellor.

"I thank you for this opportunity and will work hard to be a fair and just king for the good people of Kerwyn and the countryside," Lord Gorham said.

The room emptied, and Lord Gorham and his knights were there with Godfrey.

"I will take you through the ceremony now so you'll know what to expect, sire," Godfrey said.

"I believe you should address me as Your Highness," Lord Gorham said.

"I shall do just that the instant you are crowned," Godfrey said. "I wouldn't want to step out of protocol, sire."

"Oh, yes. Quite right," Lord Gorham said, looking at his knights. He had given the order for Godfrey, and the knights to be murdered as soon as the crown was on his head and the last coronation prayer was finished. It was looking forward to a bloody coronation room.

Godfrey took him through the order of the coronation and asked if he had any questions.

"High Councilor Godfrey, where are King Owen's knights?" Lord Gorham asked.

"They have chosen to stay at the crypt to guard the body," Godfrey replied. "We don't want any of the kings that lie there to be desiccated."

"Good idea," Lord Gorham said. "I shall eat here. Please have the kitchen servants bring me my food."

"Yes, sire," Godfrey said as he signaled for this to happen.

Lord Gorham was surprised to see all the male servants enter the room. He didn't say anything. He would demand that all kitchen servants be female, young females.

Lord Gorham and his knights finished their meal just as a messenger entered the room.

"Sire," the servant said, bowing.

"Yes," Lord Gorham replied.

"Your presence is requested in the throne room for the coronation," the servant answered.

"Where is the high chancellor?" Lord Gorham asked.

"He is in the throne room waiting for you," the servant replied. "Here are the coronation robes, sire."

The servant helped Lord Gorham into the robes and showed him the way to the throne room. They waited in the hall for a moment.

"What are we waiting for?" Lord Gorham said in a nasty voice. "And where are my knights?

"I have signaled the court musicians that we are ready," the servant said. "They will sound the trumpets. Then, you will enter and walk the length of the hall. Wait at the step for the priest to give you instructions. Your knights are waiting for you inside."

"Leave," Lord Gorham hollered.

The servant practically ran down the hall to the stairs. He had told his family to pack everything, and he would join them during the coronation. He found them on the city's outer edge as the coronation ended. They left in a hurry, traveling west to the region of one of the other kings. This king was a kind and just ruler. They would be joining his sister's family on their farm.

The trumpets sounded, and the doors opened. Lord Gorham entered the throne room and walked down the center to the waiting priest.

The priest prayed and motioned for Lord Gorham to step onto the raised platform and stand before the throne.

The scepter was handed to Lord Gorham, and the prayer for guidance and wisdom was said. The prayer for his health was said, and he was given a piece of lavender. The prayer for a long and just time as king was said, and he was handed the orb. The prayer for his soul was said, and the crown was placed on his head.

He repeated the oath of loyalty and was signaled to take his place on the throne. The trumpets blared, signaling that a new king had been crowned. The windows were thrown open, and cheers were heard from the crowd below.

King Gorham walked onto the balcony, and the cheers grew louder.

"Where is the high chancellor?" the king asked.

"New kings usually name their own high chancellor," the priest said. "Do you wish to do that, Your Highness?"

"Yes," King Gorham replied. "He is High Chancellor Lawrence."

Lawrence came to the king and knelt down. "You are now the high chancellor. Take charge. And do as I have instructed you."

"Yes, Your Majesty," Lawrence replied. "If I may, King Owen's knights are nowhere to be found, and neither is Godfrey."

"Find them and kill them," King Gorham hollered. "Bring me their heads."

"As you wish, sire," Lawrence said.

Lawrence left the room, then the castle, getting as far away as possible. He knew if he didn't get the heads of the knights and Godfrey, he would be beheaded in front of the court.

Knight Jameson rode hard along the south road to the village. He passed through the shield easily. Merlin and Feyanna felt his presence right away. They hurried to the village commons to meet the knight. He had an older woman with him.

Hamlen and Samuel greeted the knight.

"Welcome to our village," Hamlen said. "I am Hamlen, and this is Samuel."

"I recognize you, Hamlen," Jameson said. "I saw you deliver the covered wagons. Great invention."

"Thank you," Hamlen said.

"I am Samuel," Samuel said.

"I am Jameson, a knight of King Owen. This is my aunt Beatrice. She was the head cook," he said.

Greetings were made all around just as Merlin and Feyanna joined the group. They were introduced as well.

"What brings you to our village, Jameson?" Merlin asked.

"We knights are running for our lives, as is Godfrey, the high chancellor," Jameson explained. "I am headed to Avalon as instructed by my aunt here."

"Why The Lake of Avalon?" Feyanna asked gently.

"It is where we will be safe," Beatrice replied. "I will settle there for the remainder of my life."

"I understand," Feyanna said.

"What about you, Jameson? Where will you eventually go?" Merlin asked.

"I'm not entirely sure," Jameson replied. "I keep getting the feeling I should be close to this village for a while."

"I get the same thing," Merlin said. "What is it?"

"I feel a buzzing of energy here," Jameson said as his aunt smiled.

"He has the gift, too," Beatrice said. "Just like me."

"What gift, Aunt Beatrice?" Jameson asked.

"The gift of knowing The Magic," she replied.

"Me? Magic?" Jameson said in disbelief.

"Indeed," Feyanna said. "That buzzing you hear is the protective energy grid we have placed all around the village and outer areas, including Avalon. Only those with positive souls are allowed through the grid. You and your aunt passed through easily."

"This is a lot to take in right now," Jameson said.

"I know of a cottage close to the lake," Samuel said. "Have some food and drink, and then I will take you there."

"We appreciate your hospitality," Beatrice said. "We accept."

Samuel settled them on the village green with food, drink, and stories that made them all laugh. A short time later, Samuel and a couple of the villagers showed them to the cottage near the shores of Avalon.

"This is lovely," Beatrice said as they walked up the stone path to the door. They walked in and found the place ready for them.

"Everything is here. It is as if we brought it with us and set it up," Jameson said as he walked around and looked at everything.

"The Magic always takes care of its own," Feyanna said. The others agreed with her.

"What's this?" Beatrice asked as she opened the cold box door set into the little rise on the side of the cottage. "There's ice in here. How can that be?"

"We'll tell you later," Merlin said. "Time for Feyanna and me to get back home. We have lots of work to do now that Gorham is king."

"You mean protection work?" Jameson asked as they walked outside.

"Partly," Merlin said, looking at Feyanna. "We have work for you to do, too."

"We always have work to do," Feyanna said. "With a new king, it will take some time for the kingdom to get used to him."

"That's a good way to put it," Jameson said. "Thanks for everything."

"You are very welcome," Samuel said as he and the villagers headed home.

Feyanna and Merlin took the path back to their cottage home. They knew exactly what to get started on, and it included new herbal remedies and protection spells.

The coronation feast was taking place as King Gorham had ordered it—well, most of it. He wanted young girls to be servers, but there weren't any to be found. His behavior was known throughout the kingdom. Most families hid their young girls or sent them to relatives and friends in other kingdoms for safety. This made him angry, but the feast was good, so he forgot about the young girls for the time being. Most guests left well into the night or went to their rooms. King Gorham was very tired, so he retired to his chambers. He didn't have a wife and children, so he was alone. His manservant had been with him for over five years and knew just what to do for Gorham. His bed was turned down the way he liked, and he fell into bed half-dressed. The manservant helped him finish undressing, and Gorham was asleep in no time.

The manservant was dedicated to Gorham and made sure the servants knew his every wish, from his food to his activities. He loved hunting and would get back to it in a little while. First, he had to control his kingdom. He called for a public announcement for noon the next day. He was waiting on his balcony before noon, watching his subjects gather below him. He looked through the crowd for a young girl but still didn't see any. He told his manservant to bring his knights to the throne room. He wanted to speak with them. They were waiting as he made his announcement from the throne room balcony.

"My common subjects," King Gorham began. "I have a new law for the kingdom. Be it known from this day forward, there will be no talk and activities involving Magic in my kingdom. Magic is forbidden. No spells, potions, or remedies are allowed that involve Magic. Only healing herbs are allowed to be given by the healers. Witches will be burned alive. Wizards will be tortured and then burned alive. The religion that is currently practiced is now forbidden. No Magic in religion anymore. My priests will teach you all the new religion, and you will convert or be beheaded in front of your family. All dragons are to be hunted, and their heads are to be brought to me. If any of you break these new laws, I will kill you and all members of your family."

That said, he left the balcony and walked into the throne room, where he sat on his throne.

"Did you hear and understand these new laws?" he asked his knights.

"Yes, sire," they all answered, bowing before the king.

"Excellent," King Gorham replied. "Now, find those dragons. I want their heads in the courtyard as soon as possible. Just because Owen couldn't find any doesn't mean you can't. Do whatever you want to do to find them. Four of you will go now on the hunt."

The head knight, Dennison, chose the four knights and sent them on their way.

The other ten knights were told to find a young girl for him straight away. Helena had heard about this and cast a potent spell upon herself with the help of The Dark Forces. She was transformed into a beautiful young girl. The spell would last for only three days. She showed herself near the castle, and one of the knights told her the king had requested an audience. She knew what to expect. She was ready to pretend to be a virgin and act scared. She would enjoy the encounter more than the king.

The knight brought her before the king. She curtsied and kept her gaze on the floor.

"Leave us and make sure we are not interrupted," the king ordered the knight out of the room.

"Come with me," the king ordered the young girl. He took her by the arm, and she passively allowed him to take her to his bed chamber.

The king removed his clothes and told Helena to do the same. She pretended to be scared, which excited the king. Helena knew what she was doing.

"Get into bed with me," the king ordered her.

As soon as she lay down, he was all over her. He sucked her breasts while his hand played with her pussy. He took her hand and put it on his dick.

"Play with my manhood," he ordered her.

She grasped his dick and massaged it lightly, then more firmly. She began to pump it, and this made him crazy with lust.

He pushed her hand out of the way and knelt over her chest. He lowered himself so his dick was between her huge breasts. He began to rock back and forth, and his dick started dripping his juices. Helena moaned as if she were frightened, and this made him rock faster.

He couldn't take much more, so he lowered himself and licked her pussy to make sure she was wet. He raised up and began pushing into her. She moved around as if it hurt, and this made him quite happy.

"You should be scared of me," Gorham said. "I'm your king and the best lover you'll ever have."

He pushed harder and faster until he exploded. Helena exploded, too, and thoroughly enjoyed the result of the king's work. He fell away from her and slept for a short time. Helena lay there and masturbated herself. It was pure pleasure.

The king woke up a few minutes later and looked at her.

"You will stay with me for the next three days. Is that understood?" he said as he got up and grabbed his bathing gown.

"Yes, Your Highness," Helena whispered.

"I will send someone to help you bathe and dress. You will eat with the servants," Gorham said as he rang for his manservant.

Gorham left for his bathing room, and a woman walked into the bed chamber.

"Put this on and follow me," she said. "You will bathe every day before and after the king has his way with you."

She handed Helena a robe of rough wool and slippers of thin wood. Helena was taken to a bathing chamber with a tub of water ready for her. She cleansed herself and went to the kitchen as the woman had told her to do. She ate well, thanked the kitchen staff, and returned to the king's bedchamber. She was ready when he returned a few hours later.

It was late at night, and he raped her again, or so he thought, then fell deeply asleep, having pushed her to the floor. She found a bed in the next room and slept until morning.

The king had sex with her many times throughout the next two days, and he was duped into thinking he was teaching her how to please a man. Helena played along. She had taken a few pieces of the cloth he had dripped his man juices on. Just what she needed to cast spells against him.

On the third day, he sent her away, saying he was tired of her. She bowed and left the castle through a secret door that led to a passageway to the field along the back wall. The field was used during tournaments for jousting and other physical games. It eventually led to the market place which was very busy that morning. Helena needed to get home right away. The spell would be gone in about an hour. She returned home just as the spell vanished. She was once again the old-looking woman with long, stringy gray hair.

Summer moved into the fall, and the countryside was on guard. King Gorham had ordered his knights to kill anyone not practicing the new religion. The new religion recognized only one god. That god spoke through the king and gave him the power to rule as he wished. The king's priest held religious services every Sunday to worship the new god. It was similar to the old religion involving magic but without using herbs and incantations in the old language. Incense was used to purify the air to please the new almighty god. Every subject in the kingdom was ordered to attend either the morning service or vespers at sundown. The king had hired a group of religious guards to watch over the services throughout the kingdom. The people made it look like they were following this new religious law. The truth was that they continued to practice the old ways of Magic in secrecy.

Feyanna and Merlin were very busy learning new spells, potions, and ways to protect Quintan and the villagers if they needed to leave the protection shield. The shield covered an area of about forty acres, including Avalon. The Special magic had Avalon protected as it was a Magical place.

Merlin had asked Jameson if he would teach Quintan the ways of the knight, including how to be a knight's aide. A week after the new king was crowned, they started working together every afternoon. Quintan was a quick study, and Jameson enjoyed teaching him all about being a knight.

"Being a knight is hard work," Quintan said the day before his fifteenth birthday. "There was a lot of work you had to do."

"Yes, there was," Jameson said.

"Do you miss it?" Quintan asked as they readied their horses for a jousting match practice.

"Some of it," Jameson said. "I don't miss raiding villages and killing innocents. King Owen was a mean man when he thought he was being cheated on."

"I wouldn't like that either," Quintan said as he sat his horse. "I would defend my kingdom as ordered, though. I guess that's what it's all about."

"It is," Jameson said as he grabbed his jousting spear. "Defending the kingdom from evil was a good thing. There were men and women who hated King Owen and wanted him off the throne. Some of them are part of King Gorham's court now. I'm glad I ran away with my Aunt Beatrice. We feel safe here."

"I like your aunt," Quintan said. "We all love her cooking. She's been sharing recipes with the villagers, and the smells from the cook ovens are delicious."

"Yes, they are," Jameson said. "She keeps telling me to eat more, and I keep telling her I don't want to get fat. How can I be a great knight if I'm fat? She just laughs at me and keeps on cooking."

"Are you ready?" Quintan asked as he took his position opposite Jameson. "I'm going to knock you off your horse this time."

"You wish!" Jamesons said as he raised his spear, and they began the match.

Some of the village children were watching and cheering on their favorite knights. The children had decided to call Quintan a knight because he was learning how to be one.

Penny and Q were watching as well. Invisible, of course.

"He's almost ready," Penny said. "He's agile and quick."

"He is," Q replied. "His swordsman skills are excellent for a young man. Merlin keeps adding new moves, and Quintan keeps up with them. Did you see him practicing with his knife yesterday?"

"I did," Penny said. "He's getting closer to his destiny so quickly. I hear King Gorham is having his way with his subjects. He's a mean man."

"His knights brought a man to court this morning, claiming he was not practicing the new religion. When questioned by the king, the man said he was. The king asked him a lot of questions about the new religion, and the man answered every one of them. The king asked why the knight had brought the man to court and replied that he had missed the services on Sunday. When the king asked why, the man said he was with his cow, who was giving birth to twin calves. It was a difficult birth that lasted all Sunday and into the night. The calves were born healthy, and the man said he spent an hour praying for forgiveness. The king liked that answer and let the man go, demanding he return with one of the calves in six weeks. The man thanked the king for his kindness and agreed to the king's demands."

"That doesn't sound like King Gorham," Penny said. "What else happened with this farmer?"

"You're right about that," Q answered. "The king sent his knights to take all the young girls from the farm and set them to work in the castle. The knights looked for the young girls and couldn't find any. They demanded to know what the farmer had done with them. The farmer told the knights he only had three boys. His wife couldn't have any more children, so they stopped trying to. The knights believed them and returned to the castle. The king was so furious that he demanded the lead knight's head be cut off. It was in front of the people of Kerwyn."

"How horrible," Penny said.

Penny and Q watched the jousting practice for a bit, then flew off. They had heard a new set of rogue dragons was terrorizing the villages to the west and north, and they needed to see what was happening.

The next day, the village gathered at Avalon to celebrate Quintan's fifteenth birthday. The first celebration was such a great success that the villagers decided to do it every year. They celebrated Quintan's birthday, the end of a great summer, and the beginning of the harvest season. Their lives had been peacefully quiet ever since the protection grid had been put in place. The Magic was protecting them well.

It was late afternoon, and everyone was having a grand time. Clarice and Roman were watching from a distance. They remained invisible at all times when around people. The swimming races were a blast. The kids had improved, and they were working hard to win their events. The older boys and girls created another acrobatics show in the water. This included Quintan and Jameson for the final part. Quintan and Jameson threw the older kids into the air, and they dove into the deeper parts of Avalon. Everyone loved this, and the show was a success.

The kids dried off, and supper was just a few minutes away. The fires had been burning since sunrise with roast pigs and venison. Potatoes and corn had been wrapped in corn husks and placed in the hot embers a few hours ago. They were ready to be devoured. And they were. Supper was a great success, and there wasn't much left over.

Folks visited, and the children played around the shore until the sun began its descent below the treetops. Families were beginning to pack their things when the strangest thing happened. They heard what sounded like thunder, but there wasn't a cloud in the sky. Everyone looked around and found nothing that could have made that sound. So they kept gathering their things and children.

The thundering sound came again. Feyanna and Merlin looked at each other and knew what it was. Huge shadows flew across Avalon, circled around, and then flew over the gathering. As the shadows got closer, they could see what they were. Dragons. A lot of them. They were red and black in color, and they were headed right for them. They blew fire at them, but it hit an invisible barrier. The flames ricocheted off that invisible barrier and hit the dragons full-on. Three of them were severely burned. They tried to fly into Avalon but were blocked. They burned for only a few minutes, then died. As their bodies fell from the sky, they turned to ash, and the ash was taken up into the heavens. Not a trace of the dead dragons could be seen. The remaining three screamed and flew away.

People began asking questions and talking about the attack.

"Merlin, they were dragons, right?" Samuel asked.

"Yes, Samuel, they were," Merlin answered.

"Rogue dragons," Feyanna added. "Most dragons are not evil like these were."

"The grid protected us, didn't it?" Horatio asked.

"Yes, it did," Merlin answered.

"Praise be to the gods and goddesses for protecting us," Horatio said.

"Amen to that," the young Portia said.

"Do you think they'll be back?" Aunt Beatrice asked.

"No," Merlin replied. "Now that they know they can't get to us, they'll look elsewhere."

"Will the King's knights go after them?" Hugho asked.

"Probably," Jameson replied. "We tried to find the dragons when I was a knight with King Owen. Now that I've witnessed what happens to them when they die, I don't think anyone will be able to prove they killed them. King Gorham is going to be very angry about that."

"You shouldn't kill the dragons," Sarah said. "They are a part of The Magic, and most don't hurt people."

"That's true, Sarah," Glendianna replied. "But there are a few who are angry, and they want to kill as many as they can—just like the ones who tried to attack us today. They do need to be found and dealt with."

"You mean killed, don't you mother?" Margaret said.

"Most likely," Glendianna replied. "The Magic will take care of them, too."

The children were shaken by the attack, and their parents spent some time answering their questions and trying to calm them down. As night overtook the day, a million stars shone in the heavens.

"Look at that sky, children," Hamlen said to everyone. "The Magic is truly powerful enough to fill the sky with such beauty. Let's try to remember the good things we see every day. There'll be time enough to worry about the world when you are all grown up. This has been a wonderful celebration."

"I thank all of you for the wonderful gifts and the water show," Quintan said. "You are all becoming strong swimmers. I'd better practice more so I can keep up with you."

This made the children laugh as Quintan pretended to be swimming.

"We thank the gods and goddesses for this splendid summer and look forward to the harvest," Sylvannia said. "Rest well, everyone."

Folks were home and settled a while later.

"Merlin, that was horrible," Feyanna said as they walked into their meadow. Penny and Q were waiting for them.

"What the hell was that?" Merlin said in a loud voice.

"That was an attack by the rogue dragons," Q replied. We've been following them for quite a while now, and we've been able to thwart some of their plans. Today, they flew fast and hard with the plan to wipe this village off the face of the earth. We held back, knowing the grid would stop them. They killed themselves. That's three less to worry about."

"I suspect the remaining three will hide out somewhere in the north for a few days. They're probably terrified and scared," Penny said.

"Will they try to attack anyone who leaves the grid?" Feyanna asked.

"Not sure," Q replied. "If they do, they'll be seen by others who will try to kill them. I think that's what's going to stop them for now."

"Good," Merlin said. "At least we have some time to think about this."

"We loved the celebration," Penny said.

Feyanna and Merlin looked at the dragons.

"You know Quintan will be leaving us soon, don't you?" Feyanna asked.

"We do," they replied.

"He's going to join the court, isn't he?' Feyanna said.

"Yes," Q replied. "As is his destiny."

"I can understand that," Feyanna said. "Merlin, we'll have to teach him how to call upon The White Light for extra help."

"We will," Merlin said. "We will."

"Get some rest," Penny said as she spread her wings. "Things are going to speed up around here for Quintan's departure."

The dragons lifted into the sky and were out of sight in the blink of an eye.

"We have a lot of work to do with Quintan," Feyanna said. "I need to teach him about the herbal remedies he will need."

"We'll start tomorrow morning right after sword practice," Merlin said. "Let's get some sleep."

They settled for the night with the rest of the villagers. Quintan lay awake for a while. He felt restless and couldn't quite figure out why. Something was about to happen to him. He finally fell asleep and dreamed of water acrobatics that had him laughing in his sleep.

CHAPTER 17

The next morning was the beginning of a new chapter in Quintan's life. After sword practice with Merlin, he spent the next few hours with Feyanna, learning about plants and their medicinal properties. Lunch was a quick affair, and Quintan went back to the workshop to learn how to make remedies. Feyanna taught him how to use feverfew to lower a fever. He learned how to make herbal blends to lessen pain from cuts and scratches. He learned how to set a broken bone from Merlin and how to use dried catgut and a needle to close a wound. He learned how to make teas from many blends to help with illnesses.

By the end of the day, his head was full of a great deal of new information. He'd had a short break with Jameson and Hugho, practicing sword fighting technique. Jameson was teaching him how to perform a sword fight as if he were in the castle competitions.

"Miss Feyanna, how do you remember all this stuff?" Quintan asked as they ate supper.

"I have been using these remedies for years," Feyanna replied. "You'll remember them when you need them. If you can't remember one, ask The Magic to help you. Do it in your head."

"I got that," Quintan replied. "I'll recite them every day so I can remember as much as possible.'

"That's a good idea," Merlin said. "We'll make sure you have a supply of your own."

"I like that idea," Quintan said. "Miss Feyanna, this chicken is so good," Quintin said with a mouthful of food. "And the roasted potatoes and carrots are seasoned to perfection."

"Thanks," Merlin replied. "I got the recipes from Beatrice."

"You made all this?" Quintan said. "I stand corrected and apologize for assuming Miss Feyanna made this meal."

Feyanna and Merlin laughed.

"We both cook, Quintan," Feyanna said. "You'll have to learn how to cook for yourself soon. Who knows when you'll be far from home and need a meal."

"My mother has been teaching all of us to cook for the last couple of years," Quintan said. "She assigns us a day, and we have to plan the meals for the whole day. The girls get more cooking practice than I do, though."

"I'll make sure to have you assist me from now on," Feyanna said.

"I'd like that," Quintan replied.

They finished their meal, and Merlin walked Quintan home. Hamlen was waiting by the fence when they arrived. Quintan hugged his father and went into the house.

"Merlin, he's going to leave us soon, isn't he?" Hamlen said.

"Why do you think that?" Merlin asked.

"I feel it in my soul," Hamlen replied. "He's destined for great things."

"Trust your soul, my friend," Merlin said. "He's almost ready. Just a few more cooking lessons, and he should be able to fend for himself."

"His mother is going to be waking him earlier each morning to get him that practice," Hamlen replied, laughing.

"Feyanna is going to work with him, too," Merlin said, laughing as well. "Boy, is he going to be busy!"

"Indeed," Merlin said. "How are the orders for the covered wagons coming along?"

"I just received an order for two of them for the new king," Hamlen replied. "He wants them as soon as possible. I've asked the owners of the ones I'm making now if I could give them to the king, knowing how he kills people if he gets angry. They said absolutely. They should be finished in about a week. I'll deliver them one at a time on the same day. I don't want any trouble from the court."

"I agree," Merlin replied. "Let me know if you need my help with anything."

"I will, my friend," Hamlen replied.

"Time to get along home," Merlin said.

"Until tomorrow," Hamlen replied as they went their separate ways.

Merlin told Feyanna about the covered wagons for the king. She agreed with the plan.

The villagers went about their business of harvesting over the next eight weeks. Hamlen delivered the covered wagons about a week after he got the order. The king was surprised with this. He had his manservant pay Hamlen a reduced price for them. Hamlen was thrilled to be paid anything for them. He left in the evening after the delivery of the second wagon. He hurried away from the castle and didn't slow down until he was far from Kerwyn. He arrived home exhausted and tired. He ate and fell into bed, glad his business with the horrible king was completed.

The harvest was the biggest one they'd ever had. They held the harvest festival on the northern edge of the village under the protection grid. Some folks stopped just before they reached the village and turned around, deciding not to enter. Others came through the grid with ease. The festival was a great success, and the villagers got busy completing their final preparations before the winter storms arrived.

It was at this time that Quintan was asked to join the court as a lesser paige. The guard from King Owen's reign stayed with King Gorham's reign. He was asked by the other guards if he knew of a trustworthy young man who would like to work for the court. The guards and knights needed someone to run errands for them. The guard remembered Quintan and sent word about the job. If he was interested, he should report to the guard at the eastern gate as soon as possible.

"Well, father, what do you think?" Quintan asked.

Quintan's parents, Feyanna and Merlin, were gathered around the outside table near the meadow that morning.

Hamlen looked at Merlin for a minute. "Is this what you want to do, son?"

"It is, sir," Quintan replied. "Merlin, Feyanna, and Jameson have been preparing me for this for quite some time now."

"I am worried about how the king will treat you," Glendianna said.

"I won't even meet the king, Mother," Quintan said. "The note says that I will be working with the guards and the knights only. No one else."

"I remember that guard," Hamlen said. "He was kind to us."

"I remember as well, father," Quintan said. "Master Merlin, what does The Magic say about this?"

"Quintan, The Magic will never make a decision for you," Merlin answered. "The Magic will do its best to protect you from harm. But, after all is said and done, you are responsible for your mind, body, and soul."

"I understand that," Quintan replied. "I know this is a big step for me to take. I will miss all of you terribly. In my soul, I know I am supposed to do this. It's my destiny."

Feyanna and Merlin exchanged a quick look with each other.

"Then, my son, you have your mother's and my blessing," Hamlen said as he stood to shake hands with his son.

Glendianna grabbed him into a hug that only a mother could give. She had tears in her eyes when she let him go.

"Master Merlin, what will you and Miss Feyanna do with all your free time?" Quintan asked, laughing.

"Funny, Quintan," Merlin replied. "Quintan, I have something for you."

Merlin handed Quintan something wrapped in cloth. He opened it and found a knife in its sheath. It was beautiful.

"You made this for me, didn't you?" Quintan said, looking at the knife.

"I did," Merlin said. "There is Magic in it, just like your sword."

"I know you made this scabbard, Miss Feyanna," Quintan said. "The art-work is incredible."

"Thank you, Quintan," Feyanna said.

"His sword and knife have Magic in them?' Glendianna said.

"Yes, dear," Hamlen said. "Feyanna and Merlin are with The Magic."

"I'm not surprised to learn this at all," Glendianna said.

"You'll keep our secret?" Feyanna asked.

"Always," Glendianna replied. "It's good to know my son is being watched over by The Ancient Magic."

"Yes, mother, it is," Quintan said.

"When will you leave?" Merlin asked.

"Day after tomorrow," Quintan replied. "I have a few things to take care of first. Please don't tell anyone about this. I want to leave quietly. After I leave, you can tell them."

"As you wish, son," Hamlen said. "I am proud to give you Buttercup as your own horse."

"Father!" Quintan said. "I appreciate this more than you could ever know."

"He knows you, and you know him," Hamlen replied. "He will respond to you quickly."

"He's only five years old, so you will be together for a long while," Glendianna said. "We have the two new colts to train now, so we won't miss Buttercup too much."

"You have trained me well, mother, and I am grateful for that," Quintan said.

They talked for a little longer, and then Hamlen and Glendianna went home.

"Quintan, the court these days is a dangerous place," Merlin said. "Keep your mouth shut and your head down. Listen to everything you hear and find a few good escape routes. Don't show anyone your sword or knife. Keep them secreted away, wrapped up in your bedding and clothes. If anyone remembers the sword, tell them you left it at home for your father."

"Yes, sir," Quintan said. "I understand the importance of these words."

"You are going to be a lesser paige for the court. If someone wants you to learn how to handle a sword, let them give you one. They will soon learn you know how to handle one. Do not ever mention The Magic to anyone, even someone you think you trust. You could be beheaded if you so much as say the word, even joking around. Go to the religious services and be a good practitioner. Fake it well, Quintan."

"Oh, Merlin, I have already decided to do just that," Quintan said. "I will keep the prayers for The Magic alive in my heart and soul and repeat them every day as I do now. I will always be true to The Magic."

"If anyone asks where you came from, tell them you came from a farm way up in the northern foothills. That way, they will never come to our village," Merlin said.

"What if they ask the name?" Quintan said.

"Tell them the truth," Feyanna replied. "You are from a small farm that stands alone between villages."

"Ah, yes. That's a great answer," Quintan replied. "I doubt if they know all the names of the tiny Dells up there anyway."

"They don't," Feyanna said. "If they do, tell them the closest little Dell is called the Hamlet Under the Mountain."

"Great name," Quintan said, laughing with Merlin.

"Well, let's get busy with one more sword-fighting lesson," Merlin said. "Today, I will hold nothing back."

"I am ready for you, sir Merlin," Quintan said as they took their places in the meadow.

Feyanna watched this last practice. She was impressed with Quintan's skills. He anticipated a number of Merlin's moves. And, the new ones, he managed to counter well. In the end, they called a truce.

Feyanna prepared several pouches of herbs and herbal remedies for him. He wrote a word about them on parchment and put it in each pouch.

"Quintan," Merlin said when he had finished. "Please know that we are always here for you. Just send a thought, and we'll hear it."

"I will," Quintan said. "I'll have Clarice and Roman as well."

"Yes, you will," Feyanna said. "Remember, they will be invisible."

"I remember well," Quintan said just as the four dragons landed in the meadow.

"Good afternoon all," Quintan said.

"So, you are going to work in the castle," Q said.

"Yes, Q, it's my time," Quintan said.

"We will be with you the whole time," Clarice said.

"Clarice, I'm wondering how you are going to avoid everyone. That castle is a busy place," Quintan said.

"It is," Roman said. "We'll be in the field out back some of the time. Other times, we'll perch on the towers and parapets."

"I think some of the guards up there may run into you," Quintan said, smiling.

"Not if we can help it," Clarice said, laughing.

"Although it would be fun to mess with them from time to time," Roman said, laughing with them. "Merlin, we will need a purple crystal placed in the meadow every morning just after sunrise."

"I was just going to ask about that," Merlin replied. "I will take care of it, of course. I believe Penny and Q will keep me on point."

"We will," Penny replied. "Merlin, please place a crystal now."

Merlin always carried one in his pocket. He placed it on the meadow, and the four dragons disappeared. Then they reappeared.

"I love watching this," Feyanna said.

"Quintan, would you honor me by taking a ride with me? I'd like to show you the countryside from high above. You'll have a better perspective of things."

"I would be honored, Q," Quintan said. "This is wonderful."

"Please show Quintan where to get on my back, Penny," Q said as Quintan walked over to him.

"Come this way," Penny said, pointing to Q's wing next to his neck. "You won't hurt him walking on him."

"I hope not," Quintan said as he stepped onto Q's wing. He climbed onto Q's neck and sat there. "Is this good for you, Q?"

"It would be best if you could slide back a couple of scales," Q answered.

Quintan moved back a little bit.

"That's perfect," Q said. "Now, if you need to hold onto me, just grab those black, wavy scales in front of you. You won't hurt me at all."

"Thanks," Quintan said. "I'm ready."

"Here we go," Q said, spreading his wings and lifting a few feet off the ground.

Quintan grabbed hold of the shiny scales just to be sure he didn't fall off.

"You good up there?' Q asked.

"This is amazing," Quintan said. "Yes, Q, I am good. See you later."

Penny joined Q, and they lifted high into the sky just as they became invisible again.

Feyanna and Merlin were laughing as the dragons, and Quintan became airborne.

"Can anyone see me?" Quintan asked as they flew to the north.

"Nope," Penny replied. "You're as invisible as us."

"This is great," Quintan said, laughing.

They flew north to The Great Northern Mountains, then banked to the east and flew along the coast.

"That's the Ocean of The Sun down there, Quintan," Q said.

"I can't see the other shore," Quintan said, searching for it.

"You won't," Penny said. "It's about a thousand miles across to its eastern edge."

"That's enormous," Quintan said. "How do you cross it?"

"People use big sailing boats called ships," Q replied. "It's a long and dangerous journey. Stay on land."

"I think I will," Quintan replied.

"We are approaching the castle now," Penny said as they banked to the west and flew over the land.

Quintan could see the whole city of Kerwyn wrapped around three sides of the castle. A large lake was on the west side.

"I never knew there was a lake there," Quintan said as they slowed down.

"It's been here since the beginning of time," Penny said. "It's called the Silver Lake because of the way the sun shines on it in the afternoon."

The dragons flew over the city many times, pointing things out to Quintan. Quintan spotted a little cottage in the woods to the west of the castle near the lake.

"I know that cottage," Quintan said. "The evil witch lives there."

"How do you know that?" Q asked.

"Because I do," Quintan answered.

"He's tuned into The Magic now," Penny said.

"I guess so," Quintan said as they flew low at treetop level, over the cottage. An old woman came outside, looking for something she couldn't find. She was angry and kicked a bucket across the clearing before going back inside.

"That's the witch," Quintan said. "She can feel our energy but can't see us. Boy, is she mad."

"That's true," Penny said as they rose into the sky once again.

They flew around to the back of the castle to show Quintan the playing field.

"This is where the jousting and sword-fighting events occur," Q said. "There is a tunnel beneath the field accessible from stairs just inside the castle door over there. That's where the participants enter the field. It should be one of your escape routes. Once in the tunnel, it looks like it ends at a rock wall. Look to your left, and you'll see a few rocks sticking out just a little from the others. Push them, and the wall will open. Once inside, push the little gargoyle head, and the wall will close. The tunnel will take you under the castle and the city. It will open in the forest north of the city. You'll be well protected from sight by all the trees."

"Wow! Thanks for that," Quintan said. "I get the feeling I may need that tunnel."

"Time to go home, my friend," Q said.

They flew over the village a couple of times, then circled Avalon before landing in the meadow and reappearing to Merlin and Feyanna.

Quintan hugged Q before he slid off. Q helped by shaking him onto the ground. He landed with a soft thud.

"Thanks, Q," Quintan said as he stood up. "That was the most amazing thing I've ever done in my life."

"It was my pleasure," Q said. "You are a good rider. You only held onto my scales for the deep turns."

"I didn't want to fall off and land in the middle of that ocean," Quintan replied.

"I take it the journey was magnificent?" Merlin asked.

"Oh, indeed, it was," Quintan replied, stroking Q's wing. "Miss Penny is an excellent tour guide."

"I am rather good," Penny said.

"Of course you are," Clarice replied. She and Roam had materialized as soon as Penny and Q landed.

"You four are so much fun," Feyanna said.

"We try," Roman said.

"Quintan, show them the crystal you were given," Penny said.

Quintan took the tiny red dragon from his trouser pocket and showed them.

"All Quintan has to do is hold the crystal in the light, and we'll come to him right away," Penny said.

"We'll already be nearby, too," Clarice said.

"We dragons can talk to each other using Magic," Roman said.

"I figured as much," Quintan said, staring off into space for a few minutes.

"What did you see?" Merlin asked.

"What?" Quintan said, shaking his head.

"What did you just see?" Merlin asked again.

"It was weird," Quintan said. "I saw myself in the courtyard of the castle— not the servants' courtyard, but the main courtyard where people enter the castle for an audience with the king. It was as if I was watching people all dressed up for something grand. The trumpeters were on the parapets, waiting for a signal from someone. Everyone was excited to be there. That's all."

Feyanna and Merlin looked at each other for a moment, then at the dragons. The dragons shook their heads just a little bit to signal not to tell Quintan what he was seeing.

"That's interesting," Feyanna said. "I've never been to any castle. It sounds like it was beautiful."

"It was," Quintan said. "Maybe I'm just getting all caught up in everything with going to work there. My mother has always said I have quite the imagination."

"She would know," Merlin said, smiling. "Quintan, we have shared a great many things with you. Use the knowledge well. Practice your skills every day where no one can see you. Be kind to everyone, even the mean people, and you will do well."

"I am grateful for all of you," Quintan said. "Having my own dragons is a wonderful thing. I truly love The Ancient Magic, as my mother refers to it. I will always remember my humble beginnings."

"Time for us to fly," Penny said as she and Q spread their wings and flew off.

"We are staying here with you," Clarice said as she and Roman settled down.

"Well, I'm about to head home, so don't get too comfy," Quintan said, laughing.

"He's a wise guy," Roman said as the two dragons stood up.

"I'll see you tomorrow one last time," Quintan said. "Thank you for everything."

Quintan hugged first Merlin, then Feyanna. He turned and headed down the path. He didn't want them to see the tears in his eyes. He loved them as if they were his own parents, just like Hamlen and Glendianna.

His last day in the village went by like a blur. He made breakfast for his family, who were thrilled with this and teased him all day. In the late morning, he found Hugho and asked him to take a walk.

They walked down to Avalon and stood by the shore in silence for a minute.

"Hugho, tomorrow I leave home to become a lesser paige in the court of King Gorham," Quintan told his best friend quietly.

"You're leaving here?" Hugho said, surprised.

"Yes, my friend," Quintan said. "I know it's what I'm supposed to do, but I don't want to leave you and my family and all the others."

"This is difficult to hear," Hugho said. "You are my best friend. I tell you all my dreams and secrets. Who will I talk to now?"

"I'll always be your best friend, and you mine," Quintan said. "I want to know if you'll come to work in the castle with me if I can find you a job."

"Yes, I will," Hugho replied. "Of course I will. I have learned a great deal about swords and knives from you and Merlin. And Jameson, too. He really knows all about the whole being a knight thing. I've even grown some muscles this summer."

"Yes, I know," Quintan said, laughing. "I still have the bruises to show for it."

"Well, you didn't duck when I punched you. So there," Hugho said, laughing at Quintan.

"You're right, of course," Quintan said as he punched his friend rather hard in the arm.

"Now, you may have one, too," Quintan said as he stepped a few feet away.

"So that's how this is going to be," Hugho said as he splashed water all over Quintan.

"I'll remember this," Quintan said, laughing. "So, you okay with all this for now?"

"As if I had a choice," Hugho replied. "Of course, I'm okay with this. I want what you want for you. I'll keep working with Jameson and Merlin, so when it's my time to join you, I'll be ready. Probably a better swordsman than you could ever wish to be."

"I highly doubt that," Quintan said.

"We'll see," Hugho said. "I'm going to miss you something fierce."

"Take all the energy and use it to learn about the world from Merlin. He is a wise man," Quintan said.

"And a Master Wizard," Hugho said.

"You know about that?" Quintan replied.

"I sure do," Hugho said. "Always have since the minute he and Feyanna arrived. She's an amazing healer."

"She is," Quintan said. "Keep quiet about it. And, when you do join me, you'll have to pretend to believe in the new religion. You'll go to services with me and everything."

"I know," Hugho replied. "I've already thought about that and decided to fake it and remain true to The Magic—all in secret, of course."

"This is great," Quintan said. "I think you'll be ready when the time comes. It could be sooner than you think."

"Just send a message, and I'll come running," Hugho said.

They stood their in the silence of their friendship for a while.

"Well," Quintan said. "Time for me to get back and pack. Father gave me Buttercup, so I need to make sure his tac is all ready to go."

"That was generous of him," Hugho said. "He is a good man."

They walked back to Hugho's family farm rather slowly. They stood there staring at each other for the longest time.

"Always my friend," Quintan said. "I will always protect you."

"Always my friend," Hugho said. "I will always protect you."

They grabbed each other in a fierce hug and then slowly stepped back. They both had tears on their cheeks. Quintan waved as he turned and walked down the road crying. Hugho stood there crying for a bit before he went on into the pasture to help his father.

Quintan never made it back to Feyanna and Merlin's cottage home. They all knew he wouldn't. He didn't sleep much that night, thinking about his life growing up in the village and now moving on. He got up with the sun and gathered the eggs before his mother could. He milked the cow, too, before his sister could. When they came into the kitchen they found him there with a bag at his feet.

"Quintan, are you going somewhere?" Sarah asked as she stood in front of him. His father and mother were standing in the doorway.

"Yes, my sweet pet, I am," Quintan said.

"Where?" Margaret asked as she stood beside him, placing her arm around him.

"My sweet sisters," Quintan said as he knelt in front of them. "It's time for me to leave home and go out into the world. I have a job as a lesser paige with the guards and knights in King Gorham's court. I leave now."

"But you can't," Sarah said crying. "Who will be my big brother?"

"I'll always be your big brother," Quintan said.

"But you won't be here for me," Margaret said.

"That is true," Quintan said as they all cried. "I have asked Horatio to look out for you. He'll be your uncle."

"I like Horatio," Sarah said. "But, I want you."

"Me, too," Margaret said.

Quintan looked at his father for help.

"Girls, we've always known you would grow up and leave home," Hamlen said. "It's time for Quintan to do just that."

"It doesn't mean you'll never see him again," Glendianna said. "He'll come by a lot of times. He's going to miss you as much as you're going to miss him."

"It's not fair," Sarah said. "It's just not fair."

"Being fair has nothing to do with this," Hamlen said. "He's grown into a fine young man and needs to leave and see the world. This is what's best for him."

"Maybe so," Margaret said. "But I don't like it anyway."

"Me either," Sarah said.

"Sisters, if I stay, I will be very sad because I can't go out into the world and learn new things," Quintan said." You don't want me to be sad now, do you?"

Sarah and Margaret looked at each other for a minute. Then, they shook their heads.

"I didn't think so," Quintan said. "And besides, in a few years, you're going to fall in love, get married, and move away yourselves. Where would that leave me? Without you."

"He's got a point there, Margaret," Sarah said.

"He does," Margaret agreed.

"Okay then, Quintan. You can go," Sarah said. "But you have to promise to come home a lot."

Quintan stood tall, placed his hand on his heart, and said, "I solemnly promise to come home every chance I get."

"Good," Margaret said. "You can't break your promise. Bad things will happen if you do."

"I know," Quintan said as he grabbed his sisters and lifted them off the floor.

They giggled and squirmed for a minute until he put them down.

"It's time for me to leave," Quintan said. "Will you do one more thing for me?"

"What?" they both said.

"We have those two colts out there. They are going to need great trainers. Mother has her hands full with running the house and gardens. Will you promise to train those colts the best way you know how?"

"I promise," Sarah said with her hand on her heart.

"I promise, too," Margaret said with her hand on her heart.

"Mother will show you just what to do," Quintan said.

"She already has," Sarah said. "Oh, Quintan, we named the colts."

"Well?" Quintan said. "I'm waiting."

"The brown one is called Bear because he is the same color as the bears around here. And he doesn't really whinny yet. He kind of growls," Sarah explained.

"And the black-and-white one is Patches," Margaret said. "Because he was born when the moon looked like it had black patches on it. Mother says it was just the clouds passing over the moon. I say they looked like the patches she mends our clothes with."

"Those are great names, sisters," Quintan said. "I couldn't have thought of better ones. Take good care of them and their mothers."

"We will," they said as Quintan grabbed his bags and walked outside. He tied them to his saddle and turned and looked at his family.

He hugged each sister for a long while. He next hugged his mother, then his father.

"Thanks for taking me in," Quintan said. "I couldn't have chosen a better family to grow up in," Quintan said. "I love you deeply."

With that, he swung up into the saddle and rode out of the pasture. He waved without looking back. He was crying and didn't want them to see this. He paused for a moment when he passed the path to Feyanna and Merlin's cottage home. He loved them, too.

Quintan made it to the castle by mid-morning. He rode on the outskirts of Kerwyn as long as he could before he had to go through some of it to reach the gates. The guard he remembered was on duty there and smiled when he let Quintan in.

"I see you received my message," the guard said. "Your decision?"

"I accept, and thank you for thinking of me," Quintan said.

"I don't see your sword this time," the guard said quietly.

"I thought it best to keep it out of sight for now," Quintan replied.

"Excellent idea," the guard said. "My name is Russell. You may call me that when no one else will hear you. If people are around, call me guard."

"I will, Russell," Quintan said. "Now, what do I do?"

"Follow me, lad," Russell said rather loudly as if someone was watching them. "I'll show you what to do. Under no circumstances are you to enter the castle except when instructed to do so. Stay away from the royal family at all times. You are a lowly lesser paige and not worthy of the king's time and attention."

"Yes, guard," Quintan replied, looking at Buttercup.

Russell led Buttercup to the stables the knights and guards used and assigned him a stall.

"You are responsible for keeping your horse's stall clean. Food and water are in the black buckets. Do not take food from the brown buckets; that is for the knight's horses only."

"Yes, guard," Quintan replied, looking at Russell. Russel winked at him as Quintan placed Buttercup in his stall.

"I'll show you where you will sleep," Russell said.

Quintan followed Russel to the back of the stables and climbed the stairs to the loft above.

"This will be your bed and storage area," Russell said as he looked around to see if anyone else was up there. "You can have these two spaces. Don't leave anything of value up here. I'll show you where we can hide your sword."

Russell was talking very quietly. Quintan followed him downstairs and outside. They entered the building next to the stables. There were two other guards inside.

"Fellow guards, this is Quintan. He is our new lesser paige. He will be on duty this afternoon. I am assigning Karl to be his guide," Russell said.

"Welcome, Quintan," the two guards said as they rose to leave.

"Thank you, guards," Quintan said, looking at the ground.

"At least he knows to look down when he talks with us," one of the guards said as they left.

"That is a lie," Russell said after the guards left. "Don't you look down when anyone talks to you. Keep your eyes on their eyes, and you'll earn their respect."

Quintan looked right into Russell's eyes as he replied, "Yes, Russell."

"Well done," Quintan Russell said as he slapped him on the back. "Well, done."

Russell showed Quintan a spot in the floor under one of the beds.

This is my bunk," Russell said. "I made a hiding spot here after I first arrived. No one knows it's here. I got a few things stolen when I was young. I've made a hiding spot in every building I've stayed in in this castle. You're welcome to use it."

"Thank you," Quintan said. "I think I'll find my own hiding spot, though. Too many eyes would be on me if I came in here a lot."

"Oh, yes. You are probably right," Russell said. "Good thinking. I knew you were a smart one when I first met you and your father. He is amazing with his covered wagons and that sled wagon. Sure made things easier for everyone around here when we needed to move a lot of stuff. The king never used it, of course. His manservant was a wise and kind man. He ran away as soon as King Owen died. He knew the new king would have him beheaded. Smart man."

Quintan just nodded in agreement. Russell showed him a few other places around the inner courtyard. He cautioned him about befriending any of the older girls. He told Quintan they were whores and were trouble. Quintan thanked him. Russell took him to the kitchen, showing him which door to use. It opened into a small entryway that led into the kitchen.

"Good day, everyone," Russell said. "This here is Quintan, our new lesser paige for the guards and knights. Please feed him well. We have a lot of work for him to do."

"You know we will," an older woman said. "I am the head cook here, young man. Be on time for meals, and I'll be happy with you."

"Yes, ma'am," Quintan said, looking right at the cook.

"He shows respect," the cook said. "That is a good sign. Sit yourselves over there, and I'll fetch you some lunch."

"Thanks, Rosie," Russell said as he kissed her cheek.

Rosie smiled and gathered their meal. It was roasted chicken and vegetables, with fresh bread and butter.

"This is heavenly," Quintan said as he tased the chicken. "I taste a hint of rosemary and thyme with a bit of lemon."

"A young man who knows his seasonings," Rosie said. "I am hopeful for you, young Quintan. How do you know about seasonings?"

"My mother was insistent that I learn to cook and cook well," Quintan replied.

"Your mother is a wise lady," Rosie said. "You come around here anytime you're hungry, and we'll take good care of you."

"I thank you kindly for that," Quintan said as they finished their meal.

"Time to show young Quintan his work," Russell said as he kissed Rosie on the cheek again. "I love ya, my Rosie."

"Go one with you now," Rosie said as she smiled and handed them each a piece of pie.

"Thanks so much, Miss Rosie," Quintan said as they left.

"He's a keeper," Rosie said after they left. "I know people, and he's a good one. Don't tell the king about him. He'll throw him out. The king doesn't like anyone smarter, younger, and more handsome than himself."

The kitchen staff agreed with Rosie and went about their work. Word got around the castle servants about young Quintans, as he was now called. They were going to protect him at all costs. They felt something special about him. Not many got the approval of the servant class. Quintan had earned it in less than an hour.

Russell showed him the places he would need to go each day, including the specific vendors. He was told not to go to other vendors, no matter what they offered or said. They were evil people, and he was told to stay away from them.

Russell sent him to set up his living space. The stable was made of rocks and timbers. It was a place in the wall. Quintan looked around his living area and saw a place he thought he might be able to use to store his sword and knife. The walls were about two feet thick, and he found a rather loose rock nestled next to some support timbers. You wouldn't know the rock was loose unless you tried to move it. He was able to pull it away from the timber. There was a space inside between the two support timbers near the head of his bed. He ran his hand inside and found it to be a long space that would hold his sword. He heard someone coming and quickly replaced the rock.

It was a knight. Quintan stood up as the knight approached him.

"You must be young, Quintan," the knight said. "I am Harrison. I am here to help you learn how things are done around here."

"Hello, Harrison," Quintan. "I am Quintan, not young Quintan."

"I hear you," Harrison said. "I'll bet Rosie gave you that added name. It's her way of approving of you. She's a tough nut to crack. She loves Russell and me. She tolerates the other guards and knights. I hear you showed her respect, and you know a few things about cooking."

"That's true," Quintan said, smiling. "My mother taught all of us how to cook. She insisted on it."

"She is a wise and smart lady," Harrison said.

"Yes, sir," Quintan said, taking the clothes from Harrison.

"Quintan, call me Harrison," Harrison said.

"I'll be down in a few minutes, Harrison," Quintan replied.

"Okay," Harrison said as he went downstairs.

Quintan made quick work of placing his sword and knife in his hiding place. They fit well. He asked The Special Magic to keep them safe. A soft light flashed in reply. He quickly changed and was downstairs a minute later. His uniform was a navy blue tunic with dark gray trousers.

"This is an interesting uniform," Quintan said as he joined Harrison.

"King Gorham demands that all castle workers wear specific uniforms so everyone knows what the other person is supposed to be doing."

"Okay, I guess," Quintan said. "I do as I'm told."

"That's an excellent attitude to have," Harrison said as they walked across the inner courtyard, through an opening, and into another inner courtyard. The knights were gathered there, working on their fighting skills. They held their shields as they fought. Swords, knives, and mallets were being used.

Harrison let Quintan watch for a few minutes before he called out to his fellow knights.

"My fellow knights," Harrison called across the courtyard.

The knights stopped what they were doing and walked over to him and Quintan.

"Please meet Quintan," Harrison said, "He is our new lesser paige. Quintan, the knights of King Gorham's realm."

"I am honored to meet all of you," Quintan said, looking right at each one of them.

"We are pleased to have you with us," one of the knights replied.

"All right, everyone, back to work," Harrison said when they finished greeting Quintan. "Quintan, please fill the drinking buckets. There are ten of them over there."

"Where is the handcart Harrison?" Quintan asked.

"Handcart?" Harrison asked.

"Yes," Quintan replied. "It would be better for me and quicker for everyone if I used a handcart."

"That is true," Harrison said. "No one has ever used one before. Let's go into the other courtyard and ask Russell if he knows where one might be."

They walked over to Russell, and Quintan asked about the handcart.

"Good question, Quintan," Russell replied. "I see one over there. It looks like it might be able to carry your buckets."

Quintan went over to get it and was stopped by a worker.

"You can't have that boy," the worker snarled. "I use it all day long."

"Yes, he can," Russell told the worker. "This handcart belongs to the king's court, and anyone can use it as needed. We need it now."

The man snarled some kind of muttering, and Russell pointed to Quintan to take the cart. It was filthy.

"I will need to clean this before I use it," Quintan said. "It has shit and dirt all over it."

"You'll find brushes and cleaning soap just inside the stables," Russell said. "Get busy now."

Quintan spent about a half hour cleaning the bucket. It was disgusting. He almost threw up when he got it wet. The smell of piss and shit was overpowering. He knew the worker was using it to pee in instead of going to the outhouse. He would report this to Russell in a bit.

The handcart was finally clean. Quintan took the buckets to the well and filled them, returning to the knight's courtyard. The knights were thankful for the fresh water. Quintan kept the handcart near the knights when he went to tell Russell about the worker.

"That is gross," Russell said. "Thanks for letting me know. I'll take care of him. He is lazy, and it's time he was dismissed."

Russell walked over to the worker. The worker was sound asleep.

"Worker!" Russell hollered as he kicked the man. "Wake up!"

The worker stood up, saying, "What do you want, guard?"

"Worker, you no longer work for the court," Russell said. "This guard will escort you out of the castle area. Do not return. You are lazy, your work is never completed, and you used the handcart to piss and shit in. Be gone!"

"Lies! All lies!" the worker shouted as the guard kicked him out of the castle gates.

Russell saw Quintan and winked at him. Quintan did not respond. He kept busy with his work. Evening brought him to the kitchen, where he found Russell and another guard.

"Good job taking care of that handcart today," the guard said. "That man needed to go."

"Thank you, guard," Quintan said as Rosie brought him a plate of food.

"Good job, young Quintan, figuring that man's laziness out," Rosie said. "He is a good-for-nothing, and it's about time he got the boot. Not bad for your first day."

"Thank you, Rosie," Quintan said. "This mutton stew is spectacular."

"Thank you, young Quintan," Rosie said. "Now eat."

Quintan and the guards were in their beds a short time later. Quintan didn't remember falling asleep but knew he was being woken up. One of the guards threw a block of wool at him, and it landed on his head.

"Hey, knock it off!" Quintan yelled before he remembered where he was.

Quintan opened his eyes and saw the guards smiling at him.

"Welcome to the castle," Russell said, laughing with everyone else.

"At least it wasn't a bucket of water," Quintan said as he stood up. "Very funny, guards."

Quintan saw one of the guards holding a bucket of water.

"Good thing you woke up when you did," the guard said. "We always use the bucket of water as a second choice."

"I'll be sure to remember that," Quintan said. "Now, allow me to take care of things and dress. I'll be down shortly."

It took more than a few minutes to get ready, but Quintan was in the stable in good time.

"Good morning, Buttercup," Quintan whispered in the horse's ear.

Buttercup gave him a nod and hug as Quintan set up his feed and fresh water. "I'll be back in a bit."

"Let's get some breakfast," Fred, one of the knights, said.

Quintan settled quickly into his duties and the rhythm of the castle. He was teased when the guards and knights heard him call Buttercup by name. He explained that the horse had been born in a field of buttercups, and his mother deemed it appropriate to name him such. They liked that explanation and continued to tease him anyway.

He saw a beheading during his second week. A man had been accused of stealing from a neighbor and found guilty by the high chancellor. The king deemed it necessary to kill him to set an example for everyone. He was in the back of the crowd and looked away when the axman swung his ax. He ran away into the field behind the castle and threw up. Others were there doing the same thing. Not a word was said as they all returned to their work.

During the second week, the king ordered all but two of his knights to hunt and kill the dragons. The king was convinced there were hundreds of them, and the dragons were wreaking havoc on the harvest. He wasn't getting what he deemed was his rightful portion from the farmers and decided it was because the dragons were burning the fields and orchards. None of this was true. The farmers were hiding their crops from the king so they would have enough for their families for the coming year. Nevertheless, the king ordered the dragons to be hunted and killed. He wanted proof of this as well, so he ordered their heads be delivered to him.

The knights had been gone for five days, and when they returned, they didn't have any heads. The king was furious. He was told they hadn't even found any of them. The head knight gave him great details, and the king calmed down some. King Gorham decided that the knights needed more help. Three of them did not have personal aides. He ordered the guards to find them each an aide. Russell spoke with Quintan that evening on their walk back to the stables from supper.

"Quintan, how would you like to be promoted to a knight's aide?" Russell asked.

"Really?" Quintan said, stopped in his tracks. "A knight's aide?"

"Yes, indeed," Russell said. The king thinks the knights couldn't find any dragons because they were spending a lot of time taking care of themselves. There are three knights who need aides. Harrison is one of them. Interested?"

"Yes, I am?" Quintan said. "Could I be Harrison's aide?"

"He asked if you could be his aide," Russell said. "The answer is yes. As of tomorrow morning, you are to report to Harrison as his aide. You will still live, and Buttercup will still be in her stall in these stables. You will ride her when the knights go out on maneuvers."

"This is great," Quintan said as they walked through the stables. "Hey, Buttercup, you're going to get a lot more exercise from now on."

"That's for sure," Russell said. "The king has ordered the knights to be ready to return to the countryside in one week. You have a lot to learn between now and then."

"I sure do," Quintan said. "Russell, thank you for thinking about me. I greatly appreciate you."

"You are very welcome, Quintan," Russell said as they climbed the stairs. "I'll be watching you."

"Good to know," Quintan said. "Sleep well, guard."

"Sleep well, knight's aide," Russell replied.

Quintan couldn't believe his good fortune at becoming a knight's aide. This was great. He finally fell asleep and dreamed of dragons and apple pie. Must have been Rosie's apple pie that made him dream about it. That woman sure knew how to cook.

The next morning, he was awake before the guards. Harrison walked in and gave him his new uniform. It was gold, light blue, and orange, just like the knight's clothes, and it was in the king's colors. Quintan, dressed, ran across the courtyard and into the kitchen for his breakfast.

"Would you look at you?" Rosie said with a smile on her face. "All dressed up in your new clothes."

"Good morning, Miss Rosie," Quintan said as he sat at the table. "Yes, indeed. I am Harrison's aide now. Is that okay with you?"

"Oh, child, of course it is," Rosie said as she set his breakfast in front of him. "I'm right proud of you as if you were one of my own. You be careful out there, now."

Rosie squeezed his shoulder as she passed by, and Quintan squeezed her hand in return. He missed his mother immeasurably, but Rosie sure helped him get by. She was like a second mother to him.

He finished his breakfast and found Harrison in the knight's courtyard.

"Good morning, Harrison," Quintan said.

"Good morning, Quintan," Harrison said. "Time to earn your keep. First, please clean and polish my dress boots. The king wants us in his throne room this afternoon. Not you. All of the knights. Then, clean my clothes from the past few days. The soap is in the bucket near my bed. You'll find the line to hang them on just past the stables. Be sure to feed and water my horse when caring for yours. After the meeting with the king, I will need to spar with the other knights to keep in shape. Make sure my sword and knives are sharpened and cleaned. Any questions?"

No, sir," Quintan said.

"Thanks, Quintan," Harrison said as Quintan went back to the sleeping quarters above the stables.

Quintan found Harrison's boots and polish, his dirty clothes, and the soap bucket. He took them down to the stables and cared for the horses. Next, he went to find a large wooden tub to wash Harrison's clothes in. First, he put them in plain water to get as much crud off of them as possible. He changed the water, put some soap in the tub, and began to stir the clothes with a broom handle. The water became dirty after a few minutes, so he dumped out the water, poured in fresh water, and stirred it again. This time, the soap had time to work out the dirt. He dumped the dirty water out again, put fresh in again, and rinsed the clothes. The water didn't change much, so he figured the clothes were clean. He rang them out and piled them in the water buckets to take to the hang on the line.

While walking through the courtyard these past few days, he noticed that some of the clothes on the lines had fallen onto the ground and gotten dirty again. He made some clothespins from small pieces of branches and used them now to hang the clothes on the line. The courtyard became very quiet while he was hanging the clothes. He looked around, and a number of people were watching him.

"What do you have there, Quintan?" one of the washing ladies, Matilda, asked him.

"I fashioned some pins to keep the clothes from falling off the line," Quintan replied. "I've watched you all have to rewash clothes because the clothes on the lines were just hung there. A few strong breezes always seemed to come along and make the fall. I have quite a few extra if you'd like to use them."

"That would be greatly appreciated," Matilda said. "I'll wait until you're finished."

Quintan finished up quickly and gave the rest of the pins to Matilda.

"Please keep them safe, as I don't have time to make new ones," Quintan said.

"Oh, I will," Matilda said as she shared the pins with the other laundry maids.

Quintan polished Harrison's boots quickly, placing them near Harrison's bed. Next, he sharpened and polished the sword and knives. He was finished before the knight's meeting with the king. And he was starving. He had his lunch and then decided to practice his own sword-fighting techniques. He took his sword from its hiding place and went to the events field. No one was there, so he set to practicing his moves. He started with his warm-up exercises and then moved on to running through the basic moves Merlin and Jameson had taught him. He didn't know he was being watched. Harrison and Fred were in amazement at what they saw. Quintan was a master swordsman. How did he learn all those moves? It wasn't since he came to the castle. He'd had no time for all that. He must have learned as he was growing up by a master swordsman. They stayed hidden for a while longer than couldn't contain themselves.

Quintan had his back to them as they approached. He heard them just before they got to him.

"Quintan, you are a master swordsman," Harrison said, looking at Quintan's sword. "May I hold your sword?"

"With all due respect, Harrison, no," Quintan said. "A man's sword should not be handled by others."

"You are being a bit insolent, aren't you?" Fred asked.

"No sir," Quintan replied. "I speak the truth."

Harrison and Fred looked at Quintan for a moment. They'd never had an aide who spoke to them that way. They'd never had an aide who was a master with the sword, either.

"Quintan, will you spar with me?" Harrison asked.

"I would love to," Quintan said.

"Come back into the courtyard while I get my sword," Harrison said as the three of them walked across the field.

As soon as Quintan entered the knight's courtyard, everyone stopped what they were doing. They saw his sword and were shocked that a lowly aide would have such a magnificent sword. Fred stood next to Quintan while they were waiting for Harrison.

Harrison joined them a few minutes later. He motioned for Quintan to stand in the middle of the courtyard with him.

"You have sharpened and cleaned my sword to perfection," Harrison said. "I think I know how you do that now."

"Yes," Quintan replied.

"Shall we?" Harrison said.

And, they began. Quintan countered every move Harrison made again and again. He even showed Harrison a few new moves. It was when Quintan tripped Harrison, making him lose his balance and drop his sword, that Harrison knew he had been bested by a champion. He threw his hands into the air, signaling defeat.

Quintan held his hand out to Harrison to help him to his feet. Quintan was ready for Harrison to pull him to the ground, but he didn't.

"You are truly a champion," Harrison said as he grabbed his sword from the ground.

The knights and others in the courtyard who had gathered to watch this unbelievable match applauded and cheered for Quintan. Harrison raised Quintain's hand to show he was the winner.

"I thank you for allowing me to spar with you, good knight," Quintan said.

"I thank you for showing me that I need more practice," Harrison said.

"I would be happy to show you those new moves if you wish," Quintan said as people began to return to their work.

"I accept," Harrison said as the two of them got a drink of water. "Fred, this young man is amazing."

"I agree," Fred said. "Quintan, who taught you to fight like that?"

Quintan smiled for a second, then said, "There is an older man near my village who taught me all I know."

"I would like to meet him," Fred said. "I know I need some lessons."

"I would be happy to instruct you as best I can," Quintan said, bowing to them.

"Offer accepted," Fred said. "Tomorrow morning, right after breakfast, eat hearty. We are going to make you work your pants off."

"Challenge accepted," Quintan replied, laughing with the knights.

The next six days found, Quintan training with the knights. He showed them some of the techniques Merlin had taught him and held some back. The afternoons were spent taking care of Harrison's needs. Quintan went into the city a few times to get things for Harrison. The women and young girls tried to flirt with him. He just smiled and walked on. He was getting to be known as a serious man.

The day after Quintan started training the knights, they were ordered to go out into the countryside and hunt dragons. Harrison gave Quintan a list of things he would take with him and told him to be ready by mid-day.

Midday found the knights eating in one of the banquet rooms in the castle while the aides ate in the kitchen. Rosie let Quintan know she was taking good care of him. She gave him larger portions of food and drink. When the other aides left, she held Quintan back and handed him a parcel of food.

"This is for you, Quintan, "Rosie said. "You and Harrison. Do not share it with the others; keep it by your side the whole time."

"Rosie, you spoil me," Quintan said. "I appreciate you taking this special care of me and Harrison. You know he loves you. And so do I."

"I do," Rosie said. "So, make sure you don't get killed out there with those dragons. And keep a sharp eye out for bandits. You do not want to make me sad, young Quintan."

"Yes, ma'am," Quintan said, giving Rosie a hug.

"Here, enjoy," Rosie said as she handed Quintan a piece of berry pie and wiped at her eyes.

Quintan waved to everyone in the kitchen, and they wished him Godspeed. He joined Harrison in the stable and gave him a piece of the pie from Rosie.

"I love our Rosie," Harrison said as he bit into the pie. "She makes the best pies I've ever tasted."

"They are wonderful," Quintan said. "But, as I must say, my mothers are even more yummy."

Harrison laughed at Quintan. "Get the horses packed. We leave in ten minutes."

"The packs are ready," Quintan said.

"Make sure you wear your sword and have your knife at your side," Harrison said. "You may only be an aide to most people, but we knights consider you an equal."

"I am honored," Quintan said as he and Harrison shook hands. "I'll be out there in ten minutes."

Ten minutes later, Quintan walked Harrison's horse out to him, returned, and got Buttercup.

"Buttercup!" the knights said in one voice as Quintan and Buttercup joined them.

"Guys," Quintan said, bowing. He had taught Buttercup to bow and bow he did.

This made the knights laugh and cheer Buttercup on. Buttercup rose and whinnied his approval.

"That's one special horse you have there, Quintan," Fred said.

"He is indeed," Quintan replied, giving Buttercup a carrot.

The trumpets sounded, and the knights mounted their steads and rode out of the castle through the main gate. The city cheered them on all the way through its space. Once they were away from the city, they headed north along the eastern road, away from Quintan's village.

Helena watched them leave and felt Quintan's power. He was protected by The White Light, and she could not harm him in any way. At least she had the king on the throne. She was working on the spells she was going to use to taunt him for the way he had used her. She still had a great deal of work to do. She needed to harvest mushrooms and ferns from the forest. This would take her a few weeks. So, she sighed and went back inside to continue to make her plans.

Merlin and Feyanna felt Quintan's energy as he left the castle.

"I'm glad we have Penny and Q to keep us updated on Quintan's activities," Feyanna said.

"Things are moving along rather quickly," Merlin said. "He's now a knight's aide. That was fast."

"He has Clarice and Roman with him at all times," Feyanna said. "I sleep better knowing that."

"The Special Magic has made them take the eastern road to the north," Merlin said. "The village is being kept safe from travelers. They won't find any good dragons. I wonder if those three rogue dragons are flying again?"

"They are," Penny replied as she and Q landed. "They most certainly are."

"I don't like the sound of that," Feyanna said.

"Either do we," Q replied. "The dragon brigade is on constant patrol. They have split up into three groups, flying all day and night. The rogue dragons haven't attacked any villages or towns yet. I think they're trying to figure out if we, the good dragons, are on their tails."

"I take it you are," Merlin said, smiling.

"Of course," Penny replied. "I'm so glad the protection grid is in place. At least we don't have to worry too much about all of you."

"Quintan is riding with the knights," Q said. "He will be safe."

"Thanks for that," Feyanna said, sounding relieved.

"Time for us to fly," Penny said. "We just stopped in to catch you up on the latest."

"We appreciate that," Merlin said. "Take care and stay safe."

Penny and Q flew off and banked to the north. They had decided to settle in The Crystal Caves closest to Quintan for the night.

The knights spent three days looking for dragons before they found dragon tracks in the wet sand next to a small lake on the fourth morning. They had just set out a mile south of the lake and were riding north when they saw the tracks.

"They've been here," one of the knights said. "Their tracks are fresh—probably only a few hours old. The sun hasn't dried them out yet. I'll scout around and try to find more of them."

"Look here," Quintan said. "It looks like they took flight. See how the sand is messed up right next to their prints?"

"He's good," the knight scout said. "He's right. Let's ride north to the next village. I think we may find them there. If they attack the village, we can kill them."

The knights rode hard and were just coming into the village when the rogue dragons attacked. The knights drew their crossbows and fired at the dragons. One of them was hit in the chest and fell to the earth behind one of the cottages. The other two breathed fire at the knights. The knights were able to get out of the way in time.

Three of the knights readied their crossbows again and fired at the dragons. They hit a second one on a wing tip. This made the dragon crazy mad, and he breathed fire at the three knights and killed them and their horses instantly. The third dragon breathed fire on one of the fields, and it burned far and wide.

Penny, Q, and one set of The Dragon Brigade flew in and chased the two rogue dragons through the sky. The good dragons were invisible to everyone, and this made the two rogue dragons look like they were possessed by evil spirits. The knights drew on them again and let their arrows fly. One arrow hit a rogue dragon, then two arrows hit Penny, and Q. Penny was hit in the chest near her wing, and Q was hit in the back leg close to his tail. They screamed in pain and banked south to get away from the fight. They were bleeding badly and had to settle down before they got to the meadow.

"Penny, can you make it into the forest and The Crystal Caves?" Q asked.

"I don't think so," Penny answered. "I am very weak."

Penny's skin had turned gray as her life force bled out of her.

"I call upon The Special Magic to give Penny the life force she needs to get to The Crystal Caves just here in the forest," Q cried out.

"Q, you are wounded, too," Penny said. "Help Q, too."

A solid white light wrapped them in its power and floated them to the cave entrance. The faeries also helped them and covered their tracks so they wouldn't be found.

"Just one more step, dear Penny," Q said as he gave her a push into The Crystal Caves.

"Q, follow me," Penny said as she rolled down the entryway.

Q collapsed, and the faeries lifted and pushed him into the cave entrance.

Once inside The Crystal Caves, the crystals moved them into the healing space.

"We will take care of you," a voice said. "You are safe now."

The battle over the village ended when the knights killed the other two rogue dragons. They fell to the earth onto the field they had burned. As the knights watched, their bodies turned to ash, and the ash was taken into the sky by a vortex. There was nothing left of them to bring to the king.

It was a sad day. The knights retrieved the bodies of their fallen comrades. They were wrapped in shrouds and placed across their horses.

"We will take them home now," Harrison said sadly.

One of the villagers approached Harrison and said, "We thank you for defending our village. We are deeply saddened by the death of these fine knights. Please, take this food to help keep you strong on your ride to the castle."

"Thank you, kind man," Harrison said as he signaled the knights to move out.

They rode all day and through the night. It was midday when they entered the city. Word went out that knights had been killed. The castle gates opened for them, and the trumpeters played the mourning cadence.

The fallen knights were brought to the main castle entrance. King Gorham walked down the steps.

"This is a sad day," King Gorham said. "Three of my finest knights have fallen. Harrison, how did this happen?"

"They were killed by three rogue dragons," Harrison said. "We killed the dragons. As we went to behead them, their bodies turned to ash, and the ash was taken into the sky. It was the strangest thing I've ever seen. Be assured, King Gorham, that those three dragons were killed as you ordered."

The king looked at Harrison and the rest of the knights for the longest time.

"We will have a service for them in one hour," the king decreed. "Make caskets for all of them and have them placed near the altar in the chapel. All the knights will attend with their aides."

"So be it, sire," the high chancellor said.

People ran to the posts, and the carpenters got busy making the caskets. An hour later, the three knights' bodies were in the caskets, draped with the knights' colors. The surviving knights carried them down the aisle in the chapel and placed them on the stands. The priest prayed for the souls. The choir sang the mourning song, and King Gorham offered his condolences to his knights.

The King left the chapel first and signaled to Harrison to follow him.

"Harrison, we need three new knights," the king said. "Come to me in an hour with the names of three candidates you think are the best. I will order them to be tested for swordsmanship, knife capabilities, and physical endurance. We will have the test tomorrow after breakfast."

"Yes, King Gorham," Harrison said.

Harrison returned to the chapel and walked with the mourners to the grave-side to watch the fallen knights be buried. The priest said another prayer, they were lowered into their graves, and the people left. The grave diggers would fill in the grave.

Harrison returned to the knight's courtyard with everyone else.

"The king has ordered me to find three new knights this minute. He is waiting for my recommendations in the throne room," Harrison told them.

"I would like to recommend Quintan," Fred said.

"Fred, that is a grand idea," Harrison said. "Go get him. I think he's in the stable taking care of our horses."

Fred found Quintan feeding the horses.

"Quintan, I'm so sorry you had to witness that horrible ordeal today," Fred said. "The king has ordered Harrison to find three new knights this minute. I suggested you. Please follow me."

"Me?" Quintan said as he poured fresh water for the horses.

"Indeed," Fred said. "You are an excellent swordsman and quick with the knife. You are quite intelligent, and that is a good thing."

"Thank you, Fred, but aren't I rather young to be a knight?" Quintan said.

"You may be fifteen years old, but your soul is much older and wiser than most of the knights, me included. Now, come along."

"Yes, sir," Quintan said, surprised at this turn of events.

Quintan and Fred joined the knights as they talked about two more possibilities.

"Quintan, thank you for coming," Harrison said. "Fred has explained everything to you. Do you accept the challenge?"

Quintan looked around the courtyard and caught a small glimmer of Clarice sitting on the parapet. He knew what his answer was to be.

" I accept," Quintan said.

The knights cheered his decision and got busy telling him about the test of skills and endurance set for the following day.

"Let's go see Rosie," Harrison said.

The knights walked into Rosie's kitchen, and she cried with them.

"Young Quintan, so you are going to be tested to be a knight tomorrow," Rosie said as the knights left the kitchen and sat in the small room beside it.

"I am," Quintan replied.

"Well, I'll need to strengthen you up with my food," Rosie said as two kitchen maids brought plates and bowls of food for Quintan and Harrison.

"Rosie, you are incredible," Quintan said. "I am honored to sit at your table."

"He is older than his years," Rosie said. "There is something special about you, young Quintan. There most certainly is. I do believe god has blessed you."

The kitchen staff looked down for a second.

"Rosie, I do believe he has," Quintan said, folding his hands and saying a quick prayer.

"You are a good boy," Rosie said, winking at him. "Now, both of you, eat!"

After supper, Harrison and Fred prepared Quintan for the next day. He fell asleep quickly and didn't remember his dreams.

Clarice and Roman remained on the stable roof throughout the whole night. They would be on the field the next day.

Dawn brought a day full of intense work. Right after breakfast, Harrison and Fred took Quintan to the event field before the king arrived. They practiced with him for over an hour.

"I say you're ready," Fred said as the other knights entered the field.

"I believe I am," Quintan replied.

King Gorham arrived and sat in his royal seat and everyone stood at attention.

"Today, we test the skills and physical endurance of five men who think they will make good knights. I will choose the three that will join my royal court as full knights. Let us begin." Gorham said.

Quintan was held back. The other four went through the tests. Two of them didn't make it all the way. They were eliminated with the thanks of the court. The next two completed the tests and sat with their sponsors.

Quintan was the last man to take to the field. Harrison was deemed his opponent, and they began with the sword test. They fought for quite a while. It was when Quintan used a technique he had kept to himself that the match ended. Harrison was against the fence, and Quintan had his sword tip at his throat. The trumpeter sounded the end of the test. Quintan lowered his sword and shook hands with Harrison.

"That was a new move," Harrison said as they walked over to the targets for the knife-throwing contest.

"I don't show you everything," Quintan said, smiling. "If I did, you'd get complacent."

"You truly are older than your years," Harrison said.

Quintan threw his knife at the targets and placed it in the bullseye each time. Next, he had hand-to-hand combat with one of the guards. This guard was known for his strength. Quintan outsmarted him many times and had him on the ground with a knife at his throat. The king waved his hand to show Quintan had won. The guard bowed before Quintan, showing he had been bested.

"Thank you, guard, for making me work hard," Quintan said.

"You, young sire, are an amazing fighter," the guard said. "I will make sure no one bothers you as best I can."

"I am grateful for your loyalty," Quintan said, bowing to the guard.

The three competitors stood before the king.

"You have worked hard showing me your skills and endurance," King Gorham said. "I accept all of you as knights of my kingdom. We will have the ceremony in two days' time at noon."

The king left the field, and the knights gathered around the three new members.

"Quintan, congratulations," Harrison and Fred said.

"I had no doubts," Harrison said.

"The two of you will need a great deal of practice to get anywhere near close to knight Quintan's skills. We begin practice after breakfast tomorrow morning," Fred told them.

"Harrison, may I speak to you?" Quintan said.

"Walk with me," Harrison said as he took them to the open field. "What is it?"

"Harrison, I would like to return home early tomorrow morning. I would like to tell my family the news," Quintan said.

"I like that idea," Harrison said. "Your village is about a two-hour ride, so you will have plenty of time to visit. Return by midnight."

"I will," Quintan said. "Just one more thing. I will need an aide. I would like to bring my best friend Hugho back with me. He knows me well and will fit right in. He's been practicing sword and knife skills with my mentor. He's a good fellow."

"By all means, "Harrison said. "Be sure to tell him what his duties will be. I wouldn't want him to be surprised."

"Oh, I will. And thanks," Quintan said as they walked back to the castle.

They walked into the kitchen, and before Rosie could say a word, Quintan swept her up and twirled her around.

"Oh, young Quintan, you put me down this instance," Rosie said, laughing at Quintan.

Quintan set her down and kissed her cheek.

"Rosie, it was your food that strengthened me so I would win," Quintan said.

"I knew you would," Rosie said, smiling and bustling about the kitchen. "It was my food, of course."

This made everyone laugh. They talked about the events while Rosie fed the two of them.

"Rosie, I'm headed home for a visit tomorrow. I'll be back quite late. I don't want you to worry about me when I'm not here," Quintan said

"Thanks for that," Rosie said. "If you're hungry, just knock on the door, and I'll fix ya' somethin to eat."

"No need, Rosie. My mother will feed me all day long and send food along for at least five people," Quintan said.

"She's a good woman, your mother," Rosie said.

"I'm going to tell her all about you," Quintan said. "She'll be relieved that I'm being cared for by such a strong and wonderful woman."

"Ah, go one with ya' now," Rosie said, blushing. "He's a charmer for sure."

"He's right about you, my Rosie," Harrison said.

"The two of you are fit for each other," Rosie said, trying to be stern. "Now, out of my kitchen if you're finished. I have a great many things to do to plan for the knighting ceremony. Don't be late getting back here, young Quintan."

"I won't be," Quintan replied as he gave her shoulder a squeeze.

Harrison and Quintan joined the knights in their courtyard to talk about the ceremony. It was going on night when they went off to their quarters.

Quintan was up at dawn the next morning. He packed a few things and went into the kitchen for breakfast.

"I knew you'd be up early," Rosie said as she set a hearty breakfast in front of him. "Here's a little something for the journey. Be Safe."

"Thanks, Rosie. I will be safe," Quintan said.

A few minutes later, Quintan rode through the east gates with a high sign from Russell and quickly road through Kerwyn. The ride home was uneventful, and he arrived in the pasture around mid-morning.

Hamlen looked up from a wagon he was working on and let out a holler. The rest of the family came running through the door and saw Quintan. He fell to the ground as his sisters smothered him with hugs and kisses.

"Give me a break," Quintan said, standing up. "I need to take care of Buttercup. Help me."

The three of them took quick care of his horse and came back outside.

"Son, it's good to have you home," Hamlen said.

"It's wonderful to be home, father," Quintan said.

"You're wearing the king's colors," his mother said as she looked him over.

"I am," Quintan said. "That's why I came home for a visit," Quintan said. "I am to be knighted tomorrow."

The whole family cheered so loudly that a few of the chickens flew up onto the fence.

"How did this happen?" Hamlen asked just as Feyanna and Merlin walked into the pasture.

"Quintan," Feyanna said, hugging him

"Good to see you, Quintan," Merlin said as they hugged.

"Good to see you both as well," Quintan said.

Quintan told his story about becoming a knight in just four week's time. Everyone had questions for him.

"Let's go sit at the outside table," Glendianna said. "Margaret, please help me with refreshments. You too, Sarah."

"I take it a little birdie told you I was home?" Quintan said, smiling.

"They did," Merlin said. "They're resting in the meadow with the other two."

"I take it Quintan has a couple of dragons protecting him?" Hamlen asked.

"I do," Quintan said. "They remain invisible at all times."

"I wondered about that," Hamlen said. "This is good to have confirmed."

"They are wonderful dragons, father," Quintan said. "Hold on."

Quintan looked like he was having a conversation with unseen people.

"Okay, thanks," Quintan said as he turned to his father. "Father, how about you come to Merlin and Feyanna's with me later? I would like you to meet my dragons."

"I would like that very much," Hamlen said as the girls returned with food and drink.

They spent a while talking and sharing stories of the village. Then, Merlin and Feyanna stood up to leave.

"It's time for us to get back to work," Merlin said. "We'll see you later."

After they left, Quintan said, "Mother, that was just what I needed. You know me so well. I'm going to go find Hugho. We have a lot to talk about. I'll be back for the mid-day meal on time. I don't want to miss anything you make."

Quintan kissed his mother on the cheek and walked into the village.

The villagers welcomed him home. He walked north to Hugo's family's farm. He saw Hugho before Hugho saw him. He wanted to remember this moment before everything in their lives would change so dramatically.

Quintan walked closer to his friend. "Hugho," Quintan said.

"Oh my god, you're home," Hugho said as he lifted Quintan off the ground in a huge bear hug.

"I am," Quintan replied as he was set down. "You have become stronger."

"I have," Hugho said. "Merlin and Jameson are taskmasters when it comes to my training."

"I remember well," Quintan said.

"You are wearing the king's colors," Hugho said. "Why?"

"That's why I'm here," Quintan replied. "I am to be knighted tomorrow."

"You're going to be a knight?" Hugho said, surprised. "How did all this happen?"

Quintan told him, and they talked about it for a minute.

"Hugho, I am in need of a knight's aide. I would like you to be that aide," Quintan said.

Hugho stared at Quintan for a moment before bursting out with, "Yes. Of course, I will be your aide," Hugho said, jumping all over the place. "This is just what I have been praying to the gods and goddesses for. I thank you all for this great blessing."

"I knew you'd say yes," Quintan said, slapping Hugho on the back. "We leave this evening at sundown."

"Oh, yes, I suppose we do," Hugho said quietly. "We have to tell my family right now."

"Let's go," Quintan said.

They walked into the farmhouse and found his mother, father, and two brothers. One brother was a year younger than him, and the other was five years younger.

"Mother, Father," Hugho said. "I have something to tell you. As you can see, Quintan is wearing the king's colors. He is to be knighted tomorrow. Hold on a minute. There's more. Quintan has asked me to be his knight's aide. I said yes. We leave at sundown this evening."

The house was very quiet for a moment, and then everyone cheered and was excited by the news.

"I always knew you'd leave us, but I thought it would be when you were a bit older," Hugho's mother said. "It's a good thing I just finished mending your clothes."

"I am happy for you, son," Hugho's father said as he stood and hugged his son. "I know you will do us proud."

"I will, father," Hugho said.

They sat around the family table and talked for a while.

"I need to do a few more things before we leave, Hugho, so I'll be on my way," Quintan said. "I'll see you this evening."

"Understood," Hugho said. "Quintan, thank you for this."

Quintan smiled, bowed, then left.

Quintan returned in time for the family's mid-day meal.

"I'm off to Merlin and Feyanna's for a while," Quintan said.

"Enjoy the visit," Glendianna replied. "Girls, let's make a special berry cake for Quintan's supper tonight."

Sarah and Margaret liked the idea and helped make the cake.

"Hi there," Feyanna said as she saw Quintan walking towards the cottage home.

"I love this place," Quintan was saying when Clarice and Roman materialized in the meadow. A third dragon flew in at that same moment.

"What's this?" Merlin said as he walked over to the dragons.

"We have some bad news," Clarice said. "First, let me introduce Beauregard to you. He is a fine dragon and has brought us this news."

"Nice to meet you, Beauregard," Merlin said.

"The honor is all mine," Beauregard replied. "Please, call me Beau. It's so much easier than Beauregard."

"Agreed," Feyanna said.

"What is this news," Quintan asked.

"Quintan, you were at the battle in the northern village that killed three rogue dragons," Beau said.

"I was," Quintan replied.

"You saw the three dragons killed," Beau said. "What you didn't see was Penny, Q, and the Dragon Brigade."

"I knew something more was happening in the sky," Quintan replied.

"I am sorry to say, Penny and Q were hit with crossbows," Beau said.

"Oh, no," Feyanna cried out. "Are they alive?"

"They are," Beau replied. "They made it back to The Crystal Caves with the help of The Special Magic and the faeries. They have been seriously wounded and will need quite a long while to heal. They told me to tell you that Clarice and Roman are more than capable of keeping you safe."

"Is there any way we can see them?" Merlin asked.

"They said you'd ask that question," Beau replied, smiling. "They know the three of you quite well. The Special Magic has agreed for the three of you to visit now. Please stand close to us."

"I have to return to the castle tonight," Quintan said.

Feyanna raised her hand to show that she would explain the whole time thing to Quintan.

"Quintan, you are about to experience something incredible," Feyanna said. "Time in this world stands still when we are in the presence of The Special Mage, The White Light. Don't try to figure this out. Just go along with it."

"I trust you, Miss Feyanna," Quintan said. "Let's go."

A white mist enveloped everyone in the meadow, and in less than an instant, they were in The Crystal Caves.

"This place is beyond beautiful," Quintan said as he looked all around the cave. "Absolutely magical."

"Good way to describe it," Merlin said. "Where are they?"

"Follow the purple hallway. You'll find them at the end," Beau said. "They are in rough shape. Keep your visit short. They need rest and love."

"We will," Feyanna said as she led them down the hall.

They found Penny and Q lying quietly surrounded by crystals. The crystals were pulsing and humming as they covered the dragons in healing light energy.

Quintan cried as he watched them. So did Merlin and Feyanna.

"Quintan, do not cry," Penny said softly. "We are healing well. The crystals keep most of the pain away, and we are grateful for that."

"You fought well and killed the three rogue dragons," Quintan said. "I saw the arrows hit something but never imagined they were striking you."

"It is a risk we take," Q whispered.

"Q was struck in the wing near his tail," Penny said. "It hurts to move even the tiniest bit."

"No need to speak, Q," Merlin said. "It greatly saddens us to know that this has happened."

"Us, too," Penny said, trying to smile.

"At least you aren't red today," Quintan said.

"Funny man," Penny replied. "You are to be knighted tomorrow. Are you ready for this responsibility?"

"I am," Quintan said. "I don't look forward to the fighting and killing thing. But I know it is required sometimes. I follow the ways of The White Light."

"As is your destiny," Q said.

Quintan bowed to Q, and Q winked back at him.

"You dragons have the longest eyelashes," Feyanna said. "No ones are longer than Penny's, of course."

"Of course," Penny said, sounding tired.

"We will take our leave," Merlin said. "We ask The White Light and The Divine to heal our most precious dragons. We look forward to the day you visit us again."

Penny and Q winked at the three of them, then went to sleep. The humans returned to the main room.

"They are indeed gravely wounded," Merlin said to Beau. "It's been three days since it happened. I suppose we should be happy they've made it through those days. That time usually determines if a body lives or dies."

"And they have The Magic taking care of them," Feyanna said.

"They are of The Special Magic," Quintan said. "I hate King Gorham for ordering all the dragons killed. "

"Hate is a strong thing," Merlin said. "It is used by the young and the ignorant. You know better than to hate, Quintan."

"I do, Master Merlin," Quintan said. "I am so angry with that law, though."

"That is the correct thing to feel—anger," Merlin said. "Think before you voice your opinion. Determine if it comes from the moment or your beliefs."

"That is wise advice I will try to adhere to," Quintan said.

"Time to take you back," Beau told them. "Here we go."

They were returned to the meadow just as they had left it.

"You are right, Miss Feyanna," Quintan said. "Time hasn't seemed to change the whole time we were gone. We were gone for what seemed like a couple of hours."

"That's The Magic for you," Merlin said. "Now, Beau, who will be our temporary dragons while Penny and Q recover?"

"I will be that dragon," Beau said. "Clarice and Roman will continue to protect Quintan. Use caution when you are fighting as a knight. We can't interfere with most things."

"I understand that," Quintan said. "I am grateful for both of you. How will Hugho be protected?"

"So glad you asked that question," Clarice said. "Roman and I will watch out for Hugho until Penny and Q are well again. Then, Beau will be Hugho's protector. Hugho is not to be told about us for a long while. You'll know the right time to tell him everything."

"Thanks be to the gods and goddesses for protecting Hugho," Quintan said. "I will caution him about the religious aspect as we ride to the castle tonight."

"Your father is coming. Time to show him our magic," Beau said.

Hamlen walked over to them and asked, "Who were you talking with? There isn't anyone else here."

"Father, there's only one way to tell you this," Quintan said. "Watch that space in the meadow."

The three dragons appeared, and Hamlen fell to the ground.

"Dragons for real? I know they exist and all, but you seem to be friends with them," Hamlen said.

"All true, Father," Quintan said. "We are great friends. This is Clarice, and this is Roman. They are my protectors and have been with me since I left for the castle. This is Beau. He is a messenger from The Special Magic for Feyanna and Merlin. Dragons, this is my father, Hamlen."

"This is amazing," Hamlen said. "Dragons. And they come in different colors."

"Yes, we do, Hamlen," Clarice said.

"And they can talk," Hamlen said in disbelief.

"Of course we can," Roman said. "How else are we to communicate with you humans?"

"He's got a point there, father," Quintan said.

Hamlen stood and walked closer to the dragons. "You are huge! Your tails are magnificent."

"Thank you, Hamlen," Beau said. "Would you like to touch my wing?"

"I would," Hamlen said as he walked closer to Beau.

Beau spread his wing a little so Hamlen could touch it.

"You are soft and warm," Hamlen said.

"We are," Beau said. "But don't tell anyone. It would ruin our reputation."

"And they have a sense of humor, too," Hamlen said, laughing. "I can't believe I'm standing here having a conversation with three dragons."

"I know how you feel," Quintan said. "I felt the same way when Penny and Q rescued me. It was scary and amazing. They told me they were my friends and let me ride on them to get me to you through Merlin and Feyanna."

"So that's how you got here," Hamlen said. "I always wondered where Feyanna and Merlin found you."

"Hamlen, are you okay with all of this?" Clarice asked. "We won't be able to leave Quintan's side to tell you how he is. Beau can relay messages to Merlin and Feyanna."

"I am good with all of this, and I appreciate the dragon relay group," Hamlen said.

"I like that," Roman said. "The dragon relay group."

"Excellent," Beau replied. "Time for you to go home for a few more hours, Quintan. All of us dragons are close by. Just raise your Crystal Dragon if you need us for anything."

"I will. Thanks so much," Quintan said as they disappeared from sight. "That is the most amazing thing they do. Well, at least one of them."

"It most certainly is," Merlin replied. "Quintan, I have something for you. I was told to make it by The Magic."

Merlin handed Quintan a sheathed knife. It was made of steel with a bronze and gold hilt. The outline of a dragon was sketched into the hilt, and it was clear for all to see.

"This is magnificent," Quintan said. "I am honored to have this knife. You made the sheath again, didn't you, Feyanna?"

"I did," Feyanna said. "Some of the villagers have ordered them from me. I enjoy making them."

"I love you both very much," Quintan said.

Feyanna and Merlin wrapped him in a strong hug for the longest time.

"As do we," Merlin said when they stepped back.

"This knife is a work of art," Hamlen said.

"Time to leave," Feyanna said as she gently pushed Quintan toward the path. "We'll be together again before you know it."

Quintan and Hamlen waved to them as they turned to walk down the path to the south road. A surprise was waiting for Quintan as he neared the farm. The whole village was gathered there to say hello with supper and stories. Merlin and Feyanna were close behind Quintan and Hamlen as they walked home. The evening was a great success. It was near the end of the evening that Quintan asked for everyone's attention.

"Family, dear friends of my growing years, it is with great joy that I tell you that Hugho has agreed to come with me to the castle as my knight's aide."

"That's fantastic!'

"Good for you, Hugho!"

"You're leaving, too?"

"This is wonderful news!"

"We'll all help your father with the farm and all."

"He's not a schoolboy anymore."

It took a few minutes for folks to calm down before Hugho could say a word.

"I am honored and thrilled to become my best friend's knight's aide," Hugho said as he saluted Quintan.

"I am honored and thrilled that you accepted," Quintan said. "Now, we can cause mischief together like the old days of last month."

This made folks laugh and tell a few stories about the boy's adventures. Supper was shared, and more stories were told about everyone in the village. Evening gave way to night, and it was time for the festivities to come to a close. Quintan and Hugho said goodbye to everyone until only the two families remained outside.

"We must get going," Quintan said as he brought Buttercup from the barn, ready to ride.

"Father, I thank you for giving me Thunder," Hugho said. "He is a fine horse, and I'll treat him well."

Hugho hugged his family one last time before they left for home.

"Thank you for this celebration," Quintan said as he hugged his sisters. "I have kept my promise to you to return home."

"Yes, you did," Sarah said.

"Agreed," Margaret said. "Mother packed some of the berry cake for you to have on your ride back to the castle."

"That is splendid news," Quintan said. "I love that cake. I might even share some with Hugho."

"How very special you are," Hugho said as he punched Quintan in the arm.

"No matter how old they get to be, they'll still be boys," Glendianna said.

Quintan hugged his mother, and she and the girls went into the house.

"I'd like a moment alone with my father if you'll excuse us," Quintan said as he walked with his father into the barn.

"Father, don't tell anyone about the dragons," Quintan said. "And that includes Mother. I know you are soul mates, but she is not to know. Understood?"

"Yes, Quintan, I do understand," Hamlen said, looking at his son. "You have changed so much these past four weeks. You are a grown man now, wise beyond your fifteen years for sure."

"I feel like that grown man sometimes, and sometimes, I'm just me," Quintan said. "There is one thing I will always need from you: this."

Quintan pulled his father into a strong hug, holding him for a long while. Hamlen held tightly onto his son, too. He knew great changes were coming, and he wanted to remember this moment for the rest of his life.

"Be safe, my son," Hamlen said as Quintan and Hugho rode out of the pasture.

As soon as they rode past the path to Merlin and Feyanna's cottage home, Quintan explained the whole religious thing to Hugho.

"So, I am to pretend I am following the rules of the new religion," Hugho said. "I am not to talk about The Magic with anyone, including you, in case someone is listening."

"Exactly," Quintan said. "The first thing you're going to do when we return is care for our horses. I'll let Harrison know we're back. Then, we'll go up to the sleeping quarters and sleep for a while. We'll figure the rest out as we go."

"Okay, Quintan," Hugho said. "It's really dark out here."

"It is," Quintan said. "I have a dozen crystals in my bag. Feyanna said to use them in our sleeping quarters. I'm sure the others will be quite interested in them."

"What was that?" Hugho said as he reigned in his horse.

Quintan stopped, too.

"I do believe we're about to be robbed," Quintan said, smiling.

"Why are you smiling?" Hugho asked as three masked figures ran up to them with swords drawn.

"Watch," Quintan said.

A cloud of smoke came down from the treetops and caught the robbers by surprise.

"I suggest you go away," Quintan said. "This isn't going to end well for you."

"Shut up," one of the thieves said as he tried to shove his sword into Quintan's leg.

A searing pain enveloped him. He was on fire. The thief fell backward, trying to put the fire out.

"Help me," the thief yelled to his companions.

His companions ran back into the forest, and the burning thief rolled over several times until the flames were out. He was screaming in pain.

"I told you to go away," Quintan said as he looked down on the thief lying beside the road. "You did not."

Quintan signaled Hugho, and they rode on. They left the injured man to fend for himself.

"Where'd that come from?" Hugho asked.

"It must have been The Magic," Quintan said. "But we didn't see that."

"Got it," Hugho said, nodding in agreement.

Clarice and Roman smiled at this. No one was going to bother their Quintan and Hugho.

"Take this piece of berry cake," Quintan said. "My mother thinks we're going to be starved on this ride to the castle."

"This is so good," Hugho said. "It has honey in it."

"My favorite," Quintan said, pointing in front of them. "Look there, Hugho."

They stopped for a minute at the edge of the forest.

"That is the city of Kerwyn," Quintan said.

"It's huge!" Hugho said. "Do you visit it much?"

"No," Quintan said. "We have everything we need in the castle grounds. If we do need something, the lesser Paige gets it for us—not you. You stay with me."

"It's the middle of the night, but the city is busy," Hugo said as they rode through.

"There is a knighting ceremony tomorrow," Quintan said. "It's a time of celebration for everyone."

"I see," Hugho said. "There's the castle. Why are we going around to the east side? Shouldn't we go through the front gate?"

"Never," Quintan explained. "It's for the king and his special guests only. This is our gate and here's Russell waiting for us. Hello, Russell. Thanks for waiting for us."

"Hello, Quintan," Russell said as he closed the gate. "I take it this is your paige?"

"It is indeed," Quintan said as he and Hugho dismounted. "Russell, this is Hugho, my best friend. We've grown up together. Hugho, this Russell, the chief guard. He's a good guy. Listen and learn from him."

"I am honored to meet you, Russell," Hugho said, shaking hands with Russell.

"We need to take care of our horses and get some sleep," Quintan said. "We'll see you later this morning."

Harrison was waiting for Quintan and Hugho as they entered the stables.

"Good work on getting back in time," Harrison said.

"Harrison, this is Hugho, my best friend and now paige," Quintan said.

"Harrison, it's great to meet you," Hugho said, shaking hands with him. "Quintan has told me a lot about you."

"All good, I hope," Harrison said.

"Of course, Harrison," Quintan said.

"Including besting you in the sword test," Hugho said, laughing.

"He did," Harrison said. "Next time, I'll be the winner."

"You can only hope," Quintan said. "Is there anything I need to know for tomorrow morning?"

"No. Your clothes, shield, and helmet are by your bed," Harrison said. "I'll show you how to hold the shield for tomorrow's ceremony. We'll visit the black-smith after the ceremony for a minute so he can measure you for your chainmail."

"Okay," Quintan said, yawning as he brushed Buttercup.

"Oh, Hugho," Harrison said, smiling. "What is the name of your horse?"

"Thunder," Hugho said. "It's a strong, manly name fit for a horse."

"Funny guys," Quintan said as he finished with Buttercup. Let's get up-stairs."

"No candles, Quintan," Harrison said. "Just feel your way around."

"We have a better idea," Quintan said as he and Hugho took their charged crystals out of their bags and held them in front of them. The light was just the right amount to show the way.

"How'd you do that?" Harrison whispered.

"I'll tell you tomorrow," Quintan said as he dropped his clothes. "I need sleep."

Hugho and Quintan fell sound asleep as soon as their heads hit the bed. Things were quiet in the castle that night. Clarice and Roman sat on the stable roof, alert and ready to protect Quintan and Hugho. Helena was pissed! She was working on a spell all night to kill Quintan. The White Light had other plans.

Dawn arrived, and the trumpets blared. The knights were ready for the ceremony. The three new knights followed them into the throne room. The knight's aides were shown where to stand along the wall on the left. They could see every-thing.

The king arrived and was seated on his throne. The high chancellor called the ceremony to order. The priest offered a prayer of thanksgiving for the new knights.

Each new knight was called forward to be knighted.

"Quintan of the cart farm, come forward," the court bailiff ordered.

Quintan stepped in front of the throne and knelt with his head bowed. The priest said a prayer over him. The king approached him, laying the tip of the ceremonial sword of the realm on each shoulder, saying, "You are hereby accepted into the order of the knights of the realm. Stand and swear your obedience to your king."

Quintan stood, recited the oath of obedience, bowed his head, and stepped back. The king handed him the symbol of the knight: a pendant bearing King Gorham's likeness. Quintan put it around his neck for all to see.

"Let the kingdom know that these good knights are my messengers and protectors," King Gorham said. "Let no one harm them."

Quintan joined the two new knights to the left of the throne. The priest gave a benediction and a blessing on each knight's head. The court bailiff declared the ceremony concluded. The trumpeters played the knights' cadence, and the city cheered and applauded. The three new knights were told to step onto the balcony, smile, and wave. They did. As they left the throne room, the knights took the new knights to the banquet room for the feast.

Everyone had a grand time. Quintan saw Rosie watching him a few times. He winked each time, and she smiled. When the feast finally ended, it was late in the afternoon. The knights gathered in their courtyard for a little while.

"Our real work starts tomorrow morning with physical endurance training," Fred said. "Be ready after breakfast, which is at seven. Not any later. Enjoy the rest of the day as you wish as long as it's here in the castle."

As evening came along, there was a noise at the east gate. Someone was demanding to be let in. Quintan was going to go along and see what the commotion was all about, but Harrison stopped him.

"What's happening out there?" Quintan asked.

"The healer, or as most of us call her, the witch, is trying to get inside. She says she has a message for you from God's angels. We know she does not because only the priest can communicate directly with God. She is saying that if you don't get this message, you will die a horrible death," Harrison explained.

"I know that's not true for the same reason you do," Quintan said. "I'm sure the outer guards will handle her."

"That is exactly right," Harrison said, looking at Quintan. "When did you get so wise?"

Quintan smiled and slapped Harrison on the back as they went their separate ways. The outer guards carried the witch away from the castle and warned her never to return. The city finally quieted down, and most slept. Quintan lay awake for a while, thinking about his knighthood ceremony. The prayers meant nothing to him. He offered thanks and gratitude to The Magic during the ceremony. He fell asleep smiling.

CHAPTER 18

Quintan rode out with the knights several times to check on the kingdom. They stopped at farms and villages, settled complaints between folks, and continued to hunt for dragons. One particular event turned out differently than most would have expected.

The knights were riding into a village south of the castle. A messenger sent a note asking for help with an angry neighbor. Seems the farmer asking for help was being targeted by the nasty neighbor. The farmer would find his sheep running along the road with the pasture gate open. The farmer found some of his garden crops pulled up and torn about. And the most disturbing thing was that the farmer found two of his chickens dead on his doorstep with their heads chopped off. The farmer had watched the neighbor kill the chickens and was afraid for his family's lives. That's when he sent a messenger to the castle.

The eight knights stopped at the farmer's home and talked with the family. The nasty neighbor came down the road, screaming and yelling at the knights. He called them lap boys, saying the king was too afraid to handle his kingdom the right way. Before the neighbor knew what had happened, two knights rode over and lifted him off the ground, leaving him hanging there.

"You put me down," the neighbor yelled. "You can't do this to me."

"We are doing this to you," one of the knights said.

A third knight walked over, grabbed the neighbor, and held his arms behind his back. The neighbor struggled, but the knight never let go.

"Good farmer, is this the man who has been tormenting your farm?" Harrison asked.

"It is, sir knight," the farmer answered.

Harrison and Fred walked over to the man, grabbed an arm, and forced him to walk over to the farmer and face him.

"Why are you destroying this farm and the animals?" Fred asked.

"This should be my farm," the neighbor yelled.

"Please lower your voice," Harrison said.

Quintan dismounted and walked over to the group. "Why should this farm be yours?"

"I asked the farmer's wife's father for her hand in marriage, and he said yes," the neighbor said. "She refused to marry me. I should have been given the farm anyway, and she should have been given to a family that needed a servant."

"That is the most outrageous thing I've heard in a long time," Quintan said. "Tell me this, sir: Did you love her?"

"What's that got to do with it?" the neighbor said.

"Answer the knight," Harrison said, interested in where this was going.

"No," the neighbor answered. "I wanted the land. I needed the land to become the mayor of this village. Without it, I never had a chance."

"The king chooses a mayor," Fred said. "The mayor needs to be an honest and religious man. It's not awarded to the person with the most land."

"It is," the neighbor replied. "In King Owen's day, that's how things worked. This should be my farm."

"King Gorham is on the throne now," Fred said. "When did all of this happen?"

"In the spring," the neighbor said.

"This spring?" Quintan asked.

"Yes, this spring," the neighbor answered.

"King Owen died a while back. King Gorham has been on the throne for almost a year," the farmer answered. "I tried to tell him this, but he insisted King Owen was still on the throne."

"King Owen is still on the throne," the neighbor said.

Quintan looked closely at the neighbor. His eyes were very red, and his face had pox marks.

"This man was sick with the pox," Quintan said. "He has scars from the disease on his face. This illness is known to alter a man's thinking. We should take him to the local healer and see if he can take care of him or put him out of his brain sickness."

"What? You're going to kill me?' the neighbor said.

"No," Quintan said. "We are taking you to the local healer."

The knights put the man across one of the farmer's horses and followed the farmer to the local healer. She was a woman of about thirty years.

"I have the medicine ready," she said. "Open your mouth, you nasty-smelling fool."

As soon as the neighbor opened his mouth to yell, the healer pushed a spoonful of paste into it. He tried to spit it out, but the healer placed her hand over his mouth so he would have to swallow. He looked at her for a second, then passed out.

"Leave him here," the woman said. "I will keep him quiet while I bathe him. His clothes will be burned, and the women of the village will clear out his house down to nothing. We will burn everything. When I allow him to regain consciousness, he will be well. We'll deal with him then. Thank you, good knights, for bringing him here. Which one of you noticed the pox scars?"

"I did, ma'am," Quintan said.

"Good job, sir, knight. Not many would have known this," the woman said. "You were raised on a farm."

"Yes, I was," Quintan replied.

"Time for us to go," Harrison said as he handed the woman a pouch. "Thank you for your service to the kingdom."

"Blessed be the king," she replied, winking at Quintan as he turned to ride away.

"The law dictates that man was to be hung," Harrison said. "I'm glad we didn't have to do that, thanks to you."

"So am I," Quintan replied.

For the rest of the summer and fall, the knights did the king's bidding. They brought criminals to be tried. Most were hanged, and some were put in jail for a long time.

Quintan first saw her at the beginning of the winter. She was a servant in Rosie's kitchen, having arrived a couple of weeks before. She was beautiful.

She was about his age. She had long brown hair pulled back in a bun. Her skin was flawless. She had a smile that would melt snow and ice. Quintan finally met her one morning when he walked in for breakfast.

"Rosie, I'm so glad you're here," Quintan said as he removed his cloak. "This place is always warm and reminds me of home."

"You are a sweet talker, and I love it," Rosie said. "Will you be eating with the others this morning?"

"No, ma'am," Quintan said. "I'm up early to practice with Hugho. He's a tough opponent, and he works me hard."

"As he should," Rosie said as Hugho walked in. "Here he is. You keep young Quintan busy. Show no mercy."

"Yes, Miss Rosie," Hugho said as he removed his cloak. "You heard what she said."

"Sit down and eat your breakfast," Quintan said, laughing.

Then he saw her. Her beauty took his breath away. Rosie saw this and smiled to herself.

Quintan stayed back a moment after Hugho left.

"Rosie, who is she?" Quintan asked.

"You behave yourself," Rosie whispered.

"I will treat her with the utmost respect as my father taught me," Quintan whispered.

"I know that," Rosie replied. "Her name is Angelique. Her family lives in the southernmost village of the kingdom. She is your age. She has been watching you since she got here two weeks ago."

"Why haven't I noticed her before today?" Quintan asked.

"She is timid and has been hiding when you come in," Rosie said. "She asked me about you yesterday. I told her you were a gentle and kind soul, so she let you see her today."

"I appreciate you, Rosie," Quintan said. "I'd like to meet her properly."

"I will arrange it without anyone knowing," Rosie said. "I'll let you know when."

Quintan kissed Rosie's cheek. "Thank you, my Rosie."

"Now, be off and work hard," Rosie said a bit more loudly.

Quintan left smiling, and Rosie went back to running her kitchen with a smile as well.

It was late in the day when the whole court heard King Gorham yelling something fierce. They had all heard him have temper tantrums before. It was a regular, recurring thing. No one responded to these outbursts, and this one was no different. People shrugged their shoulders and went back to what they were doing.

King Gorham hollered for his manservant. It was the fifth one he'd had since he was crowned. This one's name didn't matter. He just yelled for him when he wanted them.

"Yes, Your Highness?" the manservant said as he ran into the king's bed chamber.

"Get me my wizard immediately!" Gorham yelled. He was barely covered by his sheets, and the woman under them was crying. "Suck me harder, wench!"

The manservant ran down into the lower chamber and raced into the Wizard's quarters.

"What is it?" the wizard asked.

"The king demands your presence immediately," the manservant said.

"What seems to be the problem this time?" the wizard asked again.

"Well, ah, the king seems to be having a problem with, ah, you know," the manservant said, making a crude jester.

"He can't get it up?" the wizard asked.

"Indeed," the manservant said.

"Tell him I'm coming right away. Then get the hell out of the castle," the wizard said. "He'll want to kill someone, and you'll be his first choice. Take this and go far, far away."

The wizard handed the manservant a pouch of gold coins.

"Thank you, kind wizard," the manservant said as he put the coins deep within his garments.

The manservant knocked on the door.

"Enter!" the king yelled. "You are worthless; get away from me."

The woman grabbed her clothes and ran out of the room. A servant was waiting for her, calmed her down, and helped her bathe. The servant told the woman to leave the city and go far, far away, to the west. She gave her the name of a family friend and some gold coins.

"Your Highness, the wizard is coming here right this minute," the manservant said.

And in walked the wizard.

"You are dismissed," the wizard said to the manservant.

The manservant ran out of the room and the castle and was on his way to a safe place in no time.

"You can't do that," the king said.

"Yes, I can if it means protecting you," the wizard slyly remarked. "You need to stop tormenting the women around here. They aren't your problem. You are. I have a potion here for you that will cure the disease you carry. You will need to drink this for a fortnight. No sex at all. Understood?"

"Not even a blow job?" the king asked.

"No! Nothing touches your dick except soap and water every day," the wizard ordered.

"I have to clean myself every day?" the king said.

"How do you think you got the disease?" the wizard said. "And clean undergarments as well."

The king was getting furious.

"As you say, wizard," the king said. "I want the women who have been in my bed for the last two weeks killed. They can keep their disease to themselves."

"That won't make a difference," the wizard said. "They said they got the disease from you. They were all virgins."

"I am the king! I don't have diseases," the king bellowed.

"Even kings get sick," the wizard replied. "If you do as I instruct you to, you should be well healed in a fortnight. Now, drink this."

The king drank the small vial of fluid the wizard gave him and made a face.

"I will bring a vial each morning, sire," the wizard said, then left.

The king was furious and very tired. He fell asleep for quite a few hours. The wizard had taken care of that. By the next morning, the woman and the man-servant had escaped into safety.

Feyanna was making breakfast when Merlin woke up a few days after Quintan had been knighted.

"It's always lovely to wake up to the aromas of your cooking," Merlin said as he poured a cup of tea.

"I thank you, kind sir," Feyanna said as she set breakfast on the table.

"Our Quintan is a knight," Merlin said. "This has happened rather quickly."

"I agree," Feyanna said as she set the jam in front of Merlin. "We know his destiny, but I didn't think it would happen so fast."

"Exactly," Merlin said. "I wonder if this means things are going to esca-late?"

"Probably," Feyanna said. "Merlin, I had a rather odd dream this morning. Maybe it was a vision. Not quite sure."

"Tell me about it," Merlin said.

"I was deeply asleep and found myself floating above the meadow," Fey-anna began. "I figured it was another 'thing' to be aware of. It quickly transitioned into me walking through the forest toward Avalon. It was a lovely fall day like today. As I headed toward the shore, I was turned away from the lake and found myself walking down a path I'd never seen before. I could hear the trickling of water, so I figured I was close to the shore. Not so. As I walked past an Aspen tree, I saw a brook. It was a lovely brook just flowing along away from Avalon.

"I walked to the edge of the brook and saw a few crystals in the water, glowing as they do. I looked upstream and saw that the stream was flowing away from Avalon. It was when I looked downstream that I saw it—a bridge. It was good-sized and crossed over the stream in an arch of boulders. It was beautiful. I walked over to it and tried to walk onto it, but there was an invisible force that wouldn't allow me to walk onto it. It was a benevolent force. It just didn't want me on the bridge. I bowed to the water and walked back here, where I woke up, remembering everything. That's all."

Merlin thought about this for a minute as he poured them another cup of tea.

"Feyanna, I'm not sure about this dream vision. That's what we'll call it," Merlin said. "It sounds like The Special Magic was showing you something you may need to know about in the future. What do you think?"

"That's exactly what I was thinking," Feyanna said. "It was as if The White Light wanted us to be aware of this beautiful bridge for some future thing. And, as you know, I never question The White Light's messages."

"Yes, indeed," Merlin replied.

"I know exactly where it is, but I don't need to go there yet," Feyanna said as they cleaned up the breakfast dishes. "Oh, and what about Penny and Q? Have you heard from Beau lately?"

"Not in the last couple of days," Merlin said as they walked outside and found Beau waiting for them. "And, here he is."

"Hello, Feyanna and Merlin," Beau said. "I've got some news about our Penny and Q for you."

"Do tell," Feyanna said.

"They are healing well," Beau said. "Miss Penny said to tell you both to stop worrying so much about them. The Special Magic is taking great care of them."

"That's what we needed to hear," Merlin said. "Are they able to move a bit without deep pain yet?"

"Yes, a little bit," Beau said. "The faeries are all over The Crystal Caves, working with the healing energy of the crystals. They keep them well-fed and cover them in faerie energy all day long. Q tried to sit up, but it was too much for him. He's rolling around a little bit, though. He says it helps him from getting achy."

"That's good to know," Feyanna said. "How's Miss Penny's wound? It was a deep one."

"Indeed," Beau said. "She can't move her wing much right now, although she can kind of fluff it up a bit. This is going to take a long time to heal. She's not a very patient dragon right now."

"I can understand that," Merlin said. "I think I'd be the same way if I couldn't walk around when I felt like it. We'll send her some love this morning."

"I'm sure she'll tell me all about it when I get back," Beau said. "I do have some troubling news. It seems there are a few dragons bent on burning buildings and fields. They haven't killed anyone yet. The grid here keeps everyone safe. It's just that Quintan is about to go on a journey to find those dragons, and I wanted you to know this."

"Thanks for telling us," Merlin said. "We know that Clarice and Roman are with him constantly. I faithfully set the purple crystals in the field at sunrise each morning. What else can we do?"

"Nothing for now," Beau replied. "The Special Magic wants you to be aware of this dilemma. Those pesky dragons may try to set fire around here. They'll be in for a surprise. We, The White Light and all, don't want the knights to come this way. There are a few who will not be permitted under the grid. That may make people ask questions. We don't want the king to know about this place."

"No, we do not," Feyanna said. "I wondered when Quintan and his knights might come this way. I guess The Magic will show us what to do if they come here."

"That's true," Merlin said.

"Keep your eyes and ears open," Beau said. "Time for me to fly. Take care."

"By Beau," Feyanna and Merlin said as Beau took to the air.

"Always something around here to watch for," Feyanna said.

"I just got an idea for a new herbal remedy," Feyanna said. "Something to soothe sore muscles. I'm going to gather the flowers and herbs and get busy with it. It might help Penny and Q."

"I'm working on a special potion that makes the air move at a command," Merlin said. "I'm going to practice in the meadow later."

"That sounds like fun," Feyanna said. "Make sure to tell me, and I'll come watch."

"Okay," Merlin said as they got busy with their projects.

Breakfast time found Quintan in Rosie's kitchen. She set him up at a table away from the main working area. Angelique brought Quintan his breakfast.

"This looks delicious," Quintan said quietly as he looked at Angelique. "You're Angelique. I'm Quintan, and I thank you for bringing this to me. I'm happy to meet you."

Angelique blushed a little and said, "I'm happy to meet, too, Quintan."

Angelique left Quintan to his breakfast. She was blushing when she walked past Rosie.

"He's a fine man," Rosie whispered.

"Yes, Miss Rosie," Angelique whispered. "He was kind and smiled when he spoke to me."

"He better be kind, or he'll have Rosie to answer to," Rosie whispered as Angelique went on with her work.

The knights rode out later that morning to hunt dragons in the southern part of the realm. Quintan knew they wouldn't find any. The Special Magic was keeping the dragons under control. They would be needed in the near future. It was late in the evening when they saw it.

As Harrison, Fred, and Quintan made sure their tents were set firm into the ground, Fred looked up into the sky and saw a strange thing.

"Quintan, Harrison," Fred said, pointing to something in the sky right above them. "Do you see that? What is it? It doesn't look like a star or a bird."

"What is that thing?" Hugho asked.

"It looks kind of round-shaped," Harrison said. "And it's shining."

"The sun's about to set," Quintan said. "How can it be shining? It's not moving around much. It looks like it's just sitting there."

The others heard this and walked over and looked up into the sky.

"How can it just sit there like that?" Fred said.

"It kind of looks like it's watching us," Dennison said. "Let's shoot some arrows at it. Maybe it'll move or something."

"Dennison, let's not," Harrison said. "Let's not waste our arrows on that thing. It's way too far away for our arrows to strike. We need those arrows for the dragons."

Quintan looked at Harrison and Hugho and rolled his eyes. Harrison tried not to smile, but a little one did show on his face for a second. Good thing no one saw it. Dennison was devoted to King Gorham and would not tolerate anything less from his knights.

"Good thinking, Harrison," Dennison said. "Look! It's moving closer to us."

They watched as the round flying thing began to move closer to them. It changed colors, then shot straight up into the sky and was gone.

"That was crazy," Hugho said as they all returned to setting up camp.

"Have you ever seen anything like that before?" Harrison asked.

"Nope," Quintan replied. "Wonder where it came from?"

"What do you mean by that?" Hugho asked.

"Well, we don't know how to fly. We're humans. Birds and bugs fly. That thing must have come from another universe to be able to fly like that."

"Wow!" Harrison said. "I never thought of it that way. That makes it really scary."

"It does," Hugho said.

"I don't think we should tell anyone about this," Quintan suggested. "It might sound like we believe in The Magic of Old, and King Gorham would have us beheaded."

"Oh my god!" Fred whispered. "You're right about that. Harrison, go talk with Dennison. He seems to listen to you."

"I think you mean tolerate me," Harrison said. "I'll go talk with him now."

Dennison saw Harrison walking over to him. Harrison motioned for them to walk away from the others.

"What is it, Harrison?" Dennison said.

"May I suggest we keep our voices low?" Harrison suggested. "I don't think we need the whole countryside to hear this."

"Alright, Harrison. What is it?" Dennison said.

"I was just thinking about that strange flying thing," Harrison began. "It would seem it was from some other universe since we can't fly. So, I was thinking that we, all of us, should keep quiet about it and tell no one. If the king heard about this, he might think we were practicing The Old Magic and have us beheaded. What do you think?"

"Harrison, that is good thinking," Dennison said. "I will tell the knights and their aides about this. Do you think it's part of The Old Magic?"

"Honestly, Dennison, I don't know what to think," Harrison said, shaking his head.

"Me, either," Dennison said as they walked over to the others.

"Knights, I think it would be wise not to discuss this with anyone. If our beloved king hears about this, he may feel betrayed by his most trusted knights and have us all beheaded."

They all agreed to keep silent about the flying thing. Harrison and Quintan stayed up after the others settled for the night, watching the sky.

"Do you think it'll come back?" Harrison said.

Quintan smiled and looked up into the sky. The flying thing was back.

"Shit!" Harrison whispered.

The flying thing hovered just above their heads and sent a beam of yellow light over the two of them. It lasted about a minute, and then it was gone. The flying thing shot straight up into the sky, just like the last time.

"What the hell was that all about?" Quintan whispered.

"How the hell would I know?" Harrison whispered back.

"And that yellow beam of light," Quintan said. "What was that for?"

"Why do you keep asking me about this thing?" Harrison said.

"Oh, sorry, Harrison. I was just thinking out loud," Quintan replied. "Of course, neither of us has any rational answers. This is just so bizarre."

"Agreed," Harrison said. "Now what? What do we do now?"

"Keep this just between the two of us. Period," Quintan said.

"Absolutely," Harrison replied. "Let's get some sleep."

"Good idea," Quintan said as they went into their tents and fell sound asleep.

Hugho had Quintan's breakfast ready for him when he woke up.

"Thanks, Hugho," Quintan said. "Eat with me."

"Sure thing," Hugho replied.

"Well, my friend, what do you think about all this knight stuff?" Quintan asked.

"It's a lot of work," Hugho said. "Your clothes really stink. But, other than that, I like it."

Quintan threw his helmet at Hugho and laughed. "Funny, Hugho," Quintan said.

"Your aim is off," Hugho said, setting the helmet down.

"It landed right where I wanted it to," Quintan replied. "If I'd meant it to hit you, it would have."

"Not likely," Hugho said, laughing.

"Eat your food," Quintan replied, laughing with his friend.

Harrison looked at Quintan as they readied their horses with their aides. The two of them would keep an eye on the sky all day as they rode through the countryside looking for dragons.

The next two weeks found the knights riding from south to north, then west to east. Not once did they find a dragon or any damage from a dragon. Harrison and Quintan did not see the flying machine again, either. The knights did settle a few arguments among villagers peaceably. The third week found them returning home. Harrison reported his findings to King Gorham, and the king was pleased. He told the knights to rest for the remainder of the week.

It was a month later when Quintan got up enough nerve to ask Rosie to set up a meeting with Angelique.

"Ah, young Quintan, I can see you're smitten with her," Rosie whispered.

"Rosie," Quintan said, blushing. "She is beautiful and kind. I want to get to know her better."

"Alright then, come around after the castle settles for the evening," Rosie said. "I'll be waiting for you."

"Thanks, Rosie," Quintan said, holding his hand up. "No need to tell me to be a gentleman. I got it."

"You'd better be," Rosie said as she slapped his backside with her towel, sending him on his way.

Quintan was laughing as he joined the knights for sword practice in the field behind the castle.

"What are you laughing about?" Fred asked as Hugho handed Quintan his sword.

"That Rosie," Quintan replied. "I asked for a cookie, and she gave me grief."

"Then she's doing just fine," Fred replied. "Did you get the cookie?"

"Of course," Quintan said. "Three of them, and they were delicious."

"Ready?" Fred asked as he took his stance before Quintan.

"You ready to be bested?" Quintan replied, raising his sword.

"You wish," Fred said as they set to fighting.

They practiced with each other for the next couple of hours. Quintan won all his matches except the one with Harrison. They called it equal. Harrison was a skilled swordsman equal to Quintan. Clarice and Roman enjoyed watching them practice.

"Quintan has become a fine swordsman," Clarice said.

"Indeed," Roman replied. "Harrison is his equal. They work well together in most things."

"They do," Clarice said. "I like the way they worked together to settle the arguments in the villages these past few weeks. They were wise beyond their years to suggest the villagers come to an agreement because if they were brought before the king, they would be sentenced to death."

"That was genius," Roman agreed. "The villagers quieted down after that statement and worked with the knights to settle their differences."

"I wish the knights were allowed to settle most of the disagreements," Clarice said. "Then, most of the villagers would stay alive."

"I agree," Roamn said as he repositioned himself, sending a few pieces of stone to the ground below.

"What made that happen?" the knights asked as they walked over to the wall.

Quintan knew and looked up at the parapet where Clarice and Roam were sitting invisible. He shook his head at them.

"What?" Fred asked Quintan.

"I'm just trying to figure out what would make that happen?" Quintan replied.

"My father is a stone mason," Knight Gerald said. "He says when pieces of stone fall from a wall, it usually means a lot of water got into a small crack and loosened them. We have had a great deal of rain these past two months. I'll take a look after practice and let you know, Harrison. No need to get our good king involved in something we can take care of."

"Agreed, Gerald," Harrison said.

"Good to know we have a stone mason's son with us," Quintan said. "Let's get to knife practice for a while."

An hour later, the knights finished practicing. Gerald went up onto the parapet and looked around. Clarice and Roamn moved over to another space and watched as Gerald thoroughly looked over the stonework. It was as he suspected. Water had loosened a few of the outer stones used to create a rough surface. It was an easy fix. He told Harrison about it, and Harrison sent a few workers to replace the rough stones. The problem was repaired by nightfall.

"Roman, did you have to push those stones off the parapet?" Clarice asked as they flew over to the stable roof to settle for the night.

"I didn't mean to," Roman said. "Those stones were loose."

"I know," Clarice said as she folded her wings and settled for the night. "We have to be so very careful. That's all."

"I know," Roman said as he settled down. "I'll take the first watch. You sleep, sweet friend."

Thanks," Clarice said as she dozed off.

The night was quiet, and dawn came around faster than the dragons could have imagined.

The king was in an uproar.

"This food isn't fit for my hogs," the king said as he sent the tray to the floor. "Get me new food that is edible."

A new manservant took the tray and broken dishes back to the kitchen. A maid cleaned the room.

"Rosie, he's in a temper this morning," the manservant said. "He wants new food."

"Go get the wizard right away," Rosie said.

The manservant entered the wizard's chamber and said, "Excuse the interruption, kind wizard."

"What's he done now?" the wizard asked.

"He threw his food on the floor, saying it was horrible, and sent me to get new food," the manservant replied.

"He hasn't been happy with anything since his dick got sick," the wizard replied, laughing.

"Has the medicine you've been giving him helped?" the manservant asked.

"Yes, it has, Lawrence," the wizard replied. "He's got a greater sickness than that."

"What is it, Uncle?" Lawrence asked.

"His mind is sick from the diseases he's gotten from fucking diseased women in the past. He will never recover from this sickness. He'll just get worse over the next few months."

"Then we'll have a new king," Lawrence said. "I hope he's a kind one."

"I do, too, Lawrence." The wizard said. "I'll be right up with a potion."

"You've been giving him sleeping draughts, haven't you?"

"Yes. At least this way, he doesn't bother anyone and orders anyone to be killed," the wizard replied.

"You are a wise man, Uncle," Lawrence said as he left.

"Where's my breakfast?" the king hollered as the wizard entered his sitting room.

"Your Highness," the wizard said as he bowed. "I have a potion that will take care of the horrible taste of the food. I had breakfast, and it was delicious."

"Then why does it taste horrible to me?" the king demanded as his new breakfast was brought into the room.

"I believe it is an aftereffect of the medicine from last week," the wizard said as he motioned the servant to set the food on the side table. "Drink this. It should work rather quickly."

The king drank the potion.

"How long will this take?" the king asked. "I'm starving."

"Just a couple more minutes, sire," the wizard said as he set the tray in front of the king. "Now, don't throw your things around this time. Just let the medicine take a few more minutes to work. Try the tea."

"The tea tastes as it should," the king said as he drank it.

"Try the biscuit next," the wizard offered.

"It tastes fine, too," the king said. "I will eat the rest now. You are dismissed, wizard."

"Thank you, your Highness," the wizard said. He knew the potion was working by the way the king was speaking. It was slower and quieter. He had dosed the potion with valerian root. It was a sedative that worked quietly and lasted for a long while.

The king finished his breakfast and went back to bed. He slept well into the afternoon, and the castle was grateful for the wizard's potions.

Suppertime found the knights gathered in their dining room next to the kitchen. Most left after they finished their meal. Harrison and Quintan remained.

"Quintan, I've noticed you looking at the young kitchen maid," Harrison said seriously.

"Yes, Harrison," Quintan said.

"I need to tell you something about the king," Harrison said. "He has a thing for young girls."

"You mean he likes to have sex with the young ones," Quintan said.

"You're smarter than I thought," Harrison said. "Yes, exactly that. We knights have kept the young girls hidden throughout the kingdom, and we are taking precautions with Angelique."

"I wondered why there weren't any girls my age around here," Quintan said. "He's that bad, huh?"

"He's worse than that," Harrison said. "He's pure evil."

"Why has Angelique come here, then?" Quintan asked.

"Her father needed her to be safe from some horrible men in their village, and he sent her to his sister, Rosie," Harrison explained.

"I understand," Quintan said. "I will be honorable and kind to her, Harrison. Rosie has already warned me about that."

"I've no doubt she has," Harrison said. "So, we need to keep her hidden down here."

"I agree," Quintan said.

"Don't break her heart, Quintan," Harrison warned him. "I'll have to beat you within an inch of your life if you do."

"I know you will," Quintan said as they stood and shook hands.

They left the kitchen and took care of their business for the rest of the evening.

As the evening began to meld into the night, Quintan arrived in the kitchen after most of the castle had settled for the night. Rosie was waiting for him.

"Harrison told me her real story, Rosie," Quintan said. "I will treat her with great kindness and respect."

"I know you will," Rosie said quietly. "Angelique, Quintan is here for you."

"Good evening, Miss Angelique," Quintan said. "Thanks for accepting my invitation to sit and talk."

"Good evening, Quintan," Angelique said. "Rosie says you are a gentlemen. Let's sit, shall we?"

Rosie brought them tea and pastries, then walked over to the far end of the kitchen.

"She's a love," Angelique said as she poured for them.

"She most certainly is," Quintan said. "I cherish her. She helps me not miss home so much."

"I know the feeling," Angelique said. "How many sisters and brothers do you have?"

"Well, let me tell you my story," Quintan said. He left out the part about the dragons. Time for that later.

"Your new family sounds wonderful," Angelique said. "My family is rather special, too. I have three sisters and two brothers. We love each other very much most of the time."

This made Quintan laugh and point at Angelique. She laughed as well.

"We have a large farm with animals and a huge garden," Angelique continued. "My mother has taught all of us how to sew and cook. The boys think it's a girl's job, but my mother makes them prepare one evening meal a week. They soon learned how not-so-easy it is."

"I was happy to learn how to cook," Quintan said.

He told Angelique about the sleeping sickness that forced him to learn how to prepare meals and run the farm.

"It was caused by a mean witch who didn't like our village," Quintan said as he finished the story.

"That's just crazy," Angelique said. "Is the mean witch still around?"

"She is," Quintan said. "She keeps trying to get into the castle grounds, but the guards and knights keep her out. She keeps yelling that she needs to kill me because I am evil. She is crazy, for sure."

"I know you're not evil," Angelique said. "Rosie wouldn't have allowed you in the kitchen if you were. She knows things like that."

"She most certainly does," Quintan was saying when Rosie walked over.

"It's time to end this chat," Rosie said. "Has he been respectful, my Angelique?"

"Most certainly, Rosie," Angelique said as they stood up.

"I thank you for meeting me here and hope we can do it again soon," Quintan said as he took Angelique's hand and kissed it.

Quintan winked at Rosie, and she smiled at him.

"Now, off with you, young Quintan," Rosie said. "Sleep well."

Quintan kissed Rosie's cheek as he left.

"He's a nice man," Angelique said. "I like him."

"He is a nice man," Rosie said. "Now, off to sleep with both of us. Morning will be here in a hurry."

Winter made itself known a few days later. The winds came from the north and brought a light dusting of snow. The villages were ready for the cold winter. The castle was mostly set for the winter. A few minor things were being tended to as a storm was forecast to hit in a few days. The winter solstice was a week away. The king had ordered no celebrations throughout his kingdom. The penalty for disobeying was death.

The king made an announcement from his balcony the day after the solstice.

"We will celebrate the excellent harvest on the 24th of this month. Feasting will take place, and everyone must spend the day with their families after morning prayers in the chapels across the land. Your attendance will be written down. The services are set to begin at sunrise and last one hour. Bring a gift to show your thankfulness for the harvest," the king ordered.

The knights gathered in their courtyard to discuss the new order.

"It looks like our king has a plan for us," Harrison said.

"He most certainly does," Dennison replied. "We have been ordered to travel the kingdom for the next few days to make sure everyone is preparing their gift for the chaplain. I will pick certain villages for us to visit on the day of the celebration to make sure no one is missing from the services."

The knights acknowledged Dennison's orders.

"We leave at sunrise," Dennison added. "Make ready."

The knights went about their preparations for the remainder of the day. Quintan had celebrated the solstice in his own way. Rosie had given him a small sesame cake to be offered for the solstice celebration.

By the end of the day, Quintan, Harrison, and Fred were gathered near Buttercup's stall in the stables.

"Looks like we're ready," Fred said.

"We are," Harrison replied.

Quintan looked at his two companions with raised eyebrows.

"Yes, indeed, Quintan," Harrison said. "We will follow the King's orders to the exact letter. We will deal with those that do not follow his commands as instructed."

"I agree," Quintan replied. "We are his servants, and his wishes are our commands."

"Let's get some supper," Fred said. "All this work has made me hungry.'

The three of them entered Rosie's kitchen to find one of the king's special guards arguing with Rosie.

"Rosie, you will bring the young maiden here immediately," the guard was yelling. "The king wants her for the night."

"I can't do that," Rosie explained in anger. "I told you she left three days ago to return to her family in the far east of the kingdom. Her father is gravely ill, and she's needed there."

"I saw her this morning in the courtyard, talking with the blacksmith," the guard said.

"No, sir, that wasn't her," Rosie replied. "She's not here any longer."

Rosie was very angry and trying not to let it show. She knew the guard would tell the king if she were insolent, and the king would order her beheaded.

"I know what I saw. Now, where does she sleep?" the guard yelled.

"I think I know what you may have seen," Rosie said, smiling at the knights as she turned from the guard. "Martha, would you come here, please? Bring your scarf."

Martha walked over to Rosie. She was a slightly older woman, small and graceful in her movements, but she looked far younger than her years.

"That's not the young girl I saw." The guard said.

"Martha, please wrap your scarf around your head," Rosie said as she waved her hands ever so slightly toward Martha.

Martha seemed to change in an instant. She looked as young as Angelique with the scarf on her head.

"I believe this is who you saw," Rosie stated.

The guard walked over to Martha and looked her over thoroughly.

"This is the young girl I saw," the guard replied.

In an instant, Martha returned to herself, looking somewhere in her mid-thirties.

"She looks older now," the guard yelled when he looked at her again.

"That's impossible, sir," Rosie said. "I do believe the light might have made her look younger. We all know how that can happen."

The guard looked at Rosie for the longest time, then said, "I suppose you're right. My apologies. Carry on."

The guard left the kitchen with a sweet pie for the king to hopefully calm him down. Rosie had put skullcap in his pie to make him sleep for a long time and have nightmares he wouldn't be able to wake from.

"What the hell was that?" Harrison asked as he walked over to Rosie and gave her a hug.

"The king is beside himself because he can't get a hardon," Rosie replied. The kitchen workers laughed at this, along with the knights. "The wizard says he's got a disease that makes him hallucinate. The wizard cannot cure him. He says the king got the sickness from sleeping with a whore."

"How long does he have to live?" Fred asked as Roise set the three of them up with their supper at her table in the kitchen.

"The wizard says maybe less than a year, and that was three months ago. The king will keep hallucinating right up until he dies. The wizard is trying to keep him sedated. It usually works unless the king has a temper tantrum."

"That's awful," Quintan replied. "He's going mad."

"Indeed, he is," Harrison said. "Rosie, this chicken stew is excellent as usual."

"You know I made it just for the three of you," Rosie said, smiling.

"You sweet-talker," Quintan said, laughing with Fred and Harrison.

Quintan looked up from his supper and saw Angelique peeking around the corner of one of the cupboards. He kept eating without acknowledging her. They had decided to do this to keep their secret from everyone, except Rosie, of course. Rosie saw Quintan and turned her back to him with a smile.

When the three of them were finished with their supper, Rosie gave each one a sweet tart. She whispered to Quintan to come right back to the kitchen.

A few minutes after they left, Quintan entered the kitchen again.

"Well, there you are," Rosie said, setting a large bowl on the table. "It's time to get the dough rising for tomorrow's bread. Will ya' get me a large sack of flour from the pantry, young Quintan, please?"

"Of course, Rosie," Quintan replied.

"Don't be too long, now," Rosie said, winking at him.

Quintan crossed the kitchen and went through the doorway in the back wall. He stepped into the pantry and found Angelique.

"Angelique," Quintan said as he took off his hat and bowed to her.

"Sir Quintan," Angelique said, curtseying in response.

They both laughed softly at their silliness.

"It is lovely to see you again," Quintan whispered.

"Yes, it is," Angelique whispered in return.

"The knights are away in the morning for a few days, as I'm sure you've heard," Quintan said, leaning on the door frame.

"I've heard," Angelique replied, moving a bit closer to Quintan. "Don't let anything happen to you. I'd be devastated."

"There shouldn't be any skirmishes. We knights have a plan, of course," Quintan said, reaching out to take her hand in his.

They both felt a jolt of electricity fly through their bodies as they touched. There was a swift flash of brilliant white light as well.

They stared into each other's eyes for a long moment. Quintan moved very close to Angelique as they continued to look into each other's eyes.

"Young Quintan, bring me the flour," Rosie said. She sounded so very far away.

Angelique was the first to lower her eyes and return them to the here and now.

"Straight away, Rosie," Quintan replied as he looked for the flour.

"It's over there," Angelique said, laughing quietly.

"So it is," Quintan replied, lifting the sack to his shoulder. "Until we meet again."

Quintan leaned over and placed a soft kiss on Angelique's cheek. Angelique took his hand in hers and kissed it.

"My knight," Angelique whispered as they left the pantry.

"My lady," Quintan said as he closed the door.

Angelique entered the kitchen just before Quintan.

"Here you are, my Rosie," Quintan said as he placed the flour on the table.

"Thank you, young one," Rosie said as she looked over at Angelique, then nodded at Quintan. "I'll have fresh bread for you knights in the morning before you leave."

"We appreciate your every effort, Rosie," Quintan said as he kissed her cheek. "Thanks for the sweet-tart. A great bedtime snack."

"I must keep my boys strong and healthy," Rosie said. "Now, off to the stables with you. Angelique, come learn how to make my bread. You'll need to know now that Martha has left us."

"She's well?" Angelique said as she stood next to Rosie.

"Indeed, she is," Rosie replied. "I sent her to the summer residence for a lesser strenuous position."

"I like that," Quintan replied, knowing exactly what Rosie meant.

If the king had heard that Martha was who he thought was the young maiden, he would have raped her, then killed her. Rosie knew exactly what was happening in the castle. Quintan had a thought that it was probably the wizard and Rosie who really made things happen. It certainly wasn't the crazy king. He rarely left his chambers anymore. The word around the castle was that he really was going mad.

Helena, the evil witch, loved hearing this. She had cast many spells to make him become sick and demented. She was sure that's what was wrong with him. She was thrilled about this. She planned to get another lowly lord on the throne as soon as King Gorham died. She had planned to be King Gorham's queen, but that hadn't happened. He had a lust for young girls, and she was old and ugly as far as he was concerned. She spent a lot of time thinking about Quintan and how she could kill him. Every time she came up with a spell and was ready to cast it, her potions would disappear from sight. Gone, right before her eyes. She knew there was a lot of Old Magic happening around Quintan and was worried he would get in her way.

The evening before the knights rode out before the new celebration, she called upon her minions to attack him in his sleep. She cast a strong spell to bring the rats and mice into his quarters and bite him until he bled to death. Didn't happen.

As soon as The Special Magic heard her conjuring her spells, they sent a cold wind and lightning right into her cottage, ruining everything. Everything in her cottage was incinerated, leaving only piles of ash. She was hysterical with fear. She had never experienced such powerful forces going against her. She fell to the floor, crying out in terror.

"What have I done to deserve this?" she said. "I have served the Dark Forces well."

"You chose the Dark Forces for your own gain," a voice replied. "You have tried to harm a Special One. For this, you will pay the consequences."

"Who are you? You have no power over me!" Helena screamed out as she stood up. "You will return my cottage to me at once."

"No, Helena. You made a choice a long time ago to serve The Dark Forces," the voice replied. "Now, you will pay for this choice."

In an instant, Helena was struck down to the floor. She couldn't move. She cried out in fear. "I will serve The White Light from now on."

"No, Helena. You cannot change your path," the voice said. "Your time on this Earth Plane has come to an end."

As Helena watched, three figures floated towards her. She was terrified. She knew the evil things she had done and realized her time of reckoning was at hand. The energies were transparent as they reached down for her. She felt their energy pull her to her feet. They let go of her, and she was struck with a bolt of lightning. She was vaporized in an instant, and her cottage disintegrated into ash. Not a trace of her existence was to be found anywhere. It was as if she had never been there.

As she transcended into her energy form, her guardians brought her to the high council for her reckoning. It would be a long, long time before she was free to do anything in her energy form, and she knew that she would probably not be allowed to be human again.

Quintan and his fellow knights settled for the night. Roman and Clarice had been put on high alert. They were told that Helena was trying to kill Quintan again. And, just like that, they knew Helena was gone for good.

Merlin and Feyanna had felt the energy shift as well. They were just settling in their rooms when it happened. They ran into each other as they came from their rooms.

"Sorry about that," they both said at the same time, then laughed.

"Something's up," Merlin was saying when they heard Beau land right next to the cottage home.

They opened the door, and there he was. Literally blocking the door.

"Could you move back a step or two, Beau?" Merlin asked as he nudged Beau.

"Oh. Sorry about that," Beau said as Feyanna laughed at the two of them trying to step around each other.

Beau stepped back, and Feyanna and Merlin came through the door.

"What's going on?" Feyanna asked.

"We felt the energy shift at the same time," Merlin added.

"That evil witch, Helena, was trying to conjure a potion to kill Quintan," Beau explained. "Now, now. Settle down. The White Light immediately knew about this and took care of things. Suffice it to say, Helena will not be bothering anyone on the Earth Plane or in the Energy Realm for a long, long time."

"I remember Hamlen saying something about a strange woman when he and Quintan were delivering wagons to the other king," Merlin said.

"Oh, yes, so do I," Feyanna added.

"She kept at it as soon as Quintan started working in the castle," Beau said. "The guards and knights knew she was a problem and kept her away from him. They are mostly good people."

"The Special Magic said they were protecting him," Merlin said. "We've never doubted it. Blessed be The Special Magic."

A quick flash of soft blue light enveloped all of them.

"Good to hear he's okay," Feyanna said.

"The knights will be here tomorrow evening to make sure everyone has a gift for the chaplain for the special celebration services," Beau told them.

"We all do, thanks to The Magic," Merlin said, smiling.

"That beautiful Magic set a gift of food in everyone's cottage to take to the service," Feyanna explained.

"I know," Beau said as he started to laugh. "Just wait until you see what The Special Magic has in store for every chaplain in the kingdom. I dare say there won't be any services the day after tomorrow."

"And, why is that, Beau?" Merlin asked, smiling.

"It would seem that all the chaplains will be losing their voices for two days beginning tomorrow right after mid-day," Beau said, laughing as dragons do: loud and boisterously. His laughter was heard for miles. Many laughed at this, knowing it was a dragon having a great time.

"I like the sound of that," Feyanna said as they all laughed.

"By the way, how are Penny and Q?" Merlin asked.

"They are healing wonderfully," Beau said. "Penny is getting a bit restless. She wants to fly, but she isn't strong enough yet. Every time she tries to spread her wings, she is reminded that she isn't quite ready."

"I can just imagine how she reacts to that," Feyanna said, laughing. "Miss Penny isn't used to just sitting around."

"That's the truth," Beau replied. "Q is a better patient than Miss Penny. He tried to move around a lot the other day and was reminded that his dragon self wasn't ready yet. He bellowed a bit of smoke about the place in frustration. Penny yelled at him to settle down before he burned them to a crisp. They both laughed at that, even though it did hurt some. They finally settled down, and the faeries brought them a huge pile of winterberries. This made Penny and Q quite happy. They thanked the faeries for their love and promised to try to remain calm for the remainder of their convalescence."

"I would have loved to see that," Feyanna said as she laughed with Beau and Merlin.

"Not the smoke thing, but all the rest," Merlin said. "It's good to hear they are coming along. Winter is setting in now, and we're going to need them to be healthy as soon as spring wakes up. You know how crazy the king gets in the spring."

"Indeed, Merlin. Indeed," Beau replied. "Well, it's time for me to get along. I'll let Penny and Q know you send your love as always."

"Please do," Merlin said as Beau walked into the middle of the field and spread his wings.

"Stay safe, Beau," Feyanna said as he lifted into the sky.

"I'm going to set another purple crystal in the field right now," Merlin said. "It seems to be the right thing to do."

"I'll walk with you," Feyanna said as they walked across the field to the exact center.

Merlin set the crystal in the meadow, and something new happened. A ring of purple crystals of all sizes, shapes, and shades of purple surrounded him and Feyanna. Some of the colors they had never seen before.

"This is absolutely indescribable," Feyanna whispered.

Merlin nodded as they turned around, looking at the ring of Magic. Two large baskets appeared, and some of the crystals were floated into the baskets.

"Now, that's The Special Magic showing us some love," Merlin said.

"As Beau says, Indeed!" Feyanna said as she lifted her basket. "This isn't heavy at all. I don't know why I thought it would be. Love The Magic."

Merlin and Feyanna stood in the ring while losing track of time and place. The crystals began to fade, and then they were gone.

"Time to get some sleep," Merlin said quietly.

They walked back across the meadow to their cottage home under a clear sky, which showed millions of stars. They settled again for the night and were soon asleep.

Quintan slept deeply that night, having visions of summer, coronations, and dragons. He didn't remember them the next day. But he would at the right time.

Angelique slept with a smile in her heart all night long. Rosie knew why and approved.

The knights rode out at sunrise the next morning after eating a special breakfast Rosie had made for them. The bread was like nothing Quintan had ever tasted, and he let Rosie know. She nodded and smiled.

The knights split up into four groups. Fred, Harrison, and Quintan were set together. As they rode away from the others, Harrison signaled them to follow him. As soon as they were far from everyone, he stopped.

"Fred. Quintan, "Harrison began. "We all know the king is crazy. We will not be harming anyone today. These good people barely have enough for themselves."

"What about the chaplains?" Fred asked.

Quintan began to smile as he was told about The Special Magic's plan for them and how it had provided the mandatory gift from every household. "I don't think any of that will be a problem."

"Why do you say that?" Fred asked.

"I have a hunch," Quintan said. "Shall we move along?"

They rode to all the villages they were assigned and found out that every household had a gift for the chaplain that did not cause them hardship. They also came to realize that the chaplains in all the areas couldn't utter a word. The three knights looked at each other and smiled. They reassured the chaplains that they would tell the king that all his orders had been followed perfectly and suggested the chaplains rest until they felt better. The chaplains were immensely thankful.

Quintan's home was the last village they had to go to the night before the celebration. They rode along the south road, and Hamlen saw them coming. He recognized Quintan and ran into the road. Quintan swung down from Buttercup and grabbed his father in a bear hug. Hugho had ridden ahead and found his father outside. He grabbed him likewise. The villagers heard the commotion and ran outside to see what was happening. Cheers of welcome could be heard throughout the village. The evening was spent with much joy and celebration. Harrison informed the villagers of the chaplain's illness, stating there would not be any services the next morning. He gathered the gifts and took them to the chaplain. The chaplain was not happy. Harrison told him he would tell the king the services took place, and everyone attended. The chaplain was relieved and thankful for the gifts.

Harrison returned to Quintan's home to a wonderful meal and lots of teasing. The knights were settled in many homes around the village, and the night was a quiet and cold one.

Quintan was the first to get up in the morning and got the fire going just as his mother walked into the kitchen.

"Quintan," she said as she hugged him. "You are a thoughtful man."

"I was raised right, Mother," Quintan returned. "I'll fetch the eggs while you begin breakfast."

Quintan gathered the eggs in quick time stopping to care for Buttercup.

"Thanks for gathering the eggs, brother," Margaret said. "I do not like the cold."

"I hear you," Quintan said as he twirled her around, making her laugh. "You are growing, sister."

"Yes, I am," Margaret said as he set her down. "I'll be seventeen a few months before you."

"Indeed you will," Quintan said. "You're older than me, for sure, but not any wiser."

"That remains to be seen, little brother," Margaret sassed back.

"All right, you two, let's get on with breakfast," Glendianna said, laughing with them.

"This sounds like a cheery bunch," Hamlen said as he and Sarah came into the kitchen.

"Quintan, aren't morning chores beneath the dignity of a knight of the royal court?" Sarah asked.

"Not at all, my little sister," Quintan replied. "Even though there are those who look after us when we're riding throughout the kingdom, we take care of ourselves. Our mother taught me well, so I don't have any problems. And Hugho is fantastic as well. A great friend and paige he is."

"Oh, I thought you didn't do anything simple," Sarah replied.

"All the time, little sister, all the time," Quintan replied as he pulled on her braids.

"Hey, cut that out," Sarah said as she whacked him on his backside.

"Always children, no matter what age they get to be," Hamlen said.

"And I love it," Glendianna said as she brought the egg pie and bread to the table.

"Girls, please bring the butter, cheese, and fruit to the table," Glendianna said.

"Yes, ma'am," they both replied.

Hamlen gave the blessing in The Old Magic way, and they all enjoyed their meal.

As the knights gathered at Hamlen's farm, Merlin and Feyanna walked in.

"Good morning, Quintan," Feyanna said as he gave her a big hug.

"I've missed you terribly," Quintan whispered so no one could hear him.

Merlin gathered Quintan into a big hug, too.

"Ah, Master Merlin," Quintan said, returning the hug. "How are Penny and Q?"

Merlin released Quintan and replied, "Your friends from the north are doing quite well. We should be seeing them once the winter is over."

"Speaking of winter," Fred said, "I have been told by the family I stayed with that a great storm is gathering."

"That's what I was told as well," Hugho said.

"I've been following the clouds, and that storm is going to be a long and hard one. Lots of snow and great winds will last the better part of a week. Our village is ready for it," Merlin said.

"When do you sense it will begin?" Harrison asked of Merlin.

"Sir Harrison," Merlin replied. "Tomorrow morning before first light. I hope you will have returned to the castle by then."

"Thank you for that, Master Merlin," Harrison said. "We ride in an hour, knights. Be ready and meet here."

The village met with everyone at Hamlen's an hour later as the knights prepared to take their leave. Food was given to the knights for their return journey with lots of advice on how to get through the storm.

Quintan caught a glimpse of a dragon wing as he looked toward Merlin and Feyanna's field and smiled. Feyanna saw this and sent a message to Beau to settle down. This made Merlin laugh out loud.

"I see Merlin has seen the same cloud shape as I have," Quintan said, covering for Merlin and Feyanna. Quintan had heard Feyanna's message as well.

"And what was it?" Fred asked.

"It was a duck chasing a horse," Quintan said. "The faster the clouds moved, the sillier it looked until the duck was chasing nothing."

"I love watching the clouds," Sarah said. "I could watch them for hours."

"You do," Margaret replied.

This made everyone laugh and look at the clouds for a minute.

"Those clouds have rain in them," Fred said.

"Yes, they do, sir Fred," Feyanna said. "As it begins to fall in the night, it will come through frigid air and turn to snow before it falls on the earth."

"You are very well learned, Feyanna," Harrison said.

"My mother taught me well," Feyanna replied, winking at Quintan.

"I believe Merlin may have added to that knowledge somewhat," Quintan teased.

"He tries," Feyanna replied, laughing.

"Time for us to take our leave," Harrison said as the knights and their paiges fell into form. "We thank you for taking us in and wish you all a blessed winter."

The villagers called out as the knights road along the south road back to Kerwyn.

The clouds continued to gather and become lower in the sky as they rode along. They were near the evil witches' cottage when Fred said, "I don't see the evil witches' cottage anymore. Wonder what happened to it?"

Quintan was told by his Guardians about her demise.

"I do believe I heard it burned down one night with the witch inside," Quintan said.

"I heard that, too," Hugho replied. "A new herbalist has settled on the east side of the city—well, not near the city. She is about a fifteen-minute walk from the city. Our new blacksmith is her father. She is quite gifted from what I hear around the castle grounds."

"I've heard the same thing," Harrison said as they approached the eastern gate. Russell was waiting for them.

"Good day, sir Harrison and all you knights," Russell said as they rode through.

"Thanks for being here, Russell," Quintan said. "Hugho, let's get the horses settled, and then we can get the washing done before the storm arrives."

"That's a great idea, Quintan," Harrison said. "Let's all do the same thing. We can take care of our other chores later. I'll report to the king right away."

A few hours later, the knights had cleaned their clothes and hung them around Rosie's kitchen and baking rooms to dry. As always, she gave them a bit of grief.

Harrison reported to the king's chamber. The king was sitting in his chair by the window.

"Harrison," the king said in greeting.

"Your highness, "Harrison replied as he bowed before the king.

"Report on your activities," the king bellowed.

"Your Highness will be pleased to learn that all the villagers in our region followed your law to the letter. Gifts were ready, and all attended the service."

"No one disobeyed me?" the king asked.

"Not a single one of them," Harrison replied, looking directly into the king's eyes.

"Well done, then. I don't relish a hanging during a storm. Is the castle ready for the storm, knight?"

"Yes, sire. Your every command has been fulfilled," Harrison replied.

"You are a good knight, Harrison," the king said as he closed his eyes.

"I am honored by your words, sire," Harrison said as he bowed.

The king seemed to have dropped off to sleep. Harrison stood at attention for a minute, not knowing quite what to do. The wizard came through the door a few minutes later, dismissing Harrison.

"He falls asleep quite a lot," the wizard whispered. "If he asks about you, I'll tell him he dismissed you."

"Thank you," Harrison said as he made a quick exit.

"Wizard, where's my knight?" the king asked as he suddenly woke up.

"You dismissed him before you fell asleep, sire," the wizard replied.

"Oh, so I did," the king replied. "Why are you here, wizard?"

"I have your mid-day tonic, sire," the wizard said as the king's manservant arrived with lunch.

The manservant placed the tray on the table and quickly retreated before the king could throw food at him.

"Please take a bite of your food before I give you your tonic," the wizard said. "The tonic will work much better if you eat first."

"That does seem to be how it always works," the king said as he ate some of his lunch. "I want one of the kitchen wenches in my bed right away."

"Your Highness, you know you need to be cured before you can have sex again."

"I don't care," the king yelled. "I want to fuck a wench. Send one here."

"As you desire," the wizard said as the king drank his tonic.

"Be gone with you and take that tray with you," the king said as he walked over to his bed and disrobed. "I want that wench now!"

"Yes, your Highness," the wizard said as he left the king's chambers.

The wizard would not send a woman to the king under any orders. He was riddled with disease. Anyway, the king would be unconscious in a few minutes and stay that way for many hours. He wouldn't remember asking for a wench when he finally woke up in the middle of a blizzard.

While the wizard was dosing the king, the knights gathered in their dining room for supper. Rosie was ready for them with beef stew, bread, and lots of love. As they finished and went on to their rooms, Quintan stayed back.

Rosie smiled and nodded for Quintan to follow her. She led him to a room he didn't even know existed. It was a few steps from the kitchen proper and up a winding staircase. The staircase opened into an alcove. Angelique was waiting for them.

"Be a gentleman," Rosie whispered.

"Always, Rosie," Quintan replied.

"I'll be back in a while," Rosie said. "Enjoy the tea and cakes."

"Thanks, Miss Rosie," Angelique replied, smiling.

Rosie took her leave, and Quintan and Angelique sighed at the same time. Then they quietly laughed.

"It's good to see you again," Quintan said as they sat across the table from each other.

"I look forward to our chats," Angelique said as she poured the tea.

"I see Rosie has outdone herself for us," Quintan said as he pointed to the tiny cakes.

"She had so much fun frosting them to look like snowmen and snow-flakes," Angelique said. "I offered to help, but she insisted she do this herself."

"It's just like her," Quintan said as he bit into one. "This is berry flavored. Fantastic!"

"Mine tastes of cinnamon," Angelique said.

They spent a while enjoying the cakes and tea and catching up on what each other had been doing since they last talked.

"The castle is all abuzz about this snowstorm," Angelique said. "I do hope it isn't too horrible. I worry about my family when things like this happen."

"Does your village help each other?" Quintan said as he took her hand in his.

"They do," Angelique said as she blushed a bit.

"Mine, too," Quintan said. "So, I don't think either of us has a thing to worry about. My sisters will be building snowmen and other shapes as soon as the storm ends. The whole village will be outside clearing paths to each others cottages."

"My family will do the same thing," Angelique said, stroking Quintan's hand with her thumb. "All the children have been gathering sticks and pinecones for the snowpeople's faces and hands. They keep them in their barns and stables. They'll have to shovel a path first, of course. I do believe the adults planned it that way."

"We have wicked smart adults in both villages," Quintan said, laughing. "My father insisted that we keep our treasures in the barn as well. I suggested we build a box to keep them in just outside the kitchen door so we could get to them easily. But he insisted on the barn. Now, I understand why."

They were silent as they held hands across the table. Quintan took a deep breath, stood up, and walked around the table to Angelique. He gently pulled her to her feet, and they stared into each other's eyes for a moment. Angelique thought her heart would leap out of her chest. Quintan could hardly catch his breath. He leaned into Angelique and touched her lips with his ever so softly. They stayed like that for a long while before Quintan pulled away just a little bit.

"You taste like cinnamon," Quintan whispered.

"You taste like berries," Angelique said.

Quintan put his arms around Angelique, pressing his body into hers. He felt the soft mounds of her breasts. They were quite large. This made him light-headed. He bent his head and pressed his mouth against hers. Angelique parted her lips, and they deepened the kiss. They stayed like this for a long time.

Rosie was quietly climbing the stairs as she didn't hear them talking. She peeked around the door and saw them kissing. A very deep kiss it was. Rosie stepped back to the top of the stairs and waited until she heard them talking again.

"Angelique, please forgive my rudeness," Quintan said.

"No need to," Angelique. "I've wanted to do that ever since I first saw you. I'm so glad you finally kissed me."

"Same here," Quintan said as he gave her a little kiss on the lips before stepping away from her.

"I think Rosie will be coming back any minute," Angelique said. "We ate all the cakes and drank all the tea. That will make her happy."

Rosie was thinking a little differently. She was thrilled that they had finally kissed. It was about time. She knew they were very new at all this, so she would take great care to help them along the way.

Rosie made herself known by stepping harshly on the floor as if she had just cleared the stairs. She came in, looking around, and said, "I see you enjoyed the cakes and tea,"

"We most certainly did," Quintan said. "Thanks so much for arranging this for us."

"And for keeping me a secret from the king," Angelique added. "I hear he is a monster."

"Truth. Every word, dear child," Rosie said. "The wizard assures me we have nothing to worry about. He is keeping him comfortable, if you know what I mean."

"We do," Quintan and Angelique said at the same time.

"Well, it's time for you to leave, young Quintan, and you, Miss Angelique, need your rest," Rosie was saying as she gathered the dishes.

"I'll take those downstairs," Angelique said.

"No, you will not, "Rosie said. "We don't want anyone to know about you and Quintan. Go on now, missy. Quintan, wait until I'm in the kitchen before you come down."

"Yes, Ma'am," Quintan and Angelique said at the same time again.

They all laughed at this. Angelique left first.

"Quintan, she is a sweet girl," Rosie said. "You be gentle with her."

"I will, Miss Rosie," Quintan said. "I am quite taken with her."

"And she with you," Rosie said as she walked to the door. "Wait a few minutes, then come into the kitchen so I can bother you."

Quintan smiled at Rosie as she left. He was thinking about their kiss. It was extraordinary. Holy cow! This must be what it felt like to fall in love.

Quintan walked into the kitchen from the knight's dining room a few minutes later, putting his cloak on.

"Young Quintan, get yourself to bed," Rosie said. "The storm has started. The snow is just beginning to fall, and the wind is letting us know it's here. Can ya' hear that?"

Everyone listened as they heard a gust of wind wrap itself around the castle, rattling anything that wasn't tied down.

"Indeed, Miss Rosie," Quintan said as he crossed over to the door.

"Here, take this with you," Rosie said as she handed him something wrapped in a hot cloth. "Sleep well, young Quintan."

Quintan tucked the food under his cloak, bent down, and kissed Rosie's cheek, whispering, "Thanks."

The storm had definitely begun. There wasn't much snow yet, but the wind was howling something fiery. Quintan searched the parapets and saw the shadows of Clarice and Roman. He sent them a message, hoping they would be safe in the storm. They flew down to him, showing themselves for just a minute.

"We are going to stay here in the courtyard during the storm. The winds will be fierce, and we could be thrown off the wall," Roman said.

"The Special Magic will take care of us until the storm is over," Clarice added.

"Which will be in three days, just in case you were wondering," Roman said, with a cocky smile on his dragon face.

"Always the wise guy," Clarice said.

"How are Q and Miss Penny?" Quintan asked as he walked slowly toward the stable.

"They are healing quite well," Clarice said. "They should be ready to fly when the spring arrives."

"Restless as anticipated, but behaving most of the time," Roman said. "Time for you to get inside. Be off with you now."

"You sound a bit like our Rosie," Quintan said as he opened the stable door. "Thanks for taking such great care of me."

"Always, our Quintan," Clarice said.

"Always," Roman said as they vanished.

Quintan watched as he saw their footprints going across the courtyard. He closed the door, making sure he secured it well. He checked on Buttercup, then went on up to his quarters. Hugho was waiting for him.

"You stayed in the kitchen quite a while," Hugho said as Quintan undressed and crawled into bed.

"I had some thinking to do," Quintan replied. "It's quite warm in here. What happened?"

"I suggested we build a chimney from the middle of the stables where they keep a fire going all winter long so we could have some warmth in here. The others liked the idea and worked with the masons and others to build it. It has tiny open vents on all sides for the warm hair to move through. The smoke was pulled from the room by the other vents in the ceilings.. We've done it very quietly so the king doesn't go nuts."

"I hear that," Quintan said. "Sit up and take some of this."

Quintan handed the warm cloth to Hugho. He looked at it and smiled. "I love our Rosie. Apple bread is one of my favorites."

"All food is your favorite," Quintan said, laughing at the face Hugho made at him.

Quintan and Hugho's quarters were in a corner of the room, which gave them a little privacy.

They ate the bread and finally settled down for the night.

"Sleep well, my brother," Quintan said.

"Sleep well, my brother," Hugho returned.

They fell asleep quickly as the storm raged on outside. The snow had rapidly become like a wall of white ice. The dragons were fine, settling next to the blacksmith's shop. The world outside the castle and all across the land was quickly becoming covered in a thick blanket of white. The Special Magic made sure of that.

During the second day of the storm, word got around the castle that the king was sick. He had been coughing most of the day. The wizard came into the kitchen at supper time, looking quite worn out.

"What's with you, Charles?" Rosie asked as she set a cup of hot tea in front of him. "Sit down and eat."

"The king has a lung sickness," Charles the wizard replied. "It's a bad one. I've given him some elixirs to help loosen the stuff in his lungs."

"Will he live?" Rosie asked quietly.

"Maybe," Charles replied. "His disease will make that difficult."

"Has his disease affected his brain badly?" Rosie asked.

"It has," Charles replied. "I keep him dosed with a sleeping potion most of the time. But, with this lung sickness, I'm afraid it would probably kill him."

"Put him out of his misery and everyone else's," Rosie said. "You stay sitting right there. I'll get you some supper. I know you haven't eaten much today, being with him and all."

"Rosie, you know I love ya," Charles said as he squeezed her hand.

"I do," Rosie replied, winking at him.

Rosie brought Charles a hearty meal, and he sat, ate, and talked with the kitchen folks for quite a while.

"That was splendid," Charles said as he finally stood. "I'd better check on the king. I have his manservant keeping a steam bowl next to his bed."

"Let me know if you need anything," Rosie said.

"I will," Charles said as he left.

Charles found the king sleeping.

"How long?" Charles asked the manservant.

"About an hour," the manservant replied. "He seems to have stopped coughing for a bit. Is that good or bad?"

"We'll find out when he wakes up. Go to the kitchen. Rosie is waiting for you," Charles said.

The king woke up two hours later. The manservant had the steam bowling working well, and Charles had nodded off in a chair.

"What's going on?" the king tried to holler but was consumed with coughing. "Damn. Can't you cure me?"

"It takes time, sire," Charles said. "You seemed to have slept well."

"I do feel a bit rested, and the cough seems to have stopped, but I'm having a hard time catching my breath," the king whispered as he started to cough again.

"I thought that might happen," Charles said as he mixed a potion and handed it to the king. "Drink all of this. It will help loosen the phlegm in your lungs. If the phlegm doesn't get out, you will suffocate. So, don't try to yell anymore. Just breathe as deeply as you can. You will begin to cough up the putrid stuff in a bit. Be sure to spit it out. Don't swallow it!"

"Can't you give me something to sleep?" the king asked.

"No," Charles replied. "It will kill you."

The king looked scared at this. He swallowed the potion, settled against his pillows, and dozed for a while. He was woken up because he needed to cough. He coughed hard for a few minutes, then spit green crap into the bowl by his bed.

"That was horrible," the king whispered.

"This is what's making you ill. It's horrible," Charles said as he threw the phlegm into the fire. It sizzled for a second, then burned away.

"I will give you several potions over the next week if you make it that long," Charles said. "Don't even think of yelling at me. Rest!"

"The storm," the king said. "What's happening with the storm?"

"It rages on," Charles said. "Harrison said there's already six feet of snow around the castle. It's going to take a long time to clear the castle and city out when the storm finally stops."

"Keep me posted," the king said as he closed his eyes.

The next day, the third day of the storm, the king seemed to be getting worse. He rattled when he breathed, and he could only take shallow breaths. Word got around that he was very sick and might die. The castle was very quiet, waiting for news.

The storm started to wind down by the end of the third day. The morning of the fourth day, the snow had stopped falling, and a hazy sun was seen trying to shine down on a pure white landscape.

The knights had been shoveling since dawn with everyone's help. They had cleared the gates of snow on the inside of the castle. They opened them and found about ten feet of snow in front of them. The children asked if tunnels could be made. Everyone helped, and by mid-day, you could hear the squeals of joy from the children as they ran through the tunnels.

The knights dug tunnels to the outside of the castle and found the people of Kerwyn doing the same. Some made flags and set them on the top of their tunnels. Although digging out was hard work, making the tunnels was great fun. It took five days after the storm ended to finally clear a path to the city.

The king remained in grave health during this time. Charles did everything he could, but he feared it wasn't going to be enough. The king slept most of the time. When he was awake, he coughed and spit out that horrible green phlegm. It had blood in it now and smelled horrible as it burned in the fire.

It was on the seventh day after the storm stopped that the king woke up.

"I feel so much better," he said. "I'm even hungry."

"Your Highness, that's good news," Charles said. "Take this potion, and I'll fetch you some of Rosie's chicken soup."

"I want steak and potatoes and bread," the king tried to yell but coughed instead.

"You are a bit better, but not all better," Charles said. "Do as told."

The king was about to yell, but he thought about it first and decided to remain quiet.

"Good choice," Charles said. "Your manservant has hot water to bathe you with and clean clothes. Sit here while the bed is changed. It will take all the energy you've got, so behave."

The king tried to stand up but fell back on the bed. He motioned to his manservant to help him. In a few minutes, he was in the chair and naked. His manservant bathed him and changed him into clean clothes. His bed was stripped, cleaned, and made with fresh linens.

"I can't believe how tired I am," the king said as he was helped back into bed. "These linens feel wonderful."

Charles was entering the room with his soup and heard this.

"Glad to hear that," Charles said as he and the manservant set the king's bed table in front of him with the soup and bread.

"Take your time," Charles said as he handed the king another vile of medicine.

"Tell Rosie this tastes delicious, and thanks for the bread," the king said.

Charles and the manservant looked at each other with surprise. The king hadn't said a nice word to anyone for a very long time. The king finished his meal and fell back against the pillows. He fell asleep and slept for the rest of the afternoon and night. Word got around that it looked like he was going to recover. Oh well, most thought. You can't have everything you wish for.

Harrison, Fred, and Quintan were in the stables caring for their horses after the tunnels were completed.

"I've never experienced a storm like this before," Fred said.

"Me, either, even as a kid," Quintan replied.

"Same here," Harrison said. "The king seems to be recovering. Charles says it's going to take all winter before he could be completely recovered from the lung illness."

"What about the other thing?" Quintan asked. "His brain may not make it that long."

"I was thinking that same thing," Fred said quietly.

"Charles told me he knows the king will die from the disease he carries. Charles doesn't think he will live another year," Harrison said.

"That's what he told me, too," Quintan said. "So, now what? Do we start looking for a new king before he dies?"

"That's a good question," Fred said. "We could talk privately among the three of us for now about that. I don't think any of the lords are qualified, to be honest."

Quintan and Harrison nodded in agreement.

"We should think about this very carefully for now," Harrison said. "Time to get on with our duties. We'll ride out tomorrow and check on the city."

"Agreed," Fred said. "The horses are getting restless. A ride will be good for them."

"Great idea, Fred," Quintan said. "I'll inform the others and the guards of our plans."

Quintan told the knights and the guards, and they liked the idea. Everything was ready to go the next morning after breakfast. Folks stopped their work to watch the knights ride through the courtyard and the gate. Quintan looked up at the parapets and saw a quick glimpse of the dragon's shadows. He saluted to them, making it look like he was honoring the king's colors. Angelique watched them leave from a special place near the room she and Quintan had first kissed in. They were meeting there again tonight after Vespers.

As the knights rode through the city to check on everyone, a flash was seen high above the city. As people turned and looked, they saw three silver disks hovering high above the land. As they continued to watch, the disks changed shape and became long and narrow. Their color kept changing: red, then green, and finally blue. The blue color remained as the crafts flew over the city, settling lower and lower until you could see the details on the crafts. There were ridges, lights, and strange markings. They didn't make a sound and stayed moving over the city for quite some time. As if a signal had been given, they all shot straight up into the sly and were gone in a flash.

The entire city was silent for a moment before everyone began talking about those strange things in the sky.

"Harrison," Fred said. "We've seen these before."

"Yes, we have," Harrison replied.

"Why are they here?" Fred asked.

"What do they want?" the knights all said at the same time.

"I have no idea," Harrison said, looking at Quintan.

"Don't look at me," Quintan said. "I'm as shocked by those things as everyone else."

One of the citizens was heard to say, "It's the wrath of God. He's displeased with us and has sent these flying machines to punish us."

Similar comments were heard as the knights rode through the city and into the countryside.

Rosie and Angelique had been looking out the same window when the disks appeared.

"Rosie, what are those things? Is God mad at us?" Angelique asked as she grabbed a hold of Rosie's arm.

"Dear child, they have nothing to do with the king's God," Rosie replied.

"Then, why are they here?" Angelique asked.

"I suspect something tremendous is about to happen," Rosie replied.

"You've seen them before?" Angelique said.

"Yes, I have," Rosie replied. "It was when this king banned all the old ways, The Ancient Magic, from being used. It was a terrible day for us all."

"I remember that day," Angelique said. "My mother and father cried in the night. It was horrible for the whole village."

"Child, we mustn't talk about this," Rosie whispered. "The king will have us beheaded."

"I know," Angelique said just as the disks shot straight up into the sky and were gone. "I'll be careful."

As Rosie heard footsteps approaching, she said, "We must pray to God for mercy and forgiveness at once."

The High Chancellor came around the corner and heard Rosie.

"Rosie, you are perfectly right about praying," he said. "We must have insulted God, and all need to ask his forgiveness at once."

Yes, sir," Rose replied as she and Angelique curtsied. "I will be sure to tell the kitchen staff at once."

"Good," the High Chancellor replied as he went on his way.

Rosie waited until she heard him no more and then said, "And that is why we must be very careful about what we say. Someone is always close by."

"I understand, Miss Rosie," Angelique replied.

"Let's get back to the kitchen and warn the others," Rosie said rather loudly. She whispered, "We are well protected by The Special Magic here."

Angelique nodded her head as they left the window.

Merlin, Feyanna, Goldie, George, and Beau were in the meadow when the disks appeared.

"Ah, we have visitors," George said. "It would seem something is about to happen."

"Why do you say that, George?" Feyanna asked as they watched the disks move around in the sky.

"I remember another time when they appeared just as an earthquake engulfed this region," George replied.

"I remember that, George," Goldie said. "It was frightening. I was trying to find bugs, and all of a sudden, the ground seemed to come apart around me. Afterward, there were a lot of bugs for me. I guess it turned out to be a good thing."

"Good for you, Goldie," Merlin said. "They are magnificent even if they're a ways away from here. Look at how they change color."

"And their shape," Feyanna added. "Amazing, for sure."

They watched the disks until they finally shot straight up into the sky and disappeared.

"Well, that was an interesting way to get the day going," Beau said. "So glad you cleared a path out to the meadow."

"We didn't clear the path," Feyanna said. "It was here when we got up this morning."

"Those faeries are wonderful," Beau said. "Thanks for helping out here."

The snow flashed a myriad of colors in response.

"I like that," George said. "I think I'll fly around the area and see how everyone else is making out. The villagers know me, so they won't be surprised to see me."

"Good idea, George," Merlin said. "We'll wait for your report in the cottage. It's getting quite cold out here."

George took to the air, and Goldie started down the path to the cottage. "It is cold out here. Later, Beau," she said.

"I'll be off, too," Beau said as he vanished. Feyanna and Merlin felt the air around them move as Beau took off.

Merlin and Feyanna hurried back to their cottage home and were warming themselves by the fire a few minutes later.

Merlin looked over at Feyanna and said, "I know that look. What?"

"I think this snowstorm was sent by The Magic," Feyanna said.

"I agree," Merlin said. "I agree."

"It would seem that the king is an angry, mean person, and the storm was sent to keep him from causing any more damage," Feyanna explained.

"That's a good thought," Merlin said. "I think we should be ready for anything to happen involving the king."

"Yes, we do need to be ready for more chaos," Goldie said from her place by the fire. "This is a warm and cozy fire. Thanks,"

"Oh, Goldie, you are very welcome," Feyanna said.

"Open the door," Goldie said with her eyes closed. "George is home."

Merlin walked over and opened the door just as George arrived.

George settled on his perch and said, "Thanks, Merlin. This fire is just what I needed. It's cold out there."

"How are the villagers?" Merlin asked.

"They are all dug out and doing just fine," George said. "The children are having a grand time with the snow. They have tunnels to run through and a big hill in the meadow next to Hamlen's farm to slide down. The animals have open areas as they need. The villagers were talking about the extra hay and straw they found in their barns and sheds after the storm. I heard Samuel suggest they thank the Special Ones for the gifts. They all bowed their heads and said a silent prayer to The Ancient Magic for the gifts. The sky flashed a special lavender color over the village in response. Everyone smiled and then got busy with their day."

"Thanks for the update, Geroge," Feyanna said as she stroked his wing.

"That feels nice," George said as he closed his eyes and fell asleep.

"Let's get busy, Feyanna," Merlin said.

Merlin and Feyanna spent the rest of the day working on their remedies and potions.

About a week later, Charles came into the kitchen to find Rosie.

"Oh, there you are, Rosie," Charles said as he watched her at the working table.

"Where else would I be, Charles?" Rosie sassed back.

"That's my Rosie," Charles said, smiling with the others. "I came to inform you that the king is healing not only from his lung illness but from his old disease, too."

"How'd that happen?" Rosie asked.

"I've been giving him a new potion I thought up," Charles said. "It has herbs and such to help his body heal itself. He seems to be rather clear-headed this morning."

"Well, aren't you just the clever one," Rosie said as she walked around the table to Charles. "What'd ya' do that for?"

"It's my job," Charles replied. "And, I may have another remedy to help others."

"Oh, well then, I guess that's okay," Rosie replied, setting pans of rolls in the oven. "Does that mean he's demanding young girls again to rape?"

"It does," Charles said. "I told him most of the young girls in the countryside have married and are not available. He yelled for a minute. He said to find someone and send them to him right away. I told him the snow had blocked many roads and pathways and that it would be many weeks until they were cleared. He was so angry he threw one of his boots at me. I ducked, of course. I suggested he look outside. When he did, he gasped at what he saw. He was looking out of the window that showed him the countryside, and all he could see were mountains of snow and smoke from chimneys buried in that snow. He grumbled for a bit, then dismissed me. Here I am."

"Wise ass," Rosie said, smiling at him. "Sit here and have some tea and scones."

"Thank you, my Rosie," Charles said.

"Do the knights know of this news about the king?" Rosie asked as she joined him.

"Harrison was waiting outside the king's chambers when I left. I told him everything I've just told you. He said he would tell the knights right away. Rosie, these berry scones are delicious."

"Everyone helped make these this morning," Rosie said, waving her hand to include the kitchen staff.

"Well done, everyone," Charles said.

The kitchen staff knew Charles was a good wizard and took care of him just as Rosie did.

It took almost a month for most of the snow to clear enough for travel and commerce to resume. It was now late January. The courtyards were clear, and the knights resumed sword practice. Everyone was happy to go out and about. Cabin fever had settled in weeks ago and all looked forward to the snow melting so they could get outside. The king was in good health, bellowing and hollering as he used to. He called for a city-wide proclamation on the first day of February. He demanded that all citizens appear unless they were tending to their businesses.

And, so, the citizens gathered on this first day of February. Dennison and three of the higher knights flanked the king. The others were in the courtyard below. The trumpets blared the gathering signal, and the courtyards and grounds surrounding the castle were filled with people. It was a cold day, but the sun was in full glory, so most were warm enough.

The High Chancellor called the gathering to order and said a prayer. Then, the king took his post at the edge of the balcony.

"Good citizens of Kerwyn, I am pleased to see you here. The remnants of the past storm are finally melting away, and we are back to business as usual."

A cheer was heard from the crowd. The king liked this.

"I am proclaiming the hunt for dragons to be undertaken in full force. I expect to see many dragon heads in my courtyard in the near future. A great reward will be paid to those that bring me the heads."

The crowd cheered at this, although they already knew this. The knights in the courtyard exchanged quick glances. The king seemed to think this was his first order concerning the hunting of dragons.

"We have been plagued by these monsters for a very long time. It's time we took control from them," the king shouted.

Most of the crowd cheered this statement, although many were puzzled by the king's behavior.

"I am pleased at your response," the king said. "I expect full cooperation from the good citizens of Kerwyn when the knights go on the hunt."

Everyone cheered this order as they loved their knights.

"So be it," the king said. He stepped down from his balcony riser and went back inside. He was exhausted.

"Bring me food and drink," he yelled at his manservant.

"I have it here for you, sire," the manservant replied as he set the tray on the king's table.

"Good work," the king replied as he ate his lunch. "Be gone with you. I'll call for you if I need you."

The manservant ran from the room, relieved that the king had not thrown his food across the room at him. Charles was waiting outside.

"He seems to be happy for the moment," the manservant said to Charles.

"I'm about to make sure he doesn't bother anyone for the rest of the day," Charles said. "I have his afternoon tonic here. Get some lunch."

"Thanks, Charles," the manservant said as Charles entered the king's chambers.

"Good speech, Your Highness," Charles said as he bowed before the king.

"I know," the king replied. "Tell the cook this chicken is delicious."

"I most certainly will," Charles replied. "Here is your tonic."

"Why must I keep taking this vile potion?" the king asked. "I am completely healed."

"You will if you want to stay that way," Charles said, holding the vial before the king.

"You mean to tell me I could get sick again if I don't drink this potion?" the king asked.

"Indeed," Charles replied." And we don't want you sick again. We need you well to lead the good citizens of Kerwyn in glory."

"Yes, we do," the king said. He drank the potion and made a face. "Fowl tasting stuff."

Charles took the empty vial from the king and smiled to himself.

"Is there anything else you need me for, sire?" Charles asked.

"Not at the moment," the king replied. "I'll need you to give a potion to the woman I fuck later. I want to make sure she is clean."

"Indeed," Charles said as the king yawned. "I will see to it."

"Yes, you will," the king said. "I need to lie down for a bit."

Charles helped the king get to his bed. The draught had made him a bit unsteady. Laudanum will do that to a body.

The king closed his eyes and was snoring as Charles left the room with the tray of empty dishes. He left them in the kitchen, smiling the whole time. Rosie saw this and winked at him.

That same night, Quintan and Angelique met in their secret room. The king had been dosed after supper and was oblivious to everything happening in the castle. Russell made sure the knights devoted to the king had projects to work on outside the castle until late in the night.

Angelique was waiting for Quintan. She ran to his arms when he arrived, and they settled into a long and lustful kiss. They explored each other's mouths with their tongues. Quintan felt for Angelique's breasts and played with them through her dress. This made Angelique moan. She pressed into Quintan and felt his hard dick pressing against her. He pressed against her even more. It took all his strength to pull away from her. He was about to explode.

"Oh my God," Quintan said as they settled at the table. "I fear we are going to make a mistake."

"We will not," Angelique replied. "I don't know how, but we will remain steadfast."

"I know," Quintan said as he reached for her hand and caressed it. "I think about you all the time."

"Me, too," Angelique replied, smiling at Quintan. "I've never felt like this before. It's all new to me."

"Me, too," Quintan said. "Although I have looked at some of the young girls as we've ridden through the villages. Some of them were quite lovely."

"I'll bet they were," Angelique sassed, laughing. "I've watched a few of the handsome knights and thought the same things."

"None of them are as handsome as me, are they?" Quintan teased her.

"Of course not," Angelique replied. "Although Harrison is ruggedly good-looking. Nice on the eyes. And Hugho, of course. Gorgeous!"

"You little vixen, you," Quintan said, pouting at her.

"None are as beautiful as my Quintan," Angelique said as she walked around the table and sat in his lap. She kissed him thoroughly, and he responded in kind.

Angelique ended the kiss and laid her head on Quintan's shoulder. "I like this."

"Me, too," Quintan said as he stroked her back. "What do you think of the king's latest order for us knights?"

Angelique sat back down and poured the tea as she replied, "He's mad. How can he not remember giving that order last year? I think he's lost a few marbles from his lung illness."

"We think the same thing," Quintan whispered back. "That's Harrison, Fred, and me. We only talk about such things between ourselves."

"Rosie says we should be very careful what we say," Angelique whispered. "She says someone is always around the corner."

"Rosie is right about that," Quintan replied. "That is why Fred and Harrison are keeping guard outside this room. They are on the stairs on either side. They will stop anyone from getting close to us. I trust them with my life."

"As do I," Angelique said. "Rosie, too."

"Rosie, indeed," Quintan said as he took a bite of the tea cake in front of him. "Did you make these, Miss Angelique?"

"I did," Angelique said. "Rosie says I'm becoming a great baker. She has me making most of the deserts these days."

"You are indeed a great baker," Quintan said. "What else does she have you doing?"

"She is teaching me how to make breads. There are a lot of them," Angelique explained. "The kneading of the dough takes a long time, and my arms get tired. They are getting stronger."

"I can feel that when we hug," Quintan said.

"Then, I'll keep working on the breads. I don't want to get weak," Angelique replied, looking a bit mischievous.

"Why, Miss Angelique, I do believe you have plans for us," Quintan said.

I believe I do," Angelique said, winking at Quintan.

Quintan stood up and walked over to Angelique. He pulled her to her feet and grabbed her around the waist. He backed them against the wall and pressed into her.

"Would those plans include this?" Quintan asked as he kissed her mouth and neck. He released her apron and unbuttoned the front of her dress so he could get to her breasts. He felt them through her camisole. They were soft and huge. He began teasing the nipples, and Angelique moaned deeply as Quintan started to kiss her neck and shoulders.

Angelique felt for his hard dick and began to play with it through his clothes. She felt it getting harder and hotter. All she wanted to do was strip him of his clothes and play with his dick. She wanted him to suck her breasts, too. She knew she had to pull away before things got out of hand.

"Oh, Quintan," Angelique said as she pulled away from him. "We are in trouble."

"We are indeed," Quintan said as they worked at catching their breath and calming down. "Let's drink some tea."

"Good idea," Angelique said.

They sat quietly for a few minutes. They looked at each other the whole time.

"Angelique, I need to say something to you," Quintan said quietly as he reached for her hand. "I am quite fond of you. No, it's more than that. I'm falling in love with you. That's what's happening to me."

"I'm falling in love with you," Angelique replied in a whisper.

"It is an amazing thing we have," Quintan said. "What do we do now?"

"Um, I guess we get to know each other more," Angelique answered.

"That's a good idea," Quintan said. "We know some about each other, but we don't know a lot of things. Do you want children, and how many? What are your thoughts about running the house and paying the bills? Who does that?"

"I do want children," Angelique replied. "Do you?"

"I do," Quintan said. "I love my sisters and don't know what life would have been like without them. They are a pain sometimes, but, mostly, we get along okay."

"Same with me," Angelique replied.

"As for running the house, I guess we would have to think about that. We'd have to figure out how and where we would live and what my job would be to bring money into the house," Quintan replied.

"I, too, could bring in money," Angelique said. "I am a great baker."

"Great idea," Quintan said. "It would seem we are already figuring things out. That is, if we were to marry and all."

"Well, yes, of course to that," Angelique said, blushing.

"No need to blush. I think we both know where we're headed with all of this," Quintan said. "I'll speak to Rosie about making this official. She will know the protocol for us."

"Yes, she will," Angelique said. "Including all the rules about proposing to me."

"Then you will consider marrying me?" Quintan asked.

"I most certainly will," Angelique replied. "I would have to choose between you and Harrison, of course."

"Oh, you tease," Quintan said, laughing with her.

They finished their tea and cakes and suddenly realized how late it was.

"We need to get along," Quintan said.

"We do," Angelique replied. "The night is upon us. I'll take these back to the kitchen after you leave."

Quintan held Angelique softly as they kissed good night.

"Sweet dreams, my sweet Angelique," Quintan said.

"Sweet dreams, my handsome Quintan," Angelique replied.

Quintan took his leave, smiling at Fred and Harrison. Fred and Harrison stayed on the landings until Angelique took her leave. Harrison followed her to the kitchen, smiling at Rosie.

"Well, did you behave?" Rosie asked quietly.

"It was very difficult, but yes, we did," Angelique answered. "Quintan will be speaking to you soon."

"And I will be thrilled to answer his questions," Rosie replied, hugging Angelique. "Now, let's get some sleep.

Harrison joined Quintan and Fred as they crossed the courtyard to the stables.

"Well?" Harrison asked.

"Not yet, but soon," Quintan replied. "Our secret always."

"Of course," Harrison replied, slapping Quintan on the back.

The castle settled for the night as Roman and Clarice watched over Quintan.

A week later, the knights rode out into the countryside, looking for dragons. The weather was cold, and it hadn't snowed since the storm in January. Dennison set the course of travel, heading to the far north of the kingdom. They were stopped about halfway there because there was still a great deal of snow covering everything. Dennison decided to ride southwest, and they camped not far from Quintan's home. He asked to go on and stay at home that night. Dennison granted his request, stating they would see him in the morning.

Quintan arrived just at supper time, to the surprise of his family and the village. Sarah was sent to Merlin and Feyanna's cottage to bring them to supper.

They had a grand time catching up on everything since Quintan's last visit. They talked about the storm, and the girls told their brother about the tunnels and the snow hill. He was thrilled to hear all of this. As they quieted down, his mother looked at him.

"Quintan, do you have something to share with us?" Glendianna asked.

"I do," Quintan said, looking at all of them. "I've met a young woman who I am very fond of."

"Did you ask her to marry you?" Margaret asked.

"Margaret, that is not proper for you to ask," Hamlen said.

Margaret quieted down and waited for Quintan to speak.

"No, sister, I have not," Quintan answered. "We barely know each other. I am interested in her, and we talk when we can."

"Where is she from, son?" Hamlen asked.

"I would rather not say anything more right now," Quintan replied. "We'll talk later."

Sarah was about to say something when her mother said, "Sarah. Margaret. Quintan's life is his own. He doesn't have to tell us about it. Please respect this."

"Yes, mother," the girls replied, looking disappointed.

"I will tell you that she is beautiful," Quintan said to appease his sisters.

"I would hope so," Sarah said. "I wouldn't want you to choose an ugly girl. You need someone beautiful and smart like you are."

"Thanks, little sister," Quintan said. "I appreciate your support."

They talked about the villagers, and Quintan told them why the knights were there.

"Haven't they figured out that the dragons are taken care of by The Special Magic?" Glendianna asked.

"Well, mother, talk about that topic is forbidden and punishable by death," Quintan said. "Some of us know and recognize The Special Magic, nonetheless. However, we are the king's servants and must obey his commands."

"You won't find any dragons to kill," Margaret said. "I know about these things. The dragons make themselves invisible to strangers."

"And how do you know about that?" Merlin asked, smiling.

"I just know these things," Margaret explained. "One minute, I don't know about them. Then, the next, I do."

"Sounds like you are a very wise young lady," Merlin replied, looking at Hamlen and nodding.

Hamlen and Merlin understood each other. It seemed Margaret was gifted with knowing about The Magic. Time would tell.

"It's time for us to get along," Feyanna said.

"I'll walk with you," Quintan said as they prepared to go out into the cold night. "Don't give me that face, you two. I'll be back to tuck you in just like always."

"You better be," Sarah said sternly.

As the three of them walked along the south road, Feyanna said, "You're in love."

"Yes, Feyanna, I am," Quintan replied.

"Will you marry her?" Merlin asked.

"Yes, I will," Quintan replied. "We need to be extremely careful. Rosie has been able to hide her from the king for a long time. But, with the king healed, he's demanding young girls again. The wizard told him they were married, and the storm had blocked the roads for everyone else. Now that the roads are cleared, he is screaming for sex. The wizard keeps him unconscious most of the time, but he's starting to refuse the potions. We need to protect Angelique as best we can."

"I'll set a protection grid around her this evening," Feyanna said. "The dragons are probably already keeping an eye on her."

"I know they are," Quintan said. "She was outside for only a second the other day, getting something for Rosie. It was next to the door. One of the guards saw her and was about to approach her when Roman and Clarice sent a shower of rocks down into the courtyard in front of the guard. He was quite surprised, and this gave her time to get back inside. She told Rosie about it, and Rosie told her not to go outside again during the day."

"That's terrible," Feyanna said. "That king needs to be something."

"I agree," Quintan said quietly.

"We can't interfere with his life from here, but we can protect her," Merlin said.

Just then, they heard a thud outside.

They opened the door to find Beau smiling at them.

"Of course it's you," Quintan said. "How are you, Beau?"

"Quite well, Quintan," Beau replied. "Penny and Q heard you were here and sent me to tell you they are healing quickly and have started flying about some. They are getting stronger every day. They send their love, of course."

"Splendid news. I send my love as well," Quintan said. "I can't wait to see them again."

"We all can't wait to see them again," Merlin said. "Any rogue dragons about these days, Beau?"

"Not yet," Beau replied. "They are staying in their caves for now. However, there are about six of them ready to cause trouble as soon as the weather warms. Springtime, most likely."

"Great! More trouble to worry about," Quintan said. "The king gave what he thought was a new order to kill all the dragons just a couple of weeks back. That's why we're riding throughout the countryside. The king thinks we're going to bring dragon heads to him. I truly believe he doesn't remember when we told him they vanish when the dragon dies. He won't want to hear that."

"He's an angry man," Feyanna said. "No good comes from anger."

"That's the truth," Quintan said. "Harrison has a way of talking to the king when asked questions. Dennison, the king's head knight, says things that get the king angry. Dennison makes sure the king is always angry about something. That way, the king favors Dennison, thinking Dennison agrees with everything the king says and does. I think that may be true in itself. Harrison, Fred, and I stay clear of Dennison whenever possible."

"Good tactic," Merlin said.

"I could cause a little trouble for this Dennison without him being aware of me," Beau offered, smiling.

"Not gonna happen, Beau," Merlin said, shaking his head at Beau.

"I was just offering as a good dragon should," Beau said.

"And we appreciate the offer," Feyanna said. "Now, behave yourself."

They laughed at Beau's antics.

"I could fly by and bother him," George offered.

"I could shoot my quills at him," Goldie added.

"Nice, you two," Merlin said, laughing. "Not today."

"Just saying," they both said at the same time.

"You two are definitely trouble," Feyanna said, laughing as well.

"Of course we are," Goldie said. "We're pure Magic."

"Well, that explains everything," Quintan said.

"How's Hugho doing?" Merlin asked.

"Quite well," Quintan replied. "He'll be here with all the others tomorrow so that you can ask him yourself."

"Nice way to divert the questions," Merlin said. "You're learning a lot at that castle."

"Yes, I am," Quintan said. "I've learned it's not always easy to do the right thing when ordered otherwise."

"A true statement and a difficult situation to be in," Merlin said.

"I do know that bullying people and killing them because you don't like the way they live is wrong. No one can convince me otherwise," Quintan said with strong conviction.

"You are very right about that," Feyanna said. "How do you balance the king's orders with your own morals?"

"Well, that seems to be an ongoing problem," Quintan said. "Three knights resigned their position for that reason alone. They quietly gave their notice to Dennison, and he immediately dismissed them before he told the king. He knew the king would order them beheaded for leaving his service. When Dennison did tell him, he ordered them beheaded, and Dennison informed him that they had run away like the cowards they were. The king proclaimed them enemies of the kingdom and to be killed when found. Of course, no one has or will kill them."

"That's a good point for Dennison," Merlin said. "He needs lots of good points to balance the evil things he's done for the king."

"For sure," Quintan said. "When servants quit their positions, we give them money and goods and get them as far away from the castle as possible. We have an underground network that gets them to other kingdoms so they can live safely. Dennison does not know about this."

"And he never should," Beau said. "We dragons will help as well."

"I'll be sure to let Fred and Harrison know. Thank you," Quintan said.

"It's late, and I must take my leave," Beau said as he backed away from the cottage home and spread his wings. "I'll be close by if any of you need me."

"Thanks, Beau," they all said as he lifted off and flew away.

"I hope dragons are in our lives for all eternity," Quintan said.

"Us, too," Feyanna replied.

"Well, I guess I'd better get back home," Quintan said. "My sisters are waiting for me to tuck them in."

"Hug them from us, too," Merlin said. "Be safe and well."

"Always, Master Merlin. Always," Quintan said as he hugged Merlin and Feyanna.

Quintan returned home a short time later to find his sisters waiting in the kitchen near the fire.

"You took a long time," Margaret said.

"We've been waiting for you forever," Sarah added.

"Well, then, let's get you tucked in warm and cozy," Quintan said. "Get your hot stones."

The girls grabbed their stones, wrapped them in the quilted bags, and ran to their beds in the loft.

"These are new," Quintan said. "Did you make them yourselves?"

"Yes, we did," Margaret said. "Mother showed us how."

"And we made new ones for Mother and Father," Sarah added.

"How are the crystals working out?" Quintan asked as the girls snuggled into their covers.

"Quite well," Sarah said. "They shine so brightly onto the snow that you would think it was morning."

"I never thought about that," Quintan said. "I'll have to look for that the next time it snows."

"Which will be in three days," Margaret said with authority.

"And how do you know that?" Quintan asked.

"I've been watching the clouds, and Master Merlin has been teaching me about the weather," Margaret replied. "He is very smart, our Merlin."

"Yes, he is," Quintan said, smiling at them. "You are becoming smarter and wiser every day. I'm proud of you for that."

"We're proud of you for protecting The Magic while you're working for a mean, nasty king that doesn't believe in it," Margaret said.

"I do think he believes in it," Quintan said. "I think he's scared of it because he can't control it. I think that's why he has all these weird rules."

"Brother, you are wiser than your years," Sarah said.

"Oh, my Sarah, you are so sweet," Quintan said as the two girls yawned deeply. "It's time to sleep."

"Will you be here when we wake up?" Margaret asked with her eyes closed.

"I most certainly will be," Quintan said as he leaned down, hugged and kissed her.

"That will be a good thing," Sarah said as he leaned down, hugged, and kissed her.

"May The Magic bless and keep you safe, my sisters," Quintan said.

He stood looking at them for a while as they slept. He loved them more than could ever be measured.

He went downstairs and found his parents sitting by the fire.

"Are they asleep, son?" Hamlen asked as Quintan sat between them.

"Indeed they are," Quintan replied. "I love them more than ever."

"We know," Glendianna said. "Now, tell us about Angelique. How did you meet?"

Quintan told his parents everything he could think of about Angelique and how Rosie was keeping her hidden from the king.

"I'm loving your Rosie more than ever now," Glendianna said with Hamlen nodding.

"Son, will you ask for her hand in marriage?" Hamlen asked.

"I will, Father," Quintan replied quietly. "There is a lot going on with the king right now, so I am going to wait. Rosie said we should wait until he's gone, or he'll rape her again and again and have me beheaded because I've kept her from him. He'd probably kill Rosie, too."

"That's horrible!" Glendianna said. "Just barbaric. He must be insane."

"Oh, most likely," Hamlen said. "I agree with Rosie in keeping silent about this. We won't say anything either and caution the girls about talking about Angelique to anyone."

"That's an excellent idea," Quintan said, agreeing with his parents.

"Time to get some sleep," Hamlen said as they walked toward their rooms.

"Good night, my son," Glendianna said as she held Quintan close for the longest time. "I love you dearly."

"I love more than you could ever know," Quintan said. "Both of you for taking me in. I will always be in your debt."

"My son," Hamlen said as he hugged Quintan. He had tears in his eyes.

The night came along, and the countryside slept peacefully. Feyanna felt the faintest shift of energy as she slept. She knew something was about to happen.

CHAPTER 19

Margaret had been right. The snow started again three days after the knights returned to the castle. This time, it fell straight down for two days. No wind. When it was over, the end of February arrived with five feet of snow all over the place. The king was not happy about this because he still hadn't had sex. He was possessed by the craving to have sex all the time. He hollered and bellowed as always, and everyone in the castle tried to stay far away from him.

Rosie had to hide Angelique a couple of times when the king suddenly appeared in the kitchen. Rosie and Angelique had practiced this very scenario. They planned well. Angelique was able to leave the kitchen both times because the king was heard yelling as he approached. Rosie made sure Angelique had a cloth over her face at all times to hide her youth.

Dennison had reported to the king two days before the snowfall that they had not found any dragons nor any dragon damage. He offered that the dragons were staying in their caves because of the snow and cold. The king didn't know any better. Dragons don't care how cold it is. They fly whenever they choose. The king ordered the knights out into the countryside again as soon as the spring weather arrived. Dennison said he would see to it.

The snow finally melted away by mid-March, and everyone was looking forward to spring. Now that the snow was gone, the king demanded that women be brought to him. Dennison and another of the king's devoted knights went into the city and returned with five women. All were sex workers. They were taken to Charles. He gave them draughts to clear any disease from their bodies. Well, that's what he told the king. He actually gave them potions to block the king's diseases.

Next, they were bathed and dressed in loose-fitting robes. They all knew how gross the king was and were prepared to please him. The gold they would receive was well worth putting up with the nasty ways of the king.

The king sent the maid on her way and told the women to take off their robes. They all had huge breasts, which he fondled as he walked by them. They were clean and had all their teeth. He instructed them to sit on his bed. He crawled between them and grabbed the one closest to him. He pushed her head down to his dick.

"Suck me hard, whore!" he yelled.

She did as he said. She began by licking his dick. It wasn't quite hard yet, but her licking made it harder. Next, she pulled the head of his dick into her mouth and squeezed it hard. The king moaned and began pushing into her mouth. She let him push for a minute. Then she grabbed his shaft and pumped hard. The king almost lost it. He pulled away from her and pushed her onto the floor.

"You did well," the king said. "You, and you, play with each other's tits. Lick and suck them. You play with their pussies. And, you, with the big cunt, lay here next to me so I can fuck you when I feel like it."

The women did as they were told and convinced the king that they were enjoying each other. The king told the woman lying next to him to sit up so he could suck her tits. He enjoyed sucking them and playing with her pussy. He was getting very excited watching the women suck each other's cunts. He finally couldn't wait another minute. He pushed one of the women onto her back and mounted her. He spread her legs with his and began ramming into her. He didn't care if he hurt her. He wanted a goof fuck.

"Your pussy is small, and I like that," the king said as he rammed into her again and again.

The women had been given a vinegar ointment to use on themselves so the king would think their pussies were small and tight. Charles had thought of everything. The king was getting tired, but he kept going. Finally, he hollered out as he climaxed and fell to the bed. He smothered the woman for a minute before rolling off. She lay there silent, not moving a muscle.

The king slept for a while and then woke up to find the naked woman on his bed.

"Go clean yourselves," the king ordered. "I want you all after the evening meal."

The women grabbed their robes and left the bedchamber quickly. A maid was waiting for them in the hall. She took them to a suite of rooms down the hall. Warm baths were waiting for them, and Rosie sent hearty meals to them as well.

All of the castle knew what was taking place in the king's chambers. It seemed that the king was back to being his horrible self again. He kept the women for five days, then dismissed them with the promised gold. All five were whisked away by the underground system to places far away.

The king sent his knights back out to find dragons. After two weeks, they returned, not finding any. Dennison suggested that the dragons were hiding from the hunters, knowing the king wanted them dead. This calmed the king for a while

It was the day before the Spring equinox, which the king forbade anyone to acknowledge, that all hell broke loose. It was late in the day when a cloud of dust was seen approaching the castle. Soldiers under a foreign king were riding hard straight at the castle. The lookouts on the parapets saw them killing anyone whom they rode past. The guards sounded the alarm, and the castle gates were closed, but not before a good many of the soldiers rode into the courtyard. The knights grabbed their swords and shields as the castle servants ran for cover in the castle.

The soldiers on the outside of the castle were trying to climb the walls, but the outer guards were fighting with them. Many of King Gorham's guards and the attacking soldiers were killed.

King Gorham was taken from his writing room to a secret hiding place deep within the castle. He would be kept there until the attack was over.

Quintan found himself in his first-ever real battle. This wasn't sword practice! He kept spinning around as more of the attacking knights ran at him. He killed one after the other for a long while. It was dark when one of the attacking knights set his sights on Quintan. Quintan saw him out of the corner of his eye just as the attacking knight swung his sword to attack. Quintan blocked the attempt, and the battle between the two commenced. They parlayed again and again, blocking each other's attempts to land their swords in each other's flesh. The attacking knight landed a blow across Quintan's right arm. Quintan twirled around to avoid another thrust and found himself against the castle wall. The attacking knight smiled as he aimed his sword at Quintan's chest.

In a quick second, Quintan grabbed his tiny crystal dragon from his trouser pocket and held it, pointing to the sky. In an instant, Clarice and Roman saw this and immediately came to life. They blew black smoke at the attacking knight, blinding him for a few seconds. It was just what Quintan needed. The smoke did not cover him. He swung his sword in a mighty arc and plunged it into the other knight's chest between his chainmail pieces. Quintan's sword hit home. The attacking knight looked surprised as his lifeblood rapidly flowed from his chest, pooling on the ground. He fell dead, and Quintan breathed for only a moment.

Quintan watched as Harrison swung his sword and slashed two knights across their bellies. They both bleed profusely and fell dead from their wounds. Fred was being chased by an attacking knight. Fred must have had a plan because as soon as the knight ran across the front of the smithy's shop, Fred tripped him, making him fall on his face. Fred plunged his sword into the knight's back and through to his heart. The attacking knight was dead in an instant.

Harrison, Fred, and Quintan all saw King Walter kill Dennison. They were fighting, and King Walter got close enough to Dennison to grab his arm and swing him to the ground. King Walter smiled as he drove the sword through Dennison's gut, watching him scream in pain. He then thrust his sword and knife into Dennison's chest, killing him instantly. King Walter laughed out loud as he fought more knights.

There were bodies littered all over the place. Some had their heads cut off. Others had massive gaping wounds across their bellies and backs. One attacking knight had his hand cut off. It was lying next to him. He saw it as he died. King Gorham's knights finally got the upper hand and began to round up the attacking king and his knights. The guards marched them to the dungeon. The remaining knights gathered in the middle of the courtyard, looking at the devastation. It was a horrible scene. The guards called on Charles and his helpers to gather the fallen knights and prepare them for a religious service. The attacking dead knights were taken out into a field and burned in a great bonfire.

The knights met with the king in his meeting hall.

"Who was the king that attacked me?" Gorham yelled.

"It was King Walter from the southernmost area of the continent, known as the Isles of Chalk," Harrison replied.

"Where is he?" Gorham asked.

"He and the remaining soldiers are in the dungeon awaiting your orders."

"Why are you telling me this? Where is Dennison and the other knights?" Gorham asked.

A moment of silence was felt before Harrison answered with, "They were killed defending you, Your Highness," Harrison said.

The king became furious and agitated.

"Who killed Dennison?" the king asked.

"King Walter," Harrison replied.

"Kill them all. Behead every last one of them. Save the king for last," Gorham said. "Make it happen tomorrow morning. The king will be beheaded at noon."

"Yes, Sire," Harrison said as he motioned for the knights to leave.

"Harrison, I place you in charge of the knights," King Gorham said.

"I will serve you with humility and honor, Your Highness," Harrison replied, bowing low.

"We will have a service for the knights tomorrow during morning prayers," the king said. "Tell the high chancellor and Charles and everyone else."

The king looked sad.

"Yes, sire, Immediately," Harrison said.

The knights met in their eating hall to make plans. Rosie and the kitchen servants brought them food and drink.

"I'm sad that your fellow knights have met their God," Rosie said. "The whole castle is."

"Thanks, Rosie," Harrison said, giving her shoulders a hug. "Some of the outer guards gave their lives as well. We'll be having a service for them at morning prayers."

"Thanks for telling me," Rosie said. "I'll spread the word. "I'm here for all of you."

"We love you, Rosie," the knights said as she left.

"Harrison," Quintan asked as he and Fred walked quietly away. "Why the attack?"

"Rumor has it that King Walter was told Gorham was a lunatic and demented, and overtaking him would be easy. Guess their sources didn't get the latest update."

"How could they have known? The snows have kept everyone isolated until just recently," Fred said. "Senseless slaughter."

"It usually is," Quintan said. "The greed for power is a force to be reckoned with."

"When did you get all wise and knowing?" Fred asked.

"I've seen it first hand as a child. My family was slaughtered by greedy men," Quintan quietly replied.

"Oh my god! I'm so sorry," Harrison said. "I thought your family in the village was your original family."

"No. I was taken there by benevolent and kind strangers and given to Hamlen and Glendianna. They are my second family, and I love them more than anything. Even my pesky sisters."

"I hear that," Fred said. "How wonderful for you."

"Yes, it has been," Quintan said as he looked up into the night sky and saw a shooting star. "Beautiful."

"I love seeing those," Harrison said. "It's so rare to see one. Let's decide this is a good omen for the immediate future."

"Agreed," Fred and Quintan said at the same time.

"Let's secure the grounds and get some sleep. We all have sentry watch throughout the night," Harrison said.

The night was quiet as the castle was guarded inside and out.

At sunrise, the morning prayers were said, and the service for the knights and guards followed. The castle chapel was packed, and more people stood in the courtyards and outside the castle. It only lasted a short time. Folks went on about their business in a quiet and subdued manner waiting for the beheadings. They began at ten, and all the soldiers were dead by noon. King Walter had been forced to watch each of his soldiers die.

Five minutes before noon, the guards brought King Walter to the shopping block mound. He looked at King Gorham with hate in his eyes.

"Do you wish to beg for your life?" King Gorham asked, laughing loudly.

"No, I do not," King Walter replied.

He was knocked to his knees, and his head was set on the block.

"May you rot in hell for all the atrocities you have forced on good people," King Walter said.

King Gorham gave the signal, and the ax man felled the ax. As King Walter's head fell into the basket and his lifeblood flowed out onto the chopping block, a flock of black ravens swarmed around King Gorham. He collapsed onto the balcony floor in front of everyone. The guards and knights near him grabbed him and carried him to his bed. Charles was called for and spent a great deal of time over the king. King Gorham finally opened his eyes and asked what the hell was going on.

One of the guards went back out to the balcony and told the crowd the king was doing well. He just needed food and drinks, and the wizard was caring for him.

They raised a quiet cheer for the king and left the courtyard.

Charles asked everyone to leave the bedchamber except Harrison.

Fred and Quintan stayed at the closed door, listening as Harrison had suggested they do.

"Your Highness, you collapsed when King Walter was beheaded," Charles explained. "We brought you in here right away, and now you're awake."

"I remember that," King Gorham said, sitting up. "He deserved even more torture before he died."

"Are you in need of food, sire?" Charles asked. "Rosie sent a tray up a moment ago."

"Yes, thank you, Charles," King Gorham said. "Would you bring it to me? I don't want to fall again."

Harrison carried the tray to the king's bedside as Charles set the small table across his lap. The king ate his lunch with Charles and Harrison watching over him.

"I am tired," King Gorham said. "Maybe I'm not as well healed as I thought I was. That would be your fault, Charles."

"I agree," Charles said as he held a vial of liquid before the king. "This has many healing herbs in it. I suggest you drink it all so you will not feel tired anymore."

"As you wish it, "King Gorham said. "Your potions have healed me quite well since the first winter storm."

The king drank the potion and handed the vial back to Charles.

"Now, leave me the two of you," the king said. "I have many new laws to go over."

"Yes, sire," Harrison said as he and Charles left.

Harrison walked outside into a mostly empty courtyard.

"Is he still delusional, Charles?" Harrison asked quietly.

"I believe he is," Charles replied. "He has his moments of clarity, but not many. I suspect the disease is still ravaging his mind."

"I thought it might be with him ordering all dragons killed. He was giving the order as if he had never said it before. It was quite strange," Harrison said.

"We'll keep a close eye on him," Charles said. "I do need some lunch. Let's go visit Rosie."

Harrison and Charles walked into Rosie's kitchen as the other knights were settling in their hall.

"I see you made it here," Rosie said. "I was wondering if the king was going to keep you with him all afternoon."

"No, Rosie," Harrison said. "Even he wants us to eat so we can protect him at all times."

"Besides, he's busy writing new laws," Charles said. "That's what he told us."

"New laws, my ass," Rosie replied. "We don't need any more of his laws around here. Now, get into the hall so we can feed ya."

"Yes, Ma'am," Harrison replied as he and Charles joined the others.

The rest of the day went along as usual. It's what the night brought that will never be forgotten.

It was at the stroke of midnight that King Gorham was lifted off his bed and crashed to the floor. He woke up screaming in pain. He looked around but didn't see anyone or anything that could have thrown him to the floor. He sat there for a few minutes before getting up. He was in pain and just wanted to get into his bed.

As he settled against his pillows, a black shadow fell across him. He could see right through the shadow and was terrified of it. He tried to call for his guard, but he couldn't speak. He had no voice, and he couldn't move a muscle.

"It is time," the black shadow said as it morphed into a terrifying creature.

It was iridescent black, with bright red-orange eyes that glowed with a piercing light. It had claws for fingers and smelled hideous, like rotting flesh, which even maggots avoided. Gorham would be puking his guts out right now if he could move.

More dark shadows began to appear and morph into the same hideous creature, filling the room.

"You want to know why we're here?" the largest creature said. "Oh, I can read your thoughts. Why won't I let you speak? You'll only scream for help; then we'll have to kill those humans as well."

The king looked at the creature with cold fear on his face.

"Yes, Gorham, we've come for you," the creature said. "You promised your soul to The Dark Force. You agreed to this when it made you king. The Dark Force gave you everything you asked for and more. Diseases and sickness are our specialties."

The king began to weep silently. The creature gave him his voice back.

"Why are you doing this to me," the king asked.

"Why not?" the creature replied as he ran one of his claws along the king's arm, ripping the skin.

"What do you want now?" the king asked as he watched his blood flow from his arm.

"We are here to remind you of our pact," the creature said.

"It's for real? You're going to take my soul?" the king said in disbelief.

"We are, in due time," the creature replied. "This is just a subtle reminder of that pact. For now, we leave you with this."

The creatures covered the king and ran their claws all along his body, cutting his skin. They played with his dick making him so hard it hurt. He cried out, and they just kept torturing him. His dick finally exploded, making him puke all over himself.

"Let that be a reminder of who controls you!" the creature said. "We're watching you!"

They all vanished in an instant. King Gorham lay there in his bed, bleeding. It was just little trickles. He didn't have the strength to move. The bleeding finally stopped. He was horrified. He didn't sleep the whole night long. He finally got up at sunrise, washed himself, and called for his manservant.

"Don't say a word," the king said. "I need clean bedclothes right away."

The manservant nodded and stripped the bed, taking the filthy sheets with him. A few minutes later, two chambermaids arrived and redressed his bed. They were told not to look at the king They didn't. They left quickly, and the manservant entered the room.

"Get the wizard up here now!" the king yelled.

The manservant ran to Charles's chambers and burst in, scared crazy.

"What happened to you?" Charles asked.

"Oh my god! The king looks like he's been clawed by vultures," the manservant said. "His bedclothes were all bloody. It looks like he's been fighting with a bunch of cats, and it looks like he puked all over the place. He wants you now."

Charles was surprised to hear this.

"Stay away from him," Charles ordered. "I'll take care of him for the day."

"Glady, and thanks," the manservant said.

"Tell Rosie I'll need some herbal tea for healing cuts. Ask her to bring it herself to the door and knock. I'll take it from her."

"Yes, wizard," the manservant said. "Right away."

"What the hell has the king got himself into now?" Charles said under his breath as he gathered his things and set out for the king's bedchamber.

The manservant entered the kitchen and went right over to Rosie.

"Rosie, Charles has asked that you brew an herbal tea for healing cuts. Please bring it yourself to the king's chambers. Do not enter the room. Knock on the door, and Charles will take the tray from you."

"Thanks, I'd do just that," Rosie said, looking at the manservant.

"You sit down," Rosie said. "Give him some chamomile tea and a scone. He needs some nourishment."

"Thanks, Rosie," the manservant said as he fell into a chair at the kitchen table.

Charles arrived as the chambermaids were leaving. The king was sitting in his chair by the table.

"What's happened here?" Charles said as he looked over the king and cared for his cuts.

"Don't ask," the king replied. "Don't ask."

Charles continued to care for the king. A knock was heard and Charles found Rosie at the door with the tea.

"Thanks," he said as he took the tray and closed the door.

Rosie returned to the kitchen and found Quintan there. He was eating a cookie from a freshly made batch.

"Young Quintan, is that your breakfast?" Rosie said.

"Just getting warmed up, Rosie," Quintan replied.

"Sit here this morning, and I'll fetch you your breakfast," Rosie said.

Quintan looked around and found Angelique working in the corner. She saw him and nodded. He returned the nod.

"Enjoy your meal," Rosie said, winking at him.

"Thanks, my Rosie," Quintan said.

Quintan watched everyone in the kitchen as they prepared and served breakfast to the knights and guards. It was a busy time. Quintan stayed a long while, hoping the bustle would calm down. It finally did, and he nodded to Rosie to follow him.

They walked along the wall to a place where they could see if anyone was listening.

"Can we meet? Do you think it's safe?" Quintan whispered.

"Not today," Rosie said. "Something is happening with the king, and it's not good. We'll have to wait a couple of days."

"Okay," Quintan said. "Hug her for me."

"I will," Rosie said as a guard came by.

"Rosie," Russell said, "Breakfast was scrumptious. Thanks for taking such good care of me."

"Me, too," Quintan added.

"I take care of my boys that take care of our own," Rosie said.

"And that's why we love ya," Russell said as he twirled Rosie around the corridor.

"So, it's a dance you're wanting, is it?" Rosie said, laughing.

"It is," Russell replied. "A week from now, my girl."

"As always," Rosie said. "I'll be waiting for ya."

Russell smiled as he went on down the hall to the courtyard door.

"What's he talking about, Rosie?" Quintan asked.

"We have a servant's party the week before the Spring Solstice. We call it the Spring celebration," Rosie said. "The king doesn't like the old ways, so we gave it a new name. We hold it in the courtyard and the knight's hall. There's food, drink, dancing, and fun. All the servants are invited including the knights. Now that Dennison and his few are gone, we can have a regular celebration. You have to come, too."

"Will you allow her to be there?" Quintan asked.

"No. She must remain hidden," Rosie said. "That's why I've arranged for the two of you to meet in my quarters when the celebration is going strong."

"I love ya, my Rosie," Quintan said as he lifted her and spun around with her. "You'll be saving a dance for me, will you?"

"I most certainly will," Rosie said as Quintan set her down.

"That will be most enjoyable," Quintan said.

"Now, go one with you," Rosie said, fixing her hair. "I have a great many things to do."

Rosie returned to the kitchen, where everyone was talking about the celebration.

Quintan joined the knights for their daily practice, and they talked about the celebration, too. As a matter of fact, all the castle was talking about that special day.

The attack on the king had terrified him beyond common sense. He was sure his enemies had planned the attack, and he was convinced that another kingdom would try to take over his kingdom soon. He was healing quickly. He hadn't let anyone into his chambers except his manservant and Charles. He figured that in another couple of days, he'd be able to walk around the castle without anyone noticing his scars. While he kept to his chambers, he continued to create new laws. He would have them read to the people right after the celebration.

The king was still obsessed with having sex all the time. He had ordered one of the guards, a new guy, to report to him during the celebration. He wanted all the young girls brought to him so he could fuck them.

Rosie started roasting meats and vegetables two days before the celebration. The guards had set up two roasting pits: one for a lamb and the other for a hog. The knights were busy practicing their fighting skills in the morning. The afternoon of the day before the celebration, the knights were found setting up their area for the musicians and the dancing. The knight's hall would be used for staging the food and drinks. Rosie had plenty of help with bringing the food and such out into the other courtyard near the blacksmith's shop. He was burning wood and coal to make charcoal to keep the food warm.

Throughout the days before the celebration, you could hear music playing all around the castle. Many of the servants, guards, and knights played instruments. As different groups got together, you could hear drums, wood flutes, mandolins, lyres, and tambourines. The king heard the music as well and didn't mind it. It even helped him come up with the crazy laws he was writing.

Two nights before the celebration, Angelique was walking along one of the hallways near the kitchen. It was past sundown, and she was gathering herbs for Rosie from one of the pantries. She had placed all she needed in her basket and had just stepped through the pantry door into the hallway when one of the guards blocked her way. He was an older guard. She had seen him a time or two when she was looking through the kitchen windows. She had her face covered as Rosie had ordered.

"You, there, take off that face covering," the guard ordered as he stepped right in front of Angelique.

"I'm sorry, guard, but I cannot," Angelique replied.

"And why is that?" the guard said as he stepped closer.

"I have pox on my face and do not wish to spread it," Angelique replied, looking down.

"No bother. It's not your face I'm after," the guard said as he took the basket from her and dropped it on the floor.

The guard loosened his clothes and bared his dick. It was hard and standing right up. The guard reached for Angelique's apron and ripped it from her body.

"Do not do this," Angelique cried.

"You can't do a thing about it," the guard said. "I take what I want, and I want to fuck you."

"I beg of you, sir, do not touch me," Angelique said.

The guard tried to grab the front of her dress and tear it down, but something strange began to happen.

As the guard watched, Angelique grew taller and broader. In an instant, she had morphed into a very large creature. She had blue skin, three long fingers on each hand, and her ears had disappeared altogether. She had no hair anywhere on her naked body. Her eyes were almond-shaped and black, and she had long eyelashes, too. The guard stepped back and stared at the creature.

"What the hell is going on here?" he yelled.

"Keep your mouth quiet," Angelique said.

"Where in hell did you come from?" the guard yelled, trying to take his sword from its sheath.

Angelique waved her hand across his body, paralyzing him.

"I told you to be quiet," Angelique said. "I asked you not to touch me. You refused. I asked a second time. You refused. Now you will be punished for trying to rape me."

The guard looked at Angelique. She waved her hand across his throat so he could speak.

"What did you do to yourself? This is not real," the guard said.

"It is very real," Angelique answered. "We try not to interfere with you humans. You are a vicious and mean creation. Some of you are kind and benevolent, but not all of you. Especially you. You terrorize the common people with threats and rape. You take their food and money for yourself. We know this is part of the cosmic plan. However, when you decided to attack me, you crossed the line."

"You sound like the kitchen maid, but you don't look like her," the guard said, puzzled.

"Not everything you see is as it truly is," Angelique said.

Angelique waved her hand across the guard's body as she morphed back into her human form.

"You are mine, now," the guard said as he grabbed her.

"You had your chance to change," Angelique said. "You choose not to."

"What are you going to do about that?" the guard asked as he grabbed for her breast.

In one swift move, Angelique wrapped her arm around the guard's neck and snapped it. He was instantly dead. She let him fall to the floor, picked up her basket, secured her apron, and returned to the kitchen, where she gave the herbs to Rosie.

"You found them all," Rosie said.

"They were right where you said they would be," Angelique replied.

"Let's get the dough rising overnight," Rosie said. "We have a great deal of baking to do in the morning."

Rosie, Angelique, and one of the kitchen maids mixed many different types of yeast dough and had the work table completely covered within an hour. Rosie set the fires in the three fireplaces so there would be heat to keep the dough rising until morning.

"Sleep well," Rosie said as they went to their quarters.

The dead guard would be found in the morning when the usual guard patrol walked through the castle. Angelique slept well that night.

Rosie's kitchen was bustling long before dawn the next morning. Angelique and Rosie arrived just at sunrise. The other kitchen staff were preparing breakfast for the castle.

"Ladies, we have a great deal to do today," Rosie said as she tied on her apron. "Russell is bringing us more wood so we can keep the meats and vegetables roasting slowly and begin the baking. Good morning, Russell."

"Good morning, Rosie and everyone," Russell replied as he placed wood near the three fireplaces. "It smells heavenly in here."

"Thanks, Russell, we appreciate you telling us that," Rosie said.

"Rosie, could we talk outside for a minute?" Russell said.

Angelique saw the look he gave Rosie. She knew they had found the dead guard.

Rosie followed Russell out into the courtyard near the blacksmith's shop.

"What's the matter, Russell?" Rosie asked as she warmed herself by the smithy's fire.

"We found a dead guard on the kitchen stairs this morning. His neck had been snapped," Russell said. "He was one of the older guards that had been causing a bit of trouble with the servants and city folk."

"I know the one," Rosie said. "He was a troublemaker. I wonder who did it?"

"It had to be a very strong person," Russell said. "He was a big man. Did you hear anything last night?"

"No, Russell. We were in the kitchen well into the night preparing bread dough for this morning. One of the kitchen maids went to the pantry in that hallway last night and didn't see anything. She would have been very upset if she had," Rosie replied.

"Well, I guess we'll never know," Russel said as he walked Rosie back to the door. "Get inside and get warm. I'll be by for breakfast in a bit."

"Thanks for telling me about this," Rosie said. "I'll have breakfast ready in no time."

Russell went over to the knight's courtyard to report the death. None of them knew anything about it.

"Wonder what he was doing in that part of the castle?" Harrison asked. "His area to patrol is closer to the king's chambers."

"I wonder," Fred said, looking at Quintan and Harrison.

"Let's walk," Harrison said to Fred and Quintan.

When the three of them were away from everyone, Fred said, "I've seen him eyeing the kitchen maids. I think we all know what he was doing there."

"Most likely," Harrison replied. "I don't wish anyone harm or death, but I will say I'm not surprised. He was a bully and always after the girls."

"I found him bothering one of the vegetable vendors the other day," Quintan said. "He was trying to take the vendor's pay from the king. I put a stop to it and warned him to leave the townspeople alone. He was angry as he walked away."

"I've had to warn him about leaving the women alone," Harrison said. "Now, we won't have him to worry about. I'll find a new guard this morning. I'll let you know who he is."

The knights gathered in their hall for breakfast. Rosie told the kitchen staff about the dead guard.

Quintan stopped in the kitchen on his way to the hall.

"Good morning, everyone," he called out.

The kitchen staff replied likewise.

"Rosie, are you all okay here?" Quintan asked as she walked over to him.

"Yes, we are," Rosie replied, knowing who he was asking about. "Now, get yourself into the hall. Breakfast is waiting."

Quintan winked at Rosie and left the kitchen. He caught a glimpse of Angelique as he walked across the hall to the knight's room. She smiled and went to the kitchen, replacing her face cloth.

The day of the celebration dawned clear and a bit chilly. The castle was abuzz with anticipation. Rosie's crew had everything ready. The guards had set the lamb and hog on their spits the day before, and you could smell the roasting meat all over the castle and countryside. The bonfires were set in the middle of the courtyards, and tables were ready to receive the food near the smithy's shop.

Work was completed by suppertime, and the celebration got underway. The king's meal was brought to him as usual, and Charles kept an eye on him until the draught he gave him took effect. Charles had dosed the king with a bit of opium to make sure he would be quiet during the celebration.

Folks gathered around the food tables and helped themselves to Rosie's creations. The lamb and hog had been taken off their spits and placed on platters for all to enjoy. Everyone sat with everyone. They were all equal tonight.

"Gentlemen," Quintan called out. "This lamb is fantastic! Great job with the roasting. I'll have to learn your technique."

"Quintan, it's a secret," one of the guards replied. "Rosie's secret herbal blend makes it so mouth-watering delicious."

This made everyone laugh as they all knew how the lamb and hog were prepared.

"I have no doubt about that," Quintan replied.

Folks kept eating and sharing news of the day. It was about dusk when you could hear the musicians begin to warm up. Folks moved into the courtyard set up for dancing and waited for the musicians to be ready. A signal was given, and the music began. An old folk song was the first thing played. Folks danced and sang along, enjoying themselves.

Rosie grabbed Quintan, and they danced through the next two songs. Russell asked Rosie to dance with him, and Quintan bowed and stepped aside. Quintan watched Rosie and smiled. He was glad she was taking time to enjoy the evening. The knights danced with everyone that night, enjoying the camaraderie and light-hearted flirting that was taking place.

The musicians took a break, and everyone talked, ate, and drank for a while. When the music began again, Rosie looked over at Quintan and smiled. That was the signal for him to make his way to the hallway next to the kitchen. It took a few minutes to get there, and when he arrived, Rosie was waiting for him. She nodded, and he left by the back staircase. He knew where he was going.

Angelique was waiting for him. As soon as he closed the door, they wrapped their arms around each other and fell into a deep and sensuous kiss. Their tongues danced around each other for the longest time. They explored each other's bodies through their clothes and moaned and gasped as they found each other's hot spots.

They finally stepped away from each other, breathing heavily.

"Quintan, this is crazy," Angelique said. "I can't seem to get enough of you."

"I feel the same way," Quintan said. "Let's sit and talk for a minute."

Rosie had left them tea and cakes on her small table. They enjoyed them as they talked.

"I told my parents about you," Quintan said. "They're very happy we met and can't wait to meet you. I told them it would be a long while since the king is crazy about taking young girls to his bed. I told them Rosie keeps you hidden. My mother was angry and horrified. My father liked the idea of hiding you. He thinks Rosie is great."

"She is," Angelique said. "I know we have to wait until the king isn't the king anymore. I was hoping he would die from his disease. But, Charles seems to have cured him."

"Charles thinks the disease is being quiet right now," Quintan said. "He told Rosie and me that the king still has moments when he doesn't remember the most common things. I don't wish him dead at all. I just wish he would leave the throne and someone with a more kind attitude would become king."

"Me, too," Angelique said. "It's becoming very difficult for us to find time to be together. The king wanders the castle whenever he feels like it. Rosie is doing a great job keeping me hidden from him. He showed up in the kitchen a few days ago without any warning. He wasn't hollering about anything. He just showed up. Thank the gods and goddesses, I was near the outer door. I slipped out and heard the king ask Rosie who I was. She said one of the old women who took the garbage out. He was okay with that explanation. Rosie was rather stern when she said it, so I think he knew not to ask about me, or shall we say, the old woman again."

"That must have been scary for you," Quintan said, taking her hand in his. "I wish I could have helped you."

"No way, good knight," Angelique replied. "We don't want anyone to see us together."

"That's true," Quintan said. "Sparks fly around us for sure."

"Yes, they do, and lovely sparks they are," Angelique replied, laughing with Quintan.

"I suppose it's time for me to get back to the celebration," Quintan said.

"It is," Angelique said as they wrapped themselves around each other and spent a while kissing and saying goodnight.

Quintan left Rosie's room and was back outside by the time Angelique got to her room.

Rosie saw Quintan return and smiled and winked at him. He winked back. Harrison saw this and knew something was up between the two of them. He felt he shouldn't ask and that whatever it was, it was a good thing. One of the chambermaids took Harrison's arm and led him to the dance floor. Quintan watched as they flirted and danced with the others.

Russell was watching Rosie and Quintan as well. He knew something was going on and decided he would make sure no one bothered either of them. He had a good feeling about Quintan. He was a good knight and a great swordsman.

An old ballad began to play, and everyone stood in a circle around the musicians and sang along. The harmonies were heavenly, and when it was over, there was a bit of absolute silence in the courtyard.

"We're going to play one more for you," the mandolin player said. "Be sure to grab a partner for this one and enjoy the story of the dance."

The music started, and Quintan found himself being taken to the dance floor by one of Rosie's assistant cooks. She was the age of his mother, and they enjoyed the dance. It told the story of a young couple who married, raised their family, and left the earth in their old age, happy and content. Partners were changed a couple of times, but as the pattern worked itself around, Quintan and his first partner ended the dance together. The men bowed, and the ladies curtsied.

A cheer went up for the musicians, and someone added Rosie to the cheer, and it went on for a few more minutes. Folks began to clear things from the courtyard, and a short while later, even the fires were quenched. Good nights were heard all around as the castle began to settle for the few hours that remained of the night.

The king was unconscious in his opium dreams. He hadn't heard a thing all night long.

Clarice and Roman enjoyed the festivities from their view up on the parapets. The sky was quiet that night as everyone celebrated.

The next day, the castle got back to business as usual. The king was relatively happy. Charles thought it might be due to the opium dreams he had had. He figured the king dreamed of an orgy, and when he awoke, he was sure it had happened. He was so content he didn't throw anything at his manservant that morning. The manservant was just as happy as the king.

Life was going along as usual. The knights practiced their fighting techniques. The citizens of Kerwyn took care of trade and commerce. The castle staff performed their duties as expected.

The villagers in Hamlen and Glenndianna's village were all talking about the spring planting. Although the Solstice Celebration was forbidden, the village celebrated it in its own way. It looked like they were preparing their fields for planting when, in reality, they were offering prayers and herbs to the gods and goddesses. They thanked them for the past year's harvest and asked for a good harvest this year. Foods were shared amongst the houses, and the crystals kept the fields and houses lit all night, as was customary. A bonfire had been created as well. Anyone questioned about this would answer that the fire was lit to keep the women and children warm while the fields were prepared. They were never asked.

Feyanna wasn't the only one who had felt the slight energy shift. The new herbalist who lived a bit to the east of Kerwyn had felt it, too. The local folks liked her. She was kind and caring. She never turned anyone away. She bartered for services she needed, and this made her liked by most. She was a practitioner of The Old Magic, although she never said so out loud. She followed the religious rules of King Gorham and attended services every Sunday as ordered.

She called herself Lylia. Lylia knew something was stirring in the world of The Magic. She felt the energy shift the same night that Feyanna did. Lylia knew to just wait and be mindful of what was happening each day. She had seen the flying disks with the others and just smiled to herself. She believed in life forms from other stars and planets. She liked seeing the disks that day.

People ran to her in great fear, asking for her guidance. She had to be very careful of her answers. She calmed them and said she didn't think God would send flying disks to do his bidding. That seemed rather beneath him. She offered that they were enemies from far, far away who knew so much more than they did. After all, she would say, our people aren't the only ones on this planet. We've been told that. Let's not worry about them, she would say when she finished. Folks agreed with her and went on about their day. Lylia was a sage woman.

Feyanna was sitting in the meadow a few days later when Merlin came upon her. It was the middle of April, and the weather had begun to get warmer.

"Feyanna, I didn't know you were out here," Merlin said. "You are so very quiet this morning."

"The energy is shifting," Feyanna said quietly. "It started a few weeks ago. Very calmly, but it's there."

"I felt it last week," Merlin said as he sat beside her. "What are your thoughts?"

"I know nothing will happen until Penny and Q return to us," Feyanna said. "They are needed for the next phase of time here."

"Agreed," Merlin said. "That's all I'm getting right now."

"Me, too," Feyanna said. "I just wanted to sit here and enjoy the meadow."

"I suspect you are right," Merlin said. "I'll sit here quietly, too."

They stayed in the meadow for a long, long while.

The Spring planting season was on the land. The next few weeks found the farmers busy planting their fields. Everyone in the villages helped. There were a couple of days of light rain, which everyone was thankful for. All in all, the planting season went along without any problems.

It was in late May that trouble began to brew. The rogue dragons decided it was time to attack anything and everything they could see. They had been in their cave for a long while and were ready for trouble. The first warning was seen at dusk one evening. Some of the villagers were securing their livestock for the night when they saw a great shadow pass over them. When they looked up, they saw two dragons flying to the north. The villagers waited in their fields to see if the dragons would return. The dragons did not come back that night.

The villagers went around the village, telling everyone what they had seen. This put the whole area on alert. The winter had been free of dragons, and the villagers were happy about that. But now, with this sighting, they were once again scared of what might happen. Their village was small, with only ten families. It was a routine stop for travelers seeking food and rest.

The next night, the villagers had sentries watching the sky. Just at dusk again, two dragons were spotted flying right at the village. The sentries rang the warning bells, and everyone took cover. The dragons blew fire at the village homes and burned them all to the ground. The dragons circled around, and they targeted the outbuildings next. These, too, burned to the ground with the animals inside. Not a soul survived the attack. The dragons were ecstatic with the outcome. They flew back to their cave and settled for the night.

Three days later, in the last week of May, a farmer stood at the southern gate of the castle in Kerwyn, asking permission to enter.

"What is your business here, farmer?" Russell asked.

Harrison and Quintan were standing next to Russell.

"Guard, sir, there has been a dragon attack on a village near my home. I need to report this to the knight," the farmer replied.

Harrison nodded to Russell, and the gate was opened for the farmer to enter.

"Thank you, guard," the farmer said as he spotted Harrison and Quintan.

"Come with us, farmer," Harrison said as they walked over to a table by the smithy's shop. "Where is the village, and what happened to it?"

Quintan gave the farmer a dipper of cold water.

"Thank you, sir knight. This is very kind of you," the farmer replied as he finished the water. "I live just a bit west of the village in the north country. I rode over to the village to barter eggs for my family as I usually do. When I got there, the whole village was burned to the ground. Not one building was left standing. There were partial animal carcasses near the outbuildings. I called out for the farmer and anyone else I knew. Not a soul returned my call. I walked closer to where the cottages had been and saw only ashes.

"I rode back home, and my family and I rode around to the other farmers to come help us. We buried the ashes and said prayers for their souls."

"How do you know it was dragons that did this?" Quintan asked as he looked up at the parapets where Roman and Clarice were sitting. They showed a quick shadow of themselves.

"I found these in the ashes," the farmer said as he showed the five black dragon scales he had found.

"These are indeed dragon scales," Harrison said as he and Quintan took them and looked them over. They gave them back to the farmer.

"I will say that the rogue dragons are on the attack again," Quintan said. "We should gather and make plans to find them."

"Yes, indeed," Harrison said. "Farmer, come with me. You need food and rest. We'll take you to the kitchen. Rosie will take good care of you."

"I am greatly humbled by your caring for me," the farmer said as he was shown where to leave his horse.

"Rosie," Harrison called out when they entered the kitchen.

"Yes, Harrison," Rosie replied, coming around the corner from the ovens. "What have we here?"

"Rosie, this good farmer has come to report that a village was completely burned to the ground by dragons in the north country," Harrison said. "Everyone was killed."

"That's horrible," Rosie said. "Sit here, Farmer, and allow me to feed you."

"I thank you, Miss Rosie," the farmer replied, sitting at the small table in the kitchen. "I am tired and hungry."

"I'll stay here and see to it that the farmer has a place to sleep," Quintan said. "I'll have him bed down in the stables."

"Good idea," Harrison said. "I'll gather the knights and inform them of this news. I'll tell the king right away."

Harrison entered the king's chambers on command.

"What news have you for me? Have you found the young girls I demand?" the king asked.

"No, sire. There are no young girls anywhere we have looked," Harrison said, bowing to the king. "I do come with frightful news. Dragons have completely obliterated a village in the far north country. No survivors."

The king got up and paced around the room. "That is unacceptable. How will I get taxes and goods from a dead village?"

Harrison said not a word. The king didn't have a bit of compassion for the lives lost. He was only worried about his money and possessions."

"Well, Harrison, how are we going to make up the loss?" the king hollered.

"I am gathering the knights this minute to discuss that very issue," Harrison replied, standing at attention near the door. "What do you command us to do about the dragons, sire? Any new orders?"

"Go after them at once," the king replied. "Leave at first light."

"As you command," Harrison replied, leaving quickly.

The king could be heard yelling all around the castle as he stomped around his chambers, screaming about the loss of money and young girls. Harrison went to find Charles in his quarters and informed him of the latest news.

"That's horrible," Charles replied. "What can we do about it?"

"The king has ordered the knights to ride out and find the dragons. Again."

"You will ride, of course," Charles said as he mixed a potion. "You won't find the rogue dragons."

"Agreed," Harrison replied. "And, if we did manage to kill them, their bodies turn to ashes and are taken into the heavens without leaving a trace."

"So, if you rode and didn't find any dragons, you could always tell the king the ashes were taken by his God," Charles replied, smiling slyly at Harrison.

"I do believe we speak the same language, good Charles," Harrison replied.

"We do," Charles said. "I'll take this to His Highness and try to get him to drink it. It should calm him down for a while. He won't be passed out. Just quieter."

"I'm off to meet with the knights and see what we can come up with this time," Harrison said as the two parted ways in the hallway.

The knights were gathered outside in their practice courtyard.

"What's this all about?" Fred asked.

Harrison told them about the village and the king's new orders.

"We ride at first light," Harrison said. "Make ready for tomorrow."

"Where's Quintan, Harrison?" Fred asked.

"He's with the farmer. Rosie is feeding him. Quintan is taking him to the little room in the stables for a rest," Harrison explained.

"He must be quite tired and sad," one of the knights said.

"He is, Gerald," Harrison replied. "I can't imagine what he must be feeling with all his friends killed."

"We'll offer prayers for the deceased and the farmer and his family," Gerald said.

"That's kind of you," Fred replied. "Very kind."

The knights knelt and offered the prayers for a moment, then got busy taking care of things for the ride to the north country in the morning.

"Farmer, follow me," Quintan said when he had finished his meal.

"Miss Rosie, that was delicious. Thank you kindly," the farmer said.

"You are very welcome," Rosie replied. "Rest easy and have a safe return home."

"Follow me," Quintan said as they left the kitchen and went to the stables. "Sleep here as long as you wish. I'll tend to your horse. He will be ready for your return home."

"Thank you, sir knight," the farmer said as he lay down. He was asleep in an instant. Quintan covered him with a blanket and asked The Magic to keep him safe.

Quintan joined the knights as they prepared for the next morning's ride. All was ready by midnight. The knights and their aides settled for some sleep.

"Quintan," Hugho said.

"Yes, Hugho," Quintan replied as they settled under the covers.

"Do you think we'll find those dragons tomorrow?" Hugho asked.

"I think we'll see them the day after tomorrow. It's a long ride to the north country," Quintan replied.

"Thanks," Hugho said. "Sleep well."

"You, too," Quintan answered.

The rest of the night was uneventful. At sunrise, the knights rose, had breakfast, and were sent on their way with provisions from Rosie and prayers for safety.

They traveled due north that first day and stopped to make camp just before sunset.

"Your tent is ready, Quintan," Hugho said as he set to making supper over their campfire.

"Thanks, Hugho," Quintan said. "Let me help you with this."

"You're a knight," Hugho replied. "This is beneath you."

"Hugho, no job is ever too small for me," Quintan said. "Besides, I want to make sure you don't burn Rosie's stew and bread."

"Wiseass," Hugho replied quietly. "Always the wiseass."

"That's me," Quintan said as they worked together.

The other knights had their tents up and fires going as well. Comments were heard all during supper that made them all laugh. That is until Fred's aid mentioned the rogue dragons.

"I know how you feel," Fred said to his aide. "I don't relish fighting with them myself."

"None of us do," Harrison added. "The last time we fought with them, they killed some of us. It was a very sad day."

"The strangest thing was when the dragons died; their bodies turned completely to ash, and the ash was lifted into the heavens. Not a trace of them was left. Nothing," Fred said.

"That's true," Harrison said. "When Dennison told King Gorham about that very thing, he just stared at him for a moment. He always trusted Dennison, so he believed him."

"No temper tantrum?" Hugho asked.

"Nope," Harrison replied. "It was the first time Dennison said he saw the king behave."

"It's getting late," Quintan said as he cleaned his bowl and spoon. "Let's get some sleep."

"I agree," Harrison said. "I'm sure we'll encounter those dragons tomorrow. The village that was destroyed is just an hour's ride north of here."

The knights settled down and slept fitfully. The next morning, they were up with the sun and riding north an hour later. They came upon the destroyed village and the recently dug graveyard. They bowed their heads for a moment of silence to offer prayers of peace for the souls that had perished.

"The next village is just a bit north of here," Gordon told them. "I used to visit my Uncle there. He passed a while ago. He was an old man."

"Lead us to him," Harrison said.

The knights rode on and easily found the village. It was bigger than the other one. It had about two hundred inhabitants and several farms and craftsmen. It was settled where two major roads crossed each other. It was a busy morning all along the roads. Folks were out and about taking care of business.

Harrison halted the knights just past the north boundary. They walked back into the village and talked with people about the recent dragon attack.

"It was horrible," one of the women said. "My friend and her family were all killed. No reason. Just killed out of meanness."

"We agree that it was horrible," Harrison said.

"Those dragons attacked without warning," a farmer added.

"We all go to bed, afraid of what might happen in the night," a brick mason said.

"We understand the fear," Quintan replied. "We'd like to stay here for a few days in case those rogue dragons come by."

"Would that be okay with everyone?" Harrison asked.

"Absolutely," was the response from the villagers.

"You can stable your horses just west of where you have them now," a framer said. "I'll show you the way. Follow me."

"Thank you kindly," Harrison replied as the knights walked back to their horses and followed the farmer to his home just west of the village.

"This is a large stable," Fred said as the knight's aides settled the horses.

"My father-in-law had an inn here years ago," the farmer replied. "My name is Riley. I married his daughter, and we ran the inn for a while. When my father-in-law passed, we decided to close the inn and run the stables for those who need a place to keep their horses when they stay here. We have five children who help out sometimes. We prefer them to stay in the school to learn."

"This is very kind of you," Harrison said. "Take this as compensation for your help."

Harrison handed the farmer a small pouch of gold. When the farmer looked in the pouch, tears fell down his cheeks.

"I am honored," Riley whispered. "We have a loft here if you'd like to sleep there."

"That would be excellent," Harrison said, patting Riley on the back. "Aides, get us settled in, please. We'll take care of our meals and such. Thanks for your hospitality."

"Thank you for being here," Riley replied. "Not sure what you can do against two huge dragons, but I'll sleep a bit better tonight knowing you're here."

"We'll do our best," Fred replied.

"Time for me to get back to my chores," Riley said as he waved and left the stables.

"Fred. Quintan," Harrison said, motioning them to follow him outside.

They walked a bit away from the stables before Harrison told them his plan.

"Let's set up a watch from sunset to sunrise," Harrison said. "Fred, make the assignments. Quintan, make sure everyone has their swords by their sides all night long. We'll keep the outside fires going. If those dragons are spotted, beat this kettle to wake everyone."

Fred and Quintan followed Harrison's plan, and by midday, everyone knew what they were to do. Fires were started, and lunch was prepared. Some of the villagers visited the knights, and stories were told that made everyone laugh. Pies were handed around as a token of the village's respect and thanks for the knights' presence.

The knights talked at length with some of the older villagers to get an idea of how often they'd seen dragons overhead. It seems that dragons have been seen from time to time over hundreds of years. Some of the oldest villagers told stories that were handed down for generations. They spoke about how a few dragons were bent on causing death and destruction in each generation of the families that had settled the place hundreds of years ago. Maybe thousands of years ago. No one really knew.

Supper time came, and the villagers brought a potluck for the knights. Everyone enjoyed the impromptu gathering, and the evening came along quietly. Folks began to gather their families and say good night. It wasn't long before the knights were alone.

"This is a great village," Quintan said. "It reminds me of home."

"It does," Hugho said. "I sure hope we get to those rogue dragons before they get to anyone else."

"We all do," Fred said. "Let's get settled for the night. First watch, take your places."

"Good night, everyone," Harrison said as he took his place near the front of the stables. "Stay safe."

The night was quiet, and it wasn't until well after sunrise that the watch saw the first dragon. He sounded the alarm, and the knights gathered where he stood. They looked up into the sky and saw the first rogue dragon flying straight at the village. Villagers ran for the caves back in the forest, trying to get somewhere safe.

The second dragon flew into sight a moment after the first one. Both were black and huge. The first dragon had a green streak that ran down his back to the tip of his tail. The second dragon had a silver streak that ran across his chest like a lightning bolt. They flew a pattern that caused everyone to run as far from the village as possible.

The knights aimed and let their arrows fly when the two dragons flew close to the top of the buildings. The dragons were hit in a couple of places, which made them angry. They circled around and aimed themselves at the knights. They blew fire and smoke at the knights. The knights figured this would be the dragons' next move and took action to avoid the flames. This made the dragons angry beyond belief. They circled around again, and this time, they flew very low, straight at the knights.

Just as the dragons took a deep breath, a brilliant flash appeared in the sky overhead. It blinded the knights and the dragons. The knights covered their eyes, and the dragons pulled up high into the sky. It took a few minutes before the knights regained their sight. The dragons circled around high in the sky. They kept shaking their heads as if to clear their vision.

"What the hell was that?" Harrison said as he bathed his eyes in cold water.

"I swear a star exploded," Gerald said. He was a new knight.

"I don't know what that was, but it made the dragons fly away," Quintan said. "They're still up there, though. I think their vision was affected, too."

"I think you're right about that," Fred said. "I can see just fine now. How about the rest of you?"

"We're all okay now," Harrison reported. "No lasting damage."

"I know we hit those dragons in a couple of places," Fred said. "I can't believe they're still here. I would think they'd have flown away to die and recover if they could."

"I don't know how dragons work," Quintan said. "I have no idea what makes them hurt."

"I hear ya," Gordon said.

"Oh my god, they're coming back at us," Hugho said, pointing to the sky.

"Prepare to release your arrows," Harrison ordered.

Just as the dragons got close again, two silver disks flew straight at the dragons. The dragons breathed fire at the disks, but it didn't damage them one bit. The flying disks kept in front of the dragons, making them veer off at the last minute. The dragons were beyond angry and bellowed a growling, howling sound that shook the ground and the forest. The knights had a hard time standing upright.

The dragons began breathing fire and smoke as soon as they got close to the village, moving from side to side to burn everything and everyone they could see.

As soon as the dragons let loose with their flames, the two silver disks sent a beam of brilliant light at each of them, and the dragons exploded into millions of tiny pieces as they flew at the village. The pieces were glowing red, orange, and yellow as they began to fall to the ground. The knights ran for cover under the stable overhang. The pieces of dragon never made it to the ground. As soon as the pieces got close to the trees and buildings, they were turned into ash and taken high into the sky beyond where anyone could see them. They disappeared in thin air as the knights watched the fireworks.

The two silver disks hovered low over the village for a few minutes, changing colors and humming. Then, without a sound, they shot straight up into the heavens, just as before.

"What the hell was that?" Gerald asked.

"There isn't a piece of dragon anywhere," Hugho said.

"Are those the same disks we saw over Kerwyn?" Fred asked.

"How did they know the dragons were here?" Gordon asked.

Harrison and Quintan looked at each other as they said, "I have no idea."

The knights walked out onto the pasture and looked all over the place for dead dragons. They just weren't there.

"Has this ever happened before?" Gerald asked.

"Which part?" Harrison asked.

"The no dead dragons anywhere part,"' Geral replied.

"Yes, last year," Harrison answered. "We were hunting dragons and were attacked by them. They killed some of our knights. When we shot arrows into a couple of them, they fell to the ground, died, turned to ashes, and the ashes were lifted up into the heavens. Gone. Not a trace of dead dragon anywhere."

"That's crazy," Gerald replied, shaking his head in amazement. "Just plum crazy! Now what?"

"Let's go find the villagers," Fred suggested.

The knights set out on the path the villagers had taken earlier. They soon found them just outside a cave.

"Knights, what's happened?" one of the older farmers asked.

"The dragons are dead, and the village is perfectly fine," Harrison replied.

"How can that be? We saw them coming," one of the women said.

"Come along home, and we'll try to explain it all to you," Harrison said. "We'll meet at the stables where we knights are staying."

A short time later, the whole village was gathered in the pasture outside the stables. A riser had been placed for the knights to stand on.

"Good villagers, I have asked Sir Quintan to explain what happened here today," Harrison said as Quintan stepped forward.

"We, knights, are thrilled to have told you that the village is safe and sound," Quintan began. "This is what happened. Those two rogue dragons aimed for the village, flying straight at us. We let loose with our arrows and wounded both of them. They were furious because they didn't get a chance to burn us or anything else. They circled around and took aim at us again. Just as they were about to let loose with their fire, two silver disks appeared in the sky. They shot beams of something, light or lightning or something, at the two dragons, blowing them up into a million tiny orange, red, and yellow pieces. Those burning pieces filled the sky, and right before our eyes, those dragon pieces turned into ash and were taken into the heavens by an invisible source. I swear on all that is sacred that this is exactly what happened."

There was a shocked silence for the longest time.

"So, there won't be any more bad dragons?" a boy asked.

"Child, not those two and, we hope, no others," Harrison said as he knelt to look at the child.

"Son, I would think that when those two don't return to the cave, any other bad dragons would think twice about attacking villages ever again," the boy's father said, lifting the small child into his big arms.

"Okay, Papa," the child said. "You are always right about such things."

"Well, he thinks he is," his wife said with a smile and a wink.

There was laughter and teasing from those nearby.

"I am the village mayor. My name is Michael," Michael said, introducing himself to the knights. "I say we should take a moment right here and thank the, uh, uh, powers that watch over us for keeping us and our village safe."

Harrison shook hands with Michael and nodded in agreement. The pasture became very quiet for a few moments as folks thanked the gods and goddesses for their safety.

"Now, I say, bring food and such here for a mid-day celebration," Michael said. "We should celebrate this day."

"We agree," Harrison said. "We'll help you all."

About an hour later, the village gathered again in the pasture. Tables were set up near the stables, and food and beverages were shared. Stories were told, and some of the children asked the knights if they could hold their swords.

"A knight's sword is a sacred thing," Fred explained to them. "We do not allow anyone except our aids to touch them. However, if you have a wooden few of them around, we'll be happy to show you how to use them."

Children ran to get their homemade swords, and some found sticks near the forest that would work as swords. The knights spent the better part of the afternoon teaching everyone how to hold and use swords. The children decided to have fake fights and had a blast pretending to die.

Harrison, Fred, and Quintan walked around the pasture to talk privately.

"We should head back at first light," Harrison said.

"Agreed," Fred and Quintan replied.

"I haven't even started to think how I'm going to explain this to the king," Harrison said. "Mentioning the fly disks might get me beheaded."

"He knows about them just like everyone else," Fred said.

"I know that, and you know that. However, the king may have forgotten and think I'm being blasphemous," Harrison said.

"True," Quintan said. "Let's think about this for a bit. Maybe we can come up with some kind of story. Oh, I know. How about a storm was coming, and they were hit by lightning?"

"I like that," Fred said.

"It just might be believable," Quintan said. "I think I'll say just that. Quintan, you are a genius!"

"I'll agree with that," Quintan said as they rejoined the group.

"Knights, we'll stay the night and leave at first light," Harrison said. "We humbly thank you for your hospitality villagers. Your kindness will be remembered."

The crowd applauded and cheered the knights. This was the signal for everyone to get along with their afternoon chores. It was late, and many chores still needed to be done. The knights took care of their horses and then offered to help around the village. By evening tide, all work was completed. The knights gathered outside the stable and built a small fire. They talked briefly about the dragon fight and the silver disks. No one really knew what to think about flying disks. They were sensational, to say the least.

Quintan remained awake after the others had fallen asleep. He walked across the meadow near the forest's edge. He felt at peace here. He became aware of movement just inside the forest and looked closely for the source.

"Praise the gods!" Quintan said as he recognized Penny and Q. The forest had moved apart for them. "You look fantastic!"

Quintan ran to them, hugging each of them in turn.

"You look strong and healthy," Quintan whispered. "Did you see the battle today?"

"Quintan, you've grown at least a foot since we last saw you," Penny said.

"You've grown some muscles, dear boy," Q added.

"Yes, to all of it," Quintan said, showing off his muscles and making the dragons laugh.

"Still the wiseass," Penny replied.

"Always, Miss Penny, thanks to you," Quintan said, bowing his head respectfully.

"And, yes, we saw the battle from nearby," Q answered. "It was looking quite bad for a moment. Then, the disks appeared and took charge."

"I know the answer to this already, but I'm still going to say this: you've seen them before, haven't you?"

"You are quite intelligent," Q replied.

"Now, who's the wiseass?" Quintan said, laughing at Q.

"He is right, Q," Penny said, laughing with Quintan.

"Yes, we know about the flying disks," Q answered. "Always have. They've been around for eons."

"I figured as much," Quintan said. "I suspect they are a part of the bigger universal picture."

"They are," Penny said. "I just have to ask."

"I knew you wouldn't stay quiet about this," Q said, pointing at her.

"What, Miss Penny?" Quintan asked.

"How is Miss Angelique?" Penny asked.

"She is wonderful as if you didn't already know," Quintan said. "You both know I'm going to marry her, too."

"Yes, we do," Penny said. "We heard you talking with your parents when you were in the village the other day."

"I thought I sensed a dragon about," Quintan said. "You kept your energy very quiet."

"We had to," Q said. "We promised The Special Magic we would if they would let us take a short flight to see how we were healing. We did. We are perfectly healed."

"I can see that," Quintan said. "I will wait to ask for her hand until the king is gone, dead, or disappears."

"That is wise thinking," Penny said. "We don't want him to know about her."

"Exactly," Quintan said. "Now, do Feyanna and Merlin know you are out and about yet?"

"No, just you," Q replied as Quintan yawned. "Go get some sleep. We'll visit Feyanna and Merlin in the morning and tell them all about this adventure."

"Good," Quintan replied. "I am quite tired all of a sudden. Battling dragons takes a lot of energy."

"And so does playing with children," Penny said. "You all had a great time with them, and they loved it."

"It was great fun for everyone," Quintan said, yawning again. "I'm off to sleep. Love both of you very much."

"We love you, too," Penny whispered as Quintan left the forest and found his pallet in the stables. The villagers and the knights slept deeply that night. The Special Magic was making plans for them all.

Sunrise came, and the knights bid farewell to the villagers. They made it just past the spot they had stopped at before and made camp at sundown. It was a quiet night. No one saw the swarm of flying disks in the sky that night. There must have been about fifty of them. It was a sight to behold if anyone had seen them.

The knights returned to the castle in the late afternoon. They were greeted with cheers and applause. Russell was waiting for them at the south gate.

"Welcome home, lads," Russell said. "All went well, I take it?"

"Indeed, Russell," Fred said. "We'll talk later."

The knights gave their horses to their aides and reported to the king's throne room as a group. Harrison had sent a paige ahead so the king would be there when they arrived. They bowed and stepped into their assigned places. Harrison stood before the king.

"What is your report, Harrison?" King Gorham asked.

"Your Highness," Harrison said as he bowed. "The two rogue dragons are no more. They were killed when lightning struck both of them in an approaching storm."

"Where are their heads?" the king asked.

"Sire, just like last year, as soon as the dragons were dead, their bodies turned to ash, and the ash was taken into the heavens," Harrison explained.

"I do remember that same report from last year," the king replied. "What about the villagers?"

Harrison could tell from the king's behavior that he had no recollection of the dragon battle from the past year. He would feed the king exactly what he knew the king would want to hear.

"They are all alive and well," Harrison said. "Not one of them was killed or injured. They've sent their deepest thanks for sending your knights to protect them."

"As they should," the king replied. "This is a good thing. I will still get my taxes and goods from them."

"Yes, sire," Harrison said.

The king walked around the throne room for a few minutes, lost in thought. The knights stood still and watched. It looked like he didn't know what to do next. Harrison took care of this awkward moment.

"Sire, now that those two rogue dragons are dead, I was wondering if you would wish the knights to prepare for the summer tournaments?"

"That is exactly what I command you to do," the king replied. "You have listened well to my orders, Harrison. You are a good leader for the knights."

"I am honored that you say this," Harrisons said, bowing again. "If you wish, I will send word across the land to announce the tournament and the rules."

"So be it," the king replied. "We will have the tournament on the first day of Summer, June 21st. Make it happen."

"Yes, Your Highness," Harrison replied, signaling the knights to leave the throne room.

"Harrison," the king said as the last knight left, "Make sure we win every event."

"As you desire," Harrison said as he quickly backed out of the room before the king could say anything else.

Fred and Quintan were waiting for him in the hallway. Harrison signaled them to remain quiet and follow him. They left the castle grounds and walked through the event area. No one else was around. It looked like they were checking on the grounds for the coming tournament.

"He's lost it all," Fred said.

"I agree," Quintan said. "He didn't remember the dragon battle from last year. We all saw him trying to figure out what you were talking about."

"I saw that, too," Harrison said. "That's when I put the rest of my plan to work. I decided to tell him by asking him what the next steps should be."

"Now, who's the genius?" Quintan said, slapping Harrison on the shoulder.

"As long as we have each other to talk ideas through, we should be good," Harrison said. "Now, let's figure out how to get the word out quickly. The first day of summer is only three weeks away."

"I'll give the scribes the information so they can post it around Kerwyn. We can send the carrier pigeons to the outer areas. They'll get there quickly," Fred said. "I'll take care of that, too."

Done," Harrison said. "Quintan and I will plan the events. We'll have all the knights give their thoughts on this."

"I'll gather them in our practice area this evening," Quintan said.

They saw Charles approaching them and waved him over.

"I see you are all safe," Charles said as he joined them.

"We are," Quintan replied.

"What really happened out there?" Charles asked. "I saw two silver disks flying in the north late in the day two days ago."

"Indeed, they were there," Harrison said. "They sent a beam of lightning at the dragons and killed them."

"There were millions of dragon bits burning down all over the place," Fred said. "Thing is, none of them ever touched the ground. They were turned to ash and taken aloft."

"That is what usually happens with dragons," Charles said. "The Special Magic takes their energy back home."

"That's what we figured," Fred said.

"I take it the king was okay with this?" Charles asked.

"We told him lightning struck the dragons and all the rest, just like last time," Harrison replied. "He didn't remember a thing from last year. He said he did, but we all could tell he didn't."

"I expect that," Charles said. "He's lost a lot of his memory. Just yesterday he was hollering for young girls again. I reminded him that he'd had three of them the day before and needed to rest before he had them again. He looked at me with glazed eyes and agreed with me. He hasn't fucked anyone in a long time."

"That's good to know," Quintan said. "Thanks for convincing him otherwise."

"Now what?" Charles asked as he walked with the knights to the far edge of the field.

"I asked him if he wanted me to begin arrangements for the tournaments he ordered right before we left," Harrison said.

Fred and Quintan smiled at this.

"He didn't order any tournaments, did he?" Charles said, smiling.

"Nope. We have them now, though," Harrison replied. "Just like your suggestion, I did the same. He thinks he ordered them, and that's just fine. We were just setting plans in motion. We'll need you, of course."

"Yes, you will," Charles said. "When and for how long?"

"They will begin on the first day of summer, June 21st, and end three days later with a banquet to honor the winners," Harrison said. "Fred is taking care of getting the message out. Quintan and I were just about to set the schedule of events."

"I offer my assistance," Charles said.

"Accepted," Harrison replied. "Let's get busy planning the events now."

The four of them walked around the field, setting the schedule for the events. When they finished, they joined the knights in their practice yard and told them the plans. Everyone was thrilled with the plans. Harrison gave each knight specific duties to complete in readiness for the tournaments, and everyone got busy getting ready.

Quintan walked into Rosie's kitchen after everyone had their orders and was greeted by her with a big hug.

"Good to see you're in good health," Rosie said.

"You as well, Miss Rosie," Quintan said as he stepped back. "You look tired, Rosie."

"Maybe a bit more than usual," Rosie replied. "I'm taking a potion Charles made for me. It seems to be helping some."

"Good," Quintan said. "Now, let these excellent people help you out. That's an order. Make sure she rests every afternoon and doesn't do too much."

"Look at you, taking charge," Rosie said. "I do feel quite tired right now. I think I'll take a rest. Everything is ready for supper."

Rosie walked out of the kitchen and into her room, falling onto her bed. She was asleep instantly.

"How long has she been ill?" Quintan asked the kitchen maids.

"She's been ill for three days," Angelique said as she stepped into the work area. "I told her to go to bed, but she refused. I went and got Charles, and he took her to his quarters. She came back with a vial of medicine, took it, then got back to work. I walked her to her quarters right after supper, and she fell sound asleep. I'm glad you're here. We'll take care of the kitchens as long as needed."

"Good job, Miss Angelique and everyone," Quintan said. "May I eat in here tonight? I don't want to be an added burden."

"Of course you can," Maybel said. She was one of the older kitchen maids. "We always like it when you knights eat in the kitchen with us."

The others agreed with this and set Quintan up with his supper. He told Harrison and Fred about Rosie. They agreed to make sure Rosie stayed out of the kitchen for the next few days.

"Mabel and Angelique," Quintan said as he ate. "We are planning a country-wide tournament for June 21st. Mabel, you've done this a few times. You'll be in charge with the help of everyone, including the knights. Just tell us what you need, and we'll make it happen."

"I most certainly will," Mabel said. "I'll be sure to visit Rosie and get her advice."

"Good thinking," Quintan said. "This venison stew is just what I needed. Delicious."

Everyone thanked Quintan for his kind words and got busy making early plans for the tournament.

The next couple of weeks seemed to fly by. Everyone across the countryside was excited about the tournament. A week before the tournament, people began to travel toward Kerwyn to find a good camping spot close to the castle. Rosie was still feeling a bit tired, and Charles was trying to figure out why. He decided to stay in the hallway next to the kitchen one day from before sunrise through nightfall. He wondered if something underhanded was going on.

Just before sunrise that day, he saw someone he didn't recognize deliver herbs to the kitchen. He waited until the man left and then walked in.

"Don't touch those plants," Charles said. "I suspect they're poisoned. Let me take them and test them."

"Oh, my," Mabel said. "Why do you think that, Charles?"

"Mabel, when did that man begin delivering herbs here?" Charles asked as he carefully placed the herbs in a sack.

"About a month ago," Mabel answered. "He said the regular framer was ill and offered to take care of the delivery."

"Has anyone else been ill since he started delivering these?" Charles asked.

"Now that you mention it, a few people fell ill every time Rosie used the rosemary. They felt better the next day."

"Rosie fixes a special tea with rosemary in it for herself, doesn't she?" Charles asked.

"Indeed, she does," Mabel said. "Oh my god, she's been poisoning herself without knowing it."

"Make her tea with these ingredients," Charles said as he pulled a few jars from the shelves. "Tell her I said to drink it all. It should begin to flush the poison from her right away. I'll stop by to see her in a little while after I test these herbs. Ladies, keep this to yourselves. Not a word to anyone. I want that man arrested tomorrow morning when he delivers the next batch of herbs. If I find out someone told him what I suspect, that person will be thrown in the dungeon as well."

Charles ran to his quarters while Mabel made the tea and took it to Rosie.

"Rosie, drink this, and don't give me grief about it," Mabel said sternly. "Charles thinks you've been poisoned with bad rosemary and says this tea will fix things."

"Who would do such a horrible thing to me? I haven't done anything wrong to anyone," Rosie said as she sipped the tea. "This tastes bitter."

"Charles says to drink it all and don't add anything to it," Mabel said as she watched Rosie.

"You gonna' stand there and watch me drink all of this?" Rosie asked, making faces.

"I am," Mabel said. "We need you back in the kitchen. There's going to be a tournament, and I need your help."

"I know about the tournament," Rosie said as she finished the tea.

"Charles will be here soon to talk with you," Mabel said. "He's testing the rosemary to determine what poison is in it. He threw away all the rosemary on the shelves. I'm going over to the knights to tell them about this and ask them to find new rosemary for us."

"That's a great idea, Mabel," Rosemary said. "Thanks for taking over. I appreciate it."

"You rest and do whatever Charles tells you to do," Mabel said. "We need you, and I miss my best friend."

"I know, dear," Rosie said. "I will follow Charle's every order."

"Yes, you will," Charles said as he walked into the room. "Did she drink all of the tea?"

"She did," Mabel said. "I'll be getting back to the kitchen now. Let me know if you need anything, love."

"I will," Rosie said as Mabel left.

"It was cyanide in the rosemary," Charles said. "Someone has been slowly poisoning you for at least the last month. Keep drinking the teas I send you, and you should feel much better in about three days."

"Of course, I'll do as you say," Rosie said, closing her eyes. "Why would someone want me dead?"

"The knights will find out," Charles said. "Now rest. My sweet friend."

Charles left as Rosie fell to sleep. He found Mabel with the knights and added to the story. They were shocked and angry.

"We'll take care of the man," Harrison said. "I'll be in the kitchen tomorrow when he arrives. You point him out to me, Mabel, and I'll throw him in the dungeon. No one hurts our Rosie!"

They went their separate ways, and the rest of the day was very busy with regular chores and the preparations for the tournament. The next morning, the man with the poisonous herbs was arrested and thrown in the dungeon. He was questioned by Harrison and Quintan all day, pretending he didn't know anything about the herbs. He finally broke down and told them what they wanted to know.

It seems a farmer just north of Kerwyn had asked Rosie several times for her hand in marriage. She refused him every time. He asked why, and she said he wasn't the right man for her. The farmer became very angry with the repeated rejections and decided she would pay for his humiliation. He began dosing his rosemary with poison a month before she fell ill. He had his neighbor deliver the herbs so he wouldn't be suspected of her death.

Charles tested all the herbs that day and found them laced with cyanide. He ordered all the dried herbs to be thrown away. They were. The knights found a new supplier, and the new herbs were delivered the next day. Charles tested them as well, and they were clean.

Rosie continued to improve, and four days later, she returned to her kitchen to the joy of everyone. She made scones for Charles and the knights to show her appreciation for taking such excellent care of her. The king had no idea about any of this. Harrison handed down the sentence for the delivery man: He was sentenced to six months of hard labor for the castle. The farmer who had poisoned the herbs was arrested and beheaded on his farm by three of the knights and the king's axman. His farm was given to a family nearby. They were very happy with the gift.

It was now only a week before the tournament. The countryside outside of Kerwun was filled with people ready to enjoy the event. The participants had been given places around the outer edge of the event field. Excitement was in the air as the day drew near.

Opening day finally arrived. The trumpets blared from high on the parapets, and everyone entered the event field. The king arrived, and everyone cheered as he waved to the crowds. He finally sat down, and the parade of knights entered the grounds. They were dressed in their formal colors, and the crowds cheered and cheered as they rode around the grounds. They stopped in front of the king and bowed their heads. The king acknowledged them as he held his ceremonial sword high. The knights dismounted, their paiges took the horses, and they walked to their places among the other contestants.

The official court herald announced the tournament open, and the games began.

The king was all set for blood, gore, and guts. He wanted to see people maimed and killed. That wasn't going to happen. Quintan, Fred, Harrison, and Charles decided that this tournament would be for fun. They decided they would deal with the king if he became upset.

That first day saw the knife-throwing games. Knives of all kinds were used, including spiked mallets. In the afternoon, many skilled contestants took their turns. The crowds cheered everyone on, and by the end of the afternoon, the score-board showed very close results. Quintan, Harrison, and a knight from the court of King Micah were tied.

The king dismissed everyone and returned to his chambers, where he told his manservant, Lawrence, to bring Harrison to him at once. Harrison, Quintan, and Charles were ready for this.

Harrison arrived in short time and bowed to the king.

"Your Highness, you summoned me," Harrison said.

"I most certainly did," King Gorham said. "What's with these games? No one is dying. I want to see blood and death."

"Your Highness, the event today was to show skill and agility as you ordered," Harrison said.

"Yes, I did say that," the king replied. "And you and Quintan were very good today. Make sure you stay at the top. I expect to see the losers die tomorrow when they fail."

"If I may, sire," Harrison began, waiting for permission to speak.

"Speak," King Gorham said.

Charles and Quintan walked in right on cue.

"What do you two want?" King Gorham yelled.

"I have your evening potion for you," Charles. "There are two this evening. I noticed you had a difficult time this afternoon, so I made a potion to give you more energy for tomorrow. I will give you one in the morning as well."

"Good thinking, Charles," the king said as he drank the first potion. "Disgusting!"

"It is bitter, sire," Charles said as he handed the king the second vial

"What's this one for?" the king asked.

"It's the one to keep you healthy, sire?" Charles said.

"Oh, the one that keeps that nasty disease away from me. Okay," the king said as he drank it down. "This one, I remember. No better than the last one."

"I'll work at finding a better flavor for you," Charles said as he bowed and stepped back.

"Quintan, what do you want here?" the king said, yawning.

Harrison and Charles exchanged a quick glance.

"Your Highness, I was asked to give you a message from King Micah," Quintan said, bowing before the king.

"Well, what is it?" the king asked.

"He wanted you to know how pleased he is that you invited him and his knights here for the games. He is quite happy to attend these games that will not demand death for the losers. He says showing grace and good sportsmanship is every bit as important as showing the resilience and strength of the knights without anyone dying. He applauds you for making this decision."

"He does, does he? What about the others? Do they agree with him?" King Gorham asked as he lay on his bed. "I seem to be quite tired."

"It has been a very busy few days," Harrison said.

"Well, what about the others?" the king asked as he yawned.

"They agree with King Micah," Quintan answered. "They stated that an exceptional man would order this type of tournament to show responsibility."

"Well, then, so be it," the king said as he closed his eyes. "Go away, all of you."

The king fell asleep, and the three left his chambers hastily.

"That was as expected," Harrisons said when they returned to the court-yard.

"Will he remember the whole thing about King Micah?" Quintan asked.

"No, for two reasons," Charles said quietly. "The disease is robbing him of his day-to-day memories, and I gave him a potion that will make him forget most of what just happened."

"You're a good man," Harrison said. "Make sure I stay on your good side."

"Same here," Quintan said. "It looks like we're being summoned."

Rosie was waving at them from the kitchen door.

"Yes, my Rosie," Harrison said as he lifted her and twirled her around.

"Harrison, you're a charmer," Rosie said, laughing with everyone as Harrison set her down.

"We're so glad to see you healthy and back ruling the kitchen," Charles said as he kissed her cheek.

"Same here," Quintan said as he did likewise.

"You three flatterers," Rosie said as they walked into the kitchen. "I have something special for you three and Fred. Where is he?"

"I'm right here, my Rosie, " Fred said as he kissed her hand.

"Good," Rosie said as she signaled two of the kitchen maids. "Sit over there, and you'll have your special dinner."

"Rosie, this is sensational," Harrison said as they were served roast pheasant, roasted vegetables, and Rosie's secret rolls with fresh clotted butter.

"This is fantastic," Charles said as he sampled the pheasant.

"I think I've died and gone to food heaven," Quintan said as he spread butter on one of the rolls and bit into it. "Pure bliss."

"You deserve this for the way you've handled the king," Rosie whispered with her back to the kitchen help. "Now, enjoy and save room for dessert."

"Yes, Ma'am," they replied.

They thoroughly enjoyed their special meal and the fabulous berry pie for dessert.

Harrison, Charles, and Fred hugged Rosie and went on their way. Quintan remained for a moment.

"Rosie," Quintan said.

"I know," Rosie replied. "Tonight in my quarters. One hour."

"You're a love," Quintan whispered in her ear as he kissed her cheek.

He caught a glimpse of Angelique as he stood and nodded her way. She smiled and went on with her work. An hour later, he walked into Rosie's room and found Angelique waiting for him. He locked the door, and they devoured each other in a deep and passionate kiss.

Quintan's hands found Angelique's bare breasts. She had loosened her dress and was ready for him. She moaned as he caressed them. He began kissing her neck and then the soft mounds of her breasts. They were huge and spilled out of her dress for him to see and touch. He lay them on Rosie's bed and began licking and sucking her breasts.

Angelique began to feel a wave of heat take over her and a tingling in her private parts she had never felt before. She moaned and didn't realize she was pushing her breasts against Quintan's mouth until he laughed and sucked harder. She began to get dizzy and felt her pussy getting wet. Quintan felt for her pussy through her underclothes and found them wet. He began to rub the area, and Angelique felt a rising sensation in her loins she had never felt before. She reached for his dick through his clothes and grabbed it. It was hard and hot.

She began rubbing him, and he almost exploded. He pulled away at the last second. They were both breathing hard and fast.

"I want more," Angelique said as Quintan began playing with her breasts again.

"So do I," Quintan said as he stopped. "We can't. Not until we're married. And we both know that has to wait."

"Yes, we do," Angelique said as she softly kissed Quintan on the lips. "I love the way you suck my breasts and touch me. I've never felt like this before, and I want more of it."

"I love the way you touch my hard dick as well," Quintan said. "I love sucking your breasts as much as you love having me suck them."

"I can't wait for us to be together," Angelique said.

"Now, wait a minute," Quintan said, smiling. "I haven't asked your father for your hand in marriage yet. Then, we must wait a bit while you plan the wedding with your mother."

"That's right," Angelique said as she pushed her breast against Quintan's mouth. "Until then, I suggest we keep practicing for our wedding night."

"I like the way you think," Quintan said as he took her breast and sucked it for a while.

They continued to explore each other, learning more and more about what made them feel good. Quintan began rubbing Angelique's mound through her thin cotton covering, and she began to feel those sensations again. This time, he didn't stop. He sucked her breasts harder and harder while he rubbed her faster and faster. She gasped as she felt her first-ever climax begin. She pushed against Quintan's hand, and he made her soar like an eagle. She clenched her gut and pushed faster until she held her breath and fell off the edge of reality as she reached the pinnacle of her climax.

He watched her and kept sucking her breasts as she began to relax. She fell asleep for a few minutes. When she awoke, she saw him watching her. He was licking her breasts.

"You are amazing," she said, stroking his cheek. "I don't know what that was, but I want more of it, and I want you inside me."

"I want to push into you so we can soar together," Quintan said." Keep remembering that, and we'll make it to our wedding night. Right now, we need to say good night."

Indeed we do," Angelique said as she stood and tidied her clothes. "Rosie needs me in the kitchen."

"And I need to speak with Harrison about tomorrow's events," Quintan said as they walked to the door.

They kissed deeply for a bit, then stepped aside.

Angelique left first, and Quintan a few minutes later. Their secret was still safe.

The next day was the hand-to-hand combat event. Shields, chainmail, and hand weapons were used. The sword fights were set for the morning of the third day.

The event was well attended, and everyone cheered on their favorite knight. The games were called at midday for the meal, and the rest of the event took place in the afternoon. King Gorham yelled with everyone else when one of his knights entered the arena. Some of the knights were bested, while others won their challenge.

"Charles," the king motioned to Charles, who had been standing next to him all day. "Why aren't the losers killed?"

"Your Highness, you remember you decided this tournament would not include death. It would be for skills and sportsmanship, to show respect for each other, and to build trust in case we need to go into battle together."

"That is right," the king replied. "I'm just so caught up in it. Pardon me."

"Of course, Your Highness," Charles replied. "It is rather exciting."

"Especially when our knights win," the king said as Harrison was deemed the winner of his challenge.

"He's the best," the king said as he stood and applauded Harrison.

Harrison bowed to the king, and the crowd cheered harder and longer.

The evening meal was served, and the king fell asleep after taking the two potions from Charles. The knights gathered in their hall, ate, and talked about the day. They agreed it had been a great day.

"Tomorrow will be the best," Gerald said. "I love watching Quintan handle his sword."

"We all do," Harrison said. "I'm going to enjoy you fighting with King Micah's lead knight. He's got some good moves himself."

"I know," Quintan said. "I watched him practice this morning. He didn't even know I was there. That might be his downfall, not picking up on what and who's around him."

"Well said, Quintan," Fred said. "I try to remember what you've taught us about that all the time."

"Let's get some sleep," Quintan said. "These have been busy days."

The castle settled for the night. Clarice and Roman watched over Quintan from their post on the parapets. They felt the energy shift now that Feaynna and Merlin had felt a while back. Something was stirring across the countryside.

The sun rose, and the final event of the tournament began. Most of the challenges were finished late in the morning. Harrison and his opponent were up next. They bowed to the king and each other, then took their stance. The flag was waved, and they began.

It was a rousing fight as Harrison and his opponent danced around each other and bested each other time and time again. The final blow came when Harrison jumped out of the way of his opponent's sword and fell and rolled away. He leapt to his feet while his opponent was trying to figure out what had happened, and Harrison set the tip of his sword at his opponent's neck.

His opponent smiled, and Harrison removed the sword. His opponent bowed to Harrison, showing defeat. The crowd went wild. They cheered and hollered for quite some time as Harrison and his opponent shook hands and bowed to the king and the crowd.

The last pair of the day was Quintan and King Micah's lead knight, Stanishman. The two knights met in the middle of the arena; they raised their swords to King Gorham, then to King Micah, and then to each other. They bowed and took their stance.

For every parry Stanishman came at Quintan with, Quintan outmaneuvered him. There was one time that Quintan found himself in a tough spot. Stanishman had cornered him near the wall and was about to win when Quintan remembered something he had learned from Merlin. Quintan faked defeat, then suddenly dropped to the ground, rolled a few feet away, and stood as his opponent ran at him. Just as Stanishman was about to thrust his sword at Quintan, Quintan gathered his strength and flipped over Stanishman, landing on his other side. The crowd went wild. The kings went wild. Stanishman stood there in shock at what had just happened.

This was all the time Quintan needed. He stepped up to Stanishman and placed his sword at the back of his neck. Stanishman turned and smiled at Quintan and lowered his sword in defeat. This brought everyone to their feet, and the roar of the crowd could be heard for miles around.

"Where did you learn that move?" Stanishman said as they bowed to King Gorham, King Micah, and the crowd.

"From a master swordsman," Quintan replied as they bowed to each other and embraced. They acknowledged the crowd again and were finally allowed to walk back to their fellow contestants. The crowd finally settled down, and King Gorham rose and addressed everyone.

"We have the unique honor and pleasure of hosting this tournament," King Gorham said. "Each and every one of you have performed well. I am proud of the actions of all of the contestants."

The crowds showed their approval by cheering for a minute. King Gorham pointed to King Micah to allow him to say a few words.

"You have all made your country proud. Your skills are the best, and your respect for each other is commendable. I am humbled to have been witness to these games." King Micah said.

The crowd applauded this as well.

"A feast has been prepared for the contestants and King Micah, which will take place at sunset in the main ballroom. Awards will be given at that time," the

Herald said. "Now, enjoy your countrymen and the day. You've all earned this celebration."

The crowd began to go to their areas and prepare the food for their celebrations. This was going to be one long and rowdy night.

And that's exactly what commenced as soon as the sunset. The main ballroom was full of music, food, and conversation. After the kings had eaten, the awards were presented.

Harrison, Quintan, and Fred took top awards, as did King Micah's Stanishman and two of his knights. A few others received awards for their knife-throwing skills. Applause and cheers were heard all around the countryside. The festivities went on until first light for some. Harrison and the knights quietly slipped away just after midnight. They were well guarded by Russell and his men.

When the knights came down for breakfast, there was a great deal of cleaning up going on all over the castle. Rosie was ready for them, and they showed their appreciation well. The king had managed to stay up until about three in the morning when he and King Micah called it quits. They left the ballroom to the younger group.

King Micah left around noon the day after the celebration. King Gorham sent him off with good wishes for a safe journey home. King Gorham returned to his chambers and found a hot meal waiting for him along with Charles and Harrison.

"This is great," the king said. "I'm starving, although I don't know why. I ate well last night."

"Rosie outdid herself last evening," Charles said.

"She most certainly did," the king said. "Give her a pouch of gold for her efforts."

"I most certainly will," Charles said.

"Harrison, you served me well yesterday," the king said. "I commend you for that."

"Thank you, sire," Harrison replied.

"Tell my knights I am proud of them," the king said. "That Quintan is a great swordsman."

"I will tell them, sire," Harrison said. "Is there anything you need me for?"

"No, not today," the king replied. "Be off with you."

"Thank you, sire," Harrison said as he quickly left.

"Charles, you have healed me well, and I appreciate that," the king said. "I never would have been able to celebrate so much if you hadn't taken such great care of me."

"It is my honor, Your Highness, to serve you," Charles said.

"Be off with, too," the king said. "I'll send for you if I need you."

"Thank you, sire," Charles said as he left.

The rest of the day, everyone took care of their business. King Gorham slept in the afternoon and got up for supper. He fell asleep soon afterward. Nightfall found most of the castle cleaned up and most of the visitors gone. Only a few remained. It was definitely much quieter than it had been for the last week.

By nightfall, the castle had returned to normal. Most folks had gone to sleep a little earlier than usual due to their celebrating most of the night before.

In the deepest, darkest part of the night, King Gorham was suddenly brought out of a deep sleep. He didn't know why he was awake and tried to go back to sleep. He felt something touch him and tried to brush it away. His hand was grabbed, and he was pulled into a sitting position. All of a sudden, the lamp next to his bed was lit and glowing brightly.

He looked at it and knew he hadn't lit it. He tried to reach over to blow it out and found he couldn't move. Not one muscle was under his control. He became aware of a cold stench surrounding him. As he looked around, he saw a shadow appear at the end of his bed. It was huge. It took shape and looked like it was wearing a black robe. A hood hid its face. Its hands were old and long with sharp claws at the end. King Gorham began to wonder what was happening.

"I don't know who you are, but you will be beheaded for entering my chambers without my permission," Gorham said sternly.

An evil, maniacal laugh responded to him.

"Leave!" Gorham hollered.

"No," a throaty, deep voice replied. "It is you who will be leaving."

"What kind of madman are you?" Gorham asked.

"The worst kind you could ever imagine," the creature replied as it walked to the side of the bed.

"Get away from me, you hideous thing," Gorham yelled. "Guard! Guard!"

"They can't hear you. No one can hear you," the creature said. "Only I can, and my master can hear you."

"What are you talking about?" Gorham said. "I demand you tell me. I am the king."

"That's right. You are the king," the creature said. "We made you king."

"I made myself king," Gorham replied.

"No, you did not," the creature said. "You were a pathetic, lowly lord of a manor in the middle of nowhere. You made a deal with us to give us your soul if we made you king."

"No one knows about that," Gorham said, beginning to feel uneasy. "No one knows because I told no one."

"That is correct," the creature said. "You have been king for a while as promised, and now we've come for your soul."

"That's a bunch of lies," Gorham said. "Everyone knows there's no real devil. It's a fable told to children and simpletons to make them do what we want them to do."

"You are wrong," the creature replied. "The Dark Force is real. We want our due."

The air in the room began to change as other shadows began to form. A moment later, five more hideous creatures were around the bed. Gorham became very scared.

"This is crazy," Gorham said. "I must be having a nightmare."

"No nightmare," the creature said. "This is very real."

One of the other creatures ran his claw down Gorham's arm, cutting him open.

Gorham screamed out in pain.

"Stop that. You're hurting me," Gorham said as he grabbed his bedsheet to wrap it around his arm.

"You're not going to need that," the creature said as the sheet was pulled off him and thrown on the floor.

"Get away from me," Gorham yelled out.

Gorham tried to move, but he was paralyzed. Only his mouth and voice were still working. "This is a horrible nightmare. I'll wake up in a minute, and everything will be back to normal."

"Never again," the creature said as he nodded at the five others.

The six creatures began to torture Gorham. First, they cut into his arms and legs with their claws, making him bleed. Next, they scalped him, causing him to scream. The creatures liked this response, so they kept going.

They attacked his gut next, cutting into his abdomen, making his stomach fall out onto his fat belly. He screamed out at the top of his lungs. His eyes began to bleed, and he could hardly breathe. The next thing the creatures did was to make his dick hard and bulging, then cut along the shaft. He cried out time and time again, begging them to stop.

The first creature looked at him and said, "No."

The last thing Gorham felt was his chest being ripped open. He passed out before the creatures ripped his heart out and threw the blood all over the room. Gorham died a moment later, and the creatures ripped his body apart, throwing the pieces on the walls and ceilings. His soul began to rise, and a great black fist grabbed it and pulled it into a deep, dark void that appeared in the room. The six creatures jumped into the void and disappeared. Gorham's body pieces were all over the place, with blood soaked into the bed, curtains, floors, walls, and ceilings.

Just before he died, he couldn't believe no one heard him. Oh, there were a few guards who heard him, alright. They chose not to respond to his screams.

They figured he was hallucinating again. It happened quite frequently, so they ignored it.

Lawrence, the king's manservant, knocked on the door and opened it the next morning with the king's breakfast. He took one look, dropped the tray, puked on the floor, and ran away. He ran into Charle's quarters in shock.

"What's the matter, Lawrence?" Charles asked when he saw him. He was white as a ghost, shaking uncontrollably and silent. He tried to speak, but the words wouldn't come out.

Charles knew something terrible had happened.

"Is it the king?" Charles asked.

Lawrence nodded his head and began to sob.

"Follow me," Charles said as he ran to the king's chambers.

Charles knew something terrible had happened. He could smell blood and body fluids before he opened the door. Lawrence grabbed Charle's arm and tried to keep him from opening the door.

"I think something horrible has happened to the king," Charles said quietly to Lawrence.

Lawrence nodded and dropped to the floor in the hallway.

"Guard!" Charles called out, and two guards came quickly. "Something bad has happened. Please stay with Lawrence while I take a look inside."

"Yes, Charles," the guards said as they knelt down close to Lawrence. "We're here for you, Lawrence.

Lawrence looked at them and nodded.

Charles opened the door and puked just like Lawrence had done.

"Charles, what's wrong?" one of the guards asked.

"Ring the death bells," Charles said. "The king is dead. He's been ripped into pieces, and those pieces have been thrown around the room. Ring the bells at once."

Charles sat on the floor next to Lawrence and held him close for the longest time. They heard the death bells ringing and were still on the floor when the knights arrived.

"Don't open the door," Charles said. "It's pure horror in there. Get the mortician over here to clean it up. He's going to need help. Take Lawrence to my quarters and stay with him. He saw the whole thing. Lawrence, I'll give you a draught to help you forget this horror."

"We'll take you, Lawrence," two of the junior knights said as they helped him to his feet.

Lawrence looked at his uncle Charles and whispered, "Thank you."

The knights left with Lawrence, and the mortician and his assistant arrived a moment later.

Charles spoke to all of them.

"The king is dead," Charles said. "I don't know what hell attacked him, but his body was ripped into pieces and thrown all over the place. Before you get started, sir mortician, come to my quarters with me so I can give you both a potion that will dull your senses. You're going to need it. It will take a long while to clean the room."

Two knights were left to guard the room while everyone else followed Charles to his quarters. He mixed a potion for Lawrence first. It would knock him out for a few hours, and when he finally woke up, he wouldn't remember most of what he had seen. He made the numbing potion next and had the mortician and his helper drink it in front of him. He told them to wait thirty minutes while the guards brought the wagons and tools to the hallway outside the king's chambers. Then, they would be allowed to enter and do their work. A coffin would be waiting for them to put the body pieces in.

Charles sat down hard. "This is a nightmare."

"Charles, we know no one killed the king," Harrison said. "I suspect The Dark Forces came for him because he sold his soul to them."

"I agree a hundred percent," Charles replied. "We have to find a new king and fast. The funeral will take place in about a week, now that we've rung the death bells. How do we explain this?"

Harrison and Quintan looked at each other as Quint offered," We tell them he died in his sleep. The disease attacked his heart and made it stop. That's all. Agreed?"

They all agreed by placing their hands over Charle's table in a show of agreement.

"Charles, we'll tell the guards and other knights that is what happened," Harrison said.

"The mortician and his helper will not remember any of this, and neither will Lawrence," Charles said. "I saw to that."

"Why are we here?" the mortician asked.

"The king has died of a heart attack, and we need you to clean up his chambers. His heart exploded and made a mess," Charles explained.

"Nothing I haven't seen before," the mortician said as he and his helper stood up.

"Good knight, please take them to the king's chambers," Charles said as he stood.

The mortician and his helper followed the knight back to the king's chamber and got busy cleaning up the mess.

"Uncle Charles, I'm feeling exhausted and a bit confused," Lawrence said as he yawned.

"I'm sorry to tell you that you found the king dead this morning," Charles said.

" I remember that," Lawrence replied. "He was a mess."

"Death usually is," Charles said as he guided Lawarence over to a cot at the far end of the room. "Lye here and sleep for a while. You no longer have a job."

"That's right," Lawrence said as he yawned. "He was a mean man, so I don't mind."

Lawrence closed his eyes and was softly snoring a few minutes later.

"Well, we have a lot of work to do," Charles said. "Harrison, bring Fred and Quintan here immediately."

"Can they have breakfast first? We are very hungry knights," Harrison said, smiling at Charles.

"Oh god, of course," Charles replied. "Let's take them to Rosie. I'm sure she's heard about the king and will have everything in hand."

"Right you are," Harrison said, motioning for the other knights to follow him.

"Keep guard, will you please?" Charles asked the guard. "We'll send your breakfast over shortly."

"Of course, Charles," the guard replied as he put a chair in the hall and sat down.

Rosie was waiting for them as soon as they walked into her domain.

"Breakfast first," Rosie said. "It's all set up in the knight's hall. Plans and details later."

"Yes, Ma'am," they all replied as they made their way to the hall and breakfast.

Feyanna ran into Merlin's room when The Dark Forces took Gorham's soul.

"Merlin, it's happened," Feyanna said as she sat on the side of Merlin's bed.

"What's happened?" Merlin said as he sat up.

"Gorham is dead. The Dark Forces just took his soul," Feyanna said in a rush.

Merlin held up his hand and closed his eyes for a moment. Feyanna knew he was tuning into The Special Magic to connect with them. She sat quietly.

"You are right," Merlin said. "He is dead, and his soul is gone into The Dark Forces."

"It's now," Feyanna said.

"Yes, it is now," Merlin said. "Let's get some sleep for a bit. Our lives are forever changed from this moment forward. I'd like to feel the energy of our wonderful cottage home and the meadow for a little while longer."

"Great idea," Feyanna said. "I am quite sleepy. Later."

Merlin slid back under the covers and fell asleep before Feyanna laid her head on her pillow. Penny and Q landed in the meadow and would be waiting for them when the morning arrived. There was a lot to do.

.

CHAPTER 20

The funeral week was all about preparing the king's body for internment. Quintan, Harrison, Fred, and Charles met later the day the king had died to discuss this week.

"We don't need the three days to prepare the body, obviously," Fred said.

"Correct," Charles replied. "But the country doesn't know what we know, so we need to make it look like he died of a heart attack and all."

"Quite so," Fred said, agreeing with everyone.

"We need to choose a successor, a new king," Harrison said. "The High Chancellor said he'd conduct the funeral service and leave immediately afterward. I think the priest in the small southern village of Angel's Gate would make a great High Chancellor."

"Speaking of which, what religion will we practice?" Quintan asked.

"That depends on the new king," Charles said, smiling at Harrison and Fred.

"Why are you three smiling like that? Have you chosen a new king already?" Quintan asked.

"We have," Harrison said. "We chose the new king about three months ago because we knew this day would arrive rather quickly."

"And, who have you chosen?" Quintan asked.

"You tell him," Fred said.

"No, Charles should tell him," Harrison said.

"I think Harrison should be the one to tell him," Charles said, laughing with Fred and Harrison.

"Funny guys," Quintan said. "Now, who have you chosen?'"

"You!" the three of them said at the same time.

Quintan looked at them for a minute. "What did you say?"

"You," they repeated.

"Me?" Quintan said.

"I don't know about this," Harrison said. "He seems to have lost his ability to hear and understand us."

"Very funny, Harrison," Quintan said, standing up. "Why me?"

"Seriously, Quintan, you may be young in age, but you are wise beyond my years and those of others older than me. You seem to know so much, and you make wise decisions about the people around here," Charles said. "We talked about other lords in the kingdom, and none of them are fit for the job."

"I agree with that conclusion," Quintan said. "This is so surreal."

"We need you on the throne," Harrison said. "You believe in the good that most people possess. You are a fair judge when it comes to settling disputes. You are the most accomplished swordsman I've ever known. I would be proud and honored to serve you as our king."

"Here! Here!" Fred and Charles said.

"You're serious about this," Quintan said quietly. "Will you three help me with all this king stuff?"

"Wouldn't have it any other way," Charles said.

"I need a minute alone," Quintan said as he walked outside and signaled Clarice and Roam to follow him as he swung up into the saddle and left the castle. He rode northwest into the forest for the better part of an hour.

He dismounted and turned to talk with the dragons.

"Clarice and Roman, now what?" Quintan said.

They appeared, and Clarice said, "We have some helpers for you."

Penny and Q landed right in front of Quintan.

"Praise the gods and goddesses," Quintn said as he grabbed onto their wings. "This is exactly who I need to help me with this decision. You look fabulous! Are you officially healed now?"

"We are," Penny said as her dark eyes shined with dragon tears.

"Miss Penny, please don't cry," Quintan said. "We're all here, and we're all healthy and well."

"I just never thought this day would finally get here," Penny replied.

"It has been a long and difficult recovery," Q said. "But, we are finally well."

"Indeed," Clarice and Roman said together.

"You all know what's happening, right?" Quintan said. "How do I know I will make a good king?"

"This is a decision you must make on your own. We will answer some questions, but, in the end, you will decide," Penny said.

"Okay. Let's talk," Quintan said and began the long afternoon of questions, frustrating thoughts, and a lot of laughter.

"Now that I am away from the castle, I can feel the power of The Special Magic all around me and us. I know what must be done. I'm ready to be king," Quintan said.

"What will your first order be?" Q asked.

"I will return The Special Magic as the religion for all who want to believe and practice it. It will be a choice, not a law," Quintan said.

"That is a superb first order," Penny said as the forest lit up with faerie lights as far as anyone could see.

"I do believe I have the approval of our faerie world," Quintan said. "I appreciate your kindness and welcome you anywhere you want to be. You might need to wait a few days and all."

The faeries flashed their lights at Quintan, and they all heard the faerie bells ringing.

"Excellent," Penny said.

"I'll welcome the dragons back into our lives as well," Quintan said. "We will still have to monitor those rogue ones and all."

"Indeed," Q replied. "Time for you to return and accept the offer. We'll chat with Feyanna and Merlin. They've known about this since you joined Hamlen's family. I'll be sure to have them tell your family."

"Why am I not surprised? Thank you, kind dragons," Quintan said, bowing to them all.

He jumped into the saddle and returned to the castle a short while later. He handed his horse off to Hugho and went to find Charles and the others. They were in Charles' quarters. Lawrence had woken up and returned to his room.

"Gentlemen and dear friends, I accept your offer," Quintan said. "I am ready to be your king as long as you will always be at my side."

Hoots and hollers were quietly sent around the room.

"We are thrilled with your decision, King Quintan," Harrison said, bowing.

"Not yet," Quintan said.

"I'm just practicing," Harrison said. "Let's talk details for a while. I've asked Rosie to send supper our way, and here it is."

They ate their supper and then talked into the night. That night, many important decisions were made that would positively impact the kingdom.

Charles gathered Quintan, Fred, and Harrison in his quarters the next morning for more decision-making.

"I have heard from the priest in Angel's gate," Charles started with. "He has accepted the position of High Chancellor and will arrive after the service. He knows The Old Magic will be brought back and will practice that belief."

"Excellent," Quintan said. "That's one less thing we have to worry about. Now, as for my advisors. I would like Harrison and Fred to accept these positions along with Hugho."

"I accept," Fred said.

"I accept, Harrison said. "We need to recruit new knights as well. I know three of our knights will leave right after the funeral, leaving us with only eight knights. What are your thoughts, Quintan?"

"I agree with you," Quintan said. "I will leave that area to your expertise. Fred, feel free to assist as you will."

"Yes, sire," Fred said.

"Wiseass," Quintan replied, pointing a finger at Fred.

Fred made a face at Quintan that made Charles laugh.

"This is going to be a fun kingdom with a very young king," Charles said.

"I promise to be serious when needed," Quintan replied. "I will need more help, so I'll ask Feyanna and Merlin to join me here."

"That's a splendid idea," Harrison said. "I've met them a couple of times, and they are wise and intelligent. And, they can help keep our young king in line."

"I like the sound of that already," Charles said. "Seriously, Merlin's reputation is well known around here. He is a great wizard, and I look forward to learning from him. He can take over my quarters if he wishes."

"I suspect he and Feyanna will want to have a cottage of their own that is not too far from here," Quintan said. "I think there's an area near Silver Lake to the west of the castle. It's only a ten-minute ride, so it will be relatively close."

"I know that area," Harrison said. "The cottage needs a lot of work. I'll send a detail tomorrow to have a look. We can get busy rebuilding it quietly while we wait for the funeral week to be done."

"Good idea," Quintan said. "Keep 'em coming."

"Ah, Quintan, there's just one more very important thing," Fred said. "You need to tell your family about all this."

"Yes, I do," Quintan said. "I'll ride over in the morning and return by nightfall."

"With a couple of knights as guards," Charles said.

"Oh, I never thought of that," Quintan said. "How about Hugho and Gerald? They are good at being knights."

"We'll need to swear them to secrecy," Charles said. "Can they be trusted?"

"Hugho, definitely," Quintan said. "I don't know Gerald all that well. Maybe we should pick someone else?"

"I'll go," Fred said.

"Okay then," Charles said. "Let's get Hugho in here."

Charles asked the guard outside the door to get Hugho for them. They returned a few minutes later.

"Hi, Hugho," Quintan said as his lifelong friend entered the room. "Sit here next to me. We've been making plans that include you."

"Great, Quintan," Hugho said. "What have you gotten us into now? More trouble?"

"Most likely," Charles said, laughing with Fred and Harrison.

"Hugho, I need you to take an oath of secrecy for what we're about to say to you," Harrison said.

"I swear on my honor to keep these secrets," Hugho said.

"That was easy," Quintan said.

"Now, who's the wiseass?" Fred said.

"Hugho, you know we need a new king," Charles said. "We are the committee that has chosen that very king."

"Okay," Hugho said. "How can I help you?"

"Quintan, please tell Hugho who the new king is going to be," Harrison said.

"My dearest and greatest friend, I am to be king," Quintan said, looking Hugho in the eyes.

Hugho looked right back at Quintan and knew he was telling the truth.

"Holy cow, Quintan," Hugho said, standing up. "This is amazing. I mean, it's a great choice. You are wise beyond your years. You're tuned into The Magic of old. You settle fights well with your sword or your words. Most people like you. Why, I really don't know."

This made them all laugh.

"So, will you be one of my advisors, Hugho?" Quintan asked as he pulled his friend back into his seat.

"Me? Why me?" Hugho asked, surprised.

"You know all his secrets," Harrisons said, smiling at Quintan.

"That's the truth," Quintan said. "You know me well and can calm me down in a minute when needed. We both follow The Old Magic and know there is much more going on in the world than we can see. You know my thoughts, and I trust you with my life."

The room was quiet for a minute.

Hugho stood before Quintan and said, "I accept the position as your advisor. I give you my life and my honor."

Quintan stood and grabbed Hugho into a bear hug for the longest time. They settled again at the table.

"We leave for home at first light," Quintan said, "And return by nightfall. Only you and Fred know I will be king in a few days. I will tell my parents so they can travel here for the coronation. They will be sworn to secrecy. My sisters will think that they are coming for the coronation of the new king. That part is true. They won't know who that will be until they arrive the day before. They will be given quarters in the castle. Russell is seeing to it."

"You're the new king," Hugho said. "This is going to take some getting used to."

"No kidding," Quintan said.

The five of them talked for a while longer before settling for the night. At first light the next morning, Fred, Quintan, and Hugho rode through the south gate toward home. They arrived just as breakfast was ready. Glendianna saw them first and gave a holler. She ran out of the cottage and grabbed Quintan just as he got off Buttercup.

"My son!" Glendianna said, crying and hugging her son.

"Mother, you look wonderful!" Quintan said as he held her close.

Hamlen and the girls were close behind their mother. They latched onto Quintan and refused to let him go.

"Sisters," Quintan said, trying to pry them loose. "You need to let me go so I can come inside and eat. We are starving as we left the castle before breakfast."

Sarah and Margaret looked at each other and released their brother at the same time.

"We'll let you go, but only long enough to eat," Sarah said.

"Then you're ours forever," Margaret added.

"I understand and agree," Quintan said as he kissed both of them.

"Father," Quintan said as they hugged.

"My son," Hamlen said as they separated. "You have grown taller and filled out more. You are a man now."

"Thank you, Father," Quintan said. "Hugho, get on home now. We'll see you at mid-day."

"Thanks, Quintan," Hugho said as he rode away.

"Family, you know Fred," Quintan said.

"Greetings, everyone," Fred said, shaking Hamlen's hand and nodding to the girls. "It's so nice to be here again. And, Glendianna, breakfast smells wonderful."

"Let's get inside and eat," Hamlen said as he locked arms with Quintan.

The talk around the breakfast table was about the dragon battle. News of that bizarre happening had traveled quickly. Then, the king's death came up.

"Quintan, what are the knights going to do?" Glendianna asked,

"What do you mean, Mother?" Quintan replied.

"Who will choose the next king?" Glendianna asked.

"Oh, well, I think the High Chancellor and the senior knights will decide on that," Quintan said.

"Do you know when the announcement will be made?" Hamlen asked.

"Right after the funeral service," Fred answered. "That is the usual procedure."

"So, my son, what brings you home?" Hamlen asked.

"I have been given permission to invite my family and Hugho's to the coronation," Quintan said.

"Wow!" Margaret replied. "Sarah, we need to figure out what we're going to wear."

"Indeed we do," Sarah replied. "We'll look over everything right after breakfast."

"Right after you clear up breakfast," Glendianna said, smiling at her daughters.

"Yes, Mother," both girls replied.

"You may be getting older, but you haven't changed a bit," Quintan said, laughing at his sisters. Boy, were they in for a surprise. He knew his mother would make sure they were dressed appropriately for the coronation and the festivities afterward.

"When will the coronation take place?" Hamlen asked.

"Three days after the funeral services," Fred replied. "That would be in about a week's time."

"We have a great deal of planning to do," Glendianna said. "We'll need to find lodgings and such."

"I have that all taken care of," Quintan said. "I'll tell you about it later. Now that breakfast is over, I'd like you and Father to join Fred and me on a walk over to Feyanna and Merlin's cottage. There is much to discuss."

"We're coming, too," Margaret said.

"Not this time, sweet sisters," Quintan said. "I do believe you have some chores to do?"

"They do," Hamlen said. "Let's be on our way."

The four of them walked along the south road to the path in the forest. A few minutes later they arrived at Merlin and Feyanna's cottage. Merlin and Feyanna were waiting for them.

"Good day, my dear friends," Quintan said, hugging first Feyanna and then Merlin. "This place is so beautiful and peaceful. I miss it."

"We know the feeling," Feyanna said. "Please. Sit with us here. We'll have a couple of other visitors in a few minutes."

"You know why I'm here," Quintan said. "You've always known."

"Yes, we do," Feyanna said.

"And yes, we have," Merlin added.

"What is this all about? I thought you were inviting us to the coronation?" Hamlen said.

"I am, Father. That's exactly what Fred and I are doing," Quintan said. "I am inviting you to the coronation of the new king. I am to be the new king."

Glendianna and Hamlen stared at Quintan for a moment.

"Is this true, Fred?" Hamlen asked.

"It is," Fred said. "The council chose Quintan a short while back when the king became ill. We spoke with Quintan the other day, and he accepted. We are thrilled to have such a wise and intelligent man taking the throne."

"But, he's so young," Glendianna said. "Not quite seventeen yet."

"That is true, Glendianna," Feyanna said. "The truth is wisdom is not only for older ones. Quintan was born to be king. The Special Magic has made sure of this, and we are thrilled to have been a part of his childhood."

"I am honored to be his mentor," Merlin said.

"My son, a king," Glendianna said as tears rolled down her cheeks. "I never would have thought of this."

"The special Magic knew your home was the perfect place for Quintan to be raised," Penny said.

"Oh my god! There are two dragons here!" Glendianna said.

"Yes, dear," Hamlen said. "They brought Quintan to us. He's been with The Old Magic since he was born. They're real, dear."

"We are very real," Q replied. "Now, Glendianna, don't worry about us. We're good dragons. We've been teaching Quintan many things since he came to live with you. And, these two, Clarice and Roman, are his protectors."

Clarice and Roman appeared where they had been sitting in the meadow.

"You're purple," Glendianna said, looking at Penny.

"I am," Penny replied. "My name is Penelope, and this is Q."

"Very nice to meet you both," Fred said, standing and bowing.

"Four dragons right in front of us, Hamlen," Glendianna said.

"Yes, dear," Hamlen said. "They are really here."

"Now, Mother," Quintan said as he stood beside her and touched her shoulder. "No need to worry. They will be with me as they always have been. They are great protectors and friends."

"Your sisters are going to be thrilled about this," Glendianna said.

"About all this," Fred said. "They can't know about any of this, especially the dragons, for quite some time. They cannot be told their brother is to be king until he is crowned."

"I understand," Hamlen said. "Dear, you will help them choose their clothes for the coronation."

"I will," Glendianna said.

"And for the festivities right afterward," Quintan said. "I must have my whole family with me on this extraordinary day."

"Absolutely," Hameln said. "I can see Glendianna planning everything already."

"You will be staying in the castle. You will enter through the south gate and speak with Russell. Father, he's the guard we first met when we delivered the wagons," Quintan told them.

"I remember him," Hamlen said. "He noticed your sword and commented on it. He took great care of us that time and when I returned the next day as well. It will be good to see him again."

"He has become a trusted friend," Quintan said.

"Now, Feyanna and Merlin, although you already know this, I need you to be my advisors and healers. Will you accept these positions?"

"We accept," Feyanna and Merlin's aid together.

"Splendid," Fred said. "We are building a cottage for you a short distance from the castle. It is on Silver Lake, which is about a ten-minute ride away. Please give me a list of the things you will need in the building of this cottage, and I'll see to it."

A bright blue light flashed, and Merlin said, "The cottage home is ready for us. We'll move in over the next couple of days."

"How can that be so? We haven't even started on it." Fred said.

"The Special Magic has made it happen," Feyanna said. "It's going to be glorious to have The Old Magic and The Special Magic back in our everyday lives."

"We've never been without it," Merlin said. "Now, it will be a part of the whole country's existence."

"Indeed it will," Quintan said. "I am bringing it back as soon as I am crowned. I will offer people the opportunity to follow whatever religion they choose. The royal family will follow The Old Magic."

"Splendid!" Hamlen said.

They talked a bit more about things before leaving for home.

"Now, remember, Mother, not a word about any of this to my sisters," Quintan said.

"What about Hugho?" Hamlen asked.

"He is inviting his family to watch just as I told the girls," Quintan replied. "When his family arrives, they will learn the truth during the coronation as well. They will be staying in the castle right next to your rooms."

"The funeral service is in four days, so that means we will be traveling in five days," Hamlen said. "I'll ask Samuel to care for the animals while we're gone. How long will that be?" Hamlen asked.

"A full week, Father," Quintan said.

"Quintan, will we have to call you Your Highness all the time?" Glendianna asked.

"No, Ma'am," Fred replied. "Only when others are around. We'll walk you through everything once you arrive."

"That will be wonderful," Glendianna said.

"This has been an incredible morning," Feyanna said.

"Indeed," Penny replied. "We've got you covered, Quintan. You and your family from here on out. Hamlen and Glendianna, there will be guardian dragons around you all the time from this moment going forward. This is Beau, and he's been assigned to your family. He will be joined by Magdalena this afternoon. They will meet all of you after you return home. We don't want to scare the girls."

"That is very thoughtful of you. Thank you to The Special Magic for your protection," Hamlen said, bowing.

"Our own dragon protectors? Why?" Glendianna asked, a bit puzzled.

"Mother, there are enemies of every king. They target the king's family, hoping to bully the king. That won't happen here, not with our dragon protectors," Quintan explained.

"Oh, I never thought of that. Good to have you with us," Glendianna said.

"It's our pleasure and honor," Q replied.

"Let's get home, dear. I'm getting hungry again," Hamlen said.

"When aren't you hungry?" Glendianna said as she, Hamlen, Quintan, and Fred started down the path to the south road.

Sarah and Margaret were preparing lunch when they arrived.

"Mother, we have chosen a few dresses for the coronation," Sarah said.

"They are lovely, of course," Margaret said as she set food on the table.

"I'll just bet you have," Quintan said, messy Margaret's curls.

"When are you ever going to grow up, brother?" Margaret asked.

This made the adults laugh, knowing what was about to happen.

"I'm back," Hugho said as he entered the kitchen.

"Lunch is ready," Glendianna said.

"Mother sent this berry bread for dessert," Hugho said as he set it on the table.

"I love your mother's berry bread," Fred said. "So light with lots of berry flavors."

"Aren't you the food expert?" Quintan said, teasing Fred.

"Well, with Rosie in our kitchens, you have to be," Fred said.

"She feeds us well," Hugho said. "She always has something for the knights between meals. It's as if she's afraid we'll go hungry."

"She is a wonder," Quintan said. "You'll meet her after you arrive, Mother. She's a lot like you."

"Maybe a bit tougher when needed," Fred said, smiling.

"She would have to be with a whole pack of knights running around the place," Glendianna said. "I can't wait to meet her."

A few minutes later, most of the village showed up and the afternoon was spent talking and visiting in the meadow close to the house. Teasing was a great part of the conversation. The afternoon was giving way to evening when most people went home.

"Mother. Father. It's time for us to leave. We need to return by nightfall," Quintan said.

"I have meat pies for you to take with you," Glendianna said as she handed each one a warm wrapped package.

"These smell heavenly," Fred said. "Thank you, Ma'am."

"It's always my pleasure to feed Quintan's friends," Glendianna said, winking at Fred.

"We'll see you in four days, sisters," Quintan said, hugging them. "Don't give Mother a hard time about what to wear. Be kind and respectful."

"Always, brother," Sarah said.

"Same here," Margaret added.

"Safe travels, son," Hamlen said as they hugged.

The three left the village and were back at the castle as evening turned into night. Russell was waiting for them.

"How's the family, Quintan?" Russell asked as the guards closed the castle gates.

"They are splendid as always, Russell," Quintan said as he dismounted. "A word with you, please."

"Of course, sir, knight," Russell said as Hugho walked the horses to the stable, and Russell and Quintan found a quiet spot to talk.

"Harrison told me the news, sire," Russell whispered. "I am thrilled and will serve you to my dying breath."

"I'm not the king yet," Quintan said. "I'm still just Quintan, please. We don't want people to panic."

"Panic? They'll be thrilled to have a fair and just man on the throne," Russell whispered.

"Thank you for those kind words," Quintan said. "My family will be arriving on the day after the funeral service. My father expresses his respect as he remembers your kindness. The announcement of my becoming king will be made as soon as we return from the burial grounds. Be prepared for whatever may happen. I know Harrison has briefed you on all of this. I just want to make sure you know about my family."

"I remember your father and will be happy to see him again," Russell said as they walked toward the stables. "We will make sure you are ready for your day, Quintan. I am so proud of you. You'd think you were my son."

"I appreciate you, my friend," Quintan said as they parted.

Quintan was settling for the night with the other knights.

"Anyone have any ideas about who our next king will be?" Gerald asked.

"Who do you think, Gerald?" Fred asked.

"I have no idea," Gerald replied. "Most of the lords are not, uh, ready to be king, even if they think they are. A lot of rumors are going around about this very topic. No one has any idea who might be crowned."

"I agree," Hugho said, smiling at Quintan.

"Some think it might be Harrison," Gordan said. "He knows a lot about how things are run around here."

"And he's a splendid senior knight," Gerald added.

"I agree with you on all counts," Quintan said. "He does have a lot of information about the castle, having been Gorham's senior knight. And, he's a splendid swordsman."

"Not as good as you," Hugho said.

"Thanks for that, Hugho," Quintan said. "I appreciate your support, but you don't count. You're my best friend and are prejudiced for me."

"Ah, true, my friend," Hugho said. "Very true. I guess we'll just have to wait and see."

"Now, that's a plan I can sleep on," Gerald said. "Good night, all."

The loft finally settled down, and Hugho and Quintan laughed quietly to themselves.

The next two days, preparations continued for the funeral. Quintan stopped into the kitchen on the afternoon before the funeral service. He'd been quite busy learning all about castle policies and procedures from Charles and Harrison. Meals had been brought to them the whole time.

Rosie saw him enter the kitchen and grabbed him into a big hug, tears streaming down her face.

"My sweet Rosie," Quintan whispered in her ear. "You will stay?"

"Of course," Rosie said. "Who else is going to make sure you behave?"

"Only you, my Rosie," Quintan said as he stepped back. "Good afternoon, everyone. Thanks for the splendid meals for us as we've been preparing for the funeral service tomorrow."

"Smooth talker," Rosie said under her breath. "Do ya need some tea and cakes, young Quintan?"

"I do indeed," Quintan replied. "Please have Angelique bring them to me."

"Indeed," Rosie said as she waved at Angelique.

Now that Gorham was dead, Angelique and the other young girls could move about the castle and the countryside.

"Here you are, sir knight," Angelique said as she set a pot of tea and a plate of cakes on the table in front of Quintan.

"Did you make these cakes, Angelique?" Quintan asked as he poured his tea.

"I did, sir knight," Angelique replied. "I hope you enjoy them."

"I'm sure I will," Quintan said as he bit into one. "This one is a honey cake. Delicious!"

"Thank you," Angelique replied, winking at him.

"Soon now," Quintan whispered.

"Indeed," Angelique replied.

"Time to get back to your baking, Angelique," Rosie said as she stopped by the table.

"Yes, Miss Rosie," Angelique replied as she went back to work.

"She doesn't know, Rosie," Quintan said. "Only you do."

"I know," Rosie said. "I can keep secrets."

"Yes, you can," Quintan said. "Start planning a wedding feast. I plan on marrying her one month after the coronation day."

"I've already got the plans well underway," Rosie said.

"I knew you would," Quintan replied as Harrison walked in. "Harrison, sit with me. These honey cakes are delicious."

"Is this how you get your work done for tomorrow?" Harrison asked as he sat down. "I should report you, but there's no one to report you to."

"Wiseass," Rosie said as she brought another hot pot of tea.

"Always, my Rosie," Harrison replied, laughing with Quintan.

"It's quite a light and happy atmosphere around here with a dead king and all," Rosie said.

"It is," Harrison said. "He was a mad, crazy, mean man. It's a pleasure not to worry about being yelled at or the threat of being beheaded anymore."

"Here! Here!" Quintan said.

"We'll be sure to show our respect tomorrow during the services and burial. But, as soon as that is over, we will be celebrating when the new king is announced. Are you ready, Rosie?" Harrison asked.

"I am," Rosie said. "It's time for this new beginning. Bless the gods and goddesses."

"Exactly, Rosie. Exactly," Quintan said, winking at her.

"I figured as much," Rosie said, leaning down to kiss the top of Quintan's head. "You're a good boy."

"Promise me you'll keep kissing and hugging me after all of this," Quintan said.

"Just try to stop me, young Quintan," Rosie said as she went back to work.

"She is a precious jewel," Harrison said as he and Quintan enjoyed their treats.

"My mother and Rosie are about to become best friends for all eternity," Quintan said.

"I agree with that," Harrison. "Quintan, what about marrying? Any ideas?"

"Thanks for whispering," Quintan said. "I'll be announcing that soon. Or you will announce that soon. Or whoever is supposed to announce things like this."

Harrison laughed with Quintan. "We'll figure it out. Who is she?"

"All in good time," Quintan said. "Is anyone giving a eulogy tomorrow?"

"No, just the religious service and graveside prayers," Harrison said. "It will be a short service."

"It starts at nine, so we should be done by eleven," Quintan said.

"We're planning to make the announcement as soon as we get back. The people were told that a great announcement would be made right after the burial, so I think they'll be crowded around the castle. You and I will meet in the throne room dressed as knights. When we get here, Richard, your new manservant, will have your royal clothes ready. No robes yet. Just the colors we decided on."

"That's right. You didn't even ask me about that," Quintan said.

"Sure we did," Harrison said. "You remember the time we knights were camping, waiting to fight dragons last summer? We talked about the ugly colors Gorham had chosen. You said navy blue, crimson, and silver were the colors you would choose. So, we did just that."

"I did say that, didn't I? Glad someone was paying attention," Quintan said. "Okay then. I approve of the colors."

"Cute!" Harrison said.

"Rosie, this has been a splendid treat," Quintan said as he and Harrison stood up. "We thank you for taking such great care of us."

"You are welcome, sir knights," Rosie said, winking at them.

"Time to finish a few things before tomorrow," Harrison said. "We'll see you for breakfast."

"Harrison, do you want the usual funeral breakfast prepared?" Rosie asked.

"Hell, no. Rosie. Make it your usual wonderful breakfast feast," Harrison replied. "We are celebrating the rest of the day, are we not?"

"Indeed, we are," Rosie said. "We're already baking for tomorrow."

"Thanks, Rosie," Quintan said as he and Harrison left.

The rest of the day was spent finalizing the details for the announcement of the new king. The castle settled down, and the night was quiet.

Daylight saw mourners gathering around the outside of the castle. Only the knights would be at the service, which took place as planned. The burial followed. The mourners followed the procession to the graveyard. Prayers were said as King Gorham's body parts were lowered into the grave.

The knights returned to the castle and people began gathering inside the castle grounds and outside in the city of Kerwyn. Exactly at noon, the trumpets blared, and people quieted down.

The formal balcony that overlooked the city and the inner grounds was being used for the first time since the last king was announced.

Harrison, Fred, the new High Chancellor Patrick, and Quintan stepped onto the balcony. Not a sound could be heard as all waited for the name of the new king.

"Citizens of Kerwyn and our surrounding kingdom," Patrick said. "I am here to present our new king to you."

Harrison and Quintan stepped forward. The knights had changed into Quintan's new colors. The flags flying from the castle flew these new colors.

"Dear citizens, I present to you your new king, Quintan of Hamlen," Patrick stated.

Quintan stepped forward alone. There was a second of silence, and then the good people let loose with a roar that could be heard for miles. Cheers, hollering, trumpets, and bells could be heard for the longest time.

The knights looked at each other and then bowed to Quintan. He bowed back to them. Rosie and Angelique stood just inside the balcony, and Angelique looked at Rosie.

"Oh my god!" Angelique said. "You knew, didn't you? You made cakes in his colors."

"Yes, child, I was told and sworn to secrecy," Rosie said.

"That means, oh my god! Rosie," Angelique said as she swayed a bit.

"Sit here, Miss Angelique," Fred said, smiling.

"Yes, Angelique," Rosie said. "That's exactly what it means."

"Drink this," Fred said as he handed her a glass of water. "You'll be okay. We'll all make sure of that. No one knows except Rosie, Harrison, and me."

"Okay," Angelique said. "Will I be able to talk with him today?"

"Of course, in a little while," Fred said. "You'll be joining us at the feast in about an hour."

"This is incredible," Angelique said. "I'm supposed to be serving at the feast."

"Not anymore," Rosie said. "I'll keep you busy in the kitchen as we learn about your likes and dislikes. I have a good idea already."

Harrison entered the room, saying, "The crowd is finally quieting down. Time for us to announce the coronation day."

Harrison, Patrick, and Fred joined Quintan on the balcony. Patrick stepped forward.

"Good people," Patrick said. "I take it you like your new king already."

This brought an instant roar of approval. Patrick held his hand up to quiet the crowd.

"The coronation will take place three days from today at noon. It will take two hours as knights will be sworn in as soon as Quintan has been crowned. A feast will follow. Please go make ready," Patrick said.

People erupted into cheers, making plans for the coronation day. A short while later, the castle had emptied, and people returned to their work and homes.

Quintan walked into the room from the balcony and saw Angelique. She had tears running down her cheeks. He quickly walked over to her.

"Angelique, are you okay?" Quintan asked as he knelt and took her hands in his.

Rosie, Harrison, Fred, and Patrick were the only ones in the room with them.

"I think I am," Angelique said. "This is quite the surprise."

"My family is about to rush in here. Only my father and mother knew about this. My sisters are going to be all over me. Are you ready?" Quintan asked.

"I don't know yet," Angelique said. "This is going to take some getting used to."

"We're all here to help you," Rosie said.

"No one is to know about us until I ask your father for your hand in marriage. Today, you are here helping Rosie," Quintan said.

"Good idea," Angelique said as she stood up. "Rosie, what do I need to do right now?"

"Let's get the cakes and tea," Rosie said as the door burst open, and Sarah and Margaret ran in.

"Quintan," Margaret said as she grabbed her brother. "You kept a secret from us."

"How dare you?" Sarah said as she latched onto her brother.

"Yes, I did, for the good of the kingdom," Quintan replied.

"Nice try," Margaret said as everyone laughed at the girls harassing their brother.

"It's the truth," Harrison said.

"I don't know if I believe you," Sarah said, looking at Harrison and Fred.

"Me, either," Margaret chimed in. "We are your sisters, after all."

"Let go of me for a minute, will you?" Quintan said as he untangled himself from the girls. "I'd like to hug mother and father."

The girls stepped aside as Quintan walked over to his parents. He grabbed them and gave them a long, wonderful hug.

"My son, the king," Glendianna said, crying.

"Indeed," his father said.

"You have taught me well. You have shown me, unending love, guided me growing up, and shown me how to be truthful and honest even if it meant I was wrong. You accepted me as your own. I am forever grateful for all of this," Quintan said as he stood before them. "It is because of you that I am the man I am."

"We love you, too," Hamlen said, grasping hands with his son.

"Merlin and Feyanna have arrived," Fred said as they entered the room.

Feyanna hugged Quintan for a minute.

"You have learned well," Feyanna whispered. "The Old Magic is alive within you."

"It is," Quintan whispered back.

"Merlin," Quintan said as they hugged. "Please accept my request to be the healers and wizard we need in this castle."

"We accept," Merlin and Feyanna replied, bowing.

"Your new cottage home is ready for you," Fred said. "Gerald and Gordon will take you there when you're ready."

"After the feast," Feyanna said.

"Thank you, knights," Merlin said, nodding at them.

"I love your colors," Sarah said. "They look great on you."

"Thank you, little sister," Quintan replied.

"I am older than you, little brother. Remember that," Sarah said.

"She is," Quintan said.

This made everyone laugh. Rosie and Angelique entered the room, followed by a couple of kitchen maids with tea, cakes, and grog.

"Let's eat," Fred said. "I'm famished."

The group enjoyed the tea and such for a while, telling stories about Quintan, his sisters, and some of the knights' antics. Gerald walked in to signal that it was time for the feast.

"Let's go to the throne room and enjoy ourselves with the others," Harrison said.

"Will Quintan sit on the throne today?" Margaret asked as they walked along.

"No, Margaret, not until he's crowned in three days," Patrick, the High Chancellor, replied. "The throne has been draped in his colors and will remain empty until he takes the oath of the king."

"Thank you for telling me," Margaret said as they entered the throne room.

Cheers and applause were heard as Quintan walked to the head of the table.

"I appreciate each and every one of you here," Quintan said. "Let us feast and enjoy our freedom."

The rest of the afternoon and evening were spent eating, telling stories, and enjoying each other's company. The girls began to yawn, and Glendianna motioned for them to join her.

"Son, this has been an amazing day," his mother said as she kissed his cheek. "Time for us to get some sleep. We need to be rested for tomorrow. We are going to learn all about being a king's family and the rules for the coronation service."

"Then, off with you," Quintan said, hugging his sisters. "Sleep well."

Glendianna and the girls were escorted to their quarters, where they talked for quite some time, getting ready for bed. Glendianna was finally able to quiet them down enough for them to fall asleep. She smiled as she closed her eyes in sleep. *My son is the king.*

The feast in the throne room ended a short while later. Everyone had a lot to do in the days before the coronation. Quintan was taken to a private room to talk with Angelique. They were finally alone.

"Quintan, if you're going to be the king, that would make me," Angleique hesitated.

"My queen and the queen of the kingdom," Quintan said softly as he held her.

Angelique just stared at Quintan for the longest time.

"You are the king," Angelique said.

"I am," Quintan replied. "You are the queen."

"I, I don't know what to say," Angelique said.

"I know how you feel," Quintan said as he gathered her in his arms. "Kiss me, my queen."

They enjoyed each other for a few minutes and then sat at the table.

"How will I know what to do and how to act around you?" Angelique asked.

"I have an answer to all that," Quintan said. "Harrison and Fred will be teaching both of us how to do everything for the coronation and the coronation celebration. We're going to be busy tomorrow with my family as well. I'll tell my sisters about us in the morning and swear them to secrecy until after I speak with your father."

"When will you do that?" Angelique asked.

"The knights have already gone to your farm and asked your parents to come here the day after the coronation. I will formally ask for your hand then."

"Will I be present?" Angelique asked, smiling.

"Yes, you will be there," Quintan replied. "We will become betrothed at that moment, and the wedding will be four weeks later to the day. Harrison has lined up two women of the castle who usually take care of the queen's details. They are going to prepare you for the wedding as well. It will be held here."

"Quintan, I am becoming overwhelmed with all this," Angelique said as she stood and paced around the room. Quintan walked them over to the bed. He lay Angelique down and then joined her. They kissed and explored each other for quite some time. Angelique loved it when Quintan unlaced her dress and found her bare breasts. He kissed them and sucked them until she thought she would float away. Angelique found Quintan's hard shaft and played with it until he pulled away, begging her to stop.

"Good thing we're being married in a month," Angelique said. "I can hardly wait to get naked with you."

"I know what you mean," Quintan replied, adjusting his clothes as Angelique did the same.

"It's time to leave," Angelique said. "I guess we're going to be very busy for a few days."

"We most certainly are," Quintan replied, kissing her. "Not too busy to think about us at any given minute, though."

"I agree," Angelique said as they opened the door.

Two knights were waiting for them.

"Miss Angelique, please follow me," Gerald said as he offered her his arm.

"This way, Quintan," Jonathan said. "I have been assigned to you for the next few days."

"Thank you, Jonathan," Quintan replied as he followed the knight to the king's chambers.

"These are your new chambers, Sir Quintan," Jonathan said. "There will be someone outside all the time. Sleep well."

Quintan nodded his head at Jonathan as he closed the door. Quintan looked around the chambers. They were not the ones Gorham had used. These were bigger and more beautifully furnished and decorated. His sword was in its scabbard on the desk, along with his knives. All of his things had been moved here from the stable. Everything except that note he had hidden in the eaves. He would retrieve that in the early morning hours.

The castle was busy throughout the night as Quintan and the others slept. A great event was about to take place. The dragons were even more excited than the humans. The Old Magic was about to be brought back to life. Maybe the humans would be allowed to remain on the earth with Quintan as their king. Time would tell.

Coronation day finally arrived. The countryside was awake and ready to greet their new king. The castle was ready as well. Just before daybreak, Quintan met with Merlin and Feyanna in his chambers.

"Merlin, are the dragons ready to show themselves?" Quintan asked.

"They are," Merlin answered. "They will reveal themselves along the parapets the instant you are crowned. Have you chosen a name?"

"I have," Quintan said as he leaned over and whispered into Merlin's ear.

Merlin smiled and nodded at Feyanna. She smiled as well.

"Excellent!" Merlin said. "What about The Old Magic?"

"I will proclaim its return as my first order," Quintan replied.

"That is splendid," Feyanna said.

"There will be much joy throughout the kingdom," Merlin said.

"I will instruct the kingdom not to harm our dragons as well," Quintan said. "The people need to know there are more good dragons than rogue ones. Once The Old Magic has returned, The Special Magic will be called upon to help us keep a balance in the world."

"That is exactly what should happen," Merlin said. "I know we're all going to work hard to keep that balance."

"I swear to the gods and goddesses this moment that I will strive to bring balance back to this world," Quint said as he stood and bowed.

A purple mist began to fill the room, followed by a brilliant white mist that took shape. A beautiful white and silver being began to appear. As it took its human form, Quintan, Merlin, and Feyanna bowed in reference.

The purple mist hung at the top of the room as the brilliant form spoke.

"Please stand up," the voice said. "We are all pleased with the work you have accomplished. Quintan, we thank you for following the signs we set forth for you. You have grown into a wise and intelligent man—young in human years but wise and intelligent in our focus. Merlin and Feyanna, your journey has been challenging and harrowing a lot of the time. We thank you for your perseverance in reaching this moment."

"We are honored to serve The Special Magic," Merlin said.

"The three of you face a new challenge upon Quintan becoming king," the voice said. "It will be a pleasant one for the most part. There will always be challenges and joys. Quintan, your decisions will form the very fabric of life for the next millennia. Be wise in your decisions. Heed your counsel. You have chosen your advisors well. They may not always agree with you. Discuss these differences and make your choices carefully and with conviction."

"I will honor the ways of The Special Magic always," Quintan said,

"Angelique will assist you in making your decisions," the voice continued. "She is wise beyond her years. We know the love you share is deep and genuine. We bless this union."

"I am humbled and will share this with Angelique, if I may," Quintan said.

"After the wedding, you may share this with her," the voice said.

"I understand and will obey," Quintan replied.

"Feyanna, you have learned the healing arts well. We are proud of you and applaud your every effort to ease the pain and suffering of your fellow man," the voice said.

"It is my honor to do so," Feyanna said. "I shall continue with your guidance always."

"We add this caution: Be aware that the Dark Forces will continually try to undermine your knowledge and decisions. Ask us for protection every day, and we will keep them away as much as possible. Each morning, say these six words: White Light, surround and protect me. That is all you need to do."

"We accept this gift and will use it as instructed," Merlin said. "And, we will call upon that protection in any situation that seems harmful."

"Yes, indeed," Quintan added.

"You have listened well," the voice said. "It is time for us to leave. Continue to honor The Old Magic every instant of your existence. It is The Old Magic that will bring peace and harmony to this sad world."

The being returned to its silver and white brilliance and ascended as the purple mist opened a channel for it to flow heavenward. Merlin, Feyanna, and Quintan were silent for a moment.

"That was amazing," Quintan said. "I am humbled by all of this."

"We are, too," Feyanna said.

"What a beautiful and amazing start to your day," Merlin said. "Not a word of this to anyone."

Feyanna and Quintan nodded in agreement. Just then, there was a knock on the door, and Rosie and her kitchen maids arrived with breakfast.

"Hello, Miss Rosie," Merlin said, bowing to her.

"Master Merlin," Rosie replied. "It is so good to have you and Feyanna here from now on."

"We think so, too, Rosie," Feyanna said. "You have outdone yourselves with this glorious breakfast."

"Only the best for my young Quintan," Rosie said, winking at him.

"Why, Rosie, are you flirting with the soon-to-be king?" Harrison asked.

"Of course I am," Rosie replied. "And I plan to continue flirting as long as I can breathe."

Everyone laughed at this as Quintan kissed Rosie on the cheek.

"Let's eat," Harrison said.

They all enjoyed Rosie's breakfast and were ready when Patrick, the High Chancellor, arrived to announce that it was time for Quintan to dress for the ceremony. Everyone left except Harrison and Fred. It was just before ten o'clock when Quintan was ready. He wore his colors with a sash of burgundy. They walked to the throne room and stood outside.

"Are you ready, my son?" Patrick asked.

Quintan looked around for a moment. He had never dreamed of becoming a king. This was surreal.

"I am, High Chancellor," Quintan replied.

Harrison, Fred, and Patrick walked into the throne room, up the aisle, and took their places. The door closed behind them. Everyone was waiting in anticipation. The trumpets finally sounded the processional, and the doors opened. Quintan stood alone, and as the trumpets quieted, he began a slow walk down the aisle to the front of the throne room by himself. He stood before the High Chancellor in silence. The guests took their seats, and the prayers began.

After the beginning prayers, Quintan was told to stand.

"Quintan, what name do you take as king?" the High Chancellor asked.

"I take the name Arthur Pendragon of Camelot," Quintan replied so all could hear him.

Quintan's family sat just to his right. He looked over at them and winked. His parents were crying, and his sisters winked back at him.

"Let it be known far and wide that Quintan has taken the name Arthur Pendragon of Camelot to be his royal name. I so order this to be true and in place from this time forward.," the High Chancellor said.

Quintan turned to his knights, who bowed. He then turned to face everyone in the throne room, who bowed and curtsied accordingly. Quintan turned back to face the High Chancellor.

"Follow me, Arthur Pendragon of Camelot," the High Chancellor instructed Arthur.

Arthur followed the High Chancellor and was directed to stand before the throne facing the room. The throne had been draped in his royal colors. The High Chancellor signaled, and Hugho and Fred brought the royal cape. They stood before Arthur with the cape lying across their outstretched arms.

"I deem this moment to be remembered as the time Arthur Pendragon of Camelot was draped with the royal cape of the King's Order," the High Chancellor said.

The High Chancellor nodded to Hugho and Fred, and they walked up onto the dais and behind Arthur. They draped the cape around his shoulders and set the clasp across his chest.

"I am honored to have you both place this cape upon me," Arthur said.

Fred and Hugho bowed to Arthur and returned to their places with the knights.

The High Chancellor offered the royal scepter to Arthur.

"This royal scepter I give you as a token of your office," the High Chancellor said as Arthur accepted the scepter. "It is a symbol that denotes justice and power. It is a reminder to rule with grace and wisdom," the High Chancellor said.

The moment of the crowning was at hand. The High Chancellor signaled to Arthur to kneel in front of the entire room. Arthur knelt and bowed his head for the blessing of the crown. He raised his head, and the High Chancellor stood before him. The knights had walked over to Arthur and fanned around him on both sides of the High Chancellor.

"Let it be known from this moment forward for all eternity as I place this crown upon the head of Arthur Pendragon of Camelot that he is now the rightful King of Kerwyn and the entire Kingdom," the High Chancellor said as he placed the crown on Arthur's head. "Stand and face your subjects, Your Highness."

Arthur rose and looked out over the crowd, first at his family, then Angelique, then his knights. The High Chancellor signaled that Artur was to sit on his throne. Arthur did so, which signaled that the service was over. The room erupted into loud cheers and applause. The trumpeters played the music that signaled the king had been crowned. A roar was heard as all the people in the castle grounds and the surrounding city and countryside cheered as well.

"I am honored and humbled that I have been permitted to sit here as your king. I have two announcements to make at this time. First, the name Kerwyn has been removed from the surrounding city. From this moment forward, I give the name of Camelot to the city. Secondly, I restore The Old Magic religion to all my peoples and places. You may now live in this religion free from the threat of death. You may also choose any religion you wish to worship. I implore all my subjects to be kind and accepting of people who do not follow their own religion. So be it," King Arthur ordered.

There was a moment of absolute silence across the castle and Camelot as word got out. Then, a roar of cheering and the beating of drums was heard for the longest time.

"It is time for the Coronation Feast to begin," Harrison said as food and drink were brought into the throne room and royal hall.

Arthur found his parents and hugged them and his sisters for a long moment.

"Our son, the king," Glendianna said. "I am so proud of the man you have become."

"I am blessed with you as my family," Arthur said as his sisters grabbed his arms and tried to run off with him.

Harrison and Fred laughed as they untangled his sisters.

"Now, ladies, the king has others to visit with," Fred said. "I'm starving. Let's get some lunch."

The girls went off with Fred as Arthur walked over to Angelique. She curtsied before him as he took her hand in his.

"My king," Angelique said.

"My Angelique," Arthur replied. "I will be speaking with your father in a few minutes. Meet us in my chambers with your mother. My parents will be there, too."

"Yes, Your Highness," Angelique replied as Harrison stepped next to Angelique.

"Angelique, come with me to the kitchen," Harrison said. "We need food."

Angelique laughed as she followed him, saying, "We most certainly do."

"Look who's here?" Rosie said as she hugged Angelique. "Sit here, both of you. I have a little something for you to sustain you before the feasting begins."

"Rosie, I should be working with you," Angelique said as she tried to walk over to one of the counters.

"Angelique, you no longer work in the kitchens," Harrison said quietly.

"Oh," Angelique said as she sat down and served them tea.

"No worries, child," Rosie said. "We'll get ya through all the new things."

"Thanks, Rosie," Angelique said, looking a bit uncertain.

"Miss Angelique, I know what's about to happen, and I think it's wonderful," Harrisons said quietly.

"Thank you, Harrison," Angelique said. "I'm still in shock over all of this."

"So are all of us," Harrison said. "We're all going to be learning new things together."

"You listen to Harrison," Rosie said. "He knows a great deal about the royal life. He's been through two other kings already."

"That's true, Rosie, just as you know many things, too," Harrison said, pointing at Rosie.

"And, Russell," Rosie said. "He's a wealth of knowledge. Ask him anything. He'll answer you truthfully."

"That's true," Harrison said, setting his napkin down. "It's time for us to go to the king's chambers."

"Be off with you," Rosie said, kissing Angelique's cheek. "I'll be seeing everyone shortly."

Harrison knocked on the king's chamber door, and Fred opened it.

"Please enter," Fred said.

Angelique saw her parents and ran to them. They gathered her in a hug and reassured her that everything was good.

"Angelique," Arthur said as he took her hands in his. "I am ready. Are you?"

"I am," Angelique said.

"Stephan of The Valley," Arthur began as he stood before Angelique's parents. "I thank you for coming to my chambers so that we can talk. I love your daughter with all my heart and soul. I am asking you for her hand in marriage."

Stephan and his wife Marianna looked surprised.

"We didn't know you were being courted," Stephan said.

"I know, father," Angelique said. "Forgive me for keeping the secret. We all thought it was a good idea when Gorham was king. He had a thing for young girls, and it was horrible. He never knew I worked in the kitchen. Quintan and I met one day, thanks to Rosie, the head of the kitchen. She arranged for us to meet properly with a chaperone. Quintan and I have met many times since, with Harrison or Fred close by. Our courtship has been proper and honest. I love him with all my heart and soul, too, Father and Mother."

"We can see that," Marianna said. "Your eyes are glowing, and your cheeks are flushed. I remember feeling that same thing when I met your father."

"I remember well, too," Stephan said.

"Sir Stephan of The Valley, I would like your blessing for the marriage of your daughter Angelique and me," Arthur said, standing before Stephan.

Stephan looked at Marianna as she nodded her consent.

"We gladly give our consent for the marriage of our Angelique to you, Your Highness," Stephan said as he took Angelique's hand and placed it in Arthurs.

"As is the custom in this manner, I declare King Arthur and Lady Angelique betrothed," the High Chancellor declared.

Arthur hugged Angelique as she cried. Congratulations were shared, and joy was felt throughout the chambers.

"Quintan, why am I Lady Angelique?" Angelique asked.

"You are about to be the Queen of Camelot," Arthur answered.

"Oh, my," Angelique said. "I believe I am. What do I do now?"

"You, my sweet, will be taken care of by three women here in the castle to prepare you for the duties of the queen," Arthur said. "You will be fitted for a wedding gown with your Mother by your side for the entire month. Oh, yes. We are to be married four weeks from today. I will make the announcement at the feast in a little while. One of my knights, Sir Gerald, will always be at your side, keeping you safe. That's enough for now."

"I should think so," Marianna said. "Angelique, are you happy?"

"I am beyond happy, Mother," Angelique said. "This is all so much more than I could have dreamed of, even as a child. Quintan, I am honored to be your bride."

"Ah, just one thing, Lady Angelique," Gerald said. "The king's name is now Arthur."

"Oh, my. I'm so sorry, Arthur. I have a lot to remember," Angelique said.

"No worries. We'll help each other remember all the little things that come our way," Gerald replied. "May I escort you and your parents to the feast? The king will join us in a few minutes. Protocol and all."

"Of course," Angelique replied, taking Gerald's arm and leaving the room with her parents.

"The kingdom is going to be very surprised by this news," Harrison said.

"Are you?" Arthur asked as he adjusted his clothes.

"No," Harrison said. "I knew from the very first minute I saw you looking at her that day at breakfast that the two of you were to be together for eternity."

"I did, too," Arthur said. "Am I ready?"

"You look perfect, Your Highness," Harrison replied as Hugho held the door for them.

"Oh, guys, please, lose all the Your Highnesses and stuff when we're together. Just call me Arthur," Arthur said.

"With pleasure," Harrison replied.

"Always Quintan," Hugho said, smiling.

"Cute, Hugho," Arthur said as he slapped Hugho on the back.

They were told to wait at the entrance to the great hall. The trumpeters were about to announce the king's entrance. A moment later, the trumpets sounded, and King Arthur entered the hall with Harrison and Hugho following him.

King Arthur walked to his place at the head of the table and cleared his throat.

"We have an announcement to make," Arthur said as he held his hand out for Angelique.

Angelique stepped up next to him.

"I hereby announce the betrothal of King Arthur to Angelique of The Valley," the High Chancellor said. "The wedding will take place four weeks from this day in the morning. The betrothal band is hereby blessed. King Arthur, please place the betrothal band on Angelique's fourth finger of her left hand."

Arthur took the band from Patrick and placed it on Angelique's finger.

"I bless this betrothal with the blessings of the gods and goddess and The Old Magic," Patric said as he held their hands in his. "Be happy."

Arthur placed a soft kiss on Angleique's cheek, and the room erupted in cheers and applause. Wishes and hugs were shared for quite some time. Arthur's sisters were beside themselves, and Glendianna had all she could do to hold them back. Arthur finally came over to them and was wrapped up in their hugs.

"Quintan, you kept this secret well," Margaret said as they stood apart.

"You sure did," Sarah said. "And I'm your favorite sister, and you didn't even tell me."

"I'm his favorite sister," Margaret said, laughing at Sarah.

"You are both my favorite sister," Arthur said. "Margaret is my oldest favorite sister, and Sarah is my younger favorite sister."

"Cute, brother," Margaret said.

"Always has been able to settle these two down," Hamlen said.

"I do believe handling the two of you has been a great lesson learned for being a king," Arthur said.

"It surely has," Glendianna said. "Girls, we are staying here for the month to prepare for the wedding. You'll have plenty of time to be with your brother."

"Really? This is great news, Mother," Sarah said.

"I can't wait to see the whole castle and everything," Margaret said.

"Girls," Angelique said. "We are going to learn how to dance and sing the old songs. We are going to help make my wedding gown and your special dresses, too. And you'll be spending some time in the kitchen with Rosie. She's in charge there and wants to meet you and hear all about Arthur's favorite foods and the things he doesn't like."

"We can do that," Sarah replied.

"It's time for the feasting to begin," Harrison said. "Let's all take our places for the blessing."

Patrick said the blessing, and the festivities began in earnest. Hours later, well into the night, the last knights left the great hall. It had been great fun, which the castle hadn't seen in many, many years. The night settled, and the kingdom slept well.

CHAPTER 21

The following day, King Arthur had a surprise for his knights. He called them together in the central courtyard with the castle workers and the guards.

"I'm glad to see all of you here," Arthur began. "Last evening was grand. I will remember it always."

"As we will, Your Highness," Russell said, bowing and smiling.

"I have some friends I would like you all to meet. Please clear the middle area of the courtyard. They are wonderful friends I need you to meet. Miss Penny and Q, if you please," Arthur said as he waved his hand across the area.

Penny and Q materialized from thin air, flew down from the parapets, and settled in the middle of the courtyard. The place was silent for a minute; then mild chaos took hold.

"Those are dragons!"

"They look okay."

"That one is purple. I didn't know dragons came in colors."

"Dragons are mean-spirited. They are evil!"

"No, sir, they are not," Russell said. "Some are just like some people that are mean-spirited. Get my drift?"

The man remained quiet.

"Good people," Arthur said rather loudly. "Quiet down, please."

Harrison and Fred were talking with Penny and Q.

"You knights know these dragons?" a townsman asked.

"We do," Harrison replied. "These here dragons are two of the kindest and most protective dragons I've ever encountered. And I've encountered a few nasty ones in my day. So, I know what I'm talking about."

"Thank you, Sir Harrison," Arthur said, nodding. "This is Miss Penny. She has been my protector for most of my life. She is intelligent, funny, and kind. And, be forewarned, if anyone tries to harm me and my family, Miss Penny and the Dragon Squad will intervene."

"Thank you, Arthur," Penny said.

"She can talk, too?"

"Oh my goodness!"

"Yes, I can talk, and my hearing is excellent for at least five miles," Penny replied.

"As is mine," Q added.

"This beautiful black dragon is Q," Arthur said. "He is a fierce fighter and a loyal friend."

"He helped us knights fight off those rogue dragons a while back," Fred said. "He and Ms Penny were severely injured and needed most of a year to heal in The Old Magic."

"So glad The Old Magic is always about," an older woman said. "I've never stopped honoring The Old Magic and the old ways. Sure happy you dragons are well healed."

"Thank you, Matilda, so are we," Penny said.

"Matilda, you know these two?" Russell asked.

"I do and have since I was born," Matilda said. "They are lovely indeed."

Thank you, Matilda," Q replied. "We feel the same way about you."

"I wondered if dragons were about a few months back. I found a dragon scale on the courtyard walkway after a rather nasty windstorm. Must be more than two of you. It's not your color."

"You are correct, Miss Matilda," Arthur said. "Come on down here."

Roman and Clarice flew down to join Penny and Q.

"It was the green one," Matilda said. "Thank you for the gift."

"You are quite welcome, Miss Matilda," Roman said.

"The green one is Roman, and this lovely yellow one is Clarice," Arthur said, introducing them.

The townspeople walked among the dragons and talked with them for quite some time. They were having a grand time seeing how The Old Magic was alive and well right here in the castle.

Russell called everyone to order. Arthur stepped up on the standing stone.

"I'm glad you all have met my magical friends. They will be here and about the kingdom from now on. There are others as well," Arthur explained. "Be cautious, as there are still rogue dragons about. If you hear about them or see any of them, please tell one of the guards or knights, and we'll look into it. I must go on about my day."

King Arthur and his contingent returned to the castle and the day's business. The castle workers remained outside for a few minutes more before returning to their duties.

"Miss Penny, Q, I'm glad you're healed and here to watch over King Arthur," Russell said. "I'm glad to know that Roman and Clarice have been here the whole time Quintan has been at the castle. I'm proud and honored to have known the king when he was a young lad."

"It is our honor to serve as well," Q replied. "Clarice and Roman told us that you have been a true and honest friend of our Quintan. We want you to know how much we appreciate that."

"He is very dear to me," Miss Penny said. "I am glad he has you as a friend as well."

"I see someone is in need of my services," Russell said. "Thanks for being here. I know we'll see each other soon."

The dragons nodded to Russell as he went about his duties. Roman and Clarice took to the sky to fly over Camelot and the whole kingdom to make sure everything was in good shape.

"Penny," Q said as he stretched his wings to their full length. "I do believe I need a bit of exercise. I'll be back in a few minutes. I'm going to check on Merlin and Feyanna to see if they're awake yet."

"I hope they're still sleeping," Penny said. "They were some of the last ones to leave last night."

"It was a great celebration," Q said as he lifted off.

Penny flew up to her favorite resting spot on the parapets. She could see all the castle courtyards and the southern kingdom from up there. She loved it.

The castle went back to work while the news about the four dragons buzzed around the kingdom faster than a lightning strike. The Old Magic surely was alive and well in Camelot.

Q settled in the meadow as Feyanna and Merlin finished breakfast. Or lunch. It was late in the morning.

"Q's here," Merlin said as he looked out the door and nodded to Q.

"I felt his energy a moment ago," Feyanna said. "Let's go."

"Good Morning, you two," Q said, smiling.

"Good Morning, Q," Merlin replied, yawning.

"What brings you our way, sir !?" Feyanna asked, yawning, too.

"Looks like the two of you are a bit tired," Q said. "I wonder why?"

"Wiseass dragon," Merlin replied, pointing his finger at Q and laughing.

"Indeed, we are tired," Feyanna replied. "Yesterday was beyond amazing. I'll be remembering it for the rest of my life."

"I know you will," Q replied. "It was magnificent. The Old Magic is alive and strong this day. We are very happy to be back and not have to hide anymore."

"That's right," Feyanna said. "We are happy, too."

"Now we can practice the old ways in the open and help all in need," Merlin said.

"How is Miss Penny this splendid day?" Feyanna asked.

"She is quite thrilled to be able to set upon the parapet in full view and watch over the castle and Camelot. I don't think she's stopped smiling since Arthur introduced us to the castle folks this morning," Q replied.

"That is great news!" Merlin said. "I have some things to discuss with Charles this afternoon. I'll chat with her before I go inside."

"She will love that," Q said.

"Oh, Q," Feyanna said. "What will Beau do now that the two of you are back in full force?"

"Beau is training to become a permanent member of The Dragon Brigade," Q explained. "One of his duties as such is to train young dragons in the first steps of using their powers to protect the innocents."

"That is a great deal of work and responsibility," Feyanna said.

"The Special Magic knows what it's doing," Feyanna said.

"Beau was fiercely dedicated to protecting us while you and Miss Penny were recovering. He'll make a great teacher," Merlin added.

"That's exactly the way Penny and I think about it," Q said. "Well, it's time for me to get back to the castle. I'll see you later, Merlin. Take a nap, Feyanna."

"I was just thinking that exact same thing," Feyanna said, yawning again.

Q lifted into the sky in one swift move and was gone a moment later, flying toward the castle.

"I guess I'd better gather my things and head over to the castle, too," Merlin said.

"I'll tidy up the cottage some," Feyanna said. "Then I'll take that nap."

Merlin gathered his things and set out for the castle. It was only a short ten-minute walk to the south gate. Feyanna got her chores done quickly and was sound asleep as Merlin was greeted by Russel at the south gate.

"Greetings, Sir Merlin," Russell said as Merlin walked in.

"Greetings, Russell," Merlin said. "I see things have been cleaned up quite nicely."

"The guards and castle folk worked through the night to get things back in order," Russell said. "It sure was a great celebration. We haven't seen anything like it as long as I've been here, and that's my whole life."

"It was fantastic," Merlin said. "Feyanna is napping as we speak."

"Good to hear," Russell said. "She is a special healer, and we love her."

"I'll be sure to tell her you said so," Merlin said as he looked up at Penny.

"Ah, you know Miss Penny I see," Russell said as he waved to her.

"For a very long time, Russell," Merlin said as Miss Penny flew down to stand beside him.

"Merlin," Penny said, lifting a wing.

Merlin walked over and stroked her wing.

"My Penny," Merlin said.

"It is good to see you here," Penny said as Merlin stepped back. "I suspect you are on your way to visit with Charles?"

"I am," Merlin said. "We have lots to discuss."

"Yes, you do," Penny replied. "Back up to my perch."

Penny flew up to the parapet as Merlin waved to Russell and walked into the castle to find Charles hard at work in his quarters. Merlin and Charles spent the afternoon discussing potions and remedies. Then, Merlin brought up a sensitive subject.

"Alchemy? I've heard of it but haven't looked into it," Chares said.

"It's the mixing of metals to make a pure metal," Merlin said, watching Charles.

"I've heard tales of witches and wizards trying to make gold from metals to no avail," Charles replied.

"Me, too," Merlin said.

Charles looked at Merlin. Merlin looked like he was talking with someone, but nobody else was there.

"Who are you talking with, Merlin?" Charles asked.

"Charles, you know that The Old Magic is back in our everyday lives, right?" Merlin

"I do," Charles replied. "King Arthur declared it as such."

"I tell you this: The Old Magic was never gone. It's been with us all the while the old king declared it heresy."

"I suspected as much," Charles.

"The Old Magic is part of a bigger realm known as The Special Magic. Dragons are from The Special Magic," Merlin said, smiling. "Charles, if I tell you that gold and silver can be made from other metals is fact, would you believe me?"

"These days, Merlin, I would believe you," Charles said.

"Watch," Merlin said as he set about gathering three different metals, crystals, and a few herbs.

Merlin brought a pot of water to boil and placed the herbs and crystals in separate earthen bowls. Next, he took three quartz crystals from his cloak and placed them on the workbench. They were glowing brightly.

"How did you make them do that?" Charles asked in amazement.

"Quartz has an energy all its own," Merlin explained. "When you place quartz crystals in the sun, they absorb the sunlight and store it so you can use it instead of candles. That's what's in the other bag. Feyanna sent about twenty crystals for you to have and share around the castle. We've already taken care of the king, the kitchen, the knights, and the guards. Just remember to set them in the sunlight each day to charge them. Blow out your candles now."

Charles blew out his candles and continued to watch Merlin. As soon as the water was boiling, he placed the herbs in the pot. There was a momentary hissing sound as the herbs became steam. Next, he took the metals and carefully placed them into the boiling herbs. He stood back and began chanting in a language Charles had never heard before.

"Charles, I have asked The Special Magic to bless us with the gift of gold from the blending of the herbs, water, and metals," Merlin said. "Listen."

"Charles," a voice said as a mist began to form in the room. "Merlin is a gifted and blessed wizard. All of this is good magic. Search your heart, and you will know instantly."

Charles thought about this and knew it was all good.

"I accept this gift of The Special Magic and am honored," Charles said as he bowed toward the mist.

"Charles, you have been a good wizard, and we are happy with all you have learned. Listen and learn from Merlin. You will need all that he can tell you. Feyanna, too. She will add to your knowledge of herbal healing," the mist said.

"I will do as you wish," Charles said as the mist took form.

Merlin saw the Lady of The Lake.

"I am honored at your presence, dear Lady," Merlin said, bowing.

"Hello, Merlin," the Lady said. "We are happy with all that has taken place here with Arthur. Guide him well."

"As you wish," Merlin said.

"I have visited Feyanna as she sleeps. She knows what she must do," the Lady said. "Charles, enjoy the alchemy. It can be quite fun as no one except you, Merlin, and Feyanna will know that the blessing of The Special Magic turns metals and herbs into gold and silver."

"Lady,'" Merlin said, laughing, "You do have a great sense of humor."

"Indeed," Charles said, laughing along with Merlin.

"We think so," the Lady replied. "May you all be blessed with the love of The Divine. Merlin, we will meet again soon."

"Dear Lady, "Merlin said. "Thank you for this visit and these blessings."

"I am honored by your blessings," Charles said, bowing as the Lady returned to mist and vanished altogether.

The men looked at each other and remained silent for a bit.

"That was beyond belief," Charles whispered as he sat down.

"It always is," Merlin replied, sitting next to Charles. "Not a word to anyone except me and Feyanna."

"Understood," Charles said. "Now what?"

"Let's look in the pot," Merlin said. "The water has stopped boiling, and the fire has gone out."

They stood, looked into the pot, and saw several good-sized nuggets of gold staring back at them.

"That's amazing!" Charles said.

"Always is," Merlin said as he took them out one by one with a pair of wooden tongs. "They're still very hot. They'll need a few hours to cool down. Tell no one. These are a gift for you alone. At some point, you will leave the castle and will need them to live a good life somewhere else."

"I've been thinking about that a bit lately," Charles said. "The way you've talked about the village where King Arthur grew up sounds like a delightful and wonderful place. I was thinking I might settle there one day."

"That would be excellent," Merlin said. "The cottage home Feyanna and I lived in is a solid structure and close to the village. I'll tell Hamlen when I see him next that you will take possession of it one day."

"Thank you for your kindness," Charles said. "Now, let's go visit Rosie. I'm beyond starving."

"Me, too," Merlin said as they left the room and headed to the kitchen.

Rosie was thrilled to see them and set them down to a bountiful supper. They talked about the celebration, laughing and sharing stories of the night. Rosie sent Merlin home with enough food for at least three days. She wouldn't let him refuse.

The days flew by during the wedding preparations. King Arthur and his advisors handled daily business and got ready for the wedding as well. About a week before the wedding, the knights brought a man before the king.

Sir Jacob stood with the man before the king.

"Sir Jacob, what have we here?" Arthur asked.

"Your Highness, this man was caught stealing food from one vendor and clothing from another. Their stalls are right next to each other. We have five witnesses who can verify this action," Sir Jacob explained.

"I see," King Arthur said. "And what are you called?"

"I am known as Maynard, Your Highness," Maynard replied, bowing before the king.

"Maynard, are these accusations true?" Arthur asked as he stood and walked toward Maynard and Jacob.

Maynard didn't reply.

"Sir Jacob, is there a problem here?" King Arthur asked.

"Your Highness, it seems Maynard here thinks he is to be allowed to take anything he wants from the merchants because he says he's related to you," Jacob said.

"Really, Maynard? How are you related to me?" Arthur asked.

"Your Highness, you may not remember it, but before you were taken away from your homeplace, we were cousins," Maynard replied.

"I do remember my old home perfectly," Arthur replied. "We were never cousins."

"You may have been very young then, so you don't remember me or my family. We lived on your farm and worked the land. You were probably no more than four or five when you were taken away by thieves," Maynard explained.

"I see, Maynard," Arthur replied. "I must say you have quite the imagination. My family did not have relatives anywhere near the village where I was born and raised. Therefore, Maynard, you are a liar as well as a thief."

"But, Your Highness," Maynard said, trying to convince the king of his early childhood. "You were so very young; I'm not surprised you don't remember me. It was a horrible time when the thieves attacked the village and killed almost everyone."

"Nice try, Maynard. But your story isn't true," Arthur said. "You didn't hear the whole story from your friends in Camelot. They left out a few grave details. On that note, I am ready to sentence you for your acts of theft."

"With all due respect, Your Highness, how can you believe the words of liars?" Maynard asked.

"Sir Jacob watched you steal the food and the clothes," Arthur replied. "I believe him. You have a choice here, Maynard. You can spend ninety days in the dungeons or work to pay your debt by caring for the animals on the castle farm for ninety days. The farm needs someone to clean the stalls twice a day, spread clean straw and water, and feed the animals. What is your decision?"

"I choose the farm work," Maynard said, thinking no one would be watching him.

"Good choice," Arthur replied as he sat down on his throne. "Sir Jacob, please take Maynard to the farm and place him in the hands of the Guard Joseph. Joseph will put a bell around your waist so the farm always knows where you are. It will be removed after ninety days. Maynard, if you disobey the Gurad Joseph, more days will be added to your sentence. You will live in the barn with the animals."

Maynard looked at the king and Gerald for a minute, then down at the floor, feeling defeated.

"Thank you, Your Highness," Sir Jacob said. "Come along, Maynard"

They left, and the throne room was empty of citizens. Arthur, Harrison, and Fred remained. They waited a moment to make sure that Gerald had his prisoner were out of earshot, then broke out laughing.

"Arthur, that was splendid," Fred said.

"Thanks for the heads-up," Arthur said.

"That Maynard had no idea what was about to happen," Harrison said. "Boy, was he surprised by your choice of actions. I'll bet he thought he'd be home free on the farm."

"Exactly," Arthur replied. "I love the ideas we come up with. Thanks for your help with this one. I really didn't want to have him flogged. Too brutal."

"I agree," Fred said. "There is going to come a time when that will be necessary. And, even a beheading, too."

"I agree," Arthur said. "Just not now. Let's get through the wedding before we have to dish out the more serious sentences."

"Most folks are behaving these days," Harrison said. "I think it's because of the wedding and all. They want to celebrate with you and Angelique. How's she doing with all this royal stuff?"

"She is a bit overwhelmed," Arthur replied. "I'm really glad her mother and family are here to help. My family is helping her, too. My sisters and Angelique spent two days deciding on the wedding gown design and fabric and another day on the gowns for the attendants. It's a good thing there are only three pairs of them. Us guys have it easy."

"We sure do," Harrison said. "Hugho is very excited about being your witness."

"I am honored that he accepted," Arthur said. "We have so many stories to tell. It'll take us years to get through them."

"Hugho has shared a few of them with us already," Fred said, laughing with Harrison.

"I'm sure he has," Arthur said. "Now, let's get back to the business at hand. We need to discuss the rogue dragon problem before it becomes a big one."

"The scouts tell us that there has been an attack on a church just about an hour north of here," Fred said. "The church was empty, so no one died. The church was burned to the ground. The stone foundation is still intact, and the villagers have already begun to rebuild. This time, they're going to build with rocks and boulders."

"Good idea," Harrison said. "I'll be sure to get the word out about building with more rocks and earth. That way, if attacked by dragon fire or a fire burning out of control, the buildings stand a better chance of surviving."

"Make it so, Harrison," Arthur said. "Great idea. Thanks for that."

"King Arthur, come look outside," Fred said as he held the drapes aside so the three could see the sky.

"Oh my god!" Arthur said. "Here we go again."

"It's those silver discs again," Harrison said.

"It sure is," Arthur replied as they watched more silver discs appear over Camelot.

The good people of Camelot stopped what they were doing and stared at the discs. They watched as the skies filled with discs; some hovered over Camelot and the surrounding countryside. Feyanna and Merlin were outside when the first disc appeared, and they watched it as well. Penny and Q materialized and began to fly around the airspace where the discs were. The discs didn't move, and Penny and Q made sure they didn't fly too close to them, either.

"I wonder if the entities inside those things know what's about to happen here?" Arthur said.

"You mean the wedding?" Fred asked.

"Yes, and the coronation," Arthur said.

"It makes me wonder just what kind of being is so smart they can make machines that fly," Harrison said.

"I was thinking that exact thing," Arthur was saying when one of the discs sent a beam of orange light into the center of Camelot.

Screams were heard all around as the light showed three people being taken into the sky and then into the disc. All hell broke loose. People were running for cover in homes and under carts. Another disc shot a beam of blue light into the castle's central courtyard and took two of the washing women and a guard right into its discs.

Everyone watched as a beam of yellow light took two cows from a farm on the edge of Camelot into its disc. The knights thought about shooting arrows at them, but they were all too high in the sky.

"Oh my god! Arthur, what should we do?" Fred asked as beams of light continued to take people and animals into the discs.

"I have no idea," Arthur replied. "This is beyond me."

Angelique and both families ran into Arthur's chambers.

"What is happening?" Angelique cried as she ran to Arthur.

"I don't know, everyone," Arthur replied. "I think we'll all be safe if we stay inside. Let's try to be calm. Fred, will you ask Rosie to send up some tea and such?"

"Indeed, Sire," Fred replied as he stepped into the hallway to relay the message to one of the king's paiges

"This is so crazy," Hamlen said as he looked out of the window.

"Look," Angelique's father said, pointing outside. "The discs are changing colors and beginning to spin."

The discs were changing colors, and in just a few seconds, they formed a line in the sky and shot straight upward until they couldn't be seen anymore. Screaming and crying were heard around Camelot. Rosie arrived with tea and sandwiches for everyone.

"Rosie, please stay," Arthur asked of her.

"Of course, young Quintan," Rosie replied. "I mean Your Highness."

"Rosie, you can call me young Quintan whenever you like," Arthur replied. "Let's keep some things unchanged. Are all the kitchen workers still here?"

"Yes," Rosie replied. "We lost a few washerwomen and a guard. I haven't heard from anyone else yet," Rosie answered.

"Rosie, drink and eat with us," Harrison said.

"I'd like that, Harrison," Rosie said as she finished pouring for everyone and a cup for herself.

A paige was brought into the room, followed by Merlin and Feyanna.

"Report, paige," Harrison said.

"Your Highness," the paige said as he bowed toward Arthur. "About twenty people were taken from Camelot and six cows that we know of so far. Some of the knights are riding around the outer farms to gather information."

"Thank you for your report," Harrison said. "You are dismissed."

The paige bowed again, then left.

Merlin looked at Arthur and nodded.

"Merlin and Feyanna, it's good to see you are still here," Arthur said. "I was worried you might be taken."

"We were afraid as well, Your Highness," Feyanna replied.

"Call me Arthur when it's just family and advisors," Arthur said.

"Thanks for that," Merlin said. "It all happened so fast. I haven't had time to ponder on it."

That was Merlin's way of telling Arthur that he, Arthur, and Feyanna needed to talk privately. Arthur nodded his head every so slightly that only Fred and Harrison noticed.

Russell entered just then to report to the king.

"Your Highness," Russell said as he bowed toward Arthur. "The castle is in an uproar. Everyone is terrified of being abducted. The knights are working hard to calm folks down, but I think you may need to say something soon."

"I agree with you, Russell," Arthur said. "I'll address the kingdom in one hour. Get the word out. I'll use the large balcony that overlooks Camelot."

"Feyanna and I will meet with Arthur now in a private room," Merlin said in a stern voice.

"Follow me," Russell said as he led them down the hall to a small room with a table and chairs. "I'll stay outside."

"Thank you, Russell," Merlin said as he closed the door and bolted it.

The three of them looked at each other for a moment.

"We know who they are," Merlin said.

"We do," Feyanna and Arthur replied.

"May I share my thoughts?" Feyanna asked.

"Go right ahead," Arthur replied.

"Remember when the ethereal being was telling us about the creation of Mother Earth and the first entities to be placed here?" Feyanna asked.

Both men nodded in agreement.

"I remember when Penny was telling Merlin and me about a change that was set to take place that would decide if The Divine would let humans stay here. Quintan, the ethereal being, and then Penny told Merlin and me how after many hundreds, maybe thousands, of years, the first people were damaging the earth and their own kind with recklessness and disregard for life. The Divine decided to erase them from the earth and did so with floods, fire, disease, and violent earthquakes. When the eradication was over, only a few humans were left. The Divine brought more entities to this place and let them evolve until now."

"We were told that this time would come, and a kind and strong king needed to take the throne if the people were to have any kind of chance to stay," Merlin said.

Arthur looked at Merlin and Feyanna.

"You've always known my destiny, haven't you?" Arthur asked.

"We have," Merlin said.

"We found out at the time you were rescued by Penny and brought to our cottage home,"

Feyanna said. "We were not allowed to say or do anything that might influence you as you grew up. Just the usual things about being a kid and then a young man."

"I can see it all now," Arthur said as he stared into space. "I'm glad I was chosen and rescued by Penny and placed with Hamlen. I've had a great childhood. And you, Merlin, have been a magnificent teacher and Mentor in many ways."

"It has been my pleasure and honor," Merlin said, smiling at Arthur. "Especially when you ended up in the lake trying to learn to be light on your feet."

"I remember," Arthur said, laughing with them. "It has truly helped me take the throne."

"Those swimming races with the other children were wonderful to watch," Feyanna said. "Merlin and I knew without a doubt that you would be a just and strong leader from the way you worked with the children."

"I loved those races as well," Arthur said. "Now, about these flying machines."

"I'm not sure why they've taken people and animals," Merlin said. "I have a strong suspicion that they are not the same ones that have been taking care of us. It's a strong hunch."

"You mean there's more than one kind?" Arthur asked.

"Yes," Merlin said. "There are many types of animals on our Earth. So, why shouldn't there be more than one kind of creature from the stars?"

"That's an incredible thought," Feyanna said. "It makes perfect sense. It scares me as well. I wonder if those people and animals will be returned?"

"I'm sure everyone is wondering that," Arthur said. "What do I say to the people? I'm as scared as they are."

"I think we start with trying not to panic. Don't throw things at the discs. They're too far away to waste precious ammunition on. Then what?" Arthur said.

"How about try to go about your regular day and if they return, go inside?" Feyanna said

"Feyanna, you usually see the simple things," Arthur said. "That's perfect. I may add that they should not think this is a punishment from any god and goddesses, too."

"Oh, good idea," Merlin said. "Remind them that the gods and goddesses of The Old Magic are kind and loving spirits that would not steal people and animals. Remind them to be respectful of their gods and goddesses, whomever they choose to believe in."

"Excellent, then. We're ready to address the kingdom," Arthur said.

Merlin opened the door, and Arthur stepped into the hall.

'Thanks for keeping guard, Russell," Arthur said. "You are a true and kind friend."

"Thank you, Your Highness," Russell said, bowing. "Time for you to address the kingdom?"

"It is," Merlin said. "Lead on."

Arthur, Merlin, and Feyanna followed Russell to the large balcony and waited inside.

"Word traveled fast about you speaking. The place is packed in the courtyard and in Camelot," Harrison informed Arthur.

"Good work, everyone," Arthur said. "Sound the trumpets."

The trumpets sounded, and Arthur stepped onto the balcony. The people showed their respect, cheering and applauding for a few minutes. Finally, quiet took over.

"Good and kind people of Camelot," Arthur began. "A magnificent and frightening event took place a while ago, and we are all wondering about it. I am just as puzzled as you about those flying discs and where they came from. I would like to know what kind of creature is inside of them, too, just like everyone. I have been talking with my wise advisor, and the Great Merlin, and Healer Feyanna about this. We have a few things to share with you.

"First, we should not provoke them in any way. Do not shoot arrows or such at them. They are a long way up in the sky, and we would just be wasting our precious ammunition doing such a thing,"

The people talked about this for a minute before the king continued.

"Secondly," Arthur said, "I genuinely believe we should respect the gods and goddesses we choose to believe in. We have different religious beliefs, and I firmly believe that whatever Divine Being is watching over us did not send these creatures as punishment for anything wrong we've ever done. Please be kind and thoughtful of each other.

"Lastly, I do not know if the people and animals taken will be returned. I hope they are returned quickly. Please do not let your fear control your actions. We are all a bit scared and curious about those flying discs. Even after the things that happened today, watching them change color and shoot up into the heavens was a sight to behold. Let's get back to our daily business."

Arthur and the knights went back inside, where Merlin, Feyanna, and the families were waiting for them.

"That was well said," Merlin said.

"You spoke confidently and with kindness and concern for your people," Glendianna said.

"Your Highness?" Fred said.

"Yes, Fred," Arthur replied.

"The knights just returned from their scouting mission. They report no other people were taken. There were, however, two pigs and several chickens taken from several farms," Fred reported.

"Thanks for that, Fred," Arthur said as his scribe took the notes. "I think the best thing for us to do is go about our day. It is only one week before Angelique and I are to be married. I'm sure there are a thousand and one things that need attention."

"That's for sure," Angelique said, laughing.

"We have to finish our dresses," Sarah said.

"They are beautiful," Margaret added. "You'll think so as soon as you see them, Quintan."

"I believe I will," Arthur said, ruffling Margaret's curls.

"I think your brother will have his eyes on only one person, girls," Hamlen said.

"Angelique's dress is heavenly," Sarah said, sighing.

"Not a word, Sarah," Margaret said, elbowing her sister.

"I'm not saying anything in detail," Sarah replied as she elbowed her sister in return.

"Sisters," Arthur said as he hugged them both. "I wouldn't know what to do without you."

"We love you, too," the girls said at the same time.

"Alright, everyone," Harrison said. "Let's get back to your dresses and the business of the kingdom."

They went their different ways as Harrison, Merlin, Fred, Feyanna, and Arthur returned to discussing the business of the kingdom.

"I order the knights to patrol the kingdom around the clock until the people are returned," Arthur said. "We now have twenty knights in our ranks. Harrison set a schedule for the twelve knights of the Round Table to take turns patrolling the kingdom with two lesser knights. I want eight senior knights in the castle at all times."

"As you command, Sire," Harrison said as he sat with the scribe to set a schedule as ordered. He soon left to inform the Knights of The Round Table of the new plans.

"Fred, I need you to take control of the security of the castle proper," Arthur said. "Work with Russell and his two senior guards. Ensure our families continue to have guards at their chambers and wherever they go."

"Of course, Your Highness," Fred said, signaling another scribe to walk with him as he went to find Russell and set the schedule.

That left Merlin, Feyanna, and Arthur in his outer chamber.

"We need to talk with Penny and Q immediately," Arthur said. "Let's go out to the field and summon them."

"I don't think we'll need to summon them," Merlin said. "Look!"

They all laughed as they saw Penny's face looking in the chamber window at them.

"Miss Penny, of course," Arthur said. "We're on our way to the south field. You and Q, please join us."

They went down into the castle's lower level to a secret tunnel shown to Arthur by his Sacred Guides.

"Where does this lead us?" Feyanna asked as they walked along. The tunnel was lit by charged quartz crystals that appeared as they walked along.

"Never mind," Feyanna said. "I get it. It will lead us to wherever we need to go."

The crystals flashed a rainbow of colors at them for a second.

"Love The Old Magic," Arthur said.

A few minutes later, an opening appeared. They walked up an incline, out of the tunnel, and found themselves at the far edge of the south field. Penny and Q were waiting for them.

"Did you have a nice walk?" Penny asked, blinking her long eyelashes at them.

"Very funny, Miss Penny," Merlin answered, laughing with everyone.

"Miss Penny, Q, I know those flying discs are part of something so much bigger than anything we can imagine," Arthur said. "I just want to make sure our people and animals are not being tortured."

"Quintan," Penny said. "They are from another place beyond the sky you see. There are many beings from beyond the stars. These specific discs have taken the people and animals to learn about them. The Old Magic can not interfere with the actions of living entities unless we need them for a more benevolent purpose."

"You mean we have to let things happen," Feyanna said.

"That is a good way to say it, Feyanna," Q replied. "I know this is difficult for humans to accept, but it is the way of things this time."

"Will the people and animals be returned?" Merlin asked.

Q and Penny didn't say anything for a few minutes. It was obvious they were in conversation with Divine Spirits.

"Feyanna, Merlin, and Quintan," Q said. "We are not to be privileged in knowing this information."

"We understand," Arthur replied.

"I would ask this of The Old Magic, if possible," Feyanna said. "Should they be returned, would it be possible for them to forget any terrifying things that have happened to them while taken?"

"I believe The Old Magic will help them readjust if and when they return," Penny said. "That is all we are being told."

"I am thankful for that," Feyanna said, bowing toward the dragons and raising her hands to the sky to show respect for the message from The Divine. " I have remedies to help them as well."

"Yes, you do," Merlin said. "Charles and I will help you make those potions."

"Thanks, Merlin," Feyanna said.

"The Dragon Brigade is checking on the countryside and flying over Camelot to let the people know we are concerned," Q said.

"Most of them wave at us as we fly by," Penny added. "We even fly low if we can and wave at them, too."

"That's wonderful," Arthur said. "I hope it gives them some peace."

"One of the children from a farm just south of here calls out to us, too," Q said. "He says thank you and to be careful."

"He is a sweet boy," Penny replied. "It makes us feel loved."

"Maybe when this is over, you and Q could sit down near his farm and talk with him," Feyanna said. "I'm sure he'd be thrilled with the visit."

"We most certainly will," Penny replied. "After the wedding and all."

"Of course," Feyanna said. "We are only a week away from that special day. I know all of The Dragon Brigade will be there."

"We will be there," Q replied. "Wouldn't miss it for anything."

"I'm honored that you will be with us," Arthur said. "On another note, do you think those flying discs could hurt any of us?"

"That's a good question," Penny replied. "They have knowledge beyond what you here have, so I wouldn't be surprised if they have weapons to match their flying ability."

"I was thinking the same thing," Arthur said. "We are powerless against them."

"Think again," Q said.

"Ah, yes," Arthur said, nodding as he kept thinking. "We have The Special Magic to help us. I do understand and will only call upon it if need be. I will protect these good people of Camelot and the kingdom as best I can."

"That is the perfect answer," Q said, lifting a wing to salute Arthur.

"Cute, Q," Merlin said.

"I try," Q replied.

"You most certainly are trying," Penny replied, giving Q the "Penny" look. This made everyone laugh.

"Well, it's time to return to the castle," Arthur said as he walked over and shook hands and wings with the dragons.

"I will love you always," Arthur whispered to Q and Penny.

'Time to fly," Q said as Arthur stepped back from him.

"Be safe," Feyanna said.

Penny and Q lifted into the sky in one swift move. Arthur, Feyanna, and Merlin returned to the castle through the magic tunnel just in time for supper.

Arthur spent the evening with Harrison and Fred, reviewing their plans for keeping the kingdom safe.

"That should take care of everything," Arthur said, yawning. "What a day!"

"We hear ya, Quintan," Harrison replied.

"I feel like I've been in battle for hours," Fred said. "We all need a good night's rest."

"Forgive me for addressing you as Quintan, my Lord," Harrison said.

"You both may call me Quintan as you wish when we are alone," Arthur said. "I miss hearing my birth name."

"Thanks for that," Harrison said as he and Fred stood to leave. "Sleep well."

"You both as well," Arthur said as they left.

There was a knock on his door.

"Enter," Arthur said as he stood.

"Quintan," Angelique said as she flew into his arms.

"This is the best thing that's happened to me all day," Quintan said as he held her close and stroked her back.

She found his mouth and covered it with hers. They explored each other with their tongues for the longest time.

"This is the best part of my day," Angelique said as they sat down on the bed.

Quintan opened her dressing gown and found her bare breasts. He slid down and took one into his mouth. He licked her nipple and then began sucking her. Angelique moaned as she enjoyed the touch.

"I don't want to wait a week," Arthur said. "I know we need to, but I don't want to."

"Let me explore you," Angelique said as she undressed him, then undressed herself.

They climbed under the covers, and Angelique found Arthur's hard shaft and began stroking it. He moaned as he got harder and bigger. He pulled away just before he would have cum. He slid down Angleique's belly and found her wet mound. He began licking it, and she cried out in ecstasy. He used his finger to stroke her clit as he licked her. She felt a burning start in her belly and wanted more. He brought her to her climax, and she felt like every ounce of her being exploded in a pleasure she had never before felt. She bucked and writhed in the bed until he stopped touching her. She fell silent for a few minutes, feeling the pulses going through her body until they ceased.

"Oh my god!" Angelique whispered. "That was amazing. I want more."

"You will get more the minute we're married," Arthur said. "And as much as you want whenever you want it."

"I think we're going to be very busy on our wedding day," Angelique said, giggling.

"We do have to wait until after the wedding feast," Arthur said.

"Well, the ceremony is at noon, and the feast will begin immediately after that," Angelique said. "Do we have to stay for the whole feast?"

"You little vixen," Arthur said as he licked her breast. "We do."

"Alright. I suppose it will be quite fun anyway," Angelique said. "Keep sucking my breasts. It feels so good."

"As you wish," Arthur said.

He sucked her breasts and found her clit wet and hot. He began stroking her, and in a few minutes, she began to feel that rising sensation of pleasure. She felt Arthur as he rubbed her faster, and in a minute, she exploded again. She sailed through the pleasure as her body pulsed then quieted. Angelique fell asleep for a few minutes.

"I can do that more than once?" Angelique said. "This is great."

"It is great, this lovemaking," Arthur said.

"You haven't let me please you, though," Angelique said as she grabbed his hard shaft and wouldn't let go.

"God, that feels amazing," Arthur said as he let her keep pleasing him. He didn't stop her this time as he neared his organism. He grabbed his shirt and placed it over his hard shaft just before he came. She jerked him as his seed exploded from his dick.

Angelique let go of him, and they lay entwined for a while.

"I need to go to sleep," Angelique said as she yawned.

"You do," Arthur said as they untangled themselves from each other.

Angelique dressed as Arthur did, and he walked her to the door, where they kissed good night.

"Please walk Lady Angelique to her chambers, Sir Gerald," Arthur ordered.

"Of course, Sire," Gerald said, placing Angleique's hand on his arm.

They both slept deeply that night, dreaming of their wedding night.

The rest of the week found the countryside excited for the wedding and carefully watching the sky for the return of the flying silver discs. Arthur and his advisors held meetings in the mornings. The afternoons were spent learning the rules for the ceremony. Angelique was busy accepting gifts in the afternoon with her mother. Some were thoughtful, and others were very humorous. Sarah and Margaret were learning the old dances and the rules for their part of the ceremony.

The day before the ceremony, a strange thing happened around noon. Clouds began to gather in the sky out of nowhere. The day had been warm and sunny, as most summer days had been. The clouds began to swirl slowly. It was a fantastic thing to watch. The whole kingdom stopped and watched. King Arthur, Angelique, and their families were in the courtyard, taking the air when it all started.

As everyone continued to watch, the clouds began to change colors—every color of the rainbow and then some that had never been seen before. The swirling became faster, and small rays of color began to touch down on the earth. One blue stream of color stretched down and touched the courtyard, leaving baskets full of blue flowers of every shade and shape. More streams of every color did the same thing all over the kingdom. In only a few minutes, the courtyard was filled with baskets of flowers of every color. The courtyard looked like a rainbow had come to life.

"This is beautiful," Angelique said as she started walking through the baskets.

"I think we should find vases for them and put them all over the castle for tomorrow, Sarah suggested.

"I think I will gather special ones for the bride's bouquet," Glendianna said. "If that's alright with The Magic?"

There was a flash of green light as a response.

"Great. Ladies, let's get busy," Glendianna said. "Russell, will you and the guards assist us, please? Let's take these into the banquet hall and get busy."

Russell and some of the guards helped bring the baskets into the banquet hall. As soon as the guards left, an army of faeries flew in, and in an instant, the bridal bouquet was finished. It was magnificent and set on a pedestal in water.

The faeries made bouquets for the attendants and arrangements for the ceremony area. Centerpieces were made and set along the main table and all the other tables. The men's boutonnieres were also set aside.

"This is unbelievable," Glendianna said as the faeries finished. "You are all so beautiful. Thank you for your lovely help."

"We love Quintan and Angelique," one of the faeries said. "We'll take care of them always."

"Thank you for that," Angelique said. "We love you all very much. Thanks for taking care of Penny and Q, too. I hear you never left their sides."

"Indeed, we stayed," the faerie said. "We'll see you in the morning."

And the faeries left in a flash of colorful lights.

"I knew they were real," Margaret said. "I told you they were real, and you never believed me."

"I believe you now," Sarah said, staring at everything. "I will believe in The Magic forever."

"Good idea," Angelique said, laughing with everyone.

"I see the faeries have been busy," Rosie said as supper was brought in. "They are magnificent. You've done a beautiful job here, little faeries. Thank you."

Another flash of orange light filled the room.

"I love it when that happens," Rosie said as she and her workers set things up. "Now, eat. Tomorrow is a very busy day, and we need all of you well-fed and well-rested."

"Yes, Ma'am," Sarah and Margaret said at the same time.

"You're good girls," Rosie said, winking at them.

Arthur was pacing in his outer chambers.

"Arthur, settle down," Hugho said.

"What?" Arthur said.

"Settle down. You're pacing like a caged animal," Hugho said as he took Arthur by the shoulders and pushed him into a chair.

"I, ah, I guess I'm a bit nervous," Arthur said. "I didn't realize getting married was so scary."

"Maybe it's getting married in front of a whole kingdom; that's the scary part," Hugho said. "You know, with everyone watching you and all."

"I agree with that," Arthur said. "God, I hope I don't mess up the vows."

"You won't," Hugho said. "It's my job to make sure you don't. Besides, Patrick said he'll tell you what to say if you forget."

"I do believe Patrick will have a little fun with me about those vows," Arthur said.

"Most likely," Hugho said, pointing at Arthur. "It sure will be fun to watch."

"You do know I have people beheaded, right?" Arthur replied, pointing back at Hugho.

"I'm shaking in my boots," Hugho said. "Quintan, did you ever think any of this would happen to us when we were kids?"

"None of it," Arthur replied. "The thing I wanted most was a warm home and work that I loved to do."

"Same here," Hugho said. "I thought I'd probably stay home and work the farm with my father until he couldn't do it anymore."

"I know I'm not a gifted cart maker like Hamlen," Arthur said. "I can build things like most of us, but not those amazing carts and wagons."

"He sure is special," Hugho said. "I saw the ones he made for the old king in the stables the other day. Are you going to use them?"

"I was thinking about them, too," Arthur said. "I think I'll give all but one of them to the most needy families. What do you think?"

"That's a great idea," Hugho said. "I'll talk with Harrison and Fred and see if we can find a couple of families that would get a lot of use out of them."

"Thanks," Arthur said as he stood up. "I'm starving. Let's eat!"

Rosie walked in at that exact moment with trays full of food for them all.

"Rosie, I love that you know me so well," Arthur said as he kissed her on the cheek.

"Ah, young Quintan, go on with your sweet ways," Rosie said, directing the layout of the food.

"This looks delicious," Hugho said. "Thanks, Rosie, to all of you. I know you're preparing the wedding feast, and to take the time to make these delicious foods is beyond wonderful."

"You are always welcome, Hugho," Rosie said. "Now, keep this one calm for tomorrow, will you?"

"I'm trying my best," Hugho said as Rosie and her helpers left.

Harrison and Fred walked in, and they all sat, ate, and talked for a while. Patrick walked in as they were finishing.

"Your Highness," Patrick said. "I see Rosie is making sure you don't waste away before tomorrow."

"She is," Harrison replied.

"I wanted to talk with you in private for a moment if possible," Patrick said.

The others left the outer chambers.

"What is it, Patrick?" Arthur.

"No doubt you've been counseled by your father on the ways of treating a woman on your wedding night."

"Patrick, thanks for thinking of me. I am all set," Arthur said. "Both my parents have had talks with me."

"Good," Patrick said, showing relief. "I really didn't want to have this conversation."

"I'm glad you're relieved," Arthur said. "Is everything ready?"

"It is," Patrick said, eating a cookie. "Do you have any questions about the order of the ceremony?"

"One minute, I know it, and the next, I have no idea what to do," Arthur answered.

"That's typical," Patrick said. "Hugho and I will give you your cues as we go along."

"Thanks for everything," Arthur said. "My wedding clothes are ready, and my crown has been polished. Angelique's is ready as well. Her ladies told her she would be crowned after the vows, but I think she's already forgotten about it."

"Probably. She's very nervous, as most brides are," Patrick said. "I had a talk with her about the vows and such a little while ago in the grand hall. The faeries have been very busy with all those flowers and plants. One of the townsfolk told me the whole kingdom has been busy making wedding wreaths and door garlands."

"I'll bet the place looks amazing," Arthur said.

"You and Lady Angelique are required to ride through the city after the ceremony," Patrick said. "You'll see for yourselves."

"Oh, that's right. I forgot about that part," Arthur said.

"I think you'll both enjoy the ride in one of the wagons your father made. It's been decorated just for the wedding," Patrick said.

"I wondered what he's been up to these past few days," Arthur said. "I'm sure my sisters helped, too."

"They did," Patrick said. "Now, time to settle for the night. Sleep well."

"Thank you, Patrick," Arthur said as Patrick left.

Angelique was alone with her mother.

"My sweet daughter, there are a few things I need to tell you," her mother said.

"I already know about them," Angelique said. "It's about when Arthur and I make love."

"Yes," her mother replied, surprised. "How do you know?"

"I am still a virgin, but our kissing has gotten quite passionate," Angelique said.

"It's about when he enters you," her mother said. "It's going to be painful for a few minutes. It will go away rather quickly."

"I know," Angelique said. "I've spoken with Rosie about these things."

"All of it?" her mother asked.

"All of it," Angelique replied. "I know you are very uncomfortable talking about such things, so I asked Rosie about it. And she said she will tell me everything I need to know when I am with a child."

"She is a blessed woman," her mother replied. "I won't have anything to worry about."

"Nothing, Mother," Angelique said, hugging her. "Let's get some sleep. We are getting up with the sun tomorrow."

"Yes, we are," her mother replied. "Sleep well, my daughter."

Final preparations were in place by midnight all over the kingdom, and Camelot settled into sleep.

As the sun rose, Angelique and the women of the wedding party sat down to a huge breakfast Rosie had made for them.

"Rosie, you will stay and eat with us," Angelique said.

"Yes, Your Highness," Rosie replied.

"Really Rosie? I will always be Angelique to you," Angelique said.

"In front of others, I must address you properly," Rosie said.

"Yes, I know that. It just seems so weird," Angelique said. "You have always been my superior and mentor. I hope you'll still be my mentor."

"Indeed, I will," Rosie said. "Both you and the young Quintan. Always."

"Excellent!" Angelique replied.

Right after breakfast, Angelique's ladies-in-waiting entered the room.

"Lady Angelique, we are here to prepare you for the ceremony," the older one said. "We will dress your hair first and then everyone else."

And that's just what took place for the next three hours. At the end, all the women of the wedding party were ready to put their dresses on.

"Oh, wait a minute," Sarah said as she left the room.

"Good idea," Angelique said as everyone else took care of their personal business.

"Now, I'm ready," Sarah said.

Sarah, Margaret, and the two mothers were dressed quickly.

"Whose dress is this?" Sarah asked.

"That's for my witness," Angelique said. "And here she is."

Rosie entered the room in a robe, ready to be dressed.

"This is wonderful," Glendianna said. "Does Quintan know about this?"

"Not yet, "Angelique said as she helped dress Rosie.

Rosie stood back, and everyone applauded.

"You look beautiful, my Rosie," Angelique said, tears running down her cheeks.

"Now, we'll have none of that quite yet," Rosie said, trying not to cry.

"Lady Angelique, it's time to dress," her lady-in-waiting said.

The girls and women stood back as the three ladies-in-waiting dressed Angelique. When they were finished, they stepped aside, and an angel appeared. Angelique looked stunning in a white cloak with silver and gold brocade at the edges. The ladies removed her cloak, and her white and silver wedding dress was seen for the first time.

"You are stunning!" Rosie said.

"You look like an angel," Sarah said. "At least what I think an angel would look like."

"My gorgeous daughter," her mother said as she hugged her.

"I can't believe this is me," Angelique said.

Her mother placed the wedding wreath on her daughter's head, as was the custom. It was made of white roses and white ribbons that fell down her back.

"It's time," the ladies-in-waiting said all together.

"Let's set her veil," Glendianna said. "The lace is a gift from the faeries."

"It's so long," Sarah said.

"That's a long-kept tradition," Rosie explained. "She will walk down the aisle with the veil trailing behind her, reminding everyone of her purity and innocence."

"So many details," Margaret said.

"Here is your wedding bouquet, Lady Angelique," Rosie said as she handed the flowers to Angelique.

Angelique looked at them and laughed.

"Thanks, Faeries, for the little gift," Angelique said.

"What is it?" Sarah asked.

"Look," Angelique said as she showed everyone the crystal. It was a miniature dragon glowing a beautiful purple color. "I'm going to keep it in here all day."

"That's fitting," her mother said. "Time to go."

Sir Gerald was outside with her father, waiting for her.

"You take my breath away, Angelique," her father said as he looked at her.

Angelique set her hand on his arm, and the procession to the chapel began.

Arthur was already in the chapel at the altar, waiting for his bride.

"You okay, Quintan?" Hugho whispered.

"I am," Arthur replied. "Just anxious to see my bride and hope I don't forget anything."

"You're okay," Hugho replied.

High Chancellor Patrick smiled at Arthur as he said, "Your bride is here."

The trumpets sounded the music to begin the processional, and the doors to the chapel opened. The mothers were seated first, then Sarah came down the aisle, followed by Margaret.

The doors closed for a moment. The trumpeters were signaled, and the bridal processional began. The doors opened, and everyone inside stood and turned to look at the bride.

Arthur was stunned at what he saw. She was beyond stunning—more than gorgeous. He stared at her as her father began walking her toward him. The closer she got to Arthur, the more he saw. She was breathtakingly beautiful.

When Angelique and her father arrived at the altar, Hugho had to nudge Arthur to stand before Angelique's father.

"Oh, sorry," Arthur whispered. "You are beyond stunning."

"I agree with you, King Arthur," Angelique's father said.

The High Chancellor cleared his throat to get the men's attention.

"Who allows this woman to be married to the king?" Patrick asked.

"Her mother and I do," her father said as he placed her hand in Arthur's and stepped back to sit with his wife.

Arthur and Angelique followed Patrick up the steps to stand before the altar. The faeries had also decorated it, and it was perfect for the day.

The ceremony began, and when the vows were recited, Arthur didn't miss a word, and Angelique spoke out loud and clear.

"In the presence of the gods and goddesses and these good people, I declare King Arthur and Lady Angelique married," Patrick said.

Arthur kissed Angelique as a sign of love, and everyone applauded.

The usual leaving did not take place.

"King Arthur, please step to the side," Patrick asked of the king.

"As is dictated by the laws of the land, I ask Lady Angelique to kneel before me," Patrick said. The ladies-in-waiting gathered her dress and helped her to kneel. Angelique bowed her head.

"Do you, Lady Angelique Pendragon of Camelot, promise to obey the laws of the office of the Queen of the kingdom and dedicate yourself to the path set for you as Queen by your king, King Arthur?" Patrick asked.

"I solemnly swear to uphold the laws of the office of the Queen and those dictated to me by King Arthur," Angelique replied.

"Raise your head, dear Lady," Patrick said. "I crown thee the Queen of Camelot and place all duties and responsibilities on your soul as long as you shall live."

Patrick placed the crown on Angleique's head and gave her his hand to help her stand.

"I present your Queen, Queen Angelique Pendragon of Camelot," Patrick said as Angelique faced the king.

Angelique curtsied to Arthur, took his hand, and kissed the ring of his office.

Arthur took Angelique's hand and stood beside her, saying, "I give you your Queen."

Those in the chapel cheered and applauded until the High Chancellor asked them to be seated. He gave the benediction, and the recessional began with the king and queen in the lead. As they left the chapel, the crowd in the courtyard erupted into loud cheering and applause; someone was even beating a drum. The trumpeters blared the signal that the king and queen were married, and the Queen had been crowned.

Angelique and Arthur stepped into the wagon that Hamlen had made and decorated for their ride around the city. They were greeted with love and cheering.

"Arthur, look at the houses," Angelique said.

"They are decorated with wreathes and garland from the flowers from The Divine," Arthur said.

"Beautiful," Angelique said as they waved at their subjects.

"Look!" a child hollered out, pointing to the sky. Penny, Q, Clarice, and Roman were flying around in a patterned manner.

"They're dancing," Angelique said as other dragons joined in. They blew white smoke and flew in circles and patterns for about ten minutes. People made way for them as Penny and Q flew close to the ground. They landed near the king and queen.

"Penny, Q," Arthur said as he stood. "That was magnificent. I shall call it The Dragon Dance, blessing our marriage."

"That is exactly what it is," Penny said, bowing toward Arthur. "We are thrilled for you both and Camelot. This signals a new beginning for everyone."

"It most certainly does," Angelique said, smiling at Penny.

"Please thank the other dragons for their gift of flight for us," Arthur said as he sat down. "We will remember this always."

Penny and Q returned to the sky and flew over Camelot for another ten minutes as the king and queen continued their travels around the city.

About an hour later, the king and queen returned to the castle and were escorted into the king's outer chamber.

"It's time to sign the marriage papers," Patrick said as he handed the pen to Arthur.

Arthur and Angelique signed the papers quickly and then sat down at the table. Food and drink awaited them.

"This tastes splendid," Angelique said. "Great idea of Rosie's to have this here for us."

"I think Rosie thinks of everything," Arthur said. "This is my mother's berry bread with honey."

"Your mother showed me how to make this the other day," Angelique said. "I made this loaf yesterday, my love."

Arthur leaned over and kissed her soundly on the lips.

"You can make this for me any time you want to," Arthur said.

Patrick, Hugho, Fred, and Harrison agreed as they had a loaf for themselves, too.

"Alright, everyone," Patrick said. "Are we ready to begin the festivities?"

"We are, Patrick," Arthur said as he helped Angelique to her feet.

"Just a few moments, please," Angelique said as she signaled to her ladies-in-waiting to join her.

It took a little while to get her dress all set once she was finished taking care of herself.

"Now, I'm ready," Angelique said. "Let's go."

"You heard the queen," Arthur said, laughing with the others.

Harrison signaled the trumpeters to play the entrance music, and Angelique and Arthur entered the wedding feast, walking to the head of the long table.

"Let the celebration begin," Arthur declared, and the next several hours seemed to go by in a blur.

Toasts were made by both fathers and a few of the knights. Hugho's toast was the most touching.

"King Arthur and Queen Angelique," Hugho began. "It is my honor to serve you both. I have known Quintan, if you will allow me this name since he came to the village. He and I struck up a friendship right away. It may have had something to do with getting caught when we went for a swim instead of doing our chores."

Laughter and teasing were heard all around. Arthur nodded to show he agreed with Hugho.

"Quintan was a curious child. He always wanted to know how things worked. That is an excellent trait to grow into manhood. We worked hard side-by-side on our farms and in our village, as was expected. Our fathers and mothers taught us well. We learned carpentry and farming skills from our fathers and cooking and sewing skills from our mothers.

"I remember the first time Quintan had to learn to sew. We kept tearing our clothes when we were out and about discovering our world. Quintan's mother got so tired of always fixing his torn clothes that she set him down in the kitchen one evening and showed him how to sew. Word got around, and the other mothers in the village did the same thing. That made us a little more careful when we were exploring."

"King Arthur," one of the knights said, "If I need a tailor, I know just who to go to."

Laughter followed with a good deal of teasing.

"I will never forget how I felt the day Quintan told me that Merlin had agreed to teach me how to use a sword. I am still humbled by this grand experience. It is because of my hours and hours of practice with King Arthur that I even know how to hold a sword.

"I accepted his invitation to be his paige with joy and worry as I'd never even been near a castle before. It's the best thing that's happened to me ever since he came to live in our village. King Arthur, Lady Angelique, I am honored to share this day with you and look forward to a few more mischievous outings."

Everyone raised their glasses to the king and queen to show their agreement with Hugho's speech. The traditional activities took place, and then the feast was served. The cutting of the cake by the king and queen symbolized their union to share their lives with each other. The Queen's dance with her attendants took place as was the custom. The king and his groomsmen took to the floor. They challenged each other to do silly and crazy dance moves until one of them finally fell to the ground. This signaled that everyone was allowed to dance and have a great time, which everyone did. A few hours later, the king and queen stood to say good night.

"My dear friends and countrymen, we thank you for celebrating this day with us. It is time for us to retire. Stay and continue celebrating as long as you wish," Arthur said.

The knights raised their swords in a line to form a walkway for the newlyweds to walk through. Cheering and applause followed as the king and queen left the banquet hall. A few minutes later, they entered their chambers and looked at each other.

"It has been a glorious day," Angelique said. "Please, help me get out of this dress."

"Gladly," Arthur said as he unbuttoned the dress. He untied the sash, and Angelique stepped out of the dress with only her camisole left on.

"I feel free," Angelique said. "Let's get you out of those clothes."

Arthur undressed quickly, and they fell into the bed together.

"You are beautiful," Arthur said as he lifted the camisole from Angelique and ran his hands across her body.

"Quintan, make love to me," Angelique said as she arched her back toward him.

"With pleasure," Arthur said as he leaned down and took her breast into his mouth, and began sucking her every so slowly.

Angelique moaned as pleasure flowed through her body. She reached for his hard dick, and he pushed her hand away.

Arthur found her wet spot with his fingers and began stroking her clit. Angelique couldn't believe the sensations she was feeling and moaned for more.

"As you wish, my Lady," Arthur said as he stroked her faster and faster until she hollered out as her climax rocked her entire body.

"Oh my god! That's amazing!" Angelique said as she calmed down.

"That was the beginning of the ultimate pleasure we can share," Arthur said.

"There's more?" Angelique said in disbelief.

"So much more," Arthur said.

"Make it happen," Angelique said as she grabbed Arthur's hard dick and began to play with it.

"That feels wonderful," Arthur said as he lay back and let her explore his shaft.

"You are so hard and hot," Angelique said as she ran her finger over the top of his dick.

"Oh, god, Angelique. Stop!" Arthur said as he pulled away from her.

Arthur lay her on her back and spread her legs so he could put his face between them. He flicked her clit with his tongue, and Angelique cried out in pleasure. He licked her faster and faster as his fingers entered her wet place and began to push into her.

Angelique didn't know what to do. This felt so amazing and unbelievable. She suddenly knew she wanted his hard dick to push into her wet place.

"Push into me, Arthur," Angelique said in a smokey voice. "I want to feel you inside me."

Arthur brought Angelique close to her second climax before he began to push into her. She felt a sharp pain as he pushed harder and harder, and then it was gone, and she began to feel something indescribable. It was beyond anything she'd ever known. She began pushing against Arthur as he pushed into her. She grabbed his ass with both hands and wrapped her legs around his as they began to near their first organism together.

"Faster. Harder," Angelique cried out.

Arthur pushed harder and faster and felt Angelique begin her climb toward ecstasy. As she reached the pinnacle, he met her with his own, and they soared into the unknown for the longest time. It was hours later when Angelique awoke and found Arthur watching her. She rolled him onto his back before he knew what was happening.

"My turn to make you feel good," Angelique said as she began to push onto his hard dick. She knelt forward as she pushed, and Arthur grabbed her breasts and played with them as she pushed harder and faster. He met her rhythm and held her in place as they soared again into that place of pure pleasure. Angelique fell to the side of Arthur and laughed.

"We are rather good at this," Angelique said, laughing.

"I'd say so," Arthur said, laughing with his wife. "We've only been at it one night. Just think how much better we will be after a few months."

"How am I going to get through the hours without being with you?" Angelique said mischievously.

"You little vixen," Arthur replied, kissing her.

"Is it even daybreak yet?" Angelique asked.

"Let's see," Arthur said as he got up and walked to the window. "The sun is just rising now. It's a magnificent sunrise. Join me."

Angelique wrapped herself in a blanket and went to the window.

"It is spectacular, as if we ordered it from our love-making," Angelique said as she rested her head on Arthur's shoulder. "Arthur, I know that from this night, I am now with child. I can feel it."

"I believe you," Arthur said as he wrapped his arms around her. "I'll have Feyanna visit you."

"Rosie will know the minute I walk into the kitchen, which I plan to do as soon as I'm washed and dressed a little more respectfully," Angelique said as she crossed the room to get some fresh clothes.

"I like the blanket myself," Arthur said.

"Of course you do," Angelique said. "You can take it from me tonight."

"Do I have to wait that long?" Arthur asked.

"You can have me whenever you wish, Sire," Angelique said. "I am at your beck and call."

"As I am for you," Arthur said. "Let's get cleaned up and meet our day."

A short time later, they left their chambers and were greeted by Harrison and Fred, who were just coming up the staircase.

"Good morning, Your Highnesses," Harrison said, bowing.

"Good Morning to both of you," Angelique replied before Arthur could say a word.

"Did you get any sleep?" Arthur asked as they walked down the stairs to the king's private room.

"A short nap," Fred replied. "It was a great celebration."

"Indeed it was," Angelique said. "I'm off to the kitchen to see Rosie."

"Of course she is," Harrison said.

"We all love our Rosie," Arthur replied as the men talked about a few things before breakfast was delivered to them.

"Rosie?" Angelique called out.

All the kitchen staff curtsied and bowed as she walked across the room.

"Thank you for that," Angelique said. "I appreciate the show of respect."

"Miss Angelique," Rosie said as she walked over to her and wrapped Angelique in a big hug.

"You're with child," Rosie whispered ever so softly in Angelique's ear.

"Yes, Rosie, I believe I am," Angelique whispered.

"Let's get some breakfast for the king and queen," Rosie called out.

"Harrison and Fred are with us, too," Angelique added.

"Of course they are," Rosie replied, laughing. "They love to eat."

"We love to eat your food, Rosie," Angelique replied. "I'll go back and tell them breakfast is on the way."

"Indeed," Rosie answered as she started giving orders to everyone.

Angelique returned to the private dining room and said, "Rosie is ordering everyone around the kitchen like Harrison orders the knights into battle."

"I know she is," Harrison said.

"We love her for it," Fred added.

"So, have the three of you solved all the problems of the kingdom yet?" Angelique asked as Arthur held her chair for her.

"Most of them," Arthur replied, laughing with Harrison and Fred.

"The only thing is, as soon as we solve all the problems, another one arises," Harrison said. "There's always more to do."

"We have five complaints on the docket for today alone," Fred said. "Harrison and I will take care of them. They're minor ones."

"Thank you for that," Arthur said. "We will be visiting with our families throughout the day as they leave tomorrow."

565

Rosie entered with her kitchen maids, setting breakfast for the four of them.

"This looks wonderful as usual, my Rosie," Arthur said.

"Only the best for my king and queen," Rosie replied. "And my knights, of course."

"Of course," Harrison said as Rosie slapped him on the shoulder.

"Enjoy your morning," Rosie said as her staff curtsied and bowed, and she winked at Arthur.

Breakfast was a fun time with all remembering things from the wedding feast.

Late afternoon found the king and queen visiting with their families, taking a walk across the knight's field south of the castle. Angelique was walking with her mother and Glendianna. The girls were busy talking about the cute boys they had danced with the night before.

"The girls will have last night's memories with them for the rest of their lives," Glendianna said.

"They sure had fun," Angelique said. "I watched them for a bit as they tried out the new dances I taught them. They were excellent."

"Yes, they were," their mother said. "This is the first time they've ever been paid attention to by boys other than brothers, cousins, and old friends."

"I suspect they'll be talking about this for a long, long time," Glendianna said, looking at Angelique. "Angelique, tell us."

"I am with child from last night," Angelique said quietly.

"You already know this?" her mother asked.

"We sent for Feyanna and Merlin, and Feyanna used herbs to show I was with child," Angelique said. "I can already feel the change in my body."

"Splendid!" Glendianna said as she hugged Angelique. "I'll keep the secret until you send word. Sometimes, the first few months are challenging."

"Indeed, they are," her mother said. "I was a bit sick for three months when I carried you."

"Well, my stomach is a bit unsettled," Angelique said. "Feyanna gave me some herbs to brew into a tea. They've already helped a lot."

"I'm relieved you'll be well taken care of by Feyanna and Rosie," her mother said.

"We aren't going to make the announcement until I'm in my fifth month, just to be sure," Angelique said. "Thanks for keeping quiet about this, especially from the girls. You can tell my father and Hamlen, but no one else, please."

"We promise," the mothers were saying when the girls ran over.

"I see you both had a grand time last night," Angelique said.

"We did," Sarah replied with Margaret.

"Russell's grandson is cute," Margaret said, blushing.

"He is for sure," Glendianna said. "Don't worry, my precious girls; there are thousands of cute boys in the world. You'll be meeting them every time we visit your brother."

"That's true, Margaret," Sarah said. "Dad's waving at us."

"Let's go back to them," Glendianna said.

"It must be time for tea," Angelique's mother added. "We're leaving after tea as you are."

"Yes, we are," Glendianna said. "It's time to get back home and take care of the farm. It's been an amazing time here."

Tea was a fun time. Everyone teased the girls about the boys they had danced with the night before. Margaret mentioned having a niece or nephew soon, and her mother told the girls that it was the king and queen's business alone. The girls stopped mentioning babies and talked about the castle and everything they had been a part of. The late afternoon was just beginning to flow into early evening when Hamlen stood to speak.

"Quintan, my dear son, we are very proud of you and all that you have accomplished in your young life," Hamlen said. "You know you can come home whenever you wish as the king or as just young Quintan, as Rosie calls you."

Everyone laughed at this.

"We know you are in good hands here and have friends that will defend you to their death if need be. May the gods and goddesses bless and keep you in the love of The Divine," Hamlen finished with a hug for his son.

"Our dear daughter, we love you and are beyond thrilled that you have found your life partner already. May the gods and goddesses bless you both as you walk in their love and The Old Magic," Angelique's father said as he hugged his daughter.

The families walked into the courtyard to their waiting wagons. The knights were set to accompany them home.

"We'll keep an eye on the young ones," Russell said as he shook hands with the fathers and hugged the mothers. "Be off with you now while the sun still shines."

The wagons left, and the courtyard was very quiet.

"Time to get back to business," Arthur said.

Arthur and his advisors returned to the castle. Angelique walked with Feyanna.

"How are you feeling?" Feyanna asked as they walked around the courtyard.

"I'm tired from yesterday," Angelique said. "It was a marvelous day. I don't think I've ever danced so much in my life."

"Me, too," Feyanna said, laughing. "We stayed for another two hours after the two of you left. The knights and a few others stayed on until the sun came up. Russell said he found them sound asleep on the floor."

"I don't doubt it," Angelique said, laughing with Feyanna. "My body is already changing."

"I was just going to ask about that," Feyanna said. "Rosie will see that you get the right kinds of food and teas whenever you wish to eat. Don't worry about gaining weight. That is normal. That little one needs lots of nourishment. Merlin and I would like to perform the blessing of the new soul when you're six weeks along. It will be done privately, of course. Charles is all excited about this. He knew before you called for us this morning. The Old Magic is strong with this child."

"He is tuned into The Old Magic for sure," Angelique said. "Let's go to the kitchen. Talking about food has made me hungry already. This little one already loves food!"

"I'm with you," Feyanna said as they walked into the kitchen from the outer castle door. "I can always eat Rosie's food."

"Well, looks who's here," Rosies said as she saw the two of them. "Time for a snack?"

"It is," Feyanna said. "I think my body is all off its regular time from everything we've been doing lately. Maybe I'll get back to normal in a few days."

"Don't count on it," Rosie said. "It's a full moon tomorrow night. That's always a blessing."

"It is," Angelique said. "And the animals know it. They can get very loud and feisty around a full moon."

"You got that right," one of the kitchen maids said. "I'm sorry, Your Highness."

"No worries, Nora," Angelique. "We've known each other a long time. Save the Your Highnesses for when others are around."

"Thank you, Lady Angelique," Nora said, bobbing her head. "Here's the berry cake all warm from the ovens."

"It smells delicious," Angelique said as she cut a piece and tasted it. "It tastes as delicious as it smells."

"It does," Feyanna said, winking at Rosie.

Camelot got busy finding a new normal for the city. The king was a just man and most found his sentences understandable. Only once in the first few months did he have to sentence a man to death. The man had been found guilty of killing a farmer and raping his wife and daughters, then stealing their farm animals. The daughters told the neighboring villagers of the event and word got back to the castle. Arthur sent three of his knights to the village to get details about the event. Two days later, they found the man in a house with the stolen animals outside.

The man tried to convince the knights that he owned the house and animals properly. It didn't work. Two village men had ridden with the knights and identified the house as belonging to an old woman and her son. They were away visiting family down the road. The man tried to run away, but one of the knights roped him, and they brought him back to the castle to stand before the king. Witnesses validated the information, and the man was sentenced to death right then and there. The henchman was ready, and the man was dead a few minutes later. Word got around Camelot about this, and even the petty thieves were very quiet for a few days.

The rest of the summer was relatively quiet. No one tried to take over Camelot. Summer flowed into fall. Arthur's birthday was celebrated quietly, as Angelique's condition was still unknown to the kingdom.

It was late October when the High Chancellor announced that the king and queen were expecting their first child. The countryside was thrilled with the news. The child was expected in the late spring. Two days later, all hell broke loose over Camelot!

It was late morning when one of the lookout posts at the northern edge of Camelot sounded the alarm. Dragons were spotted racing toward the city. Penny and Q took to the sky to have a look at them. They were exactly what Penny and Q thought they were: rogue dragons. There were twelve of them. They were full-size adult male dragons with a double row of scales down their backs from their necks to their tales. They were dark brown and orange in color. They were flying low over the land and breathing fire at everything on the ground. Buildings and forests burned instantly. Q sent a dragon message to the Lady of The Lake, and she relayed that message to every dragon in the kingdom. Within only a few minutes, green, yellow, blue, and black dragons could be seen coming in all directions toward Camelot.

The alarm sounded in the castle, and people ran inside as fast as they could. The good citizens of Camelot ran for cover, too. Arthur, Harrison, and Fred ran to the parapets to have a look. They stayed in the shelter of one of the towers. Smoke rose from the forests and a few places in Camelot.

"This is horrible," Fred said. "We need to do something."

"Something is already being done," Harrison said." Look!"

They watched as the Dragon Brigade flew in straight at the rogue dragons. Dragon smoke was bellowing from the Dragon Brigade to try to confuse the rogue dragons as to where they were. It worked for a few minutes until the smoke blew away. Then, Penny and her team began circling some of the rogue dragons to make them fall. One of them did and landed in a pile of boulders. It was badly hurt and couldn't get up. Q had his team bellow fire at the rogue dragons. It burned some of them bad enough to fall to the ground. Others were only cinched and circled back around to attack Q and his Dragon Brigade.

The rogue dragons were headed toward the castle. Harrison called the knights together to load their cannons and shoot on his command. He waited for the rogue dragons to get very close to the castle. Just as they began to blow fire, Harrison gave the signal, and three cannons sent cannonballs at the dragons. Three of them were hit square in the chest, killing them. They fell to the ground, and as the knights watched, they were vaporized, and their essence was taken high in the sky until it couldn't be seen anymore.

The knights cheered and readied the cannons again. Penny and her crew were chasing five rogue dragons as they continued burning buildings. Penny gave the secret signal, and her crew blasted fire at the rogue dragons at close range. All five were burned to death, and as their bodies fell to the earth, a swirling wind took their essence up into the heavens.

Now, only three rogue dragons remained. Penny and Q sent thoughts to each other using The Special Magic. They agreed to circle the rogue dragons until they couldn't fly anymore. This would force them to fall to the ground. Penny and Q's strategy was to push them higher into the sky as they circled them. This would make them fall to the earth far enough to kill them.

The Dragon Brigade got into place and began to circle the three rogue dragons. One of the rogue dragons blew fire at Clarice and burned her wing. She flew down to the earth and signaled that she was okay. She sat there in pain, and her left wing was still on fire. Some of the people in Camelot ran to her with buckets of water and threw the water on her wing. The fire was quickly quenched, and she was relieved. It was still very painful. As the people watched, faeries appeared and placed leaves over the burned wing.

"Thank you, sweet faeries," Clarice said. "The pain is gone. I'll stay here until the battle is over. Then we can try to figure out how to get me home."

They all looked up unto the sky and watched as The Dragon Brigade continued to circle the rogue dragons, pushing them higher and higher into the sky. Q raised his tail, and The Dragon Brigade closed in on the three rogue dragons.

The people on the ground were mesmerized, watching the dragons fight each other. They cheered for Penny and Q. They had accepted them as their own personal dragons and would do anything to make sure they were okay.

The Dragon Brigade had tightened the circle around the three rogue dragons to the point that they didn't have room to use their wings. One by one, the rogue dragons began to fall to the earth. As each one hit the ground, they were killed instantly. After the third one died, their essences were taken in a mighty gust of wind into the heavens just like the others. The wind calmed, and there wasn't any trace of the dragon anywhere. The damage they had done was real.

People cheered for The Dragon Brigade as it circled the countryside. Penny and Q flew over to Clarice and settled next to her.

"Dear Clarice, how are you?" Penny asked as she looked over Clarice's wing.

"It hurt like crazy. The faeries took care of that," Clarice replied.

"Really?" Penny said, smiling at Clarice.

"That's a human expression," Clarice explained.

"I like it," Q said. "It looks like the faeries are taking great care of you."

"They are, and I appreciate and love them," Clarice said, winking at the faeries as they flew around her. "I'd like to get back to our cave right away. Do you think we can do that?"

"We can right now," Penny said as Q hovered over Clarice.

The rest of The Dragon Brigade set a sling on the ground made of tree branches and grasses. Clarice stepped on it and lay down. The Dragon Brigade picked up the sling and flew her away to the forest. There, The Special Magic opened a magical door into the dragon's cave. Clarice walked in and settled on her bed. The faeries and dragons tended to her wound, and she fell asleep a short time later.

Penny and Q returned to the castle with Beau. He would take Clarice's place until she was healed.

Arthur, Harrison, Fred, and Russell were in the courtyard when the dragons returned. Penny and Q landed in the courtyard while the others flew up to their places along the top of the wall.

"How is Clarice?" Arthur asked.

"She is resting easy with the help of the faeries," Penny replied. "Her left wing is burned a bit. She will be well again in a few weeks. It won't take as long as we did."

"I'm glad to hear this news," Arthur said. "I feel horrible that she was hurt ."

"We know and we appreciate your caring so much," Q replied.

"How man rogue dragons in all?" Russell asked.

"Twelve," Penny replied. "They were the worst of the worst. They are all dead now, and it will take the Dark Side quite a while to train new ones. We should be safe for a few years anyway."

"They do have about seven in training, though," Q added. "I don't think they will attack any time soon after the defeat they've suffered today."

"I should think not," Fred said.

"I would hope not," Russell added.

"It makes sense to us," Penny said. "But rogue dragons think differently than we do. We'll keep a sharp eye out for them, nonetheless."

"And I am forever grateful for that," Arthur said. "Time to get some supper. I'm sure Rosie is anxious to hear about everything."

"She is," Russell said. "She was out here several times during the battle. I kept sending her inside to keep her safe. Charles finally took her by the arm and dragged her inside."

"That's our Rosie," Harrison said as they walked into the castle near the kitchen door.

Rosie was waiting for them.

"You're all safe," she said as she hugged the three of them.

"We are," Arthur replied. "I hear you had to be dragged inside by Charles, my Rosie."

"I did," Rosie said, standing tall. "I have to know my boys are safe. Especially you, young Quintan. You're about to be a father. We can't let anything happen to you."

"Did anyone tell Angelique I'm safe?" Arthur asked.

"We told Gerald to tell her," Harrison said. "She's worried about Clarice."

"Have Gerald bring her to my private dining room. We'll eat there, my Rosie." Arthur said.

"I'll have your dinner brought in in a minute," Rosie replied, going into the kitchen and giving orders.

Angelique joined the men a few minutes later.

"How is our precious Clarice?" Angelique asked.

"She has a nasty burn on her left wing," Harrison replied. "The faeries and dragons are taking great care of her."

"She's in the dragon cave as we speak," Arthur replied as a faerie flew in. "Hello, Bluebell. How's our Clarice?"

"Oh, Quintan, she is sleeping peacefully," Bluebell replied. "We've covered her wound with healing ointments and leaves that take the pain away. She is a dear dragon."

"She is," Angelique said.

"Angelique," Bluebell said as she flew over to her. "The babe is growing well. You are already a great mother."

"Thank you, Bluebell, for that news and the kind words," Angelique said. "This babe is a busy one. I can feel little flutters every once and again. I suspect they will get stronger as he or she grows."

"That is true," Rosie said as she entered the room with Nora to serve their food. "Hello, Bluebell. It's good to see you again. It's been quite some time between visits."

"It has been, indeed," Bluebell said as she set a faerie kiss on Rosie's cheek.

"You are a dear one," Rosie said.

"Harrison and Fred," Arthur said. "I'd like you to meet Bluebell. We've known each other since I was a young boy. She is a wonderful faerie."

"Nice to meet you, Bluebell," Harrison and Fred said.

"Nice to meet the both of you, too," Bluebell said. "Quintan, is Hugho around?"

"I'm right here, Bluebell," Hugho said as Bluebell sat on his shoulder.

Hugho gave her his finger to shake in greeting.

"Hi, Hugho," Bluebell said. "Are you staying out of mischief?"

"Me? Of course," Hugho replied as the rest of the group laughed at this.

"Cute, Hugho," Arthur said as they began eating. "Always the wiseass."

"I'm going to get back to Clarice," Bluebell said. "I'll keep you informed."

"Thanks, Bluebell," Angelique said. "Rosie, this food is just what I was craving."

"I figured as much," Rosie said. "I'll be back later to gather the dishes. Sleep well."

"You too, our Rosie," Harrison replied.

"This has been some crazy day," Fred said.

"Let's hope the night is quiet," Angelique said. "I'm so very tired all of a sudden. I'm going to bed. Good night."

"I'll be there in a bit," Arthur said as he walked his wife to the door. "Sir Gerald, take great care of her."

"I will, Sire," Gerald said as he took Angelique's arm in his, and they walked away.

Angelique was sound asleep in minutes. Arthur and his advisors sat for a while, discussing kingdom news.

"Just one more thing to talk about," Arthur said when the other business was completed. "What do we do about those flying ships that took our people?"

"What can we do?" Harrison asked. "We don't even know if they're going to return."

"You are correct," Arthur said. "When they do return, we need some kind of plan to follow."

"We can't outfight them," Fred said. "I hope the people are returned unharmed."

"We all do," Harrison said.

"I'm going to talk with Merlin and Feyanna in the morning. Maybe they'll have some ideas about the whole mess."

"Good idea," Harrison said. "I'll ask Russell if he's ever seen anything like these before. He was born and raised here, so I think he may be able to add to the conversation."

"That's another good idea," Fred said, yawning. "I apologize, Sire. It's been a long day."

"Get some rest," Arthur said as they left the room.

"Your Highness?" Hugho said. "Will you need me any longer?"

"No, Hugho, go on to bed," Arthur said as they arrived at Arthur's chamber door. "Thanks for everything, Hugho."

"Always, Quintan," Hugh replied as he went on down the hall to his own chambers.

The next morning, there was a chill in the air, even with the sun shining brightly. The harvest was mostly complete, with a few late vegetables almost ready to gather in. The apples had been picked, dried, and set in root cellars across the land for the winter.

The annual fall challenge was to take place in mid-November. This was a challenge of strength and skill between the knights of Camelot and others from surrounding kingdoms. The knights of Ocean of The Sun kingdom had accepted the challenge along with others from five other kingdoms. This was not a fight-to-the-death kind of competition. It was a time to gather, have fun, and visit with friends and family from near and far before the winter snows and winds set in. Camelot was busy preparing for this event. The city had hung banners and flags, and you could smell pastries, meats, and pies of all kinds baking for hours at a time.

Russell was overseeing the roasting of lamb, hogs, and sides of beef over pits, which started about five days before the visitors arrived. The sky had been quiet since the dragon battle, and everyone was happy about that. Arthur had ordered extra sentinels to be posted throughout the kingdom to watch the sky just in case anything appeared that shouldn't be up there: dragons and flying discs alike.

Angelique was four months along and was beginning to show a little rounded belly. You couldn't see it when you looked at her, but it was there.

Rosie made sure she had plenty to eat and drink, and Feyanna made sure she took her potions every morning as well. The castle was draped in banners and flags during this time, and everyone was excited about the event.

Visitors began arriving two days before the event started. Russell and Harrison had laid out an area south and west of the castle for them to set up camp. Some of the local folks assisted the visitors with this work.

Arthur went looking for Angelique the afternoon before the festivities and found her in their chambers, knitting a baby blanket.

"There you are," Arthur said, kissing her long and hard. "I want you this minute."

Angelique set her knitting aside and stood up. "Then, you shall have me,"

They undressed quickly and fell into bed. Arthur began stroking her wet spot, and Angelique moaned. He found her breasts with his tongue and began licking them.

"You're huge," he said as he pulled a breast into his mouth and sucked it.

Angelique pushed his head onto her breast. "Suck me hard."

Arthur sucked harder and stroked her faster.

"Fuck me, Arthur. Fuck me hard," Angelique cried out as her organism began.

Arthur mounted her and pushed into her with her guiding his dick into her wet spot. She gave his dick a hard squeeze as he pushed into her. Arthur moaned and pushed harder and faster. Angelique pushed against him and they reached the point of no return at the same time. She cried out as she bucked and writhed from the orgasm. He hollered out as well as they left this space and time, falling into that abyss of pure ecstasy together. They were quiet for a few minutes.

"I love when we do this," Angelique said.

"I'm quite sure this is how we got you this way," Arthur said as he kissed her round and growing belly.

"It is," Angelique said as she found his dick and made it hard again.

"You are insatiable," Arthur said as he let her pump his dick.

"I love your dick," Angelique said as she rolled over and began to lick it.

Arthur moaned as he let her bring him to that moment just before he would cum. He lifted her on top of him, and she pushed onto his shaft. He came right away and pushed back into her as she reached her climax. They rode each other until they finally began to quiet down.

"I swear sex is even better when I'm pregnant," Angelique said.

"I agree," Arthur replied. "Time for some food."

"It's always time for food these days," Angelique said as they dressed.

Arthur stepped into the hall and saw Hugho coming toward him.

"Hugho, Lady Angelique is in need of food," Arthur said, smiling at Hugho.

"I'll let Rosie know right away," Hugho said, bowing a bit.

The evening found King Arthur and Queen Angelique visiting with their friends in the south field. There was a lightness in the air that was enjoyed by all.

The trumpets sounded at ten o'clock the next morning, calling the games to order. The king and queen walked into their seats, and the visiting challengers followed in a parade of color and gallantry.

Once everyone was in their places, Arthur stood and announced the games open. Everyone cheered and called out to their favorite knight, wishing them the best. Harrison held up his hands and pointed to the first challengers, and the event began in earnest.

The three days of events were a great success. Knights from all the kingdoms won a variety of awards. One of the funniest events was when Russell entered the arena with a mule in tow. The mule had been dressed in the king's colors and had a headpiece on that looked like a proper hat. The mule was settled in the center of the arena, and Russell waved his hand, and the children from Camelot came running in. They wore the king's colors, too. Each child was given the chance to make the mule speak. Most couldn't make the mule talk.

Then, the last child, a little boy of about five years old, approached the mule and stood before him.

"Mr. Mule," the boy said. "I would think it would be rather kind of you to have a talk with me, please."

The mule looked at Russell, and Russell pointed to the boy. The mule looked at the boy and remained silent. The crowd laughed quietly and kept watching the boy.

"Now, Mr. Mule, why won't you talk with me?" the boy asked.

The mule continued to stare at the boy.

The boy stepped up to the mule's ear and said," I know you can hear me just fine. Here, have this apple just in case you're hungry."

The boy held an apple out for the mule, and the mule ate it in one bite. The mule belched, and this made the crowd laugh again.

"I'm glad you liked the apple, mule," the boy said. "I think I know what you need to make you talk with me,"

The boy took a wood flute from his satchel and began to play a tune. The mule's ears perked up, and the mule looked at the boy. The boy kept playing and started dancing around a bit, and the mule followed him with his eyes.

All of a sudden, the mule let out a bellow as clear as day. The boy stopped playing, walked up to the mule, and said, "Is that all you needed to hear, Mr. Mule? I'll play some more for you."

The boy played another tune, and the mule began to sing along with him. The crowd cheered and laughed as the boy and mule danced around the arena. The boy finally stopped playing, and the mule stopped moving and bellowing.

"Thank you, Mr. Mule, for singing and dancing with me," the boy said, bowing before the mule.

The mule bowed down as well, making the crowd applaud for the longest time. The boy waved as he left the arena, and Russell stood with the mule. Russell gave a tug on the rope that was tethered around the mule's neck, and the mule followed Russell out of the arena to the cheers and applause of the crowd.

The last event on the afternoon of the last day was all swordplay. All the knights gathered and gave demonstrations of different types of sword moves. Some of the knights pretended to be gentlemen and then would try to best each other with silly moves. The crowd loved this. The best part of the whole event was when the knights invited the children to join them.

Each child was given a wooden sword according to the child's size and taught a few of the moves needed to become a knight. Girls were included in this event, and the crowd had a great time cheering them on. Each child was presented with a trophy that looked like a knight's shield. The children were returned to their families, and the king stood for the closing ceremony.

The knights from all kingdoms lined up and presented themselves in front of the royal box. Camelot was the last group of knights in line.

"Dear friends and good citizens of all kingdoms," Arthur began. "This event has been a grand celebration of our love and respect for each other and our lands. I am humbled to have so many of you visit us here in Camelot. Our event has come to an end. I wish you all safe passage home, and may you all be blessed by the gods and goddesses as you go your own ways."

Applause and cheers were heard as people gathered their families and returned to their campsites. Most folks had left by suppertime, with only a few waiting for the morning, as their journeys would take most of a day.

Rosie had a hearty meal ready for the knights and guards. She had sent supper to Arthur's chambers for the king and queen. Angelique fell asleep right after she ate, and Arthur closed the door to their bedchamber. He settled in the outer room with Harrison, Fred, Hugho, Merlin, and Charles.

"I know we all saw them," Charles said.

"The whole place saw them," Harrison said.

"I think most people were surprised to see our four dragons flying around and settling on the castle parapets," Merlin said, laughing.

"Most folks think that dragons are either a child's fantasy or the work of evil," Hugho said.

"Most folks are idiots," Fred said, laughing with Arthur.

"I will agree with that statement," Harrison said, laughing with everyone else.

"Did you see the King Octavius of Ocean of the Sun Kingdon when he saw Penny?" Charles said, trying not to laugh so hard.

"I did," Arthur said. "I had all I could do not to laugh at his expression. It was when he looked at me that I laughed and smiled and told him dragons are real and that we have a few very nice ones right here in the castle. I thought he was going to fall flat on his face."

"Me, too," Harrison said. "I looked at him and waved to Penny, and she waved back. She looked right at him until he gave her a little wave. I do believe that the king of the Ocean of the Sun has learned a thing or two. His life has surely changed forever."

"This has been the best fall event I can remember," Harrison said. "And I've been through plenty. I think the citizens far and wide will fondly remember this for a long, long time."

"It has been a great few days," Fred said. "We need to finalize the winter preparation plans with Russell in the morning. We have quite a lot to do before the castle is ready for the winter storms."

"We do," Arthur said. "I'm meeting with Merlin and Feyanna in the morning. We have several things to discuss. Harrison, how about you, Fred, and Russell make a work list for those preparations? If you think we'll need extra help, hire folks that can do the work. Rosie may need extra kitchen help with the work. We'll feed them and give them a little something for their work. Talk with Rosie. She's probably ready to hire extra kitchen help as well. The harvest was exceptional this year, and there's lots of food to store for the winter. Make sure we share some of that food with our castle workers."

"As you wish, Your Highness," Harrison said, bowing.

"Cute, Harrison, as usual," Arthur said, slapping Harrison on the back. "Get some sleep. See you tomorrow."

Good nights were shared as the men left Arthur to himself. He quietly entered his bedchamber and saw Angelique sound asleep under the covers. A soft fire was burning in the fireplace. He set more logs on the fire and then banked them for the night.

Arthur thanked the gods and goddesses for his Angelique and their unborn child as he slipped into bed. He was sound asleep in no time.

Camelot settled into sleep as the dragons watched over it and the countryside. There was a soft energy flowing around the land. The dragons felt it and stayed on high alert. Something was beginning to stir, and the Realm of The Special Magic would be needed before long. First, the time of the wintersleep would take place. Then, the world as Camelot knew it would change.

CHAPTER 22

The winter settled in as the snow covered the land. Angleique's baby grew and grew as the winter months passed. She had made special clothes for herself to cover her expanding belly. She chose to make dresses that were just like her sleeping gowns. The Solstice Celebration was splendid. The homes and castle of Camelot were adorned in evergreen wreaths and holly berries. Crystals shown in windows all night long instead of candles. People loved the quartz crystals that Merlin and Feyanna had given them to use instead of candles. Using the crystals meant less time making candles and more time for other things. Some of the crystals had a touch of color, making the snow on the outside windows glow.

The expected severe snowstorm came in mid-February. The kids loved it. It took the countryside two weeks to dig out. The castle looked like something in a fairytale, with snow on all the parapets and dragons sitting alongside. There was an added advantage to having four dragons about the castle. They used their fire to clear the courtyards and roads around the castle. Everyone stopped what they were doing to watch the dragons at work. They cheered their beloved dragons to show their appreciation for helping clear the roads.

Angelique was nearing her time to give birth during all this snowstorm activity. She was due to deliver in late March or early April. The countryside was excited as her time got closer and closer. The snow was finally cleared by the end of February, and the February thaw took place. There were puddles everywhere, as usual. The spring flowers began to push through the earth and the sun shone more brightly now. Talk of spring planting began to be heard around the castle even though it was still weeks away.

It was during the second week of March that Angelique woke up in pain. She shook Arthur awake and told him to get Rosie. He threw his dressing gown on and ran down the hall to Rosie's room.

He knocked on the door and called out to Rosie.

"What is it, young Quintan?" Rosie said as she answered the door, pulling her dressing gown around herself.

"Angelique said to come," Arthur replied.

Rosie followed Arthur into the bedchamber and saw Angelique wide awake with the look of fear on her face.

"Arthur, leave," Rosie said in a stern voice.

Arthur left the room, and Rosie uncovered Angelique.

"When did the pains begin?" Rosie asked as she pulled up Angleique's sleeping gown.

"I don't really know," Angleique said as another pain started. "They woke me up. Here's another one now."

"Breathe, child," Rosie said, looking at Angelique to get her to follow Rosie's words.

"I need to look at you," Rosie said. "I've sent for Feyanna. She'll be here soon. Now raise yourself so I can take off your underclothing."

Angelique did as Rosie instructed. Rosie washed her hands and spread Angelique's legs far apart.

"I'm going to put my fingers inside you to see if you're getting ready to give birth," Rosie explained to Angelique. "This may feel uncomfortable."

Rosie did just as she said she would and determined that Angelique was in active labor.

"Angelique, you have begun the birthing process," Rosie said. "You are just a little opened up. This laboring may take hours or even a couple of days. The first child usually does. I'll get the kitchen busy with the tea and food we're all going to need. Every time you feel a pain coming along, breathe deeply, and I will coach you through it."

"It's time for the baby to come?" Angelique said as another pain started.

"It is, and I think it's going to be sooner than later," Rosie said. "The pains are only five minutes apart. This little one seems to be in a hurry."

Just then, Feyanna walked into the bedchamber.

"So, we're going to have a wee one tonight, are we?" Feyanna said as she removed her cloak and set up her herbs and potions.

"We are," Rosie said. "She's begun to dilate with pains every 5 minutes. I'm going to get dressed and get the kitchen busy with tea and food for us."

"I love you for that," Feyanna said. "Now, Angelique, let's get you a bit more comfortable if we can."

"These pains really hurt," Angelique said as another hit her harder than the last one only three minutes before.

"Let's check you," Feyanna said.

As soon as the pain subsided, Feyanna checked Angelique and found her more than halfway dilated. Feyanna went to the door and told the guards to get Arthur and Merlin quickly.

"Feyanna here's another one," Angelique said. "This is even worse than the last one a few minutes ago."

Arthur and Merlin walked into the bedchamber.

"We are going to have a baby soon," Feyanna said. "Make sure the castle is secured."

Merlin looked at Feyanna and nodded. Merlin took Arthur by the arm and walked him out of the chamber.

"Let's talk with Harrison and Fred and have them secure the castle," Merlin said.

Merlin knew this was a distraction for Arthur. Merlin also knew a magical event was about to take place.

Angelique was trying to breathe through the labor pains, but this one was just too much. She hollered out in pain, and Feyanna took her hand and told her to take short, little breaths until the pain was going away. Feyanna took one of her ointments and rubbed it on Angleique's cervix to help numb the pain. Feyanna was surprised to find the cervix fully dilated.

"I want to push," Angelique said.

"Not yet," Feyanna was saying when Rosie came back in. "She's fully dilated and wants to push. I've put the numbing cream on her to help with the birthing pain. The instruments and string are ready."

"I need to push," Angelique said as she tried to sit up and push.

Rosie and Feyanna took the bedclothes off the bed, placed a mat under Feyanna, and then told her to get ready to push. Rosie pulled Angelique's legs as far apart as possible and told her to put her feet on the bed to help push the baby out when the next pain started.

"It's time," Angelique said.

"Watch me, child," Rosie said as she took her through the breathing and pushing work.

"This is very hard," Angelique said as the pain lessened.

But not for long. The pains seemed to come none-stop for the longest time. Angelique was tired.

"We know you're very tired, sweet Angelique," Rosie said. "Just a couple more strong pushes. We can see a bit of the head now."

"The pain is horrible," Angelique said, crying.

"I'll put some more ointment on you," Feyanna said as she did just that. "I can see some dark hair here."

"Push hard, Angelique," Rosie said as the never-ending pains rocked through Angelique's whole body. "That's it. One more time. You ready?"

Angelique took a deep breath, nodded at Rosie, and pushed with all her might. There was a moment of silence as Feyanna caught the baby and cleared his mouth with a large straw to get the mucous out. The baby looked at Feyanna and gave a resounding cry.

"It's here?" Angelique said, lying back against the pillows.

"One more little push," Rosie said. "Come on now, one more time."

Angelique looked at Rosie and pushed one more time. The baby was fully born and crying loudly.

"Angelique," Feyanna said as she cut and tied the cord, "Here is your beautiful baby boy."

Rosie took the baby from Feyanna and placed him on Angelique's breasts. The little one found a nipple and began to suckle immediately.

"He's beautiful," Angelique said as the afterbirth was released. "What was that gush?"

"That was the afterbirth leaving your body, just like when the lambs and cows give birth," Feyanna said.

"I remember that," Angelique said. "He's so beautiful."

"We'll have you both cleaned up in a few minutes, then bring the king into the room. You can tell him he has a son," Rosie said.

"I'd love to tell him that," Angelique said, looking at the baby. He had stopped suckling and was sleeping on her breast. "Just like his father."

They all laughed at this, with Rosie saying, "Most men love to be on the breast at all ages."

"Don't I know that," Angelique replied, laughing.

A short time later, Feyanna cleaned up the remnants of giving birth, Angelique and the baby were bathed, and the room was ready to receive its first visitor.

Rosie opened the door and motioned for Arthur to enter. She pointed to Angelique and the bundle she held. Arthur rushed over and fell to his knees.

"My sweet Arthur, we have a son," Angelique said.

Arthur leaned over them both and gently kissed Angelique on the lips.

"He's beautiful."

"Look at all this hair," Angelique said, pulling the blanket away from his head for a few minutes.

"Oh, my. He does have a lot of hair," Arthur said as he touched it and felt his son for the first time. "It's so soft. And brown as a cow."

"I'll be sure to tell him that every day," Angelique said, laughing at Arthur.

Arthur brought a chair next to the bed and sat down, holding his hands out for his son. Angelique gave Arthur his son and watched them as Arthur cried, holding his son for the first time. Arthur kissed his head and cheeks over and over.

"I shall call him," Arthur was saying when Angelique interrupted him.

"I think we'll call him," Angelique said.

"Yes, just like we said we would," Arthur replied softly.

"Tell them, then," Angelique said.

"Rosie, Feyanna, we have chosen the name of Thomas Arthur Pendragon for our son," Arthur told them.

"That, my dear Quintan, is a grand name," Rosie said, kissing Arthur on the cheek and hugging his shoulders.

"It's a fine name, for sure," Feyanna said as she stood at the foot of the bed. "Rosie, let's leave this little family alone for a few minutes. Food and drink are on their way."

"Thank you so much, Rosie and Feyanna," Arthur said as he continued to stare at his son. "Please tell everyone that we are healthy and happy."

"We will," Feyanna said as she and Rosie left the bedchamber.

Feyanna and Rosie were stopped the minute they left the chambers and stepped into the hallway.

"Well?" Harrison asked.

"You have always been an impatient one, young Harrison," Rosie said, winking at him.

"Don't mess with me, my Rosie. Tell us the news," Harrison said.

"The king and queen have asked us to inform you of the birth of their son, Thomas Arthur Pendragon. He's a fine boy and has already suckled at his mother's breast. He's sleeping now. The birth was fast and hard for them both. Angelique is resting as well and will recover quickly."

Cheers were heard in the hallway, and everyone went to the kitchen to eat and celebrate. The official ringing of the bells to announce the birth would take place three days later, as was the custom in The Old Magic.

The faeries flew into the bedchamber the minute Feyanna and Rosie left. They hung faerie bells and garlands all around the bedchamber, making tinkling musical sounds. Thomas seemed to like this and sighed in his sleep.

"He already knows The Old Magic," Arthur said as he handed the baby back to Angelique.

"Of course he does," she replied. "It was The Special Magic that made my labor so fast. I was only in labor for an hour. His birth is a great part of The Old Magic. It has plans for us all. Please set him in his basket. I need food and sleep."

A knock on the door signaled the arrival of Rosie and Feyanna with food and drink. They sat with Arthur and Angelique for a few minutes, then left them alone. Angelique ate a good meal and was soon asleep. Thomas let her sleep for one hour before waking and demanding some food of his own. Arthur changed his diaper and handed him to his mother. He watched them as she nursed him. He was a good baby.

The next few days were bright and sunny, although the temperatures were still cold. The third day, Thomas Arthur Pendragon was presented to the kingdom. His parents stood on their balcony as the bells were rung, and the trumpeters played the cadence to signal a healthy living birth. Arthur announced his son's name, and the countryside cheered for the longest time.

This third day after Thomas's birth was also the day of the Spring Solstice. Fires were set to burn at sundown until the next morning. There was a lot of celebrating taking place. Arthur and Angelique watched the lighting of the fires across the land from the castle's balconies. It was a magnificent moment when those fires were lit as they signaled the return of The Old Magic to the kingdom.

One week after the Solstice celebration, those silver flying discs appeared in the skies over the land far and wide in mid-afternoon. Angelique had a terrible feeling and gave the baby to Rosie to watch as she stepped into the hallway. A vision began to form and take shape. It was a creature that was not from the Earth.

"Welcome, sweet friend," Angelique said as she shape-shifted into the exact creature that stood next to her. "Follow me."

They walked a few steps, and Angelique placed her hand on the pentagram and dragon symbol carved into the stone wall. A door slid open, and the two of them walked inside. They were in a room inside the walls of the castle. It was soundproof, as it had been formed from The Old Magic.

"They have returned," her friend said.

"I felt it the instant they came through the portal," Angelique replied. "We need to act fast. The child is strong and well. He will be protected. We need to inform our fellow Kygarians about the invasion and hope they can get it under control."

"The people are being returned now. Look," her friend said as she waved her hand in the air, and a circle of activity appeared.

The people and animals were being returned to the exact spots where they had been abducted months ago.

"Send the signal," Angelique said.

Her friend raised her arm and pointed into the wavering circle. The picture cleared, and waves of what could only be described as energy formed. They were silver and blue, and little lightning bolts could be seen all shooting through the circle. Her friend pointed her three-fingered hand at the circle and wiggled those fingers, sending energy bolts from himself into the circle.

The circle closed, and Angelique said, "We've sent the message. Now we wait. Back to work with you," Angelique said as they shape-shifted back into their human forms.

They walked out of what looked like a small room into the hall. Hugho was running toward them.

"Lady Angelique, the silver flying discs have returned," Hugho said as he nodded at Sir Gerald. "King Arthur wants you to stay in your chambers until he tells you otherwise."

"That is an excellent idea," Sir Gerald said. "Shall we?"

"Thank you, Hugho," Angelique replied as she and Sir Gerald returned to the king's chambers.

King Arthur and the knights were in the main courtyard, watching the silver flying discs as beams of light shot to the ground. Penny and Q flew down to the courtyard.

"Arthur," Penny said. "The people are returned. Nothing has been damaged. Look, they're already leaving."

They looked up at the discs and one after the other flew straight up into the sky and vanished.

"Let's get up on the parapets," Harrison said.

The knights and the king ran to the stairs and joined the four dragons atop the castle walls.

"It looks like an invasion took place," Fred said. "Only, they're leaving without harming anything or anyone."

"That's what it looks like," Arthur said. "I want every household and business looked at by all the knights except Harrison and Fred. You two will remain here with me. Harrison, make it happen."

"Yes, Your Highness," Harrison replied, bowing. "Men, gather in the knight's courtyard as we make plans to inspect every building in the kingdom."

The knights left, and Arthur stood alone with his dragons in the mid-afternoon light.

"This is not good," Arthur said, looking directly at Penny.

"You are perceptive, Quintan," Penny replied.

"You will be guided as you go along," Q said.

"Thanks for that," Arthur replied, bowing to the North, South, East and West. "This is a time of great change. I feel it in every ounce of my soul."

"You have connected with The Old Magic well," Penny said as she touched his arm with her wing. "We are all very proud of you."

Arthur looked at Penny, Q, Clarice, and Roman for the longest moment.

"I will never forget you," Arthur said. "Time for me to help my people."

"We will be here," Penny said.

Hamlen was outside when the flying silver discs appeared and began sending light beams to the ground. No one in his village had been taken, so the discs were a ways away.

"Glendianna, the discs are back," Hamlen cried out.

"This is not good," Glendianna said. "I feel it in my bones."

Hamlen put his arm around his wife's shoulders, saying, "Me, too."

They watched as the discs retracted their light beams, shot straight up into the sky, and vanished.

Merlin and Feyanna looked at each other at the same exact moment.

"They're back," they said at the same time.

"This is not good," Merlin said. "We need to pack our satchels and get to the castle."

Feyanna and Merlin had their things ready in ten minutes.

"Let's go," Merlin said as they walked away from their home and got to the castle as quickly as possible. No one was paying attention to them. Everyone was all over the place, talking with the returned people and caring for the animals.

"Merlin, we need to stay inside the castle, not even in the courtyards," Feyanna said.

Merlin turned and looked at her and saw she was staring straight ahead of them. Her eyes were focused on an unseen object. He took her arm and guided her to the south gate, where Russell awaited them.

"Close the gates, Russell. All of them," Merlin said.

"I feel the darkness, too," Russell said as he signaled for the gates to be closed and bolted.

The castle gates were closed and bolted, and no one except the knights were allowed in or out of the castle. When they returned, it was late in the evening. They reported to Arthur and Harrison.

"Sire," Sir William said. "The people have been returned, as have the animals. All are acting strangely. They returned and didn't seem to remember anything or anyone. They have a blank stare on their faces. When we called them by name, they just turned and stared at us as if we weren't really there. Their eyes were jet black like a piece of coal."

"That doesn't sound good," Arthur replied. "Charles, Merlin, do you have any thoughts on this?"

Charles and Merlin looked at each other for a minute.

"King Arthur," Charles began. "Many eons ago, a legend was handed down about a time that would signal a drastic change for the Earth. The legend says that an evil the likes that had never before been known would attack the Earth and try to exterminate the people. The legend says the evil would come from a place beyond the stars and infect the people of the earth. The infected would infect others until all people were killed, and the evil would take over the Earth. The legend says there is a way to stop the takeover, but only one person of The Old Magic would know how to stop the invasion. I strongly believe the legend is coming true now."

There was absolute silence in the room for the longest moment.

"Merlin, what say you?" Arthur asked.

"I have heard the same legend and agree with Charles," Merlin said. "The legend is coming true now."

"What can we do about all of this?" Harrison asked.

Feyanna and Merlin looked at each other and instantly knew what must be done.

"This is going to sound harsh," Merlin said. "We need to get all the Returned into the same place away from everyone and every animal as soon as possible. We could take them to the Castle Farm for holding."

"That's a great idea," Charles said. "I have an old potion handed down for as many years as the legend. I think it may be the thing that brings the people back to us."

"If I may?" Feyanna asked.

"Indeed, you may," Arthur said.

"The legend also says that an evil will possess the taken ones," Feyanna began. "It is the potion that will kill the evil that possesses them and free them to be themselves again."

"What kind of evil?" Harrison asked.

Charles, Merlin, and Feyanna looked at each other. Then, Feyanna looked at Angelique.

"Angelique, you must hide Thomas right away," Feyanna said. "You must leave him with those chosen to hide and protect him while the battle rages on."

"Feyanna, he is but a new babe," Fred said. "How can he be taken from his mother?"

"The Old Magic will care for him," Feyanna replied, looking at Merlin.

"She is right about that," Merlin said. "Charles and I need to get to his quarters to prepare a great deal of that old potion. We'll need to get it to the farm by this time tomorrow night."

"Come with me, Merlin," Charles said. "I have all the ingredients for the potion. I received the recipe from the last great wizard and am ready to mix the potion."

"Feyanna, you know what you need to do," Merlin said.

"I do," Feyanna said. "Charles, may the gods and goddess protect you."

"And you both as well," Charles said as he hugged Feyanna.

Charles and Merlin rushed from the room and were in Charles's quarters a few minutes later, mixing and brewing the old potion. They had several vials ready to hold the potion. The brew would take about two hours to be completed and cool.

Harrison and Fred gathered the knights and ordered them to take the Returned to the Castle Farm. They knew the sixty-seven people that had been taken and spread out across the countryside. The knights were told they should not allow the Returned to get close to them. If the people were scratched by the Returned, they would be infected with a deadly organism.

Feyanna looked at Angelique and said, "Spend the next few hours with Thomas. We will need to get him away before daybreak."

Angelique took Thomas from his bed and held him as he slept. She rocked him most of the night, nursing him, changing his clothes, and loving him.

The knights loaded many of the Returned in wagons and headed to the Castle Farm. Two messengers raced to the farm to prepare it for the Returned. They were to be placed in a barn that held no animals. The returned animals would be given the potion as soon as all the Returned people had received it.

The knights weren't able to locate two of the Returned. Their families said they had gone to bed when everyone else had and had not heard anyone leave the house.

One of the knights returned to the castle to report this information.

"Tell Russell about this," Arthur said. "He will need to add extra guards all over the castle."

Fred left and informed Russell of the new problem.

"I have already hired extra guards, and each gate has double the sentries. The parapets are guarded by the dragons. Look there, more dragons are arriving as we speak," Russell said.

Fred and Russell watched as The Dragon Brigade circled the castle and flew in different patterns to cover the countryside.

"I'll report this to the king," Fred said as he walked away. "I'm certainly glad we have you here, Russell."

"I appreciate that," Russell said as he continued to watch the dragons.

The Returned were delivered to the Castle Farm by suppertime the next day. Merlin and Charles had dispensed hundreds of vials of the old potion recipe, and Charles was just arriving at the farm with them.

Charles entered the barn where the Returned were being held and set up his table with the vials.

Two knights brought each of the Returned to the table without touching them and told them to drink the potion. The first few refused, and the knights didn't know what to do about that. Charles came up with an idea.

"Bring one of them to me," Charles said. He had poured the potion into a drinking mug and added a bit of water.

"I have some water for you," Charles said as he handed the mug to the Returned. "You must be thirsty."

The Returned person looked at Charles with those hollow black eyes and took the mug. He drank all of the potion. A few minutes later, he began to growl and jerk around. He fell to the ground and screamed out as a black, oily liquid came out of his eyes. He screamed again, then lay there quietly. He opened his eyes, and Charles saw that the black was gone from them.

"Where am I?" the man asked as he stood up, looking around at the unfamiliar barn.

Charles poured some of the potion on the black, oily liquid pooling on the dirt floor. As soon as the potion hit it, the substance vaporized and vanished.

"We'll tell you all about it," one of the knights said as he handed the recovered man over to one of the farm workers to take to a barn next door.

Charles and the knights began to mix the potion with a bit of water, and by daybreak, all of the Returned that had been gathered in the Castle Farm barn were recovered. About half of them needed a second dose of the potion. Charles suspected that might be the case and had made four times the amount required. Some were used to vaporize the oily substance once it hit the dirt floor.

The two Returned who hadn't been found were being controlled by the black, oily substance covering their brains. They were on a straight line to the castle. In the dark of the night, they arrived at the east gate and waited for the gate to open to allow the knights to enter. The two Returned walked beside the horses and got inside without being discovered. They went to the kitchen entrance and got through the door without anyone seeing them. They headed to the staircase that would take them to the king's chambers. They heard footsteps and found an old closet to hide in to wait their turn to get to the king.

The king's chambers were busy preparing Thomas for a journey that would save his life. Angelique was crying as she prepared him.

Merlin and Chares had returned by daybreak and told everyone that the potion had worked. The cured ones had been returned to their families, and the black, oily substance had been destroyed.

Feyanna looked at Charles and Rosie for the longest time.

"What is it, Feyanna?" Charles asked.

"Nothing," Feyanna said. "I think I'm getting quite tired."

"King Arthur, you are needed in the meeting hall," Harrison said.

"I will return as soon as I can," Arthur said, kissing his wife and son. "I love you with all my soul."

"As we love you," Angelique replied.

The king and his knights were discussing the matter at hand when two strange men burst into the room. They came right at the king, and four of the knights encircled the king with raised swords.

"He's ours," one of the men said.

"Look. His eyes are black," Harrison said. "He is one of the possessed. Keep him away from the king."

The two possessed men pulled swords from their belts, and a massive fight began. One of the knights was killed straightaway with a sword driven straight through his heart. Another knight was wounded on the forearm, but he kept fighting and killed one of the possessed men. That man fell to the ground, his body turned black, and a hideous creature stepped from the dead body. The beast lunged at Harrison. Harrison sliced his chest from top to bottom, and his innards fell out. The creature fell to the ground and turned into a pool of black ash. The ash sizzled for a moment, then vanished.

The other possessed man ran from the room to hide in another closet. The knights ran after him as Arthur returned to his chambers.

"There is a possessed man in the castle. Take Thomas and leave," Arthur said.

Feyanna looked at Charles and Rosie.

"Charles and Rosie, you have been chosen to take Thomas to a safe place and raise him as your own," Feyanna said. "The village is expecting you. Use the secret tunnel found at the back wall of the dungeon. As you walk to the wall, the wall will open and allow you entry. The tunnel is long and will take you to the forest by our old cottage home. You will find everything Thomas needs as you walk through the tunnel. The fairies are waiting for you. May you always be blessed by The Old Magic."

Angelique and Arthur hugged Thomas one more time and then handed him to Charles. Charles strapped him into the sling he had on and turned to Rosie.

"It's time to leave, dear Rosie," Charles said as he held his hand out to her.

Rosie hugged Angelique and Arthur for the longest moment.

"You must leave now," Merlin said.

Rosie, Charles, and Harrison left the chamber and headed to the secret back stairs that would take them to the dungeon. No one was on guard as they walked past the cells to the back wall.

"I love you, my Rosie," Harrison said.

"As I do you, my Harrison," Rosie replied, hugging him.

"Charles, you're a great man," Harrison said as they shook hands. "Now, walk to the wall and touch it."

As Rosie and Charles touched the wall, it opened for them, and they turned one last time to look at Harrison. He motioned them to move forward. As they entered the magical tunnel, the wall closed, and it looked as it always had.

Harrison returned to the king's chambers just in time to see the possessed man run at the king. Fred stepped in to protect the king, and the possessed man threw him across the room. Arthur drew his sword as Angelique and Feyanna backed away toward the wall. Harrison drew his sword, and a vicious fight ensued. The possessed man was cut several times, but it didn't seem to phase him. He kept trying to get to Arthur.

There was a moment when Arthur wasn't protected, and the possessed man saw this. He lunged at Arthur and scratched him on the face, causing it to bleed. Harrison ran his sword through the man back to front, and he fell to the floor. His body turned into black ash, which sizzled for a minute and then vanished.

Arthur fell to the floor, holding the wound on his face. Angelique ran up to him to help him.

"Don't touch me, my sweet. I am possessed by the strange black oily creature," Arthur said as his eyes turned black.

"Drink this water, Arthur," Merlin said. "You must be very thirsty after such a strenuous fight."

Arthur took the mug and drank the potion it held. A few minutes later, the black, oily substance left his body and pooled on the floor. Merlin poured more of the potion on it, turning it into black ash, and vanished.

"Now we can take care of him," Merlin said as he placed a cloth against the wound on Arthur's face. "This is a bad wound. We need to get the king into his bed so I can care for him."

Harrison and Fred helped get Arthur to bed, but both men fell to the floor. They had been badly wounded by the sword the possessed man had used, but they were not possessed. Feyanna and Angelique cared for them, and they went to their quarters to rest and heal.

Two days later, word reached the castle that the people who had been possessed were dying from disease. The good witch Lylia, who lived just south of the castle, reported this to Russell, who reported it to Harrison and Fred, who were recovering well.

Harrison went to the king to report the news. What he found shocked him. The king had the disease and was dying.

"Angelique, how can this be?" Harrison asked in a whisper.

"Feyanna has tried everything she and Merlin can think of, but it is not helping. We fear the king will die this night," Angelique said, crying.

"Harrison," Feyanna said as she entered the room with Merlin. "We have nothing else we know of to cure the king."

"Lylia reported to Russell just now that the people that had been possessed are dying likewise," Harrison said.

"Arthur," Angelique said as she stood at his bedside. "Harrison is here as you requested."

Arthur opened his eyes. They were glazed with fever. He was pale as the sheets he lay on.

"Harrison, kneel before me," Arthur said as Patrick stood beside them. "I give you all the powers of the king this day."

Arthur placed the sword on each of Harrison's shoulders with the help of Patrick.

"Do you accept the duties of the king of the realm?" Arthur asked.

"I do with honor and truth," Harrison said, crying.

Patrick placed the king's crown on Harrison's head and helped him stand.

"You are crowned the King Harrison of Camelot and all the countryside as dictated here and now," Patrick said. "Heal well, Your Highness. We have a great deal to do to recover our kingdom from this vile disease. I have just been informed that people who have not been possessed are being infected as well. Half of the citizens are now ill."

"I accept this duty and will do my best to care for my people," Harrison said. "Arthur, you are my inspiration. I will follow your lead in all things."

"Add a few of your own as well," Arthur said, smiling a bit. "The dragons know how to heal the people of this vile disease. It was brought by the sky creatures. Ask The Dragon Brigade to help you. It's too late for me and others. You should be able to save most of the people. Go, be the king."

"As you demand," Harrison said, handing the crown to Patrick. "Take care of that."

Arthur had closed his eyes, and his breathing was heavy for a bit. Through-out the rest of the day and into the night, Arthur began to fade quickly. Feyanna and Merlin never left his side and watched as Angelique said her final goodbye to him just as the sun rose. Geroge and Goldie, who had spent the night just outside the castle wall, knew the moment Arthur died.

"My sweet Quintan, thank you for loving me and giving me our son," An-gelique said. "I will always remember this time with you. Sleep now with the gods and goddesses so you can watch over Thomas."

Arthur opened his eyes one last time, smiled at Angelique, raised his crys-tal dragon in the air, closed his eyes, and died.

Angelique, Merlin, and Feyanna cried together for a few minutes. As Mer-lin was about to go tell Harrison that Arthur had died, the bedchamber door opened, and Russel ran in.

"He's gone," Russell said as he took his hat off and bowed his head respectfully. "You three need to run. The people of Camelot are angry that Merlin and Feyanna couldn't cure Arthur and are spreading rumors that you three actually killed him. Lylia has created a potion with the help of the dragons and is giving it to the sick. They are beginning to heal. Some of the citizens are sure that you killed Arthur to take over the kingdom."

"Harrison has been crowned king already," Feyanna said.

"This is crazy," Angelique said. "Maybe I could address them and tell them the truth."

"Not going to happen," Russell said. "The people are already gathering to storm the castle to kill the three of you. You need to leave now."

"Russell, thanks for saving our lives," Merlin said. "We'll leave by the south tunnel now. Take care of Arthur. See that he has a proper funeral and burial."

"I will, Merlin," Russell said. "Be safe. I'll try to hold the people off as much as I can. They're already encircling the castle."

Merlin, Feyanna, and Angelique flew down the stairs to the same tunnel that Rosie and Charles had used. They touched the wall, the wall opened, and they stepped into the tunnel. The wall closed, and they began running down the tunnel. They stopped and rested for a minute.

"Where does this tunnel open up?" Angelique.

"It opens just inside the forest near our old cottage home," Feyanna said as she stared past them for a minute. "We'll be safe as long as we are in the tunnel. We must get to the Lady of The Lake as soon as we emerge from the earth. Follow me."

They walked for quite some time and finally reached the tunnel's end.

"We will need to hurry," Merlin said. "We must get to the lake."

"That's the same message I received," Feyanna said. "Are you okay, Angelique?"

"I am, "Angelique replied. "It's been a crazy few days."

"That's one way to put it," Merlin replied. "Ready?"

Merlin touched the wall, and the earth opened into the forest just west of their old cottage home.

"The lake is only a few minutes away," Feyanna said. "Follow me."

Just as the lake came into view, Merlin heard a commotion behind them. It was some of the people from Camelot.

"I will try to bother them to slow them down," George said as he circled back to harass the people.

"I will stay with Charles and Rosie and care for young Thomas," Goldie said as they ran toward the lake. "Hurry"

"There they are," a man's voice was heard to say. "After them!"

Penny and Q circled around the crowd, trying to slow them down. They blew smoke at the crowd, slowing them for only a minute.

Feyanna looked at Merlin and Angelique, and they broke into a run. The people were catching up with them.

"We need to hurry," Angelique said as a mist began forming at the lake's edge.

"Come to me, Angelique," the Lady of The Lake appeared in the mist. "Walk out onto the water. You will be safe."

Angelique looked at Feyanna and Merlin for only a second, then walked out onto the water and stood next to The Lady of The Lake. As Merlin and Feyanna watched, Angelique shape-shifted into her original self. She waved at them and disappeared as the mists enveloped her with The Lady of The Lake.

"Look to your left," the voice of The Lady of The Lake was heard to say. "Step onto the Northridge Footbridge, and you will be safe."

Before their eyes, a bridge made of boulders, rocks, and crystals appeared. It arched across the brook that flowed into The Lake.

Feyanna and Merlin were within the grasp of the angry mob as they stepped onto the bridge. As they turned to look back, they vanished.

CHAPTER 23

Katelyn and Jordan felt a wind encircle them as they stood on the NorthRidge Footbridge, and then it was gone.

"That was weird," Jordan said.

"There wasn't any wind all day," Katelyn said. "But then, weird stuff has been happenin' to us a lot lately.

"You got that right," Jordan said. "This sure is a beautiful spot."

"This is a beautiful bridge," Katelyn said as she looked at the stones and crystals. "Look here."

"I can't believe it," Jordan said as they looked at the crystal Katelyn pointed to.

"It's a crystal dragon," Katelyn said. "It sure is small."

"It's sparklin' like crazy, too," Jordan said as he thought of his crystal dragon.

Katelyn got lost staring into the rays the crystal dragon was giving off for the longest time.

"Katelyn? Katelyn?" Jordan said a few times.

Katelyn didn't hear him.

Jordan lightly touched her arm and whispered her name again. "Katelyn."

Katelyn thought she heard someone calling her name. She looked around and didn't see anything she recognized. She thought she saw a castle with flags flying from the top walls for a second, but the air cleared, and she was back on the NorthRidge Footbridge. She heard her name again, turned, and saw Jordan staring at her.

"Katelyn," Jordan said again.

"Yeah, Jordan. What is it?" Katelyn replied.

"Glad to see you back here with me," Jordan said. "You were somewhere else for a few minutes."

"Really? How long did I ignore you?" Katelyn asked.

"About five minutes," Jordan replied. "Just as you looked at the crystal dragon there, you seemed to go off into space."

"Oh, yeah, the crystal dragon thing," Katelyn said. "It is beautiful."

"It sure is," Jordan said. "Let's get on home. I suspect we both need a great deal of nourishment."

"I agree, even if I ate before we left," Katelyn said as they finished crossing the bridge and returned to Jordan's truck.

Katelyn glanced back at the bridge and saw the little rays from the wee crystal dragon shining up into the sky.

They drove down the road and were at Katelyn's place a short time later. The Store was a bit busy for this late at night.

"See you later, Jordan," Katelyn said as she got out. "This has been more than amazin'."

"I agree. Not a word," Jordan said.

"Not a word," Katelyn promised as Jordan backed out of the driveway and went on down the road home.

Katelyn dropped her things on the porch and walked over to The Store.

As Katelyn walked in, she saw Michael talking with Hal and Sarah.

"Hey, y'all," Katelyn said as she walked back to the dining room.

"Hey, Katelyn," Hal said. "You and Jordan finished with your latest survey?"

"We are," Katelyn said. "Walking the land always makes me hungry."

"I hear ya, Katelyn," Sarah said. "That's why I'm here. I had a good supper, then decided to wander around the field, and now I'm hungry all over again."

"That's exactly why I'm here," Katelyn said, laughing with everyone.

"Well, Miss Katie, let me know what ya' want," Ted said. "I've got a few things left."

"Well, Ted, I don't want a big meal, just something to nibble on," Katelyn said.

"We all know what that means," Michael added, pointing at Katelyn.

"I do have a healthy appetite," Katelyn replied.

"You just wait here," Ted said. "I'll fix ya' up a snack."

"We're in trouble now," Hal said. "Ted's known for his 'little' snacks. They usually last for a couple of days."

"That's right, Hal," Ted said, handing a package to Katelyn.

"This smells yummy," Katelyn said as she kissed Ted's cheek.

"Only the best for you, Katie girl," Ted replied.

"Is Gina and Terry's site ready for everything?" Hal asked.

"It is, Hal," Katelyn replied. "We start decking on Monday."

"I'll take any of the wood that's cut down," Hal said as he walked Katelyn to the register.

"Ethan was talkin' about that yesterday," Katelyn said as she paid Michael for her snack. "He chose a place close to the road for all the wood for you so you would be safe collecting it."

"I like the sound of that," Hal said. "I'll check in with him at the end of the week after they've had a chance to move stuff around."

"I'll let him know," Katelyn replied. "See y'all later."

"Enjoy!" Ted hollered out from the kitchen door.

Katelyn settled in the kitchen to enjoy Ted's snack. The Store emptied out and Michael and Ted closed for the evening. They set the outside lights, locked the doors, and went on upstairs. The dragons were keeping an eye on Katelyn, Jordan, and one other special soul. The Magic was alive and well tonight.

The week flew by in the blink of an eye. Fall was settling into the Blueridge as usual. It was Saturday afternoon when the strangest thing happened. Hal was outside clearing the yard of sticks and such from a windstorm the night before. He looked out over the ridge and saw a quick flash in the sky. He thought it was a jet or something, but Crab Apple Creek was not on any flight path. He kept looking, but nothing else happened.

Katelyn was over at Jenna's, and they were walking down to the faerie house. Katelyn loved how the faerie house sat up from the creek's bank. The sun was high in the sky, and it was a beautiful, sunny fall day. Leaves were changing colors, and there was a chill in the air.

"This place is so cute," Katelyn said as they looked over the Faerie House. "I love the way you painted it."

"Thanks," Jenna said. "I love this place and thought all those colors would reflect well when the sun hits it. I used a special reflective exterior paint I created. Watch."

Jenna pointed to the roof of the Faerie House. The sun was just touching the roof line, and it glowed like crazy, sending rays all over the place.

"That's wicked awesome!" Katelyn said. "You're a genius artist for sure."

As they watched the sun dance along the roof line, a quick flash was seen in the sky high above them.

"What was that?" Jenna asked.

"I don't know," Katelyn replied as they kept watch on the sky for a few more minutes.

"Weird stuff happens in the atmosphere all the time," Jenna said. "I'll bet it was some kind of sun thing bouncing off ice crystals in space."

"Great thinkin' there," Katelyn said as they walked along the creek. "I like the way you think."

"I wonder if anyone else saw that?" Jenna said.

"I'm sure we'll hear about it if anyone else did," Katelyn said. "Things don't stay quiet around here for long."

"That's the truth," Jenna said. "Let's head back. I'm in need of hot chocolate."

"With a touch of Bailey's?" Katelyn said, looking mischievous.

"Of course," Jenna replied as they turned and began walking through the meadow toward the barn.

Matthews was in Boone for a meeting with his regional director.

"Matthews, good to see you again," Darren said.

"Good to see you, too, sir," Matthews said. "It's been a while since Yuri was taken care of."

"We're still sorting everything out," Darren said. We're still making arrests with the thousands of connections this guy had. Two of those people are here in Boone."

"That's why I'm here," Matthews said. "Is Emily in any danger?"

"We're not sure," Darren said. "So far, none of the people that have settled near The Creek and become friends with her are part of the web. They are clean. We really like your Jordan. He's a great guy. We've been following his research about the Underground Railroad. He's found things no one knew existed."

"I'm sure Washington is all abuzz about that," Matthews said.

"Oh, they are," Darren replied.

"So, what's our plan for Emily?" Matthews asked.

"What are your thoughts about this?" Darren asked. "I know you've read the intel."

"I have," Matthews replied. "I think we start with adding six agents to the detail, similar to what we had before. I'll meet with Emily and Ethan and tell them about this whole thing."

"I like that," Darren said as he picked up the phone. "Connors. I need the best six agents we've got for undercover work in Crab Apple Creek. We'll use Ethan Sutherlands' business for two of them. Yes, just like before. Have them report to me at 0900 tomorrow. Thanks."

"I'll get Ethan on board with this," Matthews said. "I know he'll be onboard."

"I think so, too," Darren said as he looked out the window of his tenth-floor office. "We'll have to move quickly. I want our people in place tomorrow. We can't use Kendra's properties. Got any ideas?"

"A couple of farmhouses have been up for sale for the past six months. I'll give Connors the info. They are only a mile or so from The Store up near Emily's place. They're on a side road past the sister's farm. They should work well."

Matthews called Connors and gave him the information.

"We'll get the digital squad out there tonight to start installing everything," Darren said. "I know this sounds like a lot, but I don't want to be taken by surprise."

"Where are the two persons of interest?" Matthews asked.

"One is working at the local feed and grain, and the other, a woman, is working at a local distribution center just south of Boone," Darren replied. "We've got people inside both businesses. We suspect the two are moving drugs from Asia and South America. We've got eyes everywhere."

"Crazy people," Matthews. "Do they know who Emily is?"

"We don't think so," Darren answered. "All of Yuri's henchmen and regional leaders were either killed or captured in the sting the day he died on the mountain. Whoever was left after that stayed quiet for a long while. We heard chatter about the current tracking situation, and his name was mentioned several times. We've been gathering intel for the past three weeks. The chatter keeps mentioning Yuri as if he were still alive. Our forensics team thinks the cartels are using his name as a code for moving contraband through the United States. We've confiscated several shipments from South America off the coasts of Florida, both sides, in the past ten days. We're confident that's how the information is passed on to the regional dealers. We just want to make sure Emily is safe."

"This is going to drudge up nightmares of the past," Matthews said. "I think I'll speak with Ethan first. Then, we can both tell Emily about this."

"Good idea, Matthews," Darren said. "We are Code Silent as of this minute."

Darren pressed a button on a fob he held, and they heard people running past the door.

"We're live," Matthews said.

"Here's a new weapon for you," Darren said as he handed Matthews a new revolver. "It has a GPS tracking system and will set off an alarm if you fire it. We'll know exactly where you are and come to the rescue."

"Cute, Darren," Matthews said as he strapped on the second weapon. "I'll be sure to let you know when I'm practicing."

"You got the right idea," Darren said.

Connors walked in with a briefcase for Matthews.

"Hey, Matthews," Connors said. "Here's the latest. Sir, I've already activated the team. They're on their way to The Creek. The farmhouses are a go. We've secured contracts with the realtor for an open amount of time."

"Fine work, Connors," Darren said. "Keep me posted."

"Yes, Sir," Connors said as he left.

"I'd better be on my way, too," Matthews said as his stomach growled. "I'll stop at Hank's Diner in Pine Ridge on my way back. He's a great asset to our team."

"Great idea," Darren said. "He's up-to-date on this. I love that diner. Stay safe."

"Yes, Sir," Matthews said as he walked to the door. "Wouldn't want to be the reason for more paperwork."

"Wiseass!" Darren said, laughing as Matthews left.

"Here we go," Matthews said as he called Ethan and asked to meet with him immediately.

"What?" Ethan yelled. "What the fuck! This was supposed to be all over. How am I going to tell Emily?"

"I feel the same way," Matthews replied. "The extra detail is already. One group is in a house near Emily's Meadow. The other is just down the Pine Ridge Road from here on the other side of Jordan's place. By the way, you have four new employees. They'll be at your place in an hour."

"This is just wrong," Ethan said as he sat at the kitchen bar with Matthews. "Is the bar open yet?

"Wiseass!" Matthews said as he poured them coffee. "I love this kitchen. You know that."

"Yes, I do," Ethan said as he looked around. "We did a great job on your place."

"Modest, too," Matthews said as he threw a potholder at Ethan.

"And, humble," Ethan said as he threw the potholder back at Matthews. It landed on his head, and they both laughed.

"Now, back to this nightmare," Ethan said. "Give me the details."

Matthews explained the possible connection with the drug and trafficking link in Boone. The two suspects were a new feature in the worldwide investigation. He told Ethan the agency didn't think there would be any trouble for Emily. They were being extra cautious and would keep the security detail in place until told otherwise.

Matthews and Ethan spent about an hour discussing the details of every aspect of this new operation. At the same time, Miss Cora was outside taking care of one of her gardens when she felt a sudden and menacing shift in the energy. She stopped what she was doing and tuned into the energy.

"We got us a problem," she said as she dropped her rake and went inside. She was on the phone with Kendra in a flash.

"Miss Cora, I know," Kendra said when she answered her phone.

"Yes, we have a problem," Miss Cora said. "Come over right away."

"On my way," Kendra said as she set her work aside, grabbed her jacket, and was on her way a minute later.

Emily was mucking out her horse's stall in the stables when she felt the sudden energy shift. Trouble stood up and barked at the air. He felt it, too.

"It's okay, Trouble," Emily said as she rubbed his head. "Somethin''s comin'."

Emily finished in the stable and went into the kitchen. Trouble was at her heels. He wouldn't leave her side.

"You are such a great protector," Emily said as she gave him a treat. "I'm gonna call Miss Cora. That okay with you?"

Trouble gave a soft woof and settled on his bed right next to Emily. She punched in the number for Miss Cora.

"Hi, Emily," Miss Cora said as she answered the call.

"I feel it," Emily said. "And it's not good. As a matter of fact, it's quite ominous."

"You're right about that," Miss Cora replied. "Kendra's here with me. Let's talk."

"It's not as bad as the Yuri thing, but close," Emily said.

"I agree," Kendra added. "It's not good. I keep getting images of people in trouble, but not The Creek folks. Other people nearby."

"Me, too," Emily said. "It's as if they're in the Boone area."

"Same here," Miss Cora said. "Let's switch to Facetime,"

A second later, they were on Facetime.

"This came out of nowhere," Kendra said.

"I agree with that," Emily said. "Just the other day, we all felt a ripple in the energy, but nothing like this. It's as if something shifted to make this happen."

"That's a good way to say it," Miss Cora replied. "I think that's exactly what must have happened. Something shifted in the universe, and now we have this."

"Yup," Kendra said. "I feel it like that, too. Now what?"

"Well, we're aware of the shift," Miss Cora began. "I think we'd better be on our toes around here and watch things very closely. Have either of you noticed anything amiss lately? Even the tiniest thing."

"Can't say I have," Kendra answered.

"Me, either," Emily said. "Although Jordan and Katelyn were over near The NorthRidge Footbridge the other day as they walked the land over at Gina and Terry's new place. They said the crystals in The Crystal Creek are amazin'."

"That they are," Miss Cora said. "Wonder why they were north of their land."

"I don't know," Emily replied. "You know how those two just get to walkin' the land and get lost in it. Katelyn said she showed Jordan how the build was taking shape, and they walked around the perimeter of the property so the cameras wouldn't pick them up. She said they didn't want to bother Ethan's security folks."

"Right thoughtful of her," Miss Cora said as her phone beeped. "It's Katelyn. Hi, Katelyn."

"You felt it, too?" Katelyn said.

"All three of us did," Miss Cora replied. "Kendra is here with me, and we have Emily on Facetime. Join us."

"Well, what do ya think, Miss Cora?" Katelyn asked as she joined them.

"I hear you and Jordan were out walkin near The NorthRidge Footbridge the other day."

"We were," Katelyn replied. "That bridge is gorgeous, and the crystals in The Crystal Creek are like nothing I've ever seen before."

"That's the truth," Miss Cora said.

"You've been on the bridge?" Emily asked.

"I have," Miss Cora replied. "I was in my early twenties when I found it. I go there once in a while when I feel the urge."

"Not many are allowed to see it," Kendra said.

"That's true," Miss Cora replied. "The Magic knows what it's doin'."

"So, The Magic needed Katelyn and Jordan to see the bridge? Wonder why?" Emily said.

"Beats me," Katelyn replied. "I know when The Magic is in charge, y'all need to follow its lead. If ya don't, it'll bother you until you do."

Everyone agreed with this.

"So, any thoughts on this new trouble headed our way?" Emily asked them.

No one had any ideas.

"I believe we should keep ourselves tuned in to the energy extra well from here on," Miss Cora said. "The Magic will show us the way."

"I agree," Kendra said. "I just don't like how it all of a sudden barreled in here."

"That's what's got me worried," Emily said. "We usually feel the changes over a few days or so. This time, it was all at once. I wonder if that means somethin's about to happen."

"I'd say so," Miss Cora replied. "Well, let's get back to our chores. I've got some clean-up to take care of."

"The pumpkins are going strong," Emily said. "The Creek is having a blast goin' out into the patch and picking their own. We've got lots of pictures."

"I heard some of the kids talkin' about it yesterday at The Store," Kendra said, laughing. "One of them said they had a pumpkin that weighed at least a hundred pounds."

"I guess it would if you were just a little kid," Katelyn said. "Time for me to get back to work. Lots to do for Gina and Terry's build. They'll be drivin' the first nail in on Monday."

"And Sami's home in a couple of days," Kendra added.

"That's right," Emily said. "Did her stuff get here yet?"

"It did, and her new design table did, too," Katelyn said. "Ethan came over, and we set it up for her. She'll be home the day after tomorrow."

"That's Friday," Kendra said. "Can't wait."

"Either can she," Katelyn said.

"Take care, everyone," Miss Cora said. "Keep in touch."

They ended the chat and went back to their work. Katelyn got lost in her thoughts and found herself daydreaming or something. She saw herself in that cave again, with the pots and plants. And the older man was there, too. And, a most magnificent looking hawk. It was quite big, and its eyes were gold. This was very familiar to her. She came back to the here and now when she almost fell off her chair. She laughed at herself and got back to her work.

Jordan found himself daydreaming at the same time. He saw the cave and the woman, just as Katelyn had. He saw the hawk with the gold eyes, too. Those eyes looked familiar. Jordan jumped up and ran onto the back porch through the kitchen door. George was waiting for him.

"It's not a dream," Jordan said. "It's a real memory. I'm the older man, and Katelyn is the woman. What the fuck have you done to me?"

A brilliant flash of white light filled the sky as three energies descended from the sky.

"What the fuck is this now?" Jordan hollered.

Geroge morphed into his human self as the energy took human form.

The three energies surrounded Jordan and covered him in a soft blue light. Jordan felt the energy touch his soul, and he became less angry but still furious.

"What the fuck is going on? Those weird dreams and flashes of visions are from a real time in my life," Jordan said. "Does Katelyn know about this yet?"

"Hello, Jordan," a woman's voice answered. "She has the same visions you have but hasn't tied everything together yet."

"And you were there, too," Jordan said, looking at George. "You were a hawk. A most magnificent-looking hawk. It was your eyes that gave you away."

"Thanks, Jordan," Geroge said as he took a few steps backward. "I always thought I was magnificent looking, too."

"Go fuck yourself," Jordan hollered. "This is beyond anything I can handle. Stop! Leave me alone."

"I wish we could, Jordan," a man's voice replied. "We can't. Your world needs you to help keep it safe. Crab Apple Creek needs your help."

"What the fuck am I supposed to do? Defend the realm?" Jordan yelled as he walked around the porch.

The three energies looked at each other, then replied together, "Yes. Exactly. Defend the innocent ones."

"Nice try with the guilt thing," Jordan said, giving an evil look at the three energies.

As Jordan stood there, confused and angry, he felt a sudden change in the air.

"You felt that," the woman's voice said.

"I did," Jordan replied. "It wasn't a good thing. It's as if the air has become heavy and oppressive."

"Exactly!" the man's voice said. "That's why we're here."

"Oh, no," Jordan hollered. "Not another battle like the one on The Rise."

"Absolutely not," the third energy's voice said. "That was a whopper of a battle, and The Dark Forces have been banished to the ends of the universes for a long, long time."

"So why do you need me?" Jordan asked.

The silence that followed was so thick you'd need a chainsaw to cut through it.

"I get it," Jordan said, sounding defeated. "Not for me to know right now."

The three energies nodded.

"Just be aware of the energy in The Creek," the woman's voice said.

"Okay, I guess I'm in," Jordan said as tears fell. "This is so beyond what I can handle."

"We'll take care of you," the man's voice said as the soft blue light wrapped around Jordan and held him close.

Jordan stood there, wrapped in the energy for a long while. He didn't remember the three souls leaving when he found himself seated in one of the porch chairs. George was an eagle again. He just looked at Geroge and nodded his head.

While Jordan communicated with the ethereal souls, Hal was busy working on his frames. He was sanding an oak frame when he felt a heavy breeze blow through his workshop, giving him the shivers.

"What the fuck was that?" Hal said out loud.

Hal stopped his work and stepped outside to have a look around the place. Nothing seemed out of the ordinary. He walked around the house and the barn. All looked good. He returned to his work, thinking about that strange breeze.

"Hey Ted," Michael hollered from the front of The Store, "Did ya feel that?"

Ted came running from the kitchen, saying, "What the hell was that all about?"

No one else was in The Store at that exact moment.

"It felt like a wave of bad stuff," Michael said, looking through the windows with Ted.

"Everythin' looks good outside," Ted said as they walked all around looking through all the windows. "Doesn't look like anything fell off the walls or the porch."

"It was more of an air thing, like a bit of wind winding through the place," Michael said.

"It was strong in the kitchen," Ted said. "I don't like this thing. It feels like somethin' bad might be brewin'."

"I hear ya," Michael replied as a couple of folks walked into The Store.

Ted returned to the kitchen while Michael helped his customers.

As soon as the customers left, Michael said, "We'd better check in with Miss Cora about this. I'll give her a call right now."

Michael was on the phone for only a couple of minutes.

"Well, what's she have to say?" Ted asked.

"She said she felt it, too, and had a Facetime meeting with Kendra, Emily, and Katelyn. Kendra was at Miss Cora's. They said to be extra vigilant and all."

"No idea why it happened?" Ted asked.

"Nope," Michale said as Ethan and Ian walked in. "Just keep an eye on things. Well, look what the cat dragged in?"

"Cute, Michael," Ethan said, laughing with Ted and Ian.

"Ted, we're in need of some supper to go," Ian said. "We've been workin' hard all day and am about to waste away."

"Just for you, Ian, or the whole family?" Ted asked.

"The kids are at a pizza party with their mom, so they're all set," Ian replied.

"I'm getting dinner for two tonight," Ethan said. "Emily's been busy with the pumpkins and all, so I told her I'd bring dinner home."

"That's nice of you," Michael said.

"We're all countin' the days until Sami's return home," Ted said. "I've got the makin's for her favorite breakfast bagel, just waitin' for her to say so."

"We're all happy she's makin' The Creek her home," Ethan said. "Katelyn, well, she's over the moon about it. She's been smiling since Sami decided to live here."

"Let's take a look at the menu board," Ted said as they walked up into the dining room.

Orders were placed, and Ethan and Ian talked with Michael while Ted prepared their orders.

"How's Gina and Terry's place comin' along?" Michael asked.

"We're ready to start deckin' bright and early Monday mornin'," Ethan replied.

"Gina and Terry will be there to drive the first nails into place on the house and barn foundations," Ian added.

"Finn's been workin' with the ground engineers getting' the thermal run ready to place the pipes. That's a major job they're doin'. You know the foundations are all set. Karl was in here last week gettin' meals for his guys. He's a generous man when it comes to his folks," Ethan said.

"That's true," Ted said as he handed Ethan and Ian their orders. "He showed a bunch of us the videos of diggin' up the ground and settin' the forms and all. Sure is a lot of work."

"He knows what he's doin'," Ian said. "Thanks for the goodies, Ted."

Ethan and Ian paid for their dinners and stepped outside.

"Somethin''s changed," Ethan said.

"I feel it, too," Ian replied.

"Be careful goin' home," Ethan said as they got into their trucks.

Ethan looked across the road and saw Katelyn and Kendra carrying boxes into Sami's new house. They all waved and carried on.

Ethan was at Emily's a few minutes later. The last of the folks buying pumpkins were just leaving.

Trouble greeted Ethan and began sniffing the bags.

"Not for you this time, boy," Ethan said as he grabbed Emily and kissed her.

"I do like the way you say hello," Emily replied. "Let's get into the kitchen. I'm starvin'."

"Me, too," Ethan said as he looked for Trouble. "Emily, look."

They saw Trouble just staring off into the night.

"Trouble, here boy," Emily said.

Trouble didn't hear her. He stayed where he was. Emily walked over to him and looked in the direction he was staring in.

"Ethan, come here," Emily said sternly. "Look. What is that?"

They watched a strange-looking cloud forming over the mountain ridge to the west. It was gathering white and gray clouds and began to cover most of the late-day sky. The air was absolutely still, and no animal or insect was making a sound.

"What the hell is that?" Ethan said.

"I'm not sure. I do know it's not good," Emily replied.

Emily began to chant as Miss Cora had taught her. The cloud stopped moving and growing. The more Emily chanted, the smaller the cloud got until it was gone. Well, not visible to the human eye.

"What was that chant thing?" Ethan asked.

"Somethin Miss Cora taught Kendra and me when Katelyn was beginnin' to fight the bad guys on The Rise," Emily replied. "I'm wicked tired all of a sudden and hungry. Let's go."

Trouble ran ahead of them and was waiting at the kitchen door.

"Good boy," Emily said as they walked into the kitchen.

"I'll feed him while you get this food set up," Ethan said.

A few minutes later, Trouble was snoring on his bed, and Ethan and Emily were enjoying Ted's creations.

"I do love our Ted," Emily said. "And you for takin such great care of me."

"My privilege, ma'am," Ethan said as he leaned over and kissed her. "You taste real good."

"It's Ted's food," Emily said, laughing.

"Some of it is," Ethan said. "Let's finish here and get upstairs. I need a long, hot shower. I think I'm covered in at least five layers of dust."

"Me, too," Emily said as they cleaned up their dishes. "I'll take mine down here and join you in bed."

"Deal!" Ethan said as he ran upstairs.

Ethan was stretched out on the bed, fully naked, when Emily walked in. She had a tiny towel that was not really covering anything.

"I do believe you need a bigger towel," Ethan said, smiling as Emily walked over to his side of the bed.

"Could be," She replied as she set the towel over his hard dick. "Not big enough for you, either. That's the way I like you. Big. Hard. Ready."

Emily leaned over Ethan and ran her fingers along his dick. Her breasts hung near his mouth.

"Hmmm," Ethan said as he began sucking her tits.

She grasped his hard dick and began slowly pumping him. Ethan moaned and sucked her tits harder as his hand found her wet pussy. He stroked her clit hard and fast. Emily fell onto the bed across Ethan, and he moved her underneath him.

"So, this is how it's going to be, is it?" Emily moaned as Ethan began finger fucking her.

"It is," Ethan replied as he sucked her breasts again.

Emily began to feel her climax growing and moaned and pushed against Ethan's hand.

"Fuck me hard!" Emily cried out as her organism got closer to exploding.

Ethan moved over her and pushed his hard dick into her again and again. His dick got harder and hotter, and he began to feel his organism growing. Emily pushed against Ethan as he rammed into her. She felt her climax spill over and cried out as Ethan rammed harder and faster into her. He met her climax with his, and they flew off the planet to that place of pure ecstasy for what seemed like forever.

It was deep into the night when Emily woke up. She felt fully satisfied and rolled over to find Ethan's hard dick ready for her. She scooched down in the bed and took him into her mouth, licking and sucking his shaft.

"Stop!" Ethan cried out as he moved away from her. "You are dangerous."

"I know," Emily replied. "I don't like to do as I'm told, either."

Emily mounted Ethan and pushed down hard onto his dick as she took him into her. This was too much for Ethan. He pushed against her thrusts. Emily hollered out as Ethan grabbed her ass and moved it against his dick. He followed her climax, pushing against her thrusts again and again. They collapsed in a tangle and lay there breathing heavily for a few minutes.

"That was beyond amazin'," Emily said. "If you pull out of me, I'm gonna cum, again."

"My pleasure," Ethan said as he began rocking her. Emily came right away, enjoying every pulse of her organism.

"Holy shit, Ethan," Emily said a few minutes later.

"Agreed," Ethan said as they lay back, trying to cool down. "I need food."

"There's pie on the counter and ice cream in the freezer," Emily said, laughing. "Why is it we're always so hungry after sex?"

"I don't know, and I don't care," Ethan said as he got out of bed and put on a robe. "Here you go."

Ethan plopped Emily's robe onto the bed as she got up.

"Thank you, kind sir," Emily said, grabbing Ethan's ass.

"Don't get me started until after my pie," Ethan said, laughing at Emily as they ran down the back stairs to the kitchen.

Pie was warmed and served with ice cream and they both were silent for a few minutes.

"What time is in, anyway?" Emily asked with a mouth full of ice cream.

"Two in the mornin'," Ethan replied.

"Great," Emily said. "It's the middle of the night, and we're sittin' here eating pie and ice cream."

"Sure. Why not?" Ethan said.

"Yup," Emily replied.

They felt the ripple of energy just as a bright flash of light lit up the night sky.

"What the hell is that?" Emily said as they ran out onto the porch and watched the sky.

Everything was quiet, and the sky was dark, with a million stars shining like crazy.

"Don't know," Ethan said. "Let's get back upstairs. We can talk with folks tomorrow. I need a few more hours of sleep."

"Me, too," Emily said as they snuggled under the covers and fell sound asleep.

They woke up late Sunday morning and laughed at each other. Trouble was looking at them.

"Let's go, boy," Ethan said as he pulled on a pair of jeans and a shirt. "We'll be back in a few."

Hal, Bob, and Ned met for breakfast that Sunday morning at The Store.

"Mornin' men," Ted said as they got their coffee and sat at the table. "What's it gonna be as if I didn't know?"

"Farmer's breakfasts for us all, as usual," Bob said, laughing with everyone.

"They'll be ready in a bit," Ted said.

"Hey, Hal," Ned said. "Did you see that strange cloud over the mountain last evening?"

"Nope," Hal replied. "I did feel some strange energy, though. Not sure how all that Magic stuff works, but I know what I felt."

"What strange cloud?" Bob asked. "Tell us about it, Ned."

"Well, it was just before true evenin', and I was out closin' things up. I saw a shadow fall across the barn roof, and I looked up and saw a strange cloud forming. It was gray and moving around in weird circles. It was getting really big then, all of a sudden, it vanished. Gone," Ned told them.

"Well, that seems odd," Bob was saying when Ted brought them their breakfasts.

"I'll get the rest," Ted said as he disappeared into the kitchen.

"These look magnificent," Hal said as Ted set the biscuits and gravy on the table.

"Enjoy y'all," Ted said.

"Oh, we will," Bob replied as they got started on their breakfast.

Katelyn and Finn walked in and saw what the guys were eating, and ordered the same for themselves.

"Gentlemen, this looks great," Katelyn said as she sat across from Hal.

Hal smiled and kept eating.

"Katie girl, ya know how great Ted's creations are," Finn said, teasing Katelyn. "Don't go bothering these men while they're stuffing their faces."

This made everyone in The Store laugh.

"I hear Gina and Terry are drivin' the first nails in the mornin'," Hal said between bites.

"They are for sure," Ethan replied. "As soon as the sun's up, we're gonna get started."

"Looks like the whole Creek's here this mornin'," Ned said as more folks walked into The Store.

"Ted, ya got some of this stuff for us?" Terry asked as places were made for them at the table.

"Of course I do," Ted answered. "I had a suspicion that this mornin would be a busy one. I'll be back in a few."

"We're obliged," Gina said as she sat next to Katelyn.

"Gina," Katelyn said. "Ya ever get that feelin' that ya know someone from a long time ago, but ya know you've never met them before today?"

"All the time," Gina said.

"That's how I feel about you and Terry," Katelyn said. "Ever since we met, I'd bet a week's pay that we've known each other before."

"Isn't that Deja Vu?" Bob asked.

"It's somethin' like that, Bob," Katelyn said. "But this time, it's wicked strong."

"I get that feelin sometimes, too," Terry said, winking at Gina. "Mostly with places more than with people."

"Oh, I guess that would be true, too," Hal said.

"I wonder if that's why the three of us are such good friends," Bob added.

"What do ya mean by that, Bob?" Ned asked.

"Well, think about it," Bob said. "Ever since we were tiny ones, we've been friends. More than friends. We've grown up together. We've gotten into mischief more than once."

"That's the truth," Hal replied, laughing and nodding.

"Sometimes, it's as if we can read each other's minds," Ned said.

"Like when we all decided at the same exact second to go looking for The Crystal Caves," Bob added.

"Yup," Ned and Hal said at the same time.

"Long-time friends, for sure," Terry said, laughing with everyone just as Ted came through the kitchen door with a tray full of breakfasts.

"Oh my God, Ted," Gina said as Ted set her plate in front of her. "This is heavenly."

"Don't we know it," Finn replied as he grabbed a biscuit and some gravy. "I think I'm in food paradise."

"You are," Katelyn replied.

There were a few moments of silence as everyone enjoyed Ted's Farmer's Breakfast.

"Ted, absolutely delicious!" Hal said. "Terry, you and Gina ready for tomorrow?"

"We most certainly are," Gina said before Terry could answer.

"Cute!" Terry said, making a face at Gina. "We haven't been out there since they started digging the foundations. Really excited to see everything."

"There are a few big holes out there," Katelyn said.

"The run for the thermal pipes is ready, too," Finn added. "We'll be laying those pipes tomorrow while the crew starts the decking on the house and barn."

"Is anyone gonna be takin' pictures?" Gina asked.

"Yes, Ma'am," Katelyn answered. "That's my job tomorrow. Take a zillion pictures of the two of you drivin' the first nails and all the rest."

"That's great," Terry said. "Be sure to send them to my phone, please."

"We'll be takin' a lot of pictures as the project moves along. We have a professional photographer on-site as well. Albums will be made for us and the two of you."

"You really do think of everythin'," Gina said.

Folks talked about the build for a bit, then began to take their leave.

"Ted, that was heaven on a plate," Ned said as he, Bob, and Hal paid for their breakfast.

"I appreciate that," Ted replied.

"I've got more frames to make," Hal said as the three men left.

"Hey, Wanda Sue," Bob said as they stepped off the porch.

Wanda Sue gave a grunt as she lay on the porch on a patch of sunshine.

"She's some pig," Ned said. "Later, guys."

"Time for us to get goin, too," Katelyn said.

"What are you two up to today?" Michael asked.

"We're gonna finish settin' up Sami's new architect drawing table, then head over to my folk's place," Finn replied. "Mom and Dad are busy makin' Sunday dinner."

"That sounds nice," Ted replied. "Send our love."

"Will do," Finn replied as he and Katelyn left.

As they crossed the road to Katelyn's house, Finn said, "Katie girl, you get the feelin' somethin' strange is about to happen?"

"I do, Finn," Katelyn said as she stopped walking. "There's been a shift in the energy, and Miss Cora, Emily, and I aren't too sure what it's all about."

"I get the same feelin'," Finn said. "Guess we'll have to stay on high alert."

"Good idea," Katelyn replied. "Let's go over to Sami's and finish with her table. She's gonna be so surprised with it."

"Sure was generous of Ethan and Ian to give it to her," Finn said as they worked on the table.

"She doesn't know it yet, but she'll be doing some work with us, too. They like her ideas and how she got the URR project goin. So, the guys want her to be a kind of consultant on a few projects as well."

"That's fantastic," Finn said as he stepped back from the table. "All done."

"It looks great, especially with that big red bow on it," Katelyn replied.

"I need warm cookies," Finn said as he sprinted over to Katelyn's house.

"I shouldn't be surprised," Katelyn said as Finn warmed up his peanut butter cookies in the microwave.

"These are fantastic as always, my Katie girl," Finn said as he ate the last one. "But not as delicious as you."

Finn grabbed Katelyn, unbuttoned her blouse, sat down, and began sucking her tits.

"Oh God, Finn," Katelyn said. "Take me here, right now."

They fell to the floor, ripping each other's clothes off, and Finn spread her legs. Katelyn grabbed his hard dick and pulled it into her wet cunt.

"God, girl," Finn said as he began pushing into her. "You are amazin'."

"Faster and harder, Finn," Katelyn hollered out.

"Yes, Ma'am," Finn replied as he picked up the pace.

Katelyn met his thrusts with a fierce power of her own, and they came at the same time.

"Oh my God," Katelyn said. "We're getting really good at this."

"It must be those cookies," Finn replied as he sat up and started to get dressed.

"Oh, I guess I forgot to tell you," Katelyn said as she dressed. "I put some love potion in them. Guess it worked quite well."

"Funny, girl," Finn said as he helped her stand up. "Let's, uh, clean up and get on home. My folks should have dinner ready just before we arrive."

"Great idea," Katelyn said as she went down the hall to her room.

They were ready a few minutes later and set out for Finn's home.

Finn and Katelyn arrived and were warmly greeted by his parents. The afternoon seemed to fly by with great food and company.

Hal was working on his frames and had a sudden flash memory of a time long gone by. He liked history and all and thought he just remembered a bit of some show he had watched. Thing was, he'd been having these flash memories for a few days now. They'd happen no matter what he was doing. He was even woken up by one of them last night. He decided to set aside his work and go have a visit with Miss Cora.

Miss Cora was digging up some of her potatoes in her garden when Hal arrived.

"Good Afternoon, Miss Cora," Hal said as he walked over to her. "How's the harvest?"

"It's a bountiful one, Hal," Miss Cora said as she pointed to a basket half full of potatoes.

"How many plants was that?" Hal asked.

"Two," Miss Cora replied, standing up and laughing. "I was thinkin maybe I'd get a full basket from the twelve plants I put in. But now it seems I'm gonna get six baskets full. Sure hope folks are in need of a few spuds."

"I'll bet Ted and Michael could find a few homes for your spuds. Ya gonna keep some in the root cellar?"

"Sure am," Miss Cora replied. "Nothin' like fresh baked spuds on a cold winter's night."

"I hear ya there," Hal said. "Can I carry that for ya?"

"That'd be right nice of you now that I've filled it," Miss Cora replied. "Set it on the back porch near the kitchen door. The root cellar door is just below the window there."

"I'd be happy to take 'em down for you," Hal offered.

"Let's do that," Miss Cora replied as they walked over to the cellar door, and she opened it for Hal.

Hal set the basket next to Miss Cora's workbench, and they went back outside.

"Now, Hal, what brings you over my way?" Miss Cora asked.

"I wanted to ask you about somethin' that's been happenin' to me," Hal replied.

"Let's get a cup of tea," Miss Cora said as she motioned for Hal to go into the kitchen.

Miss Cora poured the tea a few minutes later, and they sat in the kitchen, eating cookies and tea.

"Miss Cora, for the past few days, I've been havin' what I call flash memories of a time long gone by," Hal began. "Now, you know how much I love history and all. So, I was wonderin' if they could be just some pieces of somethin' I've watched over the years. Not sure why they're happenin' now, though."

"I like that phrase you used," Miss Cora replied. "Flash memories. Are they always the same thing, or are they from different times and such?"

"I've been thinkin' that same thing myself," Hal said. "These are really good molasses cookies, Miss Cora. I thank you for these. Well, I remember the memory when the flash happens, but right after it's done, I don't really remember any details. I know I had the flash memory, and it was of a time long ago, but that's about it."

"Have ya written' anythin' down about them?" Miss Cora asked.

"No. But I like that idea," Hal said. "I'll do that if it happens again. What are your thoughts, Miss Cora?"

"Well, I've been thinkin' about these the past few minutes," Miss Cora said. "You are very aware of The Magic around The Creek."

"Oh, yes, ma'am, I am. Especially after I was gifted that magnificent crystal last year," Hal replied.

"I thought you'd remember that whole thing," Miss Cora said. "Now, I'm thinkin' The Magic has somethin' to do with these flash memories. Not quite sure how they're all connected, but I do get a strong resolve when I put them with The Magic."

"Well, I'm not surprised," Hal said, sitting back in his chair. "There's so much of The Magic in our lives here in The Creek, I suspected they may be connected. I just don't know how."

"The Magic will tell us when it's time," Miss Cora replied.

"That's the frustrating part," Hal said. "Waiting to learn the connection."

"Ain't that the truth," Miss Cora said, laughing.

"Tell me what you remember," Miss Cora said. "Take your time and breathe easy."

Hal sat quietly for a few minutes, then began to share what he remembered.

"I remember seeing a castle with flags flying from the parapets," Hal said, keeping his eyes closed. "It was summertime, I think. No snow. Lots of people around. That's all."

"That's a lot to remember," Miss Cora said. "Was that from one flash memory or all of them?"

"Good question," Hal said. "I think from just one of them. In another, it was night, and I really didn't see much. Just the night sky with a couple of shooting stars."

"No castle?" Miss Cora asked.

"No," Hal replied. "That's all."

614

"Well, Hal, I agree with your thoughts that these may be from something you read or saw with the history stuff you like," Miss Cora said. "On the other hand, I wonder if they may be linked to The Magic for some reason. Now, Hal, hold on. I don't know the reason or any reasons for this. I'm just thinkin' out loud. One can never tell when The Magic is at work."

"I understand that," Hal said. "I would like to know the why of it, that's all."

"And I understand that," Miss Cora said.

"Well, I'd better get back to my frames," Hal said as he stood up. "Thanks so much for your time and hospitality. I am much obliged."

"And, thank you for takin' the spuds down to the root cellar," Miss Cora said. "Could ya use a few?"

"Sure could," Hal replied.

"Let's go dig up a few," Miss Cora said. "Here's a spud sack for them."

Hal and Miss Cora spent a few minutes digging up more potatoes. She cut a few squash for Hal, too.

"Thanks much, Miss Cora," Hal said as he hugged her.

"Anytime, Hal. Take care now," Miss Cora said. it

Hal drove back home and got back to working on his frames. He thought about their talk for a bit, then concentrated on his work. By nightfall, Hal had six more frames ready for Ethan and Ian.

Sami was wrapping things up in Mongomery. She was at one of the hotels she was working on, as the movers had taken her things earlier in the week. They would arrive in The Creek on Tuesday morning. Katelyn and Kendra were ready for the driver to call to tell them when they'd be arriving.

Monday morning, alarms sounded earlier than usual. Ethan's crews were at the build site just as the sun rose. Gina and Terry were finishing breakfast and ready to drive over. Katelyn and Ian were looking over the floor plans while waiting for Karl. He was going to push some of the earth back against the foundations for safety reasons before anyone got busy.

Karl arrived a few minutes later, and the earth was back against the foundations in short time. The building inspector had approved the rough plumbing the Friday before. Gina and Terry arrived, and Ethan gave them instructions on how things would be done.

"Ready?" Ethan said as he handed the hammer to Gina.

"I'm ready," Gina said.

"Okay, hit that nail as hard as you can," Ethan told her.

Gina swung the hammer and drove the first nail into the foundation of their new house.

"That was so cool," Gina said with tears streaming down her cheeks.

"It's really happenin'," Terri added, crying as well.

"Let's let the framers get to work," Ethan said. "We're off to the barn."

A few minutes later, Terry was ready with his hammer.

"Let her rip," Ian said.

Terry gave that nail a mighty blow, and it was set into the foundation just like Gina's had been.

"Now, that's a powerful feelin'," Terry said.

Gina hugged Terry, and they laughed and cried. Katelyn and the photographer caught it all on film.

"This has been so special," Gina said. "Thanks for lettin' us do this."

"Of course," Ethan said. "Let's get out of these guy's way. I'll walk with you back to your truck."

"These are huge holes, just like y'all said yesterday at The Store," Gina said.

"They look bigger than the building'," Terry added.

"That's right," Ethan said. "We have to dig bigger holes so we can get the rough plumbin' and septic drainage in place. As you can see, Karl pushed a lot of the earth back against the foundations where he could. Some areas need to be left open for a while. There are three different crews workin' here and will be here for the next month anyway. Then, once we get the buildings weather-tight, we'll change out the subcontractors for the interior work."

"This is a huge dance ya got goin' on here, Ethan," Terry said. "I wouldn't want anyone else doin' it for sure."

"Thanks, Terry," Ethan said. "We appreciate that. Time to get back to work. Now remember, ask before you come by. Safety first."

"Understood," Gina and Terry said at the same time. "See ya later."

It was about seven when Katelyn got a call from Sami.

"Facetime," Sami said.

They were live a few seconds later.

"How's it feel to be between homes?" Katelyn asked.

"Weird," Sami replied. "Although it's not gonna be as long as we thought."

"What?" Katelyn asked.

"I'm gonna be home on Wednesday afternoon," Sami said.

"Oh my God!" Katelyn said, jumping all over the place. "This is the best news I've heard since you decided to live here permanently."

Sami was laughing at Katelyn's craziness.

"Settle down, Katie girl," Sami hollered.

"Oh, yeah. Sorry," Katelyn said, laughing and crying at the same time. "How come earlier?"

"My work here is finished. Just a couple of details to take care of tomorrow, then I'm on the road. I'll get a hotel room for the night and be home by lunchtime Wednesday," Sami explained.

"I love you for this," Katelyn said. "Kendra and I have everythin' ready for the movers. This is so exciting!"

"No fuckin kiddin'," Sami said.

This made Katelyn laugh.

"That's my Sami," Katelyn said, laughing with Sami.

They talked for a while about everything. Katelyn made Sami promise to call every hour on Wednesday until she drove into the driveway.

"This is a dream come true for both of us," Sami said.

"Dreams really do come true, my Sami," Katelyn said quietly.

"Indeed they do," Sami replied. "Time to get some sleep. Sweet dreams, my Katelyn."

"Sweet dreams, my Sami," Katelyn said.

They fell asleep around ten in Montgomery and The Creek. Most of The Creek was asleep a few minutes later. Most of The Creek. Seems George was flying around to make sure everything was safe in The Creek. A few other big shadowy things had taken to the sky north of The Creek. Miss Cora stepped outside to look at the night sky and saw them. She smiled and went back inside. She offered a prayer of thanks to The Magic before falling sound asleep.

CHAPTER 24

It seemed that Monday and Tuesday would never get done, and then they flew by in the blink of an eye. It was finally Wednesday morning. Katelyn woke up at sunrise and texted Sami. Sami responded with a sleepy emoji and a few choice words. She said she was gonna sleep for a bit before heading home. Home. Her Sami was coming home.

On Tuesday afternoon, the moving company called Katelyn and arrived an hour later. They spent about two hours getting everything in place. After they left, Kendra and Katelyn tidied a few things up so Sami's new home would be ready the next day.

Katelyn was up early on Wednesday morning for Sami, of course. And she needed to get to the shop to pick up a few things for the build at Gina and Terry's. She arrived a good thirty minutes before anyone else. She parked and began walking toward the barn. She had a revised blueprint for the foreman. As she looked around, she thought she saw something fly overhead. Something huge. Oh no. Wait. It might have been Penny. She hadn't seen her in a few days. She'd have to stop by Jordan's on the way back to the shop. There it was again. This time, it was high in the sky and flying toward the sunrise. It was hard to see any details. Katelyn sighed, knowing The Magic was at work this morning.

"Terry!" Gina said as Terry came through the kitchen door. "What have you done?"

"Nothin'," Terry said. "I just went for a mornin stroll around the place."

"We promised not to leave without tellin' each other," Gina said.

618

"I'm sorry," Terry replied, wrapping his arms around Gina. "It was such an amazin' sunrise. I couldn't resist. You were sound asleep, and I didn't want to wake you."

"Cute, Terry," Gina said, laughing as she put breakfast on the table. "You didn't want to miss the sunrise. You would have if you'd have woken me up."

"Truth in that," Terry said, laughing as well.

"Let's eat," Gina said. "We've got to meet Katelyn and Ian at the shop to discuss faucets and drawer pulls and stuff like that. The details are endless."

"They sure are. But they make a big difference in the end," Terry said.

"They do," Gina replied. "Now, try to behave yourself. It's all gonna be done in just a little while."

"I know," Terry replied. "I know."

The work crews arrived a few minutes after Katelyn, and she met with the foreman to discuss the revised blueprints. She walked around the site to see how things were coming along, then headed out just as Ethan arrived.

"Everythin' in place, Katie girl?" Ethan asked, ruffling her hair.

"It was until you did that," Katelyn said, laughing. "You guys never grow up, do ya?"

"Not if we can help it," Ethan replied. "Look here, we're all playing with trucks and tools."

"Yes, you are," Katelyn replied. "Time to get back. Gina and Terry are due at ten, and Ian and I have lots of stuff for them to look at."

"I'll be back late, so lock up when you guys leave," Ethan said. "Finn's gonna be here all day as well."

"He told me this morning when he called," Katelyn replied. "I'm waitin' for Sami. She should be here around noon or so. She's already sent me three texts. The last one was a picture of her waving at me as she drove away from the hotel."

"I told her to come right to the shop to see you first thing," Ethan said.

"That's really sweet of you, Ethan," Katie said, punching him in the arm.

Get along," Ethan said as Katie got in her SUV and drove away.

Katie met Ian, and they got busy. Gina and Terry arrived at ten and spent the rest of the morning choosing all the little stuff for their build, as they called it.

Katie heard the shop door close and looked up to see Sami standing there, smiling at her.

"You're home!" Katelyn said as she ran to Sami and hugged her, laughing and crying all at the same time.

"I am," Sami replied, laughing and crying along with Katelyn. "I don't have the words to tell ya how I feel. But, I do feel whatever."

"Well said," Ian offered as he walked over to them and hugged Sami. "Welcome home, our Sami."

Sami looked over at Gina and Terry and smiled. They smiled back.

"Gina and Terry, I'd like you to meet my bestest friend ever, Sami," Katelyn said. "Sami, this here is Gina and Terry. They're the couple we're doin' the big build north of Emily's place for."

"Nice to meet ya both," Sami said, shaking hands with them.

"Same here," Gina replied. "I guess this means we're finished for the day, Ian?"

"We are because you've completed the to-do list for today," Ian said. "We should have all those fixtures here in about two weeks. I'll let ya know so you can come by and look them over."

"It'll be like an early Christmas," Terry said. "I love gadgets and stuff."

"Can't wait to see them," Gina added. "Come on, Terry. Let's get along. We've got chores to do."

"We do," Terry said as they walked through the door. "Later."

"See ya," Katelyn said.

"I propose we go over to The Store for some lunch," Ian suggested.

"Deal!" Sami replied. "I'll drive over and park in my driveway."

"That sounds just as it should," Katelyn said. "Let's go."

They all drove their vehicles to The Store. Katelyn and Sami parked in their driveways and Ian pulled up next to the building.

Ted saw Sami and Katelyn walking over and ran to meet them.

"You're finally home, our Sami," Ted said, crying and laughing as hugs were shared.

"I am, and it feels good," Sami replied as they walked into The Store.

"Give a squish," Michael said as he grabbed Sami into a huge hug.

"So glad to be home," Sami said. "Let's settle down for some of Ted's great fixin's."

They settled around the table and gave Ted their orders. Miss Cora walked in and settled at the table with them.

"Well, Sami, you're finally home," Miss Cora said.

Sami walked over to Miss Cora and hugged her. "I am."

"As it should be," Miss Cora replied. "Ted, what're we eatin' today?"

"What would ya' like, Miss Cora?" Ted replied.

"I see ya got a pulled chicken bar-b-que sandwich there," Miss Cora said. "I'll have one of those with everything."

"Comin' right up," Ted said as he disappeared into the kitchen.

You could hear Ted singing in the kitchen as he fixed everyone's lunch.

"He's a happy man when he's in the kitchen," Sami said.

"That's his happy place," Katelyn replied.

"It's one of them," Michael said, winking at them.

"That, too," Ian said with a knowing smile.

Lunch was a fun time. Everyone wanted to hear the latest news about Sami's move.

Katelyn and Sami went back to Katelyn's house for a minute after lunch.

"Ya ready to see what we did?" Katelyn asked as they walked over to Sami's house.

Kendra was there waiting for them.

"Hey, Sami," Kendra said as they hugged. "Easy ride home? Sorry I wasn't at lunch. Busy day in the real estate world."

"No worries," Sami said. "Let's see what you two have done to my place."

The three of them walked into the kitchen to find a basket full of goodies.

"Ted?" Sami asked.

"Ted and Michael," Kendra replied.

" I truly love those guys," Sami said. "Let's check out my office."

Sami stopped in her tracks when she entered her office. The table Ethan and Ian had gifted her was in place, and so were a few surprises.

"What the hell?" Sami said. "Where's the remote?"

Kendra handed her the remote, and Sami put it to use. The wall opposite the door opened, and a flat screen came forward just like the one Ethan had. It was smaller but worked the same.

"Oh my God!" Sami said. "This is beyond awesome. Where are those two Sutherland brothers?'

"Right here," Ethan said as he and Ian walked into the room.

Sami grabbed them into a group hug.

"I don't even know what to say," Sami said. "You guys are incredible."

"Well, there's just one thing that goes with the whole setup," Ian said.

"Oh, oh, the catch," Sami replied. "What is it?"

"Well, Katelyn and I are swamped with tons of design work, and we could use your help with a couple of projects," Ian answered. "How about you do some side work for us?"

"Absolutely!" Sami replied. "When do I start?"

"How about you take the rest of the week to get settled, and then we can talk?" Ethan said.

"Deal. Besides, I've got a lot of unpacking to do," Sami said.

"Yes, you do," Kendra replied. "And I'm gonna help with that this afternoon. Katelyn has a lot of work to do, so she's excused."

"Funny, Kendra," Katelyn replied. "We do have a lot to do, so I guess the three of us should get to it."

"Agreed," Ian said. "I see Ted and Michael send some goodies over. Enjoy every bite."

Oh, I will," Sami said.

"I'm gonna help with that, too," Kendra added, laughing. "See you tonight, Katelyn."

"Well, I guess I'm really here," Sami said. "Time to get some laundry done. I'll get a load goin' before we start with the kitchen stuff."

Kendra and Sami spent the afternoon unloading Sami's SUV and doing a lot of unpacking.

"I swear the days are getting shorter faster than I want them to," Sami said. "It's only five o'clock, and the shadows are getting long."

"I know," Kendra said as they settled in the kitchen for a cold drink. "I prefer the summertime."

"This has been a busy day," Sami said, yawning. "I need some food and some sleep."

"Katelyn made lasagna. I put it in her oven about thirty minutes ago," Kendra said. "It should be ready in another half hour. Take a shower, put on some comfy clothes, and wander over. She'll be home soon."

"I like the sound of that," Sami said. "Later."

Kendra went home, Sami showered, and Katelyn got home just in time to take the lasagna out of the oven.

"Smells like an Italian restaurant in here," Sami said as she walked into the kitchen.

"It does," Katelyn replied. "Here, put the garlic bread in the oven just the way we've always done it."

"Done," Sami said as she prepared the bread and placed it into the oven. "Ten minutes should do it."

"Hey, girls," Kendra said as she walked in. "I'll set the table."

They thoroughly enjoyed dinner and talked about all kinds of stuff. It was around eight o'clock when a loud bang was heard. They hurried outside and looked around but didn't see anything amiss.

"What was that?" Sami was asking when it happened again. This time, there was a brilliant flash of light from overhead.

"Holy shit!" Kendra said.

"Fuck!" Katelyn said. "What was that?"

Folks had run out from The Store and were watching the sky with the girls.

"It could have been a meteor burning up in the atmosphere," Hal said.

"Could have," Chief Charlie said.

"Do they get that close before they burn up?" Sarah asked.

"Not usually," Ted replied. "They usually burn up high in the mesosphere. Some of the bigger ones explode, and small pieces make it closer to the earth. Sometimes, they hit the earth.

"That was a huge blast," Hal said. "It didn't look like a meteor to me."

"What do ya think it could have been, Hal?" Sami asked.

"Call me crazy, but maybe it was a UFO," Hal said.

"A UFO over The Creek?" Sarah said.

"Maybe," Michael said. "Who knows? It sure was loud."

Katelyn looked at Chief Charlie. He was deep in thought.

"Chief Charlie, what are ya thinkin'?" Katelyn asked

"Just rememberin' some of the stories that have been passed down," Chief Charlie said.

"Like what?" Ted asked.

"My ancestors told a story of the sky makin a thunderous noise in the night. The sky lit up like it was noon. Shook the earth so hard a few trees and such fell over. People were frightened. The Shaman communed with the Spirits, and they told him it was a rare happenin and to be mindful of their surroundings for a while. That's all they said."

"Not much, but thanks for that," Ted said. "Nothin' else seems to be happenin', so back to work, Michael."

"Yes, boss," Ted said, making a face at Michael.

They laughed at Ted and Michael's antics and got back to what they were doing.

"It's time for me to turn in," Sami said, yawning.

"It most certainly is," Kendra agreed.

Hugs were shared, and they went into their own houses. Sami stood in the kitchen for a few minutes, tears rolling down her cheeks. She was beyond happy to finally be home.

Kendra stood on her back porch for a few minutes, watching the night sky. Katelyn found her there.

"Somethin's up," Katelyn said quietly. "Somethin big. Not with The Dark Forces, but evil anyway."

"I agree," Kendra said, placing her arm around Katelyn's shoulders. "It's not about to happen. It's here."

"Yes, it is," Katelyn said. "Let's get some sleep. We're gonna be extra busy real soon."

Katelyn walked across the yard to her back porch steps, glancing one more time up into the night sky. Something was definitely here.

Miss Cora knew exactly what that flash was. She was told not to say anything yet. Like Kendra and Katelyn, she knew something fierce was about to take place in The Creek. Again. She offered a prayer of protection for all in The Creek and went back inside to settle for the night.

Jordan awoke in the night from a vivid dream. He sat up and remembered everything that had happened in his dream. And he knew it had all been real. He had lived that dream.

"Holy fuck!" Jordan said as he jumped from his bed and ran into the kitchen. "George, get in here as a human."

George walked into the kitchen as a human and leaned against the counter. "What's up, Jordan?" George asked.

"Don't you mean Merlin?" Jordan shot back at George.

"So, you finally remembered?" George said. "Don't punch me."

"Punching you would not be enough to begin to lessen the crazy I feel right now," Jordan yelled. "What the fuck? What the holy hell fuck?"

George remained silent and still while Jordan ran around the kitchen and then outside for a good ten minutes. Cussing was heard all around the farm. Penny heard it, too. Jordan finally came back into the kitchen and stared at George.

"Well? Now what?" Jordan said as he got a beer from the frig and guzzled it down.

"What do you remember?" George asked.

"Really? You want details?" Jordan replied.

"They do," George said, pointing upward.

"Oh god! Now, what else is gonna happen?" Jordan asked.

"Talk, Jordan," George said.

Jordan sat down at the table and put his head in his hands.

"I know I'm Merlin from Middle Earth and Camelot," Jordan began. "I know you were there as a most magnificent hawk. Very huge and very colorful."

"Thanks," George said, standing taller.

"Don't even think about it," Jordan said, pointing to the chair across from him.

George sat down and waited for Jordan to continue.

"We lived in a cottage home near a village," Jordan said. "I said we, didn't I?"

"Yes," George replied. "Who is the other person?"

"It was a young woman. I've seen her in my dream visions before. She's the same young woman who was assisting me with my work," Jordan explained. "She knew a lot about plants and remedies. There's something familiar about her, though. As if I've known her before."

George watched Jordan as he thought about that young woman. It didn't take long for Jordan to figure out who she was.

"No fuckin way!" Jordan said. "Katelyn. It's Katelyn. Her name wasn't Katelyn. It was something quite different. Started with an F, like Fey or something.

No, wait! I got it. Feyanna. That's it. Feyanna. What the fuck is she doing with me in this place?"

"What place is that, Jordan?" George asked quietly.

"What place?" Jordan replied. "How the hell do I know? I just know it wasn't here. It was Middle Earth back in the days of Camelot. There were knights and a castle and dragons. Penny! Get over here now!"

They heard her land as she settled in the yard by the back porch.

"Hello, Jordan," Penny said.

"Penny, what the fuck is goin on here?" Jordan said as he walked outside and stood in front of her.

"You're figuring that out quite well," Penny said.

"So it seems," Jordan replied. "What were you doin' there besides the usual dragon stuff?"

"Keep remembering," Penny replied.

"So none of it was a dream," Jordan said. "I was really living there?"

"Yes," Penny replied.

"How can that be? I'm living here, and I don't feel any older," Jordan said. George looked at Penny, and they remained silent.

"The Magic," Jordan said, sounding defeated. "It's all about The Magic. So, I don't get to know. This is pure bat shit crazy."

"Jordan," George said. "You'll find out the why in just a very short time. Katelyn hasn't remembered yet. She needs to remember before we can move forward."

"And, then, as usual, there's gonna be a battle or somethin," Jordan said.

"The Magic has got to be protected here in The Creek," Penny said sternly and quietly.

"I understand, Miss Penny," Jordan said. "I just don't know if I can do more stuff."

"Try to remember all the things you did as Merlin," Penny said as she reached out and wrapped Jordan in her wing. "It will serve you well in what's coming along."

"Miss Penny, you feel so good," Jordan said as he closed his eyes and absorbed Penny's healing energy.

"Miss Penny, that was great," Jordan said as he stepped back. "I remember you were seriously hurt and needed a long time to heal. You all okay now?"

"Yes, Jordan, I am," Penny replied. "Thanks for remembering that. Q and I recovered after a long spell."

"Yes. Q. I remember him, too," Jordan said. "He is a mighty warrior, and his black scales always shine brightly."

"I'll tell him you said that," Penny replied. "Now, Jordan, keep remembering as much as you can. Write it all down. You'll need some of it soon."

"Thanks for the warning, Miss Penny," Jordan said sarcastically.

"Get some sleep now," George said as he morphed back into his eagle self. "I'll keep an eye on you and Katelyn."

"Thanks, George," Jordan said. "Miss Penny, you goin back to our cave?"

"Not quite yet," Penny replied. "I need to fly around the place first. Sleep well."

"You, too," Jordan said as she took to the air.

Watching a dragon take flight would never get old. Jordan went back to bed and was sound asleep in no time.

Katelyn was restless and woke up a couple of times in the night. She finally slept deeply a couple of hours before her alarm woke her.

"Hey, sleepyhead," Finn said when she answered her phone.

"Hey, Finn," Katelyn said as she yawned.

"You sound tired," Finn said.

"I am," Katelyn replied. "I kept wakin' up in the night. I didn't fall sound asleep until about two this mornin. It's gonna be a long day."

"I hear ya," Finn replied. "I hate when that happens. Take a nice hot shower and eat a good breakfast. I'll see you at the shop soon."

"Okay," Katelyn said as Finn winked at her.

Katelyn kept having those flashback kind of visions of the older man in the cave with the young woman assisting him. The man was mixing something in a pot over a fire. She was separating plants and putting them in clay bowls and cloth pouches. There was a hawk of some kind on a perch. It was huge and had an array of amazing colored feathers from head to tail tip. She had a vision in the shower, another quick one while she ate, and then a longer one when she went to the shop. She sat in her SUV for about three minutes with that one. It finally ended, and she shook her head and went into the shop. Time to get to work.

Matthews was very busy. The two people the Marshals had been watching had just left Boone and were headed to Pine Ridge. Agents followed the two of them as they drove into Pine Ridge and parked near Hank's Diner. The two suspects walked behind Hank's Diner down the block, crossed the side street, and knocked on the backdoor of a small printing shop. The door opened, and the two of them went inside.

"This is Agent Billings," Billings said. "The two are inside the small print shop we've been watching. An agent is inside at the front counter."

"Thanks, Billings," Matthews replied. "We've got cameras on the place. Stay put."

"Will do," Billings replied as he and his partner settled behind some pallettes, waiting for further instructions.

The two suspects opened their backpacks and took out a package.

"As agreed upon," Suspect A said.

"I'll count it, of course," the counter agent said.

The money was counted.

"It's all here," the counter agent said. "Bring the girls in here."

Suspect B went back to the backdoor, opened it, and a woman with two teenage girls walked out of the door next to the print shop backdoor and handed the girls over to Suspect B. Suspect B handed an envelope to the woman, pushed the girls inside and slammed the door shut.

Agent Billings stepped out from the pallets and blocked the woman's path.

"Get out of my way," the woman hollered.

Agent Conlin stepped behind the woman as she turned to run.

"Not so fast," Agent Conlin said as he grabbed her arms and pulled them behind her back. "You are under arrest for human trafficking."

"You're full of shit!" the woman yelled. "Get your hands off me."

"Yell all you want," Agent Billings said. "We've got everything on camera."

The counter agent smiled at Suspect B when he came back into the shop with the two young teenage girls. They looked terrified. They were dirty, unkept, and scared. They stood there watching Suspect B.

"You come with me," Suspect B said as Suspect A entered the room.

"We have a few men who are going to like you," Suspect A said, smirking at the girls.

The girls were no more than thirteen or fourteen years old. They became hysterical.

"Shut up!" Suspect A yelled at them as he slapped them across their faces.

The counter agent pressed his panic button, and four agents came running into the shop. Two of them were women, and they stood next to the girls.

"You are safe," Agent Hanson said. "We're with the FBI."

The girls fell to the floor, sobbing and shaking uncontrollably.

"Get the paramedics in here now!" Agent Hanson ordered.

Two paramedics came through the backdoor and went over to the girls. They wrapped them in warm blankets and gave them water to drink.

"Are you hurt anywhere?" Paramedic Jones asked. "Has anyone touched you?"

"Only that guy," one of the girls said, pointing to Suspect A. "He's hit us a few times. She has a bruise on her shoulder from where he grabbed her yesterday.

We tried to run away, but he got her and pushed her into the wall. The other guy threw me to the ground. We hurt all over."

The paramedic looked at the girl's arms and legs. They had multiple bruises and scratches on them.

"I need to ask a very private question," Agent Thompson said. "Did anyone touch your private parts and try to have sex with you?"

"No," the second girl said, sobbing. "We heard those two telling someone on their cell phones that we were virgins and would stay that way until we were sold."

"I'm glad no one touched you," Agent Thompson said. "We need your parents' information now, and we're taking you to the University Medical Center in Boone to be taken care of."

The girls gave the agents their parents' contact information, and then they were escorted through the backdoor to the waiting rescue rig. The rig was waiting on the small sidestreet for them. The rig left, and Agent Billings handed the two suspects to other agents for transport to the federal penitentiary south of Boone.

Once the scene was free of the suspects, Agents Billing and Hanson set crime scene tape around the shop and let the Crime Scene Unit get to work. Matthews was updated through all of this and was relieved the two girls were safe. The group the suspects came from had moved to a new apartment. The Marshals had this one under surveillance and were recording sound and video nonstop.

"Matthews," Director Darren said. "Those two girls are lucky your people were following them. This could have been horrible. Excellent work."

"Thank you, Director," Matthews replied.

"We have just learned that four new suspects have joined the group in Boone; their plan is to rent a house near The Creek as soon as possible. Kendra's ready for their call. We're sending two agents to stay with Emily right now. Time to talk with her and Ethan."

"Yes, sir," Matthews said. "Have we established their connection to Yuri?"

"We have, just an hour ago," the Director said. "We know Yuri had connections all over the globe. Looks like there's a new boss in charge. The thing is, we can't find any intel on the four new suspects. Nothing. It's like they're in a class of their own."

"I understand," Matthews said. "Get back to you after I meet with Emily and Ethan."

"Thanks, Matthews," the Director said as he signed off.

Matthews drove over to Gina and Terry's build to talk with Ethan.

"This place is going up fast," Matthews said as he walked over to Ethan, putting his hard hat on.

"Hey, Matthews," Ethan said as they shook hands. "It sure is. We set the first nails on Monday with Gina and Terry. They sure were excited."

"I remember that feelin'," Matthews said. "Ethan, we need to talk now."

"I figured somethin was up," Ethan said. "Let's walk over here so no one will hear us."

"Your security cameras will," Matthews said.

"Yes, they will, and that's okay," Ethan replied. "Out with it."

Matthews told Ethan about the situation and how four new suspects were trying to rent a house in The Creek.

"Kendra won't let them, right?" Ethan asked.

"As far as Kendra can," Matthews replied. "There are a few other realtors that handle rentals up here in the Blue Ridge. We're watchin' them closely."

"Shit!" Ethan said. "We gotta tell Emily now?"

"Yes, we do," Matthews said.

"Okay. Hold on a minute," Ethan said as he called his foreman on the radio. "I need to step away for a little while. Get a hold of me if anything big happens."

"Yes, sir," the foreman replied, saluting at Ethan from across the field.

"Wiseass," Ethan radioed back, laughing.

"Always a wiseass or two around," Matthews said as he and Ethan walked through the field and down the track to their vehicles. "I'll let you go first. Emily's gonna be upset soon enough."

"Thanks for that," Ethan said.

"She doesn't need to see my vehicle first," Matthews added as they got into their trucks and drove onto the road toward Emily's Meadow.

Emily heard them cross the covered bridge and stood watching them drive up to the barn. She saw Matthews and knew something was happening. It couldn't be good.

"What's wrong, Matthews?" Emily asked as he walked toward her.

"It seems a few of Yuri's old distant workers have set up shop here. Again," Matt said.

"We don't know if they know about you yet. We arrested a couple of them a short time ago in Pine Ridge. The Director has assigned two agents to be with you until this thing blows over."

"Not again?" Emily said. "When will they be here?"

"That's them now," Matthews said as he turned to look at the black SUV crossing the covered bridge. It drove right up to them and stopped. Two agents got out and walked over to them.

"Agent Matthews," the woman said.

"Emily, this here is Agent Roscowitz," Matthews said. "She is going to keep you company every single second of every single minute."

629

"Cute, Matthews," Emily said, nodding at Agent Rosenthal. "Nice to meet you, Agent Roscowitz."

"I'll be with you from here out," Agent Roscowitz stated. "This is Agent Bankowski. We'll be wherever you are."

"I know the drill," Emily said.

"Agents, this is Ethan Sutherland," Matthews said. "He owns and runs Sutherland Builders. His crew built the place."

They all shook hands as Trouble came running over and stood between Emily and the agents.

"Trouble, it's okay," Emily said, stroking Trouble's head. "These are the nice guys."

Trouble looked at Emily, then sat down.

"He's very protective of Emily," Ethan said.

"Was he trained as a guard dog?" Agent Bankowski asked.

"Nope," Ethan said. "He just showed up one day when we were building the place and has never left Emily's side since."

"That's great to hear," Agent Roscowitz said. "It's as if a higher power sent her a guardian."

"That's the truth," Matthews replied. "Emily, we need Agent Roscowitz to stay in one of your guest rooms. She'll take you wherever you need to go. No more driving yourself around until we get a better handle on things."

"Seriously? Again?" Emily replied.

"Yes," they all said at the same time.

"Okay. I get it," Emily said. "My keys are hangin' on the hook inside the back porch door. Ethan can show you the spot. Come on, Agent Roscowitz, let's get you settled."

"Agent Bankowski and I will be rotating 12-hour shifts. Two other agents will be close by as well," Agent Roscowitz explained.

"The stable has a couple of bunks in it they can use," Ethan said.

Just as they were stepping onto the front porch, a brilliant flash and a thunderous roar shook the place.

"What the fuck is that?" Emily asked as she stepped off the porch and looked to the west.

The brilliant flash came again, and this time, the thunder roar was so loud that it shook the earth. Everyone had a hard time keeping their balance.

"This is Agent Matthews," Matthews said into his watch. "Connect me with Seymour Johnson Air Force base immediately."

"This is the Command Center at Seymour Johnson Air Force Base. Who am I speaking with?" a voice said.

"This is Agent Matthews of the U. S. Marshals. Codeword Alpha Delta Zulu one niner four."

"Yes, sir," the voice replied. "I'll connect you with the Base Commander immediately."

"This is Commander Lawrence," the Commander said as he answered the call. "What can I assist you with, Agent Matthews?"

"We just experienced two brilliant flashes of some kind of energy and a noise so loud, it shook the earth like a small earthquake. Our location is Crab Apple Creek, North Carolina. What is your impression of this event? Are you in the airspace here?"

"No, we are not," Commander Lawrence answered as he gave orders to someone in his office. "I'm looking for the event right now. I see it. Holy shit! What the hell was that?"

"That's my question for you, sir," Matthews replied as they all kept watching the sky.

"Look!" Ethan said as he pointed to a strange object flying over the ridge. "Is that a UFO?"

"We don't have any aircraft in the vicinity at this time," Commander Lawrence said. "Pull up the sector screen for Crab Apple Creek. I see The Store. You're north of there a few miles, correct?"

"Yes, sir," Matthews replied. "We still see the UFO hovering over the ridge. Do you have it on your radar?"

"We do not," Commander Lawrence replied. "Scramble two F15 Strike Eagles to fly over the sector."

"Yes, sir," the officer in the Commander's office replied.

Matthews and the group at Emily's Meadow heard the order given, and within five minutes, they saw the two fighter jets fly overhead. They also saw the UFO move out of the way of the jets.

"That's crazy," Agent Bankowski said as he filmed the whole thing.

Emily and Ethan were catching the whole thing on their phones. The UFO kept moving away from the jets. It was as if the jet pilots didn't see them.

"This is just crazy," Ethan said. "We can see the UFO, but it looks like the pilots can't."

"Commander Lawrence, we can still see the UFO, but it looks like your pilots can't," Matthews said.

The Commander ordered access to the pilots' radios.

"This is Commander Lawrence," he said. "Do you see any strange objects in the sky?"

"We do not," Pilot #1 replied.

"We have U.S. Marshals that can see a UFO in your vicinity," the Commander said.

Just then, the UFO became visible to the pilots.

"Holy shit, sir, Sorry," Pilot #1 said. "We see the UFO. It's flying around us. It's cigar-shaped and about the size of half a football field. It's mostly gray but keeps changing color. We're recording this."

"Keep it in sight," the Commander replied.

"Yes, sir," both pilots replied.

"Well, I guess the military has just acknowledged the presence of UFOs," Ethan said.

"They have, but we won't be allowed to talk about this with anyone," Matthews said.

"As if no one else is watching this," Emily said. "Get real. The whole Creek is watching this. Keeping us quiet isn't gonna happen."

"She's right, sir," Agent Bankowski said.

The UFO decided to have some fun with the jet pilots. It stopped dead in space and hovered near the jets. The pilots were able to come along both sides of it and have a good look at the craft. They saw strange markings on the outside of the craft. It didn't have windows, so you couldn't see inside.

Then, in an instant, that brilliant flash of light and the roaring thunder occurred, and the UFO was gone. Vanished from sight. The energy from that flash rolled over the jets, and the pilots had difficulty controlling them. They finally got control and flew off back toward the coast, where the base was located.

"We've recalled the jets," Commander Lawrence replied. "The pilots reported that the UFO vanished, so we've got them coming back for a detailed debriefing."

"I understand, and thank you for your assistance with this thing," Matthews replied. "Let me know if you need anything from this end of things."

"I appreciate that, Agent Matthews," Commander Lawrence replied. "Make sure everyone writes down what happened in their own words."

"Will do, sir," Matthews replied. "Signing off, sir."

The meadow was absolutely silent for the longest time.

"What the hell was that all about?" Ethan asked as he walked around the meadow, trying to get a grip on things.

"You're askin' me?" Emily hollered back. "How the fuck do I know?"

"Any of you ever seen anything like this before?" Matthews asked his agents.

No, sir," they all replied.

"Strangest thing I've ever seen," Agent Roscowitz replied.

"I've heard about UFOs, but I've never seen one myself," Agent Bankowski added.

"Well, now what?" Agent Caspar asked.

"Write down every detail of what you saw," Matthews said. "First, we need to get you four set up here. Emily, please take Agent Roscowitz inside, and Ethan and I will take the others to the stables. Meet you all in the kitchen in ten minutes."

Ten minutes later, they were all in the kitchen.

"This is where you'll be headquartered until further notice," Matthews said. "Write everything down here at the kitchen table. Do not discuss the details. Just write down your impressions of the UFO thing. All the details."

"Yes, sir," the agents replied and set to writing down their versions of what had just happened.

"I'm goin back to the build," Ethan said as he kissed Emily. "Let me know if you need anything."

"I will," Emily replied. "I guess I'll keep the Keurig busy this morning." Emily set muffins and coffee mugs on the table. "Help yourselves."

"You guys are in for a real treat," Matthews said as he set a muffin next to his place on the table. "Emily here is a world-class baker."

"Thanks, Matthews," Emily said. "Flattery will get you supper every time."

This made everyone laugh as they made their coffee and settled down to write.

As soon as Ethan got back to the build, everyone asked him if he'd seen the flashes and the UFO.

"We sure did," Ethan replied. "I was at Emily's when it happened. Strangest thing for sure."

"We saw the jets fly in, and it looked like the UFO was playin' with them," Karl said. "The jets got right up next to the UFO for a minute, then the thing vanished."

"That's what Emily and I saw, too," Ethan replied. He had to be careful. He didn't mention the agents at Emily's place.

"Was Matthews with you?" Finn asked.

"He was, and he was just as surprised as we were," Ethan replied. "I've never seen a real UFO before. I've seen strange lights in the night sky. That could have been a UFO. But not really sure about those. This one was one hundred percent a UFO."

"Agreed," Karl said, as everyone agreed with him.

"Well, let's get back to work," the foreman said. "We've got lots to do."

Hal was outside when he saw and heard the flash.

"What the fuck?" Hal hollered out as he looked up.

Hal saw the UFO flying over The Creek. It looked like it had come from the ridge. What was it doing in The Creek? His phone beeped just then. It was Ted.

"Hey, Ted," Hal said as he continued to watch the sky.

"Hey, Hal," Ted replied. "You outside?"

"Sure am," Hal answered. "You see that flash and the UFO?"

"We sure did," Ted replied. "All of us at The Store did. The MacKinnon boys are here with Miss Sarah. Miss Cora is on her way over. We're watching it now. It seems to be movin' south."

"It does," Hal said. "It looks like it's comin' my way. Holy shit, that thing is huge!"

"It sure is," Michael replied. "Wonder why it's here? Got any ideas, Hal? Anybody?"

"I have no clue," Hal said.

"We've seen lights in the night sky all our lives," Don MacKinnon said. "But I've never seen a real UFO before."

"Same here," was the general reply from everyone at The Store.

"Hey, y'all," Kendra said as she joined the group. "That thing is amazin'."

Miss Cora arrived just then and got out of her truck.

"It's a big one this time," Miss Cora said.

"You've seen others?" Don asked.

"Of course," Miss Cora replied.

"Look there," Michael said as the two Air Force jets zoomed in. "I guess the Air Force knows about them, too."

"This won't be kept quiet for long," Don said. "I'll bet those news guys will be all over the Blue Ridge in short time."

"Let's hope not here," Sarah said. "The last time was a mess."

"We remember that," Ted said. "We had to order extra provisions for a week. Thank God y'all helped us, or we would have had to close The Store."

"It sure was crazy around here," Michael said.

"Hal, it looks like it's headed over your way," Miss Cora said. "You know somethin' we don't?"

"No, Ma'am," Hal replied as the ship came back toward The Store. "It looks like they're lookin' for somethin or someone."

"Sure does," Kendra said. "The jets are right up next to it."

A second flash of brilliant light and a thunderous roar happened just then, and the UFO was gone! The jets looked like they were being buffeted by a wave of air or something.

"What the hell?" Don said.

"It's gone! Where'd it go?" Ted asked.

"It's like a door opened, and it went through," Sarah said.

"Hey, y'all. It's Ethan," Michael said. "He and Emily saw it with Matthews. I told them we all saw it, too."

Jordan rang Miss Cora's phone.

"Hey, Miss Cora," Jordan said. "That UFO was huge!"

"Sure was," Miss Cora said. "What's ya think about it?" She had him on speakerphone.

"Not much," Jordan replied. "It looked like it was over The Store, Emily's and Hal's place."

"Yup," Miss Cora said. "Same here."

"Sami's with me," Jordan said. "We're gonna head over to The Store. See ya soon."

They ended the call, and Miss Cora went inside. The others followed.

"Ted, how about a cup of tea and some of that strawberry cake?"

"Yes, Ma'am," Ted said.

Folks settled around the table with their drinks and such and began to talk about the UFO. Jordan and Sami walked in and joined them. Kendra and Sami nodded slightly to each other. They knew that the UFO was real and probably looking for something or someone that was connected to The Magic in The Creek. They also knew how it had arrived over the earth.

Emily texted Kendra with the same thoughts. They would keep the information to themselves.

"I need to get back to my research," Jordan said. "I think I'll come back for lunch."

"Great idea," Ted said. "We'll be lookin for ya."

Talk returned to the UFO for a bit, and then most folks went back to their work. They promised to come back for lunch around one.

Matthews got on the phone with the Director when the UFO vanished.

"Lots of people saw this," Matthews said. "How is the agency gonna handle it?"

"Emily is to stay at the farm until further notice." The Director replied. "Multiple agencies are conferencing about this event. Craziest thing I've ever seen."

"You saw it, too?" Matthews asked.

"Boone isn't that far from The Creek, and that thing was huge," the Director replied. "We're closing down the Pine Ridge Road from Pine Ridge to The Creek. Keeping it open to residents only. We need to control things in case some of the suspects we're tracking try to get to The Creek."

"Good idea," Matthews said. "I'll inform folks that we're keeping the media and spectators away so this place doesn't become a circus again."

"Good thinking," the Director said. "The military will want statements from everyone involved. They're sending a couple of people your way. I'll get you their credentials soon. Keep me informed of everything."

"Yes, sir," Matthes said. "Did you get any pictures of the thing?

"I did," the Director replied. "You?"

"We all got tons of photos and videos," Matthews replied. "The team will send them along when ready."

"Thanks. Carry on," the Director said as he signed off.

Matthews got responses from Emily's team about the roadblocks a few minutes later.

Emily texted Ethan about the roadblocks just as he sent her the same message. They sent LOL emojis to each other.

Matthews texted the roadblock information to Ted and Michael so they could send out a Creek-wide notice.

The individuals that were involved in the drug and human trafficking conglomerate were very aware of the UFO. They had been waiting for it.

Penny was waking up when she felt the energy of the UFO. She immediately rushed from her cave and went into the air. There it was. The time was here.

She made herself invisible as she flew close to it. It was the ETs she had been expecting. She flew away from it just as the jets approached. Penny got to The Crystal Caves a few seconds before the UFO vanished in a brilliant flash of light and a thunderous sound.

Gina and Terry were outside working on one of their gardens. They were preparing it for the winter when they felt the energy of the UFO. They looked up, and there it was. Huge and looking for something or someone. The time had come.

"Terry, time to get to The Crystal Caves," Gina said as she dropped her gardening gloves on the ground.

"Let's go," Terry agreed.

They closed the farmhouse doors and got in their SUV to drive as close to the NorthRidge Footbridge as they could. They parked about a half mile east of it.

They crossed the bridge and hurried on into the woods until they came to the rock arch over the meadow. As soon as they stepped into the meadow, the door appeared in the rock wall. They ran to the door and rushed into the large room. Penny was waiting for them.

"It's time," Penny said.

"Does he know yet?" Gina asked as she stretched her arms.

"No. We don't want him to know anything for a while," Penny replied. "We need to keep him safe for quite some time yet."

"Have the other two figured this out yet?" Terry asked as he stretched his body as tall as he could.

"He has," Q replied as he entered the room. "She is about to any minute. We're keeping a close eye on her."

"Is it time for us yet? Terry asked.

"Just a few more hours, Terry," Penny said. "We know this is difficult for you two. We appreciate your patience."

"Of course, Miss Penny," Gina said as she settled down. "Terry, cool it."

"I know," Terry said as he stopped stretching.

"There is one other thing," Penny said.

"The UFO? Is it them?" Terry asked.

"It is," Q replied. "They haven't figured out the other Magical Entity yet."

"This is gonna get real crazy real fast," Gina said.

"It is," Penny replied. "Watch for the signal. Then do your thing."

"Yes, Ma'am," Terry replied.

"Time to get back to my cave and Q to remain here for a bit," Penny said. "We'll be watching the skies."

"I'm sure The Creek is buzzing about this UFO right now," Gina said.

"They are," Penny replied as she walked toward the back of the cave. "Later."

"Let's go," Terry said as Q and Penny went into the far reaches of The Crystal Caves.

Terry and Gina returned home in short time while the folks at The Store were talking with Miss Cora.

After the arrest of two of their kind, the three people left had relocated their headquarters to an abandoned warehouse along the railroad tracks just south of Boone. They were discussing the latest developments in their plans.

"Well," Chuck said, "It seems we've been found out as human scum. The two in custody will morph out tonight. Their cells will be found empty in the morning without a trace of how they got out. Our ship will come back and get them after midnight. We still have to find the person who holds all the knowledge of The Ancient Magic before they figure out who they are. We need to destroy them so they can't identify us. You know, once that happens, we will cease to exist."

"We know," Sally said. "We just can't get a read on the people in The Creek. We know it's someone there. That's where all The Ancient Magic is protected. We've been able to trace the movements of that particular energy since it left Camelot. We just haven't been able to pinpoint who it is here."

"I know," Chuck replied. "This is a particularly difficult mission. The Creek is protected by an energy shield that was set up a short time ago by those women. I know Emily and Katelyn are human, but I'm not so sure about Miss Cora. And that Sami and Kendra are hard to figure out as well. I've tried to probe their energy, but it's wrapped up really tight in a protective layer of energy. I've never seen anything like it."

"It makes me wonder if they're different," Benny said.

"Different?" Sally asked.

"Like us, from another planet, universe," Benny explained. "Ya' know, we can't get an energy read on creatures that are different than us or are not human. That's the only thing I can think of."

"That's got to be it, Chuck said. "This makes our mission a whole lot more difficult."

"Sure does," Benny said. "If the person or energy we're looking for is a creature from another planet, we won't be able to identify him."

"One more thing," Sally added. "If that person, we'll call it that for now, is protected by The Ancient Magic, we won't be able to find him or her either."

"Oh, right," Chuck said. "It could be a female human, too."

"Let's wait and see what the others have to say when they return tonight," Benny suggested.

"Alright," Chuck said. "Let's see if we can locate that human that killed our fellow creature. He was known as Yuri when he was here as a human. The human that killed him sent his energy to the deepest, darkest places in the deep universes. It will never be free again. We should be able to locate that human and kill it to get revenge."

Benny and Sally howled their agreement. They sounded like wolves in the wild about to attack their prey. A passing homeless person heard this and turned and ran back toward the center of Boone. He was scared. He was well-known to the Boone police, and a patrol car saw him running. They pulled up next to him.

"Hey, there," Officer Spindler said. "What's got you running so fast."

The man looked at the officer and stopped,

"Hey, Officer Spindler," he said. "I was on the tracks down by those abandoned warehouses south of town, and I heard what sounded like a pack of wolves ready to pounce on their prey. Ya know, I was a game warden in my youth up at Yellowstone. I know what a pack of hungry wolves sounds like. We don't have wolves around here. So, I figured someone was usin' the warehouse for a hideout or somethin. Didn't want to stay to find out."

"Good thinkin," Officer Spindler said. "We'll report on it and keep an eye out."

"Good," the man said. "See ya later."

The homeless man walked toward the center of town while Officer Spindler called in the report.

Katelyn was staring off into space in her office. She heard the boom and ran outside to see if someone had crashed into a tree or something. Ian was right next to her.

"What the fuck was that?" Katelyn said as they walked all around the property.

"Doesn't look like anything fell," Ian said. "It sounded like it was higher up than the rooftops."

"It did at that," Katelyn said as she looked over the sky. "What the hell is that?"

Ian looked where Katelyn was pointing, and they watched a strange-looking flying thing a ways north of them.

"It isn't a plane or jet," Ian said.

"It's a UFO for sure," Katelyn said.

"What's it doin in The Creek?" Ian asked as they watched it fly closer than go back north.

"Why are you askin' me?" Katelyn said.

"You know a lot about The Magic, so I figured you might know about UFOs," Ian said.

"I don't know anything about UFOs more than you do," Katelyn replied.

Two military fighter jets zoomed by, heading for the UFO.

"Looks like the Air Force knows they're here, too," Katelyn said as they continued to watch the UFO.

"The military isn't gonna be able to deny this," Ian said.

"No way," Katelyn replied.

Just then, a brilliant flash of pure white light went through the sky, along with a thunderous noise. The UFO disappeared. The jets were left alone.

"Those jets look like they're tryin' to surf," Katelyn said, laughing.

"They do," Ian said, laughing with Katelyn.

The jets flew back over the shop as they headed to the base.

"Let's get back to work," Ian said as he and Katelyn walked back into the shop.

Katelyn texted Finn, and he replied that they had all seen the UFO and the jets. Crazy shit goin on.

Katelyn was deep in thought when she saw that vision of the older man and younger woman in the cottage house. The magnificent hawk was there, and a porcupine was snoozing by the hearth. This made Katelyn smile.

"That's Goldie for ya," Katelyn said out loud. "Whoa! Wait a minute. How do I know anything about that place?"

Ian had stepped out to get something from the barn, so Katelyn was alone.

Katelyn saw the cottage home again; this time, a young man walked through the door with a sword. The young man was about thirteen years old. She knew his name. Quintan. He was called Quintan.

A moment later, Katelyn had an awakening moment.

"It's not a dream or a vision," Katelyn yelled, jumping around her office. "I was there. It's a real place, and I'm the young woman in the cottage home. What the hell am I doin there? "I need some help here."

A beautiful, soft green light appeared in front of her.

"Thanks for replyin' so quickly," Katelyn said, nodding at the light. "What the fuck is goin on? Why was I in that place? I don't remember ever bein' there before? Oh no, not another dimensional shift? Really? What the fuck?! This is just too much. The man, who is the man?"

The green light morphed into a woman floating above the floor.

"You will figure this out soon," the green woman said.

"Don't even think you can do this to me," Katelyn yelled. "I think I'm beginnin' to know how Jordan 's been feelin' with all the Magic stuff."

The woman just smiled at Katelyn.

"Oh my fuckin god," Katelyn said as she figured out who the man was. "It's Jordan. That man is Jordan. What the fuck are we doin' in a cottage home in that place? It looks like it's from old England or somethin."

"Keep remembering," the woman said. "You'll figure it out soon."

"The dragon," Katelyn said. "Penny the dragon was there, too. Oh, this is getting really crazy."

"A lot is going on, Katelyn," the woman said. "You know what to do now. So do it."

The woman morphed back into that beautiful green light and slowly drifted away.

"Holy shit!" Katelyn said as she plopped down in her office chair.

She grabbed her phone and called Jordan.

"Jordan, I need to see you right this minute," Katelyn said. "Come to the shop."

"I know why," Jordan replied. "I'll be right there. You're the only one there, right?"

"Yes. Ian was lookin for somethin in the barn and couldn't find it. Ethan had used whatever it was, so Ian went into Pine Ridge to get more or whatever. I'm here for quite a while on my own."

Jordan arrived a few minutes later. He was just down the road, after all.

"What the fuck were we doin in that cottage home?" Katelyn said as Jordan walked into the shop.

"I don't know yet," Jordan replied, sitting across from Katelyn at her drawing table. "I just remembered we were there yesterday or somethin like that."

"Penny was there," Katelyn said.

"You remember that?" Jordan said.

"I do," Katelyn replied. "A the most magnificent hawk I've ever seen. Beautiful colors and huge. And, there was a porcupine named Goldie that slept next to the hearth."

"I didn't see the porcupine. I did see the hawk, though," Jordan said, looking away.

"George," Katelyn said. "That was George."

"He was," Jordan replied. "How is this all possible? How did we get there, and where is it?"

"I think I know how we got there, but I don't know where there is," Katelyn replied.

"Well, spill!" Jordan said.

"A couple of times before The Battle on The Rise, I was transported to parallel dimensions to fight The Dark," Katelyn said. "I couldn't figure out what the hell was goin on the first time it happened. Everythin looked exactly the same as always in The Creek. Except, there were a few things out of place. It took a bit for me to figure this out. It seemed there was a rift in the space-time dimension as I crossed the road between my place and The Store. It was totally bizarre. I had a job to do in that dimension that would affect our dimension."

"That's bat-shit crazy," Jordan said.

"Tell me about it," Katelyn said. "I lived it, and I still can't get my head wrapped around it. The second time it happened was on the footbridge over the creek by the Redstone's meadow, where we had that great picnic day. You were recovering from that horrible truck crash caused by The Dark Forces."

"I remember that day," Jordan said. "It was great, and the way the guys fixed up that recliner for me was superb."

"That was pure perfection for sure," Katelyn said. "Well, I figured out I'd been through a dimensional rift pretty quickly the second time. Again, I had to do some stuff to make sure we'd be good here. Then there was The Battle on The Rise. Way too much for me to handle and I know about The Magic. You didn't. Then, there's that dragon tail tattoo on our shoulders and Sami's, too. What the hell is that all about? I still haven't figured that all out. I suspect it has somethin to do with Miss Penny."

"That's what I think, too," Jordan said. "Now this stuff. What the hell is goin on?"

"I really don't have a clue," Katelyn said. "I suspect it has somethin to do with that UFO. Somethin tells me there's a whole lot more to that story, too."

"I agree," Jordan said. "But, what do we have to do with it? I think that cottage home and the UFO are related," Jordan said. "No idea how. My imagination is not that advanced."

"Cute, Jordan, or should I say Jandor?" Katelyn said.

"I was known as Jandor for a while in that place," Jordan said. "I just know it now."

"I don't know how I came up with that name," Katelyn said. "Maybe our memories are wakin' up to that place now that the UFO has appeared."

"Oh, good thinkin," Jordan said. "One thing, though, Katelyn. I remember bein' called Merlin back in the cottage home."

"You mean like Merlin, the wizard from King Arthur lore?" Katelyn asked.

"Exactly from then," Jordan said. "But our story was different from the known stories of Camelot."

"Camelot?" Katelyn asked, looking off into space again. "We were in Camelot, too. I remember that. But we were in that cottage home for a while before Camelot. That young man, Quintan, was there, too."

"Oh God! Quintan," Jordan said. "I remember him, too. All of a sudden, it's becoming very clear."

"He was a young teenager then, about thirteen or so, and you were teaching him how to fight with a sword. You made that sword for him. You forged it from The Ancient Magic."

"I can see it clear as day now," Jordan said. "It's all comin' back to me."

"Me, too," Katelyn said. "I think the place was called Middle Earth."

"Absolutely," Jordan said. "We met at a farm stand near a village. It was as if we'd known each other a long time. Gee, I wonder how that works?"

"Holy shit!" Katelyn said. "That's it. We've been together in another dimension. No wonder we get along as if we'd known each other forever. I remember the first time we saw Penny."

They spent a long while remembering everything about their time in Middle Earth.

"Oh my god, Jordan," Katelyn said. "Camelot. That means King Arthur."

"I was known as Merlin after we left the cottage home. We were in the service of King Arthur. Holy shit."

"Yeah," Katelyn said. "That Quintan boy was there, too. Only he was a man by then. Not very old, but a man none-the-less."

"Katelyn!" Jordan said, standing up. "He became King Arthur when the old king died."

"Oh my god!" Katelyn replied. "Does that mean we were in the service of King Arthur? That would mean we were using The Magic to help him. You, as

Merlin, must have been a wizard. I kept seeing myself with plants and things. I guess I was an herbalist or something."

"I can see it now," Jordan said. "You were like a medicine woman. You made remedies and portions to help the sick and injured. That's why we kept seeing you with the clay pots and plants in our visions."

"It all makes sense to me," Katelyn said. "But, the UFO thing. I don't see how that's related to Camelot."

"Maybe we need to take a break from all these memories and get back to our work. It's been about two hours."

"Oh, crap!" Katelyn said as she looked at her phone. "Ian sent a text a few minutes ago."

Katelyn texted Ian, and he told her to meet him at The Store.

"Ian's on his way to The Store for some lunch," Katelyn said. "Let's go."

Most of the folks that had been at The Store were back for lunch. Conversation turned to the UFO.

"Miss Cora," Hal said. "Any more thoughts about that UFO?"

"I've been doin' some thinkin' on it," Miss Cora said. "I think it's been here before about four or five months back. I remember seein' a UFO of that shape in the night sky around the start of June. It seemed to hover over Boone more than here. Didn't stay long, only a few minutes. Then it left with the same light and sound we heard this mornin'."

Matthews walked in while Miss Cora was talking.

"Any idea why it's here?" Sarah asked.

"Nope," Miss Cora replied. "Matthews, you folks have any clue as to what it's doin' over The Creek?"

"No, Ma'am," Matthews said. "My Director is gatherin' info and pictures from all around tryin' to get a grip on the thing."

"It seemed to be lookin' for somethin or someone," Jordan said. "It stayed over Hal and Miss Cora's places for a bit longer than anywhere else."

"Yes, it did," Hal said. "Maybe they want some of my frames for their pictures of the places they've been around in the universe."

This brought a lot of laughter and teasing.

"If y'all are ready to order, let's do it," Ted said.

Orders were placed, and folks settled at the table and around The Store.

Katelyn was talking with Kendra about the UFO.

"Do you know anythin'?" Katelyn whispered.

"Tell me what you know," Kendra said.

"Jordan and I were in Camelot in another dimension," Katelyn whispered back.

"So, You've remembered," Kendra said, smilin' at Hal. "How's the pulled chicken sandwich, Hal?"

"Excellent as always," Hal said as he took another bite. "Mmm, Mmm."

Folks laughed at Hal, and he smiled back.

"How much do you remember?" Kendra asked.

"An awful lot," Katelyn said. "Nothin' with a UFO, though. So, I wonder if there's a connection. Hard to tell."

"That's for sure," Kendra said, looking at Sami.

"Oh my god!" Katelyn said. "Sami would know, too. Out with it, Kendra."

"Not here, and you have to figure this out for yourselves," Kendra said as a few folks walked over to them.

Katelyn made a face at Kendra and walked back into the dining room.

"Miss Cora," Katelyn said. "I have seen UFOs before, both here and in Montgomery. Sami and I saw a fleet of five of them about a month before I came home. I know they are from other planets and galaxies. For me, it just makes sense that we're not the only intelligent beings in all the universes. With that being said, I am wonderin why the huge UFO was hoverin' over The Creek. It looked like it was lookin for somethin or someone over your way. It was over your place, Hal's place, and near Lanie and Mo's place. Why? I'd like to know why?"

"That's what we're all wonderin' about, Katelyn," Hal said.

"Lanie texted me when it was over their place," Ted said. "She said she saw the same one about a week ago fly over the area and head toward Boone."

"We've all been wonderin' just that same thing," Sarah added. "Must be somethin' around the Blue Ridge they want. Sure hope it's not me."

"There's one more thing," Bob added. "I'm sure it's got the ability to cloak itself. So that brings up the thought that it may have been here a lot more than we know. It may be here right now, cloaked."

"Oh my god," Ned said. "He's right!"

"And," Michael added, "I would take this thought one step further. They must be a heck of a lot more intelligent than us humans. They can fly through space, cloak their ships, and who knows what else. I'll bet our military is wicked worried about them 'cause our technology is way behind theirs."

"Y'all saw how they played with our jets, makin' them rock and roll when they left," Jordan said.

"That was kind of funny," Sami said. "Makes me think they were just havin' fun with us."

"It did look that way," Miss Cora said. "I agree with Katelyn and Bob. They are much more advanced than us. So, here's my thoughts. It doesn't matter what we do, they're way beyond us. I guess we just watch and see."

"Miss Cora," Hal said. "That may be so. Remember, we do have The Magic here. I'm thinkin' The Magic may be able to protect us."

"That's true, Hal," Miss Cora said. "I know it will do whatever it can to keep The Creek safe. Always has."

"The Magic is so much more than we think it is," Jordan said. "It always surprises us with its amazin' protection."

"That's the truth," Ted said as he brought more orders.

"Ted, excellent as always," Miss Cora said. "If those ETs do come our way, I think we should feed them Ted's creations. Might calm them down a bit."

This brought laughter and comments all through lunch. Folks began coming up with new food names that were centered around the ETs. Someone even suggested a pie in the shape of the UFO that had just been seen. Lots of suggestions for the fillings were quite comical.

"Well, y'all," Miss Cora said as she stood up. "Time for me to get along. Keep an eye on the sky and share what ya see."

"Love ya, Miss Cora," Ted called out as he went into the kitchen.

"Love ya' right back," Miss Cora said as she put some money in the community share jar.

The others left soon after. Katelyn, Jordan, Sami, Kendra, and Ian stood on the porch for a minute, looking up into the beautiful clear blue sky.

"This gives us all a lot more to think about," Ian said. "Take care, everyone. Time to get back to the drawing board."

"Funny, Ian," Sami said.

"Always a wise guy in the crowd," Kendra added.

Katelyn and Ian returned to the shop. Sami and Jordan went over to his farm to work on a new idea for the URR project. Kendra walked across the road and caught a glimpse of a silver flash in the sky.

"I know you're here, and I know why," Kendra whispered skyward. "You can't have them."

The afternoon moved along, and it was late evening as The Creek began to settle for the night. It was nigh on to midnight when Sami walked over to Kendra's house. She was waiting for Sami in the kitchen.

"They're here," Sami said.

"They are," Kendra said. "And I know why."

"Me, too," Sami said. "They want to kill King Arthur's descendant. He can identify them. Once that happens, The Divine will take them and destroy their very essence."

"It's been comin' for a long, long time," Kendra said. "Katelyn and Jordan remember their time in Middle Earth and Camelot now. They know Penny and

George were there. They're remembering everything quickly. And there's Emily to worry about."

"Yes, there is," Sami replied. "The agencies think the people they arrested are a part of Yuri's mob. They are for sure. ETs. We have our hands full this time."

"We knew it was comin'," Kendra said. "That's one of the many reasons you and I are here. Miss Cora knows about us, and she's thinkin' there's somethin' goin' on with the ETs, too."

"The protection grid over The Creek will keep the ETs away for a bit," Kendra said. "Thing is, they have technology that will allow them to relocate inside the grid. You ready for this?"

"I am," Sami said.

A flash of silver light lit up the night sky.

"Another ship is here," Kendra said as she and Sami stood on the porch following the UFO as it settled over the area north of The Creek. "It looks like they've found the energy signature of King Arthur's descendant."

"I think they're close but haven't identified the exact person yet," Kendra said.

"I agree," Sami said. "Let's keep an eye on that person at all times."

"I've already asked one of my kind to stay close," Kendra said. "He's over there now, invisible."

"Good," Sami said. "Later."

Sami went back home. They didn't sleep much, and when dawn arrived, they knew the attack was at hand.

CHAPTER 25

Katelyn and Jordan were jolted awake at the same time, just as the sun rose above the trees.

"Jordan," Katelyn said as she phoned Jordan while she dressed. "Those ETs are after King Arthur's descendant. He's here in The Creek."

"I know," Jordan replied. "I was just callin' you."

"What do we do now?" Katelyn asked.

"We need to get to The Crystal Caves in a hurry," Jordan said. "See you at the NorthRidge Footbridge."

"See, ya'," Katelyn said as she made a hasty breakfast sandwich, grabbed her backpack, stuffed water bottles in it, and hurried out the door.

Kendra and Sami saw her leave. They knew where she was headed.

Gina and Terri were on their way to The Crystal Caves, too. It was time for them to protect the special one.

Gina and Terri arrived at The Crystal Caves first. Penny and Q were waiting for them.

"It's time," Penny said.

"We know," Gina said as she looked over at Terry. "Let's go outside."

As soon as Gina and Terri walked outside, The Magic took hold.

Jordan and Katelyn had just stepped onto the NorthRidge Foot bridge when they saw the air northwest of them change.

"Something's happin' in that meadow," Katelyn said. "Let's go."

A short time later, Katelyn and Jordan walked into the meadow and saw an amazing sight. There were five dragons in all their glory waiting for them.

"You're Roman and Clarice," Katelyn said. "I remember you from Camelot."

"We are," Clarice replied. "Nice to see you again."

"And you're Beau," Jordan said. "Wow! All of you here in The Creek."

"We are happy to see the both of you, Merlin and Feyanna," Clarice said.

"You sound familiar," Katelyn said. "I'm known as Katelyn here."

"You'll always be our Feyanna and Merlin," Roman said.

"Of course we sound familiar," Clarice said. "We were together for a long
time in Middle Earth and Camelot."

"I know that," Katelyn said as she kept looking at the dragons. "I mean,
you sound familiar here, in The Creek. As if we were just talkin' with each other ."

Just then, there was another brilliant flash of light and that thunderous
noise again. They all looked up at the sky and saw the strangest thing happening. It
was as if a hole had opened in the sky, and a UFO came through. Then, four more
UFOs followed, and the hole closed.

"What the fuck was that?" Jordan hollered.

"It's called a portal or stargate," Penny replied.

"What?" Jordan said in shock.

"Ditto," Katelyn said as they watched the UFOs hover near them. "What
the hell do they want?"

"They want King Arthur's descendant," Jordan said, suddenly knowing
what was about to happen.

"How do you know that?" Katelyn asked.

"I just do, all of a sudden," Jordan said as he turned and looked at her. "Go
back to Camelot and try to remember everything that happened just before and after
Quintan took the throne."

Katelyn looked off into space and seemed to be far away, remembering
her time in Camelot. It took a bit, but then she remembered. She remembered it all.

"Holy fuck!" Katelyn said.

"She remembers," the dragons said together.

"I do remember," Katelyn said. "We lived in a cottage home in a small
village about an hour's ride from the castle. Penny, you, and Q rescued a small boy,
Quintan, from a horrendous attack on his family's home. They were all slaughtered.
He managed to hide in a mound of hay. You and Q brought him to the village where
he grew up with Hamlen's family. Quintan learned about The Magic and swordplay
from Merlin. I taught him about herbs and remedies. He went to the castle and became a paige. He quickly moved through the ranks, and when the old king died, the
head knight and the chancellor chose him to be the new king. He was crowned soon
after and chose the name of Arthur. He was King Arthur: Arthur Pendragon of Camelot. Holy fuck!"

"Good recall," Q said.

"Shut the fuck up, Q," Katelyn said, laughing at them.

"She still has the same sense of humor, too," Beau added.

"So you're the wise-ass dragon?" Katelyn asked, looking at Beau.

"Sure am," Beau replied, bowing with a grin on his face.

"What else do you remember, Jordan?" Penny asked.

"I remember somethin about shiny silver disks in the sky before Quintan became Arthur," Jordan answered. "They were seen a couple of times. The second time, they abducted people from all over the place, and it wasn't until after Quintan was crowned as Arthur that they came back with those people. They were infected somehow with an oily black paste that made them evil. Charles and Merlin had a hard time figuring out how to get that black, oily stuff out of the affected people. Some they saved, some died, and others escaped into hiding. The ones infected went around trying to infect others. The palace was a mess. King Arthur became infected when one of the possessed tried to storm his quarters and kill him. He killed the possessed man, but not before he was wounded and infected by that man. Charles and I poured the potion on the dead possessed man, and he turned into a black glob of goo before turning to ashes and being taken into the air. King Arthur died a short time later."

"Oh my god!" Katelyn said. "King Arthur's wife, Angelique, gave birth to a boy during the invasion of the ETS. He was Thomas Arthur Pendragon. The head cook, Rosie, and Charles, the wizard, took the child and ran through the tunnels. They hid in our old cottage home near Hamlen's village and raised the boy as their own. You and I, and Angelique, had to run for our lives as soon as King Arthur died because the people thought we had killed him. We ran through the same tunnel, coming out of the earth near Lake Avalon. The Lady of The Lake took Angelique with her over the lake into the mists. She called out to us, telling us to step onto the NorthRidge Footbridge. As soon as we did, we were returned to The Creek in this dimension. Holy fuck!"

"Holy fuck! I remember it all now," Jordan said. "Holy fuck!"

The dragons gave them some time to take in all of their memories.

Katelyn looked at Jordan and said, "Hey, Merlin, how ya doin'?"

"Oh, just ducky, Feyanna," Jordan replied sarcastically. "You?"

"Same," Katelyn replied. "Just when I think nothin' as humongous as The Battle on The Rise could happen ever again, this takes hold of us. What the fuck?"

"I'm not even close to bein' able to handle The Rise Battle," Jordan said as he sat down on the meadow. "Now this. What the fuck am I supposed to do with all this? I thought I was beyond overwhelmed before, but this puts a whole new perspective on that."

"Please wrap them in comforting energy," Q asked.

A soft purple energy appeared and wrapped itself around Katelyn and Jordan for a while. They sat there quietly for the whole time. The comforting energy lifted, and Jordan stood up.

"That was much appreciated," Katelyn said. "Thanks to The Divine."

"Thanks for the comforting energy," Jordan said. "It does help, for sure. Where did Beau, Clarice, and Roman come from besides The Special Magic?"

"He's got us there," Roman said. "Should we show them?"

"Clarice and Roman protected you and me, Katelyn, in Camelot," Jordan said quietly. "Beau was there while Penny and Q were healing from a vicious attack by rogue dragons."

"Yes, Jordan, that's all true," Penny said.

"So why are all of you here now?" Katelyn asked.

"Oh, no, say it ain't so," Jordan said.

"Can't do that," Roman said.

"There's about to be another battle," Jordan said as he and Katleyn looked at the dragons.

"Truth," Beau said.

"Dare we ask why?' Jordan said.

"I know why," Katelyn said. "King Arthur's descendant lives here in The Creek. He knows about The Special Magic. He can identify the ETs that killed his ancestor. It's the ETs that are here now."

"Now? Right now? There are ETs here now?" Jordan said.

"Yes, Jordan," Penny replied. "They're in those UFOs we just saw."

"So, there are five UFOs over The Creek right now?" Jordan said.

"Nope," Q answered. "There are ten. They're desperate to find the ancestor."

"You know who he is, don't you?" Jordan asked.

"We do," Penny replied. "You and Katelyn have to figure this out for yourselves."

"Jordan," Katelyn said, holding her hand up toward Jordan. "Don't bother askin'. We'll figure it out. First, it's someone north of The Store 'cause that's where we keep seein' the UFOs. We know it's not Miss Cora."

"True," Jordan said. "I do know that to be true for some reason."

"That leaves Emily, the MacKinnon's, Lanie and Mo, and Hal and the dig site," Jordan said.

"It's not the dig site," Katelyn said. "I don't get much with Laini and Mo's either. The MacKinnon's are out as well."

"That leaves Hal and Emily," Jordan said. "And a few others."

"I'm not getting anythin' on Sarah and the others. I keep seein' Gina and Terry's build, though. Guess it's 'cause it's so close to The Crystal Caves," Katelyn said as she looked at the dragons. Clarice and Roman were looking at each other. "What's up you two?"

"Us? Nothing," Clarice said, looking into Katelyn's eyes.

"I know that dragon look," Katelyn said, laughing. "I learned it from Miss Penny. You both know somethin' about this place and the build. They're connected."

Penny nodded at Roman and Clarice.

"They are," Roman said. "Always have been."

"More Magic," Jordan said, shaking his head. "They're not gonna tell us, Feyanna."

"Looks that way, Merlin," Katelyn replied, laughing with Jordan.

"Suffice it to say The Creek now has five dragons watching over it," Q said.

"That's a lot of dragons," Katelyn said. "Those UFOs are still hovering over there."

"They are," Penny said. "It looks like they may have found their target. Time to fly."

In an instant, Q and Penny took to the air.

"What about the rest of you?" Jordan asked.

"You'll see soon enough," Beau replied.

They watched as Q and Penny became invisible. The UFOs saw them and started to move into a pattern of attack.

Meanwhile, Matthews had his hands full. The five suspects they had been watching in the warehouse south of Boone near the train tracks had vanished. The SWAT team raided the place and didn't find a thing. No one was there, and not one piece of evidence has been left to show that anyone had been there. The place was empty. As the SWAT team left, Matthews was notified that the two prisoners had vanished from their cells. Nothing showed on the cameras. One minute, the two prisoners were in their separate cells, and a second later, they were gone. The place went into lockdown, but the prisoners were not found.

An alarm was sent to the team at Emily's place, and they told her she was not to go outside until further notice.

The ETs that had been taken from the prison were in one of the UFOs, along with the five from the warehouse.

"They know about us yet?" the lead ET asked.

"No," the commander of the UFO replied. "The shapeshifters that live in The Creek know about us, and they know why we're here. Those two that traveled through the dimensional rift know why we're here as well. We're pretty sure we know who our target is. We still haven't been able to get the energy signal from him. The others in The Creek are not the target. Their energy signals are all wrong.

We are picking up on a signal that was sent a year or so ago. It has to do with the human who killed the ET, called Yuri. It's a female human, and she's close to where our main target lives."

"Excellent news," the lead ET said. "I was here when Yuri was killed and his essence destroyed. It was horrendous. The human that destroyed him had some help from the shapeshifters. If we can destroy them all, our kind will finally rule all the universes in all the dimensions of existence."

"Exactly," the commander said. "That's exactly what I was thinking. We know where that female human lives. She's called Emily and is north of The Store. We'll send a unit over there to destroy her when we attack our main target. All at the same time."

A roar of approval went through the UFOs.

"How soon before we know who that main target is?" one of the ETs asked.

"Any minute now," the lead ET said. "We only have a couple more humans to get an energy read on, so we'll know soon."

Katelyn looked at the dragons and Jordan as she suddenly realized who the ETs were.

"The ETs that are in the UFOs now are the same ones that showed up in Camelot and abducted the people there," Katelyn said.

Jordan looked at Beau.

"They are," Beau said.

"They killed King Arthur because he held the knowledge of The Special Magic within himself," Katelyn explained. "That's why they want his kin. That descendant holds that same Special Magic knowledge in himself, and he can identify these ETs as the ones who killed King Arthur. He's one of us, and he doesn't even know that he's related to King Arthur."

"Not yet," Beau said. "We're tryin' not to reveal that information yet. We just want to protect him."

"How can we help if we don't know who he is?" Jordan asked.

"You need to create that potion that you and Charles made so we can destroy the ETs," Beau said.

"Really? And where do we get the ingredients for that potion?" Jordan asked.

"In The Crystal Caves," Katelyn said as she walked over to the entrance.

"I don't even know what that potion is, or any potions for that matter," Jordan said as he followed Katelyn inside.

The other dragons walked in as The Crystal Caves enlarged to accommodate them.

"I love it when The Magic makes that happen," Jordan said.

"We all do," Clarice replied, settling on the floor.

The bench and pots of ingredients appeared in front of Jordan and Katelyn. They were exactly the same as the ones in their visions and in their cottage homes. Their recipe books were on the bench, too.

"This is surreal," Jordan said. "I'm gonna flip out if I suddenly grow a long beard and have robes on."

"That would be funny," Roman said. "Not gonna happen. You're safe."

"Good!" Jordan said. "Now, what do we do?"

"Get cookin'," Katelyn said as she opened one of the books and found the recipe. "Right here, Jordan. It says This is the recipe to use to destroy the ETs in The Creek. Get busy."

"Wise ass," Jordan said as he looked at the recipe and found himself gathering ingredients, making a fire, and setting a pot over it on the bench. "I guess I do remember how to do this."

A short time later, they had a large cauldron filled with the potion that would destroy the ETs.

"How do we get close enough to them to pour this on them?" Katelyn asked.

"The Special Magic has a few aces up its sleeve, so to speak," Roman said. "Make a large vat of the potion for now. More info later."

"I love the sound of that," Jordan said.

"You'll have to make three more big cauldrons of the potion in a hurry," Beau added. "It feels like the ETs are about to identify their target."

"They've figured out who Emily is," Roman said. "They're going to try to destroy her, too."

"Why Emily?" Jordan asked. "I thought they were after Arthur's descendant."

"They are after Arthur's descendant and Emily. Before you settled in The Creek, Emily came here to live to escape a violent person," Roman explained. "His boss was a horrendous ET named Yuri. He was in charge of all Earth activity. He was greedy and dangerous. He ran a human trafficking trade and drug smuggling business all around the globe. Emily fell for one of his henchmen, and they got married. The U S Marshals found Emily and told her about her husband and everything. They helped her escape to The Creek to start a new life. This Yuri guy eventually found her, and there was a battle in The Sacred Rock Meadow. Emily annihilated the Yuri ET, blowing him into a zillion pieces. His ET friends were beyond angry and have been trying to find Emily ever since. And now they have. She is a powerful energy in The Ancient Magic. They mean to kill her and take her energy for their own."

"Oh, shit!" Jordan said. "This is a real mess. Feyanna, let's get that potion ready. Looks like we're gonna need a whole lake full."

Jordan and Katelyn kept busy making batches of the potion.

Penny and Q buzzed the UFOs, trying to distract them from identifying their primary target. The dragons were invisible, and the UFOs could not get a signal on them.

Finn was trying to stay focused on the geothermal work at the build. He kept feeling that something big was about to happen. He walked a bit north of the build, telling the crew he was going to check on the source of one of the creeks and they could leave when they finished connecting the lines to the rough plumbing intake pipes.

As soon as Finn was out of sight of the build, Jay showed up.

"Hey, bro," Jay said, punching Finn in the arm.

"Right back at cha'," Finn said, returning the punch.

"Damn! You've been gettin' stronger," Jay said.

"Wait a minute. You're human," Finn said as he grabbed his brother and hugged the stuffing out of him.

"Whoa!" Jay said when Finn released him. "I love and miss ya', too."

"Uh oh," Finn said as he stopped walking. "If you're human, there's trouble brewing. I didn't ask for you to be human, so that only means trouble is brewin'."

"You are correct," Jay said. "You have really caught on to this Magic stuff well."

"Stop tryin' to distract me," Finn said. "Those UFOs have somethin' to do with why you're here, don't they?"

"They do," Jay replied. "Big trouble is about to explode around here. We need your help."

"Me? Why me?" Finn asked. "Wait a minute; you need me as a White Light Paladin?"

There was a quick flash of bright yellow light that answered his question.

"Yup," Jay said, nodding to the light,

"How bad are things gonna get?" Finn asked.

"Really bad," Jay replied.

"Like before?" Finn asked.

"Worse," Jay replied as two figures appeared in front of them.

"Brakendor and Cryton will be joining us," Jay said.

Brakendor and Cryton were dressed as the magnificent White Light Paladins. They wore the white and silver uniform of the White Light Paladin with the silver sword at their sides.

"You look magnificent," Finn said as Jay morphed into a White Light Paladin.

"As do you," Jay said as Finn was dressed in the uniform he had worn once before.

"You mean right now? This minute?" Finn said as he looked over his uniform and took his sword out to hold.

"Yes, right now," Jay said. "The ETs have just identified their primary target. They've identified Emily as the human that destroyed their fellow ET Yuri. He was a very powerful ET and was terrified by many. When he was killed and destroyed by Emily in The Sacred Rock Meadow, his fellow ETs made a pact to find and destroy her. They plan on torturing her for a very long time before they take her essence and destroy her soul."

"Not gonna happen while I'm around," Finn said.

"That's how all of The Special Magic feels. That's why Brakendor and Cryton are here. They will be protecting Emily while you and I protect the Special One. We'll be joined by others soon. Ready?"

"Who is the Special One?" Finn asked as they rose into the air.

"You'll see soon enough," Jay said. "We're off."

Brakendor and Cryton headed to Emily's while Jay and Finn flew over to the Special One's place. The skies began to show dark blue, orange, and red clouds swirling in a crazy pattern. All of the UFOs became uncloaked. Some flew over toward Emily's Meadow, and the rest flew to their primary target's spot.

Emily felt the energy shift.

"We should get into the shelter under the stables right away," Emily said as she grabbed Trouble's leash, fastened it on him, and walked out the back door before anyone could say anything.

The agents followed her, informing Matthews of their move to the bunker below the stables. They were inside the bunker a moment later. The agents didn't know it was protected by The Ancient Magic. It needed to be. Those ETs were bent on destroying Emily.

Kendra and Sami knew the minute the UFOs uncloaked. Kendra ran to Sami's as Sami was running to Kendra's.

"Time to fly," Kendra said as they shape-shifted into their original form, became invisible, and took to the air.

The dragons saw them and nodded as they flew to the north to protect one of their own. They saw Finn and Jay hovering over the house. Five of the UFOs moved into place to blow the house out of existence. They powered up their weapons and took aim at the house.

Just as the ETs began to fire their plasma weapons, Jay and Finn raised their swords, pointing them at the UFOs. The swords reflected the plasma energy, sending them back into the ships. The ships burst into a million harmless rays shooting up into the universe. It looked like a million silver streaks rising up into the sky.

Sami reached the man first and wrapped an energy shield around him. Kendra set a second grid of protection around the three of them as they stayed close to keep The Special One alive.

Folks across the Blue Ridge heard the energy blast and ran outside to see what was happening. They saw the streaks shooting up into space and couldn't believe what they were witnessing.

"We're in for some trouble now," Ted said to the folks at The Store.

"Let's get inside and make sure everyone in The Creek is safe," Michael said. "I'll send an alert out and ask folks to check in."

Ned was one of the people in The Store, and he felt an odd sensation looking at those sliver streaks shooting up into space. It was as if he'd seen them before. He knew he'd never seen them in his life and wondered if Deja Vu was happening here. He couldn't figure it out. But he was damn certain he'd seen something like this before. They were part of some UFOs somewhere. He was certain of it. He couldn't quite put his finger on the odd sensation, but he knew they were all connected.

And then there was the Air Force. It sent squadrons of jets to investigate. They told Matthews about this, and Matthews told them to return to base.

"Don't argue with me unless you want to lose every jet and every pilot," Matthews yelled into his radio at the Air Force commander. "This is way beyond anything you've ever seen. Now, do it!!"

He heard the commander give the retreat order. Matthews watched as the first jets circled back and left the airspace. The pilots couldn't believe what they saw. Ten UFOs hovering over the Blue Ridge. They took pictures as they turned around. Their commander wasn't gonna believe them without the pictures. One of the pilots flew closer to get better pictures, and a UFO shot a plasma beam at him. The pilot was able to dodge the beam and immediately turned and left the airspace. His cockpit camera recorded the whole thing.

When that pilot landed at the base, he walked around his jet and saw a streak of melted metal along the left side of the jet. It was as if the stuff was made of plastic and had been torched. He didn't even know how he was able to fly back. As the commander came out to yell at him, the left side outer layer of his jet fell to the ground. That stuff was about as tough as an alloy could be. It was made of a carbon-epoxy with carbon-bismaleimide in the high-heat areas. That stuff was supposed to withstand incredibly high temperatures. The whole piece of the jet that had fallen looked like a melted candle. The commander looked at the pilot and shook his head.

"Write it up and send me the video and pictures," the commander said.

"Yes, sir," the pilot replied, saluting his commander.

"Pilot, are you all right? You look like you got sunburned," the commander asked.

"I think I'm good, sir," the pilot replied.

"Report to sickbay to get thoroughly checked out." The commander ordered.

"Yes, sir," the pilot replied as he left the tarmac and headed for the medical unit.

Five UFOs settled over The Special One's house and took aim. Just as they fired their plasma weapons, Cryton and Brakendor raised their swords to block the rays, and these plasma beams were sent high up into space as a million silver streaks, just like the ones over the primary target.

The ETs were pissed! They communicated with each other and decided they needed to be on the ground to destroy the two humans.

Those on the ground in both locations saw the ETs as they landed. They were hideous! They were tall, greenish-orange-ish colored creatures with two triangle-shaped eyes, a round snout for a nose, and a large round mouth that was outlined in black. They had two arms and two legs. The arms had three fingers with bulbous tips. They had flat bellies and large butts with three tails that seemed to move of their own accord.

As The White Light Paladins watched these creatures, they saw their skin color change to match their surroundings. They were a type of shape-shifter. Kendra and Sami flew in just as the ETs landed and knew right away the battle was going to get a lot worse before it got better.

They beamed down to Emily's Meadow and began walking into the house. They were blocked by an invisible force. No matter how hard they tried to get inside, they couldn't. They turned and walked over to the stables. The same thing happened. One of them signaled to the others and shape-shifted into Kendra. It was still blocked. The UFOs sent plasma rays to the barn and stables, and they missed their targets at the last second. The rays were blocked and bent, hitting one of the UFOs instead. It exploded, sending bits and pieces of UFO and ETs all over the Blue Ridge and into space.

The ETs on the ground circled the stables. They scanned for Emily's energy and found it under the floor. Brakendor and Cryton flew in and saw the ETs at the stables. They blasted them with laser beams shot from their silver-gloved hands. Two of the ETs were killed, and the other six tried to fire their weapons at the White Light Paladins. Brakendor and Cryton flew away from the stables to draw the ETs out, and it worked. All six of them ran out into the meadow and found a fleet of White Light Paladins waiting for them.

The ETs drew their weapons and fired at the White Light Paladins. The White Light Paladins fired back and killed four more ETs. They exploded all over the place, covering their fellow ETS with body parts and bright orange goo. As the goo from them fell to the ground, it turned black and started to move toward the other puddles of ugly black goo from the already dead ETs.

Cryton sent a message to Q, and he sent a message to Beau.

"Dragon Brigade, get a pouch of the potion and go to Emily Meadow," Beau said. "They need you there."

Katelyn hung a pouch of the potion around the dragons' necks, and they took to the air. They were invisible as they arrived at Emily's a few minutes later. They saw all the ugly black goo puddles trying to gather together. They sent streams of the potion on all of them. The minute the potion hit them, they sizzled, exploded into a million black pieces of black ash, then were sucked up into space by The Special Magic, capturing their essence and destroying it for all eternity.

The ETs ran for cover behind the barn and fired at the White Light Paladins again. Brakendor came from behind the ETs and shot a ray of energy at the head of one of them. It exploded into ugly black bits and pieces that sizzled on the ground. The remaining ETs howled in anger and ran at the White Light Paladins.

The ETs in the UFOs saw all of this and sent flaming spirals at the White Light Paladins. One was hit and died and rose into the sky as a silver streak of pure energy. That pure energy hit the bottom of one of the UFOs, damaging it and causing it to fall to the ground. It landed just west of Emily's Meadow. It burst into flames, then exploded so intensely that the ground shook like an earthquake unfolding. It was felt all the way to The Store.

The ETs sent bolts of energy lightning toward the White Light Paladins. They countered the assault with balls of intense energy. When the lightning bolts hit the balls, it turned the bolt into pure energy as if it were a burst from the sun. Three of the UFOs were incinerated. This left two UFOs to continue the strike on Emily. She was safe in the underground bunker beneath the stables. The animals in the stables were being protected by faeries and gnomes.

While the battle raged on at Emily's, the UFOs over The Special One's house began their attack in earnest. They aimed their plasma beams at the house again. They heard from the remaining two UFOs at Emily's and decided not to fire their weapons but to get on the ground and attack the house and the person inside. Twelve of them beamed down and surrounded the house. The person inside had just figured out that something was happening outside and looked out a window. One of the ETs saw this and fired his laser at the window. The person inside fell to the floor and was missed by the laser. The window shattered, and the ray left a burning hole in his living room wall.

"What the hell is goin' on out there?" he asked as he stayed on the floor.

A second ET took aim at him through the shattered window but was stopped when Finn sent a beam of energy from his sword at the ET, killing it. It exploded into a mass of ugly black goo all over the ground outside the house. Finn hit two more ETs, and Jay hit three of them.

They all exploded into the ugly black goo and made puddles of the stuff on the ground all around the house. The goo began to move toward each other in an attempt to reform.

Q saw this and called for The Dragon Brigade to grab some of the potion from The Crystal Caves and drop it on all the ugly black goo it could see. Four of The Dragon Brigade dragons grabbed the goo from Jordan and Katelyn and flew out to The Special One's place.

The others in The Dragon Brigade began flying close to the UFOs over the houses. The dragons knew the UFOs were not protected as they fired their weapons and sent more ETs to the ground. Penny breathed fire at the ETs on the ground, killing many of them, while Q breathed fire at the front of two of the UFOs. The fire damaged them, but they kept going. The ground was covered with a lot of those ugly black goo puddles. More dragons joined The Dragon Brigade to dump potion on the nasty black goo and to assist Penny and Q at the two houses.

The Dragon Brigade dragons with the potion became invisible as they approached the UFOs, and the UFOs never picked up on the dragon energy. They released streams of the potion over the ugly black goo puddles that had started to gather and move toward each other. The minute the potion hit them, they sizzled, exploded into a million black pieces of black ash, then were sucked up into space by The Special Magic, capturing their essence and destroying it for all eternity.

The UFO ETs at both locations were pissed as hell at all the interference from The White Light Paladins. They hadn't counted on any resistance. They decided to fire their plasma weapons at the stables and the house again. This time, one of the beams hit each target.

The stable roof was set on fire, and the chimney at The Special One's house was destroyed. The White Light Paladins called upon the Spirit of the Water to quench the fire on the stable roof. It did, and this made the ETs even more angry.

The chimney fell to the ground and left an opening in the wall of the living room. One of the ETs got into the house and ran through it, looking for their target. It couldn't find him. Unbeknown to the ET, the White Light Paladins had wrapped an invisibility cloak around the man, and he was standing in the corner of the kitchen as the ET ran all over the place. The ET finally went outside and howled. Finn sent a bolt of energy at the ET, and it melted into a puddle of ugly black goo. The goo started to slither into the house, but one of the dragons was right there and dropped a stream of the potion on it. It was destroyed like the others and gone in a minute.

659

The UFOs over The Special One's house began to send spirals of flaming energy at the house and the White Light Paladins. Finn and Jay had their hands full, throwing energy bolts at the spirals and trying to protect the man. The man stayed in the invisibility cloak in the kitchen corner while all this was happening. The UFOs sent more ETs to both locations, and the battle raged on. The dragons went back to The Crystal Caves for refills. It was while they were gone that the man remembered he had a special crystal that had been given to him when he was just a small boy.

He took it out of his pocket and raised it into the air as he had been taught to do. It was a small crystal dragon. As soon as he raised it, The Crystal Dragon began to shine brightly. It was vibrating and sending rays of colored light all over the Blue Ridge.

Penny and Q saw this and knew help was on the way. A few minutes later, the full Dragon Brigade of over one hundred dragons flew in and began breathing fire at the ETS at both places. All the ETs that were left on the ground at Emily's and The Special One's house were incinerated in short time. Puddles of that ugly black goo began slithering to a common place to reincarnate.

The Dragon Brigade dragons arrived at their locations and dropped streams of the potion on the puddles. There was a lot of sizzling and ash in the air for quite some time. When the ugly black puddles were gone, there were no more ETs on the ground. Only two ships were left over Emily's Meadow, and four were still hovering over the house of The Special One. The Special One was still invisible in the kitchen.

The man in the kitchen began having weird visions. He saw himself in a strange place as a young man with a sword. It was a quick vision and over in just a few seconds. Some of The Dragon Brigade arrived to assist Finn, Jay, and the White Light Paladins. More White Light Paladins arrived. They all communicated telepathically, creating an attack strategy in just a few seconds., and the plan was put into action.

As The White Light Paladins watched, one of the most enormous dragons of The Dragon Brigade flew near one of the UFOs over The Special One's house and became invisible. A moment later, Finn and Jay began laughing. That particular dragon had taken up residence on the top of one of the largest UFOs. It sat there with a big grin on its face. The Ancient Magic had cloaked the dragon's energy signal, and the ETs had no idea it was there. Other dragons saw this and flew over to sit on all of the remaining UFOs all over the Blue Ridge.

The UFOs continued to send flaming energy discs at the stables and The Special One's house. The White Light Paladins managed to stop them by releasing energy streams from their swords and knives. The sky was lit up like a thousand fireworks were going off at the same time. Folks all over the Blue Ridge stood in amazement, watching the show. They had no idea what it was all about. Well, most of them didn't know. Miss Cora knew exactly what was happening.

Miss Cora was sending energy through ancient chanting songs. She was in her living room, rocking and chanting nonstop. She knew that the harmony of the ages was at risk. The Ancient Magic had given a special line of humans the energy of this Magic, and its current human had no idea he was the recipient and protector of This Special Magic. He would know soon enough whether he lived or died. He would know.

Katelyn and Jordan had just finished making another huge cauldron of the potion when Beau received a message from Penny and Q.

"Katelyn. Jordan," Beau said, turning to them. "You are needed at The Special One's house. Step outside: the dragons will fly you there."

"What?" Jordan said. "Fly us there?"

"Yes, hurry," Beau said. "We've got the potion taken care of here."

"Well, this is gonna be a first," Katelyn said as she and Jordan stepped into the meadow.

Two dragons they had never seen before were waiting for them. They had blue, green, and yellow swirled skin that looked like it was moving. It was.

"Ah, you see our changing skin colors," the larger of the two said. "I am Grindor."

"I am Stowmagnon," the other said. "We are ready for you. Climb up here."

Stowmagnon raised his front leg to show them where to climb onto their necks and back area.

"Settle near our necks where our scales start to go down our backs," Grindor instructed them.

Jordan and Katelyn stepped onto the dragon's legs and found themselves seated on the dragon's shoulders.

"We call this area our shoulders," Katelyn said as she patted Stowmagnon's back.

"You have a splendid touch, Katelyn," the dragon replied. "You ready, Jordan?"

"I am," Jordan said. "Does this feel okay for you, Grindor?"

"You are seated perfectly," Grindor replied. "Hold on to our scales. Here we go."

The dragons lifted a bit carefully and slowly to give Jordan and Katelyn a minute to adjust to being in flight. Then, they flew high and banked to the east toward The Special One's house.

Katelyn and Jordan were in awe of flying on the dragons. A few minutes later, they found themselves landing just south of the house.

"Did the ETs see us?" Katelyn asked as she stepped onto the ground.

"No, Katelyn," Grindor replied. "We were cloaked in The Ancient Magic. So, what do you think of flying on a dragon?"

"I loved it!" Katelyn replied.

"It was magnificent!" Jordan said. "I hope we can do it again soon."

"I think that can be arranged after we settle this matter," Grindor said.

"What are we supposed to do now?" Jordan asked.

"Go to The Special One's house," Stowmagnon said. "He needs your help."

"How can we help him? We have no weapons greater than the ET's weapons," Katelyn asked.

"You do," Grindor replied. "Take a moment and remember Camelot."

"Jordan," Katelyn said as she looked around the field. "Isn't that…"

"It is Katelyn," Stowmagnon replied. "But we aren't saying his name just yet. It's not time."

"Magic, huh?" Katelyn said, looking at the dragons.

"Magic," they both replied. "Now, be on your way. There isn't much time left. You'll know just what to do when you get there."

"From the dragon's mouth to the ear of The Ancient Magic," Jordan said.

Katelyn and Jordan set out for The Special One's house. It was only a moment's walk away.

"This place is a mess!" Katelyn said as they walked through the place where the chimney had been.

"Katelyn! In here," Jordan said from what was left of the kitchen.

"Oh my god! Are you all right?" Katelyn asked the man.

"What the hell is goin on out there? It sounds like Armageddon rainin' down on us," the man said as he tried to stand up.

"It looks like it, too," Katelyn replied, taking a good look at the man. "You stay on the floor, or what's left of the floor. We're gonna take a look around outside."

"Be careful," the man said. "There's some really scary-looking creatures out there. They've been tryin' to get to me. Don't know why. I never did anyone no harm. God, this headache really hurts."

A bag of ice appeared next to the man.

"Hold this on your head for a few minutes," Jordan said as he handed the ice to the man.

"Where'd that come from?" the man asked as he placed it on his head.

"Magic," Katelyn replied. "Now, stay on the floor. We'll be back in a few minutes."

"No worries," the man replied. "I think I'm just gonna stay here for a long while."

Katelyn and Jordan carefully walked back through the chimney hole to take a look around.

"The ETs don't seem to be close by," Jordan said.

"The UFOs are," Katelyn said. "Watch out!"

Katelyn pushed Jordan to the ground as an energy beam was shot at them.

"Oh shit!" Jordan said. "That was close. How are we supposed to defend ourselves out here?"

"We got ya covered," Finn hollered from above their heads.

Jordan and Katelyn looked up into the sky and saw a fantastic sight. Finn, Jay, and some others were hovering in the air. They wore pure white and silver uniforms with swords in their hands and knives at their waist. Some were on pure white horses, while others, including Finn and Jay, were hovering in the air. Even their hair was pure white. And they glowed brightly.

"Oh my god!" Jordan said, looking at everyone. "Pure Magic at its best?"

"Somethin like that, Jordan," Finn replied. "You take care of The Special One while we get rid of these pesky UFOs. Go back inside. You'll know what to do at just the right moment."

"Okay," Katelyn said as she and Jordan went back into the kitchen to sit with the man.

"You get sent home?" the man said, smiling.

"Somthin' like that," Jordan replied. "We are to sit tight for a few minutes."

"Finn said so," Katelyn added.

"Finn? He around here, too?" the man said. "This is so beyond anything I could ever imagine. I'm in total somethin about it all."

"We understand," Katelyn said.

"We've never been in anything like this before, either," Jordan added.

"But, Katelyn, you know about The Magic," the man said.

"I do know about The Magic," Katelyn replied. "But only a smidgin. Never seen anythin' quite like this before. I'm tryin to get a grip on it all, too."

Just then, there was a loud crashing sound from outside, and Finn walked in.

"You're all okay," Finn said. "It was just a tree crashin' down across the road."

Finn walked back outside and the three on the floor just looked at each other.

"I can understand a tree crashin down," the man said. "It's the rest that is unbelievable."

"I'm with you on that one," Jordan said. "Let's just sit here and listen to what's goin on out there."

That's what the three of them did for the next few minutes.

The White Light Paladins were fighting for all humanity. More UFOs appeared through the Stargate and began to attack both places. Brakendor and Cryton had an army of dragons and White Light Paladins blowing up the UFOs. The UFOs got a few plasma shots near Emily's house and barn, but none of them hit the stables.

Finn and Jay and their dragons and White Light Paladins were fighting tooth and neck. As soon as one of the UFOs was destroyed, another one came through the Stargate. The dragons had an idea and sent it out to everyone. More dragons became invisible and sat on top of the new UFOs. All the UFOs, as far as anyone could see, had a dragon sitting on the very top of it. On cue, Penny gave the signal, and the dragons breathed fire into the UFOs through a small opening that was usually hidden when the UFO was cloaked. As soon as the UFO became visible, the opening became visible. It was the UFO's only flaw—a good thing for the dragons.

As soon as the fire was breathed into the UFO, the dragons flew far away from them. Nothing happened for a few seconds; then all hell broke loose. First, the UFO began to shake a little bit from side to side. Then, the shaking intensified until the UFO was visibly moving around. A bit of smoke was seen for just a split second before the UFO blew sky-high. Not just one of them, but all of them all over the Blue Ridge.

Just as the shaking began, a huge swarm of ETs landed on the ground at both sights. They began running toward The Special One's house and toward the stables at Emily's Meadow. The ETs had the upper hand for a few minutes while the dragons stayed clear of the exploding UFOs. The ETs rushed the house. The White Light Paladins had only a split second to throw bolts of energy at them before they got inside. One after another was killed, and that ugly black goo began to creep toward the kitchen. It was trying to form a huge ET monster that would destroy the man, Katelyn, and Jordan.

At the same time, the ETs were trying to get inside the stable at Emily's place. The Ancient Magic held them off with the help of The White Light Paladins. They had to be exact when they threw energy bolts at the ETs because they didn't want to blow up the stable. Some of The White Light Paladins stepped onto the ground near the stable to lure the ETs away. It worked. The minute the ETs were safely away from the stable, energy bolts were thrown at them, and they blew up.

But there were hundreds of them. Back at The Special One's house, the battle was getting worse. The White Light Paladins had all they could do to keep the ETs away. At the last moment, the dragons returned to both places and helped kill the ETs. The ETs were shocked to see the dragons. They just stood there staring at them for a few seconds. That was long enough for the dragons to get close enough to breathe fire on them and incinerate them. As soon as that ugly black goo began to creep toward itself, other dragons dropped potion on it, and it was turned to ash and taken into the sky by The Ancient Magic. The sky was cloudy with all the ash rising into it.

Even so, there were still hundreds of ETs. They knew they would not be going home soon, so they fought with all their might. They tried to infect the humans by shooting the black goo from tentacles that they shot out of their fingers. It didn't work, though. The Ancient Magic knew about that trick and had warned The White Light Paladins and the dragons about it. They were ready. Every time a tentacle was seen, an energy razor was sent to cut it off from the ET's hand. The ET screamed something fierce and was instantly incinerated by a dragon's fire and an energy bolt from The White Light Paladins.

"Jordan, it's time," Katelyn said as she stood up.

"You ready?" Jordan asked as he took his twin crystal out of his pocket.

"I am," Katelyn replied as she took her twin crystal from her pocket.

"Right here," Jordan said as they set them, touching each other on what was left of the kitchen counter. A brilliant white light flashed and knocked them to the floor. It was so bright that people in The Creek saw it as well.

"There's some powerful Magic goin on up there," Sarah said to the others in The Store. Folks had been gathering for a while, ever since the UFOs appeared.

"Let's send some positive energy up there," Miss Cora suggested just after she arrived.

Folks set about and did just that. The ETs felt that energy wave and did not like it. Jordan sat up and then took his Crystal Dragon from his pocket.

"Hey, I have one of those, too," the man said as she showed it to Katelyn and Jordan. "It's not as big as yours, though."

"No matter," Jordan said. "It's the energy it holds and attracts that matters. Hold yours up right now."

The man and Jordan held their Crystal Dragons as high as they could. A second later, the earth began to hum, then tremble a little.

"I think we should go outside and look at what's happenin' out there," Jordan said. "Keep your Crystal Dragon held up to the sky."

Katelyn went outside first, then motioned for the two men to join her. The sky was a mess of colors and ash. The ash was from the incinerated ETs. They seemed to be dying rapidly. Finn and Jay flew over and settled to the ground.

They surrounded the man as a few ETs tried to get to him. They sent energy beams from their swords at them, and they were instantly incinerated.

"Watch. We're about to see something no other humans have ever witnessed before," Jay said. "When Katelyn and Jordan touched their twin crystals, the energy sent a signal to The Ancient Magic. When Jordan and the man raised your Crystal Dragons to the sky, their energy opened a portal in The Ancient Magic. That Magic joined The Special Magic. It's the energy needed to destroy the ETs and their UFOs for all eternity. Watch."

"Nice to see ya, Jay," Katelyn said.

"You, too," Jay said.

The sky began to change colors, and those colors swirled around in amazing patterns. The trembling of the earth increased so much that no one could remain standing all over the globe.

The White Light Paladins and the dragons settled to the earth at Emily's Meadow and The Special One's house and turned their eyes to the sky.

Those swirling clouds began to take shape, and soon, an untold number of energy tornadoes covered the earth. The tornadoes over The Creek were every color of the rainbow and then some. The ETs kept trying to get to Emily and the man, but the earth had now turned its trembling into a full-blown 4.0 earthquake. Nothing could stay standing for more than a second.

One of the ETs looked up into the sky and screamed a blood-curdling scream you could feel into your very soul. The other ETs at both sights looked skyward and joined in that scream. The sound was horrifying. The energy tornadoes were aiming for the ETs. One after another, the ETs were taken into the energy tornadoes. The tornadoes turned black for a minute, then returned to their ever-changing colors as they aimed at another ET. The sight was beyond anything anyone could comprehend. Emily and her agents were allowed to come out of the bunker and watch this from the windows of the stable. They were well protected by The Ancient Magic. The Divine wanted Emily to see everything.

One after another, the ETs were taken into the tornadoes and destroyed. No one really knew how long this went on. It was when the last tornado had taken the last ET at both sights that the tornado changed from black to beautiful colors and swirled up into the heavens. The sun returned to the sky, and the earth stopped trembling. There was absolute silence for the longest time.

"Well, I guess that's over," Emily said as she left the stables and let Trouble run free.

The agents didn't know what to think. They reported to Matthews that the battle was over, and everything had returned to normal, whatever that was. Matthews told them to hold tight. He would be there soon.

Jordan, Katelyn, and the man just stared at each other for the longest time. Finn and Jay walked over and stood with them.

"Jay?" the man said as he recognized Jay. "You're supposed to be dead."

"Hey there," Jay replied. "Well, my body did die. My Spirit is alive and well. I get to come back in a body from time to time to check up on you mortals. Good to see ya."

"I have known about and believe in The Magic for sure," the man said. "Always have. But this is a new level of The Magic I could never have imagined."

"I hear ya," Jordan said. "It's all new to me, too. I guess we'll just have to try to figure all this stuff out together."

"I'll take ya up on that for sure," the man said. "Those colors were amazin'. And you guys can fly. And those ETs were horrible. I don't think I'm gonna sleep for a long time tryin' to figure this out."

"You'll sleep well," Katelyn said.

"You can stay with me until we figure out what to do with your house," Jordan was saying when the air began to shimmer, and a kind of mist fell all around.

Kendra and Sami flew in and landed next to the man.

"You, too?" the man said. "I don't think I can take much more."

"Just a little more," Sami said. "Watch."

Sami pointed to his house, and the mist began to lift. A whole new house was taking shape right in front of them. It was bigger than the old one, and a barn appeared behind it.

"No way!" the man said as he walked over to the house and walked all the way around it. "It's bigger than my old one and all brand new. Everything inside is brand new. Oh my god! The barn!"

The man ran over to the barn with everyone in tow. He was inside and hollered out in joy.

"It's a completely equipped workshop for me. It has all the tools I usually have and a bunch of new ones I always wished I could afford. That tree that fell is here, too. Look."

The fallen tree was placed from one end of the barn to the other, just waiting for the man to use it.

"Now, that's really awesome," Kendra said. "I guess we know what you'll be doin' for a long while."

"You got that right," the man replied. "As soon as I feel better."

"We'll be here for you for a long time to help you process what you've been through. How about you go inside and get somethin' to eat," Sami said. "There's some food from Ted on the counter. Take a shower and get some rest. The Magic will heal your head and the other wounds you got."

"I appreciate that," the man said, bowing his head.

There was a soft flash of lavender light in the space.

"That's The Magic thankin' you for acknowledging it," Kendra said.

"I am so very tired all of a sudden," the man said as they all walked him to the kitchen door. "Later. And thanks."

The man walked into his new house, and the others walked a bit down the road.

"Well, that was some battle," Katelyn said. "Crazy ass shit!"

Ditto!" Jordan said. "Now, about Jay."

"Don't even ask," Jay said. "I don't even know how all this works. I just know it does, and I love being back here in The Creek with family. Most folks won't ever know about me comin' back human. But, y'all are a part of The Magic, so you'll always know. Now, Katelyn, I do believe you have a crock pot full of chicken stew. And, Sami, we need to celebrate your comin' home. I say it's time for a party at Katelyn's place."

"We agree," Sami said. "Let's go."

"How are we gonna get there?" Jordan was saying as he became airborne with the rest of them and placed on waiting dragons.

"This is awesome!" Katelyn said as they flew home. They were invisible, of course. And no one saw them suddenly appear on the lawn; Jordan and Finn's trucks were in the driveway.

"Hey, y'all," Ted hollered as he crossed the road. "Got a little somethin for ya. I would guess to say that noise and earthquake stuff had somethin to do with The Magic, and y'all may have been a part of it. Just sayin'. Here's some supper. Enjoy."

Kendra kissed Ted's cheek as she took the basket from him and handed it to Finn. Sami had the second basket and was headed into Katelyn's house.

"We love ya, our Ted," Finn said, nodding at him.

They thoroughly enjoyed Ted's goodies and the chicken stew.

"Time to get some sleep," Katelyn said as Jordan yawned.

"Absolutely," Jordan said as he stood up. "I'm gonna sleep well tonight with all this good food. I'll call ya in the mornin, Katie girl. We need to check in on our Special Person."

"Yes, we do," Katelyn said. "What day is it anyway?"

"I think it's still Friday night," Finn said as he walked Jordan outside.

"Sleep well," Sami and Kendra said.

"You're enjoyin the food, right, Jay?" Katelyn said, laughin' at him.

"You know I am," Jay said. "Superb, as always."

"Sounds like Jay's havin' a grand time," Jordan said as he got into his truck. "I don't even want to think about how all that works."

"Believe me, it's better that way," Finn said. "The Magic will take care of you tonight. Sleep well."

"Thanks, my friend," Jordan said as he backed out and drove down the road, waving at the security detail.

"Well, brother, sounds like you've been piggin out in here," Fina said as he slapped Jay on the shoulder.

"Exactly," Jay said as he sat back, smiling. "Great food, as always. Listen, this battle has been beyond anythin' I've ever been involved in. I know about bein' a White Light Paladin, but this goes way overboard with the UFOs and all. I'm gonna take a long while to think about this."

"We all are," Sami said.

"Or, is that Angelique?" Hmmm?" Katelyn said. "Jordan didn't recognize you, but I have."

"Truth, Katelyn," Sami said. "I loved Quintan as much as anyone could. He was amazin, and I will die again and again to protect our descendants."

"I know you will," Katelyn said. "Jordan and I will be going over to The Special One's house tomorrow to ease him into knowin' who he's a part of. I got the message loud and clear from The Divine to go slowly with him. He's in shock about the battle. Then, there's the fact that he watched his house being rebuilt right in front of him. That's a lot for any of us to understand. We're gonna go slowly with him."

"I am grateful for that," Sami said with tears rolling down her cheeks.

"Sami, have you always known about him since we met?" Katelyn asked as she put an arm around her best friend.

"I've had momentary glimpses," Samil replied.

"It wasn't until you and Jordan came back from Camelot that The Divine let her remember everythin," Kendra said.

"And what a memory flash that was," Sami said.

"I know how you feel," Katelyn said. "That sayin' "TMI": it's for real!"

This made everyone laugh.

"Time for me to get along, too," Finn said.

"I'll walk you out," Katelyn said.

"You two stay here," Kendra said. "We'll go on home. Jay, come with us."

"Yes, Ma'am," Jay said, winking at Finn.

"Katie girl," Finn said as he wrapped Katelyn into a big hug. "I don't even know what to say or do."

"Me, either," Katelyn said. "This is a great start."

They stayed wrapped in each other's arms, kissing deeply for a bit.

"Now, I can deal with this," Katelyn said as they finished their sweet moment.

"We'll have more tomorrow night," Finn said. "I'm stayin' over."

"Deal!" Katelyn said as they walked outside.

"It's getting chilly out here," Finn said as he got into his truck.

"Thinkin about you will keep me warm, my Finn," Katelyn said.

"Same here, my Katie girl," Finn offered as he drove off.

Jay was waiting for Finn in Finn's bedroom when he got home.

"Of course you're here," Finn said. "You stayin' a while?"

"Yup," Jay replied. "I get to surprise Mom and Dad in the mornin," Jay replied. "Get some sleep, mighty warrior."

"Love you to the moon and back, little bro," Finn said as he laid his head on the pillow.

"Love you to the moon and back, big bro," Jay said, laughing as he went to his old room and fell sound asleep.

Saturday morning dawned sunny and beautiful. Jay surprised his folks first thing, and they had a grand time catching up.

Katelyn called Jordan, and they met up at The Special One's house a short time later.

"Hey, you two," the man said. "This is magnificent. I still don't understand how all this happened. And that's okay. I am grateful for this beautiful home and barn. That barn has every tool I could think of and a few I've never seen before. Somethin' about digital engineerin'. It's gonna be fun figurin' it all out."

"How ya feelin'?" Katelyn asked.

"Just fine," the man replied. "It's as if I never got hurt."

"The Magic has a way of takin' care of stuff like that," Jordan said. "I should know."

"So, why are the two of you here?" the man asked. "And why were those horrible ETs trying to kill me?" the man asked.

"We've got a story to tell ya," Jordan said as he and Katelyn walked over to the man.

"Hal, you remember the stories about King Arthur and Camelot?" Katelyn asked.

"I do," Hal replied. "I love those stories. Why?"

Katelyn and Jordan looked at each other for a minute.

"Hal, you're gonna find this hard to believe," Jordan said. "Just remember, The Special Magic knows what it's doin."

THE END

What's Next

The Legend of the Crystal Caves

Dragon Myths

THE MYTH

Myth says that millions and millions of years of that the never-ending bombardment of asteroids and planets began to shape the galaxies. It was a supernova that triggered the final formation of what is known as The Milky Way Galaxy. The explosion crashed asteroids into asteroids, planets into planets. A new sun formed in the center of a bunch of planets, and they began circling that sun.

Myth says of all the planets, there was a small one that was shaping itself. Volcanic eruptions went on and on for millennia until the planet finally took to settling down. The eruptions became less, and the planet began to cool. A kind of goo formed in depressions that began to sustain life.

Myth says it was out of this goo that The First One was created by The Ancient Magic. The Ancient Magic had deemed this planet to be the keeper of The Magic for eternity and needed a fierce protector. The Ancient Magic began

671

to slowly mold its energy in that primordial goo. At long last, the creature was ready.

Myth says as the creature began to arise, the tips of two spikes were seen emerging slowly from the orange goo. They were black. As they pushed upward, the tips of two wings were seen, and the rest of The First One rose up from the goo, spread its wings, and took to the air. It was a solitary creature and flew for a long time. It finally settled on a volcano that had stopped erupting and cooled. This would be its home.

Myth says The Ancient Magic would keep this knowledge from all creatures that would use this planet as their home. The First One would only wake up when The Special Magic was threatened. The First One was the protector of all of The Ancient Magic.

Myths are legends passed down through the millennia.

Does The Myth hold any truth?

About the Author

Born and raised in the Midwest, Karmle L. Conrad moved to New England in 1985 and built her home on Cape Cod in 1988. Karmle completed her Bachelor's Degree from Harvard University and her Master's Degree from Suffolk University. She completed her Doctorate in Public Health through Capella University in 2022. Karmle has been Gifted as a Psychic Medium from birth.

Karmle's adult fiction series, The Crab Apple Creek Anthology, is centered in Urban Fantasy and the Paranormal. There are 5 sets of books, each with 3 separate books apiece. The Crab Apple Creek series is available now. Karmle is working on the 2nd set in the Anthology, The Legend of The Crystal Caves. Book 2 in this set is Dragon Myths.

She has a series for middle-school-aged kids entitled The TreeHouse Gang Mysteries: The first seven books are completed, and she's busy working on the next one.

Be sure to visit Karmle's website for more information: www.thecapecodpsychic.com.